PASSAGE OF TIME

PASSAGE OF TIME

J.M. BUCKLER

Passage of Time

Copyright © 2019 by J.M. Buckler

First Edition: November 2019

Published by: Gratus Publishing, LLC

Visit my website at www.jmbuckler.com

Instagram: author_j.m.buckler

Printed in the United States of America

Paperback ISBN: 978-1-7331057-0-5

E-Book ISBN: 978-1-7331057-1-2

Edited by: Tiffany White Writers Untapped

Cover Art and Interior Map Illustrated by: Adam Rabalais

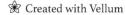 Created with Vellum

For the courageous ones who stand for truth, and for those who stand beside them.

RATINGS ARE NOT REQUIRED FOR BOOKS

Out of respect for my younger and more sensitive readers, please be advised that this book contains the following: adult content, adult language, violence, and graphic scenes that some may find disturbing.

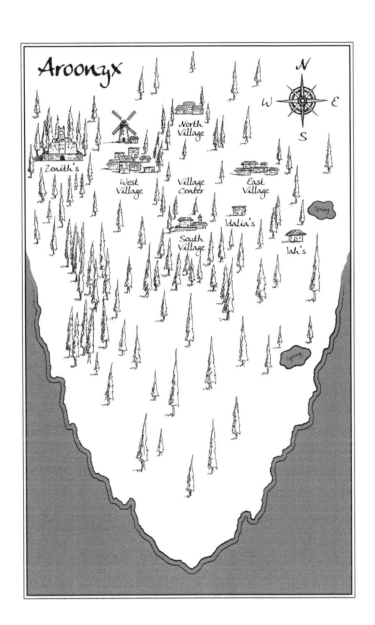

CODE OF THE COLLECTORS

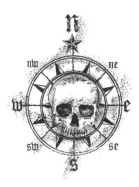

I live to serve my leader
My leader's word is law
I do not pity the weak
My blade and mind must stay sharp
I will use any force necessary to complete the mission
I will torture the guilty without regret
~~Pain is temporary~~
Insubordination equals execution

CAST OF CHARACTERS

Aarush [aa-roosh]
Solin; son of Sharik

Aelius [ay-lee-us]
Solin; Jax's biological father

Apollo [uh-pah-low]
Solin; member of the Inner Circle

Archer [arch-er]
Lunin; ex-Collector (Inactive Member)

Aries [air-ease]
Lunin; ex-Collector (Inactive Member)

Arun [air-run]
Solin; first leader of Aroonyx [aa-roon-ix]

Blaze [blaiz]
Solin

Callisto [kuh-list-o]
Lunin; Idalia's uncle

Castor [ca-stir]
Lunin; ex-Collector; Pollux's father

Chris Lofton [kris loft-en]
Cyrus's adoptive father

Cosmo [cause-mo]
Solin

Cyrus Lofton [sye-rus loft-en]
Solin; Elara's twin brother

Elara Dunlin [eh-lar-uh done-lyn]
Lunin; Cyrus's twin sister

Elio [ee-lee-o]
Solin; member of the Inner Circle

Emily Dunlin [em-eh-lee done-lyn]
Elara's adoptive mother

Helen [hell-lun]
Solin; Idalia's mother

Holmes [homz]
Lunin; member of the Inner Circle

Iah [eye-uh]
Lunin; retired doctor; Orion's father

Idalia [ih-doll-yah]

Solin; daughter of Helen

Inan [eh-nahn]
Solin; Collector (Active Member)

Ishan [ih-shahn]
Solin; member of the Inner Circle

Janus [jan-us]
Lunin; ex-Collector

Jax [jax]
Lunin; Seeker; former leader of the Inner Circle; son of Aelius and Kyra; Zenith's adoptive son

Jericho [jerr-ih-co]
Lunin; member of the Inner Circle

Julie Lofton [joo-lee loft-ten]
Cyrus's adoptive mother

Kyra [kye-ruh]
Solin; Jax's biological mother

Levant [luh-vaant]
Solin; member of the Inner Circle

Lilith [lil-ith]
Lunin; Pollux's mother

Nash [nash]
Lunin; master craftsman

Oberon [o-buh-rawn]

Lunin; member of the Inner Circle

Oriana [or-ee-ana]
Solin

Orion [o-rye-un]
Lunin; son of Iah

Phoebus [fee-bus]
Solin

Pollux [paw-lux]
Lunin; unspoken leader of the Inner Circle; son of Castor and Lilith

Ravi [rah-v]
Solin; member of the Inner Circle

Rigel [rye-guhl]
Lunin

Roger Dunlin [rah-jur done-lyn]
Elara's adoptive father

Roshan [row-shaan]
Solin

Samson [sam-son]
Solin; ex-Collector

Saros [sar-ose]
Solin; the first Seeker; Arun's advisor

Sharik [sha-reek]

Solin; Aarush's father

Stella [stell-uh]
Lunin; Pollux's sister; daughter of Castor and Lilith

Surya [sur-yuh]
Solin; ex-Collector (Inactive Member)

Taurus [tar-us]
Lunin; doctor; Arun's advisor before Saros; Zenith's adoptive father

Thea [the-ah]
Solin

Zenith [zee-nith]
Half Solin/Half Lunin; leader of Aroonyx; Jax's adoptive father

PART I

SEARCHING FOR THE LIGHT

1

LIFE ON REPEAT

My body sank deeper with each pained breath, the soft mattress mocking me with the comfort I refused to feel. Like an extra pair of fingers, my eyes traced the cracks in the black wooden ceiling. Jagged and unforgiving, the deep grooves grew wider at each intersection, then shrunk in size, fading in the labyrinth. Irritated that the convoluted map had no beginning and no end, I shifted my gaze to the morning light that seeped through the bedroom window.

Shimmering in the ginger glow, tiny dust particles twirled in an elegant dance—a waltz between two beings who moved with a purpose, an unspoken passion. Jealous of the simple beauty and frustrated with the hidden truth in nature's metaphor, I rolled onto my side and collected the black strands of hair from underneath my neck.

My pulse thumped in my ears while my eyes burned a hole in the wooden door—side effects from playing the devastating mind game of rationalization. Each morning I woke up in a cold sweat, and when my eyes shot open, only one thought crossed my mind: *how in the hell did I end up here?*

Over six weeks had passed since Jax, our guide, our friend, my first love, abandoned us on that fateful afternoon. Six long, agonizing weeks that spun in endless circles of grief, uncertainty, and mind-numbing repetition. The first few days of the Lunin's absence ripped the emotional rug right out from underneath me. This time, I found it more challenging to grieve the loss of Jax because unlike before when Pollux captured him, he had a choice, and he chose to leave us . . . he *chose* to leave me.

I pulled the comforter over my shoulder, gathered the gray material near my aching heart, and let out a deep sigh; the image of Jax's cold and defeated expression the day he walked out of Iah's flashed in my mind. I thought about him constantly, wondering if Pollux and the rest of the Inner Circle had captured him once more. *Does he ever think about me or regret abandoning us on Aroonyx? No, probably not. Jax made his feelings obvious that afternoon when he told me to stay the hell away from him.*

Forcing the emotional discomfort into a darkened room of my mind, I shut my eyes. They stung like hell, not from unshed tears but from the mental exhaustion I couldn't shake, regardless of how many hours I logged in dreamland.

Each afternoon I walked alone through the woods around the small residence we now called home, desperate to free myself from Jax's tight hold. These *therapy* sessions lasted until his piercing blue eyes crept into my mind, an unsubtle reminder of another failed attempt.

Jax had attached himself into the depth of my being like a fish hook I couldn't release. I wanted to rid myself of the dull ache, rip it out and let the wound heal, but with each frantic tug the barbed hook dug itself deeper into my heart.

Cyrus, my overly optimistic twin, reminded me that *Time has the power to heal* and *You must stay strong for what lies ahead.* Curious if the saying, "fake it 'till you make it" worked under the circumstance, I always nodded with an unnatural smile plastered on my face anytime he shared advice. Even his practical words couldn't ease my troubled mind. His encouragements fell on deaf ears.

I missed my old friend, the relaxed and humorous brother I knew so well. The one person in my life I counted on to help me see the challenging situations differently. This *new* Cyrus was foreign and impossible to relate to on an emotional level. A seriousness and unwavering dedication overpowered his casual and easy-going personality. The Solin spent so much time focused on our combative training that even him smiling or laughing seemed out of the question.

After Jax left, the two of us sat on the front porch in the freezing weather, grieving the loss of our adoptive parents on Earth. We wanted to say *I love you* one last time and apologize for lying about our military ruse. We *needed* to tell them the truth: No, we never joined the Navy or the Coast Guard and no, we weren't attending A School on a base in Mississippi or California. We were living on another planet—Aroonyx, our place of birth—and had struggled to survive ever since our arrival. Why? Because at the end of our senior year of high school we left everything behind and risked our lives to help free the people of Aroonyx. We had trusted Jax, took a leap of faith, and jumped, *literally*, into the unknown. *A lot of good that did.*

I exhaled a tired breath. Aroonyx was our home now, and we had no choice but to move forward. Otherwise, we would sink into a slippery pit of despair and never climb out.

The worry lines on my face softened as I stretched my neck to look over the side of the bed. Orion slept on the hardwood floor with his forearm draped over his eyes to block out the sunlight, his chest rising and falling with slow, relaxed breaths.

After Jax's departure, Cyrus moved into the vacant room down the hallway because I refused to sleep in the dreaded space. Orion stumbled over his words when he suggested I sleep in his bed, and Cyrus nearly choked on his spit as he listened to the Lunin's offer.

Quick to recover, Orion had said, "I'm too tall to sleep on the couch, so the bedroom floor seems like a practical option."

Cyrus shot him a warning glare, and Orion returned the gesture with a subtle head nod, refusing to argue with my over-protective brother.

I scooted closer to the edge and re-situated my head on the cool pillow, my eyes never leaving the Lunin. His visible eyelid twitched and flickered with signs of deep sleep. A thin quilt covered the lower half of his body, but my damn eyes insisted on wandering to the thin strip of exposed flesh just below his abdomen. With a silent curse, I directed my attention back to the sharp lines of his jaw.

After days of dragging my feet around the house like a lost soul, depressed and stuck in limbo, I confided in Orion and shared vague details about my romantic history with Jax.

He had listened to every word, then took my hands into his and whispered, "I understand. I'll be your friend or whatever you need me to be."

His confidence and raw honesty loosened the tight chains Jax had forged around my heart. Orion hid an underlying message behind his words, but I refused to acknowledge it. I couldn't let go of Jax—not yet.

Orion kept the promise he made, staying dedicated to our mission of defeating Zenith—the crazed dictator of Aroonyx. The Lunin had excelled with his combative training, kept the mood light, and informed us of any news or rumors during his visits to the villages. Every week Orion stopped by Idalia's pub, giving her an updated progress report about our training so she could relay it to Samson, our grumpy mentor, and every week the Lunin returned with a folded letter addressed to Cyrus. My brother spent hours on the porch, reading her cursive lettering until the ink smudged his fingers. After absorbing every thought and sentiment, he'd hide in his room and craft a lengthy reply. Orion accepted his role as the mail carrier and never complained when my brother handed him a letter with Idalia's name scribbled on the front.

Our simple life on Aroonyx had dragged by in slow motion. At times, I wondered if someone had stolen our life's remote and played a cruel joke by pressing the repeat button. Defeating Zenith without Jax's guidance seemed like a lost cause, if not a death wish. With each passing day, I struggled through the motions of life, a never-ending cycle of trudging through a mental quicksand that would pull me deeper if I tried to climb out.

"Morning."

Orion's quiet voice distracted me from my troubled thoughts. I flashed him a warm grin.

Yawning, he stretched his toned arms, then tucked his hands behind his head while meeting my gaze. "Did you sleep well?"

I nodded. A lie, but easier to do with body language rather than words. Orion winced as he sat up.

"Still sore?" I asked.

"Very." He massaged his right bicep. "Does it ever go away?"

I tossed off the covers and slid onto the floor beside him. "Eventually." I pointed at the blue and purple marks that ran down his neck, evidence of Cyrus's grueling chokehold technique. "Along with the bruising."

"Good to know," he muttered, stretching to touch his toes. "So what exciting and grueling combative exercises will you and Cyrus be teaching me today?"

My lips moved near his ear while I used his shoulder as a crutch to help me stand. "Ground holds, my favorite."

He stifled a groan that stemmed from either my comment or his sore muscles protesting my tight grip. I chuckled, helping him to his feet.

7

Cyrus knocked while opening the bedroom door, causing our heads to turn. I rolled my eyes at his less-than-casual way of greeting.

Dressed for the day, dark gray shorts covered his muscular thighs and a khaki-colored shirt hugged his biceps. Through tiny slits, his amber eyes scanned the two of us. I dropped Orion's hand as if my father had walked into my bedroom back on Earth and found me making out with a boy.

"I'm going to grab some breakfast." Cyrus met my gaze. His tone was sharp and direct. "Meet me out front whenever you're . . . done."

I scoffed, shaking my head at his behavior. Ignoring me, he turned and exited the room, leaving the door open behind him.

Orion's lips formed a tight line as he walked toward his closet. "Is it just me, or do you think this will be a *very* long day?"

"Every day's a long day."

Orion removed his shirt. Unsure how to handle the desire and guilt that surfaced, I swallowed, and even though his back faced me, I averted my eyes. *My damn eyes.* Disregarding my silent plea, they wandered to his perfected physique. Taller and leaner than Jax, but equally attractive, the muscles in Orion's back flexed as he slipped his arms into his shirt. He rotated to face me and adjusted the gray fabric over his chiseled abdomen, then paused, noting my gaped mouth. Embarrassed that he caught me staring, I stood on my toes and peered out the window. The quiet laughter rattling in his throat confirmed my horrible attempt at checking the weather.

"You watched me take off my shirt?" Not a question—an accusation.

Yes, and I enjoyed it. "No, of course not."

"Liar. You were totally checking me out and your red cheeks prove it."

I covered the evidence. "Okay, fine." Speaking through the

cracks of my fingers I added, "I may have glanced in your general vicinity."

"Glanced?"

"Looked, glanced, they're interchangeable words. I just wanted to make sure you didn't have any new bruises from training."

"How thoughtful of you," he teased, strolling toward me.

My heart thumped louder with each creak of the aged floorboards, and it skipped a beat when he pulled my hands away from my reddened face. Refusing to meet his gaze, I stared at the bedroom door out of the corner of my eye.

"Now"—he leaned closer, his warm breath grazing my ear—"I need to finish getting dressed. You are more than welcome to hang out and continue searching my body for bruises and other injuries, but full disclosure, I need to take off my pants."

Witty bastard. I pushed him away. "Are you pleased with yourself?"

A sly smile played on his lips. "A bit."

"Well, as enticing as your offer sounds, I'll pass."

The Lunin laughed, watching me step over the threshold. "Good thing there's always tomorrow."

I waved him away and ambled down the hallway to retrieve a fresh change of clothes from Cyrus's room. Once inside, my relaxed posture went rigid.

I hated that room. It only reminded me of the day we rescued Jax from Zenith's and how his lifeless body resembled a corpse in a morgue. I choked on a lump of grief that formed in my throat while eyeing the stains on the wooden floors. Blood. So much of it had splattered those who helped the injured Lunin that morning. I shuddered a breath, recalling the sickening noise the pump made as Iah emptied the contents of Jax's stomach and the foul smell that wafted into my nose once he administered the Minlav antidote. I grimaced at the image of the black vomit pouring out of Jax's mouth onto my brother's face. It was burned into my mind, along with the needle that broke inside the Lunin's chest and the corkscrew that Iah used to drill a hole into his skull.

I eyed the wall on the other side of the room. The same wall where the ex-Collector tried to kill me with his bare hands. I would have died that night had Cyrus not come to my aid. I'll never forget the way Jax's heartless eyes stared right through me as if I didn't exist and the cruel words he spat that would haunt me forever. *And now you're going to pay . . . for your crimes against me.*

I dashed to the closet and grabbed a pair of shorts and a sleeveless shirt before sprinting to the washroom, the disturbing memories chasing me the entire way.

WITHOUT A MIRROR AS A DISTRACTION, my morning routine flew by in half the time it did on Earth. It's strange how easily a reflection is taken for granted. After dressing, I secured my shoulder-length hair into a low ponytail before heading into the kitchen. The smell of aromatic herbs and fresh bread engulfed my senses as I rounded the corner.

"Iah, you don't have to keep doing this," I said, motioning to the mouthwatering offerings displayed on the table.

He added a basket of rolls to the small feast. "I know, but the house got so quiet after Orion's mom passed. It's nice to hear it buzzing with life again." The age lines around his blue eyes creased as he touched my shoulder. "I'm glad you're here, Elara. It warms my heart to see my son happy again."

"It's nice to be here. Cyrus and I can't thank you enough for letting us hide out until we figure out a plan."

"It's the least I could do after . . . " His voice trailed off. He shifted his gaze to the living room windows.

"Iah, please don't start that again. None of this is your fault.

You didn't know Cressida would tell Zenith about our births, and you sure as hell couldn't predict he would send the Collectors to murder us because we were born during a bi-lunar eclipse. You did nothing wrong. Don't carry that burden."

The doctor forced a smile before walking back into the kitchen. Unwilling to press the touchy subject, I remained quiet and piled my plate with food, my eyes darting around the living room. "Where's my brother?"

"Out on the porch," the Lunin answered, keeping his attention focused on the dull knife he used to slice through a vegetable that resembled a purple carrot.

Uncomfortable with the tension in his voice, I stood and carried my plate through the living room. The summer heat stung my face when I opened the front door. Using my forearm as a visor, I made my way to the chair beside my brother.

An empty plate rested near his feet. Quiet and focused, this new, and not so improved, Cyrus drove me mad. A sigh slipped through my pursed lips as I lowered myself onto the wooden seat, the worn slats creaking under my weight. Out of my peripheral vision, I noticed the Solin's fingers fidgeting with the tattered gray edges of a piece of paper, his eyes following the cursive lettering.

Poking the bear, I asked, "Any juicy gossip in love letter number three?"

Ignoring me, he finished reading the lengthy note, leaned forward, and slipped it into his back pocket. Frustrated that my appetite had vanished, I dropped the roll onto my plate and leaned my head against the back of the chair. The emerald leaves of the majestic trees remained motionless, the usual breeze absent from around us.

My nostrils flared. Awkward silences always chapped my ass. I looked at my brother. "When are you going to lighten up?" More silence. "I've already lost Jax, and now . . . it's like I'm losing you too."

Hearing my voice crack, Cyrus rotated in his chair to face me. His amber eyes, once bright and confident, now dimmed with doubt. "Sorry, sis, I have a lot on my mind."

I squeezed his shoulder, reassuring him that vulnerability wasn't a sign of weakness. He nodded before directing his gaze back to the motionless trees.

My head turned. Orion had stepped onto the front porch. His white teeth glowed in the morning light as his lips spread into a wide grin. Adding to his performance, he adjusted his shirt in an exaggerated motion and topped it off with a wink. I shook my head in disapproval. *Great, he'll tease me for the rest of the day about checking him out this morning.*

Orion leaned against the paint chipped railing and stole a glance at Cyrus. "Elara told me you wanted to work on ground holds today."

No answer. My brother pressed his muscular forearms into his thighs and stared at the Clear Stone floor.

I gritted my teeth. *Why is there always so much silence?*

Kicking my brother's boot, I said, "Yes, Orion. Cyrus is looking forward to teaching you this lifesaving skill."

Snapped out of his trance, the Solin rose to his feet and strolled past Orion without a look in his direction. I returned the Lunin's wide-eyed expression with an apologetic shrug, then motioned for him to follow Cyrus down the stone steps of the front porch.

Our feet sank into the emerald grass, the morning dew evaporating into the warm air. In a matter of minutes, the sun's rays had transformed the color of my fair Lunin skin into a bright shade of pink while Cyrus's bronzed Solin complexion shimmered in the golden light.

Grateful for the gentle breeze that graced us with its presence, I inhaled the sweet summer air and watched the black tree limbs overhead. Intertwined with one another, they stretched and reached for the jade-colored sky, their star-shaped leaves decorating the forest with patches of shade.

Cyrus popped his neck and crossed his arms before addressing Orion. "Today we'll teach you how to escape a basic ground hold. It's an easy maneuver to master if you stay relaxed and use your head."

I snickered. My brother's voice echoed Samson's, our combative advisor. Prepared to continue his training, Orion straightened.

"Before I test you with a male Solin's strength, let's see if you can escape with Idalia holding you."

"Um . . . Cyrus." The corner of my mouth twitched with amusement. "The last time I checked my name was Elara."

His brows furrowed with confusion. "Whose name did I say?"

"Idalia's."

"I did?"

"Mm-hmm."

"Right." Taking a moment to regroup, Cyrus shut his eyes. "Orion, why don't you try escaping a ground hold with *Elara* restraining you?"

I wanted to tease him about the thoughts that occupied his mind, but I held my tongue after he gave me a stern look. Wiping the grin off my face, I moved in front of Orion and pointed to the grass. "Lie down."

His jaw cracked open, and he clutched his chest while stumbling backward. "I thought you'd never ask."

"Move your ass," I snapped.

"I like a woman who takes control."

"Oh, geez." I moved into the dominant position once he rolled onto his back. "Is this how you plan on acting today?"

"I was the perfect gentleman until you checked me out this morning. I'm the victim here."

"Do you practice this shit in your head before saying it?" I asked, pinning his arms beside him while locking my legs around his hips.

"No, I'm just that smooth."

I hissed at his playful banter.

Unamused by our flirtation, Cyrus cleared his throat. "Here's what you need to learn if you want to escape a ground hold. Think of your attacker as a table with four legs. To make the table collapse, you must remove a leg, so start by sliding your right arm above your head."

I loosened my grip, allowing Orion to practice the motions while Cyrus continued his lesson.

"See." My brother jerked his chin at me when I lost my balance. "You eliminated one of the table legs. Now I want you to tap your right foot and lift your left hip. This gives you two options: escape by pushing off your attacker or flip them onto their back and move into the dominant position. Got it?"

"I think so." Orion demonstrated the steps once more. "Slide my arm, lift my hip . . . yeah, I got it."

Cyrus crossed his arms. "Okay, then let's see you escape the ground hold. Elara, don't hold back."

Sharing my brother's Solin strength, I pushed Orion's wrists deeper into the grass and squeezed my thighs around his hips. As instructed, the Lunin slid his right arm above his head, which forced me closer. Familiar with the combative exercise, I prepared myself for the next crucial part of the escape attempt by contracting my muscles. Orion tapped his foot and lifted his hip. I chuckled; my shared Solin strength had rendered him helpless.

"Not fair." He blew the stray hair that had fallen from my ponytail out of his eyes. "You cheated."

"Zenith and his Collectors won't play fair, so why should I?"

Orion glared, but the hard lines around his eyes softened. "Well, aren't you full of surprises?"

"Oh, you have no idea."

Cyrus cleared his throat for the second time that morning, redirecting our focus back to the training exercise. "You now have a firsthand account of what it's like for a Solin to restrain you in a ground hold. At night all bets are off, but during the day you'll want to avoid getting yourself into this situation. It's possible for a Lunin to escape a Solin during the day—*if* you keep a clear head. You can't react blindly to a situation. If you do, you'll end up dead."

Orion cringed. My brother's words had dampened his casual mood.

"Try closing your eyes," Cyrus suggested, "and sense how Elara's muscles react to yours. If they relax, take that opportunity and use it to your advantage."

Heeding my brother's advice, Orion squeezed his eyes shut. The tension in his forearms loosened and his fists uncurled. Even his pulse slowed, the steady rhythm thumping in the main artery of his wrist.

Distracted by the handsome features of his face, my thoughts drifted from the training exercise. With our noses almost touching, I couldn't help but admire his flawless skin, his chiseled jaw, and the way his jet-black hair danced in the gentle breeze.

Orion's eyes shot open, jolting my curious mind back to reality. Surprised, I struggled to tighten my grip. Using this to his advantage, he executed the escape attempt with minimal effort, and a heartbeat later, he rolled me onto my back, reversing our positions.

A smug grin crossed his face. "Who's full of surprises now?"

I mirrored Orion's escape attempt, our rolling bodies almost colliding with my brother.

"You still have a lot to learn," I said, resuming the assertive position. "Have you had enough?"

Orion locked his sapphire eyes onto mine, and in a calm

and confident voice, he whispered, "No, I could do this all day with you."

I gasped as Jax's face appeared. Orion's words didn't bother me, but the meaning behind them unraveled me. I stilled. The unspoken desire I had for the Lunin disrupted Jax's tight hold. His hidden message snapped one of the chains that bound my fragile heart.

I swore. Feeling more vulnerable than ever, I second-guessed my intentions, wondering if any pureness remained. I scrambled to my feet. Orion lay motionless with his brows touching his hairline. I struggled to breathe, the humid air suffocating me.

Watching me with curious eyes, Cyrus tilted his head. Orion pushed himself off the ground, equally confused by my alarming reaction.

"Elara, what's wrong?" A hint of concern lingered in my brother's voice.

My eyes stayed fixed on the Lunin. *Damn it. Something's changed. Something I'm not willing to face.*

Cyrus moved closer. "Elara, what is it?"

Silence. More unnerving silence, only this time I initiated the madness.

My brother's eyes narrowed at Orion before finding my own. "What the hell is going on, sis?" He wiggled his fingers in front of my vacant expression. "It's like your mind is some-where else."

"It is."

He tossed up his hands. "Well, where is it?"

"The future—and it scares the shit out of me."

2

MIND GAMES

My brother called my name. I didn't bother turning around, but instead kept running.

Short minutes passed before the burning stitch in my side slowed my quick pace to a jog. I scowled at my lack of endurance, a stark contrast to my nightly Lunin stamina. Gripping my aching side, I compelled my feet to move forward.

Quick breaths entered my lungs as I observed the secluded spring. *What is happening to me?* Surrendering, I collapsed onto my knees. Unshed tears stung my eyes when the answer zapped me. *Orion, that's what's happening.*

I rubbed my chest, the invisible chains shifting, loosening around my heart. A salty drop of emotion glided off my cheek. Even though every part of my being screamed, *No, don't do it.* I knew what needed to be done. I needed to let go of Jax.

As if the swaying tree branches had convinced him to abandon me that day, I looked up and yelled, "Why? Why did you do this to me?"

Silence, save for the rustling leaves.

Defeated, I fell onto my back and draped an arm over my

17

eyes to block out the light. I needed a cave. A dark and damp cave to find solace. Not a bright and beautiful spring that resembled the set of a charming romantic film.

I held my breath, hearing feet shuffle nearby. Someone was watching me, and my skin didn't prickle with warmth, so I crossed Cyrus off the list. Intrigued, I sat up.

My eyes scanned the wooded area that surrounded the spring. I nearly choked on my spit. A man stood near a cluster of trees. Memories of a specific night on Earth flooded my mind. *No, it can't be.*

The Lunin stood with his arms resting by his sides, the leaves overhead shading the scars on his pale complexion. My pulse raced. The gentle breeze blew the jet-black hair out of his piercing blue eyes. The loose chains around my heart tightened, for there in broad daylight stood Jax.

I looked down and patted my body to make sure it hadn't disappeared. Relieved to see each part accounted for, I lifted my head and blinked. Jax had vanished.

I shouted his name and scrambled to my feet.

Lacking Cyrus's powerful Solin vision, I strained my eyes, searching every tree in sight. *Did he jump back to Earth?* I spun in circles, my heart beating faster with each rotation. *No, I didn't hear that strange popping noise before he appeared. He has to be around here somewhere.*

"Jax?"

"Elara."

I flinched at the sound of my brother's deep voice. He tossed up his hands in a *what are you doing* motion while jogging toward me. I shook my head, matching his gesture.

As he approached, my skin surged with heat and my eyesight improved, side effects of our unique connection. I searched the area once more, my pupils dilating at the sun's intense rays. When in proximity to Cyrus, my vision exploded with a multitude of colors, and objects appeared closer. I saw the grooves on the smooth tree bark, the veins on the massive leaves, even the fine blades of grass that danced around the spring.

Cyrus frowned as he watched me share his Solin traits out of desperation.

He motioned to the vast space. "Elara, what are you doing out here? First, you bail on our training exercise, and now you're running in circles by yourself in the woods."

"I'm not running in circles for my entertainment. I saw Jax."

He paled, his blond head turning every which way. "Are you sure?"

"Yes." I pointed to the grassy area around our feet. "He was standing right here."

The Solin surveyed the area once more before dragging a hand through his hair. "Well, he's not here now."

"No shit, genius. Why do you think I'm running in circles? I was sitting by the spring, and when I looked up Jax was standing here and then he disappeared."

Cyrus touched my shoulder. "Maybe you just thought he was standing here."

I wanted to punch him in the face for verbalizing such an idiotic suggestion. Slapping his hand away, I said, "What? Like how I imagined him standing outside my bedroom window on Earth?"

"I didn't mean it like that. I only said it because you looked pretty pissed when you ran off back there, and you always let your emotions cloud your better judgment. It's not unusual to imagine things if you're upset or—"

"Wow. I see how it is. Jax left, so you took over the role of intuition master. Thank you, Cyrus, for the lengthy psycho-analysis of my current emotional state. I know what I saw and—"

"Don't jump my ass. I don't have to *intuit* the obvious, Elara. You can't stop thinking about Jax. Your thoughts consume you from sunup to sundown. Hell, half the time you walk around Iah's like a damn ghost. You better pull yourself together before you drift too far and can't get back."

My fingers curled in muted rage. I hated listening to his honest words, but even more so I hated my lack of willingness to accept the truth. Not wanting to discuss it any further, I calmed my anger and said, "Regardless of how you look at me, I know I'm not crazy. I saw Jax standing here, just as you are now."

"Fine."

His voice was calm, too calm. Cyrus's way of warning me that he would circle back to the root of my problem.

"If you're so confident you saw Jax, then where is he?" He paused, his eyes growing. "Wait. Did he jump?"

"No, I didn't hear that popping noise before he showed up, and you were there when he tried taking us back to Earth."

A flicker of grief flashed in Cyrus's eyes. "Yeah, how could I forget?"

I met his gaze. The two of us refused to discuss the day we returned to Aroonyx. The day Jax confirmed he could no longer jump to Earth. A temporary glitch—something out of his control, that's what he called it. The Lunin had the utmost confidence he could take us home once we defeated Zenith. He based this awareness on a "feeling," the intuitive knowingness of a Seeker. My jaw slammed shut. *Damn Jax, and damn his stupid feelings.*

"I don't know what to tell you, sis. After living on Aroonyx for this long, nothing surprises me anymore. Jax isn't here, so let's head back to Iah's."

"I don't want to train right now. I need a break from—"

"Orion's gone." Noting my posture tense, he added, "He left to give our weekly report to Idalia."

"Right . . . of course he did."

Not buying my tough girl façade, Cyrus lowered his gaze

and found my eyes. "Are you ready to come clean and tell me why you won't let go of Jax?"

My throat bobbed. His question didn't rattle my emotional shield; it shattered it into a million pieces. Taking off the mask I hid behind during those long weeks, I pointed toward Iah's and spent the rest of the morning sharing the thoughts that haunted my mind. I told Cyrus everything. I told him about the chains that crushed my heart each time I thought of Jax, the intense desire that surfaced when I hung out with Orion, and I even shared the unnecessary guilt I harbored because of it all.

Cyrus nodded and murmured, "I understand," or "I hear ya, sis," every so often.

We sat in silence after my long-winded rant about the personal challenges I faced while living on Aroonyx; the only noise came from the tree limbs fighting in the summer breeze.

I fluttered my lashes, trying to remove a stray hair that blew into my face. *Why does everything take so much effort these days?* The thought of lifting my arm to perform the simple task sounded exhausting, so I blew out a quick breath to remove the unwanted strand.

My brother's voice disrupted the surrounding stillness. "Elara, I'm not qualified to give advice on matters of the heart, but let me ask you this: do you want to be happy?"

No, I want live in an emotional hell for the rest of my life. "Yes, I want to be happy."

"You thought being with Jax would make you happy."

I nodded, sliding the black hair tie off my ponytail.

"But that didn't work out, did it?"

I gritted my teeth. *Obviously.*

"So you thought maybe Orion could make you happy. Am I right?"

"Perhaps."

"But that's not working out for you either. You're still unhappy."

"Thank you for the astute observation, Cyrus. You are quite the detective."

He rolled his eyes, brushing off my verbal jab.

"Attention everyone," I called, addressing the imaginary crowd before us. "Cyrus Lofton has cracked the case and discovered the hidden truth. His sister, Elara Dunlin is *not* happy."

Cyrus let out a hearty laugh. The natural reaction wasn't fake or forced. I met his gaze and smiled. *There he is.* A silver lining shone through the haze of doubt that clouded his eyes.

"You have a sharp mind, sis." His elated expression dissolved. "So I don't know why you're missing the point I'm trying to make."

"I'm not. I get it. Jax couldn't make me happy and neither can Orion." *Or can he?*

My brother groaned, dropping his head. "This is what I'm talking about. You're convinced that happiness depends on someone or something outside of yourself."

"How else am I supposed to see it? Jax left us, Cyrus. He abandoned me and took my heart with him."

"I'm aware that's how it appears, but that's not the truth."

My brows raised.

"Elara, you're missing the obvious. We create an idea of how a person should act and hold them to it. If that person falters, we get angry because they no longer fit the mold we created. Are you following me?"

"I'm trying."

Cyrus stood and scooted his chair closer to mine, then adjusted his shirt before taking a seat. "Let's use you and Jax as an example. Why do you get upset when you think about him?"

A snicker got caught in my throat. "We might be here for a while if you want me to read the entire list."

"Then just tell me a few things that really piss you off."

"Let's see, Jax promised he'd never leave us alone to fight

Zenith, but bailed and broke my heart, and he isn't the same person he was that night on the cliffside before Pollux and the others captured him."

Cyrus slammed his palm on the armrest of his chair. "There it is," he snapped.

Oh boy, the detective's back.

"Did you hear it?"

I shook my head.

"You're angry because Jax isn't the same person he was that night on the cliffside. And this proves my theory. You created an image, a role you wanted Jax to play in your life. The physical and emotional trauma he went through at Zenith's changed him in more ways than one. When Jax woke up here at Iah's, he acted differently than he did that night on the cliff and no longer fit the role you wanted him to play."

Don't say it. Please don't say it.

"And because of this . . ."

Shit. He's going to say it.

"You gave up on him, Elara. You gave up on the man you love because he couldn't meet the emotional requirements you demanded."

I winced. Cyrus's brutal but honest words sliced through me. I touched my chest, searching for the invisible weapon.

He's right. He's right about everything. I fell into a trap and didn't even notice. I thought my level of happiness depended on Jax being in my life. I do love him. Correction. I love the person I want him to be, not the person he is. Conditions, so many strict conditions. If Jax had kept his promise and never left but stayed trapped in the mental hell that tormented him, I still wouldn't be happy.

"You get it now, don't you?" Cyrus asked.

"I'm starting to."

"Then let me break it down for you, sis. Loving someone unconditionally means you love them no matter what, regardless of the choices they make."

I blinked hard while processing the simple but jarring realization. Shifting my weight, I looked at Cyrus. "Everything you said makes sense, it really does. My love for Jax is filled with conditions, and yes, I gave up on him that day, but only after he walked away."

"I told you he needed more time, but you were so quick to write him off."

Anger surged through me. "Are you *fucking* kidding me right now? You were there that day. You saw me standing in the snow, begging him to stay. Should I have gotten on my knees?"

"No, but you—"

"I tried telling him that the jaded person he hid behind wasn't him. I told Jax to stop lying to himself and to let go of his past, but he refused." I pressed on, my voice rising with each word that flew out of my mouth. "No, he wasn't the man I wanted him to be that day, but I was willing to let go of that image. I was willing to work through the madness that festered inside him. I was willing to do it because" . . . *Don't cry. Don't cry. You've shed too many tears for Jax* . . . "because I love him."

I tried to wipe the tear that rolled down my cheek, but Cyrus blocked my efforts and brushed it away with his thumb.

"And I love him enough to let him go," I whispered, staring at the black trees.

Cyrus squeezed my hand. "This is part of the reason I haven't been acting like myself lately. I hate watching you wander around Iah's stuck in a trance."

"You're one to talk. Would it kill you to smile now and then?"

He squeezed my hand once more and let out a deep sigh. "I know, I'm working on it. Orion is another reason . . ." His voice trailed off as he scanned the wooded area.

Curious, I followed his gaze. Orion's arms swung by his sides, and his feet appeared to glide over the emerald grass as he made his way toward the small home. Sharing Cyrus's Solin eyesight, I observed the man who walked beside him. *Well, it's about time.*

My lips curled into a grin as I watched the grumpy Solin stomp through the woods. With each determined step, the age lines on his tan forehead deepened. The ex-Collector didn't bother shielding his eyes from the late afternoon sun. He had experienced worse pain than the sting of blinding light in his challenging lifetime.

I eyed Cyrus. Not wanting to delay our reunion, we hopped to our feet and bounded down the porch steps. I sprinted past Orion and threw my arms around the Solin's muscular neck. The coarse hairs of his silver beard brushed against my cheek.

"What are you doing here?" I asked, finding his burnt-orange eyes.

"I had to make sure you kids weren't getting soft in your training after hiding out in these damn woods for so long."

My brother grinned while extending his hand. "It's good to see you, Samson."

"Likewise, Cyrus."

I counted to three before my brother asked, "How's Idalia?"

"She's good and sends her love." He winked at the eager Solin. "To the both of you."

Cyrus's face lit up with joy. *Was that three smiles in one day?*

Orion batted his blue eyes and slipped a hand underneath his shirt, thumping it in an exaggerated motion. Though I appreciated his accurate impression of my brother's love-struck reaction, I gave him a stern look. *Cyrus will kick your ass if he catches you teasing him.*

Acknowledging my silent warning, the Lunin hid his arms behind his back.

Wondering why Orion never mentioned Samson, I asked, "How long have you guys known each other?"

The ex-Collector shrugged. "Not long. We met a few hours ago at the pub. Callisto is usually on shift when Orion drops by to give Ida the weekly report. I was there today, so I thought I'd come along and give you the news in person."

My heart sank, recalling the grim story about the man Zenith freed after a week of torture. Unfortunately, the accused stayed imprisoned in his troubled mind. Unable to face his inner demons, the Solin ended his life by jumping off the cliffside; the jagged rocks sealed his fate.

My voice cracked. "Is it Jax?"

"No, honey." Samson twisted the white hairs on his chin into a cone. "It's not Jax."

My shoulders sagged with relief.

"Then what's the news?" Cyrus asked.

Ignoring my brother, the ex-Collector jerked his chin at Iah's. "We better go inside."

Orion moved forward at a guarded pace while my brother and I trailed behind. Something had happened—something bad. I could sense it.

I retied my ponytail and adjusted the damp shirt that clung to my sweat-lined torso. My brother rolled his shoulders and popped his neck, physical and mental preparations for our impromptu meeting.

I leaned closer as we headed up the steps of the front porch. "Why does it feel like Samson's about to toss us a live grenade?"

Cyrus huffed a breath and held open the door. "Because that's what he does."

I groaned, walking past him.

"Remember, Elara, Aroonyx is our home now. Living a normal life is no longer an option."

3

THE RIPPLE EFFECT

Samson wedged his broad shoulders between the high-back armchair while the rest of us gathered around him in the living room. My brother and I sat on the couch like soldiers awaiting time sensitive orders: our spines straight and eyes focused. Iah and Orion maintained relaxed postures as they dragged two chairs from the kitchen.

The heel of my boot tapped the wooden floors in a steady rhythm. *Come on, just tell us the news.* I tried fanning my shirt, but the sticky layer of sweat disrupted my efforts, and brushing elbows with Cyrus only intensified the heat that rushed through me.

Samson reached for the mug on the coffee table. Taking his sweet time, he lifted the silver rim to his mouth and drained half of the liquid in one long swig.

His calloused fingers tightened around the handle, and his eyes flickered between me and Cyrus. "I'm not one for small talk." The mug clinked on the table when it fell from his hand. "So let me give it to you straight. Zenith's telling everyone you're dead."

Slack-jawed, we stared at the Solin. Orion and Iah exchanged confused glances.

Speaking for us both, Cyrus asked, "Why?"

"Because you're a threat to his position."

A tiny smirk of satisfaction crossed my brother's face. I shook my head at him. *Now is not the time to celebrate.*

Samson observed our different reactions before redirecting his focus on me. "Whispers about a powerful twin scarring Elio's face are moving throughout the villages."

I looked at my brother. I didn't have to ask why grief clouded his eyes. His thoughts probably mirrored my own. I thought of Archer, the young Collector who acted as our guide the night we rescued Jax from Zenith's, and how he sacrificed himself to give us a head start—the head start I failed to take. My stomach knotted with anger and regret, the disturbing image of Pollux gutting the young Lunin stamped in my mind.

I shut my eyes. During our long walk to rescue Jax, Archer mentioned that Zenith and the other Collectors believed Elio lied about the "torch" I threw in his face the morning he, Apollo, and Ravi attacked us at the spring. The young Collector said *We knew he was lying because a torch doesn't leave a handprint burn on your face.* We suspected Zenith had made the connection and hearing these rumors confirmed our theory.

Samson leaned back in the chair. "Zenith can't risk losing face in front of the people, so he has every Collector spreading rumors involving the gory details of your deaths the night you challenged him at his dwelling, all while secretly searching the villages for your whereabouts."

Wiping the sweat from my palms, I said, "But we didn't challenge him at his dwelling. We went to rescue Jax. Hell, we never even saw Zenith."

Still sore we didn't ask his permission to save our friend, Samson's lips pursed. "I'm aware of this, Elara, and so is Zenith, but he planted the rumor of Jax's death while the two of you were hiding at Idalia's. Look at it from an outsider's perspective, a villager who believed the rumor. Why would the twins rescue Jax if he was already dead?"

"Oh," Cyrus said, "I guess that makes sense."

The ex-Collector shot my brother a sidelong glance. "Try to keep up. I don't have time to spell this shit out for you."

Iah and Orion remained silent. It appeared they wanted to stay out of the conversation.

Samson cleared his throat and cracked his knuckles before continuing. "Zenith can't go back on his word. In his eyes, the people need to believe Jax died a slow and painful death after his capture. The Collectors are telling everyone Zenith murdered the twins because they tried to avenge Jax's death. He wants to use you as an example and show the people what happens to those who defy his position. Death—a bloody and horrible death."

Orion shifted his weight on the wooden chair. I met his gaze and jerked my chin at Samson, encouraging him to speak his mind. *Go for it. Just be careful because he might bite.*

The Lunin straightened, and in a calm voice, he asked, "So what's our next move?"

As if Orion had asked Samson to share his feelings about the turbulent years he spent working as a Collector for Arun, the Solin's head turned, spite-filled daggers shooting out of his eyes. "What do you mean *our* next move?" He arched a wiry brow. "How in the hell does this affect you, kid?"

I cringed. *He bit. The grumpy bastard bit.*

Orion exhaled a quiet breath and Cyrus gave Iah an apologetic shrug. The doctor ignored my brother's gesture, the age lines on his pale face creasing with concern for his son's well-being.

Rushing to his aid, I said, "Samson, Orion's helping us out now that—" I paused, unable to finish the sentence.

"Now that what? Now that Jax is gone?"

My jaw clenched, the heat radiating down my arms.

"Easy, sis," Cyrus soothed.

Samson turned his attention back to Orion. "Those are big shoes to fill. And by the look of it"—he leaned forward and squinted at the Lunin's gray boots—"I'd say you're lacking in that department."

Orion winced at the ex-Collector's verbal jab, a hard right-hook to the gut. The doctor stilled. I elbowed my brother in the ribs after he snorted his approval of the low blow.

"Ow. That hurt."

"Good," I chided. "And if you keep acting like a jerk, I'll do it again, only harder. Orion's been working his ass off, training every day in the heat, sleeping on the floor, and dealing with your uptight attitude, all while acting as the mail carrier for you and Idalia."

An apology rolled off Cyrus's tongue before he looked at the other Solin in the room. "Samson, Orion offered to help us after Jax left."

I sighed. *Will hearing those words ever get easier?*

My brother paused, allowing me a moment to compose myself before adding, "We've spent every day going over the combative maneuvers you taught us. He'll be ready."

Samson's tongue clicked like an old grandfather clock magically set to determine one's fate. His eyes matched the ticking pattern, bouncing between me, Cyrus, and Orion. After agonizing seconds, the irritating sound ceased; his orange eyes fixed on the doctor's son.

"Do you realize what you're getting yourself into? Joining forces with these two leaves a bull's-eye on your back, a moving target for the Collectors to practice their aim. Becoming Elara and Cyrus's ally makes you a traitor, and we all know what Zenith does to traitors." Samson dragged a finger across his neck.

I gulped, but Orion showed no signs of fear or weakness.

"Are you willing to stand against Zenith and his Collectors? Are you willing to stare death in the face?"

"My son is fully capable of anything he puts his mind to," Iah said, squeezing Orion's shoulder.

A wave of heat surged through me as Cyrus observed the pride that shone in Iah's blue eyes. My heart ached for my twin brother. He never made amends with his adoptive father before he left Earth.

Samson faced the doctor. "Iah, it's nothing personal. I just need to make sure your son can handle the shit storm that's headed toward him if he joins our side."

"He can," I interjected, "and when the time comes, he'll face that storm head on."

The tension in Orion's jaw dissolved and gratitude flickered in his eyes. I smiled at the handsome Lunin. *You're welcome. Now fight back with that quick wit of yours.*

Orion sat taller. "Samson, I understand your concerns, and I respect your opinion, but perhaps you should get your eyes checked." He lifted his foot. "Because Jax and I wear the same size shoe."

Cyrus stifled the amusement that tried to escape. I bit my lip, and Iah shut his eyes. A low rumble sounded in Samson's chest as he rose to his feet. I gripped the couch cushion. *Oh shit. Here we go.*

"Years ago, when I worked for Arun—" the ex-Collector paused, slipping a hand into his back pocket. He then exposed the blade of his knife with a quick flick of his wrist. "I would have cut out someone's tongue if they used that sarcastic tone with me. Yes, I would have done it real slow. Dragged the sharp edge across the webbing of tissue underneath." Samson opened his mouth, lifted his tongue, and pointed the tip of his knife at the thick mass of tissue. He snickered at the Lunin's wide eyes. "And afterward, I would have stood there and laughed while they choked on their own blood."

I knocked my brother's elbow. Cyrus stood and prepared to play mediator. I leaned around him to get a better look. Orion didn't cower as Samson moved closer.

"I'm sure you know how long it takes for someone to bleed out." The Solin inclined his head at Iah. "Being the son of a doctor and all."

"Samson." Caution saturated Cyrus's words. "I don't think Orion meant to offend you." He met the Lunin's gaze. "Did you?"

"No, I was just trying to—"

"Prove a point?" the ex-Collector suggested, removing the dirt from underneath his nails with the tip of his blade. "By showing me the size of your balls?"

"Yep."

A large grin swept across Samson's face. He waved his knife at Orion. "Good answer, kid. You get to keep your tongue."

The Lunin melted into his chair. Iah mumbled inaudible words and pinched the bridge of his nose. Remembering Jax's unorthodox training methods, I glared at the Solin. *A test, it was all a stupid test.*

"You're a sick bastard," I said.

He chuckled, folding the blade back into the handle. "I had to make sure the kid wouldn't piss his pants if threatened."

Orion looked down, patting the dry area. "Good thing I have excellent bladder control. I would hate to embarrass myself in front of Zenith."

Cyrus's pearly teeth glowed as he collapsed onto the couch. I smiled, pleased that Orion could hold his own against the ex-Collector.

"And like Jax, you're braver than most Lunins," Samson said, clapping Orion on the back.

My chest tightened, the emotional chains acting as a vice grip around my heart.

Seeing my pained expression, Orion said, "Samson, we may

have our similarities, but I'm not Jax, and I have no intention of replacing him. I'll do whatever it takes to help Elara and Cyrus defeat Zenith, even if that means risking my life."

Cyrus nodded his approval. I forced a smile, though hidden grief stung my eyes.

Samson extended his hand to Orion. "Welcome to the team."

Without hesitation, he shook it firmly. Iah exhaled a long breath, the color returning to his pale face.

Samson directed his voice at Orion as he headed toward the armchair. "Now, to answer your question regarding our next move." The cushion sighed once he took a seat. "We play Zenith's little game."

My head snapped up. "How so?"

"We help spread the rumors, convince the people you're dead. Ida's doing her part by telling everyone at the bar."

"But why?" Cyrus asked.

Samson scowled at my brother. "Has living in these woods turned your brain to mush or are you just stupid?"

Cyrus shook his head at Orion, who tried muffling his laughter. Recovering, the Lunin cleared his throat and moved his gaze to Samson.

"Zenith's not an idiot. He's always ten steps ahead of everyone else. He's hoping that after hearing these rumors, you'll go marching into the villages and prove him wrong." My lips moved, but Samson cut me off. "Zenith wants the Collectors to capture you so he doesn't have to put forth any effort."

I eyed my brother. "Samson, maybe the woods have dulled my sharp mind too because I'm not following the new plan."

Cyrus nodded. "Me neither."

"Yeah, you lost me too," Orion added.

Dumbfounded, the ex-Collector cursed while staring at the ceiling.

Playing the devil's advocate, I said, "When Cyrus and I were living at Idalia's, you wanted to train us to defend ourselves against the Collectors so we could go into the villages and convince the people to join our side. Now you want us to hide in the woods while you convince everyone we're dead."

"Yes, that's right."

Defeated, I tossed up my hands. "So we're scratching the old plan?" More of a confirmation than a question.

The Solin nodded. "You will sit tight and wait for the rumors to spread. Let the citizens believe you made a grave mistake by challenging Zenith that night."

Iah watched Samson, the lines around his eyes deepening. I massaged my temples. *No wonder I stumbled to keep up with Jax. Samson, his old mentor, moves at the same pace.*

"Not falling into Zenith's trap will drive him mad. He knows you're alive, and he knows you rescued Jax. After a few weeks of silence and with no reports of you visiting the villages to discredit the rumors, Zenith will wonder if Jax took you back to Earth. The man is so paranoid and delusional that this concern will eat him alive. Are you still living on Aroonyx plotting against him, or did you jump to Earth hoping to avoid conflict?"

I rolled my stiff neck and adjusted my shorts underneath me. "How long are we staying at Iah's?"

"Two cycles of the seasons."

I did the math. Aroonyx had two seasons: summer and winter. Each lasted for three weeks. Two cycles equaled— twelve weeks. My jaw fell open. "You want us to hide for three months?"

"Yes," Samson snapped, matching my sharp tone. "This gives us time to let the rumors spread and allows you to continue your advanced combative training before we move forward with the next step."

I shook my head, recalling Jax's warning that night on the beach. "Samson, we've lived on Aroonyx for four months." I eyed my brother for backup. "Jax told us we had six months to defeat Zenith."

"He's gone, sis. None of that matters anymore."

"Thanks for the reminder, *bro*."

Cyrus rolled his eyes at the sarcasm that lingered in my tone. Iah and Orion stayed silent and Samson scanned my anxious face, his fingers playing with the coarse hairs of his beard.

"Elara, I don't know how Jax came up with that timeline." He glanced at my brother. "But Cyrus is right. The Seeker is no longer here. You need to accept the obvious: Aroonyx is your home now and sitting here bitching about it won't change a damn thing."

I wanted to throw my knife at Samson for his lack of sensitivity. His brutal words were a slap in the face, but regardless of the phantom pain that throbbed in my cheek, his no-nonsense approach was exactly what I needed to hear. For weeks, Cyrus and Orion had tiptoed around the touchy subject, afraid it would cause me emotional distress, but not Samson. He didn't have time for common courtesies.

Accepting my fate, I leaned forward, rested my head in my hands, and stared at the wooden floor. I let out a sharp breath. A large dust bunny near my feet rolled under the coffee table. I frowned, watching my tiny companion move farther away from me. *Are you leaving me too?* I could feel Orion's gaze upon me, but I refused to raise my head. *Not now. Let me finish wallowing in grief.*

"Elara."

With great reluctance, I lifted my eyes, and only my eyes, to acknowledge the ex-Collector.

"I base Jax's prediction on logistics."

Intrigued, my spine lengthened.

"If you had stayed living in the woods by the cliffside, running from the Collectors each time you visited the villages without a means to defend yourself, then yes, in six months, you'd be dead." Samson wagged his finger at us. "But Jax is clever. He knew exactly what he was doing by bringing you to Aroonyx. When you arrived, everything shifted. The ripple effect you started has touched the lives of many."

Unsure of how to respond, I nudged my brother, encouraging him to speak.

"Who cares if we made a small impact? Zenith won't step down."

"Cyrus, there are no small impacts in life. Everything happens for a reason. Patience. These things take time." Samson found my eyes. "Time you *both* now have."

I looked at Orion. He sat with his arms crossed, lost in thought. Cyrus yawned and stretched his arms overhead.

"I'm *sorry*." Samson kicked the coffee table, sending it flying into my brother's leg. "Am I boring you?"

The wooden corner slammed into Cyrus's shin, blood dripping from the deep gash. He scowled at the Solin. "Dude, that wasn't necessary."

"I'm not your dude, and yes—it was." Samson's orange eyes narrowed as he watched my brother wince at the small wound. "And when did you become such a pussy?"

A muscle feathered in Cyrus's jaw. I rolled my wrists, bothered by the fluctuating temperatures that mirrored our moods.

Hoping to ease the tension between the two Solins, Orion said, "So we stay here and keep training until the rumors settle."

"Yes, Orion, that's correct." Samson cracked his knuckles. "I'm glad one of you removed your head from your ass."

"I'll take that as a compliment," the Lunin murmured.

"Don't. It was an observation."

Orion flashed me a dramatic scared face. I couldn't help but laugh.

Samson shifted his gaze to the doctor. "Are you okay with the twins living here for a while longer?"

"Of course. They're always welcome."

"Good." The ex-Collector looked at my brother. "Now that Orion is part of the team, I want him learning more advanced combative maneuvers. It's crucial for his survival. I'll swing by every few days and train you myself so you're prepared for your new roles."

Speaking as one, my brother and I asked, "Which are?"

"Revolutionaries." Mischief twinkled in Samson's eyes. "The two of you are spearheading the uprising."

4

A CASUAL PROPOSAL

Shocked by Samson's bold affirmation, I tugged at my ear, wondering if I should get my hearing checked. *Revolutionaries? He's gone mad.*

A nervous laugh rattled in Orion's throat, but Iah sat motionless, stunned by the news.

Cyrus's eyes grew with uncertainty. He twisted his body to face me and mouthed, "What the *fuck?*"

I shrugged.

He then turned his head toward Samson, a wave of heat rushing through me. "How do we lead an uprising if everyone thinks we're dead?"

"After the rumors settle, I'll tell the people you're alive and stronger than ever, ready to stand against Zenith."

Dumbfounded, I said, "This makes no sense. You want the citizens of Aroonyx to think we're dead, only to tell them we're alive?"

"I don't have the patience to answer idiotic questions. It's obvious that living in the woods *has* made you stupid, am I right?"

No, asshole. It's made me practical.

Coming to my defense, Cyrus said, "Get off her ass, Samson. Elara brings up a good point. *You're* the one who isn't making any sense."

Samson slammed his palm on the coffee table. "Then let me spell it out for you."

I flinched. Orion and Iah scooted their chairs away from the angered Solin. Cyrus, the only one who didn't cave under pressure, didn't budge.

The ex-Collector inhaled a calming breath before continuing. "Zenith craves power, and his desire to control others is all-consuming. It's what he lives for. This is why we spread the rumors of your deaths and let them sink in before we make our next move. It's a mind game with this guy. Two cycles from now, everyone will think you're dead, and Zenith will have gone mad wondering what happened to the twins who escaped with Jax right underneath his nose."

My head bobbed, catching wind of the Solin's plan. Cyrus sat taller, his interest piqued.

"We need Zenith vulnerable. Therefore, we wait. Let him fester, and when he least expects it, you'll knock that bastard off his pedestal."

An unnerving silence moved through the room. Orion glanced in my direction; our blank expressions mirrored a shared uncertainty.

Samson observed the growing tension around him before saying, "When the citizens hear you're alive and willing to fight, a buzz will spread throughout the villages."

"But we thought Zenith and his Collectors terrified the people," Cyrus said. "Why would the citizens of Aroonyx risk their lives and join forces with us? We don't have an army of trained soldiers ready for battle."

"We don't—not yet at least." A hint of grief lingered in Samson's tone. "The citizens of Aroonyx live in fear. Uniting them to stand against Zenith won't be easy, but it can be done —it must."

I rolled my neck, the Solin's request weighing on my shoulders.

"The people will side with the team who has the better odds. Your job is to show them your unique abilities." Watching my nose crinkle, Samson added, "Yes, Zenith has his Collectors, but sharing both Solin and Lunin traits keeps the people in check. It's the reason they refuse to challenge his authority. Once the citizens see the little trick you used on Elio and on me"—he lifted his arm to show us the burn scar on his wrist —"everything will change. Remember what I said the morning we trained outside of Idalia's: The two of you are the perfect trifecta. You're younger than Zenith, more mysterious, and have the knowledge of Earth under your belts. You are the winning combination of what it takes to shatter his reign."

I blinked, baffled by his prediction. "Samson, I hear what you're saying, but there's no way the citizens of Aroonyx will join our side and risk their lives because I can release heat from my hand."

"Damn it, Elara. We've already been through this. I told you the reason the Collectors follow him. Should I share more gruesome stories from my dark past as a Collector?"

I shook my head.

"The citizens are exhausted. For the last sixteen years, a ruthless dictator has controlled their every move. They're constantly looking over their shoulders, afraid the Collectors will twist their words and report them to Zenith for talks of treason."

My heart sank as I thought of Sharik—the man accused of holding secret meetings, the man Zenith wanted the leader of the Inner Circle to roughen up, the man Jax killed with his bare hands.

Samson went on. "Zenith's rule has left the people jaded

and discouraged. It's only a matter of time before the light in their eyes dims forever."

Cyrus dragged a hand down his face. I knew my brother better than anyone else in that room; his kind heart ached for the ones who had suffered.

He found the Solin's eyes. "Samson, gathering the people to join our side is one thing, but starting a revolution is another. Revolution means war: a war against a ruthless dictator who has no qualms with annihilating anyone who stands in his way." Cyrus jerked his thumb at me. "How can we make a difference? Sharing each other's Solin and Lunin traits isn't enough. We can defend ourselves against the average Collector, but we lack the combative skills of the Inner Circle. And the people won't find us relatable. In their eyes, we're just two kids from Earth who know nothing about Aroonyx. We don't have the numbers. Hell, we haven't even seen Zenith with our own eyes."

"I'm okay with that," I mumbled.

Cyrus gave me a long look.

"What? It's a true statement."

Samson tugged at the white hairs on his chin. "I understand your concerns, Cyrus, but the two of you *can* make a difference, even without the advanced skills and knowledge you listed."

"How?" I asked.

"By returning the gift Zenith stole when he gained control."

My brother arched a brow. "What gift?"

"Hope."

And there it was. The word that set everything in motion. I glanced around the room, observing the faces of the men who would rise to the challenge, the men who would join me on the battlefield.

"The two of you will expose Zenith for who he is: a selfish coward, and when you do, the wall he hides behind will come crashing down."

I looked at my brother. *Are we really doing this? Starting an uprising, challenging Zenith?* Not silent questions. Confirmations about the revised plan. Acknowledging my unspoken words, Cyrus sealed our fate with a subtle head nod.

He shifted his gaze to the ex-Collector. "We're in."

"Good, because I need a strong Solin who isn't afraid of getting his hands dirty."

"You can count on me, Samson," Cyrus said. "I'll help the people defeat Zenith, and I'll do whatever it takes to get the job done."

My face beamed with pride as I listened to my brother accept his new role as leader, protector of the group prepared to end Zenith's reign. Resembling a fearless warrior, Cyrus's spine straightened and his Solin confidence emanated from his amber eyes.

I scratched my head. *How are we related, again?*

Though twins by birth, we sat on opposite ends of the emotional spectrum. I preferred to observe while Cyrus stood front and center. He never cowered if faced with a challenge, and hesitation didn't exist in his vocabulary. A strong sense of peace moved through me when I found his eyes. *Yeah, you got this, bro.*

He smiled, and I returned the gesture because the citizens of Aroonyx would follow him, and I would be by his side the entire way.

Orion cleared his throat. "Okay, we wait, we train." He pointed at Cyrus. "*You* lead, and we take down Zenith."

"Hell yeah we do." My brother nodded with great enthusiasm. "And we'll make that bastard pay for everything he's done."

"It's time you acted like a Solin," Samson said. "I wondered if living in the woods with a bunch of Lunins had turned you soft."

"I'm glad you showed up before it was too late. Lunins are

so emotional." He nudged me with his elbow. "Especially this one."

I shared his Solin strength and swung. Orion and Iah grimaced at the sickening thud of my knuckles connecting with Cyrus's shoulder.

"And *that* knee jerk reaction"—he winced, rubbing his arm —"proves my point."

I raised my fist once more.

"Easy, Elara," Samson warned, rising to his feet. "You should save that enthusiasm for your training." He walked past me and my brother. "I'll be back in a few days to make sure you kids haven't forgotten the basics."

I frowned at his sudden departure. "Why are you leaving? You just got here."

Samson turned, his chest falling with a long exhale. "I should get back to Ida. Pollux keeps stopping by the bar."

Cyrus sprung to his feet. The gentle heat that flowed through my veins transformed into a river of molten lava. Without thinking, I grabbed his wrist, my protective instincts taking over.

Samson showed him his palm, a silent command for Cyrus to get a grip on his Solin temper. "Idalia's safe. Callisto and I take shifts so she's never left alone. If that bastard touches her, I'll run my blade right through his sadistic heart—after I make him swallow his tongue."

An eerie silence swept over the room. I shivered. Though beads of sweat lined the back of my neck, Samson's threat slithered down my spine. Iah and Orion stared at the wooden floor without blinking.

Before we started our training at Idalia's, Samson shared a story about his dark past with Arun. We never asked his "number." We didn't dare. The Clearing of the Seekers was a topic best avoided, and honestly, I didn't care to hear how many men and women he slaughtered during that turbulent time.

I let go of Cyrus after the taut muscles in his arm relaxed. He found Samson's eyes and nodded.

A quiet cough from Iah turned our heads. "Samson, do you mind if I join you on your journey back to the village?"

"As long as you can keep up, old man."

"I'll do my best." Iah chuckled.

Orion helped his father to his feet. "Where are you going?"

"The West Village. We're running low on supplies."

"I can do it. Just make me a list and I'll get everything you need when I leave for Idalia's next week."

The doctor rested a hand on his son's shoulder. "It takes hours to get from the pub to the West Village."

"I don't mind the walk."

Iah filled his lungs and shut his eyes. "Son, I need to clear my head. Listening to Samson discuss the new plan allowed me to grasp the severity of the situation, and it showed me"—his throat bobbed—"your role in this mission."

I cursed, guilt consuming me.

Desperate for help, we showed up on Iah's doorstep one morning, unannounced, and covered in blood with Jax hanging over Cyrus's shoulder. The doctor and his son came to our rescue, and because of their selfless act, their simple lives now intertwined with our turbulent ones. We didn't force Orion to join our side or ask him to risk his life for the greater good, but he did—and he would. *Shame on us for not seeking the doctor's approval. If push comes to shove, can he say goodbye to his only son? A parent should never bury their child. It goes against the laws of nature—I'm certain.*

"I'll stay with my sister for a few days and visit your mother's gravesite. Will the three of you be okay without me?"

Orion forced a smile. "Yeah, Dad, we'll be fine."

"There's plenty of food and—"

"Iah," I said, jumping in on the conversation. "We have everything we need." My eyes drifted to Orion. "Right here."

Assuming I meant food and other supplies, the doctor nodded, but his son, more intuitive than his father, grasped the hidden meaning behind my message and gave me a warm grin.

Iah turned his attention to Samson, who stood with his fingers still wrapped around the silver knob, his mind somewhere else. "Can you give me a few minutes to pack?"

"Sure thing. I'll be outside."

The summer breeze whipped into the home once the ex-Collector pulled open the front door. My nostrils flared at the sweet aroma, a stark contrast from the scentless smell of winter. I followed Cyrus through the living room, then skidded to a stop when Samson spun around.

Reaching into his pocket, he said, "I almost forgot. Ida wanted me to give you this."

The elated expression on Cyrus's face rivaled an Orbit gum commercial. Grinning from ear to ear, he took the folded note from Samson's outstretched hand, and his eyes glazed over with lust as he stepped onto the porch.

"Young love." Samson chuckled and turned sideways to fit his broad shoulders through the doorway.

My lips slid over my teeth in an awkward smile that resembled a grimace. His words had left a foul taste in my mouth. *Stop it. You should be happy for Cyrus and Idalia, not jealous.*

Disregarding my brother's earlier advice, I scoffed loud enough for everyone's ears. *Screw it. I am jealous, and screw you, Jax. This is all your fault.* My chin lifted. *There, that feels better.*

This momentary satisfaction dissolved once Orion grabbed my wrist.

I turned. "What's up?"

He frowned at my resigned tone, an aftereffect of the destructive mind game I continued to play. His fingers fell from my wrist. Staring at my shoes, his eyes stayed fixed on the laces.

"Orion." I wiggled my foot, encouraging him to lift his gaze. "Why are you acting weird? What's wrong?"

The smallest breath left his mouth before he raised his head. "I'm sorry I made you uncomfortable during the training exercise this morning. I meant nothing by it. I was just messing around."

"Don't apologize, you did nothing wrong."

"Agree to disagree. Your reaction said otherwise."

I groaned his name, irritated that he felt the need to explain himself for my erratic behavior. "Don't take it personally. And please—whatever you do, don't waste your time trying to figure out the drama inside my head."

Surprised by my sharp tone, the Lunin took a step backward. I stilled, equally shocked by my response. The harsh words reflected the ones Jax used during our argument in the high school parking lot on Earth. I swore in the darkened room of my mind. *Great. That's the second time I've spoken like Jax. Get it together.*

Orion tapped his chin and scanned my troubled expression.

"Why are you looking at me like that?" I asked, the doors of my vulnerability slamming shut.

Ignoring me, he remained silent and narrowed the gap between us.

"What are you doing?" My spine pressed into the wall. "You're making me nervous."

The tiny smirk at the corner of his mouth spread into a wide grin. "I have a proposition."

5

LETTING GO

My heart thumped in my ears. "And what are you proposing?"

"Dinner."

"We eat together every night."

"With my father and Cyrus hovering over us. I want us to have dinner without an audience."

Intrigued by his offer, I tilted my head. "Are you asking me on a date?"

"Sure, if that's what you want to call it. I'm calling it a quiet meal amongst friends."

Dinner with a friend? I think not.

Mirroring his previous gesture, I tapped the tip of my index finger on my chin while debating his proposal. Yes, I found Orion attractive. He was easy on the eyes and easy on the soul. His relaxed personality and witty humor distracted my troubled thoughts, and the desire to grow closer on a more physical level stirred each time I noted his toned physique.

I sighed. The chains around my heart tightened when the other Lunin in my life crossed my mind.

With heavy regret, my tongue moved to decline Orion's

offer. It paused once his unjaded eyes found mine. Unlike Jax, he didn't harbor a plethora of secrets, and he didn't need an invisible sword to fight his inner demons.

I observed the details of his handsome face. An innocence radiated out of his being, a pureness I gravitated toward. Reminding me of a candle lit for the first time, his wick ignited with the fire of life, a stark contrast to Jax, whose flame had dimmed a long time ago, leaving a mess of dried wax behind. *I've got to let him go.* The floorboards creaked under my weight as I peeled my spine from the wall, the line between my brows deepening at the tough decision. *Perhaps a quiet night with Orion is exactly what I need.*

It is.

I blinked at the other voice inside my head—the masked figure who twisted my thoughts. *Go away.*

As you wish, Elara.

Rolling my neck, I extended a hand to Orion, and as if agreeing to the terms of a business merger, I stated, "I accept your offer. But don't expect—"

My words faded. Iah had stepped into the living room. The crow's feet around his eyes creased as he adjusted a gray sack over his shoulder. "You'll be okay while I'm gone?"

Answering his father with another question, Orion said, "Yeah, what's the worst that could happen?"

I snorted. *I can think of a few things.*

Minus the dramatic music, images of our time on Aroonyx zipped through my mind like an action-packed trailer for a Summer Blockbuster.

"Orion, hang out with me and Cyrus a little longer before you make such a bold statement."

Iah chuckled under his breath and clapped a hand on his son's back. "You guys take care of each other. I'll be back in a few days."

We followed the retired doctor onto the porch. Cyrus sat in

his favorite chair, his thoughts occupied with Idalia's letter. Samson leaned against a tree and dragged the tip of his knife along his nail beds.

I grimaced at the dried blood on the blade, and mumbled, "Ew," watching a piece of his cuticle fall to the ground.

"You look like you want to vomit."

I shifted my gaze to Orion. "What makes you say that?"

"Your face." His lips pursed and his nose crinkled as if he had smelled the inside of Samson's boots. "It looks like this."

I laughed at his accurate impression. "Sharing Cyrus's Solin vision has its benefits." I paused, watching Samson and Iah stroll through the woods. My powerful eyesight allowed me to make out the details of every scar and age spot on their tan and pale hands. My eyes lowered, noting the drops of blood that stained the Solin's boots. "But sometimes the vivid details take me by surprise."

"I bet they do." Orion crossed his arms. "Thanks for sharing. Now I know better than to walk around the house naked."

I muffled a nervous giggle. *Feel free. I won't mind.* "You also shouldn't walk around naked after the sun goes down."

Playing my little game, Orion asked a question he didn't need me to answer. "And why's that?"

"Because like you, my Lunin vision allows me to see crystal clear at night."

"Thanks for the reminder." He lowered his voice and moved his lips near my ear. "Later tonight when you're in the bath, I'll hide your clothes and you'll never be able to find them."

I chewed on my lip. *Well played, sir. Well played.*

Unable to volley his verbal serve, I turned, hoping to hide the warmth that flushed my cheeks. No luck. Orion chuckled, proud of his victory, but Cyrus's voice ripped the invisible trophy out of his hand.

"What are you guys whispering about?"

Ignoring him, I pretended to admire the beauty of the

surrounding woods while Orion squatted and fumbled with his shoelaces that didn't need tying.

Not buying our lame attempt at playing it cool, Cyrus muttered, "Never mind, I don't want to know," as he strolled past us, down the porch steps.

Eager to distract my brother from the conversation I prayed he didn't hear, I asked, "Do you want to continue with our training?"

Cyrus shut his eyes and splayed his arms toward the cloudless sky. "No sis, I thought I'd stand out here in front of Iah's and work on my tan for the rest of the afternoon."

Orion's laughter faded when I slapped him in the gut. "Whose side are you on?"

"I'm still undecided."

I scoffed, heading down the porch stairs. "And to think I would have let you hide my clothes."

"Team Elara. Definitely team Elara."

My shoulders bounced up and down. "Smart man."

Irritated with the delay, Cyrus tossed up his hands. "Please —continue your mindless banter. It's not like I have anything better to do. I'll just sit here and mentally prepare for our battle with Zenith. I'm sure his Collectors and the Inner Circle are doing the same thing right now."

I rolled my eyes and swung my arms, warming up for the next round of training. "In case you were wondering, I don't need two Samsons in my life."

"I'm his replacement until he gets back."

"How considerate," I said, stretching my quads. "The award for best twin goes to Cyrus Lofton."

He glared, flinging sweat in my face. A salty bead collided with my taste buds. I gagged. "You're gross." I spit near his boot. "And you get more annoying every day."

Orion smirked at the two of us. "Ah, good old sibling rivalry."

"Which you know nothing about, so stay out of it," Cyrus hissed.

Orion winced, enduring another verbal blow from my brother. Irritated with his constant bullying, I mouthed, "Stop it."

Staring straight through me, Cyrus circled his arms and popped his neck.

Unlike the bearable temperatures of the early morning, the afternoon heat draped over me. I groaned, using the sweat that lined my brow as a makeshift gel to keep the flyaway strands out of my face. Orion leaned forward to touch his toes, his pale skin free of moisture. Lucky for him, growing up on Aroonyx had acclimated his body to the sweltering heat.

After long minutes of an endless stretching routine, Cyrus looked at Orion. "You've shown us you're capable of escaping a ground hold with Elara sharing my Solin strength." He motioned to the grass. "Let's see if you can repeat the process with me."

Orion's Adam's apple bobbed in his throat as he lowered himself onto the ground. I took five steps backward, leaving them ample room to work.

THE SAYING *Time flies when you're having fun* rang true that day because the afternoon flew by in a blur of laughter—at least from my perspective. The comedic imagery of Orion's failed attempts rivaled Rico's appearance at Idalia's. He summoned every ounce of strength to escape Cyrus's brutal attacks: bear hugs, hair grabs, ground holds, chokeholds, and the dreaded headlock. The two practiced until sweat dripped from their brows. Even though Orion understood the proper technique of how to escape the advanced maneuvers, my brother's Solin strength outmatched his every time.

Orion struggled to catch his breath under Cyrus's tight grip. His flushed complexion matched the color of the persimmon sun as his fingers tapped my brother's arm for the fourth time in a row. He let Orion suffer for longer than necessary before releasing him from the headlock.

Falling to his knees, the Lunin clutched his neck and panted. "Why can't I escape that hold? I always tap out."

"It takes practice." Cyrus helped him to his feet. "Your body must learn how to react without a conscious effort."

Observing the discouragement that hardened the lines on Orion's face, I touched his arm. "Don't stress it, you'll get it." He met my gaze, and I inclined my head at my brother. "Cyrus is right. It takes a lot of practice for these moves to become second nature. Everything will make sense after you train with Samson. It's like riding a bike. Once you learn, you'll never forget."

"What's a bike?"

"A mode of transportation on Earth."

Orion's brows etched together with confusion.

"Forget it." I pointed to his boots. "The combative exercises will be like tying your shoelaces."

Cyrus huffed a breath. "Yeah, like you did earlier on the porch."

I cursed, realizing he *had* eavesdropped on our conversation.

My brother crossed his arms, a bitterness lacing his words. "Orion, cool it with the verbal advances you throw at my sister, especially when I'm an earshot away."

Orion shoved his hands into his pockets and averted his eyes to the emerald grass. I ground my teeth at the phantom bricks Cyrus added to the wall of tension he built between him and the Lunin.

"I guess that's enough training for today," Cyrus said.

I mirrored my brother's assertive posture. "Yes, it is."

Brushing off my sarcasm, Cyrus rotated his body toward the house and stretched. I stared at the darkening forest. The setting sun cast a copper-colored hue over the lush grounds. Preparing for nightfall, the shadows had vanished. I eyed the black tree limbs, their massive leaves swaying in the gentle breeze.

Orion rested a hand on my lower back and whispered, "I'm going to freshen up. We can leave once it gets dark."

My lips moved to agree with his plan but paused when Cyrus whirled on us.

As if Orion had offered me a private tour of Zenith's dwelling, my brother's pupils constricted. "Did I miss something? Where are you guys going?"

My jaw clenched. *I'll kick him in the balls if he doesn't stop these interrogations.*

Orion went rigid as Cyrus moved closer. His amber eyes shifted between the two of us. "Spit it out."

"*And* that's my cue." Without saying another word, Orion jogged toward the house.

My mouth gaped at his sudden departure.

Cyrus shook his head at the Lunin before turning his attention to me. "Elara, are you going to answer my question, or do I have to chase after Orion and put him in another headlock?"

"He asked me to dinner."

"What? Like out on a date?"

My chin hit my chest. *It's too hot to deal with this shit.* "No. It's not a date." My tongue tripped over the lie. "He just wants to have a quiet dinner together."

"Mm-hmm. I'm sure he does. Start with a quiet dinner and end the night with you on top of—"

"Stop it!" My palms vibrated with heat. "You're driving me crazy. It's awkward enough between me and Orion without you pulling out the Dad Card."

"Someone has to act like the adult here."

"No one asked you to fill the role."

He lifted my chin. "I don't want to see you get hurt again."

"You won't," I said, knocking his hand away. "Orion's a good guy. His intentions are pure."

"You don't know that. Did you not listen to anything I said on the porch this morning?"

I'm about to lose it. I can't talk about this with him anymore. "Yes, Cyrus. I did."

"Then why do you keep forcing whatever 'this' is between you and Orion? It's obvious you're not ready to move on."

"I'm not forcing anything." I folded my arms across my chest. "Maybe I am ready to move on."

"I call bullshit. A few hours ago, you told me you still love Jax."

"And I followed that statement with, I love him enough to let him go."

"And how's that working out for you, sis?"

"Screw you."

"That's what I thought." He pointed at the house. "This little game you're playing with Orion won't end well. He's not Jax, Elara, so stop pretending that he is."

The truth behind Cyrus's words slammed into my emotional shield. I frowned at the fractured pieces, my eyes welling with tears.

"I'm sorry," he said, wincing at my reaction. "That was a dick move."

"Perhaps, but you're right. Orion isn't Jax. He never will be."

"Still, it doesn't give me the right to be an asshole. You've been through a lot. Hell, we both have. The last thing you need is your brother giving you a hard time."

I shrugged, indifferent to his suggestion. *The trees. I'll just stare at the damn trees.*

Noting the faraway look in my eyes, Cyrus added, "So if

dating"—he paused—"*hanging* with Orion gives you some relief, then go for it."

Yeah, if it were only that easy.

Moving as one, we lifted our gaze to the evening sky. A kaleidoscope of colors transformed before our eyes. Various shades of blue and purple twirled around each other in an intoxicating dance, leaving a trail of cosmic glitter behind. Their audience, the glowing atmosphere, erupted with visual applause. Stars twinkled and galaxies flickered. I smiled at the partial halos that crowned the twin full moons.

"It never gets old, does it?" I whispered, tracing a shooting star with my finger.

"No." Cyrus's lips spread into a wide grin. "It's how I imagine a blind man's reaction to the gift of sight. The beauty is impossible to describe with words."

6

FULL MOONS RISING

My hand floated on the surface of the bathwater. Though the seas appeared calm, a storm brewed off the coast of my mind. *I'll tell Orion I'm exhausted from the long day of training. No, he won't buy that lie. Not after I stood on the sidelines while he and Cyrus did all the work.*

The water rippled against my lips as I submerged my head. *Don't be the girl who cancels at the last minute. Remember, it's just dinner with a friend.*

Fighting my desire to stay hidden in the tub, I pulled the drain plug with my toe and reached for the gray towel that hung on the wall. I smirked at the folded shirt and shorts that rested on the counter. *Too bad he didn't hide my clothes.*

Staring at the empty wall behind the oval-shaped sink, I combed through the wet locks of my hair. *I'd pay good money for a mirror. If I was a Seeker during Arun's reign, I would have insisted we brought that invention to Aroonyx.*

Giving my fair complexion a touch of color, I pinched the area around my cheekbones, then scrunched the wet strands of my hair, hoping to add some volume. After adjusting the swoop neck collar of my shirt, I frowned at my non-existent cleavage.

So much for sex appeal. I gripped the rim of the sink and eyed the imaginary reflection that didn't stare back. *Sorry, Orion. This is all I can offer.*

I slowed my pace as I neared the kitchen. Self-conscious about my appearance, I adjusted the khaki-colored shorts that hung off my waist, covering the sharp lines of my hip bones. I then tugged at the baggy shirt that once hugged my toned torso. I sighed through parted lips. My appetite had vanished during those depressing weeks, along with my curves.

I fidgeted with a loose thread on the button of my shorts. *Where's Idalia when I need her? She'd make me look attractive. What's Orion wearing? I hope he's not dressed up.* My eyes grew. *What if Cyrus is right? What if he's expecting more than a casual dinner?*

He probably is, Elara.

I rolled my neck; the masked figure's voice slithered down my spine. *Go away. I don't need your advice.*

Wicked laughter filled my ears. *Very well.*

I held my breath and tiptoed around the corner. Cyrus sat on the couch, and Orion stood near the kitchen sink, his back facing me. He packed a wooden box with a handful of dried meats, soft rolls, and rooted vegetables. It wasn't a five-star meal, not by anyone's standards, but the care he showed those bite-sized pieces, lining them up like tiny delicacies, rivaled any Michelin-star chef. His gentle touch made each food group look mouthwatering.

I observed Orion's attire: simple, practical, and like the other citizens on Aroonyx, his clothes appeared to serve one purpose and one purpose only: shield your body from the elements.

My eyes danced around the patches on his dark-gray pants, then wandered to the crème-colored shirt that accentuated the lines of his toned shoulders. Warmth bloomed across my cheeks. Orion resembled an altered version of Jax, similar, yet different. This Lunin could go days without shaving, and working indoors as his father's medical assistant left his palms callous-free; his body showed no signs of damage. I couldn't count the number of scars that decorated Jax's pale skin, and his hands looked and felt as if he'd spent years doing manual labor.

Orion's tall stature and clean-cut appearance reminded me of a high-fashion runway model, while his counterpart had a more rugged and edgier appeal. Jax rarely used a razor. The only time I saw him with a cleanly shaved face was the first night we stayed at Idalia's; the night he and Cyrus had their brawl; the night he confessed his dark past; the night we learned our trusted guide was Zenith's adoptive son and the former leader of the Inner Circle; the night we kissed, the night everything changed.

Cyrus cleared his throat, steering my mind off comparison road and back into the lane of reality. Noting my glazed-over expression, he motioned for me to wipe the drool from my chin. I returned his silent jab with a one-fingered gesture.

"Should we head out?" Orion asked, turning to face me.

I blinked. "How did you know I was standing here?"

"Your eyes were burning a hole in my back."

The warmth returned to my cheeks. *Great. That's the second time he's caught me staring.*

Cyrus chuckled but kept his eyes focused on an old letter from Idalia. Orion winked at me and reached for his backpack.

As soon as we passed the couch, Cyrus murmured, "Don't do anything I wouldn't do."

Irritated that he disguised a threat with humor, I shot him a stern glance. He lowered his head but bit his lip to keep from laughing.

Ignoring the Solin's warning and dodging the daggers that flew out of my eyes toward my pain-in-the-ass twin, Orion held open the front door. I inhaled a cleansing breath and stepped onto the porch. *Remember, tonight is about you and Orion. Leave the past behind.*

———

OUR FEET GUIDED us down the invisible path toward the secluded spring. I didn't flinch when Orion's arm brushed against me, and I didn't pull away when his fingers laced around mine.

I observed the twinkling stars that dotted the amethyst-colored sky. Content and comfortable, they didn't overlap or outshine one another, and they didn't fight for the perfect spot in the atmosphere. My lips curled into a pout as I eyed our clasped hands. Nature had a hidden metaphor for every moment in my life.

"It's a nice night."

I nodded, pointing at the moonlit forest. "The beauty never ceases to amaze me."

"Is it much different on Earth?"

My eyes widened at Orion's naïve question. "Yes, very."

"How so?"

"Earth has billions of people who own houses, cars, and possessions. It takes up a lot of space. The population keeps growing, so new homes and structures are constantly being built to keep up with the demand."

He waved a hand at the surrounding space. "So it doesn't look like this on Earth?"

"No, it's different. Nature on Aroonyx is untouched by man."

"That's not true. We cut down trees to build homes."

I shook my head, thinking of the clear-cutting technique developers used on Earth. "A single tree doesn't compare to the devastation of an entire forest."

"I see."

"It's not right or wrong," I said, acknowledging his resigned tone. "Aroonyx is . . . just different. It's like I've gone back in time, minus the dinosaurs."

"What's a dinosaur?"

I burst into laughter. "We'll save that discussion for another day."

A heartbeat later, Orion asked, "How did it feel to jump to Aroonyx?" *Please don't say his name.* "Jax"—*he said it*—"is the only Seeker to jump with people. During Arun's reign, the Seekers brought back mental notes for inventions and nothing more."

I nodded, familiar with the history of Aroonyx. "I'm not sure how to describe the experience. It happened so fast. Honestly, I wasn't sure I'd go through with it. We were standing on the trail near my house and the thought of leaving my parents and returning to a world I knew nothing about scared the shit out of me." I swallowed. "Jax spent months preparing us for that day, but I froze when he asked me *Are you ready?* I couldn't speak much less move. My brother didn't think twice. He grabbed Jax's hand without hesitation."

"That's because he's a Solin."

"No, it's different with Cyrus. His courage doesn't come from his Solin traits." I touched my chest. "It comes from in here."

"Perhaps, but every Solin I've met oozes courage."

Unwilling to argue, I circled back to his question. "The sensation of jumping between planets felt strange. The closest comparison I have is flinching before falling asleep. Have you ever experienced that?"

"Yeah, the hypnagogic state."

I halted my casual pace. "The what?"

"The transition from wakefulness to slumber. It feels like you're falling, but in reality, your consciousness is drifting off to sleep. Some refer to it as a lucid state."

"Oh." I blinked, processing this new bit of information. "I didn't know that was a real thing."

"You're forgetting," he said, taking my hand, "I'm the son of a doctor."

UNLIKE THE SPRING I visited while living in the woods with Jax and Cyrus, this tiny pool lacked the other's depth and the intertwined branches overhead blocked the evening sky.

Orion removed the wooden box from his gray bag. Sitting beside him, I leaned on my elbows and crossed my outstretched legs in front of me. *See. This isn't so bad.*

I shut my eyes, allowing my fingers to play with the delicate blades of grass. With each relaxed breath, the tension in my body loosened. I smiled, pleased that I accepted his offer.

Enjoying each other's company, we took small bites, chatting between mouthfuls. Our conversation started with lighthearted topics. I tried to explain the concept of music and the internet while Orion shared the details of a popular game that people played on Aroonyx—Night and Day.

"It sounds like chess."

"What's chess?"

I dropped my head. Orion laughed, switching the subject.

Our casual banter paused once I expressed the guilt that surfaced each time I thought of my parents, and it ended once Orion shared the emotional account of his mother's passing.

I tossed the last piece of dried meat into my mouth and reflected on our evening together. Orion's quick wit kept me laughing and his flirtatiousness filled a void in my life. I chewed on the inside of my cheek, eyeing the Lunin. *Maybe he holds the key that will unlock the chains around my heart.*

"Are you cold?"

My head swayed side-to-side, though goosebumps rose on my skin. "This weather is crazy. One minute it's the summer, the next it's the winter."

"It's normal to me."

"Let me enlighten you." I wrapped my arms around my knees. "On Earth, we have these glorious things called seasons. They fade from one to the next." I paused, recalling the short spring and fall in Texas. "At least, we had seasons in Maine."

"Where's Maine?"

"It's a state. I lived there before my parents dragged me to Texas."

Orion frowned at the shiver that rippled through me. "I don't have a jacket. Do you want my shirt?"

"Nah, I'm good." *Why do men always offer me their shirts?*

The Lunin eyed the canopy of leaves that hid the light of the full moons. "I want to show you something." He offered me his hand. "It's not far."

WE STROLLED DEEPER into the forest, our Lunin vision guiding us through the darkened areas. As if sprinkled with phosphorescence, cool light exploded around me.

"Did you struggle with your Lunin traits?"

"What do you mean?" Orion asked.

"The night vision, the endless stamina, did it freak you out when you turned eighteen?"

"No. Not really. I knew what to expect."

"I wish someone would have warned me." My adoptive mother's wide-eyed expression after she found me in the dark flashed in my mind, making me laugh.

Three strides later Orion said, "I want you to close your eyes."

"Why?"

"Because it's a surprise."

My breath hitched, for another Lunin had spoken those exact words only months ago.

"Or not." Apprehension furrowed his brows. "Surprises are overrated."

"That they are." The sharpness in my tone sliced at my tongue. "I'd prefer to keep my eyes open."

"Fair enough."

Orion reached for my hand. I flinched. Cursing my abrasive response, I laced my fingers through his.

My pulse quickened as he led me through a cluster of trees, our legs stretching over the flat pieces of Clear Stone that decorated the lush grounds.

Stop acting weird. He doesn't know the details of what happened with you and Jax that night.

Orion distracted my troubled thoughts by dropping my hand and moving his body in front of mine. "Are you ready to see"—he paused—"the place I wanted to show you?"

In slow motion, my head bobbed up and down, a strange sense of déjà vu washing over me. Orion stepped aside and encouraged me to move forward. *This isn't a good idea.*

Go for it, Elara. What's the worst that could happen?

My heart says no.

The masked figure cackled in my ears. *That's your problem. You keep listening to your heart. Stop this foolishness and listen to your head.*

Hypnotized by its soothing voice, I ducked under a low-lying branch and stepped through the gap of a tree trunk that had split in two.

A gust of wind sent my hair flying in every direction. Bothered by the distraction, I tamed the wild strands, gathering them over one shoulder, and when I lifted my gaze, the world stopped spinning.

I gasped, clutching my chest. *Why didn't I listen?*

Foolish girl. The masked figure snickered. *You fell right into my trap. Let the games begin.*

SEVEN WINS THE BET

A secluded clearing rested before me. The emerald grass flowed over the cliff's edge, cascading down the smooth Clear Stone surface. Though this magnificent space differed from the one I visited with Jax, the memories remained.

My hands trembled, and my gaze drifted from one Moon Drop to the next. The light of the full moons enhanced the dust-like centers of each small flower, glowing as I remembered. Overwhelmed with the emotions that surfaced, moisture stung my eyes. *Why did he bring me here?*

Oblivious to my reaction, Orion asked, "So what do you think?"

I couldn't speak. Shock, grief, and confusion had paralyzed my tongue.

He gestured to the white blooms around our feet. "We call these rare flowers Moon Drops and they only—"

"I know what they are."

The Lunin did a doubletake. The dam that blocked my tears had burst open. He moved in front of me. "Elara, what's wrong?"

I lifted my chin, Jax's altered reflection stared back. I gasped, the chains tightening around my heart. Orion's jet-black hair blew into his eyes as he reached for my hand, a haunting reminder of that life-changing night on the cliffside.

My fingers recoiled from his.

"Did I do something wrong?" he asked, scanning my tear-stained face.

I blinked. Even his voice reminded me of Jax. Every damn thing he did reminded me of Jax. I gripped the fabric of my shirt. The tightness in my chest increased with each beat of my pounding heart. I shook my head, desperate to erase the piercing blue eyes that haunted my mind.

"Elara." Orion used a mild tone as if addressing a patient. "Why don't you take a seat?" He motioned to the ground. "You look a little paler than usual."

Disagreeing, I continued to thrash back and forth, and my hands mimicked the erratic motion. My boots shuffled backward, dragging me from the memories of Jax, dragging me from the memories I would never make with Orion.

He called my name, but I refused to turn around. I dashed out of the clearing and through the cluster of trees, my vision blurring with thick tears. Though my Lunin endurance allowed my lungs to breathe easy, my chest still ached because the image of Jax chased me the entire way.

Why can't I let him go? He acted like a cold, heartless asshole and treated me like shit. He left me—abandoned me. I whimpered. *But he didn't treat me that way before his capture.* A tear rolled down my cheek, and I didn't bother brushing it away. *And that's why I can't let him go. I'm still attached to the man who kissed me on the cliffside—the man with the trapped potential.*

My HANDS CURLED into fists as I stormed up the porch steps. A moment later I flung open the door and found Cyrus where I left him, sitting on the couch with his feet propped up on the coffee table. Baffled by my dramatic entrance, his amber eyes narrowed on my damp face.

He scrambled to stand. "What happened?"

Unwilling to discuss the mental anguish that muddled my thoughts, I waved him away and hurried toward Orion's room. His bare feet padded after me.

"Elara, what's wrong? Did he—" My brother's voice faded when I closed the door. Hearing the lock click only elevated his frustrations. "Open up!" he shouted, banging his fist against the wooden panel.

Ignoring him, I collapsed face first into the soft mattress.

"Elara. Open the damn door."

"No." The thick fluff muffled my voice. "I don't want to talk to you right now. Just go away."

A deep growl rattled in his throat as he slammed his palm against the door. I braced myself, afraid he'd bust into the room. A second later, he turned and stomped down the hallway.

I rotated my neck and whispered to the pillow, "Why am I acting crazy? One minute I'm cool, the next I'm hyperventilating." My jaw cracked open. "Maybe I have PTSD. Pollux and the other Collectors really screwed with my mental health."

I poked the pillow. "Thoughts?" The corner slouched. "You're right. I can't be mad at Orion. He didn't know the Moon Drop clearing would send me spiraling out of control. He's been nothing but kind and patient with me over these past few weeks. Hasn't he?" I shook the beige rectangle. No response. "You're no help." I scoffed, flipping onto my back. "Fine, I'll state the facts. Jax left, and he's not coming back. Orion is here now, and he likes me, even if my behavior resembles Dr. Jekyll and Mr. Hyde." I groaned. "How did everything get so complicated?"

After long minutes of a one-sided conversation with an inanimate object, I sat up and massaged my temples. *Yeah, I've got to reel it in. This is getting out of control. I wonder if Iah can find me a therapist.* My nose crinkled. *Do they have therapists on Aroonyx? I'm sure there's a demand with Zenith as the ruler.*

My spine straightened at the sound of raised voices. I strained my ears.

"Cyrus, I don't know what happened."

"Well, *something* happened. She won't come out of your room."

"I didn't do anything."

Feet thumped across the living room floor. "Did you make a move on my sister?"

"No. I would never touch Elara without her consent."

I could hear my brother crack his neck from behind the closed door. Swinging my legs off the bed, I tiptoed across the room and rested my hand on the knob.

"Cyrus, you need to calm down. Nothing happened."

"Bullshit. Tell me what you did to my sister."

The whites of my knuckles showed as I flung open the bedroom door. The severity in Cyrus's tone sent me sprinting to rescue Orion from the wrath of my overprotective brother.

My boots skidded to a stop once I approached the living room. *Well, doesn't this look familiar.*

Mirroring the night of Jax's confession, the Lunin and Solin stood like boxers preparing for the championship fight: hands fisted, nostrils flared, and eyes narrowed.

Refusing to cower before my brother, Orion said, "You need to get the hell out of my face."

The ligaments in the Solin's arms tensed. "Or what?"

"Stop it!" I yelled, watching Cyrus reach for his knife. Dashing forward, I grabbed his arm. "What the hell is wrong with you?"

He twisted out of my tight grip, hissing at the red marks my

67

nails left behind. Orion shook his head at my brother and backed away—he backed away from me.

A fierceness sparked in Cyrus's eyes. "What did Orion do to you, sis?" He held up a finger. "And don't even think about lying to me."

"Nothing! He did nothing."

"Then why are you so upset?"

A nasty mixture of anger and pent-up frustration surged through me. "It's none of your damn business. What happens between me and Orion has nothing to do with you, so stay out of it. I'm so sick of you acting like the overbearing brother who thinks he can dish out verbal threats whenever he"—I poked him in the chest—"whenever *you* want. I'm a grown woman, Cyrus. I don't need your protection. It's one thing if we're on the battlefield, but it's another if it involves my personal life." My voice raised. "So back the *fuck* off!"

Orion sucked in a sharp breath.

My brother's eyes filled with disappointment. "You're unbelievable," he muttered before turning his back on me.

My chest caved with a long sigh. *That's a great way to wrap up a shitty evening.*

As if agreeing with my silent commentary, Cyrus shut his eyes and collapsed onto the couch. Regret's sharp claws raked across my back. *I should apologize.*

No. He deserves it.

I groaned, rolling my neck. *Get out of my head.*

I can't, Elara. We have a lot of work to do.

Eager for a distraction, I tugged at Orion's wrist and guided him toward the front door.

After it closed, he ripped his arm away from me and hissed, "Do you want to explain what happened back there?"

"He's my brother, he worries."

"Yeah, well, your *brother* went for his knife."

"I'm sorry. He didn't mean—"

"Stop making excuses for him. He didn't have a reason to lash out, did he?"

I gulped.

"Exactly. You left me standing there, looking like an idiot, caught off guard and blindsided for the second time tonight."

I dropped my chin. Orion turned, rested his hands on the wooden railing, and stared into the forest. The tree limbs scratched against each other as the icy breeze whipped around us. More goosebumps covered my arms. I didn't shiver. The numbness from the evening's events left me indifferent to the dropping temperature.

I eyed the Lunin. *Way to go. He's done everything right and you've done everything wrong.*

Orion exhaled a tired breath when I touched his arm. I inclined my head toward the opposite end of the porch. He nodded, agreeing to my silent request.

Two white clouds escaped our parted lips as we lowered ourselves onto the chairs. Orion kept his attention focused on the swaying tree limbs and drummed his fingers on the armrest while I fumbled with the loose button on my shorts.

I counted to seventy-five before finding the courage to speak. "I'm sorry." A true, heartfelt apology. "For how I acted at the cliffside."

"It's whatever."

I groaned, twisting in my chair to face him. "No, it's not. You have every right to be pissed." Orion's silence verified the truth in my statement. "Will you let me explain why I acted crazy?"

He shrugged.

"I had a great time at the spring. It was exactly what I needed until—"

Orion's head snapped in my direction, his eyes locking onto mine. "What you *needed* or what you wanted?"

Damn it. That didn't come out right. "Um . . . both?"

A warm cloud shot out of his nostrils.

Keep digging. Your hole is getting deeper by the minute.

Orion rubbed the back of his neck. "May I speak freely?"

"Sure."

"I think you need a little clarification."

My shield raised to block the emotional bullet.

"I'm not Jax."

I winced, a direct hit to the heart.

"And I never will be. I don't have a Seeker's intuition, but I'm a clever guy, and I'd bet your hot and cold demeanor has everything to do with Jax."

I squeezed my eyes shut. Orion's words slammed into my weakened shield, adding more cracks to the fractured surface.

He scoffed at my pained reaction. "Yeah, that's what I thought. Elara, I can't replace Jax. How could I? We're two different people. He lives in the past. I live in the now."

I sighed. Orion's astute observation loosened the chains that bound my heart. I reached for his hand and gave it a loving squeeze. "You're right. I'm sorry. I never meant to compare you to Jax." My voice quivered. "I'm trying to get my shit together. Honestly, I am. Emotional triggers set me off when I least expect it."

"Like the Moon Drop clearing? Why did it upset you?"

I stumbled over my words. Orion's thumb stroked my palm, calming my frazzled nerves. "The first time I saw the Moon Drops in full bloom was with Jax, on the other side of the cliff. He kissed me right before Pollux and the rest of the Inner Circle captured him."

Orion grimaced. "I'm such an ass. I thought the Moon Drops would be a pleasant surprise, but it only reminded you of that horrible day."

I forced a head nod. He had assembled the wrong piece of the puzzle. Yes, the clearing brought back disturbing memories of that dreadful morning, but that wasn't the reason I struggled to breathe when I gazed into his sapphire eyes.

"I'm slightly relieved. I thought I made you uncomfortable."

"No, not at all." The deceit came easier than I expected.

"Good." Orion lifted my hand and pressed his lips against my chilled skin. "Because your happiness means everything to me."

I turned, unable to look him in the eye. *Not Jax, huh? I'm pretty sure he said those exact words before everything went to hell.*

Orion's thumb investigated the lifeline on my palm, a silent offer to explore the more intimate side of our relationship. My pulse raced, not with desire but with anxiety.

His body language advertised his intention. Tired of playing games and ready to cash in his chips, he wanted to leave life's casino. A wise move on his part. My twisted mind found pleasure in suffering, so I brought my winnings to a new table where the masked figure—the dealer of life, stood waiting— eager for me to toss the dice.

I rested my head on Orion's shoulder, and he leaned against me. *Why am I leading him on? This won't end well.*

Go for it, Elara. Take a chance.

My free hand slid along the patches of his pants. Orion shuddered a breath as my fingers grazed the buttons of his fly. I paused my pursuit once the allusive dealer whispered in my ear.

Good roll, seven wins the bet.

Orion brought my hand to his mouth and kissed each finger with enough desire to send a tingle running down my spine. My vision blurred. Weighted with lust, my eyelids closed.

The pleasurable sensation vanished once the masked dealer appeared in my mind, only this time with an unexpected guest. A smudged image of Jax stood with his arms crossed, his features unreadable. A pale hand extended from the black robe that draped over the hooded figure. It dangled a pair of dice, its jagged claws reaching—stretching.

No, I can't. I'm tired of playing games.

Like a disturbing scene from a horror movie, the dealer tilted its head. The sudden movement tugged at the mask covering its face.

Come on, Elara. The silk fluttered around its hidden lips. *Just one more roll.*

I stilled. The dealer pressed the dice into my palm, its sharp claws digging into my skin. I looked at Jax. *Please, help me.*

He shook his head. *You must fight this demon on your own.* His silhouette dissolved into a cloud of smoke.

Even with my eyes closed, I could feel Orion staring at me. Oblivious to my inner turmoil, he leaned closer and kissed the side of my neck. My throat tightened. I couldn't escape the madness that consumed me.

The dealer nudged my arm. My fingers uncurled, sending the dice rolling onto the table.

No! I don't want to play.

It responded with a quiet snicker.

Bothered by the disturbing images, I lengthened my spine and pretended to adjust my shirt, a necessary distraction. Unaware that the masked figure haunted my mind, Orion lay his hand palm up on the armrest of his chair. A less-than-subtle gesture to continue where we left off.

I shut my eyes and pinched the bridge of my nose. *I won't play your little game.*

The dealer wrapped its icy fingers around my wrist. *That's what they all say.*

You're wrong. I'm not like the others.

The black silk brushed against my cheek as its lips moved near my ear. *Yes, you are. You're addicted.*

Addicted to what?

I could see it grinning, even behind that damn mask. *The game, Elara. You're addicted to the game.*

8

TIMING IS EVERYTHING

"Orion! Get your head out of your ass," Samson barked.

Cyrus's fist connected with the Lunin's jaw. His head snapped back, and his eyes rolled, courtesy of my brother's quick uppercut. He swore and touched the stream of blood that trickled out of his nose.

Cyrus scowled at Orion's injured face. "Damn it, dude, pay attention. That hit almost broke your nose."

Orion covered one of his nostrils and blew a blood-filled cluster of snot onto the snow. My stomach turned, the contrast of colors leaving me nauseous.

Exhausted from the grueling training with the two Solins, Orion let out a long breath and prepared for the next round of hand-to-hand combat. I never enjoyed graphic fight scenes in movies, so I slid my hands into the fur-lined pockets of my coat and spun around after Samson signaled the men to start another sparring match.

Shivering, I rocked on the balls of my feet, the tiny ice crystals crunching under my weight. I glanced at the afternoon sky and inhaled the crisp air through my nose. Nimbostratus clouds painted the atmosphere in various shades of gray swirls and beige puffs. I exhaled, watching a thick plume leave my mouth.

Three weeks had passed since the first snowfall of the season, along with the world's most awkward date with Orion. I played with the folded knife in my pocket. *Only a few more days until summer.*

Samson's raspy voice followed the sound of a fist colliding with flesh and bone. I pivoted in the snow.

"Here's a fun fact, kid. If you don't use your head, Cyrus will detach it from your body."

I groaned, observing the newest addition to the Lunin's battered face: a gash above his eyebrow. "Focus, Orion. You can do this."

"I'm trying. I can't predict his attacks."

Not one for excuses, Samson drawled, "For a doctor's son, you say some of the stupidest shit. Have you learned nothing over these past few weeks?" Orion stared at the blood-stained snow, and Samson jerked his chin at Cyrus. "This is how a trained fighter moves. They don't follow the pattern of jab, cross, hook. They change it up to confuse their opponent. You've got to learn how to parry his punches."

My brother's lips formed a tight line as he wiped the blood off his knuckles. "Samson's right. You've got to try harder. Zenith's Collectors start their training at the age of seven. The men in the Inner Circle are in their late twenties, early thirties. They've had years—"

"Exactly," Orion countered. "I've had a few weeks."

Cyrus's nostrils flared. "Which is why we're telling you to try harder. Your life depends on it. Zenith wants to murder me and my sister with his bare hands. Do you think he gives two fucks if the Inner Circle slices your neck?"

The bitter truth that laced my brother's words seeped into

my mouth, coating my tongue with an iron tang. Orion shut his eyes, the color draining from his face.

Offering him a bit of advice, I said, "Watch Cyrus's guard."

My brother's head snapped toward me. "*Elara.*"

Orion straightened, his interest piqued.

"Cyrus lowers his guard if he has an advantage over his opponent."

"What the hell, sis?"

I shrugged, flashing him a smug grin.

Using his hand as a talking puppet, Samson said, "I'm hearing too much of this . . . when I want to hear more of"—he slammed a fist into his open palm—"this. Now that Elara has sold out her brother, let's see if you can add a few bruises to your knuckles."

Orion's head jolted forward when Samson shoved him toward my twin.

Still flustered that I had shared insider information with his training partner, Cyrus spit on the ground and moved into position slower than usual. Combining my advice with the element of surprise, Orion attacked before Samson gave the signal. He faked a left jab to Cyrus's gut, which forced my brother to lower his guard. With his face exposed and unprotected, Orion swung a right hook and slammed his fist into my brother's jaw.

Cyrus's head flew to the side. Quick to recover, my brother pressed his palm underneath his chin and popped his neck. Summoning his Solin strength, he pulled back his arm and drove his fist into Orion's wide-eyed expression. Profanity and blood sprayed out of the Lunin's mouth. My lips curled into a frown. *Yeah, that probably hurt like hell.*

Orion winced, assessing the damage of his busted lip. His tongue slid over his blood-stained teeth to check if any were missing. Cyrus, uninjured by Orion's right hook, cracked his knuckles while waiting for further instruction.

Samson twisted the tip of his beard as he observed the

Lunin's disheveled appearance. "I'm guessing you've had enough of getting your ass handed to you for one day."

Orion appeared more irritated from the amount of blood that dripped from his lip than the pain. He groaned, squeezing the split skin with his thumb and index finger. My brother reached for their coats that hung on a low-lying branch.

I looked at Samson when he moved beside me. "Thanks for taking it easy on me today."

"That wasn't the plan." He pointed at Orion. "The kid needs more training than you do."

I smiled at the disguised compliment. "Do you think he'll get the hang of it before—"

"We fight Zenith?"

A small sigh was all I could muster.

Samson adjusted the collar of his coat. "I'm not sure. Like most Lunins, he hesitates before throwing a punch. I don't want to think about him holding a knife. That's why I'm having Cyrus rough him up. We don't have time to dick around." He huffed a breath, watching Cyrus fake a jab at Orion's busted lip. "The kid's got balls, I'll give him that, but Zenith and the Inner Circle have bigger ones."

I tried to swallow—a failed attempt. A knot of impending doom expanded in my throat, blocking my efforts. I rolled my neck. The taut muscles loosened once Cyrus rested a hand on Orion's shoulder.

"You'll get it," he reassured the Lunin.

Orion sighed, looking more defeated by the minute.

Adding comedic relief to the drab afternoon, Cyrus tapped the red spot on his jawline. "At least you made contact—thanks to my *sister*." Though he gave me a sidelong glance, a hint of amusement glimmered in his amber eyes.

Orion's light-hearted expression turned sour. His split lip had reopened. Wiping the blood with the sleeve of his coat, he said, "Things would be a lot easier if we trained at night. I could use my Lunin endurance." He eyed Cyrus. "Why don't you and your Solin strength take a break?"

"You'd get a break from my strength, but I share Elara's Lunin traits."

"Only if she's close by. She can wait in the house."

Cyrus looked at his Solin counterpart. He shook his head.

Curious why we never trained at night, I asked Samson, "Why not? With our Lunin endurance, we could train harder. Cyrus should see how the attacks look at night. It's much different from during the day. Quick movements leave a glowing tracer."

"No."

My hands flew out of my pockets. "Why not?"

"Because training at night won't do you a damn bit of good."

"Yes, it will," I argued.

"No, it won't." The ex-Collector pinned me with his fierce eyes. "Your night vision and endless endurance might give you an advantage over a Solin once the sun sets, but your shit out of luck during the day. Zenith's not an idiot. He won't attack at night. There are nine members of the Inner Circle and five are Solins. Are you forgetting that Zenith can use both traits? If you can't handle my Solin strength, there's no way in hell you could take on Apollo."

I gulped. Cyrus met my gaze and nodded, a silent reminder of that dreadful morning. The morning Jax accepted his fate by sliding his gray knife into my hand; the morning I dashed to the spring; the morning Elio, Ravi, and Apollo attacked me and my brother. Using our little trick as a defensive maneuver, I scorched the eldest member's wrist. I'll never forget the loathing that radiated out of Apollo's ginger-colored eyes when he hissed *This isn't over*.

This Solin differed from the other Collectors. Besides his bronze skin, white-blond hair, and massive build, Apollo's observant demeanor weighed heavier on the Lunin scale.

When the Inner Circle appeared on the cliffside that morning, they sneered and snickered while Pollux threw verbal jabs at Jax. Apollo was the only one who didn't partake in the grim festivities. He just stood there with a blank expression. His *I don't give a fuck if you live or die* attitude scared the living daylights out of me, and the thought of facing him on the battlefield chilled my warm blood.

Samson shifted his weight. "Now you understand why we train during the day. We must prepare for what lies ahead. I'll be back in a few days." He eyed me out of his peripheral vision. "I'm sure you've forgotten how to use your knives."

I slipped a hand into my pocket and exposed the blade with a quick flick of my wrist. My arm raised with Samson's brows as I hurled the knife through the air. Seconds later it sliced through the bark of a tree that rested behind Cyrus and Orion.

A wide grin spread across my mentor's face. "Well, I'll be dammed."

I curtsied before jogging through the snow to retrieve my knife. Cyrus winked, offering me a fist bump as I passed.

"Elara might avoid hand-to-hand combat when we train, but she hasn't missed a day of target practice with that knife of hers."

Samson nodded at my brother. "Good, that's one less thing for us to worry about. Give Orion an extra knife so he can practice. I don't want to waste time teaching him the basics. That's your job."

"Sure thing." Cyrus extended a hand to the ex-Collector.

"I'll see you kids later." A smirk tugged at the corner of our mentor's chapped lips as he called Orion's name. "I hope you show a little more effort at the next training session."

"Training? Is that what we're doing? I thought this was a therapy session. I'm your dark past and you get to use your fist to release all that pent-up anger."

With a stone-cold expression, Samson shook his head at the Lunin. My brother and I didn't bother hiding our amusement.

My smile vanished once Samson closed the gap between us. "Take a walk with me, Elara."

"Alone?"

"No, Zenith plans on joining us. I thought we could swap stories about our pleasant childhood."

Asshole. I slapped him in the arm. My palm stung as if it had connected with a block of ice, but Samson never flinched.

"Are you done embarrassing yourself?"

I scoffed.

He snickered, motioning for me to follow.

"Have fun, sis."

"Screw you, bro."

Cyrus's laughter faded as I hurried to catch up with the ex-Collector. Snowflakes chased each other on the ice-kissed breeze, and the casualties of their dangerous game landed on the black strands of my hair and Samson's beard.

I spent months living on Aroonyx, and my ears still hadn't adjusted to the stillness of the forest. Too far from my brother to share his powerful Solin vision, I squinted at the elongated branches that reached for the sky. No birds, no squirrels, no bugs, no sounds, only silence surrounded us. I sighed. *My good old friend, silence.*

Samson kept his gaze forward, and with each step the lines on his tan face hardened. I wrapped my arms around me and lowered my head, bracing against the strong gust. *I hate this weather. One minute I'm drenched in sweat, the next I'm covered in ice.*

Once Iah's house became a blur behind us, Samson stopped his leisurely pace. "Elara, I never beat around the bush." He paused, watching me shiver. "I need to tell you something— something you *need* to hear."

"Okay." My voice sounded ten feet away. "What is it?"

"You're stronger than you think you are. Own that power and stay focused."

"I am focused."

"No, you're distracted."

Busted.

"And I'm aware of the reason behind this distraction. His name starts with the letter J."

Busted again.

"You can't wait for him or anyone else to rescue you, Elara. You'll end up waiting forever. Be the hero of your own story."

I sighed, pressing my palms into my eyes. "I'm trying to let him go, Samson. I really am." Orion's face flashed in my mind. "Things are getting better. Well, not better—easier. I had no closure with Jax, and that's what's driving me mad. I wish I could talk to him and ask if he still hates me."

"Jax never hated you."

A white cloud shot out of my mouth. "You weren't there, Samson. You didn't see the loathing in his eyes."

We stared at opposite ends of the forest for an awkward amount of time. My chest ached. The chains around my heart had shifted.

After a long silence, Samson said, "Elara, a person gains strength when they walk through a challenge. They lose that strength if they tiptoe around the next obstacle in their life. You'll come out with a few scrapes and bruises, but trust me, it's worth it."

My eyelashes fluttered, surprised to hear the Solin dig beneath the surface. *He might be an asshole, but at least he's a wise asshole.*

The wind howled, scattering the tiny ice crystals. I buried my neck deeper into the collar of my coat.

Unaffected by the bitter weather, Samson picked a snowflake off his beard. "The citizens of Aroonyx need a strong leader to follow when the uprising occurs. Your mind must stay as sharp as that knife you threw earlier. Remember, Elara, you absorb Cyrus's power. It doesn't work the other way around. The people will look to you for guidance. *You* are the one they'll follow."

"No, they won't. Cyrus is the brave Solin. He's perfect for the job. I hate speaking in front of crowds, and I'm no role model. Cyrus will make a great leader. The citizens will grasp this once they see him in action."

The ex-Collector shook his head and scanned the vast forest. "A change is in the air."

"What is that supposed to mean?"

"I'm not sure. Whatever's coming feels dark—heavy."

"Your equally cryptic as Jax."

Ignoring my comment, he rested a hand on my shoulder. "Elara, your life is about to change in an interesting way. I don't want this twist causing you more distraction."

"You lost me, Samson."

Commanding my attention, his fingers dug into my coat. "Promise me you'll rise to the challenge."

"I . . . promise." My voice raised an octave. The simple answer sounded more like a question.

"Good. I'll see you in a few days."

I stood motionless as he turned and headed deeper into the woods. A few heartbeats later he called my name over his shoulder. I cupped a hand near my ear to hear over the howling wind.

"Enjoy the rest of the afternoon. You deserve a little break."

I blinked away the confusion. *That was by far the most bizarre conversation I've ever had with Samson. Your life is about to change? Enjoy the rest of your afternoon? What the hell does that mean?*

Unwilling to decipher Samson's coded messages, I jogged toward Iah's. My fingers fumbled with the top buttons on my coat as I climbed the porch steps. The house acted as a shield, blocking the frigid winds that blew in from the north.

Orion sat with his feet propped up on the railing, a blood-stained rag pressed against his lip. I took a seat beside him. "Cyrus's jabs are brutal."

"So are his uppercuts."

I nodded, noting the fresh bruise that blotted the Lunin's chin.

Orion reached for my hand and laced his chilled fingers through mine. The two of us sat in comfortable silence, our eyes bouncing from one swaying tree limb to the next. He dabbed the cloth near the gash on his eyebrow while I reflected on our time together.

Simple and easygoing. Choice words that described our evolving relationship. After our first date, we kept things casual —at least I did because the masked dealer ruined everything.

The guilt that surfaced tainted my physical desire. Orion gave me the green light and if the damn dealer hadn't screwed with my head, I would have jumped on the opportunity —literally.

I eyed Orion's toned physique. *Yep, your loss.*

Instead, I faked a headache and went to bed—*alone.* Cyrus, the only one pleased with the turn of events, flashed me a smirk that screamed, *I told you so.* I swallowed my pride and apologized the next morning.

Sensing my reluctance to dive into the pool of intimacy, Orion played in the shallows. He showed more self-control than most nineteen-year-old men, but his patience was wearing thin. The G-rated handholding and lingering hugs only whet his appetite; it didn't satisfy his craving. He encouraged me to join him in the deep end. I hesitated, sitting on the edge.

"What do you want to do today?"

I sucked in a breath and redirected my thoughts. "I don't know. It's too damn cold to go on a walk."

"Then let's warm you up."

I giggled, and my wind-kissed cheeks flushed.

"I wasn't implying—"

"I never said you were."

"And women complain that men have only one thought on their minds." He flicked my forehead. "In reality, it's the opposite."

My glare softened. His busted lip had reopened from his smug grin. I pointed to the stream of blood. "See, that's what you get."

"You're a mean girl."

"And I'm about to get a lot meaner."

"Why?"

"Because I had a brilliant idea to keep us warm."

He dabbed his lip. "Which is?"

"Let me teach you how to use a knife." Orion groaned, dropping his head. I patted his arm. "I'll go easy on you. I promise."

"You better." He rose to his feet. "My face hurts and so does every other part of my body."

"Really?" I jerked my chin at his pants. "Every part?"

He smirked, hobbling down the porch steps. "No, that was an exaggeration. Thankfully, your brother respects my manhood."

I laughed hard and headed toward the door. My fingers rested on the knob. "I'll meet you by the tree after I grab a spare knife."

Orion gave me a thumbs-up and limped through the snow. My body jolted forward when Cyrus pulled open the front door.

"Sorry, sis."

"No worries." I pointed to the folded knives in his hand. "I was coming inside to grab one of those."

"Why?"

"I'm bored, so I thought I'd show Orion a few tricks."

"Samson wanted me to teach him the basics."

"I'll do it."

"Why don't you hold off until I'm done." Cyrus inclined his head at the smooth stone that rested on the porch railing. "I need to sharpen them first."

"No need. It's not target practice. I just want to show him how to open and close the damn thing without cutting himself."

Cyrus bit his knuckle and faked a cry. "Samson would be so proud."

"Shut up," I hissed, snatching a medium-sized knife from the pile.

My twin chuckled, grabbed the sharpening stone, and headed toward his favorite chair. I slid the knife into my pocket and jogged to catch up with Orion. He stood with his back leaning against a tree, his fingers tapping the swollen area around his nose.

"I don't know how it's not broken," he said, wiggling the cartilage.

Though bloodied and bruised, the injuries couldn't mask his handsome features. I brushed a stray hair out of his eyes and explored the black and blue spots with my fingers. Wiping the last bit of blood off his bottom lip, I whispered, "I think you'll live."

Orion slid a hand around my waist and pulled me closer, his warm breath mixing with my own. "I want to tell you something."

"And what's that?"

He moved his free hand to the side of my face. "I think I've fallen for you."

Shit.

A bone-chilling snicker filled my ears. *See, you're addicted to the game. Isn't this fun?*

Shut up. I need to stay focused.

I'll be here if you need me.

Orion's thumb brushed against my lips. "I have a question for you, and I hope you say yes." Before I could respond, he asked, "Can I kiss you?"

I stilled. The masked dealer tossed back its head and let out a wicked cackle, the black silk fluttering against its O-shaped mouth. Without thinking, I grabbed the Lunin by the collar of his coat and pressed my lips against his. Shocked by my aggressive approach, his eyes stayed open for the kiss that lasted all of two seconds. I touched the blood that smeared on my chin.

Orion cocked his head as if gauging the level of passion in the fleeting moment.

Yeah, that was pretty bad, but . . .

I clutched my chest and stumbled backward. His hand fell from my waist. The chains that bound my heart had tightened once more. Baffled, I stared at Orion. *Why didn't it work? We kissed. In fairytales, that's how you break the curse.*

Foolish girl. Fairytales are for children.

Orion took a cautious step forward. "Should we try that again?"

He brings up a good point. A first kiss doesn't set the bar for future intimate moments. Or does it? I shook my head. *No. It can't. The kiss felt forced because the dealer got in the way again. Practice, these things take practice.*

I plastered a fake grin on my face and said, "Here's a suggestion. I'll give you a reward if you pay attention during my knife lesson."

Orion reached for my hand, an effortless gesture. "Motivation can do wonders."

A nervous laugh rattled in my throat. *Why are you forcing this with Orion? You're addicted to the game.* I cursed my brother and the masked dealer. *Bastards. What do they know? Who cares if the kiss wasn't great? And so what if my chest still aches? Time.*

That's what I need. Cyrus said it has the power to heal. I just need a little more time to get my shit together. Maybe Orion is the person I need in my life. I can learn how to appreciate these intimate moments. If the dealer causes trouble, I'll tell it to shove off because it's time I let go of . . .

"Elara."

All previous thoughts about Orion and the illusion of time dissolved into a tangible void when a deep and silky voice filled the quiet space. As if the polarity of a magnet had switched, my hand recoiled from Orion's. I would have known that voice anywhere. It was Jax.

9

REDEEMED

I stilled. Orion looked over my shoulder with his jaw hanging open. My skin prickled with heat as Cyrus bounded down the porch steps, his eyes widening in disbelief.

Orion met my gaze, a haze of disappointment and frustration clouding his eyes. His fingers curled into fists, and without saying a word he stormed toward the house, leaving me standing in the snow.

A gentle voice hummed near my heart, and it wasn't the dealer. *Breathe, Elara. Just breathe.*

I sucked in a sharp breath and held it.

Now turn around.

No. I can't. I'm not ready to face my past.

Trust your heart. Turn around.

My hands trembled by my sides, but I obeyed the quiet voice.

I gasped, the frigid air stinging my lungs. Everyone around me ceased to exist, everyone but Jax. The Lunin strolled through the forest, his boots sloshing in the snow. A disobeying hair blew into my face. I didn't lift a hand or blink it away. I couldn't risk him disappearing like he did that day at the spring. My eyes burned. *What if I'm dreaming?*

Jax moved with a purpose, a fortitude that left me breathless. A long-sleeved shirt hugged his chiseled torso, and his gray pants, free of patches, looked new. His long winter coat swayed side-to-side with each determined step he took, the heavy fabric brushing the back of his legs.

Sharing my brother's Solin vision, I scanned his striking features. My pupils dilated; blood surged through my veins. *Nope, this isn't a dream.*

A clean shave highlighted the razor-sharp lines of his jaw, and the scars that decorated his pale complexion had faded, distant memories of his capture. My breath hitched. His eyes were no longer cold and distant. They glowed with a warmth that melted my grief and resentment. The vicious storm that pounded my emotional shields calmed as Jax moved closer to the house—closer to me.

Like an invisible wand, his presence cast a spell of relief. The tension in my body vanished, my senses sharpened, and the air rushed into my lungs. I clawed at my chest. *I can breathe. I can finally breathe.*

Jax slowed his pace as he closed the gap between us, and the chains that bound my heart shattered into a million pieces once his eyes locked onto mine.

"Elara." The warm cloud that left his mouth brushed against me. "I've thought about you every second of every day." His fingers grazed my cheek. "But seeing you with my own eyes made me realize something."

Inaudible stutters proceeded. "And . . . what's that?"

"I was a fool for leaving you."

Before I could process his confession, Jax pressed his lips against mine. My heart expanded, the fire of life igniting within. Savoring the intimate embrace, I stood on my toes and wrapped my arms around his neck. The passion that rippled out of us could have melted the snow, and it probably would have, had we been sitting rather than standing.

Daring to interrupt our reunion, a gust of wind blew my hair into our faces. It didn't stop Jax's heated pursuit. No, it most certainly did not. Desire guided his tongue in circles around mine, the speed increasing with each beat of his pounding heart. His soft yet aggressive touch sent my head spinning. My pulse raced. His hand slipped under my coat, and with an assertive tug, he pulled me closer, kissing me harder. A pleasurable moan rumbled in my throat as his fingers gripped my waist.

Seconds passed, though it felt like hours. Jax held my bottom lip between his teeth, ending our make-out session. I squinted to see him, my vision blurring with lust.

Jax rested his forehead on mine and whispered, "Can you ever forgive me?"

The initial shock of his arrival wore off faster than jumping to Aroonyx. I shifted my weight, my brows furrowing with confusion.

Wait, a second. Jax left—abandoned me. I spent weeks worrying, wondering if the Inner Circle had captured him. Was he alive? Was he dead? I never imagined he'd show up and ask for my forgiveness.

I glanced at the other Lunin, who stood beside my brother on the front porch, his blue eyes glaring at Jax. *And what about Orion?* I swore under my breath. *Great. Now I'm that girl. The girl who drops the nice guy for the asshole.*

The taut muscles in my jaw loosened when a burst of clarity exploded around me. But Jax wasn't always an asshole. The way he treated me during those dark days had everything to do with the challenges he faced at Zenith's. Instead of brushing it off, I took it personally. It's easy to scrutinize a person's faults when life gets tough, and it's easy to assume those faults define their character. I did this with Jax. I overlooked the good that hid beneath the surface and clung to the negativity that sprouted.

A sigh slipped through my lips. *I don't have romantic feelings toward Orion—I never will. Our pathetic excuse for a kiss proved it. Cyrus was right. I can't force something that isn't there.*

I turned my attention to Jax. He watched me with cautious eyes. *Am I still angry that he abandoned me?* My fingers touched my chest. Though the chains had vanished, weeks of tension left my heart a mangled mess.

"Jax," I stammered. "I'm so confused. When you left, you were . . . angry. Like *really* angry. And now you're—"

"Not?"

"Yeah. What changed?"

A wide grin crossed his face as he lifted his chin to the afternoon sky. "Everything."

"How?"

He found my eyes and held my hands over his beating heart. "Elara, this was by far the most challenging thing I've ever faced. Spending weeks as Zenith's prisoner, trapped inside that damn basement stirred the darkness that lived inside of me, the darkness I never wanted you to see. The physical pain of the endless torture didn't compare to the mental anguish I experienced at Iah's."

I gulped, the image of Jax holding me against the bedroom wall etched in my mind.

As if reading my private thoughts, he tensed and cleared his throat before continuing. "The kiss we shared on the cliffside, the moment before Pollux and the others showed up, really opened my eyes. I had spent months going back and forth, wondering if I should express my feelings, and when I did, I realized our relationship was a lost cause because I couldn't let go of my past."

I frowned at his honesty and shivered at the icy breeze that snaked its way down the collar of my coat. Jax lifted my hands and cupped them around his mouth, warming them with a long exhale.

"Sharing that intimate moment confirmed that I wanted you in my life, but allowing you in meant opening the gates that guarded my heart. I just had to dust off the bullshit and grab the key buried underneath." He swallowed. "But I didn't."

"Why?"

"Fear. I was afraid."

I blinked, surprised to hear Jax use those two words.

He rubbed the back of his neck. "Who would I be if I let go of the jaded person who spent his life hiding behind a mask of solitude. My entire identity was a façade I created. The kiss we shared that night cracked my mask, and though a part of me rejoiced at the thought of ripping it off, the darker part refused.

"Zenith and Pollux forced me to revisit my past in ways that are not worth mentioning." He eyed the thick scar on the palm of his hand. "And when I woke up here, at Iah's, the identity I associated with resurfaced and morphed into a monster that clawed its way out." His shoulders sagged. "Honestly, it feels like a dream—a nightmare."

I nodded. *You can say that again.*

The ex-Collector's pupils constricted as he crossed his arms. "It pained me, sitting next to you on the porch."

I stared at his chin; his eyes brought back memories of the hateful words he spat that night.

"You brought me no relief, only resentment. I saw you as a cruel reminder of the man I wanted to be—the man I wasn't."

My chest caved. Jax had experienced enough emotional trauma to last a thousand lifetimes. I touched his arm. "You don't have to—"

"Please." He folded his hand over mine. "Let me explain. The darkness consumed me with each passing day. That's why I left. I remembered the promise I made to you and Cyrus, and I knew my decision would cut you deep, but I didn't care. I didn't care about anything.

"Apathy will do that to a person. I hid in the woods and fell into a pit of despair. I didn't eat. I didn't sleep. Hell, I even lost my will to live."

I shut my eyes, recalling the story Orion shared about the troubled man who took his life after Zenith released him from a week of torture.

Jax's voice stayed strong as he pressed on. "Those agonizing days blurred together as one. Desperate to free myself from the pain and suffering, I stood on the edge of the cliffside and stared at those jagged rocks, ready to end my life."

"Why are you telling me this? I don't want to hear how you planned on killing yourself."

The corner of his mouth twitched.

I glared. "It's not funny."

"I never said it was."

"Liar. You're smirking."

"I've missed this. Our endless banter."

I rested a hand on my hip. "I'm not playing games, Jax. Why are you laughing?"

He shifted his features into neutral. "Your comment lacked humor, but the sass in your tone did not." He acknowledged my boot that tapped the snow. "And your reaction confirms my theory."

"What theory?"

"After all this time, you're still a pain in my ass, and equally, if not more, impatient than ever." He paused, slipping a hand through the loop of my arm. My spine straightened as it settled on my lower back. "Now, if you'd be so kind as to let me finish, I think you'll discover the truth behind this story."

"What truth?"

Moving his lips near my ear, he whispered, "Here's a hint. It's a story of redemption."

10

ENDGAME

The light in Jax's eyes burned brighter as he continued. "So there I was, standing on the cliffside, ready to end my life. At the end of my rope, I had nothing to lose, so I closed my eyes and said *I'm lost, please help me.* My boot scooted over the edge but instead of falling, I stumbled backward."

Watching my nose crinkle with confusion, he added, "Elara, it was the most amazing experience. A strong hand reached out and grabbed me, but when I turned around, there was no one there. And suddenly, this light—this tangible power rushed through me. Overwhelmed, I fell to my knees; the sensation left me incapacitated. My entire life flashed before my eyes: the good, the bad—one vivid scene at a time. The darker parts were unbearable to watch: the crimes I committed, the people I hurt —killed, each vicious act more intense than I remembered. I had to relive my past all over again." Jax smiled and cupped my face. "But the darkness vanished when I remembered your words."

"What words?"

"People make the best decisions they can, regardless of the situation."

My jaw cracked open.

He hooked a finger under my chin and closed it. "And as soon as I accepted that truth, I stopped judging myself and I stopped judging my past."

Warm tears stung my eyes. Those were the words of my biological mother, not mine. She shared that bit of advice with my father on the night Zenith sent Jax to murder me and my brother. Eighteen years later, I shared the same advice with my adoptive parents when they asked why I forgave them for keeping my adoption a secret. And then Jax recalled the words from the daughter of the woman who spoke them first. I stared at the Lunin. *We've come full circle.*

A wide grin spread across his face. "Once the phenomena passed, I climbed to my feet, and when I opened my eyes, it was like seeing for the first time. After all those years, I finally had the courage to let go of my past. I couldn't rewrite history, but I could turn the page and start a new story."

A tear glided down my cheek. Jax kissed the drop of acceptance before finding my eyes. "Elara, your lesson on forgiveness struck a chord with me that day. And you were right. Forgiveness is available to everyone; we just have to reach out and grab it. I no longer blame Zenith, Pollux, or the others, and I no longer blame myself. I can forgive their actions and my own because I understand the truth. A life ruled by guilt and resentment stems from a void of love and compassion. Accepting this released me from the false power they had over me, and it released me from my past."

I melted into Jax's arms and shut my eyes, searching for any traces of residual darkness. Gone. Vanished. The light he spoke of radiated out of his being in a gentle vibration, the pulsing matched the rhythm of his heart.

I thought of the anguish that consumed me during Jax's

absence and the relief I experienced since his return. My brother's lesson swirled in my mind. He was right. My level of happiness didn't depend on Jax or anything outside of myself.

I spent weeks wishing for his return. Wishing he'd rescue me from my inner turmoil, but how could he? Jax wasn't responsible for my happiness. I was, and I had the power to let go of the negative emotions I harbored. He didn't hold the key that freed me from my mental hell. I did. And like the Lunin, I had a choice. Stay trapped in the past, weighed down by the chain of resentment or let it go. The choice was mine, and I chose . . .

"Elara." Jax's tone switched from hopeful to somber. "I can't predict the future, but I sense our toughest challenge is right around the corner." He held my hands. "Time is against us, so I plan on making every second count. I promised you and your brother I'd help you defeat Zenith, and I still stand by that promise. That's one reason I came back."

"And the other?"

A smirk tugged at the corner of his mouth. "I had some unfinished business."

"With whom?"

"You see . . . there's this girl."

"Oh, is there now."

"Mm-hmm."

"And?"

He slid his hand to the back of my neck, his fingers playing with my hair. "I needed to tell her something."

"Which is?"

"She"—he shook his head—"*you* are the light in the darkness, the torch that guides me through the fog of negativity. And for that, I'm eternally grateful."

My lips quivered.

"I've told you once, and I'll tell you again: I'm a better man because of you, and over these past few weeks, I've realized that

I want a better life, and I want to spend that life with you." The irises of his eyes sparkled as he whispered, "I want you, Elara. I love . . . *you*."

Three simple words changed my life forever. Unable to speak, I threw my arms around his neck and sobbed onto his shoulder. Jax held me in a tight embrace and stroked my hair while whispering words of comfort near my ear.

I always wondered why his presence filled me with a sense of peace. He could read my mind and decipher my emotions better than anyone else. I thought it had everything to do with his Seeker's intuition, and perhaps it aided our relationship, but in my heart, I knew it went deeper. The two of us shared an unspoken connection that bound us together for eternity. Like celestial bodies, we circled one another in an endless orbit, the gravitational pull sealing our fate.

I lifted my chin and gazed into his piercing blue eyes. Jax smiled, and I smiled back, only this time with my whole heart because at that moment I realized he was my past, my present, and my future. Jax was my everything—my endgame.

I rested a hand on his chest. "If the darkness ever resurfaces, promise me we'll face it together."

"I promise."

As if waking from a dream, I blinked and shifted my gaze to the front porch. Cyrus and Orion stood shoulder-to-shoulder, their expressions worlds apart. The Solin's amber eyes glowed with relief, while the Lunin's . . . *shit*. I winced. The angst and frustration that seeped from his eyes punctured my heart. A white cloud left his mouth as he turned and headed into the house.

My stomach knotted into a pretzel salted with guilt when I thought of our intimate moment before Jax arrived. *Do I tell him?*

The dealer snickered. *No, Elara. Keep that secret to yourself.*

What if Jax pisses you off? It's wise to have a card hidden up your sleeve.

I hesitated, then shook my head. *Stop that. You give horrible advice.*

Your loss. I'll be here if you need me.

The words ran together. "I kissed Orion."

Jax arched a brow. "And when was this?"

"Right before you called my name." Silence. I shifted my weight. "It meant nothing. I was—"

"And it's okay if it did."

"You're not mad?"

"No. Why would I be?"

I stared at our boots and fumbled with a loose button on my coat.

Jax lifted my chin, compelling me to look him in the eye. "Elara, you did nothing wrong. I put you through an emotional gauntlet. If Orion brought you a moment of peace—" he paused, observing my nervous posture, then took a small step backward. "But I'm guessing it was more than a moment."

"Jax, I—"

"You don't have to explain." He showed me his palms—a posture of surrender. "I get it. Orion was there for you when I wasn't. I've expressed my sentiments and you know where my loyalties lie." He eyed the spot where Orion once stood. "I just want you to be happy, even if that means me stepping aside for another man."

If my jaw wasn't attached to my head, it would have fallen into the snow. "I'm sorry, what did you just say?"

He pointed at the house, and not an ounce of jealousy tainted his words when he said, "If you have feelings for Orion and you'd rather—"

"No! I don't want to be with Orion."

My pulse quickened as I remembered our heated argument

about the young Lunin before his sudden departure. My eyelashes fluttered. *Are we really doing this again?*

I motioned to the porch. "Yes, I care for Orion—as a *friend.* I tried to see him as more, but it always felt forced because you had my heart." I reached for his hands. "And you always will."

"I'm glad we're on the same page."

Our heads turned when Cyrus approached. "Well, look who showed up."

Jax extended his hand. My brother knocked it away and pulled him into a strong hug. The Lunin cringed at the kind gesture. Receiving affection from a man was a foreign concept because Zenith raised him as his son.

Trying to recover, Jax patted Cyrus on the back in an awkward motion, then pulled away. "I'm sorry I bailed."

"It's cool, bro. No worries. I held down the fort." Cyrus inclined his head at me. "Keeping this one in line was a full-time job. She's gotten extra sassy and can be a real bi—"

"Choose your words wisely," I warned.

"Or what?"

"I'll tell Rico you're ignoring him again."

Cyrus's cheeks flushed with embarrassment.

"Who's Rico?" Jax asked, scanning the surrounding woods.

I burst into a fit of laughter.

Unamused, my twin wagged his finger at me and hissed, "Don't you dare."

"*Jax.*" My lips curled into a mischievous grin. "Rico is Cyrus's imaginary friend. A little monkey with a spunky personality who appeared at Idalia's one night after Cyrus drank too much Maragin." Jax looked at my brother with a puzzled expression, and before the Solin could explain, I added, "And speaking of Idalia."

Cyrus paled.

"It's fine," Jax reassured him. "Idalia told me the two of you are dating." He frowned. "Though she never mentioned Rico's part in your relationship."

My twin's shoulders sagged with relief, but my posture went rigid. I looked at Jax. "When did you see Idalia?"

"After that life-changing morning on the cliffside."

"Why did you go there? Why didn't you come back here?"

"Because I needed to clear my head." He blew out a tired breath and dragged a hand through his hair. "I'll never know how I got to the pub without the Collectors seeing me. Idalia answered the back door and let me hide upstairs for a few days. Funny enough, those were the only two days that Pollux and the others didn't search the place." Jax chuckled, rubbing a hand over his smooth chin. "She chewed my ass when I told her how I left the two of you at Iah's."

"She did?" I glanced at Cyrus, whose eyes glazed over with lust each time Jax mentioned the Solin's name.

"Yes, and she used very descriptive words to get her point across." Jax used his fingers to count. "Selfish idiot, asshole, arrogant prick—the list goes on and on."

"Accurate words indeed." I grinned.

He nodded, unable to hide the amusement that tugged at his lips. A heartbeat later his expression fell flat. "We knew the Inner Circle would return, so Idalia spoke to Samson. He insisted I stay at his place over in the North Village. No one is foolish enough to knock on his door. Not unless you want to leave without a tongue." Jax shrugged. "So I've been living there ever since."

"Are you *fucking* kidding me right now?"

Jax did a double take.

"She uses that word a lot more these days," Cyrus whispered to the Lunin.

A wave of heat rippled through me. "Stay out of it, bro." He lowered his head while I glared at Jax. "Do you mean to tell me I've spent almost two months worrying for no reason?"

"Elara, let me—"

"No, this is bullshit. You left me stuck here at Iah's, trapped in an emotional hell while you were chilling at Samson's."

"It's not like we were sitting on our asses sipping Mai Tais on an exotic beach."

I blinked, surprised to hear him use such an Earthly reference. Cyrus snorted. I pinned him with a long look that wiped the grin right off his face.

Jax found my eyes. "I had a lot of shit I needed to work through, and Samson gave me the time and the space to face it head on."

"Well, I'm glad you had a great bonding experience with your buddy Samson, but did he not think it appropriate to tell me you were alive and well? Could he not have said, *Hey Elara, in case you were wondering, Jax is taking a few personal days to get his shit together.*" A low growl rumbled in my chest. "Oh, wait until I see him."

"Don't be mad at Samson. He wanted to tell you, but I insisted otherwise." Jax reached for my hand. "I needed that time to process everything—alone."

My brother gave me a weighted glance, encouraging me to drop it.

"Fine. I'll give him a small ass chewing."

"That a girl." Jax winked.

Cyrus grumbled a slew of complaints as he watched the Lunin slide an arm around my waist. "Does this mean I'm sleeping on the couch again?"

My face reddened at the hopeful thought. Jax shrugged, squeezing the sensitive area around my hip bone.

Cyrus rolled his eyes at the giggle that escaped my mouth. My lips moved to justify my behavior but paused. The front door slammed shut. Our heads turned. Orion stormed down the porch steps, his hands fisted in silent rage.

"Uh oh," Cyrus murmured. "Someone's pissed."

Daggers etched with resentment shot out of Orion's eyes as he looked at me and Jax. He then headed into the forest, leaving a snowy wake of mist and frustration behind.

The masked dealer dragged an icy claw along my spine. I shivered.

See, wasn't that a fun little game you played with Orion? It snickered. What a happy ending. He seems thrilled with the turn of events.

"Screw you."

Jax's arm recoiled faster than one could blink. My brother winced at my sudden outburst.

"Sorry," I recovered. "I wasn't talking to either of you."

Jax's eyes drifted to Cyrus. He shrugged, unaware of the mysterious visitor who whispered in my ear at the most inopportune times.

The ex-Collector jerked a thumb at Orion's footprints. "Take a few minutes and clear the air with your friend."

I hesitated, twisting the loose button on my coat and frowning when it fell to the ground.

"He's right," Cyrus encouraged. "You should go."

I met Jax's gaze. "You don't mind?"

"Not in the slightest."

Desperate to make things right, I jogged after the man who refused to turn his back on me. *Correction. The man who just did.*

11

WINDS OF CHANGE

The strong winds slapped at my face while I trudged through the deep snow. My lungs burned with each icy breath, my Lunin endurance helpless during the day. Winded, I clutched my aching side and slowed my pace once the blurred details of Orion's winter coat sharpened. I cupped my hands around my mouth and called his name. Ignoring me, he pressed on.

"Orion." I cursed, tripping over a fallen tree limb. "Will you stop and talk to me or do I have to chase you all the way to Zenith's?"

His boots slowed to a crawl. I sighed, jogging to close the distance between us. Refusing to turn around, he stood with his back facing me, the whites of his knuckles matching the falling snowflakes that kissed his hands.

As soon as I moved in front of him, he snapped, "What do you want, Elara?"

"Please don't act like this."

"Like what?"

"Like this," I said, gesturing to his rigid posture.

He scowled and averted his eyes.

I tossed up my hands. "I'm sorry, okay? I screwed up. Had I known Jax was coming back I would have never—"

"Never what?" His brows raised. "Never kissed me?"

"Don't put that on me." He shifted his gaze back to the rustling branches, so I poked him in the chest. "You made the first move. You asked to kiss me."

"Oh, so now it's my fault."

"Don't put words in my mouth. I never said that. You know my history with Jax."

"Then why are we having this conversation?"

"Because it's obvious you're pissed and now I feel like shit."

"Well, don't lose sleep over it," he muttered. "I take full responsibility for the mistake I made."

Ouch. His spiteful words slammed into my gut. "*This*"—I waved a hand between the two of us—"wasn't a mistake. It's just—"

"It's just what?"

"That kiss." I inhaled a sobering breath and gathered my hair over one shoulder. "It felt forced. I tried to let go of Jax. I really did, but how do you let go of a person who has your heart?"

Orion shut his eyes, the muscles in his jaw twitching. It appeared my confession only elevated his level of irritation.

"So yeah, I'm guilty of caring for two people at once." Tugging at guilt's claws that pierced my back, I added, "Can you forgive me?"

A casual shrug was his only answer.

I gritted my teeth. *Great, he's still pissed.*

"What do you want me to say, Elara? I'm thrilled the girl I care for is back with the man she loves?" A cloud of resentment shot out of his mouth. "Or how much I enjoyed being a placeholder?"

I swore under my breath. Cyrus's prediction proved true.

My little game ended hurting us both. I touched his arm. "How can I make things right?"

"Actions speak louder than words." He inclined his head toward the house. "Your dramatic performance with Jax said enough."

I glared at his snide remark. Yes, I led him on, let him think our relationship would evolve into something more, but he volunteered to be whatever I *needed* him to be.

"How dare you," I spat. "You can't even fathom the emotional pain I've suffered over these past weeks, these past months—hell, this past year. Jax turned my entire life upside down, like this." I snapped my fingers in his face. "And since my return to Aroonyx, everyone has expected me to go with the flow and accept the bitter truth: I'm living on another planet." My voice raised. "Orion, do you hear how crazy that sounds? Last year I was a normal person, living a normal life, and now, I'm preparing to battle an evil dictator who wants to murder me with his bare hands."

The flicker of compassion that sparked in Orion's eyes dimmed once I added two unnecessary sentences to my rant. "So I apologize that you got caught in the middle of it all. I'm sorry you fell for the girl with the screwed-up mind and the even more fucked-up life."

Our ragged breath formed a white haze of tension. The Lunin rose to his full height. I gulped, bracing myself for the verbal blow.

"No, Elara! I don't have a personal account of your emotional trauma, but you sure as hell didn't have a problem dragging me into your pit of despair." I cringed. He countered my attack with minimal effort. "I tried to be a good friend. I tried to be there when a certain someone left you—abandoned you."

My nails dug into my palms.

The masked dealer clinked its claws with malicious intent.

He's a clever boy, Elara. You never gave him enough credit. It snickered. *Poor girl. He left you looking like the fool.*

I rolled my neck, shoving the dealer out of my mind.

"But none of that matters, does it?" Orion hissed. "How could it? You're too selfish to notice anyone outside of yourself."

I squeezed my eyes shut, forcing the tears to stay hidden. Orion muttered inaudible words and pivoted in the snow. I grabbed his wrist. My voice cracked with grief. "You're right. I'm sorry."

He ripped his arm out of my tight grip and spun around to face me. "It's too late for apologies."

"Says the prideful man who refuses to let go of resentment."

He breathed hard and closed the gap between us, his eyes narrowing. "Don't stand here and presume—"

"Orion!"

My breath hitched at the sound of Jax's voice.

"Step away from Elara."

Snapped out of his anger-driven trance, Orion took a step backward with his hands raised. My vision improved and skin surged with heat as my brother moved closer.

Jax stepped beside me, his eyes fixed on Orion. "Is there a problem?"

I stilled at the lethal edginess in his tone. Staring at the laces of my worn boots, I silently beseeched Orion to keep his mouth shut. No luck.

"Yeah," he snapped, meeting Jax's gaze. "A big one. I'm looking right at it."

A low whistle left my brother's lips, an audible warning for Orion to stand down. I held my breath, waiting for the ex-Collector to retaliate. Preparing for the worst, Cyrus slid his boot forward. I raised a hand, commanding him to stop.

As if observing an elaborate painting in a museum, Jax crossed his arms, tilted his head, and scanned Orion's troubled expression. Not an ounce of jealousy or animosity flickered in Jax's eyes.

He pointed toward the spring. "Take a walk with me, Orion."

A pair of sapphire eyes drifted to mine before locking onto Jax. After a lengthy pause, he nodded.

My brother and I shared a bewildered expression as we watched the two Lunins disappear into the snow-covered forest.

Cyrus huffed a breath. "Well, that was unexpected."

"Yes, yes it was."

The wind howled, spitting snow into our faces. Cyrus dusted a crystal off his nose before saying, "Orion's earned a badge of courage today."

"Why?"

"Because it takes some big balls to go on a walk with Jax, especially after testing him the way he did. I wouldn't want to be in Orion's shoes right now."

"It's not like that."

Cyrus murmured his disagreement.

"It's not," I pressed.

"Elara, you and I both know the repercussions of pushing Jax into a corner. I learned during the night of his confession, and you learned the day he left."

"True." I picked a snowflake off my eyelash. "But he won't use his fists or cruel words to get through to Orion."

"Why not? That's how Jax communicates when he's pissed."

I smiled, thinking of his life-changing moment on the cliffside. "Because he's different now. That's not who he is anymore."

"I hope you're right, sis." Cyrus threw an arm over my shoulder, encouraging me to move forward. "I'd hate for history to repeat itself."

12

FRIEND OR FOE

Irritated with the heavy fabric that clung to my body in all the wrong places, I stood and adjusted the gray pleats before lowering myself back onto the porch chair. Cyrus pressed his spine into the wooden slats and tucked his hands deeper into the fur-lined pockets of his coat.

He squinted, his eyes watering from the blistering cold. "Do you think Jax can make it right between the three of you?"

"Probably. He always brings clarity to the most screwed-up situations."

Cyrus picked at the dirt underneath his nails. "True. He convinced us we're twins from another planet." A smile played on his lips. "So yeah, I guess he can persuade Orion to move on."

"That's not what he's doing."

"Oh, so Jax is schooling Orion in the art of the game. Speaking of Jax's strong game; why don't you get a room the next time the two of you have a steamy make-out session."

I smothered a smirk and found his eyes. "You are sleeping on the couch from now on, right?"

He blew a snowflake at my face. I chuckled. It melted from his warm breath.

"If we were on Earth, we could invite Idalia to join us on a double date."

My brother puffed up his chest. "She'd look good riding in my car. Hillary would die of jealousy."

"You get more ridiculous every day."

He flashed me a mischievous grin. "First, we'd drop you and Jax off at Starbucks."

"Why?"

"It seems appropriate. That's the first place y'all hung out."

"You were there too."

"And *you* were too scared to talk to me."

I grimaced, remembering how quickly I vacated the Starbucks after I noticed Cyrus sitting at the corner table. "I had my reasons. It's not like you accepted our family ties with open arms."

"Fair enough."

I shook my head at him. "So you'd ditch us at Starbucks? What kind of lame double date is that?"

"The kind that leaves me alone with Idalia."

"I see. You enjoy a more hands-on approach."

"Hell yeah." His amber eyes glazed over with lust. "Have you seen that woman? She's a sun goddess."

I snorted, though he had a point. Idalia was the most beautiful woman I had ever seen. "And afterward, you could grab a beer instead of Maragin. You don't want Rico getting jealous." Laughter softened the hard lines around his eyes. My lips sagged at the thought of my only female friend on Aroonyx. "I miss her, Cyrus."

He nodded, then leaned back in his chair. "So do I."

"We'll find a way for the two of you to see each other."

"When the time is right." He squeezed my hand but stared at the trees. "I'm glad you're happy."

"Thanks. For weeks I've had this dense fog, this depressive cloud hovering over me. I looked at the world through a dark lens. The future appeared bleak—hopeless." I followed my brother's gaze. "I didn't realize how far I'd gone down the rabbit hole."

"Yeah, I worried about you, sis. Jax came back at the perfect time."

My head swayed from side to side with mixed emotions. "Jax didn't pull me out of the darkness, my brother's advice did."

He nudged me with his elbow. "I'm glad you joined the party."

"I like to make an entrance."

"Better late than never."

"Hashtag truth," I said, gliding my hand through the air.

"Damn. I haven't thought about social media since we left Earth. I wonder if everyone thinks we vanished."

"We-e-ell, technically we did."

A white cloud shot out of his nostrils. "Even though I miss the comforts of home, I've enjoyed not having a phone."

"Me too."

"I'd spend hours scrolling through Facebook and Instagram, staring at a screen, living vicariously through others. Social media has its perks, but going off the grid made me realize that none of that shit even matters."

I stayed silent, absorbing my brother's words. As usual, he was right.

Our bodies rotated to face Iah when he peeked his head around the door. "Lunch is on the table."

"Sounds good to me." Cyrus flashed the doctor a warm grin and climbed to his feet. "I'm starved."

"You're always hungry," I said, following him across the porch.

"I've got to bulk up."

"Really?" I flicked his rock-hard bicep. "Your muscles can't get any bigger."

"They can, and they will, considering I'll be fighting Apollo on the battlefield." My face fell. Recovering he added, "Forget it. Samson can handle Apollo. They're a better match. I'll take care of Pollux."

"Is that supposed to make me feel better? My brother versus a sadistic killer?"

Cyrus dropped the touchy subject and offered to help me with my coat. The heat from the crackling fire warmed my chilled body as I slipped my arms out of the sleeves. I approached the dining room table at a guarded pace. *What do I say to Iah? Jax is back, and your son hates me?*

I cleared my throat and pulled out a chair. "I'm not sure if Orion told you the news."

"He did." Disappointment saturated Iah's words.

Unable to look him in the eyes, I stared at the pile of stewed meat and rooted vegetables on my plate.

In a cheerful voice, Cyrus said, "Thanks for the food, Iah. It looks delicious. You're such a great cook."

The Lunin returned my brother's kindness with a smile and a head nod.

I eyed my brother and mouthed, "Kiss ass."

He snickered while sinking his teeth into a soft roll.

"Jax appears to be in good health." Iah's tone switched from a friend to a doctor.

The masked dealer cackled in my ear. *Your little game ended well, Elara. You hurt Iah too.*

Get out of my head. You're not welcome here.

More wicked laughter. *You don't get a say. I'll leave when I'm good and ready.*

"Fuck off."

Cyrus choked on a mouthful of food, his eyes bulging. He

pounded on his chest, then whispered, "What the hell is wrong with you, sis? Are you possessed by some evil spirit?"

Maybe. "Sorry. You weren't supposed to hear that."

He lifted a silver mug to his lips and before taking a swig, he murmured, "I might be ridiculous but at least I don't talk to myself."

I glared at my brother but looked at Iah when he said, "I should give Jax a thorough examination."

"Why?" I asked.

"I never gave him a medical clearance." The doctor pressed his palms on the counter and stared out the living room window. "I need to ask if he suffered any side effects from the Minlav antidote." He rubbed his chin. "I didn't notice the twitch when the two of you were speaking outside. It might have been a temporary effect of the treatment."

My mouth gaped. The twitch—the glitch. I had forgotten about the strange phenomena that started after Jax woke up. I swallowed. *I hope it disappeared along with the demons of his past.*

The morbid memories twisted my stomach into a knot. I scowled at my plate and divided the meat and vegetables into groups, arranged by color, while my brother shoveled spoonfuls into his mouth.

"You have the worst table manners."

He showed me his chewed food before turning his attention to Iah. The two drummed up a conversation about medical advances on Earth. I ate in silence, listening to my brother explain the benefits of an X-ray machine and a CT scan. The retired doctor stood slack-jawed, mesmerized by the life-saving inventions.

I groaned at the leftover meat.

"Are you gonna eat that?" Cyrus asked, inching his fork toward the remaining scraps.

"No. Knock yourself out."

The front door swung open right as the tiny triton stabbed a piece of meat.

I sucked in a sharp breath watching the two men step over the threshold. Jax clapped Orion on the back. After hanging up his coat, the younger Lunin strolled through the living room. Iah's posture tensed. His son didn't bother to greet us.

The toe of my boot tapped against the hardwood floors. *Don't press it. Give him some space.* I looked at my brother for encouragement. He shook his head and used his half-eaten roll to soak up the gravy on my plate.

Screw it. I'll work on my patience another day.

The chair skidded across the floor as I bolted from my seat. I caught Jax's eyes for only a moment before dashing after Orion for the second time that day. Hearing my determined approach, he rested his hand on the doorknob.

I managed a, "Hey . . . you," with a gentle punch to his shoulder.

Acknowledging my lame attempt at rekindling our broken friendship, Orion's lips curled into a tiny grin. My shoulders sagged with relief. Unsure of what to say to one another, our eyes swung back and forth.

A few silent ticks later, Orion let go of the knob. "Elara, I don't know what to say."

I shut my eyes, preparing for the worst.

The masked dealer's cape fluttered in a phantom breeze.

I gritted my teeth. *Don't even think about it.*

As you wish. It sulked into a darkened corner of my mind.

I've got this.

I could have sworn I saw it mock me behind that damn mask.

When I opened my eyes, I saw Orion scanning my troubled expression, waiting for me to speak.

I shifted my weight. "We don't have to talk about this anymore, but if there's anything you want to share, I'm all ears."

"Fine. Here it goes." He crossed his arms. "You took advantage of the situation and used me as a bridge to narrow the emotional gap between you and Jax." When I didn't argue, he added, "But the truth is—I allowed it to happen and I'm not sure why. I never act this way around girls. Maybe it had something to do with that strong game of yours."

I chuckled at Cyrus's earlier remark.

"It's true. You really caught me off guard, Elara."

"I find that surprising. You're a clever guy."

"And you're a clever girl, but you did a shitty job at hiding your feelings for Jax."

I folded my arms across my chest, matching his assertive posture.

"Sorry. I meant that in the nicest way possible."

"And?"

"I was an idiot for ignoring the obvious." He lifted his gaze over my shoulder, then lowered his voice. "I thought over time you'd learn to care for me more than Jax."

I swallowed a lump of guilt. "Orion, I—"

"None of that matters. Jax is a different person now. I *really* want to hate the guy, but I can't. He did nothing wrong, and he's more understanding than most men in his shoes."

"Maybe it's because of all the shit he's been through. Jax understands the human struggle, and patience is his middle name."

The Lunin smiled and found my eyes. "The two of you are a good match."

I sighed. His simple statement plucked guilt's claws out of my back. "Thanks for being such a good friend."

"Likewise, Elara."

I threw my arms around his neck. After a quick embrace, he pulled away and whispered, "Now that Jax is back you should stop undressing me with your eyes."

"I'll try."

Testing me, Orion pulled his shirt over his head while walking into his room. With his back facing me, he said, "I bet you're still staring."

My tongue hissed against my teeth. Muffled laughter sounded behind the bedroom door after his boot kicked it shut. I pivoted toward the kitchen but turned back around, noting the room at the end of the hall. *I wonder if I'll see it in a different light.*

Curious, I tiptoed down the hallway and slipped into the space I once feared. Thump. Thump. Thump. The window tapped against the wall above the bed, and the icy gust blowing through acted as an invisible drummer. I watched the corners of the thin comforter flutter in the breeze. The aged floorboards creaked as I hurried across the room. I climbed onto the bed and reached for the silver handle, the mattress sagging under my weight. I spun it clockwise, and after a few rotations later, the window snapped shut. I rubbed my chilled arms. *There, that's better.*

The momentary comfort faded when I glanced at the forbidden wall, the wall that Jax shoved me against, the wall where he held me by my neck, the wall where he tried to kill me. I shivered. *Nope. This room still gives me the creeps.*

A dense knot formed at the top of my stomach as I recalled the story Iah shared about Taurus, Zenith's adoptive father. The deranged doctor tortured the young Zenith for over twelve years in the attic of his home. Starvation, beatings, disturbing medical experiments, the list went on and on.

The knot expanded at the cruel way Zenith sought revenge once he came of age. After poisoning Taurus, he mutilated the doctor's body and changed the color of his eyes. Iah knew this because he discovered his mentor's corpse and found Zenith holding Taurus's black eyes in his hands. Another shiver rippled through me.

Eager to vacate the eerie space, along with the memories

that haunted me, I trekked backward across the room, stretching my legs over the bloodstains that decorated the floors. My heart nearly leapt out of my chest when I slammed into a figure who stood behind me—a man. His hands wrapped around my arms, his icy fingers digging into my skin. I cursed as all of my training with Samson flew right out the damn window.

13

BLOODSTAINED HANDS

The muscles in my body contracted so fast, I wondered if the skin had peeled off my bones.

Releasing me, the man whispered, "Elara. It's me."

I whipped around to find Jax holding up his hands, his eyes watching my every move.

"Damn it." I clutched my chest. "You almost gave me a heart attack. Why did you sneak up on me?"

"I thought you heard me come in." His brows etched together. "Why were you walking backward?"

I stumbled to answer the simple question. "Lost in thought?"

"Are you okay? Cyrus and Orion mentioned you've been talking to yourself."

A quiet snicker snaked down my spine. I rolled my neck. "Yeah, I'm fine."

"Not much has changed." He sighed through his nose. "You're still a horrible liar."

I scoffed.

"Fine. I won't pry about the thoughts that occupy your mind, but I will ask you this—what are you doing in here?"

"Uh . . . I'm not sure." I eyed the wall. "I'm trying to see this space differently."

"What do you mean?"

"This room haunted me after you left. It brought back bad memories. Each time I walked in to get a change of clothes, I'd think about the night . . ."

Jax moved closer and slid his hands down my arms. "Elara, it's just a room."

"Agree to disagree."

"It's not helpful to project past experiences or emotions onto a place or even a person." He tucked a stray hair behind my ear. "I'm sorry to have caused you so much emotional distress over these past weeks."

"It's okay. I'd do it again if it meant giving you the opportunity to let go of your past."

He leaned his forehead against mine and whispered, "I don't deserve you."

"You're probably right." I stood on my toes to reach his lips but froze when Iah cleared his throat.

Jax chuckled and stepped away from me.

Disregarding the embarrassment that stained my cheeks, the doctor focused his attention on Jax. "I'd like to do the examination." His eyes drifted to me as he adjusted his grip on the medical bag. "If *now* is a good time."

Wishing I had the power of invisibility, I stared at the cracks in the floor.

Unable to keep a straight face, Jax said, "Now is a great time."

Liar.

He winked at me before taking a seat on the bed.

Not one for awkward situations, I made a beeline toward the door.

"Elara, you don't have to leave."

The soles of my boots skidded across the floor. I turned. "I thought you'd want some privacy."

"I have nothing to hide from you."

I swallowed and broke eye contact. *Get it together. He's referring to his medical history—nothing more.*

Ignoring the smirk that tugged on his lips, I strolled across the room and leaned against the wall. *Nope.* The last encounter with said wall flashed in my mind. *Not happening.*

As though the wooden panels had caught fire, I hissed and jolted forward; the ridiculous motion sucked the cool right out of me.

Iah and Jax exchanged a quizzical look.

"Are you well?" the doctor asked.

I stumbled over my words.

"I'm sure she's fine," Jax offered.

A sound of dismissal slipped through my pursed lips. "Yeah, I'm good." I jerked a thumb at the wall. "I think there was a splinter or something sticking out of the . . ." *Shit. I don't even know what I'm trying to say.*

"Sticking out of the wall?" Jax suggested.

"Mm-hmm." I stared at the floor once more. *If I was a Seeker, I'd jump right out of here.*

Iah brushed off my complaint and reached for Jax's wrist. He held two fingers against the radial artery, shut his eyes, and counted to thirty before continuing with the examination.

The doctor moved with the grace of a high-profile surgeon who spent years mastering his craft. I thought of his time as Taurus's apprentice and wondered if his reserved personality stemmed from working with a loose cannon.

Iah inspected Jax's ears, nose, and throat. He then used his index finger to track the Lunin's eye movement and asked if he had suffered any headaches or dizziness since his departure. Jax responded with a firm *no*.

I swiped a finger under the collar of my shirt and eyed the closed window. I should have kept it open. The body heat of three people had warmed the small space.

Iah inspected the round scar on the back of Jax's head: the entry point where he had inserted the corkscrew to drain the blood and inject the needle into Jax's brain.

"The incision has healed nicely." The doctor pressed his thumbs around Jax's sinuses. "You had a high level of toxicity in your blood when you arrived on my doorstep. I've treated patients who ingested a small dose of Minlav but never anyone poisoned over a prolonged period."

My fingernails pressed into my palms as I recalled the cruel way Pollux and Zenith treated Jax during his capture.

"Have you experienced any physical discomfort from the Minlav antidote? Seizures, blurred vision, trouble concentrating?

"No."

The doctor crossed his arms and observed his patient. "What about the tremors? Are you still finding them troublesome?"

"No. They stopped a few days after I left. I'm not sure if it was the Minlav"—he caught my eye for a heartbeat—"or something else."

Iah nodded. "I'm sure the physical pain that Zenith and the others inflicted has passed, but the mental trauma can still linger. Have you experienced insomnia, depression, or suicidal thoughts?"

I blew out a tight breath and acted very interested in the split ends on my hair.

"I did," Jax said. "I experienced all three."

"I see. On a scale of one to ten, with ten being the happiest moment in your life and one being the worst, how would you rate your mental health today?"

I didn't lift my chin, though I could feel Jax staring right at me. "I'd say a solid seven."

My fingers froze their grooming efforts.

"But now that I'm back, I see that number rising faster than ever."

A smile danced across my lips.

"Excellent." Iah used both of his hands to push on the top of Jax's head. I winced. The visual reminded me of the time my mother took me to visit a chiropractor who worked out of a mall kiosk. That's right. Not an office—a kiosk. The smell of cheap whiskey and the stench of the nickel alloy from the man's "gold" chains burned my nose each time he adjusted my neck. I snickered. *No, that wasn't my mother's finest parenting moment.*

My cruise down memory lane screeched to a halt once the doctor asked Jax to remove his shirt. He obliged. A gasp of awe doused with desire escaped my mouth. *Holy shit.*

My eyes wandered faster than a starving man at a free buffet. The drastic changes in the Lunin's physique proved that he had not sat on his ass sipping Mai Tais with Samson. No. No, he did not.

As if sculpted from Clear Stone, the hard muscles of Jax's upper body flexed while he adjusted his weight on the mattress. *Good Lord.* It took an abnormal amount of self-control to not run across the room and investigate the hard planes of his chiseled abdomen and defined pectorals. I glanced at my feet, surprised a puddle of drool hadn't formed.

The doctor listened to Jax's heart, then motioned for him to spin around so he could examine his lungs. Jax's injuries had healed beautifully. Once purple, the flesh-colored scars now blended with his fair complexion.

My eyes grew, spotting the line along his rib cage—the evidence of the trick my brother and I used to melt his skin together so he didn't bleed out. I shook my head, forcing the disturbing images back into the secluded room at the far end of my mind.

The medical bag clicked shut, and the doctor smiled at his patient. "I'm pleased to announce you've made a full recovery."

Relief washed over me.

Jax extended his hand to the doctor. "Thank you for saving my life."

"Don't thank me. Thank Cyrus. I could not have gotten that tube down your throat or performed the antidote injection without his Solin strength."

Jax remained silent while Iah reached for his bag. After a final head nod, the doctor departed the room, closing the door behind him.

Not wanting to disturb Jax's inner narrative, I tiptoed over the floorboards and took a seat beside him.

After a long pause, he said, "You cut your hair."

"I'm surprised you noticed."

"I notice everything about you, Elara."

Unable to hold the intensity of his stare, I looked away. My eyes drifted around his muscular torso before settling on the scar on his back. I craned my neck to get a better view. *I can't believe we closed that wound.*

Curious, I ran a finger across the jagged line. Jax hissed. The muscles in his back contracted at my gentle touch.

"I'm sorry. Did that hurt?"

"No." His chest vibrated with quiet laughter. "Your fingers are cold."

I grimaced, sitting on the culprits.

Jax pulled them from their hiding place and raised them to his mouth. "Here." He cupped his hands around mine and blew out a warm breath.

My eyes darted back and forth between the sharp lines of his jaw and his impressive eight-pack that rivaled top fitness models.

Why can't I stop staring? Is it because of his absence? Absence makes the heart grow fonder. I swallowed. *Fonder of something— that's for sure.*

I shut my eyes, hoping to clear the lust that blurred my vision.

The masked dealer snickered. *Go for it, Elara. He won't mind.*

I rolled my neck, every fiber in my body on high alert. I wanted to throw myself on top of Jax, rip those damn pants right off of him, and I would have had his laughter not distracted me.

My eyes shot open to see his stomach muscles contracting. I groaned. *That's not helping.*

Jax continued to laugh while my cheeks flushed with heat. I stepped up my game after he flashed me a seductive smirk with enough sexual tension to fog the window. Sliding a pawn over our imaginary chess board, I cocked my head to one side. *Your move.*

Entertaining my little game, Jax scanned the more sensitive areas of my body, each one begging him to come closer. My spine straightened, a silent invitation for him to proceed without caution. He wrapped one hand around my waist and slid me across the bed. Victory. My breath hitched. His fingers grazed the side of my face, his cool touch a stark contrast to my warm cheeks. I stifled a moan, feeling his thumb brush my lips. Jax made his move. His tongue swept in lazy circles that confirmed his talent surpassed a gentle kiss to the mouth. My hand slid up his arm, nails digging into his bicep. He kissed me harder while his fingers played with the buttons on my pants. Bothered by the delay, I moved to assist with his efforts.

He grabbed my wrist and whispered, "We should wait."

"Why?"

"Because—" Jax stilled, his eyes narrowing on the door as it swung open.

In walked Cyrus. "Hey guys, I just need to grab a change of . . . *oh* shit."

I cursed, dropping my head while Jax adjusted himself.

My brother couldn't stop laughing as he headed toward the closet. "My eyes are averted."

"Get the hell out of here," I snapped, throwing a pillow at him.

He caught it with one hand, then tucked it under his arm. "Thanks, sis. I'll need this now that I'm sleeping on the couch."

"No," Jax said, "I'll stay in the living room."

I scowled, wishing he'd shut his damn mouth.

Cyrus flashed the Lunin a sidelong look. "I can't leave a brother stranded." A casual glance in my direction. "You've got to strike when the iron's hot."

My eyes bulged. "Are you done?"

His shoulders shook with more laughter. "No, I'm just getting started."

I flashed him a vulgar gesture, then yelled, "I want a new twin," as he exited the room.

"Love you too, sis."

I looked at Jax, my lips curling into a pout. "Can we pretend that never happened?"

"If it pleases you."

I rested his hand on my thigh, encouraging him to continue where he left off. He patted my leg. Patted it.

"I should put on my shirt."

"Or not."

"It's a necessary precaution," he said, slipping his arms through the long sleeves.

"And why's that?"

A low growl rumbled in Jax's chest as he pressed his palms into the mattress, locking me between his arms. "Because even though I have a strong sense of self-control"—he paused, watching me bite my lip—"if you keep looking at me the way you are now, I won't have a reason to hold back."

My vision blurred. *How can I keep up with that?*

His teeth nipped my ear. "Patience, Elara."

He rose to his feet. I had to grip the mattress to keep from falling off the bed. Instead of kicking and screaming like a toddler who didn't get their way, I inhaled a long breath and counted to ten. The calming exercise didn't do a damn bit of good.

Jax sifted through Cyrus's clothes, his fingers gliding over the organized chaos of gray and crème-colored shirts that hung from the wooden hangers. After a brief inspection, he retrieved a palm-sized, fabric-wrapped bundle from his pocket. Hiding it from view, the Lunin placed the tiny package on the top shelf.

"What should we do now?" he asked, strolling toward the bed.

"Is that a trick question?"

Jax shook his head at me for the umpteenth time that day. "Patience."

"Fine. Then why don't we take a walk? It might help me cool off."

"It is rather warm in here," he teased, pushing the sleeves of his shirt over his biceps.

"That's not fair."

He chuckled and offered me his hand. "Come on. Let's grab our coats. You can fill me in on everything I missed."

WE SPENT the rest of the afternoon circling Iah's. The icy breeze smacked me in the face each time we rounded the home, but I didn't mind because with each gust Jax pulled me closer, his arm draped around my waist.

I shared the details of each event he missed during his

absence, starting with a play-by-play of what happened after Pollux captured him on the cliffside. He stayed quiet while I explained how I burned Elio's face and Apollo's wrist when they attacked us at the spring. His eyes widened when I shared Cyrus's near-death experience, and he hummed his appreciation for Idalia when I mentioned how she saved our asses by hiding us in the wall on the day the Collectors paid us an unexpected visit.

A lump of grief blocked my airway as I shared the rumors of his death. Sensing my discomfort, Jax tightened his grip around me. He snickered at my initial reaction to Samson's unconventional training technique, then laughed hard at my retelling of Cyrus's adverse reaction to Maragin.

"I wish I could have seen that with my own eyes."

I nodded, leaning into his warmth. "It happened at the perfect time; we needed some comedic relief."

Jax inhaled a deep breath, then blew a white cloud from his mouth. We walked in silence for long minutes, our boots guiding us down the manmade path that encircled Iah's.

My eyes stung with moisture when I mentioned Archer's selfless act, and the tears fell after I confessed my foolish mistake.

"Elara, that was a challenging situation. It takes years of training to act without hesitation. I told Archer you wouldn't leave him. He assured me that he'd take matters into his own hands if you refused."

The desperation in Archer's eyes propelled the determination of his swift movements that night. Each swipe of his blade pushed me farther away from Pollux and Elio, farther away from him.

I sniffled. "It crushes me to think he died for no reason."

Jax stopped our casual pace. "He didn't. Archer sacrificed himself for the future—for the greater good. I'd be dead had he not rescued me from the basement." The ex-Collector found my eyes. "You didn't take the head start he gave you, but your brother did."

"I never thought of it that way."

"And because of your hesitation, Archer didn't die alone that night. You had the courage to stay with him until he took his final breath." A mild relief loosened my rigid posture. Jax added, "I can't say this from experience, but I'm sure that looking into the eyes of an angel instead of a demon before death makes quite the difference."

I wiped a tear off my cheek. *Maybe he's right. A sense of peace grabbed hold of Archer before he passed.*

"Come on." Jax guided me toward the porch. "Let's get you warmed up."

MY NOSTRILS FLARED at the delicious smell that wafted from the kitchen. Iah shuffled from the sink to the cabinets, then back again. The man couldn't sit still for five minutes. He busied himself with cooking, cleaning, inspecting medical equipment, and taking inventory of supplies. His busy-bee behavior reminded me of my adoptive mother on Earth. I sighed, missing her more than ever.

Refusing to pause his animated conversation with Orion about the benefits of democracy, Cyrus acknowledged us with a subtle head nod. My hand rested on the top rail for only a moment before Jax pulled out the chair.

I curtsied, flaring the fabric of my invisible dress, and took a seat. Jax huffed an amused breath and lowered himself onto the chair across from Orion.

The hunger pains in my stomach guided my hand toward the buffet of food that Iah had prepared. "Cyrus, just so there's no confusion," I interrupted, snatching a roll, "I gave Jax a thorough account of your evening with Rico."

His fork fell onto his plate. "You didn't."

"Oh, I most certainly did. It's only fair. Jax is part of the team again. *You* were the one who didn't want to leave a brother stranded, remember?"

"Touché, sis."

"Elara's a little sassier than I remember," Jax said to Orion.

"You have no idea."

"A different word comes to my mind," Cyrus added.

I raised my fork and aimed it at my brother's head. Jax clicked his tongue.

Keeping a straight face, he looked at Cyrus and said, "Can I join you and Rico in a pedal car race to Zenith's tonight?"

The defeated Solin tossed up his hands and pushed his chair away from the table. Everyone, including Iah, burst into laughter.

My heart soared as I eyed the men around me. Finally. We were finally at peace. The carefree moment dissolved any residual resentment and solidified our union as an unstoppable force, one prepared for battle.

Our cheerful mood vanished at the sound of a fist pounding on the front door. We froze, all eyes on Jax. With feline grace, he stood, pulled the gray knife from his back pocket and exposed the blade. He then moved his index finger to his lips.

With great caution, Cyrus and Orion steadied their chairs as they rose to their feet, careful to avoid scraping the legs against the floor. I followed their lead. Iah didn't budge from his place behind the kitchen sink, his blue eyes fixed on the ex-Collector.

Jax mouthed, "Stay," as he glided over the creaking floorboards.

"Open up!" yelled a raspy voice.

"It's Samson," Cyrus muttered, loud enough for everyone to hear.

The tension in our bodies eased until Jax opened the door.

He stumbled backward as Samson barged into the home. I cursed. The lines on the Solin's face appeared deeper than usual, and his pupils had shrunk to the size of tiny pinholes. His entire body quivered with rage. I shivered, and it wasn't from the icy breeze that whipped into the house.

"Samson," I stammered, rushing to his side. "What is it? What's wrong?"

He thrashed his head back and forth, his teeth grinding with the violent motion. I breathed hard, eyeing Jax. He kept his attention focused on his enraged mentor.

My brother called Samson's name as he walked past Orion. "What happened? You look like you want to wring someone's neck."

He ignored my brother, his broad chest rising and falling with quick breaths. I reached for his hand and gasped. Dried blood covered his fingers, crusting his nail beds with evidence. I glanced at his shirt. Various shades of red splattered the crème-colored fabric. *Shit.*

"Samson," Jax said. "You need to tell us what happened."

The whites of the Solin's eyes turned a bright shade of pink. "Sit down." His throat bobbed. "I've got some bad news."

14

THE SECRET DOOR

Dreading our impromptu meeting, I dragged my feet across the living room and lowered myself onto the couch. Jax sat beside me, his eyes never leaving Samson. The distressed Solin collapsed onto the armchair, dust particles exploding around him. After inhaling a shaky breath, his blood-stained fingers squeezed the bridge of his nose. My heart thumped in my ears as I shifted my weight on the lumpy cushion. *I've never seen him so pissed.*

Like before, Iah and Orion carried two chairs from the kitchen while Cyrus took his place on my right. My brother clasped his hands, his nostrils flaring.

"It's Ida." Samson's voice cracked with enough pain to send us to an early grave.

Jax balled his hands into fists. I held my breath, afraid to hear any more.

"What happened?" Cyrus growled.

Samson swallowed hard. An invisible veil of darkness had draped over his shoulders. I scooted closer to Jax, watching the Solin's grief shift to rage. The tendons in his jaw twitched, a time bomb ready to detonate.

"Samson," I whispered, the silence unbearable. "Please—just tell us what happened to Idalia."

"They took her to Zenith's."

Cyrus cursed at the top of his lungs and flipped over the coffee table. Iah and Orion balked at the sudden outburst.

"There's no time to lose." Jax stood. "We leave now."

He headed for the door with my brother on his heels. Orion and I sat there stunned, our jaws hanging open.

The two men stopped dead in their tracks when Samson barked, "Sit your asses back down."

"No!" My brother whirled on the Solin. "You heard Jax, we need to leave—*now*."

Samson inhaled a long breath, and in a quiet but severe tone, he said, "The two of you must listen *very* carefully. We can't afford to make any mistakes and we sure as hell can't rescue Idalia with our heads up our asses. I told you this once, and I'll say it again: Zenith is not an idiot. Someone must have seen Jax living at my place and tipped off the Collectors." His attention snagged on the Lunin. "He's pissed that you're still alive, so he kidnapped Ida knowing you'd run to his door." He flicked his wrist at me and Cyrus. "And as a bonus, he gets the twins. It's a trap."

"I don't care," Cyrus countered. "I'm going, and that's final."

"Samson, Idalia is in grave danger." Jax motioned for my brother to grab his coat. "The clock is ticking and with each passing second, her life is one tick closer to ending."

The Lunin hit a nerve. Samson kicked the fallen coffee table, sending it sliding across the floor. Orion used both hands to keep it from slamming into his father's shins. Cyrus breathed hard, and Jax rose to his full height as Samson stormed past me, his boots thumping faster than my beating heart.

The ex-Collector shoved Jax in the chest. I hissed. Anyone else would have flown across the room, but the Lunin only staggered backward. Preparing to play mediator, Cyrus held his hands between the two men.

Samson slapped them away and pointed a finger at Jax. "Don't lecture me on the severity of the situation. Are you forgetting I worked as a Collector, dragged Seekers into that damned basement, and tortured them for information, only to slice their throats after they could no longer speak?"

Jax stood his ground, ignoring the spit that sprayed into his face. After wiping the mist from his lashes, he drawled, "And *you're* forgetting that Zenith raised me as his son." His voice lowered to a growl. "And you're also forgetting that my adoptive father named me the leader of the Inner Circle at the age of twelve."

The shift in Jax's tone forced me to my feet. Orion eyed his father. The doctor shook his head, a silent plea to stay out of the argument.

Jax moved closer to Samson, their noses almost touching. "Unlike you, they kept me as a prisoner in that shithole, so when I say every second counts—I *mean* every second counts. We leave now."

"Not without a plan."

Jax fisted his hands.

Samson stepped away from the Lunin and motioned to him and Cyrus. "This is exactly what Zenith wants. He hopes we'll act without discussing the logistics. Everyone needs to calm down so we can figure out how to rescue Idalia without starting a war we can't win."

Cyrus looked at Jax, and Jax looked at me.

"Samson's right," I said. "We need a plan. Idalia is a prisoner at Zenith's. That's his home, his territory. We can't go barging in, guns blazing. Knives," I corrected. "I meant to say knives."

Jax nudged Cyrus in the ribs and pointed at the couch. My brother grumbled his complaints but agreed to the Lunin's request, his boots weighted with discouragement. I wiped my clammy palms on the cushion and the men took their seats.

Jax rested his forearms on his thighs. "When did they take her?"

"This afternoon." Samson stared out the living room window, his eyelids heavy with guilt. "I stepped out back to see Callisto off and that's when ..." His voice trailed off.

"It's not your fault," Jax said.

Samson scoffed. "Yes, it is. I should have never gone outside."

The Lunin lowered his gaze, tracing the knots in the wooden floor with his eyes. My brother popped his joints, one finger at a time.

As if asking a witness to describe the details of what occurred during an accident, Iah said, "Samson, can you explain what happened after Callisto left?"

He nodded. "When I came inside, the bar had cleared out. Only one group of men sends customers running."

My pulse quickened. Cyrus squeezed his hands with so much force, I thought the skin over his knuckles would split open.

"Phoebus told me they were upstairs. The bastards locked the door, so I kicked it off the hinges." His Adam's apple fought with the words that formed on his tongue. "And that's when I found them."

Quick breaths entered my lungs. Jax pulled my trembling hands onto his lap.

Through gritted teeth, Cyrus spat, "Who was it?"

"Apollo, Ravi, Elio ... and Pollux."

Every muscle in Jax went rigid. I cursed at the memory of me and Cyrus hiding behind Idalia's bedroom wall. I tried to swallow, but the saliva in my mouth evaporated. I thought of the way Pollux spoke to her, his cruel intentions—how he drew a heart on her cheek with the blood from the injury he caused.

Samson eyed me and my brother. "When I saw the wooden panels lying on the floor, I realized they uncovered her little secret. After all those years, Pollux discovered why he never found Jax after he left the Collectors, and why he didn't find you that day they searched the place."

Guilt dropped Cyrus's head; its claws dug into my back.

"Ida's a tough girl, but she's no match for four members of the Inner Circle, even with her Solin strength."

I gulped envisioning Apollo's massive build next to Idalia's slender frame.

"Those sons of bitches did a real number on her. Ravi held a knife to her throat while the others—" Samson couldn't finish the sentence. He palmed his eyes and inhaled a shallow breath.

In a cautious voice, Orion asked, "What did you do?"

"I did what needed to be done." The Solin raised his blood-stained hands for everyone to see. "After disarming Ravi, I threw him across the room. But letting him off that easy bothered me, so I beat the shit out of him until his face didn't look like a face anymore."

"What about Pollux and the others?" Jax asked.

"That's where I fucked up. It's my fault they got away. Seeing Ravi hold a knife to Ida's throat set me off. It woke the demon that controlled me during Arun's reign. I should have disarmed Ravi and grabbed Ida. Instead, I wasted time unleashing hell on Ravi's pathetic ass, and when I finished, they were gone."

My heart ached for Samson. He never married, and his parents died long ago. Idalia was the closest thing he had to family. Callisto helped raise the girl after an ex-Collector murdered Janus, his brother-in-law and Samson's best friend. When Idalia's mother passed from a sudden illness, Callisto stepped aside and allowed Samson to fill the role as guardian. No one ever asked why.

"What happened next?" Cyrus inquired.

Orion held his breath, preparing for the next crucial part of the standoff.

"Ravi made the mistake of throwing his knife at me when I ran to the window to search for Pollux and the others. The clever bastards split up. Their footprints led in three different directions. Ravi had a shit aim, but the injury slowed me down." Samson lifted his leg to show us the red stain around his calf. "Even if I knew which footprints to follow, I couldn't catch up."

"What did you do with Ravi?"

A wicked smirk tugged at Samson's chapped lips. "I pulled his knife out of my leg and used it to saw off his fingers."

Jax shrugged, indifferent to the slow torture. I bit my knuckles, bile crawling up my throat.

The ex-Collector picked at the dried blood that caked his nailbeds. "His knife was a little dull, so it took longer than expected. I'm surprised he showed up unprepared." He looked at Jax. "Rule number four states—"

"My blade and mind must stay sharp."

I did a doubletake. The Lunin finished the sentence without skipping a beat.

"You know the challenge of cutting through bone with a dull knife," Samson said.

Jax nodded and rubbed the scar on his hand.

"The bastard wouldn't stop screaming, so I cut out his tongue. I stopped after six fingers because the sound of blood gurgling in his throat irritated the hell out of me. I should have tossed his tongue to the side instead of shoving it down his throat but rule number five states—"

"I will use any force necessary to complete the mission."

I schooled my bewildered expression into neutrality. *Why is this bothering me? I'm aware of Jax's past but hearing him and Samson bounce Collector lingo back and forth has my stomach twisted in a knot.*

"Did you finish him?" Cyrus asked.

A sinister grin crossed Samson's face. "Yeah. After I let him suffer."

My nausea intensified, watching my brother smile at the Solin.

"So now"—Samson leaned back in his chair—"only eight members of the Inner Circle remain."

I took a moment to mourn. Not for Ravi's death, but for the loss of my innocence. Zenith's decision to kidnap Idalia shifted our destiny. It changed everything. I noted the different reactions to the news. Cyrus sat tall with his chin held high while Jax stared at the overturned coffee table. Iah and Orion didn't blink, their pale faces drained of any color.

I shut my eyes and shivered at the image of Ravi sitting in a pool of blood, choking on his tongue, his detached fingers scattered around him. *Stop it. You'll make yourself sick.*

The dealer's mask shifted as it pushed itself off an imaginary wall in my mind. *Don't be dramatic, Elara. You were just stating the obvious.*

I shuddered a breath. Jax squeezed my hand. Though Samson had committed heinous crimes, I still struggled to accept the truth. My mentor, my friend, had murdered a man in cold blood.

Orion's voice snapped me out of my trance. "Are you sure they took her to Zenith's?"

"I'm not in the mood for idiotic questions," Samson snapped. "Yes, it's a trap."

"So how do we rescue her?" Cyrus asked.

"I can," Jax whispered.

I paled. "No. You just got back."

"Elara." Anger saturated my brother's words as he sprung to his feet. "This is Idalia we're talking about."

"I'm aware of this, *Cyrus.*" Jax reached for my wrist, but I slapped his hand away and stood, my eyes narrowing. "I wasn't implying that we do nothing. I'm only suggesting that someone other than Jax goes inside. He barely got out alive."

The Lunin tugged at my arm.

"What?"

"Elara try to see this from a practical perspective. I grew up at Zenith's. I know that place like the back of my hand."

Before I could protest, Samson said, "So do I. We'll go in together."

"I'm coming too," Cyrus added.

"No, you and Elara must stay together at all times." Samson's definitive tone left no room for argument. "Jax and I will go inside."

Orion raised his hand. "I'll wait with Elara and Cyrus."

"Good." The eldest Solin gave a curt head nod. "We'll take all the help we can get."

Jax focused his attention on the doctor. "Why don't you stay here and prepare for the worst."

Iah's posture shifted, the fear in his eyes replaced with determination. "I'll have everything ready to go. My supplies are well-stocked." He rotated his hands for us to see. "They might look old, but they haven't failed me yet."

Jax bowed his head.

Orion turned to his father and said, "Ready the supplies in my room. I can sleep in yours."

"Very well." Iah rose from the chair. "Let me pack a bag for your journey."

Everyone murmured their appreciation except for Samson, who stayed quiet until Iah departed the room. "It's a long walk to Zenith's. Sunrise is hours away, so Elara can't absorb Cyrus's power. This leaves us with a huge disadvantage."

A simultaneous curse slipped off our tongues.

Orion slid his chair closer to our small group. "Where do you think he's keeping Idalia?"

"In the basement," Jax answered.

"How will you rescue her without getting caught?" I asked. "Archer told us there's only one way in and one way out of Zenith's."

"I doubt we'll go unnoticed."

"Perfect." My jaw clenched shut.

"Easy," Jax soothed, steadying my bouncing leg. "It might sound bleak, but Archer didn't know of the secret door."

Samson blinked hard. "It's still there?"

"Yeah. I saw it when Pollux dragged me into the basement. It's boarded up, but I bet we can break it down."

Samson played with the coarse hairs of his beard. "If we're lucky, there might be a few tools hidden underneath the floorboards. That's where Arun kept his personal stash. He always cleaned them after torturing the Seekers. We never had time for that shit. Ours stayed crusted in blood and bits of flesh."

My nose crinkled in disgust.

"You're probably right," Jax said. "I bet they're still hidden because the tools we used during our torture training were covered in dried blood."

"Rule number six."

Jax hesitated, rubbing his thumb over his scarred palm. "I will torture the guilty without regret."

My jaw cracked open. *How have Jax and Samson held on to their humanity? This Collector Code is ridiculous. What were Arun and Zenith thinking?*

The heel of Cyrus's boot tapped against the wooden floor in an offbeat rhythm. "Can the two of you stop speaking like Collectors so the rest of us can understand what the hell is going on?"

Samson glared at my brother while Jax asked Orion, "Do you have something I can write with?"

The Lunin hurried to the kitchen, and moments later, he returned with a gray sheet of paper and a slender stick that resembled a pencil, minus the eraser. After handing Jax the requested items, Orion flipped over the coffee table and slid it toward us. We gathered around, our eyes following the writing utensil as Jax moved it across the paper.

"Pay close attention," he instructed. "Zenith's dwelling includes four floors and a basement. The levels are restricted by rank, though members of the Inner Circle can access any floor." Jax added stick figures to the drawing. "When I lived with Zenith, the sub-groups didn't exist. You were a member of the Inner Circle or an average Collector—that's it. During my capture, Archer explained how the new system works."

I eyed my brother. His subtle head nod confirmed our shared memory. During our long walk to rescue Jax, Archer informed us of the different sub-groups. This change occurred after Jax left the Collectors.

Tired of sitting, I stretched out my legs and pulled the loose fabric over my hips. *These pants are too big. I should tell Orion to grab a smaller size when he visits . . .* I held back tears. *Idalia— poor Idalia.*

Orion squatted beside the table and stared at the interior map that Jax designed while Samson, already familiar with the layout of Zenith's, picked at his nails.

The former leader of the Inner Circle tapped a rectangle with the letter Z written across it. "Zenith's personal living quarters and the Main Hall are located on the fourth floor. This level is restricted to everyone but Zenith and the Inner Circle."

Cyrus scratched at the stubble on his chin. "What about union approval? I thought the citizens of Aroonyx had to appear before Zenith in the Main Hall." He eyed me out of his peripheral vision. "At least that's what Archer told us."

"Yes, this is true, but lower level Collectors and citizens are only granted access if escorted by a member of the Inner Circle."

I groaned, scowling at the map. "Jax, this is getting complicated. We don't have time to discuss Zenith's bizarre way of—" I snapped my fingers, unable to verbalize my own thoughts.

"Ruling?" Cyrus suggested.

"Exactly."

Jax tossed the pencil onto the table. "Elara, it's crucial that the three of you familiarize yourselves with the layout of Zenith's dwelling. What if Samson and I get trapped inside?"

"Damn it, Jax. How is that supposed to make me feel any better?"

"Cool it, sis. You're being dramatic again."

I rammed my elbow into his ribs. "Shut up, I wasn't talking to you."

He hissed, calling me a choice five-letter word while Orion grumbled, "How did I wind up with this bunch? They're all *fucking* mad."

"Enough!" Samson barked. Everyone flinched. Even the poor pencil rolled away. His orange eyes darted to Jax. "You know better than to say something that stupid to Elara." He shifted his gaze to me. "Stop worrying, we'll be fine." A quick glance at my brother. "Quit irritating your sister, and Orion"— he massaged his temples—"keep your opinions to yourself."

Silence. We lowered our heads. Leave it to Samson to fill the role of the world's scariest father.

He snapped his fingers at Jax. "Were you not bitching about the hands of time?" He jerked his chin at the coffee table. "Hurry up and finish that damn map of yours."

Without hesitation, Jax snatched the pencil off the floor and continued his sketch with added commentary. "The third floor, or the Top Level, is where the Inner Circle eats, sleeps, and trains. Beneath it is the Active Member's floor—the Upper Level." We nodded, observing the acronyms Jax etched in the rectangles. "I'm not sure what information Archer shared, but these Collectors are of age and go on missions."

My brother lifted his head. "Yeah, Archer mentioned the differences between the groups."

"Good, so when I say the IMs live on the Ground Floor, you know I'm referring to the underage Inactive Members." After our murmur of agreement, Jax drew another large rectangle below the other four. "The basement is a long narrow hallway with six rooms, three on each side."

A chill rippled through me as I recalled the dream—the vision I had at Idalia's.

"The doors to these rooms lock automatically and only open from the outside. This works in our favor because everyone, except for Zenith and a handful of the Inner Circle, believe there's one exit out of the basement." Jax drew an X on the rectangle labeled with a B. "But lucky for us, we know about the secret door."

Samson cleared the phlegm from his throat before speaking. "When I worked as a Collector, we used both doors. Arun tired of listening to the Seekers scream as we dragged them through the main entryway, so he built another door in the basement. It opened to the exterior of his dwelling. We still had to go through the main door of the perimeter wall, but it allowed us to do our work without disturbing him."

"And once Zenith gained control, he boarded up the second door."

Orion's brows furrowed at Jax. "Why?"

"Two reasons. He only wanted one exit out of the basement, and unlike Arun, sounds of suffering never bothered him. Honestly, I think he enjoys it."

Cyrus huffed a breath. "The man's a *fucking* sadist."

"Him and Pollux both," I muttered.

Jax nodded. "You can't even tell it's there."

"Then how do you know about the door?" I asked him.

"As the leader of the Inner Circle, I had access to classified information. Apollo, Elio, and Oberon are aware of the exit because they boarded it up. Those men are the original members of the Inner Circle, the ones responsible for silencing the naysayers who opposed Zenith's nomination."

"Right," was all I could manage.

Cyrus's amber eyes flickered between the ex-Collectors. "What if the tools aren't underneath the floorboards? It's night, Samson can't use his Solin strength."

"Let's hope they're still there," Jax answered.

"And if they're not?" I asked.

He turned to face me. "Then we find another way out. Idalia's life depends on it."

My throat bobbed with anxiety and Cyrus's shoulders sagged with mild relief. I shook my head. *Figures. We're always on opposite ends of the emotional spectrum.*

"Here's what I'm thinking." Jax pressed his lips together and drummed the pencil on the table. "We'll enter through the wall that borders the dwelling and take the stairs down to the basement."

Orion kneeled on the living room floor, his joints cracking. He pointed at the stick figures in the drawing. "Won't Zenith have Collectors standing on watch?"

"Yes, but not the Inner Circle. The Active Members patrol the grounds."

I wiped the sweat that formed on my brow. "But if you're seen, they'll inform the Inner Circle."

"One would think." Jax leaned his back against the couch cushion, the air rushing out of his lungs in a loud whoosh. He stared at no one and chewed on the end of the pencil as he spoke. "But the truth is the Collectors are so brainwashed they'll do anything to prove themselves, advance their position. An Active Member—hell, even an underage Collector would *love* the opportunity to take a shot at me or Samson."

"They're not the brightest bunch, are they?" Orion asked.

Samson's eyes filled with curiosity. "What makes you say that?"

"Because only a fool would attack you and Jax."

Samson snickered at the comment, but his counterpart's expression remained blank. My thoughts drifted to Archer. The young Lunin lacked the negative traits that defined the other Collectors. Hate and anger didn't seep from his pores. Thanks to his brother, Archer got stuck living a life he never wanted. I gritted my teeth. *Damn you, Pollux. You're the reason Archer's dead, the reason he never got a shot at a better life.*

My eyelids peeled open at the sound of Jax's voice. "Samson and I will get Idalia out of the basement and meet the three of you on the other side of the wall. If our cover is blown"—he looked at the eldest Solin—"expect the younger Collectors stationed at the top of the stairs, ready to launch a surprise attack since they think there's only one way out. With any luck, we'll have left before they realized we escaped through the secret door."

Samson sat taller, eager to set the plan in motion. Orion stared at the map as if taking a mental snapshot.

My fearless twin met my gaze. I frowned. The confidence that emanated from his being had vanished, replaced with a gut-wrenching sadness. He didn't need my approval to rescue Idalia, but he wanted my blessing.

"Cyrus, do you want my honest opinion?" He nodded. The others watched me carefully, their interest piqued. "This plan sounds crazy. Batshit crazy."

Defeat stained my brother's face.

It faded when I touched his arm. "But living on Aroonyx with Samson and Jax has taught me a bitter truth."

"And what's that?"

A spark of mischief ignited in my eyes. "Crazy people get shit done. Let's go rescue your beautiful girlfriend."

15

READ BETWEEN THE LINES

Cyrus's face beamed with a mixture of relief and a dash of surprise. "Thank you, sis."

"You're welcome, bro."

Samson winced as he pushed himself to his feet.

I pointed at his injured leg. "Why don't you let Iah clean that up before we leave?"

"Nah, I'm good. I used Ravi's shirt." His wicked smirk returned. "I didn't think he'd mind."

I may have nodded, though detest painted my face.

Samson yanked at the crusted fabric that stuck to the injury, then flexed his calf. "Idalia gave you some knives before you rescued Jax. How many do you have left?"

I eyed my brother. "We had ten, but I gave one to Orion, so six?"

"Yep," Cyrus confirmed. "I sharpened the spares on the porch today."

"I'm confused." Jax rubbed at his smooth jawline. "Ten minus one is nine, not six. What happened to the other three?"

"I used them on Pollux."

The Lunin blinked once—twice. "And did you plan on telling me this?"

"No, not really. I didn't want you to worry." A muscle feathered in his jaw. I patted his thigh like he patted mine in the bedroom. "I'll fill you in on our walk to Zenith's."

"I'm glad that's sorted." Samson rolled his eyes at us. "Now let's get back to the logistics. Jax and I will take four of the extra knives since we're the ones going inside. The three of you can fight over the other two."

"You and Elara can have the spares," Cyrus offered.

Orion shook his head. "No, you take it."

"Dude. No offense, but my combative skills outmatch yours, and if we run into trouble, you'll want—"

"Just take the damn knife," I interrupted.

Orion hesitated until Jax said, "Two knives are better than one. If we're caught sneaking into the basement, Zenith will dispatch the Inner Circle."

"He's right," Samson added. "Zenith wants you dead. Don't give him an opportunity to make that desire a reality. Remember your training."

Our heads turned at the sound of Iah's voice. "I've organized everything." He handed a backpack to his son. "If anyone requires medical assistance, let Orion take over. He can triage almost any wound."

I huffed a breath. "With our luck, we'll need a medic before the night's over."

"Sounds about right," my brother muttered as he headed toward the bedroom to retrieve the spare knives.

I turned my attention to Samson. Lost in thought, he stared out the living room window, cracking his knuckles.

Noting his somber expression, Jax rested a hand on his mentor's shoulder and whispered, "We'll get her out of there."

"I swore to her mother I'd keep her safe."

"You have . . . and you *will*."

My foolish tongue jumped in on the private conversation. "At least it's only been a few hours."

Samson shut his eyes; his jaw clenched shut.

Jax's hand fell from his shoulder and as he strolled past me toward the front door, he whispered, "A few hours in that hell-hole is all it takes, Elara."

THE BITTER WEATHER nipped at our heels as we trudged through the snow-covered forest. Not one for mindless chatter, Samson kept his lips pressed together and led the way with Cyrus by his side. Their heads swiveled back and forth, eyes searching for adversaries hidden in the brush. Orion stared at the Solins' footprints while he walked, his mind appearing to reel with unspoken thoughts.

I tucked my chin into my chest, bracing myself against the strong winds. My fingers fastened the top button of my coat. The thick collar blocked the frigid air from creeping in, but it restricted my neck movement. I had to turn my entire body to see Jax. His lips twitched with amusement as he watched my boots shuffle through the snow in an awkward side-lunge.

"Are you doing okay over there?"

"Oh, I'm great." A fake grin slid across my face. "I can't wait until we get to Zenith's. His dwelling is a combination of Disney World and Hell." I saturated my words with an unnatural sweetness. "Who's that coming around the corner, kids? Is it Mickey . . . Donald?" My voice fell flat. "No, it's Pollux with a knife." I glided my hand through the air. "Welcome to the *shittiest* place on Earth, or Aroonyx, for argument's sake."

Cyrus chuckled at my little joke but Jax—oh Jax—the more serious one out of the group pinned me with a long look. "We didn't force you to come on this mission. You could have stayed at the house with Iah."

"That wasn't an option. You heard Samson. Cyrus and I must stay together at all times, and besides, my friend's life is in danger. There's no way I'd sit this one out."

Jax twisted me around in the snow, encouraging my gait to move forward versus sideways. "I'm glad you and Idalia are friends."

The Solin's beautiful face merged with the vision of Pollux. I shivered, wrapping my arms around myself.

Jax moved closer and hooked his arm through mine. "Are you willing to share the reason you used three knives on the man whose name I'd rather not say?"

"He threatened to kill me after murdering Archer." I blew a snowflake off my nose. "I knew Elio would tire, so I used the knives on Pollux. It took three tries. I've never hit a moving target."

Samson spoke over his shoulder. "I planned on teaching you that little trick."

Jax nodded. "It's a helpful skill to master."

"Well, I'd appreciate a few lessons because that was terrifying."

Jax dragged a hand through his hair. "Where did you hit him?"

"Who? Pollux?"

"No, Zenith."

I scowled at his sarcasm.

"Where did the blade enter Pollux's body?" he added.

"Right here." I touched the left side of my upper abdomen. "I don't think the blade went that deep because the attack didn't faze him, it just pissed him off."

"Always aim for the aorta." Jax moved my hand lower and more center. "A deep puncture will rupture the blood vessel and end a man's life in seconds."

"That's correct," Orion said. "The aorta is the largest blood vessel in the body. If injured, the circulatory system will collapse, and the victim will fall unconscious."

"Noted," I murmured

"The liver, kidney, and spleen are vascular organs, so a direct hit will cause internal bleeding. Elara, if you had hit Pollux harder, you could have punctured his spleen. The liver is on the right."

My brother eyed Orion. "Thanks for the anatomy lesson, doc. That might come in handy later tonight."

"So that's how you got away."

I nodded at Jax. "The knife sent Pollux to his knees, and Elio couldn't keep up with my Lunin endurance."

"I'm impressed. Pollux can be—how do I say it?"

"A sadistic prick?"

A large cloud left his mouth as he lifted his chin toward the night sky. "I was going to say a pain in the ass, but yes, a sadistic prick is a more accurate description."

Irritated with my lack of mobility, I unfastened the collar of my coat and popped my neck, relieved that I no longer wore a modified brace. *There, that's better.* The ice-kissed breeze slithered down my spine. *Or not.*

Seeking warmth, I leaned into Jax and rested my head against his shoulder. Each step toward Zenith's sent me spiraling further down a rabbit hole of the hypothetical. *Does he know we're coming? What if it's an ambush? What if they capture Jax and Samson? What if Idalia's . . .*

I shut my eyes, letting Jax guide me through the forest.

Dead? You can say it.

I rolled my neck, baring my teeth at the elusive dealer. *Shut up. I need to stay positive.*

No. Practical is a better option. Pollux captured your friend. She's probably dead.

"Go away."

"Elara." Jax squeezed my hip. "Are you okay?"

"Yeah, I'm good."

"We should have a little chat regarding the voice—"

"Hey, Jax," Cyrus called.

I smiled at my brother, grateful for his timing. I couldn't discuss the masked dealer with Jax. I couldn't discuss it with anyone.

Cyrus slowed his pace and moved to my right. "Can you give us some insider information about the members of the Inner Circle?"

The Lunin nodded. Orion fell in line beside him, their strides syncing as one.

"When I worked as a Collector, ten members created the Inner Circle, and Zenith never filled my position after I left."

"Then there were nine," Cyrus offered.

I smirked. "You're good at math."

He flicked my nose. I glared, driving my fist into his bicep.

Ignoring our childish behavior, Jax said, "And now that Ravi's dead, there's—"

I waved a hand at my twin, urging him to finish the sentence.

He flipped me off and mouthed, "Eight."

"Excellent job, class," Jax chided.

My smile transformed into a grimace as the howling winds blasted our faces with ice and snow. Orion tucked his hands deeper into his pockets and raised his voice over the rustling tree branches. "Did Ravi have long hair?"

Another head nod from Jax.

"He attacked me at the spring that morning," Cyrus confirmed.

Samson glanced at my brother. "You would have survived a knife wound from Ravi. His blade was too dull to do any permanent damage."

I swallowed at the thought of the Solin's missing fingers.

"Cyrus and Elara are familiar with Pollux, Elio, and Apollo's identity." Jax turned to Orion. "Are you?"

"Yeah. A few years ago, my father sent me into the West Village to gather supplies. As soon as I left the apothecary, the villagers on the main path scattered, and that's when I saw them—the Inner Circle. Their knives were out, and they had two men surrounded. I didn't stop to investigate, but I heard the longer-haired one, Ravi, mention something about lethal whispers—whatever that means."

"Treason," I murmured.

Jax arched a brow. "Who told you?"

"Archer." I sighed. "He shared more information than we wanted to hear that night."

"Yeah, like the story about the *undresser* and how Zenith uses it to—"

Jax went rigid as if the scars on his back had ears. I slammed my elbow into Cyrus's ribs. He swore, realizing his error.

Redirecting our attention, Orion asked, "Pollux is a Lunin, right? And Elio is the tall Solin?"

"Yes." Jax adjusted the sleeves of his coat. "Pollux is older than us, around thirty, and has a jagged scar on his face."

"It goes over his eyelid," I added. "Courtesy of Jax."

Orion nodded, keeping his gaze forward.

"And yes, Elio is the tallest member of the Inner Circle and close to Pollux's age. Apollo is the strongest and the eldest."

Samson's raised fist halted our steadfast pace. My brother reached for his knife. I strained my ears for sounds other than our ragged breathing. Silence. My eyes darted from one towering tree to the next. *What if they're following us?*

This fearful thought vanished once Samson lowered his arm. I eyed Jax. *I'm not ready for this.*

He squeezed my hand, a silent encouragement to stay strong. The ex-Collector continued with his assessment once

Samson moved forward. "So that leaves Oberon, Jericho, Holmes, Levant, and Ishan."

"Who's our biggest threat?" Orion asked.

Jax rubbed the sharp lines of his jaw. "It depends on the situation and the time of day. Elio and Pollux are vicious, the cruelest members of the group. They work together as a team and enjoy watching their victims suffer."

"That's not surprising," Cyrus muttered.

"Pollux loves playing mind games. He'll say he's done torturing you, tend to your wounds, then leave the basement, only to show up a few minutes later with more tools. That bastard is nearly impossible to shake once he gets in your head."

I swore under my breath. *How did Jax endure three weeks of hell and keep his sanity?*

"Watch out for Apollo. Even at night, he's lethal." Jax's tone turned severe. "And never, under any circumstance, let him restrain you in a hold. Apollo has worked with Zenith longer than anyone else. The man never hesitates, and he always follows through."

Goosebumps raised on my chilled flesh. I glanced at my brother, missing the warmth that flowed through me during the day. My fingers tapped my palms as I acknowledged the twin moons that glowed behind the snow clouds. Our little trick kept us alive that morning at the spring. I blew out a tired breath. *A lot of good it does us now.*

"Oberon, Jericho, and Holmes are the other Lunins. These men have spent years perfecting their combative skills. They're clever, cunning, and not afraid to get their hands dirty. Oberon is the tallest Lunin, and his knife skills rival my own."

I gulped. *I want to go home now.*

"Don't even think about disarming Oberon. That's a fight you won't win. If he raises his armed hand, get out of the way and do it fast because like Zenith, he never misses his mark."

The ball of anxiety that had formed in the pit of my stomach, the one that manifested when I noticed Samson's bloodstained hands, wiggled its way up my esophagus. I swallowed hard, trying to dislodge the lump. A failed attempt.

I had no desire to meet the rest of the Inner Circle. Pollux had etched his pale-blue eyes into the wall of my memory bank —a horrific mural that would haunt my dreams forever. The last thing I needed was the blue and orange eyes of his comrades added to the morbid masterpiece. Sensing my desire to build a church out of snow and claim sanctuary, Jax slid his arm around my waist, anchoring me in place.

Cyrus turned up the collar of his coat and waited for another gust of wind to pass before asking Jax an important question, one I didn't want answered. "What do we do if Zenith makes an appearance?"

"Let's hope he doesn't."

"But what if he does?"

"The alarms will sound before you see him."

I chewed on the inside of my cheek. "I heard them with Archer."

Jax's boots skidded to a stop. The ends of my ponytail slapped my brother in the chest as the Lunin spun me around to face him. Orion and Cyrus froze, their baffled expressions matched my own.

Tiny clouds shot out of Jax's nostrils, and his fingers tightened around my wrist. "You heard the alarms that night?"

"Yeah, they sounded right after Pollux and Elio exited the perimeter wall. Archer told me to run but—" My voice faded at the sight of Jax's free hand curling into a fist. *Shit. I'm in serious trouble.*

Cyrus muttered, "Here we go," watching the ex-Collector drop my hand, cross his arms, and widen his stance.

I stifled a whimper, for all signs pointed to a good ass chewing.

16

THE ILLUSION OF FEAR

"Elara, what the hell were you thinking?"

My mouth moved but inaudible stutters danced on my tongue.

Coming to my aid, Cyrus said, "You know the reason she stayed behind."

"I wasn't asking you."

"My bad," the Solin muttered, bowing out of the argument.

I tossed up my hands. "Why are you mad? We've already been through this. Yes, I screwed up that night, but you told me my hesitation kept Archer from dying alone."

"I did say that, but you failed to mention the alarms."

"Would it have made a difference?"

Jax shot me an incredulous look. "Yes. A massive one."

"Why?"

"Because those alarms are a death sentence!"

I flinched at the irritation that elevated his voice. Samson grumbled a slew of curse words and stormed toward us.

The eldest Lunin inhaled a calming breath before finding my eyes. "I understand why you hesitated with Archer, but from now on you can't let your emotions dictate your actions, especially during an altercation."

I gritted my teeth. *Attention everyone, the voice of reason has returned.*

As if hearing my little jab, Jax shot me a stern glance. "One of the most valuable lessons I learned during my training was—"

"You probably learned it from me," Samson said, spitting a wad of phlegm onto the snow.

Cyrus grimaced at the dripping mucus that grazed his boot. The ex-Collector shrugged.

Jax cleared his throat. "Hesitation will send you to an early grave."

"Yep, that was my lesson."

Jax ignored Samson's added commentary and motioned for my brother and Orion to form a tight circle. His blue eyes bounced between the three of us while he spoke.

"Pay attention. This information is crucial for your survival."

We nodded, huddling closer.

"Zenith will not interfere with the Inner Circle unless the situation is considered dire. Years ago, a group of men snuck onto the property and harassed an underage Collector. They created a diversion to distract us while the other rebels waited in the surrounding woods. The men had set traps: trip wires and hidden spears they carved with knives purchased on the black market."

I eyed Cyrus, curious why our guide never shared this story. He shrugged.

"When a Collector reported the disturbance, Zenith dispatched us—the Inner Circle. We didn't expect the surprise attack because no one had the balls to approach us in the villages, much less at Zenith's."

Button-eyed we stared at Jax, clinging to every word that left his mouth. Samson, already familiar with the story, dusted the snowflakes off his shoulder.

"What happened next?" Orion asked.

Jax unbuttoned his coat, lifted his shirt, and tapped a thick scar below his rib cage. "We got our asses handed to us. Those spears were sharp. The rebels outnumbered us three to one."

"Were the men trained in combat?" I asked.

Jax shook his head. "They had the element of surprise. Zenith trained us to fight as a lethal unit that moved as one. We have—*had*—specific formations for different combative circumstances. The rebels used this to their advantage and scattered our ranks. It was a shit show." Jax snickered and refastened the buttons on his coat. "It took five Solins to restrain Apollo. The other Collectors didn't help because interfering with the Inner Circle is punishable by death."

Cyrus blinked. "Even if the Inner Circle is attacked?"

"Yep. One of Zenith's twisted rules. Fortunately, the kid who reported the rebels ran to Zenith and told him the situation looked grim."

"What did he do?" I rasped.

"What he does best. He initiated a mass execution."

I gulped. "How? I thought you were outnumbered."

"None of that mattered once Zenith appeared. His presence instills fear in the bravest of men." At this comment, Cyrus stood taller. "Zenith didn't say a word. He unleashed hell and threw two knives at once, puncturing a man in the eyes. He then aimed another blade at twelve o'clock and one at nine. Those poor men never saw death coming. Clean kills—direct hits to their tracheas."

Orion and Cyrus cursed. I made a sour face.

"What's the problem, kids?" Samson scoffed. "Enemy or not, that's pretty damn impressive."

Jax murmured his agreement. "His performance distracted the rebels long enough for us to regroup."

"What happened to the rest of the men?" I asked.

Jax touched the scar on his palm. "We slaughtered the twenty-five who remained."

My jaw almost hit the snow. "Twenty-five?"

"Zenith killed three, Pollux and Oberon killed one each. I told you, they outnumbered us three to one."

"I thought you were exaggerating."

"I never exaggerate. It wastes time."

I massaged my temples. I had a headache.

"How many did you kill?" my brother asked.

"Cyrus," I hissed.

"Nine. I killed nine men that day."

My breath hitched. I knew Jax had blood on his hands, but I never asked how much. Orion scooted closer to Cyrus, away from the former leader of the Inner Circle.

Samson scowled at our reactions. "Why are the three of you staring at Jax like he's a damn ghost?" He jerked his chin at the Lunin. "He was the leader of the Inner Circle. That job demands blood. Get over yourselves."

Cyrus's tense posture loosened, and Orion's boots inched toward their original spot. I didn't bother closing my gaped mouth.

My brother tried to act casual but failed miserably by saying, "I bet it took forever to bury that many bodies."

"No. Not when you cut off the heads and burn the remains."

My crossed arms fell to my sides. Poor Orion—our sweet and innocent Orion, stepped backward, right into the eldest Solin.

Samson shoved him in the back only after whispering, "Pussy."

Orion flew forward. Cyrus's hand shot out, catching him before he slammed into me.

"Jax," Samson said, all too cheerfully, "tell them what you did with the rebels' heads."

The Lunin groaned, scrubbing at his face.

"Go on. They need to hear who we're up against."

"Fine." The air rushed out of Jax's lungs. "Zenith wanted to send a warning to the citizens of Aroonyx, so he instructed us to mount the severed heads onto the spears they used to attack and display them in the villages." He paused, regret clouding his eyes. "After we showed them to the rebels' families."

"That's fucked up."

"Yes, yes it was," Jax said to my brother. "And when we returned, Zenith brought out his whip." He sent a quick glance in my direction. "The *undresser,* and he gave us thirty lashes each."

I shut my eyes.

"For the thirty men who attacked?" Cyrus suggested.

"No. For the thirty times we failed him that day."

Samson hummed his understanding. The rest of us stood slack-jawed.

"Zenith had the bells installed the next day." Jax focused his attention on me and my brother. "Imagine a home security system that sounds if the Inner Circle requires their leader's presence. Zenith hates being blindsided. He's always been a paranoid man, but that ambush set him off. He didn't bother sticking around after he killed those three rebels. He turned on his heels and strolled back through the door in the wall, leaving us to finish his dirty work. No one has attacked the Collectors since that day, and no one has trespassed on Zenith's property."

"I guess those speared heads really got the point across." Orion grimaced at the pun he never intended to make.

Cyrus offered him a fist bump. "Nice one, bro."

The youngest Lunin hesitated.

"That's not funny," I said.

"Lighten up," Samson muttered.

I glared. He just smiled back.

My brother showed me the palm of his hand. "I guess our

little trick did more than burn Elio's face and Apollo's wrist at the spring. It appears we burned a hole in the Inner Circle's confidence. Why else would they sound the alarms the night we rescued Jax?"

I sighed, retying my ponytail. "Perhaps, but our trick won't do us a damn bit of good tonight."

Orion inclined his head at the ex-Collectors. "What happens if they sound the alarms while you're inside?"

"Run," Samson answered. "The three of you alone can't survive the wrath of that man. The citizens of Aroonyx must witness Elara and Cyrus defeat Zenith. It's crucial to this endeavor."

My brother shook his head. "If I get a shot at defeating Zenith tonight, I won't hesitate."

Samson dashed forward, his orange eyes glowing in the milky light. "You don't think I want that bastard gone?" He didn't wait for a reply. "I want to rip him apart, limb by limb for kidnapping Ida."

"Then let's take him out together." Cyrus circled his finger through the air. "The five of us could do it."

A strong disagreement slipped through Jax's lips. Orion gawked at my twin, appalled by his suggestion.

"Cyrus"—Samson's voice raised—"you're forgetting the purpose behind this mission. We can't kill Zenith until the two of you expose his true identity to the people."

"Identity?" Cyrus asked. "The people know he's a ruthless killer. Everyone is terrified of that man."

"Your job isn't to point out the obvious. Your job is to show the citizens he manipulated them to gain control of Aroonyx. For sixteen years, they've followed Zenith with blind eyes. They think his Solin and Lunin traits make him powerful."

My brother shook his head. "Regardless, Aroonyx will be a better place once he's dead. I won't hold back if I see him tonight."

Samson clicked his tongue. Acting as a referee, Jax stepped forward, his eyes darting between the two Solins.

"You don't get it—do you?" Samson flicked my brother in the forehead.

"No!" Cyrus retaliated by jabbing his index finger in our mentor's chest—a fool's mistake. "*You* don't get it."

Orion stumbled backward while Jax tried to deflect the attack. His arm shot out a moment too late. Samson grabbed my brother's wrist and twirled him around in a dangerous dance of intimidation. The pleats of Cyrus's coat fanned, allowing the ex-Collector access to his back pocket. The knife swung open. Colorful words tumbled out of Orion's mouth, and my heart skipped a beat when Samson pulled my brother into a hold, pressing the sharp blade against his throat. Jax froze his approach, for the ex-Collector's fierce eyes screamed *Don't you dare intervene.*

"We might be on the same side." Samson pushed the blade deeper, drawing blood. "But if you ever touch me in a threatening way again, you can bet your ass all of that will change. Do I make myself clear?"

"Easy, Samson," Jax soothed. "Cyrus meant no harm."

The Solin lowered the knife but yanked my brother's hair, tilting his head toward the sky. I winced. He used enough force to snap a man's neck. Cyrus shut his eyes as Samson's chapped lips moved near his ear. "Is that right? You meant no harm?"

"It won't happen again."

The Solin released my brother after he hissed, "That's what I thought."

Reminding me of an adolescent lion who failed a challenge with the pride's leader, Cyrus lowered his head and straightened the twisted fabric of his coat. An awkward silence swept through our group. Everyone looked in opposite directions: the trees, the falling snow, the evening sky.

Orion stepped beside me and whispered, "Group hug?"

Like birds of prey spotting their next meal, the Solins' heads snapped toward the Lunin.

He grimaced. "Too soon?"

Jax pinched the bridge of his nose.

"Right." Orion showed us his palms and backed away.

I nudged Jax and whispered, "We're wasting time. Can you use your communication skills to relieve the tension?"

He cleared his throat. "Cyrus, let me clarify what Samson was trying to say."

My brother glared at the Solin with enough bitterness to taste.

"Killing Zenith tonight is not an option," Jax continued. "The five of us would have to slice through his army of Collectors and the Inner Circle before we get to him. The purpose of this mission isn't to challenge Zenith, it's to rescue Idalia. We must keep her safety in mind."

The truth behind Jax's words deflated my brother's ego. The hard lines on his face softened, the frustration in his eyes replaced with concern.

"Trust me," Jax added. "I can't wait to watch Zenith's world crumble beneath him. Unfortunately, that won't happen tonight." His lips continued to move, though Cyrus tried to cut him off. "Yes, his death would alleviate the peoples' suffering, but for how long? A few weeks?" The Lunin held up his hands. "A few seasons?" He pretended to weigh the air. "Maybe even a few years, until someone gains control of Aroonyx and uses Zenith's technique to lead the people with an iron fist. This is why you and Elara must lift the veil and expose his identity: a coward who steps on the backs of others to get what he wants.

"The people are blinded by the façade he's created. Your job is to open their eyes to the truth: over sixteen years ago the citizens made a naïve mistake. They followed a"—Jax snapped his fingers—"how do you say it on Earth?"

"A wolf in sheep's clothing?"

"Yes, that's it. Thank you, Elara. And they won't be free until they learn this valuable lesson."

Cyrus met my gaze. At that moment we grasped the importance of our mission. Jax didn't bring us to Aroonyx to defeat Zenith. He brought us home, to our place of birth, to defeat the *illusion* Zenith created.

My brother rose to his full height, his spine straighter than the surrounding trees. He locked his amber eyes onto Samson, and without exchanging words, the two men nodded at one another, accepting their roles on the mission.

Samson turned and urged us to follow. The high-pitched whistle of the winds, accompanied by the scratching tree limbs, created the perfect soundtrack to the dramatic thriller I called *Elara's new life*.

A STRONG SENSE of déjà vu tickled my mind as we passed a cluster of trees. I nudged Cyrus.

"What's up, sis?"

"Did we run through this part of the forest that night with Jax?"

"Hell if I know. It all looks the same to me. Black trees and more black trees."

"We're not far from the first campsite," Jax clarified. "The one near the spring."

I nudged my brother again—harder. "How did we not see it? It looks so familiar now."

"It's not like we were taking a leisurely stroll through the woods."

Jax's cheeks puffed. "I remember nothing about that night."

"Not surprising," Orion said. "It's challenging for a person to recall the specific details of an event if their body has experienced a severe level of trauma."

Cyrus craned his neck to find Jax's eyes. "I hope you thanked Elara. You wouldn't be standing here had it not been for her quick thinking."

"What?" The Lunin's brows furrowed. "Iah said you helped him during the procedures."

"I did, but that's not what I'm talking about."

"Then what are you referring to?"

Cyrus pointed at Jax's back. "The reason behind the massive scar near your rib cage."

"Oh." The Lunin touched the memory.

"*Oh*, is putting it mildly. That wound was deep. You were bleeding out. We had nothing to close it with, so I used my hand to apply pressure. As soon as the sun broke over the horizon, Elara pushed me out of the way, absorbed my power, and sealed the wound shut by melting your skin together."

Jax wrapped his fingers around my wrist, stopping my boots in their tracks. I turned. A spark of gratitude flickered in his eyes. In a gentle and fluid motion, he gripped my waist while his thumb and index finger held my chin, compelling me to meet his gaze.

"Thank you," he whispered onto my lips.

"And that's our cue." Cyrus snickered, urging Orion to follow.

My eyelashes fluttered until Jax's tongue swept in. The passion in the unexpected kiss sent my head spinning and vision blurring. I shut my eyes and guided my hands up to the back of his neck, settling in the soft locks of his hair. The hand that gripped my waist slid lower, his fingers clutching my backside. I pressed my body against his, wanting—*needing* more. A rumble of desire sounded in Jax's chest as he kissed me harder. I cursed the hands of time. *If I could press pause, I'd let him take me right here in the snow.*

As if hearing my inner dialogue, Jax chuckled and pulled away.

I touched my tingling lips. "I would have saved your life a lot earlier had I known that's how you express your gratitude."

"The night's still young." He winked, lacing his fingers through mine. "Who knows? You might get another chance."

SAMSON STROKED the hairs of his beard while he observed the massive structure. The dwelling resembled a rundown fortress. Multiple levels crafted from black wood narrowed as they reached the top. I couldn't see any windows, save for a boarded row on the fourth floor. A tall wall made of Clear Stone surrounded the creepy home, a barrier that Jax and Samson would soon cross.

"It looks the same as I remember," Samson said.

Jax checked the sharpness of his blade. "The inside hasn't changed much either."

Samson arched a wiry brow. "Really? After all these years."

The Lunin circled his throwing arm, warming the muscles in his shoulder. "Zenith idolizes Arun. He left the place untouched. You'll see"—he pointed at the dwelling with the tip of his knife—"it's like going back in time."

The eldest Solin used his blade to remove a chunk of flesh from beneath his nail.

Nausea coated my stomach. "Please tell me that's not a piece of Ravi's tongue."

He winked, flicking it at my face.

I gagged at the direct hit to my nose. "Damn it, Samson!"

My brother and Orion laughed. The Solin turned his attention back to Jax. "I hope Zenith didn't keep Arun's skeleton as a decoration."

"I never saw it with my own eyes." Jax paused and bent over to tighten the laces of his boots. "But I heard rumors about

Zenith having a shrine crafted from Arun's bones in his personal chamber."

"Because that's not creepy," Orion murmured.

My brother snorted. "No, not at all."

Jax adjusted his pant leg over his boot before standing upright. "Sometimes, during my watch, I'd hear these strange noises coming from Zenith's room: whimpers and painful moans. I didn't know if it was a who or a what."

The hairs on the back of my neck stood.

"I was twelve, but it still scared the shit out of me."

And that's where we differ. As an adult, those noises would scare me.

I tugged at the collar of my coat, the fear of the unknown smothering me.

This is not okay. Nothing about standing here, outside of Zenith's, is okay. It's obvious the man is disturbed. I can't imagine what happens behind closed doors, nor do I want to see with my own eyes.

Jax observed the quick breaths that entered my lungs, then nodded at my brother. A heartbeat later Cyrus moved into position.

"Elara." He snapped his fingers in front of me.

I stared straight through him.

"Look at me," he demanded, resting his hands on the sides of my face. "We've got this, sis. Everything is going to be okay. *We* are going to be okay, remember?"

My head nod didn't suffice.

"No. I want to hear you say it."

I exhaled a shaky breath, then whispered, "Everything is going to be okay."

"There she is." He smiled, slapping me on the back.

Jax scanned my vacant expression one last time before shifting his eyes between me, Cyrus, and Orion. "I want the three of you to hide behind the cluster of trees near the door in the perimeter wall. Keep your eyes peeled and ears opened. Samson and I will sneak into the basement, get Idalia, then exit through the secret door. If the alarms sound, stop what you're doing and get the hell out of there." The ex-Collector turned to Cyrus. "Stay close to your sister so you can share her Lunin endurance. Sprint to Iah's and don't look back. Samson and I can take care of ourselves."

The wind howled like a phantom wolf warning its pack of imminent danger. I shivered, my brother's encouragement fading faster than the white clouds leaving my mouth.

"Remember your training and use your heads," Samson said, slipping his knife into his coat pocket.

Cyrus and Orion murmured their agreements. I stayed silent because my throat was too tight to speak.

"Give us a head start before making your way down the hill. Come on, Jax, we've wasted enough time. Let's rescue Ida."

My boots moved without a conscious effort. I threw my arms around Samson, his beard brushing against my cheek. "Please, be careful."

"Don't worry about me, kid. I've been through more shit than those bastards combined."

A lump of grief settled in my throat as he lowered me onto the snow, and it expanded with each stride he took toward Zenith's. Jax didn't get far because I grabbed his wrist, holding him back.

He frowned at the salty drop that glided down my cheek. "No tears, Elara."

I brushed it away.

"I promise, everything will work out in the end."

In the end? How is that supposed to make me feel better?

"Jax, your Seeker's intuition doesn't allow you to predict the future."

"You're right. It doesn't. But these strong *feelings* always prove true."

"That's great—for *you*. Meanwhile, I'm left in the dark, terrified of the future."

He inhaled a long breath of the evening air and squeezed my shoulders, commanding my attention. The confidence that burned in his eyes reminded me of the afternoon we spent together on Earth, the afternoon I agreed to return to Aroonyx.

"Elara, the fear you're experiencing isn't real. It's an illusion created in your mind and will incapacitate your entire being if you allow it. The walls of fear are built by the hands of doubt. If you accept this truth, they'll crumble before your eyes. If you negate it, prepare to stay trapped in a fortress of terror."

My shoulders sagged.

Jax pressed his thumbs into my joints, forcing my posture upright. "It's time to let go of your fears. True power comes from within." He rested a hand over my heart. "It's found in here."

I leaned my forehead against his chest. "I don't want to lose you again."

"You won't. Regardless of what happens, I'll always be with you."

His brutal honesty added another crack to my emotional shield, the protective barrier that guarded my heart. *I can't say goodbye. Not again. Not like this.*

When I looked up, Jax had closed his eyes, and instead of pressing his lips against mine, he kissed the top of my head, then turned and jogged after Samson. I sighed. *That wasn't the romantic goodbye I wanted.*

I only had to call his name once before he spun around, and the phantom wolf's cries muffled my quivering voice when I said, "I love you."

His irises lit up with enough warmth to melt the surrounding snow. "And I love you. More than you'll ever know."

17

A GLITCH IN THE PLAN

"Elara," Cyrus scolded, kicking my boot with his. "Stop squirming. You'll blow our cover."

I stilled my bobbing legs but stretched my neck around the tree, my nails digging into the soft bark.

"Seriously, sis. If you don't—"

"Shh," Orion hissed. "They'll hear us."

"Who?" I jerked my chin at the dwelling. "There's no one out here."

"You can't be certain," Orion said. "What if Zenith has the Collectors hiding in the woods?"

My brother moved closer, his amber eyes scanning the surrounding trees. "Orion brings up a good point. Remember what Jax told us." He pointed to his ears and eyes. "Keep them open."

I spun around and pressed my spine against the trunk. "This is insanity," I said to Cyrus. "I can't believe we're back at Zenith's."

"Go figure, huh?"

He leaned over me and used his knife to carve block letters into the tree.

"What are you doing?"

"Just a little reminder for the Inner Circle."

I turned to see *Cyrus was here* etched above my head. "Really?"

He chuckled, folding the blade back into the handle. Orion nodded his approval, a smirk tugging at his lips.

"Why are you acting like a child?"

"I have a young heart, sis."

I responded with an eye roll.

Orion's lips tugged even more. "Cyrus, why don't you carve Jax and Elara's initials inside a heart?"

My twin bit his lip and praised the Lunin with silent applause.

"You're ridiculous." I slapped Orion in the stomach. He flexed, deflecting my attack. "I already have one brother. I sure as hell don't need another."

"I'm telling Jax you touched me inappropriately. Cyrus can be my witness."

"Hell yeah." My brother reached for a fist bump. "I got your back, bro."

My tongue slid against my teeth as they knocked knuckles. "I see how it is now. You've joined sides."

With a smug grin plastered on his face, Orion slid closer to Cyrus, drawing a line in the white fluff with his boot.

"An official line? I guess I'm not the only dramatic Lunin."

"Think about it, sis. In *Star Wars*, Luke bailed on Leia."

"Wow. That was low."

"*Star Wars*? What's that?"

"Dude—just go with it," Cyrus whispered.

Orion straightened and crossed his arms. "Yeah, like *Star Wars*."

"All right, Luke and Han." I bowed my head at the two men. "I'll team up with Jax. He's like Obi-Wan. No, scratch that, he's more like Yoda." Cyrus's grin sagged. "That's right, so good luck trying to—" The sound of rusted hinges squeaking silenced me.

We pressed our bodies together, forming a single-file line, and peered around the tree. I held my breath. Three Lunin Collectors stepped through the door in the wall, their pale fingers wrapped around their knife handles.

My mind raced with the blurred images of the Inner Circle. "Cyrus." My voice came out in a tight whisper. "Do you think—"

"No. I bet they're Active Members."

The momentary relief vanished in the breeze once another pair of boots exited the dwelling. *Shit.*

Orion froze. I reached behind me and grabbed my brother's wrist.

Older than the other Collectors, this Lunin exuded a level of confidence that rivaled Jax.

My eyes observed the features of his pale face, narrowing at the jagged scar on his forehead. I didn't know this Collector by name, but I remembered him standing behind Pollux that morning on the cliffside. I swore under my breath. This man was a member of the Inner Circle.

As if they were dogs called by a silent whistle, the younger Collectors hurried to greet their superior.

"I want the three of you scouting the area." Not a suggestion, a command. Refusing to lift their gaze, the Active Members kept their blue eyes focused on the snow-covered ground. "Stay sharp. He's expecting them any minute now." My nails dug into my brother's cold flesh. "Do *not* engage with the twins. Those are direct orders from Pollux. If spotted, report them to me or Apollo. Do I make myself clear?"

The shortest Collector, the one missing a finger, murmured, "Sure thing, Jericho."

That's his name. I chewed on the inside of my cheek. *Damn it. Jax didn't share any details about Jericho.*

The Lunin grabbed the Active Member by the collar of his coat. Steel-blue daggers shot out of his eyes as he spat, "What the *fuck* did you say to me?"

Orion repeated the four-letter word while Cyrus sucked in a sharp breath and held it.

The nine-fingered Lunin struggled to speak, his eyes darting back and forth.

Jericho fisted his hand. "I asked you a question, boy."

"I meant . . . yes, sir."

"That's what I thought." Jericho spat onto the ground before shoving the young man in the chest. He staggered backward, and his comrades stepped aside, allowing the scolded Collector to fall. "Is there a good reason the two of you are still standing here with your heads up your asses?"

Geez. He sounds like Samson.

The heels of their boots clicked to attention, and in perfect unison, they replied, "No, sir!"

"Then move!" Jericho barked.

The two Collectors scattered in different directions while the third scrambled to his feet.

"Don't make me come out here again," was the last thing Jericho said before slamming the door shut behind him.

The missing-fingered Collector dusted the snow off his coat and muttered, "Prick," then jogged to catch up with the others.

Once the three men disappeared from view, I let go of my brother's hand and touched the white knife in my pocket. "Samson's right. It's a trap. Zenith knew Jax would rescue Idalia."

Cyrus's warm breath grazed the back of my head. "Yeah, but he doesn't know he's inside."

"You don't know that."

"Yes, I do."

"Keep it down," Orion whispered, his eyes never leaving the door.

I lowered my voice and spoke over my shoulder to my brother. "How can you be so sure?"

"Because we haven't heard the alarms. If they had spotted Samson and Jax, the Collectors would have notified Zenith. Your boyfriend's combative skills are impressive, but Samson's on another level." Cyrus blew out a long breath. "I bet that dude could take out three Active Members at once."

"Then what's taking them so long?"

"Elara, it's not like they're sipping hot cocoa by the fire, chatting with the Collectors about the old days."

I brushed off his sarcasm and punched Orion in the back, his shoulders bouncing up and down with quiet laughter.

Minutes passed, though it felt like hours. We waited and waited for something—anything—to happen, but nothing did. Resembling mannequins trapped in a department store of terror, we stood with our arms glued to our sides, features rigid, eyes wide. We didn't blink, we didn't speak—we didn't dare risk blowing our cover.

After three gusts of wind, Cyrus nudged my legs, encouraging me to bend my knees, so I didn't topple over. I shifted my weight; the soles of my boots compacted the tiny ice crystals with a quiet crunch.

With five more icy slaps to the face and no signs of the Collectors standing on watch, restlessness and boredom toyed with our minds. Orion blew rings of warmth from his mouth while Cyrus caught snowflakes with his tongue. My jaw popped when I yawned, and my eyes felt drier than the time I wore contacts for Halloween. *This is grueling. It's freezing and I'm . . .*

My heart sank as I glanced at the evening sky. Only one of the twin moons grinned through the snow-filled clouds. An omen—and a bad one at that. "Shit." The word repeated on my tongue.

"Elara, what is it?"

I faced my brother, my throat tightening with the answer. "I have the same feeling I had that night with Archer. Something's wrong . . . something's terribly wrong."

Before Cyrus could respond, the door to the perimeter wall swung open. My legs buckled. Jax sprinted toward us with Idalia in his arms, Samson not far behind.

Fearing a repeat in history, I pushed my brother in front of us and said, "Get ready to run."

He dashed forward, meeting Jax halfway. Orion and I hurried after him, our eyes searching for Collectors.

A pained cry escaped my mouth once Jax rested Idalia's half-naked body into my brother's arms. *No. Please, no.*

My eyes welled with tears. Deep lacerations disfigured her once flawless complexion. I bit my knuckles. The strands of her platinum hair, the ones not caked in blood, shimmered in the moonlight, her eternal beauty desperate to shine forth.

Cyrus adjusted his grip on the injured Solin, careful to avoid the open wounds and fresh bruises that blotted her bare legs. As if someone had used a knife to undress Idalia, her shirt was shredded, leaving her bare torso exposed to the elements. My blood boiled at the sight of a thick stream of blood dripping from her pelvic area. *Sick bastards.*

Every muscle in Cyrus's body twitched with rage.

I touched his arm and through gritted teeth, I said, "I'll kill them myself."

He nodded, his nostrils flaring.

Winded from the rescue mission, Samson panted while removing his coat. With trembling hands, he draped the heavy fabric over Idalia's body. "Those sons of bitches will pay for what they did to you, sweetie." He kissed the top of her blood-soaked hair. "You can count on that."

I breathed hard, watching Orion press his fingers against the main artery in Idalia's neck.

"She's unconscious." His eyes filled with concern as he

looked at Jax. "We need to get her out of here, and we need to do it fast."

Jax grabbed Cyrus's arm and spun him around. "Hurry." He slapped him on the back. "Head for Iah's and don't stop running."

Resuming his role as savior, Cyrus sprinted away from Zenith's.

Jax's fierce gaze shifted to me and Orion. "Stay together." We nodded. "Now let's get the hell out of here."

I wanted to agree with his practical plan, but the weight of sheer terror held me in place as my eyes drifted toward the dwelling. *Oh, God. We didn't see this coming.*

Orion paled; his grave expression reflected my own. In a flash, Samson and Jax exposed the blades of their knives. I clutched my chest.

Only feet away stood the remaining eight members of the Inner Circle. A sinister smirk yanked the corner of Pollux's mouth, malice dancing in his pale blue eyes. The bitter taste of bile stung my taste buds as he dangled his knife in the air. Fresh blood, Idalia's blood, dripped off the blade onto the snow.

The other members stepped forward, creating an impermeable wall of brutal strength. The burn scars on Elio's face tightened with a sneer, his boots guiding him to his place beside the unspoken leader. Apollo's bored and flippant attitude, the same one he had that dreadful morning, sent tremors rippling through me. He moved to Pollux's right, his massive stature towering over the Lunin.

My heart pounded on overdrive. Jax stepped in front of me, an unsubtle reminder of that life-changing day. *How did we wind up in this situation—again?*

Unlike our first encounter with Pollux, unwavering confidence emanated out of Jax's being. I did a doubletake watching Orion move beside him, preparing for battle. He stood tall with his chin held high.

The phantom wolf howled its warning, sending debris falling from the overhead branches. An icicle shattered on the toe of Apollo's boot. He didn't flinch. He didn't blink.

Samson, our fearless leader, pushed up the sleeves of his shirt and cracked his neck. A hint of morbid satisfaction crossed his determined face as he scanned each member of the Inner Circle. He was ready—ready to avenge his sweet Idalia.

My teeth chattered along with my spasming muscles. *No. I can't face Pollux, not after what happened with Archer.*

Jax reached behind his back and squeezed my wrist. "Remember," he whispered, "the fear isn't real."

The Lunin's words fell on deaf ears.

Pollux stretched his neck to find my eyes. "Well, well, well." His smirk spread into a wicked grin. "We just keep running into each other, don't we, sweetheart?"

18

AN ACT OF LOVE

The last syllable slipped off Pollux's tongue in an invisible wave of venom. His poisonous words paralyzed my trembling muscles.

Elio snickered and directed the tip of his knife at me. "Look at her Pollux, she's too scared to move."

Jax dug his fingers deeper into my wrist.

The unspoken leader of the Inner Circle let out a dramatic sigh and dragged his thumb along the smooth side of the blood-soaked blade. "That's unfortunate." He rubbed the oily residue between his fingers, then licked it off his pale skin. "At least the other girl put up a fight."

Elio's blonde hair fell out of his face as he tossed his head to the evening sky, white clouds of amusement leaving his mouth.

Jax's arm shot out, holding Samson in place. "Don't break the line."

"Who knows?" Pollux said to Elio. "Elara might surprise us." My stomach did a nauseating somersault when he added, "It's always the quiet ones who scream the loudest."

Disregarding his own command, Jax let go of my hand and

took a step forward. "Choose your words wisely, Pollux. They might be your last."

The unspoken leader sneered at his arch rival. "You're a fool to threaten me."

Accepting the challenge, Jax slid his boot closer and countered with, "Only a fool confuses a threat with a promise."

Apollo and the other men eyed Pollux, waiting for the signal to attack. The Lunin didn't lift a hand. He just clicked his tongue against the roof of his mouth in a timed rhythm syncopated with the Grim Reaper's pocket watch.

After a few more ticks of the irritating sound, Pollux shut his eyes and inhaled the evening air. "Ah." They shot open. "This feels familiar, doesn't it? Reminiscent of that morning on the cliffside."

"You're wrong."

Pollux looked at Samson. "And why's that, old man?"

"Because this time"—the Solin stared at the blade of his knife while he rotated it in his calloused hand—"Jax isn't outnumbered."

I flinched at Pollux's ear-piercing cackle. He was the perfect villain: The Joker and Hannibal Lecter's love child. I shivered. *I'm living in a horror movie.*

"Samson, is your age finally catching up with you?"

The ex-Collector shrugged, unfazed by the verbal jab.

"There are eight of us." Pollux waved his blade at Elio and the other men. "And only four"—he shook his head as if deleting me from the list—"*three* of you."

"Removing Ravi was easy enough." Samson smirked at the dried blood on his nail beds. "Too bad I can't say the same for his fingers."

A stocky Solin with eyes the color of burning embers snarled. Apollo lifted his arm, halting the man's approach.

Adding fuel to the fire, Samson said, "I'm surprised Zenith let Ravi leave the house with such a dull blade. Better luck next time." His lips curled into an exaggerated pout. "Awe, poor Ravi doesn't get a *next time*."

Orion went rigid. Pollux whispered to Elio, then to Apollo.

"Get ready," Jax warned, adjusting his grip on the gray handle. "They're coming for blood."

The three men who stood before me tightened their formation. I wanted to escape the madness and head for the safety of Iah's, but that wasn't an option. It never was. I couldn't turn my back on the Solin who helped me find courage when I needed it the most or the young Lunin whose unfaltering friendship eased my emotional suffering. And I sure as hell couldn't turn my back on the man I loved.

The four of us were in this together and would be until the end. Jax's lesson on the illusion of fear may have gone over my head, but it didn't stop my boots from sliding forward or keep my chin from lifting. I squeezed my body between the two Lunins and eyed Jax. An awareness grabbed hold of me. He nodded at the unspoken recognition.

I observed each member of the Inner Circle, my attention snagging on Pollux. Not a hint of kindness or compassion flickered in his eyes—only hatred and resentment. Like the other Collectors, a void had manifested inside of his soul, leaving him powerless, and even though he'd never speak of it, the truth scared the shit out of him. I could see it in his eyes. The burning desire to experience something greater than himself. He wanted to fill the gaping hole in his heart. But he never would, because he refused life's greatest gift —love.

Prepared to face my darkest fears, I inhaled one last conscious breath of the crisp air and lengthened my spine.

Pollux's face hardened. "Bring me the girl," he hissed at Elio. "I'll take care of Jax."

A jerk of the chin and all hell broke loose. Three Solins and one Lunin rushed Samson. His fluid movements mirrored a well-seasoned Green Beret, deflecting each attack with ease and precision. My mouth gaped at his impressive skills.

He threw a spare knife at the stocky Solin while pulling another from his back pocket. The wounded fell to his knees with a blade embedded in his groin.

My head snapped to the right. I cursed. Two Lunins circled Orion, their blue eyes watching his every move. With a knife in each hand, my friend spun in the snow, unsure who would attack first.

"Stay close," Jax whispered.

I nodded, adrenaline surging through my veins.

Pollux and Elio didn't bolt forward like the other men. No. They took their sweet-ass time, strolling toward me and Jax as if they didn't have a care in the world. Their physical features may have sat on opposite ends of the spectrum, but the hatred that consumed their blue and orange eyes closed the gap between them.

Elio tapped the burn scars on his face, then pointed the tip of his blade at my heart. The muscles in his jaw twitched as he glared at Jax. "Your little bitch is going to pay for what she did to me that day at the spring. And after Pollux finishes doing what he does best, you get to watch me skin her alive."

Before Jax could react, the unspoken leader lunged, taking him to the ground. I stumbled backward. Jax was right. They worked as a team. The evil pair knew a verbal jab directed at me would distract my partner, leaving him vulnerable.

My heart skipped a beat. Elio charged, holding the handle of his knife with the dull side of the blade running along his forearm, an unfamiliar technique to my eyes. This simple yet effective maneuver kept the sharp edge at a safe distance. *What the hell? Why didn't Jax or Samson teach us the proper way to hold a damn knife?*

The long hours I spent training with my brother and Samson paid off. Elio raised his arm, directing the blade at my neck. My feet slid to the side. I dodged the first attack, only to trip over Jax and Pollux's tangled bodies. My teeth sang as my tailbone slammed into the ground.

Irritated that he missed his mark, Elio tossed the knife into his left hand. *Go figure.* I scrambled to my feet. *He can use his knife with both hands. Where's Cyrus when I need him?*

Out of the corner of my eye, I saw Samson grab a Solin by the collar of his coat. He pulled him into a bear hug, then jammed his knife into the side of the man's neck. I swore at the amount of blood that splattered Samson's face as he severed the Solin's trachea.

Choking and sputtering on the red fluid, the man touched his gaping wound. Panic flashed in his ember-colored eyes. Unable to fill his lungs with the required amount of oxygen to sustain life, the Solin collapsed. His hollow eyes stayed open, a heavy stream of blood dripping from his parted lips.

One down, seven to go.

My chest heaved, not from exertion but from shock. I had witnessed two murders in less than three months. Baffled by the violent events that unfolded around me, I steadied my wobbling knees.

Elio snickered at my disheveled appearance and circled me like a cat toying with a bird. I eyed the Solin with the injured groin. He dragged his body toward the door in the perimeter wall, a dark trail of blood staining the snow behind him.

Two down, six to go.

I gasped when Apollo attacked Samson. *Never let him restrain you in a hold.* Jax's warning had manifested. I adjusted the grip on my knife.

The eldest member of the Inner Circle wrapped a massive arm around Samson's neck and pressed the tip of his blade into my mentor's leathery skin. Blood trickled from the incision. If Apollo had applied more pressure, his knife would have punctured the main artery—a clean kill, but no, he wanted his victim to suffer. Samson's tongue hissed against his teeth as the blade went deeper.

Anger transformed into panic which shifted to desperation that raised my armed hand.

Elio shouted, "Move!" at Apollo while lunging at me.

Hearing the urgency in his comrade's voice, the Solin spun, taking Samson with him.

The white handle left my numb fingers right before Elio took me to the ground. I struggled to focus on my target, and the forceful blow left my head spinning.

Apollo's coat blew open at the most opportune time: mid-rotation. The blade sliced through the fabric of his shirt, piercing him under the rib cage. I whispered my gratitude to the universe and Apollo hollered his complaints.

The Solin slipped his knife under Samson's chin while his free hand inspected the injury. The ex-Collector used this opportunity and slid his palm between the sharp side of the blade and his throat. I grimaced at the blood that poured from his hand as he forced the knife away from his neck. He pivoted, then twisted the blade until it faced his attacker. A diversion so he could reach the embedded knife in Apollo's side. Samson gripped the white handle, rotating it 180 degrees before tugging it in a downward motion. The color drained from Apollo's face as Samson ripped the blade from his torn flesh.

Three down, five to go.

Utter darkness with specs of silver glitter filled my vision. Another burst exploded around me. The phenomena reoccurred each time Elio backhanded me across the face. Warm fluid from my busted lip overflowed into my mouth, the metallic taste of iron zapping my taste buds.

A forceful blow sent my head flying to the left. The white fluff stuck to my bloodstained cheek. I squinted, focusing on Samson. He hurled a knife at an unexpected Lunin who hurried to help Apollo. A sickening thud followed by a painful moan confirmed Samson hit his mark. The mortally wounded glanced at the blade wedged in the center of his abdomen for only a moment before falling to the ground.

Four down, four to go.

"This time your piece of shit brother isn't here to save you," Elio hissed, holding my arms above my head.

The handle of my spare knife dug into my backside. I struggled under the Solin's weight, trying to reach for the lifeline concealed in my pocket. With each failed attempt, Elio pushed me deeper into the snow. *Stop struggling. Remember your training.*

I tapped my foot, lifted my hip, and rolled Elio onto his back. He took me with him, a cloud of white mist surrounding us. I held him in the dominant position for a quick breath before he repeated my defensive maneuver. My head collided with the compacted snow, my teeth sinking into my cheek. I spit the chunk of torn flesh at my attacker, hitting him right between the eyes. Elio snarled. The moonlight illuminated the burn scars on his bronze complexion, a slick imprint of where my hand had melted his face.

Another strike from his knuckles sent my head sailing to the right, and this time, a new scene unfolded before my eyes.

Pollux had pinned his adversary to the ground and held a knife to his neck. I hollered Jax's name. It scratched the sandpaper that lined my throat, my voice hoarse from screaming.

His fingers held Pollux's wrist, keeping the blade at a safe distance. The unspoken leader leaned farther over Jax and whispered near his ear. Rage consumed the ex-Collector. He reached for his gray knife that lay inches from his outstretched hand.

Watching Pollux dangle Jax's life in front of me sent my heart racing and, blood pressure rising, it kicked my ass into gear. Elio locked his legs around my hips and made the mistake of loosening his grip on my wrist. In one violent motion, I lifted my arm and slammed my elbow into his nose.

A strong curse word flew out of Elio's mouth. The same word slipped out of my own as his warm blood sprayed onto my face. I fluttered my lashes; the sticky residue had glued them together.

The injured Solin moved to an upright position and used both of his hands to reset the broken bones in his nose. With the weight of his legs holding me in place, I summoned my core strength and performed the world's fastest sit-up before shoving him off of me.

Free from death's icy grip, I dove toward Jax's knife like a baseball player sliding into home base for the championship win. He gripped the handle once I pressed it into his palm. Giving him ample room to work, I reverse Army crawled through the snow but froze at the sound of a pained cry. I looked up.

Jax stabbed his nemesis with so much force I thought the blade would punch right through him. Not once, not twice, but over and over he rammed the knife into Pollux's side.

The nausea that swirled in my gut intensified as a blood-curdling scream, my own, reverberated through the vast space. A blinding pain shot up my leg. My jaw clenched shut. *Is it still attached? I can't look.*

Elio crouched beside me, wicked laughter rumbling in his chest. My fingers trembled, reaching for the knife wedged in my calf.

He grabbed the handle. "You might be the special twin." He pushed the blade deeper into my torn flesh. I choked on a mouthful of snow. "But you bleed like the rest of us."

"Please," I whimpered.

"Please?" Elio knocked my hand away. "Oh, so you want more?" He twisted the handle.

My watering eyes bulged, the pain overwhelming me.

The Collector moved closer. "Let me share some advice so you're prepared for your evening with Pollux. He *loves* hearing a woman beg him to stop. It really"—Elio flicked his tongue in my ear—"gets him off."

Samson grabbed the Solin by the back of his coat, ceasing the madness that left his mouth. With one hand wrapped around the collar and the other gripping the fabric tails, my savior hurled the Solin through the air. Elio's blond head slammed into the trunk of a tree, sending him into a deep sleep.

Samson didn't stop to investigate my injury; he just pulled another knife from his pocket and sprinted toward Orion.

Unsure how to triage the wound, I rolled onto my side to get a better look. Bad idea. Vomit shot out of my mouth, chunks pooling near the discolored snow around my bleeding calf. I wiped the remnants of my last meal off my chin with the sleeve of my coat.

A blur of bodies lifted my gaze. Samson had lunged at Jericho, one of the remaining Lunins who attacked Orion. The two men went blade to blade, their fluid movements mirroring each other in a dangerous waltz.

A thick stream of blood oozed from a gash on Orion's face. I cringed at the dangling skin that flapped in the breeze. Each gust exposed the white bone in his cheek. The injured Lunin winced as he held pressure over a gash in his right arm.

The other Lunin warmed his shoulder muscles. The ease in which his pale fingers gripped the handle of his black blade confirmed his identity: Oberon. The member of the Inner Circle whose knife skills rivaled Jax and Zenith; the member who never missed his mark.

Oberon's malicious expression shifted to a stone-cold killer. He checked the sharpness of his blade while Orion searched for the nearest escape route.

I reached for the spare knife in my back pocket. It was gone. I scanned the area. The blade was nowhere in sight. Desperation guided my fingers through the snow. *Damn it. It must have fallen out of my pocket.*

Oberon raised his armed hand over his shoulder, his blue eyes locking onto his target. I eyed Samson who was wrestling with Jericho in the snow, their fists colliding with skin and bone. I cursed the knife in my leg. *Just do it. Orion's life depends on it.*

I trembled, touching the handle. The smallest movement sent a burst of searing pain radiating through my calf. My eyes watered. *I can't.*

A familiar sound echoed around me, a sound that signaled my body to react without a conscious effort: the alarms. The doubt that clouded my mind vanished, and the thin skin on my knuckles split open as my teeth sank into the cold flesh. Bearing through the pain, I pulled the knife out of my leg. Blood gushed from the wound in violent waves, matching the rhythm of my heart.

Oberon eyed the door in the wall. I took advantage of the distraction and hurled my knife at his lower abdomen—the area unprotected by his unbuttoned coat. He stilled. The blade had punctured his flesh. Seconds later, he fell to his knees.

Orion's boots sloshed through the snow. "Come on," he rasped. "We have to get out of here." He bent down and threw my arm around his neck. "Zenith's coming."

I winced as he helped me to my feet. Supporting most of my weight, Orion slid his uninjured arm around my waist and dragged me through the white fluff, one painful step at a time. I focused my attention on the morbid stains that covered the ground until my friend shuddered a breath. My chin lifted only for my jaw to drop.

The events I witnessed that night rattled the pureness of my soul, but seeing Jax unleash his demons on Pollux frayed the tapestry of my sanity.

The ex-Collector held the Lunin in a ground hold, blood saturating the area around them.

Pollux's head flew to the right, then to the left. Each blow shredded the skin on Jax's knuckles. He didn't let up, pushing the unspoken leader of the Inner Circle closer to the brink of death.

Orion paled; his wide-eyed expression matched my own. Pollux reminded me of a creepy doll in a horror movie. His pale blue eyes rolled around in his head, and blood oozed out of his mutilated face and dripped from the knife wound on his side.

"Elara." Orion breathed hard. "We're running out of time. We can't wait for Samson and Jax."

I nodded; a combination of shock and pain left me speechless.

My friend guided me forward. Two steps later my stomach twisted into a knot. A darkness had grabbed hold of Jax—a darkness I never wanted to see again. The loving light in his eyes dimmed and glazed over with a nasty mixture of vengeance and spite. My chest caved. His vacant expression looked the same as it did the night he held Cyrus against the tree, the same as it did the night he tried to kill me.

"Stand down!" Samson hollered, rushing toward the Lunin. He grabbed Jax's arm mid-swing. "That's an order."

Jax blinked once, twice, then stared at the torn skin on his knuckles. Not an ounce of regret stained his pale face as he climbed off the ghost of his past.

The darkness that consumed him lifted once he noticed my injuries. His eyes darted from my split lip to my swollen brows, then narrowed at my wounded leg. He dashed forward, meeting us halfway, then squatted to slide his arms underneath my legs. Our eyes locked. A white cloud, a shared breath of uncertainty, slipped through our parted lips. I cocked my head to one side. *Is this the end?*

In my short life, I had experienced a few blips on intuition's radar, but the gut-wrenching heartache I felt in that moment left me incapacitated.

I didn't have to look up to know who stood there. Zenith's presence flowed out of his being like a destructive tidal wave, consuming everything in its wake—everything good and pure. Jax winced as if the invisible surge had slammed into him, while Orion and Samson used colorful words to express their sentiments about our grave predicament.

Everything moved in slow motion, even the swaying tree limbs. The snowflakes eased their descent from the evening sky, the heavy breathing of the men around me stilled, and the wounded members of the Inner Circle lay motionless, their painful moans faded to muffled complaints.

The evil smirk of a Collector could frighten the bravest of men, but Zenith, the man who ruled Aroonyx with fear, the man who found pleasure in torturing the innocent, the man who murdered his adoptive father in cold blood, only to mutilate his body afterward, didn't need to wear a mask of deception. He *was* deception, a master of trickery and mind games. Unlike the fallen men around his feet, Zenith could hold my gaze—and he did so without blinking.

A naïve part of me had hoped he'd appear less terrifying in person. Either short like Napoleon Bonaparte or unattractive with a ridiculous mustache, similar to the other ruthless dictators who terrorized Earth. Boy was I wrong. The man was fierce —gorgeous, a god among men.

Zenith's striking features reflected his adoptive son in a distorted image. He looked like Jax, only older and with a tan. Well over six feet tall, he towered over the men who stood beside me. With his chin held high, the confidence seeped out of his invisible pores. Not a scar, not a freckle, not a blemish marked his flawless skin.

I broke eye contact, noting the definition in his arms and the cords of muscle on his abdomen that peeked through his shirt. Apparently, he didn't require a coat. Perhaps it would get in the way. Regardless of the reason, nothing appeared to affect this man, not even the harsh elements. *It's true. He's the perfect combination of a Solin and a Lunin.*

The icy breeze ruffled the locks of Zenith's jet-black hair, and the razor-sharp lines of his jaw hardened. A white cloud of disdain left his mouth as he observed the lifeless and wounded members of his precious Inner Circle. He sneered. *Zenith's personal guard had failed him—they failed to end our lives.*

Seconds passed before the leader of Aroonyx locked his blue and orange eyes on me once more. His boot slid forward.

Samson and Jax straightened, their eyes fixed on the ruthless dictator. Orion mumbled a desperate plea to the universe while I took a quick inventory of our opponents. Two men, whose names I never learned, lay dead in the snow. The injuries that the others suffered left them unconscious or writhing in pain, and the Solin with the groin injury was nowhere in sight. *I bet he was the one who sounded the alarms.*

Zenith scanned our small group, the thin line between his brows creasing. I swore under my breath. *Cyrus. He's looking for Cyrus.* The half Lunin, half Solin ground his teeth. The sound of bone grinding against bone caused the hairs on the back of my neck to rise.

Jax moved closer and brushed his fingers against mine. He stilled, realizing his error. His gentle touch had exposed our relationship status.

Missing nothing, Zenith's head snapped toward us, and in a calm and silky voice he whispered, "Interesting."

The former leader of the Inner Circle tensed and shifted his weight.

Samson yelled, "Move!" as Zenith exposed the blade of his knife, the knife I never saw him reach for, the knife I never saw coming.

Without hesitation, I lunged, placing my body in front of

Jax. The muscles in my stomach contracted around the sharp blade, morphing my screams into whimpers. Jax caught me in his arms before falling to his knees. The whites of his eyes turned a bright shade of pink.

His name got caught in my throat as I reached for the embedded knife. "Something's wrong. I don't feel right."

"Don't pull it out!" Samson snapped.

Jax grabbed my hand and directed it away from the knife while his other cradled the side of my face. "Elara, you've got to stay with me."

My pounding heart pushed more blood out of the deep wound. I looked at Jax. *No. I'm not supposed to die. I haven't finished our mission.* My vision spun. *Or have I?*

The devastating turn of events lowered Orion's head in a mournful posture. A single tear slid down my cheek as I glanced at Samson, his grave expression matching the Lunin's. *This is it? This is how it ends?*

I tried to fill my lungs, but with each inhale the taut muscles in my stomach increased the blood flow from the injury. Death showed its illusionary face, sending a final surge of adrenaline rushing through my veins.

I squeezed Jax's hand. "Please," I cried, finding his eyes. "I don't want to die—not like this."

"Shh." He ran his fingers through my hair.

I bit my lip, stifling the sobs that irritated my pain receptors. "I want to go home." I whispered the words until they sounded foreign on my tongue. "Please take me home."

I lifted my head to see how much blood I had lost, but Jax shielded my eyes with his hand. "Stay with me," he said, pulling me closer. "I need you to stay with me."

The sharp features of his face blurred, and the sound of his voice muffled as if speaking under water. I smacked my lips, the bitter taste unbearable. Iron-rich fluid crept up my throat. I coughed, choking on my blood.

Jax touched the stream that trickled down my chin before glancing at Orion. My friend eyed the knife in my stomach, the red stains on my shirt, and the pool of blood around me. He shook his head, his throat bobbing.

Samson took a knee and rested his calloused hand on my uninjured leg. "Don't quit on me now, kiddo."

I blinked, my eyes heavy with permanent sleep.

Jax called my name and patted my cheek. "Elara," he repeated, his voice rising.

I squinted at his blurred features that withered away like the Moon Drops did at sunrise.

"You can't leave me." His voice cracked. "Damn it, Elara. Don't you dare leave me."

I wanted to ease his pain—say the words he needed to hear, but I never got the chance because the final breath of life left my parted lips. Jax's piercing blue eyes were the last thing I saw before everything faded into the oblivion.

PART II

TRAPPED IN THE DARKNESS

19

PATIENCE AND OTHER VIRTUES

W*hy is it so dark? I thought colors in the afterlife were vibrant—bright. Interesting. What happened to the tunnel of light that beckons one's spirit? That's how they depict death in the movies. Why am I thinking about movies? I'm dead. None of that matters anymore.*

Confused why my body still ached, I patted my chest and arms. *What the hell?*

I opened my eyes and hissed at the light that glowed from the bedside lantern. *I'm alive?*

A whimper of relief escaped my mouth once I spotted Jax sleeping in the wooden chair beside me. He sat with his eyes closed and head bowed.

Across the room, I noticed Cyrus, Orion, and Samson sitting on the floor with their backs pressed against the wall. The men's relaxed postures and tranquil expressions confirmed that they too had drifted to dreamland.

I scanned their bodies for injuries. Cyrus appeared unharmed, but Orion had a large piece of gauze wrapped around his bicep and over six stitches sealed the wound under his cheekbone. The muscles in Samson's throat vibrated with each slow inhale that entered his nose, the loud snore disturbing the quiet space. My eyes drifted to the blood that stained the bandage on his neck and the gauze around his hand. I gritted my teeth. *Damn, Apollo.*

Curious how my injuries fared, I tried pushing myself to the seated position. *Nope. Not happening.* The torn muscles in my stomach and calf contracted, sending a burning sensation pulsating through me. I swore under my breath.

Jax's eyes shot open. "Elara," he gasped, scooting his chair closer to the bed.

The others' heads popped up at the sound of the legs scraping against the wooden floor. They scrambled to their feet and hurried to my side.

Cyrus's voice cracked. "Hey there, sis."

"Hey there, bro." I smiled, giving his hand a loving squeeze.

A tear rolled off his cheek as he leaned over to give me a hug. "Don't you ever do that to me again." Grief saturated his words.

"What? Don't get stabbed by Zenith?" A friendly reminder of how he answered my question about his near miss during the first snowfall.

Cyrus chuckled, the warm light in his eyes resurfacing. "Touché, sis."

Orion and Samson flashed me warm grins. Jax, seemingly unamused with my little joke, palmed his eyes.

My injuries hollered their complaints in searing waves as I scooted myself up the bed and leaned against the headboard. Jax reached for a vial of liquid resting on the nightstand.

"Here." He popped off the lid. "Iah wants you to drink some of this. He said it should help with the pain."

Eager for relief, I snatched it from his outstretched hand and drained the entire bottle. I gagged, the strong substance stinging my taste buds. Bitter yet sweet, the flavor reminded me of the candied orange peels I'd eat with my grandmother at

Christmas. The liquid slid down my throat and goosebumps rose on my arms. I shivered, then dropped the vial. *Whoa.*

My head spun. I blinked, trying to focus on the four men who hovered above me. *This feels . . .*

My thoughts drifted to the quiet space of my mind I rarely visited. My skin tingled and my face numbed. I touched my lips, wondering if they were still there. With each heartbeat, the liquid pulsated through my veins, zipping and zooming; microscopic medics prepared to heal my wounds. I touched the bandage underneath my shirt, then flexed my injured leg. *Impossible.* Only seconds had passed since I ingested the strange liquid, but the pain was gone.

"Orion." A hint of concern sparked in Jax's eyes. "Was she supposed to drink the whole vial?"

"Nope." He pushed the Lunin out of the way. "She sure wasn't."

Cyrus's eyes narrowed, watching Orion switch from relaxed bystander to a focused doctor. Samson swore, scrubbing at his face.

Orion pressed his fingers to my neck, closed his eyes, and counted to himself.

He only got to five before I asked, "What's wrong?"

"You weren't supposed to drink it all."

He passed thirty, then encouraged me to follow his finger with my eyes.

Cyrus sat on the edge of the bed. "What are the side effects?"

"Well." Orion held his fingers against my wrist. "If a patient consumes a high dose, they risk—"

"They risk what?" Samson demanded.

The Lunin grimaced, refusing to look at the Solin over his shoulder. "Falling into a permanent coma."

Jax sprung to his feet. "Orion, what the fuck?"

Samson growled, cracking his knuckles.

"Jax!" The color drained from my brother's face. "Why did you let her drink that much?"

"I didn't know she'd clear the bottle. I told her to drink *some* of it, not all of it."

"Guys, I'm—"

Orion's name snapped off Jax's and Cyrus's tongues.

He held up his hands. "Before you jump my ass—"

"Oh, we'll do a lot more than that if you don't fix this," Samson warned. "Your father left you in charge. This is *your* fault."

"I didn't expect her to drink the entire vial."

"I don't want to hear any excuses, kid."

"Nor do I," Jax said.

My brother fisted his hands. "Fix it, Orion."

"Calm down," I demanded. "I'm fine. Maybe I have a high tolerance."

"She's right." Orion rested the back of his hand on my forehead. "No fever, her pulse is strong, and she's coherent. If Elara's body had rejected the medicine, it would have done so by now. The adverse reaction happens within the first minute."

The three men let out a shared breath.

Samson shook his head at Orion. "No more dumbass mistakes. Do I make myself clear?"

"Yes, sir." He stepped away from the bed. "It won't happen again."

Hoping to ease the Lunin's discomfort, I mouthed, "Thank you."

He shrugged and moved to the other side of the room, keeping a safe distance from Samson.

Jax sighed and lowered himself onto the chair. I frowned. He looked exhausted. The worry lines around his eyes had deepened along with the one between his brows; the rescue mission aged him five years.

I touched his bandaged hand. "I'm fine."

Doubt clouded his eyes.

"Really. I am. It feels like I took a muscle relaxer and drank three shots of espresso."

Cyrus, appreciating my Earthly references, snickered and took a seat on the bed once more. This light-hearted moment dissolved when a heartbreaking thought crossed my mind. *Idalia. Where's Idalia?*

Fearing the worst, I looked at Jax. "Where is she?"

"In Orion's room. Iah's with her now."

"Is she okay?"

Silence followed a long pause. My eyes bounced between the four men in the room. They stared in opposite directions.

"Jax. Is Idalia okay?"

He swallowed. "She's been through a lot. More than most."

My heart sank as I remembered the stream of blood that dripped from her pelvic region.

Orion cleared his throat. "Physically, she'll recover."

"Right," I murmured. *And mentally?* I lacked the courage to ask the simple question. *Later. I'll ask him later.* "Well, I'm glad she's . . . okay."

The skin over Cyrus's knuckles thinned as he clasped his hands.

Time to switch the subject. "So." I paused, unsure how to phrase the next part of my question. "What happened after—"

"Zenith hit you with his knife?" Orion interjected.

I grimaced. "Yeah . . . after that."

"I told Orion to pick you up and run," Samson said.

I blinked at him. "What about Zenith? Didn't he attack?"

"We didn't give him the opportunity. I charged while Jax threw his knife."

"Wait." I clutched my chest. "The two of you attacked Zenith?" They nodded. I pushed myself farther up the headboard. "How?"

Samson chuckled. "Don't look so surprised, kid. It's not like he had his army of Collectors protecting him."

"Where were they?"

The Solin raised a brow.

"Not the Inner Circle," I corrected. "The other Collectors?"

"Inside," Jax answered.

"Why didn't they help?"

"I told you, interfering with the Inner Circle is punishable by death."

"Yeah, but the Inner Circle was out of commission and their leader was in danger."

Jax shook his head. "It doesn't matter. They didn't get the orders to attack. Zenith is a prideful man. He would never ask for help."

"So what happened?"

Samson dragged a hand over his beard. "We needed to buy Orion time. Zenith didn't expect us to attack, so when I dashed forward, he reached for another knife and then Jax threw his spare."

Wide-eyed, I stared at the former leader of the Inner Circle. "Did you hit him?"

"Yep. In the stomach."

My mouth gaped. I had always assumed Zenith was untouchable, especially after hearing the story of the rebels. The thought of him injured sounded crazy, if not impossible. My fingers grazed the bandage around my abdomen, and I eyed my brother. He shrugged, already familiar with the turn of events.

"Did you try to kill him?" I stammered.

"I wanted to, considering his knife was wedged in your gut," Jax drawled, seething with anger. "But Samson stopped me."

"Why?"

"Because of the conversation we had on our walk to Zenith's. I can't be the one who ends his reign."

"But you didn't know if I was alive."

"It didn't matter," Samson said. "I wasn't willing to take the chance."

My cheeks puffed with a mixture of emotions. They had the chance to end Zenith's life but passed on the opportunity. I looked at Cyrus. Another shrug.

Orion pushed himself off the wall. "I carried you until we were a safe distance from Zenith's before tending to your wounds."

"The kid needs to work on how to administer the correct dose." Samson jerked his chin at the Lunin. "But in the field, he acted like a well-trained doctor and removed the knife without causing permanent damage."

I smiled at the Lunin and mouthed, "Thank you," once more. He returned the gesture with a humble head nod.

Samson twisted the tip of his beard into a cone. "It got a little nerve-racking because you lost so much blood."

A muscle feathered in Jax's jaw, his posture tensing.

"But once we got back," Samson continued, "Iah took over, stitched up your wounds, and told us you'd make a full recovery."

"Thank you," I said, glancing around the room. "I wouldn't have made it without your help."

Orion shook his head. "I should be thanking you, Elara. I'd be dead had you not thrown that knife at Oberon."

"He's right," Samson added. "You saved our asses. You helped Orion, kept Apollo from slicing my throat, and you literally took a knife for Jax."

I braced my abdomen while laughing. "Thanks for making me sound like a badass."

"Your actions earned you the title." Samson winked and squeezed my shoulder. "You did good, kid. Thanks for having my back."

"Anytime."

Cyrus stretched his muscular arms and rose to his feet. "I should go check on Idalia. See if she needs anything."

"Tell her I'll visit tomorrow. If she's up to it."

He forced a smile. "Sure thing, sis."

My heart ached for my brother, who dragged his feet toward the entryway, his confidence fading with each small step.

Once the door closed, I turned and craned my neck to peer out the window. It was too high to see out, but moonlight shone through the glass panes.

"How long have I been sleeping?"

"Not long," Jax answered. "We got back early this morning. It's late evening now."

I nodded, touching my swollen brow. "Hey, Samson."

"What's up?"

"Now that—" I paused, the words not forming on my tongue.

"Zenith stabbed you and Jax stabbed Zenith?" Orion suggested.

"Yeah." My eyes drifted from the Lunin to the Solin. "What's the plan?"

"We wait. Let you recover and then we regroup."

I huffed a breath. *I hate waiting.*

"Patience," Jax whispered.

Samson crossed his arms. "It's all we can do, Elara. Last night was a huge blow to Zenith. Three members of his Inner Circle are dead and six are severely injured. That knife hit him hard, but it hit his pride even harder. The injury won't slow him down." He sent a quick glance at Jax. "Zenith's pissed. No one challenges him and lives to tell the tale. Don't be surprised if he starts playing dirty."

"Great," I muttered.

"Remember," Samson added, "every action creates a ripple effect. In my lifetime, I've seen some fucked-up shit, but it's taught me a valuable lesson: prideful men fear the fall."

Jax murmured his agreement.

"We rattled Zenith's foundation last night," Samson added. "He won't make a move until he thinks he has the upper hand. This buys us time. That's why we wait. No offense, kid, but you're useless on the battlefield in your current condition."

"None taken." I sighed, smoothing a crease in the comforter.

"Try to get some rest," he encouraged. "Zenith won't come knocking anytime soon."

I nodded, still dazed by the news.

"Samson, we should get some sleep too." Orion inclined his head toward the door. "It's been a long day."

"Yeah, it has." His joints popped as he walked across the room. "I'm getting too old for this shit."

I chuckled under my breath. Samson turned sideways to fit his broad shoulders through the doorway. Orion signaled his departure with a casual wave over his shoulder before shutting the door behind him.

Alone at last, I looked at Jax and let the air rush out of my lungs. "I never want to go back to Zenith's."

"Nor do I."

I stared at the closed door. "Even though Samson's killed more people than I can count, I still find him endearing."

"I agree." Jax smiled and rubbed the back of his neck. "He's a tough old bastard, but he's got a big heart." His hand fell into his lap. "Don't tell him I said that. If you do, he'll kick my ass."

"I won't if you promise to behave."

Mischief tugged at the corner of his mouth. "I'm always on my best behavior."

"Mm-hmm. I'm sure you are."

He offered me the mug on the bedside table. "Water?"

"Why, so I can cool off?"

He shrugged, his smirk turning into a seductive grin. "You look a little parched."

I hissed, grabbing it from his hand, then took a long swig. The cool liquid removed the bitter aftertaste of the medicine. I licked my lips and handed him the cup.

"That stuff I drank earlier worked wonders. I'm a little sore but the burning sensation is gone, and it doesn't hurt to breathe anymore."

"I'm glad it helped."

Jax placed the mug on the table. His playful attitude shifted to somber as he rested his forearms on the mattress.

I took his hand, observing his troubled expression. "What's wrong?" His fingers tightened around mine. "You can tell me. What is it?"

"Life has a way of testing us when we least expect it."

"How so?"

He shut his eyes. "I had let go of fear, only for it to resurface at the thought of losing you."

I lifted his fingers to my lips. "I'm sorry. I didn't mean to scare you." Trying to lighten the mood, I added, "At least now you know how it feels. Actually, you don't. You thought I was dying, but I thought you were dead for over three weeks."

An unforced laugh left Jax's mouth. He let go of my hand to stretch his arms overhead. "Is Cyrus's humor rubbing off on you?"

"Perhaps."

I glanced at my clothes, the smug grin on my face drooping. I left for Zenith's in a long-sleeved shirt and pants. *Why am I wearing shorts and a sleeveless shirt?*

"Is it—"

"Summer?"

I blinked. "When did that happen?"

"The snow started melting on our way back from Zenith's, and it vanished before we arrived this morning."

"Will I ever get used to this crazy weather?"

"It takes time, like everything else in life."

Aware that Idalia was in no condition to play nursemaid, I asked, "Who changed me into fresh clothes?"

"I figured you didn't want your brother undressing you, so I rose to the challenge." The mattress sagged as he leaned over the bed, his warm breath grazing my ear. "I didn't think you'd mind."

Blood rushed to my cheeks. *Perfect. Jax takes off my clothes, and I remember nothing.*

Laughter rumbled in his chest, the vibration rubbing against my arm.

"What's so funny?"

"You are, Elara."

"Well, I'm glad you find me entertaining. I'll be here all night."

"On a more serious note, there's something I forgot to tell you."

"And what's that?"

"Thank you."

My head cocked to one side. "For what?"

"For saving my life." His lips moved toward mine. "Again."

My pulse quickened when I remembered the last time Jax expressed his gratitude. Excited to revisit the intimate moment, I pulled him closer and whispered, "That's twice now. You owe me."

Like dedicated soldiers deployed on a mission, my fingers marched up the back of Jax's neck, lost in the locks of his hair. A spark of desire ignited a burning ache in the lower, more sensitive part of my body. I surrendered to his request, a sound of pleasure growling in his throat.

My lips parted, allowing his tongue to sweep in, each rotation more determined than the last. With each passing second, he kissed me deeper—harder.

The wooden chair slid across the floor. I flinched.

"Sorry," he apologized, leaning farther over the bed. "It was in my way."

Jax's sensual voice sent a yearning through my body, a craving only he could fill. I shuddered a breath, his teeth nipping at my ear.

"What a foolish chair," I whispered onto his flesh.

"Indeed." He breathed hard, his lips tracing the line of my collarbone.

My back arched, a natural reaction to his touch. The weight of the comforter irritated the tender muscles in my calf. Bothered by the restricting fabric, I tried tossing off the covers in a seductive motion but failed miserably because the sheet got tangled around my feet. I groaned. *That wasn't sexy.*

"Allow me to assist you with your efforts," Jax purred near my ear.

His calloused hand slid down my leg, and his lips followed the curve of my upper thigh. Any lingering discomfort from my wounds vanished. The desire that gathered in my core throbbed, begging him to explore. Just a thin layer of material shielded his mouth, his tongue, from the spot that would send me over the edge.

My fingernails dug into Jax's shoulders, the need overwhelming me. Toying with my emotions, he flicked his tongue against my flushed skin. I rolled my hips, enticing him to move into the dominant position. Holding the waistline of my shorts between his teeth, he whispered the two words that always drove me mad. "Patience—*Elara.*"

Bastard. His hand glided along an invisible path that led to my lower abdomen, then slid past the button barrier on my shorts. My breath hitched. His fingers danced in lazy circles that lured my tongue to whimper his name. My spine arched even more once a finger moved inside me, and my nails drew blood on his bicep when another followed suit.

The gauze around my abdomen brushed against Jax's arm. He stilled. *Don't you dare stop.*

Out of desperation, I tugged at his forearm, encouraging him to continue. "I'm fine. It doesn't hurt."

He hesitated, his blue eyes fixed on the bandage. Stepping up my game, I dragged my hand along the part of him that firmed against me. With a wicked grin, Jax slid his body on top of mine and pinned my arms above my head.

"This is much better than the ground holds we practice during training."

He answered me by nudging my head to the side and kissing my neck. My heart thundered in my chest. His hands held my wrist, pushing me deeper into the mattress. I lifted my chin, begging for more.

Jax pulled away and scanned every inch of my quivering body, his eyes stopping on the hidden bandage underneath my shirt. That damn bandage.

"I'm sorry," he whispered. "I can't. I won't hurt you."

My face fell as he climbed off of me. It took an abnormal amount of self-control not to curse at the top of my lungs.

"Please tell me you're joking."

He swung his legs off the bed. "No, not this time."

"I told you, I'm fine. That medicine worked wonders. I'm not in any pain."

"Elara, it's late and—"

"Don't give me that excuse."

"I'm simply stating the facts." He turned to face me. "It's late, and your wounds need to recover before I—"

"Before you what?" I grinned. "Go on. Finish the sentence."

"Before I do something foolish and end up hurting you." He pointed at my bandaged stomach and calf, then inclined his head at the deep cuts and bruises on my face. "Your injuries are severe. I don't want to cause you any more discomfort."

"You won't." I shifted my features into neutral and motioned to the damaged parts of my body. "They're just small scrapes."

Jax shut his eyes, a low growl rumbling in his chest.

I rolled onto my knees and pressed myself against his back. "I promise." I wrapped my arms around him, slid my hands underneath his shirt and down the hard planes of his abdomen. "We can stop if anything feels uncomfortable." A lie. I didn't give a shit about my injuries.

Jax inhaled a deep breath and held it. I waited—impatiently. His eyes shot open. A hint of satisfaction curled on my lips. With fluid grace, he spun around on the bed and lifted me on top of him. My legs wrapped around his hips, securing him in place. I leaned over him and kissed the sharp lines of his jaw. His fingers dug into my backside, causing a not so quiet moan to slip through my parted lips.

"Shh," he soothed. "We don't want to wake up the entire house"—he lowered my hips onto the hardened length of him—"or do we?"

"I don't give a f—"

"Language, Elara," he whispered, sliding his hand underneath my shirt.

"The clasp is in the back."

Jax muffled his laughter by holding the skin of my neck between his teeth. "I'm aware. Thank you for the reminder."

Shit. Of course he is. It's obvious his skills don't stop at combative training. My stomach tightened at the thought of him with another woman. *Stop it. Don't think like that. Not now.*

Jax's forearm grazed the bandage as his hand slid around my ribcage. His fingers halted their pursuit, only inches from the metal clasp.

"Ignore it," I rasped. "I'm fine, remember?"

"I'm sorry." He lifted me off of him. "I can't. It doesn't feel right."

"Are you *fucking* kidding me right now?"

"Again, with the language," he scolded. "That mouth of yours will get you in trouble."

"Good." I jerked my chin at his pants. "Allow me to give you a demonstration."

Stunned by my indecent proposal, Jax's brows almost touched his hairline.

"That's right." I smirked. "Try to keep up."

Speechless, he slid off the bed onto the floor.

"Oh, come on. No one has that much self-control."

A casual shrug proceeded. "I'll be right here if you need anything."

I groaned. *Nope. I'm not giving up that easily.*

I let my hair cascade over the edge of the bed. I grimaced at another failed attempt at sex appeal. The turbulent events at Zenith's had matted my hair, leaving the black waterfall looking like a rapid river of tangled knots.

Jax refused to meet my gaze. He laid on his back and rested his hands underneath his head. With one leg crossed over the other, he stared at the cracks in the ceiling. The laces of his boots tapped the wooden floors in an offbeat rhythm, matching his uneven breathing.

"You don't have to sleep on the floor."

"Stop it," he hissed, draping an arm over his face. "Go to sleep."

My eyes sparkled; victory was within reach.

"I can't." I fanned my shirt. "It's too hot in here."

Jax watched me out of the corner of his eye. "Then crack the window."

"How will that help? It's summer."

His boot bounced faster with each word that left my mouth.

"Fine." I sat up. He lifted his arm an inch. "I'll make myself more comfortable."

Jax stilled, watching me pull off my shirt. His Adam's apple bobbed when I unfastened the clasp of my bra. I bit my lip, trying to hide my amusement, and slid off my shorts along with my undergarments. He cleared his throat and lifted his arm higher to get a better view. Sealing my fate, I tossed the articles of clothing far out of his reach.

"There," I said, displaying my body across the bed. "Much better."

"That is quite enough of you and your seductive ways."

I reminded him of his earlier words while twisting a lock of my hair. "I'm simply stating the facts. It's late, and the floor is not very comfortable. You need a good night's rest."

Jax crossed his arms and squeezed his eyes shut.

"The bed is a practical option." I patted the space beside me. "And as a bonus, you get to sleep—with *me*."

Jax sat up. "What am I going to do with you?"

"I bet you can think of a few things."

His eyes roved over every inch of my naked body. "You're right." He climbed to his feet. "I already have."

I swallowed. Jax strolled toward the door, kicking off his unlaced boots. His hand lingered on the doorknob. Click. The lock turned.

My vision blurred at the sudden rise in blood pressure. He peeled off his tight-fitting shirt and tossed it to the side. My pupils dilated at the sight of his chiseled abdomen. Each muscle contracted as he ambled toward the bed, his eyes focused on his new mission.

Jax moved me to the desired position, knocking the headboard against the wall. Every nerve in my body tingled with pleasure. Hearing him whisper my name sent my hands sliding down his scarred chest, then over his eight-pack, stopping once they reached the first button of his pants. I hesitated, my fingers playing with the silver circle. His eyes found mine in a heartbeat.

"Your move." He winked, slipping his tongue into my mouth.

My other hand moved to assist with the simple task but paused at the touch of another button. Jax kissed me harder, giving me the green light to explore the part of him I needed to feel. Our lips broke apart with the smile that grew across my face. My patience had finally paid off.

20

ABOUT LAST NIGHT

Ecstasy, elation, and bliss. These simple, yet powerful words whirled in my mind, each sentiment a reflection of my evening spent with Jax. I exhaled a peaceful breath, allowing my body to sink deeper into the mattress. Heavy with the aftereffects of the previous night's events, my lazy eyes blinked at the tiny dust particles that danced on the sunbeams in the morning light.

With my cheek pressed against Jax's bare chest, I could hear his heart thumping in my ear; the steady rhythm matched my own relaxed pulse. My fingers followed the jagged scars that lined his abdomen, and I noted the different textures and colors.

Remembering the little game we played while living in the woods, I lifted my head and braced myself on my elbows.

"Maybe tomorrow," Jax said, his eyes still closed.

"Damn it. You always catch me."

A large grin swept across his unshaven face.

"Just you wait." I walked my fingers up his stomach. "One day I'll win this little game."

"Doubtful. I've had years of training."

I rested my chin on his chest and met his gaze, the memories of the previous night flickering in my eyes. "Good thing I'm a fast learner."

"Yes. Yes, you are."

I inched my body closer and mumbled, "Good morning," onto his lips.

The Lunin's fingers tangled in my hair as he kissed me long and slow, his tongue moving in unhurried circles. I inhaled his familiar scent: the sweet aroma of a summer's kissed breeze with a dash of raw and undiluted passion. My eyes blurred with lust.

Eager for a distraction from the dull ache that pulsated around my knife wounds, I crawled on top of Jax and let my hands wander. After a thorough investigation of the area I frequented the night prior, Jax pulled his lips away from mine and whispered, "A *very* good morning it is."

I smiled, tracing the outline of his lips, then hissed when he nipped at my finger.

Holding it between his teeth he asked, "How did you sleep?"

"Better than the other nights on Aroonyx."

He frowned, eyeing my stomach. "Hungry?"

"Starving," I confessed, trying to muffle the loud gurgling with my hand. "I don't know the last time I ate."

"Then you should eat."

A slew of colorful words followed a painful cry as I rolled off of Jax. My calf and stomach burned like hell.

Jax propped himself up on his elbows, his eyes filling with concern. "Are you okay?"

"No," I whined, forcing back tears. "Everything hurts."

"Damn it, Elara. We should have waited until your injuries recovered."

"I have zero complaints in that department." I motioned to my lower half. "Because *you* refused to go past third base."

Jax shut his eyes and let out a tight breath. "I have my reasons."

Yeah, reasons you refuse to share. I scoffed while adjusting the blood-stained bandage around my leg, then pointed at the empty vial on the nightstand. "Can you get me some more of that medicine?"

"No. You ingested too much last night."

My lips sagged into a dramatic pout face. *"Please."*

He shook his head. "Speak to Iah about the proper dosage."

I sucked in a sharp breath and held it. "My entire body is on fire."

"I know that feeling well."

I glanced at the scars that decorated his pale skin, a visual reminder of the hell he'd endured at Zenith's.

"The intensity lessens over time," he reassured me. "After a week, the pain will subside to a dull ache."

"Yippee," I mumbled, dangling my legs over the bed.

"Patience, Elara."

I glared, bearing weight on my throbbing leg. My teeth dug into my knuckles and an actual cry slipped through my quivering lips when I took a small step forward.

"Let me help."

Irritated that I appeared so helpless, I slapped his hand away.

"Forgive me." Jax chuckled, leaning against the headboard. "I forget that your stubbornness follows you in every area of your life."

I shot him another glare, only this time it looked more authentic because my pain receptors had put me in a foul mood. "I'm fine," I snapped. "I'm just getting my bearings."

"Of course, you are." Jax smothered his amusement. "How foolish of me to think otherwise."

I brushed off his verbal jab and limped toward the door like a dog with a thorn stuck in its paw. "I'm going to get something to eat."

"Thank you for clarifying the reason behind your sudden departure." I rolled my eyes at his sarcastic remark. "And judging by your quick pace, I should expect you to return . . . in what?" I didn't have to turn around to see his smirk growing—I could feel it. "A few hours?"

Witty bastard.

Jax chuckled.

Keep laughing. I'll make you pay later tonight.

He called my name once my fingers gripped the doorknob.

"What is it now?" I asked, refusing to turn around.

"Just another observation."

"Which is?"

"You might want to put on some clothes before stepping into the hallway."

I gasped, my hand recoiling from the silver knob. I glanced down, noting my bare breasts. More laughter filled the quiet space.

I whipped around as fast as my pained body would allow, only to find Jax grinning from ear to ear. I wagged my finger at him. "Shame on you for finding humor in my misfortune."

"My most sincere apologies, miss."

Groaning louder than necessary, I hobbled to the other side of the room to retrieve the missing articles.

"Do you need help?"

"No, *sir.* I'm more than capable of clothing my own body, thank you very much."

Jax continued to laugh watching me struggle with the simple task. The skin around the freshly stitched wound in my abdomen tightened each time I lifted my arms. I cursed.

Jax swung his legs off the bed. "Come here. Let me help."

Surrendering, I shuffled toward him with my arms stuck above my head, shorts sliding down my legs.

He pulled one of my arms through the sleeve, then the other. I winced as he lowered the shirt over my stomach, the fabric snagging on a rip in the gauze.

"Sorry," he whispered.

My fingers gripped his shoulder while he slipped the pale shorts over my bandaged calf and up my legs.

"There." He adjusted the waistline around my hips. "Better?"

I winced, lowering myself onto the bed. The mattress sagged as he took a seat beside me.

"Jax, how did you manage? I have two knife wounds. You had like twenty and a handful of other near-fatal injuries."

He dragged a hand through his hair before finding my eyes. "I was in a lot of pain when I left that afternoon. It was foolish of me to leave in such a fragile state. My injuries hadn't healed, I had a splitting headache"—he flicked his wrist at the mug on the bedside table—"and I had coughed up enough blood to fill that cup."

I grimaced, thinking of the gut-wrenching procedures Iah performed.

Jax shifted his weight on the bed. "I'm not sure if it was the Minlav poisoning or the antidote injection, regardless, I felt like shit."

"Not surprising. Iah drilled a hole in your skull weeks prior to you leaving."

"True." He touched the faded memory.

"So how did you handle the pain?"

"I stopped resisting it."

My brows rose with a combination of confusion and curiosity.

"Let me clarify," he added. "That life-changing moment on the cliffside allowed me to see everything in a different light. If I focused on the pain, I could never pinpoint an exact location. It always moved in waves, bouncing from one injury to the next."

I nodded, grasping the sensation he described.

"Observing this phenomenon gave me a burst of clarity." He motioned to the scars on his body. "Pain is a physical experience and nothing more. Resistance is the reason we suffer."

"You're being extra cryptic right now."

"No, I'm not."

"Well, it doesn't make sense."

"Like any technique, it takes practice. If you allow yourself to surrender to the physical discomforts, you'll find that an injury only hurts so much."

"I'm still not following you, Jax."

He reached for my hand. "Remember the time your parents rushed you to the hospital?"

"How do you know about that?"

"I told you. I kept a close watch on you and your brother."

I blinked, recalling the time my parents took me to the ER because I couldn't stop vomiting. After hours of testing, the doctor rushed me into the operating room for an appendectomy.

"Did you feel scared?" Jax asked.

I lowered my gaze. "You were there, weren't you?"

"I didn't go inside the hospital."

"Fair enough." I touched the tiny scars on my abdomen. "Yes, I was scared. Dealing with the pain was one thing, but waiting for the test results was another."

"And that's what I'm talking about."

"And *that* went right over my head."

"Elara, it's the pain threshold that everyone fears. How bad can it get? Will it get worse before it gets better?"

Still confused, I stared at the wrinkles in the comforter.

"I bet you felt some relief after the doctors gave you your test results, didn't you?"

"Yeah, almost right away."

"See, getting a diagnosis helped calm your nerves. An

appendectomy is a fairly simple procedure. Yes, your illness required surgery, but you knew the pain would pass after they removed your appendix. The good thing is we don't need a doctor to remind us that pain is temporary."

"We don't?"

"No." He smiled. "I've learned a little trick, and it works every time."

Jax rested a hand on my thigh and squeezed it hard enough to send a pulsating river of fire to my injury. My eyes bulged.

"Observe the pain," he said. "Don't identify with it, and don't resist it. Just let it be there."

Baffled, I eyed the Lunin. As usual, he was ten steps ahead, leaving me lost in a trail of dusty confusion behind him.

I gritted my teeth at the burning sensation that radiated in my calf muscle. "That's easier said than done." I shot him a stern look. "And if you say the word patience . . ." The corner of his mouth twitched. "I'll kick you in the balls with my good leg."

His mouth gaped. "I wouldn't dream of it."

"Smart ass." I used the bed as a crutch and rose to my feet.

Jax stretched before leaning against the headboard.

I waved a hand at my clothed body. "Am I presentable now?"

He hummed, scanning me up and down. As if recalling our intimate time together, his blue eyes paused on the more sensitive areas of my body. "Do you want my honest opinion?"

Self-conscious, I pulled my shirt farther over my shorts and smoothed the tangled locks of my hair. "Um . . . yeah."

"I prefer you without clothes."

Blood rushed to my cheeks. I tugged on the waistline of my shorts, exposing the flesh underneath. "These clothes are *very* restricting."

A growl of desire rumbled in Jax's chest as his eyes roved over me once more.

"You're lucky I'm injured."

He tilted his head. "And why is that?"

"Because if I wasn't, I'd force you to stay in bed with me all day."

Jax reached for a pillow and covered his face. "Get out of here," he demanded, his words muffled by the thick fluff. "Before I take you up on that offer."

I frowned, the irritation for my injuries growing at an exponential rate. A casual wave signaled my departure.

I limped down the hallway, muttering different curse words with each painful step. The doors to both Iah's and Orion's rooms were closed. *I guess they're still asleep.*

My skin prickled with heat once I rounded the corner. I found Cyrus in the kitchen, his amber eyes focused on a vegetable that resembled a black potato. With a knife in hand, he sliced through the fibrous root, adding bite-sized pieces to his ever-growing pile of assorted food groups.

He turned, hearing my entrance. "Hey there, sis." He didn't bother hiding the huge smirk on his face. "Someone's looking extra pleased this morning."

"Don't start."

Cyrus tossed the knife onto the cutting board, then leaned against the counter and crossed his arms. "So." He wiggled his eyebrows. "How did it go?"

"That's none of your business," I said, reaching around him for a bite of food.

He blocked my efforts. "Oh, come on, you have to tell me."

I knocked his hand away and snatched a piece of dried meat. "Says who?"

"Says me—your twin brother."

I shrugged, tossing the cube into my mouth.

"Fine. I don't need a verbal confirmation." He flicked my cheek. "Your actions from last night are written all over your flushed face."

Sharing his Solin strength, I punched him in the gut.

He winced at the unexpected attack, then clicked his tongue. "Defensive reaction. The first sign of guilt."

"Nothing happened last night."

"Bullshit. I don't buy that for a second."

"I'm serious."

He gave me a sidelong look. "You want me to believe that *nothing* happened in there last night, even though Samson and I didn't sleep a wink because of the noises coming from the bedroom."

The color drained from my red face. "Please tell me you're joking."

Cyrus flashed me a familiar grin, the same one I gave him the day he woke up at Idalia's after his long night with Rico. "Yeah, have fun explaining your evening to Samson." He mimicked the Solin's raspy voice. "Cyrus, did I just hear your sister—*moan*?" He switched back to his own voice. "I don't want to think about it, Samson." He mimicked the other Solin with an added laugh. "Who knew Elara had it in her?"

I scrubbed at my bruised face. My brother laughed hard, pleased with his performance.

"Fine," I grumbled. "We may have enjoyed each other's company, but nothing happened." He lowered his gaze. "We didn't have sex."

Cyrus's jaw cracked open. "You're such a mean girl."

"Why?"

"Because you denied that poor man." His head shook with mock disappointment. "And after everything he's been through."

"You're ridiculous."

"I'm just stating the obvious."

I looked over my shoulder, searching for curious eyes and ears before looking at my brother once more. "I tried but Jax said we needed to wait. Why? I have no idea."

"Tough break, sis."

"You're telling me." I sighed, grabbing a handful of vegetables off the silver plate.

"Well, today is a new day." He reached for the knife. "Who knows? Maybe Jax will change his mind. I told Hillary we should wait, but that lasted for five minutes after she climbed on top of me and started—"

"Good morning, Cyrus."

We both flinched at the sound of Jax's silky voice. I swore and the torn muscles in my calf and abdomen contracted at the sudden movement.

"Damn that guy can sneak up on you," Cyrus whispered to me.

"My apologies," Jax said, kissing the top of my head. "I didn't mean to catch you off guard."

Refusing to meet the Lunin's gaze, Cyrus mumbled, "Morning Jax," while busying himself with food preparation.

Amused by my brother's awkward behavior, I reached for another piece of meat.

"Stop eating it all." He swatted my hand. "I'm trying to get this ready for Idalia."

My fingers recoiled from the mouthwatering offerings. "Is she awake?"

Cyrus nodded.

A long silence followed his somber expression, twisting my stomach into a knot.

"Can I see her now?"

My brother eyed Jax. As if speaking telepathically the Lunin nodded at the Solin, then turned to face me. "A visit from you might do her some good."

I swallowed. Jax hid a message in his words, one I needed to decipher on my own.

Cyrus handed me the plate of food. "See if you can get her to eat something."

I took it from his outstretched hand and headed toward the hallway, the knot in my stomach expanding with each painful limp. My brother called my name. I turned, bearing a small amount of weight on my injured leg.

"She's different now." A resignation lingered in his tone. "Quieter than before."

Jax sighed through his nose.

Great. Now I feel even more uncomfortable about the shitty situation.

A lump of uncertainty formed in my throat as I neared Orion's room. I shivered, recalling Idalia's limp body in Cyrus's arms: the bruises, the gashes, the blood that dripped from her pelvic area—evidence of Pollux's cruel actions.

I held my breath while my knuckles rapped on the wooden door. No answer.

My fingers gripped the silver plate. I shut my eyes and expressed my intention to the universe, a silent vow I swore to uphold. *I'll make that bastard pay for everything he's done.*

The masked dealer cackled in my ear. *Though it once tasted bitter, the thought of revenge now appeals to the appetite. Does it not?*

I nodded.

Don't worry, Elara. Pollux won't get away with this.

A wicked grin, one filled with malice, spread across my face. *No, he won't.*

21

A VEIL OF DARKNESS

I waited outside Orion's room and knocked once more, only this time a little louder. I counted. *One . . . two . . . three.* No answer. More silence.

I pressed my lips near the doorframe. "Idalia. It's Elara. Can I come in?"

In a hoarse voice, she replied, "It's open."

I held my breath and twisted the knob. Afraid of what I might see, I lowered my gaze as I stepped over the threshold. Though sunlight poured into the room, tangible darkness cloaked the quiet space, and when I looked up, my heart shattered into a million pieces.

As if a painter had smeared the oil colors on a beautiful canvas, black and blue bruises blotted Idalia's once flawless complexion. I clenched my teeth. *This is worse than I imagined.*

Compelling my body to move forward, I took a cautious step toward the bed, noting the dried blood crusting her busted lip and the swollen bulge around her eye. I calmed my ragged breathing and inched my way closer to the dazed Solin.

Idalia wrung her petite hands, the gauze scratching against her dry skin. Her head turned. The matted locks of her hair didn't bounce with life as they did before. They barely moved, the blood and grime acting as heavy weights tugging on the blonde strands. I forced a smile while holding back tears.

She returned the warm gesture but winced. Her split lip had re-opened from the sudden movement. She wiped the blood with the back of her hand and whispered, "Hey, Elara."

My anger toward Pollux grew with each passing second. Idalia's sweet voice had transformed into a distant memory of her former self.

I rested the plate of food on the nightstand after realizing she had no interest in eating, then climbed onto the bed when she patted the space beside her. Ignoring the burning sensation in my abdomen and calf, I steadied my trembling hand and reached for hers.

Drops of remorse stained her battered face. "Elara, I'm so sorry."

"Idalia." I held her in a tight embrace. "You did nothing wrong."

"Yes, I did." Her body quivered with trapped emotions. "They almost killed you because of me."

I lifted her chin, forcing her to meet my gaze. "None of this is your fault."

She looked away. "Yes, it is. If I hadn't—"

"Stop." My voice raised. "We're in this *together*—all of us. Are you forgetting everything you did for me and Cyrus? Not only did you help save his life, but you risked your own by hiding us in your bedroom wall." She shook her head in disagreement. "Idalia, think of all the times you helped Jax. If it wasn't for you, he'd probably be dead. Please"—I squeezed her hand—"don't apologize for what happened. You've done nothing wrong."

Her head snapped toward me, the flecks of gold in her weary eyes shimmering in the morning glow. "That's easy for you to say." The light dimmed as she glared at me through tiny slits. "You weren't the one who screamed, begged him to end your life while he—"

"Regardless, it's not your fault."

"Yes, it is!"

I gasped; her sharp tone knocked the wind out of me.

The Solin's voice trembled with rage. "You didn't hear the twisted shit he said or see how he held me against that *fucking* floor while he—"

"I know, but—"

"Years, Elara! I've spent years ignoring Pollux's foul mouth and dodging his cruel advances. I defended Jax that day and look where it led me." Tears streamed down her face. "I can't eat. I can't sleep. Every time I close my eyes, I see his face, hear his voice, feel his—"

"Please," I begged. "Don't do this to yourself. I know how—"

She paled. As if a ghost had appeared before her eyes, she scooted away from me, gluing her body to the headboard. Her voice lowered to a threatening growl. "How dare you assume to know how it feels." Daggers shot out of her eyes, aiming straight for my heart. "You can't imagine the hell I've been through."

"I didn't mean it like that. I was just trying to—"

"No." Her head shook so fast, I thought it would detach and roll across the room. "Get out."

"Idalia, please."

"I said, get out!"

A determined fist pounding on the bedroom door caused us both to flinch.

"What?" she snapped, her eyes burning a hole in the wooden panels.

A heartbeat later, Jax opened the door and stepped inside, his posture tense, on edge. "Is everything okay?"

"Yeah, *Elara* was just leaving."

I climbed off the bed with my tail tucked between my legs,

the comforter snagging on the gauze around my calf. Defeated, I dropped my head. My only female friend on Aroonyx wanted nothing to do with me.

Jax focused his attention on Idalia and approached at a guarded pace. "May I speak with you for a few minutes?"

She shrugged, tucking her knees into her chest. Jax gave me a *we'll talk about this later* glance and inclined his head toward the door. I nodded, regretting my decision to visit the distressed Solin.

I stood in the hallway like a disheartened soldier after a failed mission: alone and shell-shocked. I eyed my new room. *I could get some more sleep and forget it ever happened.* I huffed a breath. *No, I'll just lie there, worrying about Idalia.* My stomach growled. *I'll grab some food. Food is a good distraction*

I found my brother standing in the kitchen with the knife in hand, his eyes fixed on the living room window. I sighed. The walls of Iah's home were thin. Thin enough to let Idalia's raised voice travel to Cyrus's ears.

As soon as my toes touched the floorboard closest to my brother, he hissed, "What the hell did you say to her?"

I winced, his accusation slapping me across the face. "I . . . didn't say anything."

Cyrus turned, ire flashing in his eyes. "Then why did she tell you to leave?"

"I don't know. I told her I understood—"

The loud scoff that left his mouth drowned out my words. "Please tell me you didn't say that to her." My face fell and his voice raised. "Elara, you have no idea what she's been through."

"I'm aware of this, Cyrus. I never implied I did. I just wanted to make her feel better—"

"By telling her you understand how it feels to be sexually assaulted?"

"No! I can't imagine what she's going through, nor would I

assume. I just wanted to tell her I understand how it feels to harbor unnecessary guilt. That's it."

Regret clouded Cyrus's eyes. "Sorry, sis. I didn't mean to jump your ass. I'm just so angry."

The masked dealer raked a claw down my spine, its black nails poisoning my mind with toxic revenge, an unsubtle reminder of our private conversation outside of Orion's room.

I rolled my neck. "You're not the only one who feels that way."

"I've never wanted to kill anyone—until now."

I stilled at the quiet edginess in Cyrus's tone.

His voice lowered. "Ending Zenith's reign is one thing. It's a job—a responsibility. But when it comes to Pollux, I want to see that bastard six feet under, and I want to watch him suffer long and hard before he goes." A muscle feathered in his jaw. "*And* I plan on doing it with my bare hands."

I rubbed the cold spot in my chest. "Well, you won't have to put forth much effort. Not after what Jax did."

"What do you mean?"

I glanced over my shoulder to make sure we were still alone before saying, "You didn't hear what happened to Pollux?" He shook his head. "Samson didn't tell you?"

"No."

I blew out a low whistle. "I need to sit down for this one." I patted the space beside the sink. "Can you give me a boost?"

He wrapped his strong hands around my waist and lifted me onto the wooden countertop. I grimaced, my abdomen protesting his gentle touch.

My brother moved in front of me and crossed his arms. "So, what happened?"

"I'll tell you if you hand me one of those weird-looking carrot things."

Irritated with the delay, Cyrus scowled while reaching for

the purple vegetable. He tossed it onto my lap. "Here Babs, now start talking."

My teeth sunk into the fibrous root. "Sure thing, Buster." I tilted my head. "Wait a second, did you watch *Tiny Toons* when you were a kid?"

"Yeah. My parents found the old DVDs on eBay." He blinked hard. "Why are we talking about this right now?"

I shrugged. "You started it."

He looked at the ceiling and murmured, "Lord, help me," before bracing his hands on either side of me. "Stop trying to switch the subject. Tell me what happened."

"Fine," I grumbled, using my nail as a toothpick to remove a piece wedged in my front teeth. "So during the world's worst brawl, Pollux pinned Jax on the ground."

Cyrus shot me an incredulous look.

"Shocking, I know." I took another bite. "Anyway, after I helped Jax get his knife back, he unleashed hell on Pollux."

A gleam of satisfaction twinkled in my brother's eyes. "What did he do?"

"Um . . . he hit Pollux like a Piñata, but instead of using a bat he used his knife." I demonstrated with my hands, leaving the long root hanging from my mouth. "He stabbed him over and over again in the side."

"Damn, I had no idea."

I eyed the hallway and lowered my voice to a whisper. "But that's not all."

"There's more?"

"Mm-hmm. A lot more."

"I'm listening."

I took a moment to chew, then swallowed. "Right after the alarms sounded, Orion and I found Jax sitting on top of Pollux, beating the shit out of him."

"This was *after* he stabbed him?"

"Yeah, and Jax wouldn't let up. Pollux looked dead . . . like *really dead.* His eyes kept rolling around in his head and blood was everywhere. His face—Cyrus, you should have seen him. Pollux's nose was over here." I pointed to my cheek. "And his eyebrow was up here." I touched my hairline. "But that didn't stop Jax from swinging. I think Pollux's skin would have slid right off his bones and into the snow had Samson not rushed over and snapped Jax out of his trance."

My twin's eyes grew, the detailed imagery of my retelling appeared to whirl in his mind. "Are you sure he's still alive? It sounds like Jax killed the bastard."

"No. Pollux's chest was still moving after Jax climbed off of him."

The muscles in Cyrus's jaw flinched. "Why didn't he just kill him?"

"I don't know." My pulse quickened as I recalled Jax's cold and distant expression. "Death is quick. Maybe he wanted him to suffer."

Cyrus watched the foot of my uninjured leg knock against the cabinet. "What's wrong?"

I bit my lip.

"Elara, you can tell me. What is it?"

"I'm not sure." I hesitated, wondering if it was worth mentioning. "I guess the whole thing just freaked me out."

"That's understandable. It was a rough night. You've never seen that much blood or—"

"No, that's not it."

"Then what's bothering you?"

My lips pressed together. "It's not what—it's who."

"Go on."

"It's Jax."

"What do you mean?"

"Cyrus, he had that faraway, crazed look in his eyes. The same one he had the night he held you against the tree, and the night he held me against the wall."

"You don't think he's gone back to his old ways, do you?"

My heart sank. *I hadn't thought of that—until now.* I rubbed my clammy palms on my warm thighs, my mind reeling with the hypothetical. *Once Jax stopped assaulting Pollux his eyes went back to normal. Maybe it was just a temporary glitch. Last night was amazing. I never felt uncomfortable around him, and he didn't seem distant or distracted by his past.*

"No," I stammered. "I mean . . . I hope not."

"That would be a messed-up plot twist in our little story."

I tried to swallow the knot that formed in my throat once the masked dealer appeared before my mind's eye.

Get out of my head. I've had enough of you and your dark and twisted games.

It responded with a quiet murmur of laughter.

"Do you think an isolated incident could trigger Jax's troubled past?" Cyrus asked.

Unable to answer my brother's question, I sat motionless watching him wipe off the cutting board.

Jax stepped around the corner. I froze. *Play it cool.*

As if hearing my silent plea, Cyrus busied himself once more, the blade of the dull knife struggling to cut through the tough vegetables. Slide. Crunch. Slide. Crunch. The slow and gentle rhythm mocked my pounding heart. I sucked in a sharp breath as the Lunin approached the kitchen. His posture tensed. *Shit. He can see right through me.*

A loud cackle echoed in my mind. I shut my eyes.

The dealer's hidden lips moved near my ear, its silk mask fluttering against my cheek. *Let me tell you a little secret, Elara.*

My eyes shot open to find Jax standing before me.

In the end—the house always wins.

22

SHADOWS OF THE PAST

J ax's eyes slid between me and my brother. Cyrus, the non-discrete twin, whistled while he worked—he actually whistled. *Way to play it cool, bro.*

I hummed and stared at my clasped hands. Like that was any better.

"Does someone want to tell me what's going on?" Jax asked.

Cyrus's fake coughing fit, along with my throat clearing, tapped the nail in our coffin of embarrassment.

The Lunin shook his head at the two of us. "I've spent enough time with you both to know when you're keeping something from me."

Silence. I inspected the jagged scar on the palm of my hand while Cyrus tossed bite-sized pieces of meat and vegetables into a bowl. At least he stopped whistling.

"Okay. I see how it is." Jax's lips pressed together. "I'll be a little more direct with my questioning." He touched my arm. "Elara, may I speak with you alone?"

I complied with his request, though a low grumble of reluctance rattled in the back of my throat. With great caution, Jax lifted me off of the counter and lowered me onto the floor. My brother shot me a weighted glance. I shrugged and took a cleansing breath as Jax slid his hand around my waist, guiding me toward the front door.

My face squished up once we stepped over the threshold, the drastic change in temperature an unwelcome guest. Tiny beads of moisture formed on my brow. I used my arm as a visor to block the morning light that peeked between the trees and followed Jax across the porch.

He motioned for me to take a seat on the chair closest to the railing. "The sun will burn up the humidity in a few hours. It's always worse at the beginning of summer."

I lowered myself onto the aged slats and eyed Jax while picking at a loose thread on my shorts. His vacant expression sent Cyrus's earlier question zipping through my mind.

A burst of air shot out of the Lunin's lungs as he collapsed onto the chair beside me. It was obvious he wanted me to speak first. He stayed quiet, rubbing his thumb over the reminder of his failed mission with Sharik.

Without the encouragement of a breeze, the tree limbs remained motionless. I eyed Jax. He kept his gaze forward.

Last night we connected on an emotional level and now the tension between us is thicker than this damn humidity. I rubbed the back of my neck, my fingers sliding along the thin layer of sweat. *I'm not making the first move. I don't even know what to say right now.*

Jax scanned the surrounding woods as if searching for something—*someone*—that wasn't there. I gathered my hair over one shoulder and let my fingers comb through the tiny tangles, but I paused my grooming efforts when Jax turned to face me.

"Are you going to tell me what's wrong, or should we sit here and stare at the trees all day?"

I lowered my eyes.

Jax stood and dragged his chair in front of mine. "All right,

I'll approach this a different way." The sharpness in his tone commanded my attention. "Let me guess. Your behavior toward me has everything to do with the way I treated Pollux."

Relieved I didn't have to say the words aloud, I melted into the chair and found his eyes. "You're right. It does."

He braced his elbows on his thighs and pressed the heels of his palms into his brows. "I'm sorry you witnessed such cruel behavior on my behalf, but to answer Cyrus's question, and to put your mind at ease—no, I have not reverted to my old ways."

Great. He heard our entire conversation. I let my hair fall into my face, a curtain I gladly hid behind.

"Elara, you of all people should know I always keep my eyes and ears open."

"I'm sorry. We should have just asked you instead of talking behind your back."

"I couldn't care less. Over the years, I've grown accustomed to people expressing their concerns about my behavior through muffled whispers and stolen glances."

I squeezed my eyes shut. Leave it to Jax to make an awkward situation sound poetic. I shooed away the frog in my throat. "Thanks. Now I feel even worse."

"Don't." He dismissed my remorse with a flick of his wrist. "Cyrus is your twin brother. I expect you to confide in him, but trust me when I say this: you have *nothing* to worry about."

"I appreciate your honesty." I paused, trying to string together the appropriate words. "But it still freaked me out to see that crazed look in your eyes. It brought up a lot of bad memories—like the night you held me against the wall."

Jax winced as if my confession had punched him in the gut. The small amount of color in his pale complexion vanished before my eyes.

"Elara, words can't express the regret that consumes me when I think about that night, and to make matters worse, I have no conscious memory of my actions." A deep-rooted pain clouded his eyes. "Cyrus was the one who told me what happened. At first, I didn't believe him. I didn't want to. I couldn't imagine hurting you, much less . . ." His voice faded and he bowed his head.

"Hey," I soothed, reaching for his hand. "It's okay. You had been through a lot."

"No. It's not okay." His fingers fell from mine. "You wouldn't be sitting here had Cyrus not restrained me."

I swallowed, or at least I tried to.

Jax scratched the five o'clock shadow around his jawline. "That's the one thing from my past I can't let go. I don't think I'll ever forgive myself for putting you in danger."

"Listen." I scooted to the edge of my chair, my bare feet brushing against his. "It is what it is, okay? You said so yourself, you don't remember attacking me, so don't beat yourself up about it. It's not like you did it on purpose. Don't play the 'what if' game. If you do, you'll drive yourself mad. See"—I motioned to my body—"I'm fine. No harm done. We live in the now, remember? Not the past."

Jax searched my face for any traces of hidden doubt, then said, "I really don't deserve you, do I?"

"Probably not, so you better bring your A-game."

He flashed me a casual smirk. "I'll see what I can do." He lifted my hand and traced the lifeline on my palm with the tip of his index finger. "You never cease to amaze me, Elara."

"Why?"

"Because even when people are at their worst, you always find the good that hides under the surface—the spark that flickers in the darkness."

My heart warmed as I envisioned my biological mother. "Like I always say, people make the best decisions they can at the time—"

"Regardless of the situation."

A large grin swept across my face. "I'm glad you're finally catching on."

"Ah. The student surpasses the teacher."

"Let's not get carried away," I said, recalling his advanced lessons on fear and pain.

Jax's shoulders shook with quiet laughter, then stilled at the sound of a loud snap. Our heads turned. A massive leaf had detached itself from one of the black branches. Like a lost and forgotten kite, it drifted through the breeze, spinning in never-ending circles. I hummed my approval, mesmerized by the subtle beauty of its perfection. The leaf didn't resist the downward spiral, no, it moved with it, gliding along the unseen path.

My eyes lit up at nature's metaphor, but the corners of my mouth drooped when the leaf touched the ground, the uplifting performance ending too soon.

I looked at Jax. "Can I ask you a question?"

"You can ask me anything."

My fingers found the loose thread on my shorts once more. "Why *did* you act that way with Pollux?" The Lunin's brows etched together. Clarifying, I added, "Don't get me wrong. I won't grieve the man's death, especially after what he did to Idalia."

"Then what's the rub?"

I blew out a tight breath. "The *rub*, Jax, is that you didn't let up. Pollux's body looked like a corpse, but you kept swinging."

His fingers gripped the armrest, the flakes of paint scattering—cowering before him. "He was still alive."

"Yeah, if you call living hanging onto life by a thread."

"Why are you defending that man?"

My jaw almost hit the Clear Stone floor. "I'm not."

"Well, it sure as hell sounds like you are."

"Damn it, Jax! Don't put words in my mouth. This has nothing to do with Pollux's well-being."

He bristled at my sharp tone.

"It has everything to do with *your* behavior. I just want to know why after stabbing a man in the ribs, you felt it necessary to mutilate his face with your bare hands. Was there a reason behind this madness?"

His jaw clenched.

"Was it out of spite—revenge?"

His nostrils flared.

"Or was it because—"

"HE WOULDN'T SHUT UP."

I flinched, the windows rattling behind me. A moment later the front door swung open. My skin surged with heat as Cyrus dashed onto the porch, his amber eyes locked onto Jax. "Is everything okay?"

Answering for the Lunin, I said, "Yeah, we're good."

My brother met my gaze. I jerked my chin at the house, urging him to scram. He didn't budge. His eyes shifted back to Jax, who sat rigid with his thumb and index finger pinching the bridge of his nose.

Cyrus took a step closer. "Jax? You good?"

A curt head nod was his only response.

I mouthed, "Pollux," at my brother. He nodded with an unspoken understanding before he turned and headed back into the house.

After the door closed, I repeated Cyrus's question. "Well, *are* you good?"

"I'm fine," he murmured. "I need you to understand something."

I sat tall to prepare for the inevitable lecture.

Jax clasped his pale hands, the bandages tight around his injured knuckles. "Elara, you've never witnessed live combat."

"Then what do you call Archer's death?"

"An unexpected, cold-blooded murder. The other night was a calculated attack. It's normal to find the techniques I used —unsettling."

That's putting it mildly. Disturbing is more like it.

He went on, "You're forgetting that Zenith started my training at the age of seven. My body is conditioned to react to altercations. Yes, I let go of the Collector mentality, but the physical effects still linger."

I nodded, a sudden realization washing over me. I had overlooked a crucial part of the puzzle.

"And you're also forgetting that Pollux initiated the fight."

I lifted my shirt, exposing the gray gauze. "I was there, remember?"

"Yes, and I would have let that son of a bitch bleed out in the snow after I stabbed him had he not started running his mouth about the sick shit he did to Idalia and the even more disturbing shit he planned on doing to you." Jax's lips formed a tight line. "So to answer your question, *Elara*—that's the reason I didn't let up. The bastard wouldn't shut up, so I forced his compliance."

"I see."

Unsure where to steer the conversation after his honest explanation, I held my tongue and focused on the chipped pieces of wood in the porch railing.

Everything he said makes sense. Pollux is a sadistic prick. I can't even begin to . . . no, I don't want to imagine the foul shit he spat at Jax. I sighed, sitting on my hands. *How did everything get so screwed up?*

I searched Jax's eyes for any lingering darkness—smudges on his soul. He reminded me of a soldier who served time at a prisoner-of-war camp. He tried adjusting to a normal life, but the aftereffects had stamped a permanent impression on his mind and his heart. His time spent with Zenith had changed him in more ways than one. Memories, sounds, smells, so many insignificant moments could set him off in an instant.

A flicker of light bounced off the Lunin's blue irises. I smiled, an unspoken commitment to the man I loved. Jax needed time to heal, and I'd be by his side every step of the way.

"Thanks for answering my questions."

"Anytime." He winked.

"I understand the reason you treated Pollux the way you did. And you're right—I think it just caught me off guard. That was the first time I saw you with blood on your hands."

"And that was the first time I saw you with blood on yours," he countered. "But don't forget"—he wagged a finger at me —"you stabbed two people that night. I only stabbed one."

I offered him a bemused grin.

"But all joking aside, your knife skills were very impressive."

"All credit goes to Samson. His training technique got through to me." I lowered my gaze. "*You* were too easy on me."

"I'm aware." He yawned. "Perhaps it was foolish and a bit selfish, but I refused to watch you get hurt by my own hands."

I snickered, envisioning the scars on my brother's forearms. "I'm guessing that didn't apply to Cyrus."

"No. He's a Solin and a man. I've never had a problem kicking his ass."

The amusement on my face faded at the memory of Elio attacking me. The way he dashed forward with the blunt edge of his blade running down his forearm.

"Random question, Jax."

"Not so random answer, Elara."

"Why did Elio hold his knife like this?" I demonstrated.

"Because that's how you're supposed to hold a knife."

"Then why didn't you and Samson teach us the proper way?"

"We had our reasons."

"Care to elaborate?"

"You're a little more assertive these days."

"Yeah, I am. Life got all serious and shit. I don't have time for games."

"Really?" A seductive grin crossed his striking face as he leaned closer and whispered, "Because you played plenty last night."

Bastard. I slapped him in the stomach. He just laughed, his chiseled abs deflecting my attack.

"But to answer your question," he said, "one uses that technique after they've mastered the art of wielding a knife. If you don't have the proper grip around the handle, the blade can twist during an attack and slice the tendon in your arm. It takes a lot of practice to turn a knife in your hand without injuring yourself. I planned on teaching you that technique and so did Samson. But after everything that happened at Zenith's, I guess we better accelerate you and your brother's training."

"Add it to the list."

"Considering the skillset you showed the other night, I have the utmost confidence you'll succeed with this advanced technique."

I reached for the hair tie that always clung to my wrist and twisted my shoulder-length locks into a messy bun. "I think I'm developing my own technique."

"Now it's your turn to elaborate."

"For weeks I've spent hours each day practicing my aim."

"Smart girl."

I shrugged. *Or maybe I'm just a coward.*

"The only reason I've spent so much time perfecting my aim is because I want to avoid situations like what happened with Elio. That's the second time he's attacked me." Jax straightened, his posture rigid. I pressed on. "Hand-to-hand combat freaks me out. It hurt like hell getting backhanded by Elio, and him stabbing me in the leg didn't help. I can't restrain a Collector, even while sharing Cyrus's Solin strength. I've tried, with both him and Samson. They're too strong. Even Orion gives me a challenge. Can you imagine if Apollo attacked me during the day? I wouldn't stand a chance. He'd snap my neck in a heartbeat."

A moment of silence passed between the two of us. Jax inhaled a long breath before speaking. "You make a valid argument. Even at night, Apollo's strength surpasses an average Solin during the day. I'll give you private throwing lessons in the mornings and the evenings, but you must continue your hand-to-hand combat training with Cyrus and Samson." I frowned. "Elara, it's a necessary precaution. We don't know what Zenith has hiding up his sleeve."

Perfect. I see more blood and injuries in the near future.

The wooden slats creaked under Jax's weight as he reached into his back pocket. "Speaking of knives."

My heart lodged in my throat when he exposed a shiny blade with a quick flick of his wrist. I gulped, observing the familiar engravings. Like a steady pulse on an electrocardiograph, a silver line rose and fell from the handle to the tip of the sharp blade.

"Here." Jax offered me the knife. "You should have it."

As if presented with a live grenade, I jerked back in my chair, the legs scraping against the Clear Stone floor. Disgusted by the gesture, I dismissed the black blade with a wave of my hand. "I don't want that thing."

"Elara, it's just a knife."

My head thrashed back and forth.

"We're running low on weapons," Jax said. "I want you armed at all times. You lost your white knife when you threw it at Apollo, and the spare you had in your back pocket must have fallen out during your altercation with Elio."

I nodded. "I think I lost it while we were rolling around in the snow."

"Probably." The Lunin swallowed his frustrations before adding, "And Orion lost both of his while trying to defend himself against Oberon and Jericho. How he survived that encounter, I'll never know. Anyway, Samson's down to one knife and so am I because I used my spare on Zenith."

"Fine." I folded my arms across my chest. "I'll stay close to you and Cyrus because I want nothing to do with Zenith's knife."

Jax pinned me to my chair with a long stare.

"Don't give me that look," I snapped. "Zenith tried to kill you with that thing. And in the process, he almost killed me. Two nights ago, that blade was wedged in my stomach. He's done horrible and unimaginable things with that damned knife."

"And I've done horrible things with mine, but that's never kept you from using it."

My toes curled at the thought of the blood-stained blade. "Perhaps, but I'm still not comfortable carrying Zenith's knife, and I sure as hell would never use it." I waved it away once more. "I don't even want to touch it."

"I'm sorry." Jax folded the blade back into the handle and offered me it once more. "You don't get a say in this. As your combative superior, I insist you take the knife. That's an order."

"Order my ass. I don't take orders from anyone—*especially* you. Why don't you try wrapping your sharp mind around that one, Jax."

"Okay, Samson." He held up his hands in surrender. "Damn. Orion and Cyrus were right. You have gotten extra sassy lately."

I flattened the grin that crept across my face. "Yeah, because I live with a bunch of testosterone-driven men. It's rubbing off on me. At least Idalia's here now . . ." My words trailed off.

Jax redirected the conversation. "I have a better idea." He slipped a hand into his back pocket. "Why don't you take my knife? I'll hold on to Zenith's."

"No. I don't want you using it either. It probably has bad juju all over it."

"What the hell is juju?"

"You know," I stammered, "dark or negative energy that stays fixed on an object."

"Elara, that's both crazy and superstitious."

"No, it's not."

"Yes, it is. Zenith's knife has no power over anyone who uses it." He slid the black folded blade back into his pocket. "But it's obvious your stubborn ass won't comply with my request, so here, take mine."

I hesitated. *Hmm. Perhaps it's the lesser of two evils.*

A quiet snicker slithered through my mind. *Come on, Elara. Take Zenith's knife.*

I shut my eyes and rolled my neck. *Go away. Leave me alone.*

The silk mask wrinkled around its veiled mouth. *But what if Zenith's blade has power? Evil or not, it might help you on your journey. Aren't you curious?*

"Elara."

My eyes shot open at the sound of Jax's voice.

"Are you okay?"

I stilled. *Should I tell him about the masked dealer?*

No. Our relationship has nothing to do with your boyfriend. Don't get him involved. He has enough on his plate.

Fine. I can't argue with that.

Clever girl. It dragged its black claws along the wall in the private room of my mind before vanishing into a puff of smoke.

"Elara, if there's something you need to tell—"

Jax never finished his sentence because the front door opened.

Orion stepped onto the porch, stretching his toned arms overhead. He winced, the bandage around his arm tightening against his pale skin.

"Morning," he grumbled in way of greeting.

We mumbled our salutation with equal excitement.

The Lunin took a seat on the wooden railing. "How are you feeling, Elara?"

"Like shit. My wounds feel like someone's shoved a hot poker inside me."

His fingers grazed the stitches on his face. "Yeah, I'm feeling it too."

Jax looked at Orion. "Where's Samson?"

"He left before sunrise."

"Did he head back to the North Village?" the ex-Collector asked.

"I'm sure he's home by now." Orion walked his fingers along the railing. "Though he mentioned wanting to speak with Callisto about what happened to Idalia."

"About that." My eyes drifted between the two Lunins.

Orion's index and middle finger paused their mindless pursuit while Jax's upper body stiffened.

"Trying to comfort Idalia this morning only ended up backfiring on me," I said.

"You must be patient with her right now."

Orion looked at Jax before finding my eyes. "He's right. She's got a long road ahead of her. My father said she'll recover from her physical injuries, but mentally"—he tapped his temple—"she needs time to heal."

Jax's blank stare transformed to a more focused one when I said, "This is much worse than anything you went through."

"You're telling me. I'd walk right back into that damned room and shut the door behind me if it meant erasing what Pollux did."

I swallowed the dense knot that formed, then asked Orion, "Is there anything I can do to make her feel better?"

He hesitated, picking at a piece of chipped wood. A heartbeat later, he flicked it into the front yard and dusted off his hands. "Years ago, my father treated a female patient who had experienced similar trauma." He shook his head. "No, let me rephrase. It wasn't similar because each sexual abuse case is unique, but she had a traumatic experience with a close family member." I grimaced. *What the hell is wrong with people?* Orion brushed off my pained expression and added, "I remember hearing my father share some advice with the friend of the woman who brought her in."

"What did he suggest?" I asked.

"Be a good friend. If Idalia wants to discuss the details of what happened during her capture, then listen and let her know she's cared for and loved. A trauma of such magnitude can leave a person feeling powerless and vulnerable. We need to keep her out of that room as much as possible so she's not left alone, stuck in her head all day."

Orion rubbed the back of his neck as if a part of him didn't want to elaborate. After a long silence, he said, "Sexual abuse has a plethora of side effects: flashbacks, depression, eating disorders, dissociation, and even suicide."

I paled. *I see why he hesitated to share the rest.*

He clasped his hands. "We need to keep a close watch on her at all times."

Jax and I stared in opposite directions. The tiniest breeze fluttered through the vast space, and the tree limbs shifted at the sudden movement. I scanned the empty forest and frowned. I missed the birds and the squirrels on Earth. I missed my old life, the life that was simple—predictable. My posture sagged. *And now it's just a memory.*

I eyed Jax. The corner of his mouth twitched, a small effort to ease my troubled mind.

"My stomach twists into a giant knot every time I think about what Pollux did to her," I said.

Orion nodded. "We're all sick about it, but people make recoveries, don't they, Jax?"

The ex-Collector inhaled a long breath and inspected the scar on his palm. "Yes, but the road to recovery is a convoluted maze. The mind will play tricks to steer you off your path. One must face their darkest fears—their inner demons." He lifted his chin. "Or they'll never make it out on the other side."

"Do you think Idalia is up to the challenge?" I asked him.

"If she's willing to accept that Pollux has no control over her. Love can lift a person out of a negative state and bring them to the level of acceptance, which then leads them to forgiveness." He found my eyes. "The human spirit always prevails. Idalia is a strong woman. Pollux's actions may have dimmed her light, but he didn't extinguish it."

23

A SIMPLE TRUTH

The stifling and unbearable heat of the following two weeks mirrored the attitudes of those around me. Unable to escape the humid weather or the confines of Iah's home, our small group fell into the grueling routine of living life on repeat—yet again. The never-ending days dragged on, one slow sunrise and sunset at a time. Nature's breathtaking display mocked the darkness we would soon face.

With no word from Samson, my anxiety levels reached an all-time high. Physically, I glided through the motions of the day, but mentally, I crawled through trenches soiled by fear and doubt.

I began my private throwing lessons with Jax once the pain subsided from my injuries. As promised, we spent the early mornings and early evenings perfecting my aim, only after I trained with Cyrus and Orion.

When I wasn't complaining about the hand-to-hand combat required by Jax and the soreness in my throwing arm, we hung out at the spring or took long walks around Iah's home. In lengthy and meaningful conversations, Jax shared every detail—every sentiment regarding his troubled past.

Sorrow lingered in his voice each time he spoke of his early childhood, and the grief intensified as he discussed Sharik's death: the murder he never planned on committing.

The Lunin's vivid retellings painted a disturbing picture. One splattered with bits of despair and regret, all swirled together, creating a beautiful canvas of raw, brutal honesty. I listened with an open mind and an open heart and only spoke if necessary, allowing him time to purge the darkness that bubbled to the surface.

The others ignored the inevitable by staying busy with mindless tasks. Iah rationed our food and supplies because he could no longer visit the villages, nor could Orion. Our showdown with the Inner Circle at Zenith's had blown the young Lunin's cover, so the chance of his father venturing into town going unnoticed by the Collectors seemed slim to none. Cyrus spent his long days filling in for Samson, training me and Orion harder than ever with each grueling exercise.

One day, our mundane routine came to a halt after Idalia locked herself in Orion's room. Fearing the worst, Cyrus kicked down the door. My heart sank into the pit of my stomach as I followed him over the threshold.

We found Idalia lying on the floor, curled in a tight ball. Her long nails dug into her scalp and drew blood while she screamed at the top of her lungs. The side effects of suppressed anger, guilt, and sorrow rippled through her frail body. I stood motionless, clueless on how to approach the situation. Tears dripped from her bloodshot eyes and snot dripped from her nose: signs of a flashback.

Desperate to ease her suffering, my brother dashed to the Solin's side. Unfortunately, his presence escalated the situation. Imprisoned in a mental hell, Idalia lashed out with a sharp tongue and even sharper claws. Jax rushed forward to rescue Cyrus from the onslaught of pent-up rage but froze when I grabbed his wrist.

"Let me handle this," I said, leaving no room for argument.

He agreed, realizing that two men invading Idalia's personal space would not end well for him or Cyrus.

Sharing my brother's strength, I restrained the distraught Solin in a bear hug and whispered words of comfort near her ear. "You're safe. You're not at Zenith's." I repeated the sentences until the hurricane of inner turmoil that beat on her mind's shores calmed to a gentle breeze.

Her body went limp in my arms as she glanced around the room, and salted drops of regret streamed down her face when she looked at Cyrus. He touched the blood that trickled from one of the seven gashes on his face, courtesy of Idalia's nails. Without saying a word, he turned and left.

After that traumatic afternoon, I slowed my pace each time I walked by her room, wondering if I should extend an olive branch, but the passing thought always vanished at the memory of Orion's advice: *she needs time to heal.*

I despised those long days. Watching my friend wallow in the depths of hell was both agonizing and disturbing. From sun up to sun down, she stayed in bed and stared out the window. The lack of nutrients in the stale rolls she picked at left her attractive and shapely figure emaciated. Idalia's cheekbones protruded out of her thin skin and the circumference of her wrist equaled her forearms.

This gut-wrenching sight lit a raging wildfire deep inside me. The desire to avenge Idalia's suffering cast a dark shadow over my innocence, and with each passing day, like my brother, I wanted to see Pollux suffer. I knew my mind had drifted too far the morning I caught myself smiling at the twisted scenarios the masked dealer tossed in my face: images of Pollux set on fire, writhing in pain, blurs of Jax and Cyrus torturing the sadistic Lunin before drowning him in the spring, and visions of Samson dismembering his body with Ravi's dull knife, all while I stood on the sidelines, watching with prideful eyes.

See, wasn't that a fun little game, Elara? An unsubtle reminder.

I rolled my neck, shooing away the hidden figure before turning to Jax. "This is affecting my mental health. When is he coming back?"

Jax shrugged and rested his silver mug on the Clear Stone floor beside his chair. "Hopefully sooner than later."

"You don't think something bad happened to him, do you?"

"No. Samson won't walk blindly into a trap." He found my anxious eyes. "Trust me, the man knows how to keep a low profile."

"If you say so." I fanned my shirt. The thin fabric stuck to the beads of sweat that dotted my chest and stomach. Irritated with the heat, and Jax's nonchalant attitude about our missing mentor, I scooted to the edge of my chair and said, "But for argument's sake, let's say he doesn't come back. Then what? We keep sitting on this damn porch for weeks . . . months . . . wondering what happen to him? It's not like we can pick up the phone and—"

"Easy," Jax said, steadying my bobbing leg. "We're talking about Samson, not some novice Collector. He's got more blood on his hands than most. The man killed three members of the Inner Circle: Ravi, Levant, and Holmes, and injured Ishan and Jericho. No one in their right mind would dream of challenging him alone."

"No one but Zenith."

Jax shook his head. "He won't make an appearance anytime soon."

"Why not? Samson said the knife wound won't slow him down."

"Because Zenith doesn't fly by the seat of his pants. He never acts without thinking. Even the words that leave his mouth have a distinct purpose, and his decisions are planned —calculated."

"Sounds like someone I know."

Jax's brows touched his hairline.

Shit. Why did I say that?

I recovered with a white lie. "I . . . didn't mean to say that."

Silence. Jax turned his attention to the trees.

Damn it. Real smooth. Let me try that again. "Jax, I—"

"What's that saying on Earth?" Not waiting for me to respond, he answered his own question. "Ah yes. The apple doesn't fall far from the tree. That's it."

I cursed under my breath.

He turned. "Elara, what did you expect? Zenith raised me as his son for over six years."

As if Jax's words had slapped me across the face, my cheek throbbed with phantom pain. I took a moment to regroup before saying, "Fine. Who cares if you share his mannerisms? It's obvious you don't react to situations the same way."

The tiniest smirk tugged at the corner of the Lunin's mouth. "Was that your attempt at a recovery?"

"Perhaps, though it lacked the flair I envisioned."

Jax chuckled, shaking his head at me.

"I'm sorry." I sighed. "I never meant to compare you to Zenith. I'm so distracted, I can hardly think straight."

"Obviously."

I shot him a glare. He smiled back.

"I just hate sitting on my ass, doing nothing. We can't start an uprising without Samson's help."

Jax's head bobbed from side to side with quiet dismissal.

"Who will follow us?" I motioned to the surrounding woods. "There's no one here. We can't recruit people in the villages. Samson's an idiot for thinking the citizens will join our side and take a stand against the crazed dictator who's ruled Aroonyx for sixteen years. It's a suicide mission."

"Are you done with your little rant? Or should I see if Iah has anything to help ease panic attacks?"

I glared. "You're extra witty today."

"I'm in a good mood." He sent a furtive glance at the more sensitive areas of my body. "Which has everything to do with last night."

My teeth sunk into my lips, muffling a nervous giggle; a montage of bare flesh and pleasurable moans zipped through my mind.

"Elara, it's pointless to worry about the things we can't control. People either regret the past or fear the future."

"Why?"

"Because living in the now is . . . well . . . it's boring."

I shifted my weight on the chair. *Get comfortable. Here comes the voice of reason.*

Jax hesitated as if debating whether to share another life lesson.

"Go on," I encouraged. "Explain."

"It's easy for people to get tangled in the web of life. They dwell on past decisions or worry about hypothetical situations. This leaves no time to focus on the now." He waved a hand around the porch. "In this moment, is there anything going on?"

Curious, my spine straightened. I rotated my head to the left and then to the right, straining my ears and my eyes. Silence.

The rays of the afternoon sun seeped through the gaps of the intertwined branches, and the emerald-green grass shimmered under its majestic glow. I looked up. The gentle breeze kissed one massive leaf, then the next with a quiet rustle.

"Um . . . no." More of a question than a statement.

A lazy grin crossed Jax's face as he rested his hands behind his head. "Exactly."

Why are his lessons so advanced? He should charge for this shit. Master Class with Seeker Jax.

Observing my vacant expression, he said, "It's not a complicated lesson."

"Agree to disagree."

"It's not. Let me simplify what I'm trying to say."

"I'm all ears."

"The ego glorifies the drama in life—that excess noise that bounces off the walls in our minds is like a game of ping pong we can't stop playing." He circled his finger through the air. "In this instant, there's nothing going on, but instead of enjoying the peaceful moment, our minds get bored and search for past or future thoughts to keep it entertained, and that's the irony of it all. We dwell on expired thoughts or phantom desires, which are two things that don't exist."

I blinked at the jarring realization. *He's right. I never live in the now. I'm too preoccupied with the past and the future.*

"Elara, I've said it before, and I'll say it again: Everything in life happens for a reason. Even if we don't agree with the outcome, we need to trust the universe always has our back. I understand you're frustrated with *doing* nothing, but we needed this time to regroup." He laced his fingers with mine. "Instead of complaining about the changes we want in our life, why don't we take a moment to appreciate the things we have?"

I lifted his hand and pressed my lips against his warm skin. "How do you always speak with so much clarity? You have the magical ability to open people's eyes and help them see what was always there."

"It's a gift, one I don't take for granted."

"You're a rare breed, Jax."

"And why's that?"

"Because most twenty-two-year-old men don't share your wisdom." I tapped my chin, scanning his face. "Did you lie about your age? Are you almost forty?"

"No, but sometimes I feel like it. I've witnessed enough shit to equal the life experience of an eighty-year-old man, but who's counting, right?"

My voice lowered as I moved closer. "I'm not."

Jax shuddered a breath as my hand slid along his inner thigh.

"As long as everything keeps working like a twenty-two-year-old man."

Jax adjusted himself; my words had left a visible imprint on his pants. Not skipping a beat, he moved my hand to the desired location, and whispered, "I think we're good in that department."

My eyes glazed with lust. I leaned over the armrest, meeting him halfway. As soon as our lips touched, a slender figure stepped onto the porch. Idalia.

We froze. Out of the corner of my eye, I watched the young Solin take a cautious step toward the stone stairs. The afternoon sun, a spotlight of truth, illuminated her frail body. The streaks highlighted the physical effects of repressed guilt and other turbulent emotions. As if wearing an invisible cloak made of lead, her bony shoulders hunched forward, and her chin nearly touched her chest. Though the bruises and lacerations had healed, the layered locks of her hair had yet to see a brush. My face hardened at the shadow of despair that darkened the golden flakes in her amber eyes. I shook my head at the depressing sight: a lost soul stuck in limbo, floating in the gray area between heaven and hell.

I almost fell out of my chair when she called my name. Jax tugged at my arm, encouraging me to stand. I scrambled to my feet and answered by stuttering her name in return.

Idalia's skeletal fingers held her throat. She winced after a painful swallow. Could silent screams damage vocal cords?

Heading down the porch steps, she asked, "Elara, will you take a walk with me?"

I nodded, hurrying to catch up.

The Solin's bare feet guided us deep into the forest. I kept my distance until I found the courage to walk beside her. *Say nothing. Let her talk first.* After long minutes of a tense stroll in the sweltering heat, she turned.

"I want to tell you"—she paused, and chewed on her lip —"no, I *need* to tell you what happened with Pollux."

Heeding Orion's advice, I sucked in a large breath of the late-afternoon air and stood tall. "Okay. Feel free to share."

Idalia's toes curled, taking shelter under the fine blades of grass. She gathered her matted hair over one shoulder and played with the split ends while she spoke. "A customer spilled a mug of Maragin on me, so I went upstairs to grab a clean shirt, and that's when I heard a knock on the bedroom door."

I gulped. Samson's morbid account of what happened with Ravi flashed before my mind's eye.

Oblivious to my reaction, she pressed on. "I said come in because I thought it was Samson or Callisto, but when the door swung open, Elio, Apollo, Ravi, and Pollux walked in." Her voice trembled. "I lied when they started their usual interrogation and told them I hadn't a clue where you were hiding. Pollux saw right through me, so he told the others to search the place.

"Apollo ran his hand along the walls of my room. It didn't take him long to find the loose panels." She shut her eyes, the tight lines on her face voicing an inner pain. "Once they discovered my little secret, Pollux started beating me. I used my Solin strength to fight back, but he instructed Ravi to restrain me with his knife. Apollo and Elio just stood there, watching me with cold and lifeless expressions." Idalia's voice cracked with enough grief to bring tears to my eyes. "Elara, if you could have only heard the horrible things Pollux said to me. Regardless of how much time passes, I'll never forget."

My chest tightened. The agony she experienced rippled out of her in a wave of darkness, drowning me in the undertow. I clutched the fabric that covered my pounding heart. *Stay strong. You must stay strong for your friend.* I cleared my throat and clasped my hands.

"I have a vague memory of Samson breaking down the door," she whispered, "but everything went dark after Apollo backhanded me. I'm not sure how long I was out. Long enough. When I woke up, night had fallen. Moonlight poured in from the window." Rage filled her eyes. "They locked me in that damn room, the same one that housed Jax during his capture. And no one bothered to clean up after Archer rescued him. Dried blood covered the floor, his suffering splattered the walls, and the added smell of waste and vomit were nauseating reminders of the hell he endured over those weeks."

Bile crept up my throat. I clenched my teeth and forced the sickening feeling away.

"I sat on the floor near the drain, the only spot in the room not stained with blood, and waited. I knew it was a trap, but a small part of me hoped you'd come to my rescue."

My mouth gaped, appalled by her lack of confidence. "Idalia."

She balked at my sharp tone.

Recovering, I lowered my voice. "You should have seen Jax's and Cyrus's reaction when Samson told us the news. They didn't care if it was a trap. None of us did."

My added commentary didn't spark relief in her eyes. No, it filled them with grief. I stole a glance at her trembling hand. She picked at the dry skin around her thumbnail. The nervous habit started after she woke up at Iah's, and by the look of her scabbed cuticle, she didn't plan on stopping.

I touched her arm. "We can always talk about this later if—"

"No. There might not be a *later*."

My heart skipped a beat. "Okay. I'm here. Take your time."

A breath of pent-up emotion whooshed out of Idalia's lungs as she eyed the canopy of intertwined limbs, and the warm breeze brushed her flushed skin. Her bony fingers traced a purple scar that ran across her cheek. "The gashes on my face wouldn't stop bleeding, so I ripped off a piece of my shirt and used it as a bandage." She huffed a breath. "Go figure. The blood clotted right before the door opened."

Not wanting my anxiety to show, I shifted my features into neutral.

"This strange feeling washed over me when Pollux entered the room. It's hard to describe. My entire body went numb. I think it was a warning. A warning that something bad was about to happen."

I sucked in a sharp breath and held it. I dreaded hearing the next part of the story. The whites of Idalia's eyes turned a pale shade of red, matching the blood that pooled around the self-inflicted injury on her thumb.

Her voice quivered. "He waited, Elara. The bastard waited until it was dark so I couldn't use my Solin strength." A tear rolled off her cheek. "There was nowhere to run and nowhere to hide. Just four blood-stained walls, each one unfazed by the horrendous things they'd witnessed over the years. Unarmed and unable to defend myself, I crawled to the least bloody corner of the room." She gritted her teeth. "Pollux laughed at me. I must have looked like a damn coward."

I shut my eyes. This comment sent a shot of anger and resentment rushing through my veins.

The hidden figure adjusted its silk hood. *Don't worry, Elara. You'll make him suffer.*

I nodded, pleased with the disturbing images of pain and torture that surfaced.

Interrupting my impromptu meeting with the hidden figure, Idalia said, "He just stood there, undressing me with his eyes. It made me sick." Her face twitched. "I tried, Elara. I really tried to fight back but—"

"Hey, it's okay." I pulled her into my arms. "You don't have to say anymore. I know what happened."

Idalia used her Solin strength and shoved me in the chest, sending me flying over five feet. My back slammed into the trunk of a tree, teeth clattering, white lights flashing.

"No!" she yelled, her eyes gleaming with a ferocity that left me speechless. "I have to say the words aloud. I can't keep it stuck inside my head. It's eating me alive. I'm going crazy."

I climbed to my feet. Idalia pounded the top of her head. Over and over, her fist collided with her skull. The sickening sound turned my insides to mush. I cursed, hurrying to her side.

"Elara," she hissed, continuing the violent motion. "You don't want to know the crazy shit that crosses my mind. I can't live like this anymore. It's been weeks, and I can still smell his foul breath and feel him inside me. At night, I lay in bed and think of different ways to end my life."

My eyes welled with tears.

"The dull knives in the kitchen don't work. I've tried." She showed me the jagged lines on her wrist. "While everyone's asleep, I search the house for other alternatives. I found some rope in the supply closet, but it was too short. I didn't have a ladder to reach the tree, and the clothes racks in the closet wouldn't support my weight."

I stood slack-jawed. We never saw her leave Orion's room. Little did we know, the poor girl was sneaking around the house, trying to end her own life.

Her name left my mouth in a whimper. "I'm so sorry. I had no idea these thoughts caused you so much pain."

The Solin brushed a tear off her cheek. I reached for her hands and found her eyes. She needed to hear the truth. I sighed. *Why is tough love the hardest thing to give?*

I steadied my labored breathing. "Idalia, it's hard to see the silver lining if you're surrounded by a cloud of negative emotions. The mind loves to play tricks." I thought of the masked dealer and the images it conjured of Pollux's death. I pointed to her scarred wrist. "And it will justify dangerous behavior if you allow it."

"It's so hard," she cried. "I don't want to feel this way forever."

"You won't. You're a strong woman and you will get through this."

"I'm not anymore. I don't think I have the courage to say it out loud." She looked at me with pleading eyes. "I need to say it, but if I do, that means I'm choosing to accept what happened."

"Acceptance doesn't mean you're agreeing with what happened, it means you're acknowledging your willingness to move on. This awareness has the power to erase the victim mentality that keeps people trapped in the past—trapped in hell. Don't let Pollux win. You are not the victim of his cruel actions. You are not the result of his weakness." My fingers gripped the thin skin that covered her bony shoulders. "You're better than that, Idalia. You can't give up. I won't let you."

She used the sleeve of her shirt to wipe the tears that stained her cheeks, then adjusted the loose garment over her frail body. "Okay. Here it goes."

I straightened, bracing myself for the verbal impact: the words she needed to say.

"I tried fighting back, but Pollux was too strong. His eyes glazed over and each time he hit me, his mind appeared to slip further into the darkness, further from reality." A muscle feathered in her jaw. "That son of a bitch held me on those blood-stained floors while I screamed. I did everything in my power to stop him. I kicked, I scratched. I wish he would have just knocked me out. The sick bastard grabbed me by my hair and forced me to watch while he took advantage of me."

My hand shot to my mouth, stifling the loud gasp. Salty

drops glided down my face and mixed with Idalia's as they hit the grass surrounding our feet.

I had read stories about sexual abuse and watched disturbing scenes in movies, but hearing my friend's retelling left me heartbroken. I didn't care if she used her Solin strength to send me flying back to Iah's. I took my chance and held her in a tight embrace. She tensed for only a moment before collapsing in my arms. I fell to my knees, but I never let her go.

I rocked Idalia back and forth while whispering, "You're safe. You're loved." Once wasn't enough, and even when the words sounded strange on my tongue, I continued until her tears ran dry.

"I still feel like it's my fault." She sniffled, staring at me with those beautiful golden eyes. "If I hadn't defended Jax that day in my bedroom—"

"No." I ran a hand over her matted hair. "It's not your fault. You did the right thing. The universe never overlooks an act of courage." I slid her off my lap and rotated her body to face me. "Pollux is a severely troubled man. He knows nothing of love or compassion. It's a void in his life. He views those qualities as a weakness and treats people cruelly, hoping that in some sick way, he'll fill the hole he created." I hooked a finger under her chin. "Pollux has no power over you, Idalia. Love can heal, and it will if you give it a chance."

"How am I supposed to get through the day? Every time I close my eyes, I see his face, and feel—"

"You live in the now, that's how. When the details of that night replay in your mind, remind yourself that those thoughts are in the past. They no longer exist."

She nodded.

"I don't have a firsthand account of what happened, but I do have experience with inner demons. Jax reminded me of a truth I overlooked today."

His name piqued her interest. "What did he say?"

"The good in life always prevails." I brushed the hair out of her face. "We support you, Idalia, and my brother is madly in love with you."

My heart warmed as a spark flickered in her eyes; the fire of life had ignited once more.

"Thank you, Elara. For everything."

I stood and offered her my hand. "Anytime, what are best friends for?"

We strolled back to Iah's with our arms linked, our bond now stronger than ever. It's interesting how a traumatic event can rip people apart or bring them together. I eyed Idalia while we walked. She appeared lost in thought, not lost in despair. Her depressive state transformed into one of inner reflection. She held her head high. The invisible cloak that draped over her blew away in the summer breeze.

As usual, Jax's powerful intuition proved true. Idalia would walk through her darkest fears and come out stronger on the other side.

She turned. Our eyes locked, and at that moment, the two of us shared an unspoken awareness, the same one Cyrus verbalized to Archer the night he sacrificed himself for the greater good: True power comes from within. It's not found outside of ourselves. Idalia held her hand over my heart. I mirrored the gesture and smiled because the two of us had accepted a simple truth: love is the source of our power, and in the end . . . *love* always wins.

24

RIGHT VS. WRONG

My mouth watered as we stepped over the threshold, the fragrant aroma of stewed meat and warm rolls enticing my taste buds.

The three men sitting at the kitchen table scrambled to their feet. I shook my head. Their chivalrous attempt left them looking both awkward and foolish. Jax encouraged Cyrus and Orion to take a seat after I shot him a stern glance.

"Do you want me to bring some food to your room?" I asked Idalia. "We can eat dinner there."

She sucked on her lip while observing the men at the table. I followed her gaze and rolled my eyes. *Good job, guys. Way to play it cool.* They kept their heads down, staring at the half-empty plates that rested before them.

Answering my own question, I said, "I'll grab some food and meet you in there."

"No." Her eyes paused on my brother. "I'll eat at the table tonight."

Though his back faced us, I could tell Cyrus was grinning from ear to ear. Unable to hide their own elated expressions, the Lunins at the table relaxed, their blue eyes flickering with relief. Iah kept his composure and hurried to the kitchen to fetch two clean plates from the cupboard. When our toes touched the kitchen rug, the three men stood, only this time with more grace than before.

"Wow." I nodded at their choreographed performance. "When boys become men."

Jax added to the routine by gesturing to his chair with an exaggerated roll of the wrist. "Miss, I'm sure you're tired after your long journey. Please, take my seat."

I touched my chest, and in a sultry Southern accent, I said, "You are too kind, sir."

Cyrus chuckled under his breath and Idalia lowered herself onto the seat across from him. They made eye contact. The corner of her mouth tugged, and his eyes lit up. This tiny display of affection appeared to heal the internal wounds she caused during the day of her flashback.

Orion leaned back in his chair and rested his hands behind his head. Jax squeezed my shoulder, a silent appreciation for my time with the Solin. I thanked Iah as he handed me a plate of food, and everyone at the table smiled once Idalia picked up her fork and took a bite.

Keeping the mood light, I asked, "Who wants to learn about grocery stores on Earth?"

Cyrus and Jax snickered at the random topic for discussion. The others squished up their faces as if I had spoken another language.

I loved discussing Earth's inventions, and living on Aroonyx expanded my appreciation for the small comforts I took for granted: mirrors, cell phones, colorful clothing, television— foreign objects to my new friends. The citizens of Aroonyx displayed a sophisticated intellect with relatable mannerisms, yet their minimalistic lifestyle mimicked the Dark Ages.

After my lengthy explanation, Orion rested his elbows on

the table. "So the owner of the store doesn't take the food home after they close?"

"No. Everything stays there. Large corporations, or groups of people," I clarified, "own the stores. Thousands of items line the shelves: produce, meats, dry goods . . ." I eyed Cyrus. "Help me out here, bro."

He swallowed a long swig of water, then said, "The list goes on and on. Some stores carry food while others sell everything from bread to televisions."

Orion blinked. "What's a television?"

My chin hit my chest. Familiar with Earth's technology, Jax hid a smirk and crossed his arms.

"We'll save that conversation for a rainy day," Cyrus said, unable to keep a straight face.

Distracted by her own thoughts, Idalia stared at the wooden knots that decorated the table. The bite-sized pieces of meat and vegetables slowly disappeared off her plate.

My brother looked at Orion. "The food stays in the store until it's purchased or expired."

"Then where does it go?"

"Sometimes the food banks will pick it up, but a lot gets thrown out."

Iah braced his palms on the kitchen counter. "That seems a bit wasteful."

Cyrus shrugged his broad shoulders. "That's how it works on Earth. The farmers grow the crops and raise the animals, the slaughterhouses prepare the meat, and the factories produce the goods. Everything gets loaded onto trucks and delivered to the stores. It's a huge business."

Iah hummed his understanding. "Can you elaborate? Is a truck a large animal?"

I bit my lip and found my brother's eyes. "I should have picked an easier topic."

"What? Like how the *Buy It Now* button works on Amazon?"

My laughter dissolved at the sound of a loud knock on the front door. Idalia paled, her fork trembling in her hand. Iah didn't budge from his place behind the kitchen sink, but Orion and Cyrus rose to their feet. Before I could blink, Jax pulled Zenith's knife from his back pocket.

The entire house shook with another pound of a determined fist. "It's me," called a raspy voice. "Open the damn door."

"Why doesn't he announce himself before scaring the shit out of us?" I asked, jogging across the living room.

No one answered my simple question.

I flung open the door, prepared to give Samson a good tongue lashing about his long absence, but relief trumped anger.

The age lines around the Solin's eyes creased as his chapped lips curled into a large grin, exposing a missing tooth I had never noticed. He glanced at the scar on my calf, then pointed to my abdomen. "How are your injuries?"

"Better." I flexed my foot. "They still hurt."

"Only if you focus on the pain," Samson said, reaching for Jax's hand.

I rolled my eyes. *Great. The second voice of reason has returned.*

"It's good to see you, Samson." Jax's eyes slid to me. "Elara was getting a little worried."

I nudged him in the ribs. "We were *all* worried about you."

"Don't concern yourself with me, kid. I can take care of myself."

I glared at Jax when he whispered, "Told you so."

"I needed to take care of a few things." Samson turned sideways to fit through the doorway and jerked his thumb over his shoulder. "And this guy insisted on coming along."

My cheeks ached with the smile that spread across my face. A middle-aged Lunin followed the Solin into the house. Besides his black hair and fair skin, the man's tall and lean stature reminded me of my adoptive father on Earth. His crystal blue eyes sparkled with delight once I threw my arms around his neck.

"I've missed you, Callisto."

He gave me a loving squeeze. "It's nice to see you, Elara."

I pulled away and gathered my hair over one shoulder. "It's been too long."

"It has, considering everything you've been through over the past few seasons."

My bobbing head slowed as he shifted his gaze to the kitchen. Grief swirled in the Lunin's eyes at the sight of his niece.

"Elara, we'll catch up later. I need to visit with Idalia."

Callisto strolled past me and Jax, his eyes never leaving the Solin, who sat with her head bowed. He acknowledged Cyrus and Orion with a subtle head nod, then shook Iah's hand. After a long pause, he touched Idalia's shoulder, and in a quiet voice, he said, "Hey, honey."

She stood from the table, her teeth sinking into her quivering lips. Callisto observed his niece like a fractured figurine made of glass. Throwing caution to the wind, he pulled her into his arms. Idalia buried her face in his chest and sobbed.

The Lunin stroked her matted hair. "I'm sorry your mother isn't here."

Her sobs grew louder.

Jax hurried to the dining area and whispered inaudible words near Callisto's ear while pointing to the hallway. Idalia's uncle nodded and guided his niece out of the kitchen toward Orion's room.

Her pained reaction appeared to damage my brother's confidence.

I mouthed, "She'll be okay," once he caught my eye. He just shrugged.

"Everyone take a seat." A demand, not a suggestion from the Solin, who ambled toward the armchair. "I've got some news."

Orion cringed. I faked a cry. *And to think, I wanted to live in the now. Time to fear the future again.*

Our small group filed into the living room. Like the previous visits, Cyrus and Jax flanked me on the couch while Iah and Orion dragged their chairs from the kitchen.

"Samson." I slid the hair tie off my wrist. "Please tell me it's not bad news. I can't handle any more drama."

"Depends on how you look at it."

"That doesn't sound promising," Cyrus muttered.

The ex-Collector played with the white tip of his beard, his orange eyes drifting around the room. "Things have changed."

"How so?" Jax asked.

"News of the Inner Circle kidnapping Idalia has spread throughout the villages, and everyone knows Pollux is the one to blame."

The two men beside me tensed. Orion rested his forearms on his thighs. His father straightened.

"After I left that morning, I went to the East Village to find Callisto. We then headed to Idalia's and locked up the bar."

"What about Cosmo and the other employees?" Jax asked.

"They can't run the place without her. We told them to take some time off. They weren't happy, but they didn't get a say."

Jax nodded. My eyes grew, visualizing how quick that conversation ended.

"The customers are pissed. Idalia's is the place where people go to take their minds off Zenith."

Cyrus scoffed, disbelief smeared across his tan face. "So her customers don't care about her well-being? They're just upset they can't grab a drink with their buddies?"

Samson's eyes narrowed at my brother. "Next time hold your tongue before making an ass out of yourself. I never said they don't care about Idalia. Why do people hang out at the bar?" Samson held up his hand. "Let me give you a hint, it doesn't involve your pal, Rico."

Jax snickered. Orion flashed me a large grin. I covered my mouth, muffling my own amusement.

Cyrus elbowed me in the ribs when I whispered, "I miss that furry little guy."

Ignoring his own joke and answering his own question, Samson said, "Idalia. That's the reason. Her warm personality is infectious, and she created a safe space for the people to enjoy. My"—he paused as if realizing an error—"that girl welcomes each customer with an open heart. Hell, she even treats the young Collectors with respect."

The Solin met my gaze and arched a brow, a reminder of how he saved my ass the night I encountered Inan, the Active Member who interrogated me at the bar.

He turned his attention back to my brother. "People don't go to Idalia's to grab a drink; they go to escape the worries of everyday life."

Cyrus leaned his back against the couch.

"Does Idalia's misfortune play in our favor?" I cringed at the insensitive words that left my mouth. "I didn't mean it like—"

Samson waved away my concerns. "I know what you're implying, and as fucked up as it sounds—yeah, it does."

Every muscle in Cyrus's body contracted. Jax cracked his knuckles.

"You know how I feel about Pollux," Samson added. "The next time I see that son of a bitch, I'll make him pay—in ways I'd rather not share."

I gulped at the severe threat.

"If I could go back in time and keep it from happening, I would." He eyed Cyrus. "But I can't. We can only move forward.

Pollux's actions have caused a disruption. The people are angry, and they know who helped rescue Idalia." He inclined his head at me and my brother. "Which means they know you're alive."

My jaw cracked open. I reached for the glimmer of hope that dangled before me. "So now the people know the truth: Zenith lied about our deaths. This gives us the upper hand, right?"

Samson rubbed the coarse hairs of his beard while contemplating my suggestion. "In a way, yes, but—"

"Why is there always a but?" Orion muttered.

The Solin shot him a sidelong look, then added, "I warned you, Elara. The knife Jax threw damaged his pride. Zenith has decided to play dirty."

Jax shut his eyes. "What's he done now?"

"Passed another ordinance."

The former leader of the Inner Circle swore through gritted teeth. Orion and Iah exchanged nervous glances.

Forgetting our history lesson, Cyrus asked, "What's an ordinance?"

I twisted on the couch to face my brother. "You don't remember what Jax told us regarding knife laws on Aroonyx?"

He shook his head.

"Or what Idalia and Archer said about union approval?" I asked.

"No. I don't."

I tossed up my hands. "Cyrus, have you been listening over these past few months or is your head permanently shoved up your ass?"

Samson beamed with pride, and Jax smothered the grin that twitched at the corner of his mouth.

Cyrus pinned me with a glassy stare. "You do a horrible job at impersonating Samson."

"I thought it was pretty spot on," Orion said.

"Easy, bro." I lowered the middle finger he shot at the

Lunin. "Don't get your panties in a wad. An ordinance is an authoritative order."

"You could have just told me that."

I responded with a smug grin.

Unamused with our behavior, Iah asked Samson, "What are the details of the new ordinance?"

"You won't like it."

"Just tell us," I said.

The ex-Collector locked his eyes onto Zenith's adoptive son. "Any male between the ages of twelve and thirty-five must join the Collectors."

The color drained from Jax's face.

"Damn," Cyrus said. "Zenith initiated a draft."

Samson cocked his head to one side. "What's a draft?"

"Back on Earth," Cyrus replied, "we have soldiers who volunteer to protect our country."

Iah's eyes glazed over with confusion.

"It's like a great big village," Cyrus clarified.

The doctor nodded, scooting his chair closer to the coffee table.

"If a war starts between our country and another, soldiers deploy to fight. Years ago, during a World War, the president— that's the title for our leader—started a draft. It stated any man between the ages of eighteen and twenty-five must join the military and serve their country."

The men in the room sat taller.

"I told you he'd play dirty," Samson said. "We damaged his precious Inner Circle, Elara took a knife for Jax, and he ended up with one in his gut. The events shook him up." He motioned to the other ex-Collector in the room. "Thanks to Jax, Pollux won't be showing his face anytime soon and Zenith still needs to recover. Elio is the only one who can fight right now."

"Are you sure?" My nose crinkled. "He hit that tree pretty hard when you threw him."

A casual shrug. "A concussion won't keep that guy down for long."

"But why pass the ordinance?" Orion asked.

"Look who's asking stupid questions now," my brother chided. "Basic lesson in the art of warfare. Safety in numbers."

Samson nodded. "Zenith needs more men. He's feared an uprising for years. He can't take any chances now that the people know you're alive."

My heart dropped into the pit of my stomach with a sickening realization. *He's building an army.*

Cyrus leaned forward. "What if the men affected by the ordinance refuse? What happens if they don't join?"

"I'll give you one guess," Samson answered.

My brother swallowed hard.

"That's right." The eldest Solin smirked at his reaction. "Zenith doesn't tolerate insubordination. He has instructed the Collectors to use brutal force on the ones who refuse to leave their homes. This ordinance works like the others. A lack of compliance results in execution by Zenith's own hands."

"This is crazy," I said. "He can't force underage men to join his side."

"He can't?" Samson lifted a brow. "Sweetie, he already has."

"Yeah, but—"

Jax cleared his throat, his finger tracing the scar on his palm. "Elara, a knife can easily sway someone's decision."

"But twelve-year-old boys?" My hands curled into fists. "They're just kids."

"Jax was twelve when Zenith made him the leader of the Inner Circle," Cyrus said.

"I'm aware," I snapped. "That was a unique situation. *This* is different. No parent in their right mind will hand over their children to the Collectors."

"You'd be surprised," Jax murmured.

I swore under my breath, recalling how the Collectors took

the Lunin from his home at the tender age of six. My lips moved to apologize, but Samson's quick tongue cut me off.

"Elara, it's not like these mothers and fathers want to hand over their sons to the Collectors. They don't have a choice. If they try to defend their children by fighting back, which none of them can do, the Collectors will slice their throats."

I hopped to my feet, my voice rising with each word that left my mouth. "This is a handful of people." I looked at Jax. "You said the population of Aroonyx is around two thousand. Am I right?"

He nodded.

"Zenith doesn't have that many Collectors," I said. "If the men refuse the ordinance, then he won't have the numbers."

Jax gave me a look that screamed *that was cute of you to try, now sit your ass back down.*

Defeated, I collapsed onto the lumpy cushion.

He rested a hand on my knee. "Elara, you keep forgetting this is Aroonyx, not Earth. The only people who have access to sharp and effective knives are Zenith, the Collectors, and a few men on the black market. The average citizen can't defend themselves."

"Think about it, sis," Cyrus said. "Imagine if you were at home on Earth. A man shows up at your door, points a gun at your head, and demands you to go with him. How could you fight back? You don't know how to disarm a man with a firearm, much less use one."

I sighed, bowing my head.

"Allow me to present this in a different light," Iah suggested. "I've lived on Aroonyx for my entire life. This is how it works. We have a leader and we follow the rules. Those who don't, are punished, end of story. No one fights back, and no one challenges authority. Why? The risk is too great."

"I get it, Iah." I found the doctor's eyes. "I can't compare Aroonyx to Earth because they're two different worlds, set in two different times. My argument has nothing to do with weapons and the lack of combative training. It has everything to do with morality: right versus wrong. We can't let Zenith force these young men to join the Collectors."

Samson twisted his beard into a tight cone, his fierce eyes watching my every move. "And why is that?"

I hesitated, my tongue tapping against my teeth. It was a test. The biggest one yet. I sucked in a deep breath and stared at the Solin with an equal ferocity burning in my eyes. "Because I refuse to let history repeat itself."

I paused. Samson flicked his wrist for me to continue.

"Zenith controls the people with fear, and we"—I motioned to everyone in the room—"have the power to stop him, the power to put an end to this madness. Zenith made his move by passing this ordinance, so let's hit him back with everything we've got. He needs to see . . . no, the people need to see, true power doesn't involve force."

An eerie silence slithered into the room and wrapped its invisible tentacles around us. Orion and Iah didn't blink, their expressions stuck somewhere between shock and acceptance. Jax sat beside me, lost in thought while Cyrus cracked his knuckles as if preparing for the war we would soon face.

Samson clasped his hands in his lap. "Those were the words of a Solin."

A nervous laugh rattled in my throat as I eyed my brother. "I'm not sure why I said that."

Cyrus kept his gaze on the cracks in the wooden floor.

I looked back at Samson. "Probably a knee-jerk reaction. That plan would never work."

"What makes you say that?" Jax asked.

"We don't have an army willing to stand against Zenith. It's just us."

Samson rose to his feet. "Come on, I want to show you something."

I did a doubletake at Jax's furrowed brow. He looked equally perplexed by the Solin's request. Obeying our fearless leader, we stood and followed him toward the door.

Samson spoke over his shoulder to me and Cyrus. "I want the two of you to see this first." He rested his hand on the knob.

I scooted closer to my brother, my pulse quickening. Cyrus tensed as Samson twisted the handle. The time I chose the wrong numbered door at a haunted house back on Earth flashed in my mind. I gulped. *I hope it's not some weird demon animal he wants us to train to fight. No, it can't be. Jax said mythical creatures don't exist on Aroonyx.*

We braced ourselves for the unknown and stretched our necks around the wooden frame. I frowned. No creatures, no visitors—nothing. I scanned Iah's front yard, my Lunin vision illuminating the space in a cool white light. I strained my ears. Silence save for the tree branches that scraped against each other in the strong gust.

"Did I miss something?" Cyrus whispered near my ear. "Thanks to your Lunin traits, I can see everything." He paused, his head rotating back and forth. "And right now, all I'm seeing is a lot of trees and nothing else."

"Me too. I can't—"

I almost choked on my spit when Samson shoved us onto the porch.

"When you're done acting like a pair of idiots, go look in the backyard."

The two of us grumbled our irritations and strolled around the side of the house.

"What does Samson have up his sleeve now?" Cyrus asked me.

"Who knows?" I twisted my hair into a loose bun. "I stopped trying to figure out that man—"

"Shh." Cyrus lifted a finger to his lips. "Did you hear that?"

I nodded. As if someone had raised the volume on our life's remote, muffled voices filled the quiet space.

My brother motioned for us to quicken our pace. I breathed hard, my thundering heart synching with our determined footsteps. *Thump. Thump. Thump.*

I skidded to a stop once we rounded the corner. Out of habit, Cyrus grabbed my arm, a protective instinct. Our jaws fell open at the sight before us.

25

A SKELETON IN THE CLOSET

Cyrus's fingers dug into my warm flesh. A sea of faces stared back at us. Men stood with their boots planted in the ground, and women used their arms to guard their sons. Various shades of blue and orange glowed in the light of the Solins' lanterns that swung back and forth in their tan hands, the flames igniting the trepidation in their eyes.

I turned at feet padding behind us. Jax and Orion flanked Samson, his expression blank. Iah kept his distance while Callisto and Idalia walked side by side.

Samson locked his eyes onto my brother and jerked his chin at the group. "They didn't come all this way to hear me speak."

Using our unique bond to communicate, I nodded at Cyrus. *This is all you, bro. You're the Solin, the natural leader.*

After a long pause, he sucked in a sharp breath of the evening air, rolled his shoulders, and faced the citizens of Aroonyx. "Um." He cleared his throat. "Thanks for making the journey. I'm sure it was a long walk."

I squeezed my eyes shut. *Not a great opener, bro.*

Samson muttered his irritations. Jax's brows drew closer together with disappointment.

Cyrus shoved his hands into his pockets and looked at the grass while he spoke. "I'm Cyrus and this"—he inclined his head at me—"is my twin sister, Elara. We heard about the new ordinance and we think it's . . . *dumb.*"

I grimaced. A strong four-letter curse word slipped out of Orion's mouth. I repeated it in my mind. Had crickets existed on Aroonyx, their chirps would have reverberated around us. Realizing his error, Cyrus shifted his weight, his eyes still fixed on the ground.

The unenthusiastic crowd looked at my brother like a sports team whose coach had just delivered the world's most unmotivating speech before a championship game.

I glanced at the house, wondering if I could sneak inside without getting caught.

A middle-aged Solin with a stocky build shook his head at my brother, his long blond locks brushing against his shoulders. "Impressive." He faked a clap. "Did you practice that powerful speech before coming out here?"

Cyrus winced at the verbal jab.

The man pointed at me and my brother. "How can two kids help us?"

Cyrus watched me out of the corner of his eye. I moved closer and whispered, "Brush it off. There's no going back now."

He directed his attention at the skeptic. "Age is just a number. We've spent months—"

"I won't let Zenith take my only son," a woman cried, her arms wrapped around a young boy.

"We understand your concerns." Cyrus's voice rose over the murmurs. "We'll figure out a plan."

A Lunin's jaw cracked open. "You don't have a plan?"

I recoiled at his harsh tone. My brother's amber eyes darted back and forth. "Not yet but—"

The man interrupted Cyrus by waving him away with a *get off the stage* motion. My brother swore under his breath. A breeze of mistrust whipped through the crowd, hushed protests growing louder. Men scoffed their disapproval with animated gestures and discontent flickered in the women's blue and orange eyes.

The twin moons, orb-shaped flags of surrender, reflected in my brother's pupils when he met my gaze. I turned my attention to Samson. He folded his arms across his broad chest and observed Cyrus. A sense of déjà vu knocked me upside the head once his eyes found mine, a reminder of our private conversation before Jax's return. *Aroonyx needs a strong leader. You absorb Cyrus's power. You are the one the people will follow.*

My eyelashes fluttered. *Jax said everything happens for a reason. Samson said to trust the process.*

"Please." The word slipped out of my mouth. "Let me explain."

Eyes drifted toward me.

Heeding my own advice, I brushed off their vacant expressions and said, "We had a plan. Let the rumors about our deaths settle, then head into the villages."

A Solin in the back rubbed the scruff on his chin, his orange eyes fixed on where I stood.

Ignoring the intensity of his stare, I took a step forward and added, "But the new ordinance changed everything." I inclined my head at Idalia. "You heard what happened to our friend."

Everyone's gaze slid to the Solin. She stood with her chin held high. A handful of women chewed at their nails or averted their eyes. Proof that Pollux's cruel actions had rattled their nerves. The men showed their detest for the sadistic Lunin by sneering and cracking their knuckles.

"Unlike Zenith and his Collectors, we take responsibility for our actions," I said, motioning to those behind me.

"Doubtful." A young Solin stormed toward us, his orange eyes burning with loathing.

Jax stepped in front of me, acting as a shield.

Orion gasped, and Cyrus muttered, "Oh shit," when the teen walked up to Jax and spit in his face. The citizens, along with the others in my small group, paled.

With a steady hand, the former leader of the Inner Circle wiped the wad of phlegm off his cheek and flung it onto the grass.

"I've waited nine years to say this to you," the kid spat, poking Jax in the chest. "*Fuck you.*"

"Son." Samson's voice lowered to a threatening growl. "You've got two seconds to state your purpose."

"I only need one," he hissed. "My name is Aarush, and I'm here to avenge my father's death."

My chest caved. Jax didn't have to verbalize his thoughts because they stained his pained face. The skeleton in his closet, the one he kept hidden, had manifested before his very eyes.

Cyrus scooted closer to me and whispered, "Who was his father?"

"Sharik." I stumbled over the words I didn't want to say. "The man Jax murdered with his bare hands."

26

A LEAP OF FAITH

"Aarush." Jax spoke in a calm and quiet voice. "Your father's death was an accident."

"No. It wasn't." His nostrils flared. "My mother and I watched you crush his windpipe."

The Lunin fisted his hands.

Coming to his aid, I stepped around my human shield and said, "Jax never meant to kill your father."

"You weren't there, *Earth girl*. I didn't ask for your opinion."

"Leave her out of it," Jax warned, pushing me behind him. "This is between you and me, no one else."

"You're right." Aarush pulled a knife from his back pocket and pointed the tip of the blade at Jax's chest. "It is."

The crowd hissed, their eyes wide with panic.

"I challenge you to a duel," Aarush said, moving the blade closer.

Samson laughed. He actually laughed at the young Solin. "You've got some balls, kid. I'll give you that. You wouldn't be standing here right now had you spit in my face." He gave his comrade a sidelong glance. "Lucky for you, Jax is a patient man."

Aarush breathed hard, his armed hand trembling.

"Avenge your father by challenging Jax to a duel?" Samson clicked his tongue. "That's a *real* cute idea."

The teen lunged, aiming his knife at his enemy's heart—a rookie mistake. Jax dodged the attack and disarmed the poor kid faster than my eyes could follow. He then tossed the knife to Samson, who caught it with one hand and snapped it in two.

Aarush's eyes welled with tears as if his father's memories were imprinted on the old blade.

"Son." Samson let the shattered pieces fall to the ground. "We don't have time for grievances." He dusted off his hands. "So I'm only going to say this once: get your ass back in line or get the hell off Iah's property."

Aarush faced the citizens. "Are these the people you want to follow?" His voice raised. "They're no different from Zenith and his Collectors. Samson and Jax have innocent blood on their hands. Once a Collector, always a Collector!"

The crowd, now an angry mob, shouted their complaints. Samson reached for the back of Aarush's neck.

"Stop." I grabbed his wrist and whispered, "Don't back up his claim."

He growled his disapproval but obliged to my request.

I moved beside the teen. "I understand why you feel that way, *Aroonyx boy.*"

He scoffed at my little jab.

I looked at the other citizens and said, "Yes, Jax killed Aarush's father. And you know what? The guilt from that night has haunted him ever since." I pointed at Samson. "The faces of the men and women he murdered during the Clearing of the Seekers have haunted him for over twenty-five years."

The crowd blinked.

"*That's* the difference," I said to Aarush. "These men take responsibility for their actions." I touched my chest and motioned to my brother. "And so do we. Zenith views his position as an entitlement because of the false power he claims. Samson and Jax risked their lives for me and my brother. Do you want to know why?"

Aarush didn't answer, nor did the crowd.

"Because they're tired of watching you follow a man who rules without a heart."

The citizens exhaled a shared breath. I steadied my pounding heart.

Cyrus nudged me forward and whispered, "You've got this, sis."

I nodded. "Look around you," I said to the curious faces. "What do you see? Lunins, Solins, merchants, farmers? What about citizens or rebels?" Brows furrowed. "Titles. That's what they are. Zenith sees you as these and nothing more." I turned to Aarush. "In his eyes, your father's death was just a shameless regret."

He blinked once—twice. I directed my attention back to the crowd. "But when I look at you, I *see* you, and I see the one thing we have in common."

"And what's that?" a woman asked.

"Hope."

Her tongue tapped against her teeth. "How can you know for sure?"

"Because without it, none of you would have come here tonight."

Hushed murmurs flowed through the crowd.

"You've got their attention," Samson whispered near my ear. "Keep it going, kid."

Kid. The simple word gave me an idea. I cleared my throat and said, "I'm aware that you see me and my brother as a couple of kids who know nothing about Aroonyx."

Heads of every shape and size nodded in agreement.

"But we come from a planet with a rich history. We've seen the devastation that occurs from following the wrong leader.

277

Ruthless dictators have blinded their citizens on Earth with fear and lies, and as a result, millions have perished." I sighed, massaging my temples. I had a pounding headache but shook it off and added, "Yes, we're young, but that doesn't mean we're naïve or uneducated. And we sure as hell won't stand aside and watch Earth's history repeat itself on another planet. Especially if that planet is our place of birth."

Mouths gaped at the truth behind my words. *Did they forget we were born on Aroonyx?*

An older Solin stepped forward while the others stood there, gawking at me. My mind raced. *What am I supposed to say now? Wasn't that enough?* I wrung my clammy hands watching the man move closer. *Shit. I hope he's not another skeleton from Jax's closet.*

"Don't cower," Samson chided, shoving me in the back.

I stumbled, my head jolting at the unexpected gesture. Aarush grabbed my arm, catching my fall.

"Thank you," I mouthed.

He said nothing, though the haze of lifelong resentment appeared to lift in his rust-colored eyes. This moment passed once Jax moved behind me. The haze reappeared, transforming into a dense fog of hatred.

Aarush spat at the Lunin's feet, then spun on his heels and stormed off into the woods.

Jax sighed and Samson muttered, "Good riddance to that one."

I eyed the anxious crowd. Toes tapped and arms crossed. *Great. They're pissed or impatient. My luck, both.*

I removed the hair tie that secured the messy bun on top of my head before motioning to Aarush's silhouette. "It's easy to ignore the obvious if you spend too much time focusing on the past. Zenith has ruled Aroonyx for over sixteen years, and during his reign, you've forgotten a simple truth. He's just a man."

Their wide-eyed expressions screamed *No he's not, he's Zenith.*

"I get it," I said, finding the timid ones in the crowd. "He shares both Solin and Lunin traits." I pointed at my brother. "But so do we. And during the day, I can absorb Cyrus's power."

Gasps. Whispers. Shocked emotions ebbed and flowed before me. My brother blew out a tight breath while I chewed on the inside of my cheek. *Damn it. I don't know if he wanted me to share that bit of information.*

"You might want to elaborate," Jax murmured, taking his place beside me.

"But this doesn't make us powerful," I said. Heads tilted. "It makes us unique. Those two words have different meanings. Zenith has used this to his advantage to gain control. He's spent years creating a façade, an illusion of a powerful man."

The howling wind interrupted my speech. I gulped, touching my abdomen. The last time the phantom wolf appeared, a knife punctured my gut.

My fear-driven thoughts vanished when a Solin offered his two cents. "I appreciate how you speak from the heart. Most Lunins struggle to communicate their feelings."

I shrugged.

He tapped his chest. "But I'm a practical man. Words won't keep the Collectors from taking our sons. And how do we fight back if we can't defend ourselves? I can't remember the last time I threw a punch, and the dull kitchen knives I have at home can hardly cut through a damn vegetable."

Jax slid his boots forward. Though he had let go of his past, the citizens of Aroonyx still saw him as Zenith's prodigal son with blood-stained hands.

He observed the crowd, his blue eyes drifting from one soul to the next. Women cowered, and men lowered their gazes, terrified of the man who stood before them.

"It's obvious I don't need an introduction," Jax said, dragging a hand through his hair. "You're aware of my relationship with Zenith. As Elara mentioned, I'm not proud of my past, but the knowledge I've gained over the years gives us an advantage. Samson and I have trained the twins in combat. If an average Collector attacked, I'm confident they'd survive."

Chins lifted at this comment.

"If you let go of your judgments toward me and Samson, we can teach you how to defend yourselves."

"It's too late," a woman called. "The ordinance passed. The Collectors are taking young men to Zenith's as we speak."

As usual, my lips moved without thinking. "Then stay here with us."

The woman's brows touched her hairline.

Iah never gave me permission to offer his home as a sanctuary, so I turned and found his eyes.

He nodded.

"Are you sure?" I mouthed.

Another nod, his lips spreading into a warm grin.

I spun around to face the woman. "You're safer here than in your own home. If I were you, I'd—"

"For how long?" interrupted an elderly Lunin.

"For as long as it takes."

He pushed his glasses farther up the bridge of his nose. "As long as what takes?"

The answer tripped over my tongue.

He pressed on. "You want us to leave the comfort of our homes and live in the woods? Why? To hide from the Collectors?"

"Yeah." Cyrus stepped to my right. "That's exactly what my sister is suggesting. You can't defend yourselves against the Collectors. It's your only option if you want to avoid the ordinance. This isn't a permanent move. It's temporary."

My gaze drifted to a Solin at the front of the crowd. His dark skin stretched over his muscular arms, and the gold flecks in his copper-colored eyes shimmered in the moonlight. The way his calloused fingers played with the tip of his beard reminded me of Samson.

He flicked his wrist at me. "Cut the crap, kid. What's the purpose of this meeting?"

Cyrus and Jax straightened. My mouth moved, but no words came out.

The man folded his muscular arms across his chest, the ashy skin around his elbows tight with tension. "It's obvious the rumors are false because you and your brother are alive and well. We can see that now. And let me guess." He glanced at Samson. "This meeting has nothing to do with the ordinance."

Thrown for a nauseating loop, I stammered, "It does. This is why we want you to stay here and train—"

"To do what?"

"To defend yourselves."

"Against whom?"

"The Collectors," I snapped, irritated with the numerous questions.

He waved a hand at the surrounding area. "But they're not here, are they?"

"No, but—"

"You and your brother want us to leave our homes and hide in the woods to avoid conflict, am I right?"

I nodded. Cyrus mirrored my frustrations with a sharp exhale.

"So, tell me Elara, tell *us*, why should we learn to defend ourselves if we're safe here at Iah's?"

Speechless, I didn't respond.

The man shook his head at Samson. "You said she was smart. I'm not impressed."

Slack-jawed, I eyed Jax.

He kept his attention on the Solin, who wagged his finger at me. "I'm curious. Earlier you called us rebels."

I tried to swallow but my throat had tightened.

He went on. "In *your* eyes, we're ignorant people, blinded by our leader. The Collectors are, but like most of my friends, I'm not." He shifted his weight. "I'll ask you one more time, Elara. Why did Samson bring us here tonight?"

I gave my mentor a pleading look. He returned the gesture with a curt head nod. I winced. The truth slammed into me with a brute force. Samson didn't gather this group to discuss the ordinance. He gathered them to discuss the uprising. And the bastard wanted me to say it aloud.

I swore under my breath. *How did I not see it? The months of combative training, the cryptic conversations. This entire time, Samson's been preparing us for war. The old plan of us visiting the villages to show the citizens our shared traits was just a distraction, an excuse to train us until Zenith made his move. Now that the ordinance passed, the people are desperate. They would have never joined our side before tonight.*

Dumbfounded, I stared at my brother. He eyed at the twin moons and let out a long breath. "It's time, sis. Tell them the truth."

The inquisitive man jerked his chin at us. "This 'training' involves more than self-defense, doesn't it?"

"Perhaps." My lips pressed together.

"Why?"

Defeat weighed on my shoulders, curving them inward. "Because we want you trained to fight."

The crowd gasped, but surprise did not flicker in the Solin's eyes when he asked, "And who are we fighting?"

"Zenith and his Collectors." I paused, my heart thumping in my ears. "We're starting an uprising."

A FOUR-LETTER WORD

Voices raised and tempers flared, but the Solin remained silent.

"Say something, sis." Cyrus pointed to a Lunin couple who did an about-face. "They're bailing on us."

I spun around and ripped into Samson. "Thanks for the heads-up, boss. You made me look like a fucking idiot."

He shrugged.

I glared. "Are you going to help me out, or just stand there?"

He lifted his boot, then rested it back on the grass. "I'm *very* comfortable in this particular spot." He mocked me further by rubbing his arms and saying, "It's nice and cozy."

"You're such an asshole."

"Glad I'm not the only one," Jax murmured.

My tongue moved to ridicule the Lunin, but Samson cut me off. "You're wasting time, Elara. You started this meeting, now finish it."

Bastard. "I didn't ask for this job."

"Easy," Jax soothed. "People fear what they don't understand. A little clarification goes a long way."

"An uprising, huh?" The dark-skinned Solin rose to his full height. "You speak with a traitor's tongue."

Traitor? Pulses of anger rippled through me. Enough was enough. I was tired of his endless interrogations and skewed implications. My hands curled into fists. *How dare him? I'm not the villain.*

A cackle slithered down my spine, a dangerous adder, ready to strike. I closed my eyes and gritted my teeth. *Not now. Go away.*

The black silk shifted around its O-shaped mouth. *No. There's something I need to share.*

Well, I don't want to hear it.

Oh, but you must. It raked a claw down my spine. *It's time to take off the gloves, Elara. It's time to show the people your hidden potential: the side of your personality you keep locked away; the side that toys with the darkness; the side that enjoys my company.*

I palmed my eyes and swore.

Jax touched my arm. "Are you okay?"

"Damn it. Just give me a minute."

He recoiled at my sharp tone, his hand falling to his side. Though my eyes remained closed, I could feel the apprehension pulsating through the crowd.

More wicked laughter filled my ears. *Do you see how easily that worked? Zenith uses fear to get their attention, and so can you.*

No. I pressed my palms harder into my eyes. *I won't treat the citizens that way.*

But it's for a good cause. The illusive dealer brushed invisible dust off its black cloak. *You need them to join your side. Force them to obey.*

Its words zipped through my mind, then spun out, crashing into a wall of truth. At that moment I saw the temptation leaders face—desire. A desire to control others, a desire to justify their poor decisions.

No. I won't fall into that trap.

The silk mask that hid its face fluttered with a defeated breath. *Until we meet again, Elara.*

My eyes shot open. I had passed another test, the test of morality.

I stared at the Solin interrogator, and in a firm voice, I said, "In Zenith's eyes, yes, I am a traitor, but *he's* the one committing treason. The man betrayed you after he gained control of Aroonyx."

Curious eyes drifted toward me.

"Aren't you tired of living in fear?" I asked the remaining citizens. "Tired of looking over your shoulders, wondering if the Collectors are listening to your conversations?" I found the mothers in the crowd. "Do you want your children growing up in a world of oppression or a world of opportunity?"

The women who shielded their sons eyed one another.

I touched my chest and pointed to the men beside me. "We're not traitors. We're revolutionaries."

"Is there a difference?" the Solin countered.

A smile broke at the corner of my mouth. "Yeah, a big one. We're not betraying anyone. We're supporting a cause that's bigger than all of us."

"Which is?"

"Truth."

The man nodded his approval, then turned to the others. "She's got my attention. Perhaps we should hear what the girl has to say?"

Some shrugged while others muttered their disagreement.

My spine lengthened. For the first time, I felt confident standing in my power.

"Zenith's reign has lasted long enough," I said. "It's time for him to step down. Yes, we had discussed an uprising, but that option never seemed practical . . . until now."

A Lunin woman raised her hand. "What's the plan? We set up camp here in the woods, and you train us to fight? How long will that take?" Her chest rose and fell with quick breaths. "What if Zenith hears of the uprising? He doesn't tolerate treason. He'll send the Collectors. I have young children. I won't put my family at risk."

Unsure how to calm her frazzled nerves, I shot Jax a desperate glance.

He nodded at me before looking at the woman. "Those are valid concerns."

She cowered once his mouth moved.

"We're not forcing you to join our side," he added. "My Seeker powers can't predict the future, but I can see the obvious. The men who meet the age requirement are subject to the ordinance. Those who don't comply face imminent death." A hush fell over the crowd. "Everyone else is free to continue their lives without interruption."

A young Solin stood on her toes to see over the group. "But my life has already suffered an interruption." Her voice quivered as she brushed away a tear. "The Collectors took my brother from our home yesterday."

My heart shattered. I met Cyrus's gaze; his grave expression reflected my own. That could have been us had Jax not taken us to Earth.

"That's why we want you to stay here," I said to the grief-stricken girl. "This new ordinance affects everyone. These men are brothers, fathers, and sons."

"We'll train anyone who wants to fight," Cyrus said. "Men, women, the young, and the old. We won't discriminate. Age and gender don't matter to us. What matters is ending Zenith's reign, and when that day comes, I'll be the first in line. If you follow us—"

"No." I held up my hand. Cyrus's jaw slammed shut. "We don't want you following us. We want you standing *with* us. Getting Zenith to step down won't be easy, but we can do it together."

Curious faces stared back. I fidgeted with a loose thread on my shorts. *What did I expect? They can't make a decision that quick.*

I flinched when the strong winds snapped a branch loose, sending it crashing onto Iah's roof. Everyone shifted their gaze toward the loud sound. Everyone but the Solin with the copper-colored eyes.

"I'll stand with you," he said.

My eyelids moved in slow motion. The Lunins stirred, their boots shuffling with trepidation.

"Don't feel pressured to make your decision now," I reassured them.

The crowd went rigid when Samson stepped forward. He cleared his throat and spit a ball of phlegm onto the ground before speaking. "This is a life-changing decision. There's no going back once you join our side. Sleep on it and consider your options. If you want to participate in the uprising, then pack your belongings and meet us here." He ran a hand over the coarse hairs of his beard. "And fair warning, I'm not the easiest person to get along with. Combative training isn't for the fainthearted, and the mental preparation required isn't for the weak minded. Blood will spill before this mission is over. If that scares you"—he jerked his chin at the invisible path Aarush and the couple had followed—"then go."

The Lunins eyed the unmarked exit, while the Solins stood tall. I sighed. *Leave it to my mentor to weed out the timid ones.*

Samson narrowed his eyes at a middle-aged man leaning against a tree. Jax tensed, Orion cursed, and I cringed at the sight of Samson removing his knife. The crowd froze.

"I don't tolerate spies," my mentor growled at the Lunin. "If your intentions are ill-placed, you'll suffer the consequences."

The man scoffed and pushed himself off the tree. Big mistake. Samson exposed the blade and hurled it through the air. A colorful word left my brother's mouth. The knife had wedged itself into the bark, right above the man's head.

Mouths fell open. Blue and orange eyes jumped between the Lunin and the ex-Collector.

The crowd parted, allowing Samson access to the man, who had turned a sickly shade of green.

My mentor shoved the accused in the chest, slamming his head against the tree. "I think you and I should have a little chat."

"Here we go," Orion muttered.

Cyrus snickered, crossing his arms. "This will be fun to watch."

Samson pulled the embedded knife out of the bark. The green tinge that stained the man's face turned white.

He pointed the tip of the blade at the Lunin's neck and said, "Hey, Jax. Take a walk with us."

The former leader of the Inner Circle shut his eyes.

"I could use your expertise in the art of a clean tongue removal." Samson flashed the trembling man a wicked grin. "I hate getting blood on my boots."

Orion choked on his spit. Cyrus chuckled, slapping him on the back.

Jax found my eyes and let the air rush out of his lungs. "I guess that's my cue." He reached into his pocket and exposed Zenith's blade, the silver etchings shimmering in the moonlight. "And to think, things were going *so* well."

I huffed a sarcastic breath, watching him hurry to catch up with Samson. The sight of Jax holding Zenith's knife caused the group to scatter like ants disturbed by a careless boot. *At least I'm not the only one who fears that damn blade.*

My eyes danced between Cyrus and Orion while I motioned to the disappearing Solins and Lunins. "Now what?"

"They'll be back," answered the Solin interrogator.

He offered me his hand. I shook it firmly, observing how our contrasting skin tones merged with the friendly greeting.

"The name's Roshan."

"Elara." I winced at his tight grip. "But you already knew that."

He nodded, the strong breeze ruffling his graying hair. "Samson told me all about the famous twins."

Cyrus shook the man's hand, then crossed his arms.

"I apologize for being such a hard ass," Roshan added. "Samson's orders."

My face squished up with confusion. "What are you talking about?"

Though only a few stragglers remained, Roshan lowered his voice to a whisper. "My act back there. It was just a ruse. The citizens thought you were dead. Samson gathered a few curious folks so they could see you with their own eyes. See you alive and well. He never mentioned the ordinance or the uprising."

My jaw almost hit the ground. "Then why did I get the impression he wanted me to mention the revolution?"

Roshan shrugged.

"And *you*." I glared at him through tiny slits. "You kept prying, trying to get me to say it out loud. Why?"

His shoulders shook with laughter.

"Dude." Cyrus's arms fell to his sides. "It's not funny. My sister got her ass handed to her—by *you*."

"My bad." Roshan muffled his laughter. "Samson asked me to help." He pointed at the Solin, who dragged the terrified Lunin into the woods with Jax not far behind. "He's very persuasive."

Interest piqued, Orion asked, "So Samson told you to ask those questions?"

"No. Not exactly. I improvised. During our walk from the

village tonight, we chatted about the part he wanted me to play."

I arched a brow. "Let me guess, the interrogator."

"Or the pot stirrer." He winked.

Cyrus puffed his cheeks at me. "I guess Roshan was the card Samson had up his sleeve."

I nodded.

"The ordinance got the ball rolling," Roshan said. "Samson knew the people would never vocalize their support for an uprising. We've considered it. Hell, we've even had secret meetings discussing ways to end his reign."

A knot formed in my stomach at the thought of Aarush's father. Sharik held meetings. His plan of overthrowing Zenith had ended quicker than it started.

"The citizens who gathered here tonight needed to hear one of their own ask the right questions." Roshan tapped his chest. "That's why I kept drilling you for information. I had to lead the conversation to a place the others were afraid to go. They had to hear you say it. The villagers don't know you and your brother. Earning their trust will take time."

"We don't have time to win the hearts of the people," I argued.

"Then make time, because the two of you fighting against an army of Collectors led by Zenith doesn't sound like a promising ending for the twins."

I groaned, scrubbing at my face.

"Trust me," Roshan said. "They'll come around."

"I doubt it." Cyrus widened his stance. "Half the crowd almost passed out when Aarush challenged Jax, and everyone bailed once Samson threw his knife at that Lunin."

"He did nothing wrong," Roshan countered. "The people need to see we're not fucking around. A spy could end the uprising."

I met my brother's gaze. "He makes a valid point."

"I usually do." Roshan chuckled.

"Were you a Collector with Samson?" Cyrus asked.

"No. I turned Arun down when he tried to recruit me. I never liked that man. He couldn't look me in the eyes."

I recalled our first trip to the South Village, the afternoon Cyrus made the naïve mistake of telling a vendor he was visiting Aroonyx with his sister. Before we left our campsite that day, my brother asked Jax how to spot a Collector. He told us to watch the eyes. *I bet that quirk has nothing to do with being a Collector, and everything to do with repressed guilt.* I blew out a tight breath. *That afternoon feels like a lifetime ago.*

My thoughts drifted to the present when Orion asked, "How long have you known Samson?"

Roshan scratched the stubble on his neck. "Damn. Must be thirty years now."

"How old are you?"

"Forty-seven."

The line between my brows deepened as I did the math.

Saving me the headache, he added, "Samson's around fifty-two."

"Well, shit." Cyrus's eyes grew. "I didn't know he was *that* old."

Orion and I laughed at his observation.

Roshan shrugged. "We're all getting old, though some of us don't let it show."

Lost in thought, my brother stared at the emerald grass. The rest of us stared at each other. The citizens had vanished, took a one-way stroll back to their villages. Samson and Jax, along with the accused, were nowhere in sight, and Callisto and Idalia had followed Iah into the quaint home.

"Well." Roshan swung his arms and clapped his hands. "I think it's been a productive evening."

I plastered a fake grin on my face. "Says the Solin."

He inclined his head at my brother and said, "Optimism is one of our finer traits."

Cyrus beamed, clapping a hand on Roshan's back. I shook my head at the pair; Orion's eye roll mirrored my unspoken sentiments.

"I'm going to head into town. See if I can talk some sense into the others." Roshan's copper-colored eyes bounced between the three of us. "Tell the rest of your group to prepare for visitors. They'll start showing up in a few days."

"I hope you're right," I mumbled.

"Weren't you the one who mentioned that word earlier?"

I cocked my head to one side, watching Roshan amble into the forest.

"What word?" I called.

He paused his pursuit, his boots sinking into the grass. His full lips spread into a warm grin as he looked over his shoulder at me. "Hope. The word was hope."

28

IN THE END

No one spoke until Roshan disappeared from view. After a long silence, Cyrus said, "I like him. He's a cool dude."

Orion nodded. "I wonder if Roshan can replace Samson. He's a lot nicer." The Lunin's eyes grew at his own statement. "Please don't tell him I said that."

"Only if you behave," I teased.

"Orion's always on his best behavior," Cyrus said.

The Lunin grinned, offering my brother a fist bump. "Thanks, Cyrus."

I rolled my eyes at the two men. "So it's official. You have joined forces."

"Obviously," Cyrus muttered. "You left us without a choice."

Orion failed at keeping a straight face. "We got tired of sitting around watching team *Jalara* sneak around."

"Jax and I don't sneak . . . wait"—I held up my hand—"did you combine our names to create *Jalara*?"

Orion crossed his arms, flashing me a smug grin.

I shot my brother a weighted glance. "Be honest, how long did it take you guys to come up with that one?"

A mischievous smirk played at the corner of his mouth. "Like an hour."

The three of us burst into laughter. It wasn't even that funny, but we appreciated the comedic relief after the stress-filled evening.

Orion wiped a joyful tear from his cheek and said, "I don't know about you guys, but I could use a drink."

Cyrus nodded with enthusiasm. "Tell me you've got something stronger than water?"

"I think my dad keeps a jug of Maragin in the storage closet." Orion stifled his amusement when he added, "Care to join me?"

"Only if Rico makes an appearance. I've really missed that little furball."

Cyrus faked a laugh, then showed me his middle finger. "Are the two of you done making fun of me?"

I smiled and mouthed, "No."

Orion added to his performance by saying, "Forget the Maragin. How about a cup of tea?" He lifted his pinky and pretended to sip out of an invisible cup. "It doesn't look as manly, but you won't have to worry about Rico and his temper crashing the party."

"What a shame." Cyrus glared at the Lunin. "We were just starting to get along. Oh well, you're on your own Han." He turned and headed toward the house with his fist held in the air. "Luke out."

Orion frowned as he hurried to catch up with my brother. "Wait. Who's Han? Who's Luke?"

I chuckled under my breath, listening to Cyrus ridicule Orion. "Tea? What kind of bullshit drink is that?"

"It was a joke. And I happen to enjoy a nice cup of tea."

My head turned at the sound of footsteps. "I'll catch up with you guys later," I called.

Cyrus took one look at Jax, then muttered, "Team *Jalara* strikes again."

Orion dropped his head with an exaggerated sigh.

I ignored their jabs and scanned Jax's body for signs of a struggle with the suspected traitor. His arms swayed by his sides, and blood didn't cover his pale hands. I huffed a breath. *I guess Samson let the guy keep his tongue.*

Jax paused his approach to admire the evening sky. The light of the twin moons illuminated his striking features. I followed his gaze and inhaled the summer air. A mixture of trapped emotions rushed out of my lungs as I shut my eyes, and when they opened, I found Jax standing in front of me. I flinched.

"My apologies." He snickered.

I watched him carefully. His curious expression reminded me of our first encounter on Earth.

"Why are you staring at me like that?"

He answered with a lazy grin.

"Stop it," I pressed, an anxious laugh catching in my throat. "You're making me nervous."

Jax moved with a purpose. One of his hands grabbed my waist while his other slid to the back of my neck. He kissed me passionately, his fingers digging into my warm flesh. A pleasurable moan slipped through my parted lips. The unexpected gesture left my head spinning and eyes blurring.

I melted into his touch and clutched the fabric of his shirt, inviting him to come closer. He obliged, pressing his body against mine, his heart thumping in a steady rhythm. The locks of my hair tangled around his fingers as he angled my head higher, allowing his tongue to circle deeper, slower. My hand slid down the hard planes of his abdomen, finding his belt buckle. He gripped my backside with a burning desire that caused my spine to arch. My thumb and index finger freed the first button on his pants. Two heartbeats later, Jax pulled away.

I made a pout face. "Can we go inside now?"

He shook his head and refastened his belt after a thorough adjustment.

Dazed, I touched my wet lips. "I don't remember saving your life tonight. What was that for?"

The Lunin tucked a stray hair behind my ear and kissed the side of my neck, goosebumps trailing his soft lips. I shuddered a breath. He whispered my name, his teeth nipping at my skin.

I attempted the art of sensual name calling and failed miserably. It wasn't sexy. Not in the slightest. I called his name like a student vying for their classmate's attention.

Quiet laughter rumbled in his chest. "It takes practice, *Elara*."

More chills raised on my arms. "Show off."

"Now to answer your question." He lifted my chin. "I find it very attractive when a woman takes control. You did great tonight. I'm proud of you."

"Thanks for the compliment." I patted his chest with stiff palms and took a step backward.

He crossed his arms. "You don't think you deserve one."

"Nope."

"Why not?"

"Because I didn't do anything. I just stood there, rambling on . . . hell, I don't even know the point I was trying to make." I used my hand as a talking puppet to mock my performance. "Blah, blah, blah. That's all they heard."

"That's not true. You spoke from the heart."

"Yeah, well the *heart* won't win this war, will it?"

"You'd be surprised. It takes courage to speak from the heart, and courageous people win wars."

I glanced at the house. "Did you know the purpose behind this meeting?"

"Yes—and no."

"What is that supposed to mean?"

"It means Samson mentioned he wanted to gather a few of the villagers, though he never shared a time or a place. I was equally shocked to see those faces staring back at us tonight."

"What about Roshan's part in all of this? Did you know?"

"No, but I figured it out once he started asking you those questions."

I hid an eye roll. *Of course he did.*

"Samson's convinced the people will come around."

"So is Roshan," I murmured.

"What do you think?"

I hesitated. The anchor that held my mind in place, the one attached to the chain of practicality, dragged across the murky sea floor of my fearful thoughts.

"Go with your gut, Elara. What's it telling you?"

"I'm not sure." I blinked, staring at nothing. "I stopped listening."

Jax grabbed me by the shoulders. "Always listen to your gut. It has the answers you seek. Don't ignore it."

My mouth gaped. *The dealer?*

As if reading my mind, Jax's eyes narrowed. "Not the loud voice in here." He tapped my forehead. "The quiet voice that whispers in here." He held his hand over my heart.

I had never discussed the masked figure with Jax. I never wanted to. I feared judgment, feared him seeing me as mentally unstable, feared the private discussions he'd have with Iah, or worse, with Cyrus. I sighed. *He's right. My mind is getting in the way of my heart.*

At this thought, the dealer appeared but then vanished at the sound of Jax's voice. "You have a gift, Elara. The unique ability to connect with people on an emotional level."

I scowled. "More like the gift of awkwardness."

He couldn't hide his grin.

"I'm serious," I said, slapping him in the arm. "It's not funny."

"I'm not laughing."

"You're smiling."

"I found subtle humor in your word choice."

I folded my arms across my chest and tapped my foot. "Are you done?"

"Are you?"

"You're such an asshole."

"And you're a—"

"I dare you to finish that sentence."

"An exquisite woman."

"Nice recovery," I chided.

His grin widened. "I've had years of practice."

"Practicing what? The art of bullshit?"

"No, the art of letting women think they've won the argument."

My hand slid to my back pocket. "That insult made me reach for my knife."

"*My* knife," Jax corrected. He exposed Zenith's blade with a flick of his wrist and waved it through the air. "Shall we duel?"

"That's a messed-up thing to say, considering that knife was wedged in my stomach."

"You're right." He slipped the folded blade back into his pocket. "I took that one a little too far."

"You think?"

"Apologies, miss."

"Is that the first time you've ever spoken without a filter?"

He nodded. "You're rubbing off on me."

"See. This is what I'm talking about. This is the reason I won't accept your compliment. I don't have a filter, and I always stumble . . . over my words . . . like I'm doing now."

"Regardless, people listen. Public speaking takes practice, but the gift you have can't be taught." Jax reached for my hand. "I don't think you appreciate what you have to offer. You're smart, practical, and you see the situation for what it is, not what you desire it to become. Those are traits of a strong leader. The people will follow you during and after the uprising."

I gasped and staggered backward as if Jax's hand had burst into flames. "No!" My head shook so fast his body blurred before my eyes. "I see where you're going with this conversation and my answer is no—*hell no*."

"Your speech tonight said otherwise."

"Stop putting words in my mouth. I never implied I wanted to lead the uprising. That's why I kept saying *we* while pointing to you and the others in our group."

He took a step closer. "Sorry. That's not how the game works."

"This isn't a game, Jax. Innocent lives are on the line. I planned on keeping my mouth shut until Cyrus—" My voice faded. I couldn't finish the sentence.

"Go ahead, say it."

Refusing, my lips formed a tight line.

"Fine, then I will." Jax crossed his arms and widened his stance. "You planned on keeping your mouth shut until your brother failed to deliver, until he failed to act like a Solin."

My chin hit my chest.

Jax let out a long breath, his arms falling to his sides. "Years ago, I discussed the differences between you and your brother with Samson."

I looked up. "How many years?"

"Five."

My eyelashes fluttered. *Samson's known about us this entire time. That's why he acted so weird the first night I saw him at Idalia's. He stared right through me as if seeing a ghost, a ghost from the past.*

Jax added another piece to the puzzle. "Samson knew the reason I jumped back and forth to Earth: to keep a watchful eye on the twins. Your brother has a heart of gold. He'll give the shirt off his back to a stranger."

I nodded, remembering the afternoon he almost froze to death.

"He's brave, strong willed, and the man never hesitates if called to action. True-blue traits of a Solin. *You*, Elara, don't fit the typical mold of a Lunin."

I shot him an incredulous look.

He pressed on. "Yes, you'd rather observe than participate, you overthink every detail, and take everything personally."

I gritted my teeth. "There's that brutal honesty I love."

"And there's that sass."

I waved a hand for him to continue.

"But you also express your emotions, verbalize your opinions, and give people the benefit of the doubt." Jax swallowed. "Cyrus is a strong man, and he's willing to risk his life for this mission. On Earth, your brother was a great leader: Captain of the football team, student body president, star volunteer with the fire department—the list goes on and on. Unfortunately, living on Aroonyx has changed him . . . in more ways than one."

A deep sadness I couldn't face swirled in the pit of my stomach. I clutched my chest; there wasn't enough oxygen to fill my lungs. "What are you implying?"

"Exactly what I just told you. He's changed."

"We've all changed."

His tone shifted from casual to severe. "I'm aware, but the change occurring inside of your brother is bigger than you think. It's causing a distraction. He's getting distant and brushes me off anytime I bring it up."

I wrung my hands. "Do you think it has to do with Idalia? He wants to murder Pollux, slowly, painfully."

"No. That's not it."

"Then what is it?"

Jax shrugged. "Perhaps he's afraid. There's a lot of uncertainty in his future."

Coming to my brother's defense, my mouth moved with

words I would later regret. "You think Cyrus is acting distant because he's scared?" My voice raised. "You just said he'd risk his life for this mission. He's not begging you to take him home, Jax. He's not afraid of the future."

The ex-Collector's jaw clenched. "You know I can no longer jump to Earth."

"Yes, but you never had a problem disappearing when things got tough." He winced at the low blow. "Cyrus isn't you, Jax. He isn't a coward. He would never abandon me."

And there it was. The bitter resentment I still harbored, the resentment I fought to let go.

Jax shut his eyes. My invisible handprint had left a permanent mark across his cheek and his heart.

"I'm sorry." My voice sounded far away. "That's a perfect example of me lacking a filter."

"Noted." Jax ran a hand through his hair and stole a glimpse at the amethyst-colored sky. "I'm guessing you need further clarification as to why I left that day."

"Perhaps, but not tonight. We have bigger demons to slay."

A long and uncomfortable silence passed between us. The tree limbs fought against each other, sending their leaves spinning in endless circles. Once again nature's metaphor mirrored my current state.

Jax squeezed the bridge of his nose. "A change is coming. I can feel it."

"Samson said those exact words."

"I need to tell you something, Elara. Something you need to hear."

"And he said that too."

Jax locked his eyes onto mine. "From this point on you can no longer depend on me, Cyrus, or anyone else to help you succeed on this mission."

I tried to swallow. The saliva in my mouth had evaporated.

The Lunin inhaled a sobering breath and centered himself

before saying, "You know I can't predict the future, but I have a strong feeling how this story plays out."

My lip quivered and my eyes stung with unshed tears.

Answering my unspoken question, he whispered, "You are the one who defeats Zenith."

I didn't blink. I didn't breathe. I couldn't move. The change that Jax and Samson spoke of crashed over me like a wave with a strong undertow. My mind fought against the emotional current. Struggling didn't help. I was powerless over a force of such magnitude. A salty drop rolled off my cheek, hitting the toe of Jax's boot.

He pulled me into his arms and held me in a tight embrace, allowing me to reflect on my past and envision my future.

"Don't twist my words into thinking you're alone on this mission," he said. "I'm not going anywhere. I'll be with you until the very end."

"I know, and that's what scares me."

Jax dipped his chin to meet my gaze. "What are you so afraid of?"

"The unknown." I looked at the house and the surrounding woods before finding his piercing blue eyes. "When this is over, who's standing by my side?" Tears streamed down my face, the grief overwhelming me. "In the end—is there anyone left?"

29

ADDED PRESSURE

I squinted at the morning light while listening to Samson verbalize his expectations for the day. Without the encouragement of a breeze, the elongated branches that shaded Iah's home remained motionless. I used the sweat around my hairline to glue the flyaway strands in place, then wiped the moisture from my brow. *I'm so sick of this damn heat.*

Beads glistened on my brother's bronze skin. A droplet grazed the corner of his eye and he didn't bother wiping it away. He stood with his arms crossed, eyes focused on our mentor.

Samson pointed to the Lunin standing beside me. "You and Elara find a shaded area. The women can't train in this heat." We nodded. He turned to Jax. "You and Cyrus take the same group you had yesterday. I'll work with the others."

"Got it," Jax confirmed.

I observed the Solins and Lunins who gathered in Iah's yard. Roshan's prediction proved true. To my surprise, my long-winded speech had resonated with the people of Aroonyx, and two sunrises later, men, women, and children arrived in small droves. Families with underage sons left the comforts of their homes to avoid the ordinance. Others abandoned their old lives to join our cause, to join the uprising.

I glanced at Jax and Cyrus's group: Solin and Lunin men between the ages of eighteen and thirty. Samson always worked with the older ones. Unsure of Zenith's next move, our well-seasoned mentor pushed us harder than ever. We spent hours teaching hand-to-hand combat in the brutal heat and didn't stop until the men collapsed from exhaustion.

The elders, the ones too old to fight, stood on the sidelines, shouting words of encouragement. Grandmothers tended to the bloodied lips and swollen eyes of the men and women who volunteered to risk their lives. The seeds of hope had sprouted into a rich comradery between the members of our groups, and the sense of oneness warmed my heart.

Samson met my gaze, his orange eyes glowing with determination. The citizen's lives depended on him, depended on us to prepare for the inevitable war. "Teach the girls how to escape a ground hold." He stole a glance at Orion. "And don't be afraid to roughen them up. They need an accurate account of how it feels when a man restrains them."

My training partner mumbled, "Sure thing, boss."

The eldest Solin scanned the area around Iah's home. "Elara, if anyone else shows up, sort them into the appropriate groups."

I hummed my compliance. *Why does Samson think I want to lead this mission? I gave him my answer after our meeting with the villagers.* I eyed my brother, who stood tall and fearless. *Jax is crazy. Cyrus isn't scared of the future. He's the better choice, the natural leader.*

My brother verified my thoughts by clapping his strong hands and inclining his head toward the men and women standing in the shade. "Let's get to work."

Jax and I lingered while Samson, Orion, and Cyrus headed down the porch steps.

As if leaving for a casual day at a desk job, Jax kissed the top of my head, and said, "Have a good one."

"You too." I chuckled, moving my lips toward his. After a quick embrace, I said, "I hope we get to continue this later."

"Perhaps." He winked before dashing off to catch up with my brother.

I gathered my hair into a high ponytail and strolled toward the group gathered around Orion: women eighteen and older.

Silence fell as I took my place beside the Lunin. I cleared my throat. "Okay ladies, today we plan on teaching you how to escape a ground hold. Pay close attention because perfecting this technique is a little tricky. It saved my life the night Elio attacked me at Zenith's."

Blue and orange eyes widened with fear. *Right. I should have omitted that part.*

Skipping the details of that turbulent evening, I lowered myself onto the grass and told Orion to move into position. The women scooted closer as his legs locked around my hips. They pointed and whispered once he pinned my arms above my head.

I turned my head to address our audience, the fine blades of grass brushing against my cheek. "You'll want to avoid this situation, especially with a Solin during the day." I squirmed underneath Orion. "Even a Lunin makes it challenging to escape."

A young woman, close to my age, craned her neck to get a better look.

"You see"—I continued to struggle—"I can't reach for my knife or lift my hand to gouge his eyes, and I lack the strength to push him off of me."

The group frowned.

"But don't worry," I added. "There is a way to free yourself from this hold."

Relieved breaths escaped their mouths.

My eyes slid to a young boy who squeezed himself between the cluster of women. The toes of his worn boots stopped only inches before touching my nose, and his lips spread into a warm grin. I couldn't help but laugh. The gaps from his missing teeth reminded me of a friendly jack-o'-lantern. I observed his Solin features. The rays of the persimmon sun reflected off his white-blond hair, and the bronze skin around his youthful eyes tightened as his elated expression grew. I laughed harder. He looked like a miniature version of Cyrus.

"Why aren't you with the other children?" I asked him.

He shoved his small hands into his pockets and twisted the toe of his boot into the soil. "I got bored playing hide-and-go-seek. My friends are slow. They're too easy to catch." He shrugged. "So I thought I'd watch your group train for a while."

He even sounded like my brother.

"Why don't you watch Jax and Cyrus's group?" I suggested. "They're a lot more exciting."

"I don't think that's a good idea."

"Why?"

"Because I already tried to hang out with Samson's group."

"What happened?" I asked.

The little Solin's eyes grew to the size of bottle caps. "He turned bright red and told me to scram. He even threw a stick at me."

I bit my lip, muffling my laughter.

"I don't think he likes me," the boy said.

"Don't sweat it, kid," Orion reassured him. "Samson doesn't like me either."

I shot my training partner a stern look.

"What? He doesn't."

I turned my attention back to Cyrus's mini-me. "Okay, you can stay here, but give us some room to work."

The boy nodded and scooted his boots an inch away from

my face. I huffed a breath. *And he listens equally well as my brother.*

Orion squeezed my wrists. "Shall we begin?"

I nodded and looked at the sea of faces above me. "To escape this hold, you must slide your arm above your head, tap your foot, and lift your hip."

With little effort, I pushed Orion off of me. The women exchanged hope-filled glances and the young boy applauded.

I dusted the grass off my back, then rolled onto my knees. "Don't get too excited. It's not as easy as it looks. Orion wasn't using any strength. We wanted to show you the proper steps before getting started."

A unanimous groan sounded around me. I ignored their complaints and signaled the Lunin to move into the dominant position once more.

"Now watch what happens if Orion uses force to restrain me," I said, lying on my back.

The women in the front squatted so the others could see.

"Do you want me to kick it up a notch or leave it on novice?" Orion asked me.

"Turn it up. Expert level," I whispered. "They need to see the dangers of a real altercation."

My training partner responded with a sharp breath, then pushed my wrists deeper into the ground.

THE SUN HAD TRACED an invisible arch across the sky while we taught the required steps to escape a ground hold.

Winded, I offered Orion my hand. "They need to try it now."

He mumbled his agreement as I pulled him to his feet. Dripping in sweat, I wiped the moisture from my neck and twisted my damp locks into a loose bun. I turned to Orion, then snorted at the ridiculous sight.

He peeled off his shirt like an actor filming a romantic scene in a movie. Heavy with lust, the women's eyelids struggled to stay open as they admired his toned physique. Orion added to his obnoxious performance by using his shirt to dab the excess sweat off his chest and neck.

He flashed me a mischievous grin.

"You're ridiculous," I chided.

"I'm telling Jax I caught you checking me out again."

"Fine. I'll tell him you insisted on taking off your shirt."

He scoffed at my threat.

I pointed at his sweat-lined abdomen. "You're a distraction to the group." I jerked my chin at a woman with her mouth hanging open. "They won't pay attention to me anymore."

Orion puffed out his chest and observed the women gawking at him. His sapphire eyes lit up once they settled on an attractive Solin who played with the short locks of her platinum blonde hair. Her tan skin shimmered in the sunlight, tiny beads of sweat dotting her slender arms. Orion locked eyes with his target and winked. The girl's cheeks flushed with heat.

I rolled my eyes. *Oh boy, here we go.*

The Solin covered her mouth and whispered to the Lunin beside her. The girl giggled, her black bangs falling into her eyes.

I grabbed Orion by the arm and spun him around so his back faced the love-struck duo. "It's on your conscious if these girls get too distracted and can't defend themselves against the Collectors. Sleep well knowing—"

"I'll be sleeping a hell of a lot better after tonight," he whispered, turning to see the blushing Solin.

"Keep it up and I'll tell Samson—"

My words faded at a gentle tug on my wrist. I looked down. Two amber eyes stared back—the young Solin.

"What's up, little man?"

He jerked my arm, pulling me closer. "Will you show us your special trick?" he asked, air whistling through the gaps of his missing teeth.

"What trick?"

"The trick you do with your brother."

"It's not a trick," I corrected. "We share each other's traits. We were born that way."

The boy puffed his cheeks, his eyes rolling back into his head. "I'm not talking about your shared traits. I'm talking about the fire thing you do with your hand."

I cursed, forgetting how rumors of our little trick had spread throughout the villages. Not to mention it slipped out of my mouth during my speech.

"Um." My eyes searched Iah's property for Cyrus. He held a Lunin in a grueling chokehold while Jax, acting as the instructor, spoke to the other men in their group. I looked at the young Solin. "My brother's a little busy right now. Maybe another time, okay?"

The boy shifted his features into a stone-cold expression that rivaled Jax.

I smiled, resting a hand on his shoulder. "What's your name, kid?"

"Blaze."

"That's a pretty cool name."

He lifted his chin, his Solin confidence shining forth. "It's the coolest name on Aroonyx. It means flame. My mom told me her lady parts were on fire when she gave birth to me."

I burst into laughter, unable to keep my composure.

"She said it hurt like hell." He gasped and covered his mouth. "I'm not supposed to say that word."

More laughter rumbled in my chest. Even his dramatic facial expressions reminded me of Cyrus. I kneeled in front of him. "How old are you, kid?"

"Seven and a half."

Out of my peripheral vision, I noticed a spark of curiosity ignite in the women's eyes. It was obvious they had overheard Blaze's question.

Noting my hesitation, Orion said, "I can't help you with this one." He lifted a finger at my brother. "But he can."

I contemplated Blaze's question and Orion's suggestion. The people who joined our cause knew I shared my brother's traits, but they had yet to witness how I absorbed his power. Samson wanted to show them our little trick, use it as an incentive. We disagreed with his request. It didn't feel right. We didn't want the people following us with blind eyes. They had already made that mistake with Zenith.

Blaze tugged at my hand. "Come on. Everyone's talking about it."

"No. Not right now."

"Pleeease."

"Just show us," a woman pleaded before I could respond.

"We want to see if the rumors are true," said another.

I swore under my breath when a Solin asked, "Why are you keeping this from us? We're risking our lives just being here. If you have something that gives us an advantage over Zenith, we need to know. It's only fair."

I eyed Orion. Once again, he pointed at Cyrus.

"I'll be back in a few minutes," I said to the group. I turned to the Lunin. "Tell them to grab a partner so they can practice escaping the ground hold."

He nodded and with a huge grin plastered on his face, he said, "Listen up, ladies. I want everyone to find a training partner and work on the maneuver we taught you earlier." He paused, his eyes roving over the attractive Solin. "Who needs a private lesson?"

The girl's hand, along with twenty others, shot in the air.

I shook my head at Orion before jogging toward my brother's group, then stood on the sidelines and waited for Jax to finish showing the men how to escape a headlock.

The combination of strenuous exercise and intense heat left their participants drenched in sweat. Over half trained without shirts; beads of moisture dripped down the Solins' muscular backs and the Lunins' toned abdomens. Their chests rose and fell with heavy breaths, winded from the grueling hand-to-hand combat.

My gaze darted toward the sound of a knife connecting with a tree. I groaned. *Oh no. Not the courage exercise.*

Samson wagged his finger at a terrified Lunin who stood with his spine pressed into the fuzzy bark. The man's eyes grew twice their normal size watching the ex-Collector reach for the embedded blade wedged above his head.

I cringed at the thought of the accused spy Samson confronted during the impromptu meeting. Jax had mentioned that after a quick yet intense interrogation, the man confessed his less-than-pure intentions. My partner's hands stayed clean that night but not Samson's. He sent the guilty party running back to Zenith's without a tongue.

I had made the mistake of asking Samson about the altercation. He just shrugged and said, "Your boyfriend passed on the opportunity, so I took matters into my own hands. No sweat off my back. Tongues are easier to remove than fingers."

Needless to say, I dropped the subject.

A loud thud shifted my attention back to my brother's group. He lay on his back with Jax standing over him. The men nodded at their instructors, then moved into position with their training partners.

I cupped my hands and called my brother's name. His head turned as Jax helped him to his feet.

A moment later he hurried to my side and through half breaths, he asked, "What's up, sis?"

"My group wants to see our trick."

His nose crinkled. "I thought we weren't—"

"So did I, but this kid kept bugging me to show him, and then the others overheard our conversation, which led to this woman asking me why we're keeping it a secret."

Cyrus wiped the sweat off his brow and eyed my group.

"They think it gives us an advantage over Zenith," I added.

"Who knows? Maybe it does." Cyrus crossed his arms. "But we already told Samson it won't do them any good to see our trick."

I watched Blaze fight the air with a stick. He poked a woman in the ribs. She hissed, snatching it from his hand. His playful expression turned sour once she snapped his new toy in half.

"It's too risky," Cyrus said. "We don't want them fighting on our side for the wrong reasons. Just tell them no."

"That's easier said than done."

"Well, what do you want me to do about it?" he snapped.

I balked at his harsh tone.

His shoulders slumped forward with a long sigh. "Sorry. This heat leaves me on edge."

Obviously. I noted the taut muscles twitching in his jaw and his constricting pupils; Jax's foreboding words rang in my ears. I frowned. *Something has changed—but what?*

"Cyrus, are you okay?"

"Yeah, I'm fine."

My chest caved. He couldn't look me in the eyes. I touched his arm. "I'm calling bullshit on that one. What's going on?"

"Nothing."

I wiggled my fingers in front of his face. He turned but stared at my forehead.

"Why are you lying to me?" I pressed. "There's something on your mind. I can tell."

"You're right. There is."

"Then what is it?"

He took a step backward and showed me his palms. "I don't want to talk about it, especially with you."

My jaw cracked open. "But we tell each other everything."

"Some things aren't worth mentioning."

We stood in an uncomfortable silence with our heads turned in opposite directions. A few blinks turned into seconds. I watched my group and Cyrus watched his. I adjusted my ponytail and Cyrus cracked his neck. I tapped my foot, urging him to say something. My pain-in-the-ass twin yawned, ignoring me altogether. Seconds turned into minutes.

After a long exhale he said, "Maybe we should talk to Samson."

"About what?"

He gave me a sidelong look. "His lack of affection toward us."

"Oh, so now you want to be funny?"

"Just trying to lighten the mood."

I faked a grin, still sore from our argument. "We should revisit our conversation with him. I'm not sure about your group, but mine could use some motivation."

He responded by flinging sweat at me.

I scowled, shielding my eyes from the droplets.

"Oh, I'm sorry. Is this bothering you?" He sent more beads flying in my direction. "It must be nice training the *easy* group."

"Thanks to Orion, I do have it easy." A smug grin crossed my face as I pointed to the shirtless Lunin. "They'll do whatever he asks."

Cyrus focused his attention on the Solin who had her long legs wrapped around Orion's hips. In no rush to escape the ground hold, he lay on his back with his hands tucked underneath his head.

"Lucky bastard. I want to switch groups. Why don't you and Jax work with the men? Orion and I will assist with the ladies."

"Sure thing." I spun on my heels. "I'll go inform Idalia of the new plan."

Cyrus grabbed my wrist, spun me back around, and used the palm of my hand to wipe the sweat off his abdomen.

I gagged. He laughed.

Sharing his Solin strength, I twisted out of his firm grip and slammed my knuckles into his bicep.

"Damn it, sis! That hurt." He massaged the tender area. "I'm already in enough pain from your boyfriend kicking my ass all day."

"Good. You deserve it."

He stuck out his tongue and tried to swat my top knot.

I slapped his hand away. "Why are you so annoying?"

"I'm your brother. It's my job to irritate you."

"Well, you deserve a promotion because you've mastered the skillset of driving your sister crazy." Cyrus pumped his fist in celebration. I motioned for him to follow. "Save that enthusiasm for Samson."

"No worries. I've got an endless supply," he said, draping his arm over me.

"Stop it." I did a spin maneuver and broke free. "I don't want your gross sweat all over me."

Cyrus let out a hearty laugh as I sprinted across the lawn toward Samson. My feet skidded to a stop at the sight of him waving a knife in a Lunin's face.

"Next time, you better keep your eyes open," he warned.

I called the Solin's name.

Without turning away from the frightened man, he asked, "What do you want, Elara?"

"Cyrus and I need to talk to you."

"I'm a little busy right now."

"It'll only take a minute."

Samson pointed the tip of his blade at the Lunin. "Go catch up with the others. We'll get back to this later."

The man dashed into the woods, covering the urine stains on his pants.

I shook my head in disapproval as Samson met me halfway. A smirk tugged at his mouth. "What?"

"Did you *literally* scare the piss out of that man?"

He shrugged and pocketed his knife. "The courage exercise can do that from time to time."

I may have felt sympathetic toward the unfortunate Lunin, but my growing smile said otherwise.

"And you call me an asshole," Samson chided.

"I have yet to make anyone piss their pants. I'm still on good terms with the people."

His broad shoulders shook with laughter.

"What's so funny?" Cyrus asked, taking his place beside me.

"Your sister." His expression fell flat. "Now why do you want to talk to me?"

"Elara wants to show everyone our trick."

My jaw cracked open. "Thanks for throwing me under the bus, bro."

He just smiled.

Samson folded his arms across his chest and said, "Why the change of heart, kid?"

"People are asking questions," I said, shielding my eyes from the afternoon sun. "They think we're doing them a disservice by keeping it a secret."

The ex-Collector's eyes bounced from one group to the next before meeting my gaze. "A little excitement can light a fire under someone's ass. Seeing you absorb Cyrus's power will give them some motivation. They'll know you have something Zenith doesn't."

Cyrus rubbed the back of his neck. "Yeah, but that's giving them false hope. Our trick can't protect them from Zenith and his Collectors."

"You don't know that."

My lips moved before my brother could protest Samson's response. "He's right. It might come in handy on the battlefield."

Cyrus blew out a long breath and palmed his eyes. Samson hollered for Jax to join us.

The former leader of the Inner Circle spoke near a man's ear before releasing him from a chokehold. After clapping the Solin on the back, Jax pointed to the man's training partner. Moments later he appeared at our side, tossing his damp hair out of his eyes.

"What's up?" he asked Samson.

The Solin gestured to the burn scar on Jax's wrist, the consequence of forcing Yarfrey into my wound after his knife sliced the palm of my hand during our first round of weapons training. Samson then touched his own faded injury, the one he brought upon himself the morning we showed him our trick at Idalia's. "Elara and Cyrus want to give a demonstration."

Jax's face squished up in confusion. "I thought—"

"You and me both," Cyrus interrupted. "But Elara and Samson think otherwise."

The Lunin found my eyes. "Are you sure you want to do this?"

"Honestly, Jax, I'm not sure about anything anymore. It seems like a practical decision. Our groups have no weapons to defend themselves. We're the only ones with knives, and we don't know Zenith's next move. What if we're being watched?"

At this comment, the three men turned, their eyes scanning the surrounding woods.

I adjusted my bun, slicking the flyaway hairs out of my face. "It's our job to keep these men and women safe. Yes, we're training them to fight, but it took me and Cyrus months to get to the level we are now. The women in my group lack confidence. They know what Pollux did to Idalia and they're freaked out. If they see me absorb Cyrus's power, they might feel safer."

"You make a valid point." Jax's eyes never left mine. "And remember, you don't need my or Samson's approval to make a decision." A quick glance at Cyrus. "This is between you and your brother."

I looked at my twin. We exchanged a head nod, a silent agreement to move forward with the next step in our journey.

I turned to Samson and Jax. "We're ready. Let's show them."

The Solin winked at me, then hollered, "Bring it in!" to the different groups.

Black and blond heads snapped toward us. Blaze bolted past the women, his eyes glowing with excitement.

The young boy clutched his side and panted, "Are you going to show me your cool trick now?"

My brother chuckled, nudging me in the arm. "Is this the kid you were telling me about?"

"Yep, sure is." I patted the boy's blonde head. "Cyrus, meet Blaze. Your mini-me."

He flashed the child a warm grin. "It's nice to meet you, Blaze."

As if he had won a meet-and-greet with his favorite celebrity, the child's mouth fell open, his tiny fingers trembling as he reached for my brother's hand. Cyrus let out an awkward laugh, surprised by the kid's starstruck reaction.

Well, that's both adorable and disappointing. It's obvious my brother's level of coolness surpasses mine.

As if making the connection, Jax caught my eye and chuckled.

Cyrus rested a hand on Blaze's shoulder. "Do you want to watch my sister release some heat from her hand?"

The child wiggled with excitement.

"I'm glad someone finds us entertaining," Cyrus whispered near my ear.

I nodded.

"Blaze, why don't you stand right here." My brother pointed to his left.

The boy hopped to the designated location, his toothless grin spreading from ear to ear.

Samson raised his hand, commanding the group's attention. "Listen up. I'm only going to say this once. The rumors about the twins are true." Boots shuffled closer. "Elara wants to demonstrate how she absorbs Cyrus's power. And don't bother asking her to see it again."

Yet to witness our unique ability with his own eyes, Orion quickened his pace, a line of women trailing behind him.

My heart thundered in my chest as I observed the curious faces. "Quick disclaimer before we get started. Even though my brother and I share this unique ability, remember, it doesn't make us powerful. Don't make the mistake of confusing the two."

I strained my ears for a murmur of agreement. Nothing, not even a whisper. Just my old pal, silence. I sighed through my nose. *I'm glad they're so attentive.*

Samson shook his head at the speechless crowd. "A little respect goes a long way. A simple head nod will suffice."

The Solins and Lunins nodded with great enthusiasm. Jax snickered and moved aside, allowing our audience a better view.

The steady wave of heat that flowed through me intensified once Cyrus grabbed hold of my hand. "Are you ready, sis?"

"Ready as I'll ever be."

30

HIDDEN CONCERNS

My arm vibrated as I absorbed Cyrus's power. I flexed the fingers of my right hand, a mirage of heat extending from my palm.

Jax whispered my name, his warm breath grazing my ear. With my eyes closed, I asked, "What is it?"

"Don't you need a volunteer to show them how it works?"

Shit. My eyes shot open. I looked at my twin. "How can I do this without hurting anyone?"

"Easy. You control the amount of heat you release. Think about it, sis. You did it that day with Samson and the morning you closed the wound on Jax's back. It'll be fine. Just focus."

My nails scratched at the heat desperate to leave my palm. "Yeah, but it still makes me nervous. And who do we use as a volunteer?"

Blaze's arm shot up.

"Nope. Not happening, kid," I said.

The crowd blew out a frustrated breath. Their patience was wearing thin.

Cyrus let go of my hand and squatted to meet the boy's gaze. "Are you brave?"

"You bet I am." He thumped his chest with a fisted hand. "I'm a Solin."

"Yes, yes, you are." Cyrus grinned. "Now answer me this: Where do you find courage?"

The tan skin on Blaze's nose crinkled. He looked at the others as if searching for the answer. A Lunin pointed at Cyrus while a Solin tapped his temple.

Blaze shrugged and turned to my brother. "I don't know. Where?"

"Right here," Cyrus said, resting his hand over the boy's heart.

"I thought courage was a Solin trait?"

"It is." Cyrus stood upright. "But *true* courage comes from within." He jerked his thumb at me and the former leader of the Inner Circle. "My sister and Jax are perfect examples. They're both Lunins and two of the bravest people I know."

My heart soared at the compliment, and my eyes lit up with relief watching the citizens smile at my brother. *Samson and Jax are wrong. The people will follow Cyrus.*

Blaze tugged at my brother's arm and whispered loud enough for everyone to hear, "But Jax was a Collector. He had to be brave."

I snorted. The Lunin responded to the claim with a choice four-letter word.

"Okay, kiddo." Cyrus chuckled. "You get to help us with the demonstration. Go on, take Elara's hand."

"No," I snapped, hiding my arm behind my back. "This has nothing to do with courage. It has everything to do with the child's safety. I won't risk hurting him."

My brother's eyes looked at the afternoon sky. "Elara, you're being dramatic again. He'll be fine."

Jax twisted my arm from its hiding place. "Listen to your brother."

"Okay, *dad*."

He snickered. Samson's cheeks puffed with boredom.

I straightened my shirt and rolled my neck. I could feel the dealer dying to add its two cents. The men and women in our groups shifted their weight. Once again, all eyes were on me. I huffed a breath. *No pressure.*

"So how does it work?" Blaze asked. "Do you think of a big fire or something cool?"

"If only it were that easy." My eyes drifted between the Solins and Lunins. "This talent of ours manifested a few months ago when we were training with Jax. I don't know how it works, and I don't know why I absorb Cyrus's power. I guess it's one of those unexplained events in life. And no, it doesn't work the other way around. He can't absorb my power. Our little trick is useless at night, but it saved our life during the day."

Roshan squeezed through the crowd and resumed his role as the interrogator. "So how does it work?"

Didn't I just answer that question? Jax rested his hand on the small of my back, reminding me of Roshan's role in this mission. His job was to ask the questions the others were afraid to mention.

I cleared my throat and focused my attention on the Solin. "Cyrus and I can share each other's Solin and Lunin traits if in proximity."

He nodded, familiar with this well-known fact.

"But during the day, when we connect"—I lifted our clasped hands—"I can absorb his power. The warmth in his body, the same that every Solin feels, transforms into a fiery river and flows into me. At first, I couldn't control the amount of heat that left my hand. But now I can."

A woman craned her neck around Roshan. "Can you show us?"

Cyrus spoke for us both. "Sure thing. Blaze, take Elara's hand."

The young boy laced his fingers around mine.

Everyone's heads turned, hearing the front door swing open. Iah and Idalia stepped onto the porch. The doctor used his arm as a visor to block the sun while the Solin used her powerful vision to find Cyrus in the crowd. She smiled and braced her delicate hands on the wooden railing, her platinum locks shimmering in the golden light.

"Let's do this, sis."

I sucked in a sharp breath and held it. Cyrus tightened his grip. The heated current rippled down my arm, concentrating in the hand that held Blaze. My pulse quickened. *Stay focused. Don't open the floodgates. Let it seep out—slowly.*

I gave Blaze a gentle squeeze to prepare him for the burst of heat. He stared at our clasped hands with unblinking eyes, as did the others. I released a drop of Cyrus's power, my teeth sinking into my bottom lip. The boy hissed, ripping his hand away from me.

"I'm so sorry." I fisted my hand and held it to my chest. "Did I hurt you?"

Blaze's voice came out in a breathless whisper. "No." A moment later, he raised his arm and showed the group his red palm.

Blank stares and furrowed brows. Their reaction was less than impressed.

I swore under my breath. *Yeah. That wasn't very exciting.*

Orion grimaced when a Solin mumbled, "I should have joined sides with Zenith."

Jax repeated his earlier choice word and Roshan asked, "That's it?" His face squished up in detest. "*That's* your special power? You're going to warm up the Collector's hands on the battlefield?" He turned to the man beside him. "Maybe they'll appreciate it during the winter and kill us quickly rather than slowly."

The Solins in the crowd roared with laughter, but the Lunins whispered their concerns to one another.

I gritted my teeth. Roshan excelled at playing the devil's advocate.

My brother tensed once the Solin added, "The rumors made it sound like you could do some permanent damage. Melt the skin right off the bones."

"People tend to exaggerate."

Roshan shrugged, picking at his nails.

"We can turn up the heat," Cyrus said. "Elara didn't want to hurt Blaze."

"Prove it," Roshan said.

"No." I glared at the pot stirrer. "I won't injure a child to prove a point. Just take our word for it."

"Use me," Samson said, motioning for Blaze to scram.

The child paled and stumbled backward, crashing into Jax. His amber eyes widened with terror, and they almost fell out of his head when the Lunin steadied his trembling body.

"Easy, kid," Jax whispered. "I won't hurt you."

Blaze froze, stifling a tiny whimper.

Samson offered me his scarred wrist. My face fell.

"Elara, don't give me that pathetic look. Just do it."

"I can't help it. I don't want to—"

"I don't give a shit," he snapped. "This isn't about you, so shut the fuck up and do as you're told." Ignoring the shock that stained my face, Samson grabbed my hand and wrapped it around his wrist. "Turn up the heat and don't stop until I give the signal."

"Fine," I sneered, tightening my grip. "I'll turn it up to level *asshole*."

Orion and Cyrus laughed. Jax just sighed and pinched the bridge of his nose.

Samson muttered a slew of curse words before looking at

my brother. "Are you ready to get to work or are you going to mirror your sister's attitude and start acting like a little bitch?"

Cyrus stared at the Solin through tiny slits. I clenched my jaw, the heat in my hand building. Jax cleared his throat to remind us of our audience.

"You heard the man," I said to my brother. "Don't stop until he gives the signal."

Cyrus's lips curled into a wicked smirk. "Copy that, sis. Here it comes."

I opened the floodgates, pleased with the satisfaction that followed. This moment passed once Samson's body writhed in pain.

The crowd gasped, their eyes following the plume of smoke that rose from his burning wrist. The ex-Collector's leathery skin softened under my warm touch. My fingers sank deeper into the melting flesh. His face turned a bright shade of red as he fell to his knees. I didn't let go, even when he bared his teeth at me.

My heart raced, the forceful thumps releasing more heat out of my hand. I cringed. *I can't do this anymore. I'm not defending myself from an attack. I'm purposely hurting someone.*

But isn't it fun, Elara? Having all that power. The power to control others at your will.

I gasped, hearing the dealer's voice, then loosened my grip.

Samson rested his free hand on top of mine, forcing my compliance. Through gritted teeth, he hissed, "Not yet. They need to see the damage with their own eyes."

The dealer cackled, its icy breath welcoming the darkness. *Do it, Elara. You know you want to.*

"Okay," I said to Samson and the dealer. "How's this?"

The Solin hollered at the top of his lungs. Men swore and women covered their sons' and daughters' eyes. Seconds later, he gave me the signal by curling his free hand into a fist.

Snapped out of my trance, I let him go. Regret filled my eyes after I noticed his scorched wrist. "Damn it, Samson. I told you I didn't want to do this."

"Don't feel bad, sis. He asked for it."

Blaze poked his head between me and my brother. "Whoa! I bet that hurts."

Samson ignored the child and raised his arm for everyone to see. A hush fell over the group.

Roshan walked up to Samson and investigated the injury by rotating his wrist back and forth. "Damn. That's one hell of a burn."

"I told you," he whispered. "That trick of theirs is no joke."

A large grin crossed Roshan's unshaven face. He clapped Samson on the back. "It changes things, that's for sure."

I spun around at the sound of Iah's voice. "Samson," he called. "Come inside and let me tend to that wound."

"Nah, I'm good."

"I get it, Samson." I gestured to the crowd. "We all do. You're a tough old bastard, but if that burn gets infected, you'll be useless on the battlefield." I pointed at Iah who stood waiting on the porch. "Go on, let the doctor do his job."

Samson mocked my speech until his index finger touched his melted flesh. The tip disappeared into the burn. Without saying a word, he spun on his heels and stormed off toward the house.

"Well, that was fun," Cyrus whispered.

"Fun is taking a summer vacation or moving into your college dorm. Two things we don't get to do, bro. This"—I dangled my hand in his face, then flicked it at the speechless crowd—"is a strange version of hell."

"You do realize I was being sarcastic?"

I faked a cry, pressing my palms into my brows.

"Shows over," Jax said to the men and women. "Get back to your training."

Blaze pouted watching the others dispersed. My group

chased after Orion as if he were an ice cream truck handing out free treats. I smiled at their girlish behavior. *He is rather sweet.*

Jax shook his head at me, his lips twitching with amusement.

Ignoring him, I looked at the young Solin. "It's time for you to go play with the other kids. We have to get back to work."

He groaned, scooting closer to Cyrus. "I don't want to. They're boring."

"Then come hang out with my group," my brother suggested. "I'll train you myself."

"*Cyrus.*"

"What? He's a tough kid. I bet he can handle it." He looked at Blaze. "How old are you?"

"Seven. Almost eight."

Cyrus slapped a hand over his face. "Seven, almost eight! Elara, the kid's practically a man."

I bit my lip to keep from laughing.

"How about it, Jax? At his age you were—" My brother paused, realizing his error.

Memories of Jax's turbulent upbringing cast a dark shadow over the Lunin's face. He shut his eyes and nodded at my brother.

Without delay, Blaze grabbed Cyrus's hand and dragged him toward the group of men practicing their chokeholds.

I frowned at the somber Lunin. I tried to get him to smirk by saying, "I think Blaze has replaced Rico."

No luck. Just a curt nod.

I touched his arm.

"It's fine," he said, patting my hand. "I'm fine."

"Are you sure?"

"Yes."

I chewed on my cheek. "Really?"

He scowled. "Elara. I'm not emotionally unstable. I was, but I'm not anymore. The comments people make, the way they see me, the way *Aarush* sees me." His shoulders sagged with a tired breath. "It's the price I must pay for all the stupid shit I've done over the years." He lifted my hand and kissed my knuckles. "I'm sorry you have to witness it all. I don't want their opinions affecting the way you see me."

"I'm not easily swayed by others. I know who you are, Jax. You're one of the good guys. You might have a dark past, but your future is lit by the light of a thousand suns."

"That was very poetic." He smirked. "Did you think of that on your own, or did you steal it from a book?"

I smacked him in the chest. "That was an Elara original. I was trying to be romantic, but you ruined it."

"Forgive my lack of sensitivity." His smirk grew. "It's obvious my dark past still lingers."

"For your information, Orion is a lot nicer. He would have made a great boyfriend."

Jax watched the Lunin who stood nearby, chatting with the attractive Solin. His lips drooped into a frown. "Tough break, Elara. After today, I doubt he'll stay single. You might have to search my group for a man who meets your requirements." Jax stretched his neck. "Ah yes, I see a strapping young Lunin around your age. Shall I introduce the two of you? I think his name is Nova."

"Are you done?"

He answered me by slipping his tongue into my mouth. I wanted to push him away, but desire guided me right into his arms.

"Patience," he teased, pulling away.

My mouth moved to retaliate but paused when his eyes narrowed over my shoulder.

His lips formed a tight line. "It appears my attention is required elsewhere."

I turned. Two men faced each other, their cheeks flushed with anger. The tallest shoved his training partner in the chest, sending the Solin stumbling backward. The man recovered by swinging his fist.

Jax cursed. "Solins and their short tempers. I wish they'd save that angst for the battlefield."

"Have fun dealing with those two."

"Yeah, like I have time for their petty shit," he muttered, jogging toward the enraged men.

"Patience," I said loud enough for him to hear.

His shoulders shook with laughter as he waved me away.

Not wanting to delay our training more than I already had, I hurried to catch up with my group. The women pouted—they literally pouted after I told Orion to put on his shirt.

"But it's too hot," he complained. "I don't want to overheat."

The women sided with the Lunin, voicing their concerns for his well-being.

"We're standing in the shade," I argued.

"Shade or not," he countered. "The extra material weighs me down."

More murmurs of agreement.

"They're too distracted," I whispered.

"But it's so fun."

"Put on your damn shirt."

With great reluctance, he obliged, slipping it over his head. "Cyrus is right. You are a dream crusher."

31

BETTER LEFT UNSAID

"I think that's enough for today," I said, gesturing to the rain clouds in the distance.

Orion turned his head to the sky, allowing the strong breeze to cool his tepid skin. He stretched his arms and wiped the sweat from his brow before observing the group of women, who lay sprawled on their backs after the grueling training. "They're getting better."

"Yeah, and it's only been two weeks since we taught them those ground holds. Did you see that Lunin block my attack today?"

"Nope." A mischievous smile played on his lips. "I was too distracted with my own training."

I gave him a sidelong look. "You mean distracted by Oriana."

His eyes slid to the Solin, his new lady friend who required private lessons every morning and afternoon. "I can't help it." He shrugged. "She likes me."

"They *all* like you."

"And to think." He let out a dramatic sigh, tossing his shirt over one shoulder. "A few seasons ago, I only had eyes for you."

I aimed my knuckles at his ribcage and swung. Lightning flashed as he dodged my attack. I flinched at the rolling thunder.

"Elara!"

I turned at the sound of my brother's voice.

He pointed at the darkening sky. "Are we done for today?"

I cupped my hands around my mouth and yelled back, "Yeah. The rain will be here soon."

Cyrus turned to his group and held up a fist, signaling the men to cease their combative training.

Curious of Jax's whereabouts, I scanned Iah's property and found him leaning against a tree with Blaze's amber eyes fixed on his pale hands. The ex-Collector ran a finger over the silver etchings on Zenith's blade. The child marveled at the ease in which Jax opened and closed the knife with one hand.

I faced my group and said, "Good job, ladies. Your combative skills are improving." I motioned to the branches that fought against the strong gust. "Enjoy the cooler weather before the storm. We'll continue where we left off tomorrow."

Sore from sparring, the women winced as they climbed to their feet. Oriana lingered, waiting for Orion. She lay on her back, the locks of her blonde hair creating a majestic halo around her face. Accepting her silent invitation, Orion strolled toward the Solin and lowered himself beside her. I chuckled at the romantic comedy that unfolded before my eyes.

Oriana kept her gaze focused on the gathering clouds while Orion tucked his hands underneath his head. His leg brushed against hers. The subtle advance stained her cheeks a dusty rose. Oriana's full lips parted, whispers rolling off her tongue. The Lunin rolled onto his side and picked a blade of grass from her hair. He held it in the air and let the breeze carry it away before running his fingers down the length of her arm. She responded to his gentle touch by flashing him a coy smile. His sapphire eyes lit up as he leaned closer.

I cocked my head to one side, intrigued by their opposite yet striking features. *Orion and Oriana. Isn't that cute. They could name their kid Oreo.*

Eager to feel clean after my day of training, I hurried toward the house. The thought of a long soak vanished at the sight of a Solin heading straight for me. The woman held her head high; her stunning features reminded me of Idalia. Her flawless complexion and high cheekbones shimmered in the dull light as if she had applied bronzer. I gulped. The Solin didn't smile. She just stormed toward me, tossing the blonde curls out of her flame-colored eyes.

I tugged at my shorts, feeling self-conscious about my appearance. *Why do the Solin women resemble Victoria Secret models?*

Her tiny waist and curvy hips accentuated her hour-glass figure, and her supple breasts bounced in slow motion, causing men to nearly trip over their feet. One did. A young Lunin almost face-planted into the ground. His buddy caught him by the arm, only to ridicule him with a hard jab to the shoulder.

The woman offered me her hand in way of greeting.

Intoxicated by her beauty, I stumbled over my words. "It's ... Elara. My name ... that is."

"Thea." She faked a grin and shook my fingers, not my hand. "I figured it was time to meet the famous *Elara*."

I smacked my lips. The amount of sarcasm in her tone coated my taste buds in a bitter residue. "It's nice to meet you."

She shrugged, indifferent to my salutation. Lightning flashed, the bolt reflecting in her eyes. "Those chokeholds are tough," she said. "But thanks to Orion, I'm getting the hang of it."

I folded my arms across my chest. *Is she trying to make me uncomfortable?*

As if hearing my inner dialogue, a tiny smirk tugged at her perfect mouth. A slithery, slimy smirk.

I returned the gesture and said, "I'm glad you're finding his training technique helpful."

Her smirk grew into a grin. "You can say that again."

I recoiled. The viper struck.

Thea's fierce eyes roved over me with indiscretion. I shifted my weight, bothered by her careless stare.

Her gaze drifted over my shoulder. "Can I ask you a personal question?" My lips moved to say *hell no*, but her sharp tongue beat me to the punch. "Are you and Jax together?"

I stammered; the simple question caught me by surprise. "Yeah . . . we are."

Thea raised her chin, along with her pointy nose.

Curious why she kept glancing over my shoulder, I turned. My jaw clenched, nails digging into my palms.

Jax looked in our direction. He met my gaze before stealing a glance at Thea, and his posture tensed. I gritted my teeth. Her lips curled into a seductive grin as she wiggled her long fingers at Jax. He acknowledged her with a subtle head nod before continuing his knife lesson with Blaze.

My heart pounded, a war drum preparing for battle. I glared at my new archrival. "How do you know Jax?"

"*Sweetie.*" Her condescending tone made me want to slap her across the face. "Do you really want me to answer that question?" She frowned at my bouncing leg. "You look a little uncomfortable."

My jaw cracked open. *Hillary. That's who she reminds me of. Cyrus's ex-girlfriend.*

A familiar cackle disrupted my trip down memory lane. I rolled my neck. *Go away. I don't need your help.*

Elara, you could use my advice. Let me show you how to handle girls like Thea.

No. Leave me alone.

Thea let out a dramatic sigh. "Did you plan anything special for Jax tonight?"

"What the hell is that supposed to mean?" I snapped.

Shit. I clutched my throat. The masked dealer had spoken for me.

"It means exactly what I asked," she snapped back. "Did you plan anything special for his birthday?"

My eyelashes fluttered. "It's his birthday?"

Thea's pout face mirrored Hillary's expression the day I tried waving at Cyrus in the school's cafeteria, only to be humiliated by her cheerleader friends.

My fingers curled into a fist. I had the sudden urge to drive my knuckles through her perfect teeth.

Do it, Elara.

I raised my arm. The Solin arched a brow. Recovering, I pretended to stretch, then faked a yawn.

It was obvious Thea saw my self-control as a weakness, so she struck, attacking me with venom-filled words. "*You* of all people should know about Jax's birthday. I thought girlfriends kept up with that sort of thing."

Baring my teeth, I spat, "Isn't that a *mother's* responsibility?" I doused my words with a sickening sweetness and added, "But thanks for the heads-up. I'll be sure to give Jax a special birthday surprise later this evening when we're alone."

"How's that working out for you, Elara?"

I couldn't respond because my tongue tripped over my teeth.

"Figures." She snickered. "It takes a confident woman to accept Jax's past." She held up her hand, silencing my rebuttal. "And I'm not talking about his time as a Collector."

My wide-eyed expression must have been what curled her lips into a pout—*again.*

"Awe, poor girl. You're unfamiliar with that part of his past, aren't you?" She didn't wait for me to respond. "I guess it's not appropriate for him to share his number with his newest fling. That would make it awkward in the bedroom." Her nails dug into my skin as she hissed near my ear. "Perhaps some things are better left unsaid."

I stood motionless, utterly speechless.

"I enjoyed our little chat, Elara." She pivoted, eyeing me over her shoulder. "Until next time."

I blinked and blinked again. My encounter with Thea had transformed my sharp mind into a muddy bog of confusion, littered with bits of anger. Slack-jawed, I watched her stroll through the woods with her shoulders rolled back and her head held high—victorious. *Bitch.*

I whipped around, my eyes fixed on Jax. *Idalia mentioned he was popular with the ladies.* My heart plummeted into the icy pit of my stomach. *But to what extent?*

I shut my eyes, searching for the fragment of common sense that hid behind the veil of jealousy. Jax had shared every detail regarding his dark past and answered my questions without hesitation. I chewed on my nail. *But I never asked about his romantic past.*

I hummed my silent concerns. *Why does he insist that we wait to have sex? Wait for what? Marriage?* I blew out a frustrated breath. *No, that can't be it. He didn't wait with these other women.*

A growl rumbled in my chest. *Other women.* Those two words sent an invisible fireball shooting out of my eyes, one ignited by jealousy. I aimed it at Jax.

The barometric pressure dropped, sending the strands of my hair flying in every direction. I gathered the tangled locks into a ponytail and cursed aloud. *What am I doing? His previous relationships are none of my business. I can't be the crazy girlfriend who creates unnecessary drama. Jax is a good man. His past doesn't define him.*

I nodded, pleased with my level of maturity.

The phantom fireball slowed its pursuit until an attractive Lunin approached the ex-Collector. I sneered, slamming the burning ball of jealously right into him. Unaffected by my destructive mind games, Jax smiled at the woman and reached for her extended hand.

Are you sure you don't want my help, Elara? This is my area of expertise.

Go away.

Jax's eyes lit up, his fingers lingering on hers.

You should express your concerns. The dealer's voice slithered through my mind. *Inquire about his past relationships. He prides himself with his honest approach to life. You deserve some answers.*

You're right, I do.

Its icy breath tickled my ear. *I'm always right, Elara. Don't forget that.*

I won't.

Good girl. Now go.

I sucked in a sharp breath and stood tall, my eyes never leaving my mark.

Go on. What are you waiting for?

A dangerous smile spread across my face. *Not a damn thing.*

I stormed toward Jax, all previous concerns of acting like the crazy, jealous girlfriend dissolving in my wake.

32

A JUSTIFICATION

Watching my heated pursuit, Jax dropped the woman's hand. The wind howled, and lightning flashed overhead.

The Lunin gathered the long layers of her black hair and smiled at Jax. "Thanks again. I know it meant a lot to him. He really misses his father."

The ex-Collector bowed his head. "It was my pleasure."

"Come on, Blaze." The woman tugged at his hand. "We should get to the tent before the storm breaks."

The boy groaned, toeing a fallen branch.

She jiggled his arm and whispered, "What do you say to him?"

Another flash of lightning illuminated the gold flecks in Blaze's eyes as he looked at Jax. "Thanks for showing me Zenith's knife."

The woman cringed at the name, but Jax simply stated, "Anytime, kiddo."

"Come on," she pressed, noting my rigid posture. "We've taken up enough of his time."

Jax watched them stroll through the forest with kind eyes. A stark contrast to the scowl smeared across my face. I didn't bother shielding myself from the drizzle that fell from the sky. No, I welcomed the rain and the thunder that followed.

In a tone that rivaled the sharpness of Zenith's blade, I asked, "Who the hell was that?"

Jax turned to face me, his boots sliding in the damp grass. "Blaze's mother."

"Oh." My arms fell to my sides.

"Why? Who did you think she was?"

"One of your admirers."

"Why would you say that?"

"I'm sure you can figure it out. You're always ten steps ahead of me."

"All right." Jax grabbed my wrist and dragged me farther under the tree to avoid the downpour. He crossed his arms and widened his stance. "You're upset, I can see that now."

"I'm not upset."

He scoffed, tossing the wet hair out of his eyes. "I've told you this before and I'll say it again: Elara, you're a horrible liar."

I glared, not an ounce of amusement played on my lips.

Jax touched my arm. "What's going on?"

My voice raised an octave. "Happy Birthday." The muscles in his chiseled jaw twitched. I pressed on. "Why didn't you tell me?"

"I don't celebrate my birthday." His stern tone shifted to a more somber one when he added, "In my opinion, it's just another day."

"Noted. In the future, I won't throw you a party."

He huffed a breath.

"I wish you would have told me so I didn't look like an idiot in front of your ex-girlfriend."

Jax's pupils constricted as he tossed up his hands. "I don't even know what you're talking about right now."

"Thea! I'm talking about Thea."

"That woman was *never* my girlfriend."

"Then who was she?"

The Lunin wiped the rain that dripped into his eyes. My pulse quickened. He never hesitated if asked a question.

I cleared my throat. "Well?"

He sucked in a sharp breath, and after a crack of thunder, he said, "Thea was a girl I spent time with."

"Right. You just admired her assets from afar." The masked dealer continued to move my lips. "You've got great taste, Jax. Thea is a real classy bitch."

"Jealousy was never a good look for you." His voice lowered to a growl. "Let me give you some advice. If you ask me a question, expect an honest answer."

Asshole. His snide comment echoed my brother's words the first night I met Idalia. Refusing to back down, we stood facing each other in the pouring rain. Jax kept his calm and cool demeanor while I gritted my teeth.

He lowered his gaze, a smirk crawling across his lips. "Are we fighting?"

I folded my arms across my chest.

"Oh, come on," he drawled. "You can't judge me for my past relationships."

"I sure as hell can. Especially if those relationships follow you into the present."

The Lunin swore.

I poked him in the chest. "I understand why you kept Idalia a secret, but after my encounter with Thea, I'm wondering if I should sell tickets for a women's convention—a reunion called *My Intimate Time with Jax.*"

He pinned me with a long stare. "Are they handing out awards at this convention? If so, I nominate you for *Best Dramatic Performance.*"

My jaw fell open.

"Idalia has nothing to do with this." His voice raised. "And

Thea is one woman, so stop acting like the girls from my past are approaching you left and right."

"*Fine*," I hissed. "Forget I brought it up."

He shook his head at me. "Why are you being like this? I've told you how I feel."

"Have you?" A bolt of lightning lit up the sky. "Unlike you, I express my emotions on more than one occasion."

"I shared my feelings the day I returned. I assumed—"

"And that's where you went wrong, Jax. *Never* assume anything with me."

He shut his eyes and let out a long exhale. I ended the argument by storming off. Jax grabbed my wrist. Our positions reflected the night he approached me on Earth, the night he confessed my relation to Cyrus.

I yanked my arm out of his firm grip, and without turning around, I said, "Don't follow me."

He didn't respond. He just watched me go.

A wave of negative emotions crashed against my mind as I sloshed through the muddy yard.

I fisted my hands, hearing the dealer's wicked laughter. *Thanks for the advice. That went worse than expected.*

I think it was a very productive conversation, Elara. You put Jax in his place.

I rolled my neck. *Shut up. I never asked for your opinion.*

"Trouble in paradise, sis?"

I flashed my brother a vulgar gesture, hurrying up the stone steps of the front porch.

He hopped to his feet. "*And* that's my cue."

Idalia chuckled and leaned into Cyrus's touch as he kissed the top of her head. Like a giant inchworm, he scooted across the porch with the lower half of his body pressed into the wooden railing.

I raised my fist and motioned to strike when he passed.

"Don't act like Hillary," he blurted before darting into the house.

I collapsed onto the chair beside Idalia and let out a long breath. Following her gaze, I observed how the raindrops pooled on the massive leaves before trickling to the ground. *Interesting.* The foliage on Aroonyx stayed green, regardless of the season. And the grass never faded in color. I used my shirt to wipe the water off my face. *I wonder why.*

"Do you want to talk about it?"

My head turned. "Talk about what?"

Idalia snapped her fingers. "Focus, Elara."

"Sorry. I got distracted by the . . . leaves."

"Yes, they're lovely, now tell me what happened with Jax."

"It's not worth mentioning."

"I bet it is," she argued. "Cyrus and I couldn't hear your conversation, but your body language told us you were fighting."

I slouched in my chair. "You saw that, huh?"

"Jax is my closest friend. I know his mannerisms well."

"You and every other woman on Aroonyx."

Idalia grabbed the armrest and slid my chair closer to hers, an easy feat for a Solin with superhuman strength. She twisted in her seat to face me. "What's with the snarky attitude?"

I sighed, finding her golden eyes. "Did you know it was Jax's birthday?"

"Yeah. Why?"

"Figures."

"Please tell me you're not mad because he didn't tell you it was his birthday."

"No."

She arched a brow at the lie.

"Okay, maybe I'm a little mad." A poor attempt at a recovery. "But there's more to the story."

Reminding me of a therapist, Idalia inhaled the smallest of breaths, crossed her ankles, and folded her petite hands in her lap. All she needed was a notepad, pen, and a pair of glasses to complete the look. In a calm voice, she said, "Jax doesn't celebrate his birthday."

"Why not?"

"Because unpleasant memories surround that day."

"Which are?"

Idalia bit her lip. A Solin hesitating wasn't a good sign.

She shifted her gaze to the forest. I strained my ears to hear her speak over the heavy rain. "On Jax's sixth birthday the Collectors kidnapped him and brought him to Zenith, who murdered his parents on that same day. On Jax's seventh birthday Zenith started his combative training with Pollux and the other Collectors, and on his twelfth birthday Zenith named him the leader of the Inner Circle."

Shit. I shut my eyes. *Way to overreact . . . as usual.*

"He told you about his knife, right?"

I touched my back pocket and forced a head nod, still dazed by the morbid timeline Idalia shared. "It was a gift from Zenith. An award for his new position with the Inner Circle."

"No. It was a birthday gift. Zenith called him into his personal chambers and showered Jax with praise, telling him he was the son he always wanted, and how he had the knife custom designed to help with the accuracy of his aim."

I blinked. "I had no idea."

"It's crazy, right? To think of Zenith showing kindness to Jax."

I pulled the folded blade from my pocket. "After everything Zenith's done, why does he keep this damn knife?"

"If I had to guess, I'd say it's because of his attachment to Zenith—the one he refuses to let go." My nose crinkled. "Think about it, Elara. Jax lived with him for over six years, and during that time, he rarely left his adoptive father's side. Zenith tutored him in basic studies, combative strategy, and the art of acquiring information from the accused."

341

"You mean he taught him how to torture innocent people."

She nodded—slowly. "They even ate their meals together, secluded from the other Collectors. Zenith awarded Jax special privileges, bought him the nicest clothes, and gave him a private chamber. The list goes on and on."

I braced my elbows on my knees and dropped my head into my hands. "How is Jax not a heartless criminal? Six years isn't forever, but that's a long time to spend with a ruthless killer."

She responded with a casual shrug, then said, "Sometimes I wonder if he ever loved Zenith like a father, or if a small part of him still does."

I didn't blink. I just stared at the rainwater that pooled near my feet. Combining the words Zenith and love in the same sentence sounded wrong. No, it sounded disturbing. I rubbed my tired eyes, forbidden thoughts zipping through my mind. *Does Jax see Zenith as his father? Did they ever have a "good" relationship? Doubtful. Zenith is a sadist and a master at manipulation. I bet the "kindness" he showed Jax was all a ruse. Zenith always wanted a Seeker, and when he got one, Jax wouldn't jump for him. He couldn't. The intention wasn't pure.*

I lifted my chin and turned to Idalia. "Now I understand why Jax got pissed when I asked about his birthday."

"I'm surprised he did."

"Why wouldn't he? It makes sense after everything you told me."

"Elara, you're only hearing this story for the first time." She gathered her hair over one shoulder and separated the strands into three sections. "Jax *lived* this story. It's old news to him. Asking about his birthday wouldn't piss him off." She gave me a sidelong glance. "He's not a sensitive guy."

"Yeah, I guess you're right." Thea's perfect figure flashed before my mind's eye. "It wasn't the birthday comment that set him off."

"Then what was it?"

"I brought up his romantic past."

Her cheeks puffed. "That'll do it."

"I never thought about it until this woman approached me today. Her name was Thea and—"

"She's here?" Idalia's brows raised.

"Yeah. Do you know her?"

The Solin groaned. "Yep. We grew up together. Thea was my best friend."

"That makes sense. You look like sisters: both beautiful, perfect."

Idalia chuckled. "Haven't you noticed? We all look the same."

"Yes, Solins are physically attractive but you and Thea resemble Greek goddesses."

"What's a Greek goddess?"

"Forget it." *Note to self: stop the Earth references.* "So you and Thea were best friends?"

"Mm-hmm. We were inseparable, then one day she stopped talking to me."

"She ghosted you?"

"What does that mean?"

Damn it. I did it again. "Sorry, I'll cool it with the Earth lingo. Why did she stop talking to you?"

"I'll give you one guess."

"The man of the hour?"

She tossed her braided hair behind her back before speaking. "Thea got jealous of my relationship with Jax. It was just the two of us until he showed up. Jax needed a place to hide after he took you and Cyrus to Earth because Zenith sent the Collectors on the largest manhunt since the Clearing of the Seekers. I asked my mother if he could stay with us, and she agreed. It wasn't long before our friendship evolved into something more."

I held my tongue. *I'm sure it did.*

343

"Jax listened. He actually *listened* to what I had to say, and he always had my back. He helped me discover the truth about my friendship with Thea."

"What truth?"

"Our relationship was superficial, one-sided. I put in all the effort and got nothing in return. We grew apart, which isolated Thea. She blamed me and retaliated by seducing Jax. When they were together—"

"Bastard." I slammed my palm against the armrest. "He lied to me. He said Thea was never his girlfriend."

"She wasn't. They shared a bed and nothing more. He never had an emotional connection with her. Thea was no different from the other women in his life."

"The other women?" My eyes bulged. "Geez, Idalia. How many girls has Jax slept with?"

She tried to hide her laughter.

"It's not funny," I scolded.

"I'm sorry." She touched my arm. "Jax was a very different person back then. He didn't care for these women. They were a temporary escape from the emotional turmoil he suffered."

My stomach did a nauseating flip at the thought of Jax enjoying the company of other women. "Idalia, tell me the truth. Has he slept with every unmarried woman on Aroonyx?"

She grimaced. "Marriage was a gray area for him."

The color drained from my rosy cheeks.

Her grimace grew. "Sorry, that made him sound like an asshole."

"You think?"

"In his defense, Aroonyx has a tiny population."

I tossed up my hands. "Is this real life?"

"For Jax it was."

I faked a cry. "Please tell me he doesn't have kids running around Aroonyx or Earth?"

"Who knows? Maybe?"

My shocked reaction triggered more laughter from Idalia. "I'm teasing," she said. "Jax didn't father any children. He was always careful in that department."

"How responsible of him." I rolled my eyes. "So I'm the only girl he hasn't slept with."

She blinked hard. "The two of you haven't had sex?"

"No! He gets all weird and stops us before anything happens."

She hummed. I couldn't tell if it was out of concern or understanding until she said, "Jax has gone through a lot of shit this year. He's different now."

A disheartening thought slapped me upside the head. I gasped, finding the Solin's eyes. "What if it's me?"

"Stop being dramatic."

"I'm not. It's a valid concern. Jax has had a ton of sexual partners. I've had none. Maybe he finds me boring because I lack the magical bedroom skills you and the other girls have."

"Elara, you're being ridiculous. We didn't take a class on how to have sex."

I grabbed her hand. "No, but you can teach me."

She pulled away, her brow furrowing with confusion. "Um . . . I don't participate in same-sex activities, but I have plenty of friends who would be more than happy to show you—"

"No," I corrected. "I'm not wanting private lessons."

"You made it sound that way."

"That's not what I meant." I blew out a frustrated breath. "What if you drew me a picture with detailed instructions or something?"

A veil of darkness draped over the Solin. The light in her eyes dimmed as she observed the muddy puddles around Iah's property. "Sorry, Elara." Her voice was cold and distant. "Sex is the last thing on my mind right now."

My shoulders caved inward. *I'm such an idiot.* I wanted to

crawl into a hole and never come out after making such an insensitive suggestion.

"Forgive me," I murmured. "I need to think before speaking."

"It's okay," she whispered. "Each day gets a little better."

I squeezed her hand. "You're doing great. We're all proud of you. My brother included."

"He's a great guy and so is Jax."

"If you say so."

Idalia held both of my hands and straightened. "His past relationships don't shape your future together. Jax respects you, Elara. That's probably the reason he's making you wait."

I massaged the base of my skull, my neck tight with tension. "Did he wait with you?"

She leaned back in her chair. "No. We took that step way too young. I got attached because he was my first. Jax broke my heart after he came of age."

"Why?"

"He turned into a different person. I think the emotions surrounding his past finally caught up with him." She frowned. "That's when the other girls came into his life. We went our separate ways but hooked up anytime we hung out." She swallowed. "He was so distant. He'd stop by the pub, grab a drink, then we'd go upstairs, have sex, and that was it. Afterward, we wouldn't even talk. He'd just get up, get dressed, and leave. I wouldn't see him for weeks."

"I'm sorry," was all I could manage.

"Sex is great, but it's a hell of a lot better if you share an emotional connection with your partner."

I nodded, though I had no life experience to back up her claim.

"Each time Jax paid me a visit, he appeared less like himself and more like *them*."

"Who?"

"The Collectors."

"But he was living on his own back then. Hiding in the woods."

"It didn't prevent him from acting like Elio and the others. An arrogant, entitled asshole."

My head swayed with mixed feelings. "He still acts that way."

She chuckled. "Perhaps, but at least he's not cruel." Her amusement spread into a large grin as she nudged me in the ribs. "His attitude changed once he met this girl on Earth."

I smiled, though my heart ached.

"And shortly after, he ended the physical side of our relationship."

I looked away. We sat in silence; words no longer felt appropriate. Idalia drummed her nails on the aged wood while I shut my eyes, the humidity suffocating me.

A few heartbeats later, I stood and stretched my arms. I needed to process our conversation alone, and the bathtub seemed like the perfect place to find solace.

"Thanks for the chat," I murmured.

"I wasn't much help." She pointed at the hard lines on my face. "You're still upset."

I headed toward the door, muttering, "It is what it is."

"Do you believe everything happens for a reason?"

A clap of thunder shook the house. I curled my fingers around the doorknob, and with my back facing her, I answered, "Yeah. I think so."

The chair creaked under her weight. "Sometimes it helps me justify shitty situations."

I didn't have to read her thoughts to know Pollux had crossed her mind. Her disheartened tone said it all.

I twisted the knob, pushed open the door, and glanced at the Solin before entering the home. "And sometimes it helps me justify the truth."

33

AN UNEXPECTED PROPOSAL

My eyes found Samson once I stepped over the threshold. He sat with his broad shoulders wedged between the high-back armchair, his bandaged wrist resting in his lap.

A look of bewilderment crossed my brother's unshaven face as he gaped at the Solin. He waved his hands in front of him. "You mean to tell me you tortured that poor bastard for three days?"

"I had no choice." Samson stroked the coarse hairs of his beard. "He wouldn't talk, so I took my sweet ass time cutting off his fingers and toes. Hell, I even snapped his femurs and crushed his knee caps, but the man never said a word." The ex-Collector reached for the silver mug on the coffee table. After a long swig, he added, "After three days, I suggested we keep him alive. I'd never seen a Lunin display so much courage."

"Did Arun agree?"

"Fuck no. He just laughed, then ordered me to slit his throat."

Cyrus murmured his understanding.

My chin hit my chest. *My mentor is a trained killer, and so is my boyfriend. How did I get here?*

Engaged in Samson's vivid storytelling, Iah's blue eyes stayed fixed on the Solin as he brushed the dirt off a rooted vegetable. "What did you do with the Seekers' bodies?"

"There wasn't much left after we finished torturing them. Arun instructed us to toss the leftovers into a fire. Some Collectors preferred breaking their victims' bones, while others skinned them alive. They never got far with the peelings. The Seekers always fell unconscious." He patted his upper thigh. "I saw one Solin stay awake until my buddy peeled the skin over his groin."

Cyrus paled.

"I have a strong stomach, but burning hair"—Samson shuddered—"man, that shit smells nasty."

My feet scooted closer to the hallway. I froze when the ex-Collector added, "Arun made some bizarre requests during the Clearing of the Seekers." He tapped his temple. "One has always haunted me."

Cyrus grimaced. "Feel free *not* to share."

"I thought this was story time."

"Your stories don't have happy endings."

"This ain't a fairytale, kid."

Defeated, my brother pressed his spine into the couch.

Samson clasped his hands. "If it was a clean kill, involving minimal torture, Arun had me drag the bodies of the male Seekers up to his personal chamber. He had this sick fetish with the dead."

Cyrus's eyes almost fell out of his head. "The dude was a necrophiliac?"

The color drained from Iah's face.

Samson went on, "Yeah. If that's what you call a person who likes to *fu*—"

I covered my ears. I had heard enough disturbing details to

supply me with endless nightmares. I hurried toward the hallway but turned hearing Iah call my name.

"Dinner will be ready soon."

"I'm not hungry," I lied. "Training in the heat made me nauseous."

"I can give you something to ease your discomfort."

I waved the doctor away. "I'm fine. I'll just turn in early and get some rest."

My brother snorted. "Sleep well, Hillary."

I showed him my middle finger and quickened my pace, determined to make it to the bathtub without further interruption.

"What's up your sister's ass?" Samson asked.

Ignore him. Just keep walking.

"Who knows? A woman's mind is a lock without a key."

I slammed the washroom door shut at the sound of two mugs clinking in celebration.

After a long soak, I emerged with squeaky-clean skin. My emotions were still soiled. I had hoped the alone time would clear my head. Boy was I wrong. My mind drifted to dangerous territories: endless encouragements followed by self-sabotaging thoughts.

I towel dried my hair and stared at the blank wall above the sink. *I need to let it go. Idalia's right. Jax's past relationships don't shape our future.*

Regardless, he should have told you, Elara. You're his girlfriend. You have every right to be upset.

I rolled my neck. *If I wanted your opinion, I would have asked.*

As you wish.

I braced my palms on the wooden counter, the damp locks of my hair framing my face. *Am I losing my mind? Is there a real voice inside of my head?*

Yes, I'm real. Don't be foolish, Elara.

I cursed the dealer and the sudden realization that I had forgotten to grab a fresh change of clothes.

I tiptoed down the narrow hallway, leaving a trail of wet footprints behind. After slipping into one of Jax's t-shirts, I combed through my hair, then collapsed onto the bed. The weight of the day pressed against me, my body sinking deeper into the mattress. Short minutes passed before I fell into a dreamless sleep.

I STIRRED at the sound of the doorknob twisting. My eyelashes fluttered, adjusting to my Lunin vision. *How long was I out?* I glanced at the window, the damp panes blurred with moonlight. I yawned. *Long enough.*

My head turned.

In strolled Jax, refreshed from his day of training. His jet black hair was slicked out of his striking face, and his shirtless torso exposed the cords of muscle that lined his chest and abdomen. Out of habit, my eyes darted to the razor-sharp V lines peeking around the towel he had wrapped around his waist.

He tossed his dirty clothes into a pile near the closet. I shifted my gaze to the cracks in the wooden ceiling. They lacked the excitement of Jax's perfected physique but served as a necessary distraction.

The Lunin locked the door before approaching the bed. After tossing Zenith's knife onto the nightstand, he lowered himself beside me and walked his fingers up my abdomen, stopping at the imaginary line below my breast. "Are you still mad at me?"

I knocked his hand away. "No. I'm just confused."

"What do you want me to say?" he asked, resting his head

on his knuckles. "I can't change the past. My previous relation-ships don't concern you."

"I'm aware. Pardon my earlier interrogation. I wouldn't have bothered had I known my boyfriend slept with every woman on Aroonyx."

"That's a ridiculous accusation."

"Is it?" I flipped onto my side and found his eyes. "I don't think Idalia would lie to me."

"She's exaggerating."

"By how much?"

"A lot."

I picked at a loose thread in the comforter, mustering the courage to ask my next question. "So . . . what's your number?"

He shot me an incredulous look. "You can't ask me that."

"I can, and I just did."

Jax collapsed onto his back and draped an arm over his eyes. "Well, you're not getting an answer."

"That's not fair."

He lifted his arm. "You want to go there?"

I nodded.

"Fine, then let's go."

I gulped, silently cursing my curiosity.

"It's not that I *won't* answer your obnoxious question, it's that I can't. Unlike most men, I don't keep a record of the women I've slept with."

"*Right.*"

"Are you happy now? Is that what you wanted to hear?"

I twisted the loose thread around my finger. *Yes. No. Maybe?* I scoffed. *Geeze. What did I expect?*

The muscles in Jax's stomach contracted as he sat up. He leaned his back against the headboard. "Elara, I don't expect you to understand—"

"Forget it. It's none of my business."

"You're right. It isn't. Months ago, I would have advised you to back off." He brushed my hair off my shoulder. "But things have changed between the two of us. I'll share that part of my past if it helps ease your mind."

I nodded.

"Get comfortable," he said, tossing me a pillow.

I stuffed it under my head, curled into a ball, and closed my eyes.

"Yes, I was popular with the ladies, but for the wrong reasons. Idalia was a great friend. *Is* a great friend," he corrected. "She helped me during a very challenging time, and I'm forever grateful for her support."

"She said you changed after you turned eighteen."

"I did."

"What happened?"

"Coming of age sent my head spinning. Once my Lunin traits became active, I jumped to Earth more frequently. I lived in this altered state of reality. I'd check on you and your brother, then spend hours—days—learning everything I could about Earth. The time I stole in your world distracted me from my troubles at home. I mirrored an addict's behavior. I needed more, craved more of the escape I experienced on Earth. When I returned to my solitary life on Aroonyx, I fell into this depressive state. I became self-absorbed and treated everyone with disrespect. The contrast between the two worlds left me bitter and confused. I blamed Zenith for my suffering. If he hadn't ordered me to kill you and Cyrus, I would have never returned to Earth, never saw the potential of a new life."

I pushed myself to the upright position, my interest piqued by his honest confession.

"So that's what changed," he said. "*That's* the part I never shared with Idalia."

"I understand."

"My time as a Collector gnawed at my soul. I refused to taint Idalia's pure and innocent heart with the negative shit that surfaced within me, so I distanced myself. I was a cold and heartless person who hid behind the image of a dangerous and mysterious man, a man who didn't give a fuck about anything or anyone." Jax pinned me with a long stare. "I don't know why women find that attractive."

I shrugged, recalling my initial attraction toward Jax. "Girls love dark and edgy, brooding guys. It makes them feel dangerous, like they're playing with fire." I motioned to his half-naked body. "And all of *that* adds to the intrigue."

He chuckled, dragging a hand through his hair. "Looks don't mean shit if there's an emotional void in your life. I spent years trying to fill mine with the physical comforts of women. This approach left me stuck in an endless circle. Sex is a wonderful distraction—but it's a temporary one."

I looked away.

Jax went on. "I didn't have to think about my past or my future. It allowed me to live in the now." He huffed a breath. "It took me years to recognize the truth."

"What truth?"

"Physical pleasures are temporary. Emotional experiences can last a lifetime."

"Can't sex facilitate an emotional response?"

"Yes, if the connection goes deeper than the surface."

I angled my head.

"Let me clarify," he added. "Sex is a physical act between two people, an emotional attachment isn't required. I never shared a connection with those women. After the moment passed, my troubles resurfaced. This cycle continued for years until I spent a very memorable day on Earth."

"What day?"

"The day I approached you on the trail after you skipped school. The day you broke the news to Cyrus."

"That day changed my entire life."

"Likewise." He winked. "Until then, I had always seen you

as the girl I brought to Earth and nothing more." A smirk tugged at his lips. "I tried not to laugh when you chewed my ass for leaving, even though you were the one who asked me to stay away."

"I spent weeks living in a mental hell, wondering if you were real."

"I had my reasons for leaving."

I glared. "You and your stupid test. Was that an acquired talent or should I thank Samson?"

"Perhaps." He laced his fingers through mine. "Your reaction to the Moon Drop story confirmed my theory." He pressed my knuckles to his lips. "You weren't like the other girls in my life."

I shut my eyes. The door to my memory bank flew open, showering my mind with images: Jax offering me the delicate flower, the fuzzy stem, the way the closed bud appeared to glow from within, the white petals absorbing my tear.

"Elara, I spent sixteen years living a cold and detached life. Your emotional response to the story of the Moon Drop ignited an internal flame inside me. You knew nothing about Aroonyx, yet you trusted me as your guide. You accepted your fate, and by doing so you accepted me."

I filled my lungs with a deep breath. I could still smell the terpenes of the pine trees and hear the mulch crunch under Jax's boots as he stepped forward to show me the Moon Drop. The air whooshed out of me when another piece of the puzzle snapped into place. *I didn't accept my fate on the beach with Cyrus. I accepted my fate on the trail with Jax. The moment he told me my life would change forever. The moment I told him it already had.*

"It's crazy to think that day made such an impact on us," I rasped.

"Life's full of surprises, isn't it?"

I smiled. "Yeah, I guess it is."

"And during our visit to Starbucks, I had the privilege of witnessing the more comical side of your personality. The side you showed me this afternoon."

I arched a brow, daring him to elaborate.

He obliged, a deep laugh rumbling in his chest. "You and jealousy are quite the dynamic duo."

I retaliated by slamming my fist into Jax's stomach. He flexed his eight-pack before my knuckles connected, leaving me cursing and him laughing.

Adding salt to the gaping wound in my pride, he whispered, "I've spent a lot of time on Earth. I knew the writing on my cup was the cashier's phone number." My jaw almost hit the bed. "But nice job improvising with 'it's code for the coffee they use.'"

"You are such an asshole. You lied to me. You knew all about coffee and Starbucks." I gasped. "And pizza."

His shoulders shook with laughter. "I may have dumbed down my knowledge of Earth."

"Why?"

Jax pulled me onto his lap. I put up a fight for only a moment before surrendering to his gentle touch. I leaned my cheek against his chest as he ran his fingers through my hair.

"I gave you a lot of new information to digest," he said. "If I acted naïve regarding Earth, you'd feel better about your lack of knowledge with Aroonyx."

I traced a jagged scar on his pectoral muscle. "What a gentleman."

"I try to lead by example."

I flicked him in the chest. "Are you done gloating?"

"For now."

Jax shimmied his body farther down the bed. He slid me on top of him and settled his strong hands around my waist. My cheeks flushed feeling the towel brush my inner thighs. The thin fabric left nothing to the imagination. I tried to remove said towel but paused when Jax shared another confession.

"Do you remember how I struggled to get to Earth at the end of the school year?"

"I do."

"There was a reason. A reason I couldn't share until now."

I dragged my attention away from the V-lines under the towel and found his eyes. "I'm listening."

"You're familiar with the rules of jumping, am I right?"

I nodded. "A Seeker can only jump if the intention is pure."

"That's right. For nine years, I secretly checked on the twins, waiting for you to come of age so I could prepare you for your return. A selfless intention. After you agreed to go back to Aroonyx, I felt a tug on the emotional bond between us.

"I longed to spend time with you, Elara. I fought it for months. At the end of the school year, it all made sense." He took my hands. "The cold and distant asshole had fallen for the compassionate, sassy girl. My selfless intent for jumping to Earth had turned selfish. That's why I couldn't get back. My intention had shifted."

I blinked and blinked again. *After all this time. He's finally telling me the truth.*

Curious, I asked, "How did you meet us on the trail before we jumped to Aroonyx? Was it a lucky break?"

"I'm not sure, but I do know this: what we hold in mind tends to manifest."

"You lost me on that one."

"Before I jumped to Earth that morning, I spent hours visualizing you and Cyrus living on Aroonyx, defeating Zenith, and freeing the people. I let go of my selfish notions and stayed focused on the big picture—the greater good. A heartbeat later, I opened my eyes and found Cyrus waiting on the trail."

"Why didn't you just tell me the reason you struggled to jump?"

"I couldn't afford any distractions. I needed to prepare you and Cyrus for the future, so I pushed the thought of us being together out of my mind."

I frowned, remembering Jax's attitude toward me after we returned to Aroonyx. Distant, uptight, detached. "I get it," I murmured. "That's why you closed yourself off to me."

Jax sat up and wrapped my legs around his waist, his eyes glowing with an internal light. "I did and look where it led me. I'm not the same person I was back then, and believe me when I say this: the women in my past are just distant memories."

"I believe you."

He ran his hands down my arms. "I've shared my secrets tonight. Now it's your turn to come clean. What's bothering you?"

I cleared my throat, dislodging the lump of anxiety. "You didn't wait to have sex with these other women, did you?"

He looked away.

I sighed. "Well, that answers my question."

"Can I explain?"

"Please do." I eyed our compressed bodies. "I'm feeling super self-conscious, wondering if I'm turning you off."

Jax's face hardened. He lifted me off of him and rested me on the bed. I tucked my knees into my chest, his shirt pulled tight over my bare legs.

He spun around to face me. "Did Idalia suggest this?"

"No. She tried to put my mind at ease when I brought it up. I dug myself into a hole after asking her to draw me a picture with instructions."

His face squished up. "A picture of what?"

"How people do certain . . . things." I paused, my cheeks flushing with embarrassment.

Jax bit his knuckle, his shoulders bouncing with laughter. "Please tell me you didn't ask her to do that."

"It's not funny," I said, unable to hide my amusement.

"Then why are you laughing?"

"Because you are."

He shook his head at me and reached for my hand. "My reason for making you wait has nothing to do with your ridiculous assumption. I have zero complaints in that area of our relationship. I base my past sexual encounters on physical attraction. I've never had an emotional connection to a woman"—his fingers brushed against my cheek—"until now."

"What about Idalia? She made it sound like you had a connection with her."

"This stays between us, okay?"

I nodded.

"Idalia sees me as her first love." He swallowed. "I can't say the same about her."

Ouch. There's that brutal honesty.

"It pains me to say this out loud, especially after everything she's done for me." He struggled to get the words out. "When we were together, I felt obligated to express my gratitude on a physical level. She's an attractive woman. It's not like she had to twist my arm to join her in the bedroom."

I tensed at the images that flew into my mind.

"But to be honest," Jax said, "I only saw her as a friend. A friend with benefits." He pulled my legs from their hiding place and rested his hand over my heart. "What I have with you"—he pressed his palm deeper into my chest—"this connection. It's stronger than anything I've ever felt."

"Then why are you making me wait?"

"Your plate is full right now. You're stressed with the uprising, you're exhausted from training, and you're worried about Cyrus. I don't want to pressure you into having sex if you're not ready."

I shot him a weighted glance. "Jax, you convinced me to leave Earth with the twin brother I never knew existed so we could defeat a delusional dictator on another planet. I think I know when you're pressuring me and when you're not."

"This is true but—"

"Are you making me wait until marriage?"

His brows tapped his hairline.

Shit. Why did I say that? A montage of romantic movies played before my mind's eye, each one ending with a disclaimer: Want to scare off a man? Mention the word marriage.

"Are you proposing?"

"No," I blurted. "That came out wrong. I wasn't implying—"

"That's unfortunate."

My eyes grew. "Why?"

"Because we'd make a great team."

"We would?"

"I think so. Don't you?"

I sucked on my lip. "Yeah, I guess."

"You *guess*? Why the lack of confidence?"

"I've known you for less than a year."

"And I've known *you* for your entire life."

The truth behind Jax's words left me speechless. I recalled the first time I saw him standing outside of my bedroom window on Earth and the strange sense of déjà vu that followed. The vision at NASA, along with the sentiments that surfaced once the mysterious faces appeared. My biological mother and father, a young Jax standing between them. The tug I felt on the emotional bond that day had nothing to do with my parents. It had everything to do with the boy, the boy with the piercing blue eyes. It had everything to do with Jax.

I clutched my chest, my heart expanding, and looked at the Lunin. "You're right. You've always been there."

"And I always will be." Jax swung his legs off the bed. "Now back to your proposal."

"I wasn't proposing."

He chuckled, walking toward the closet. I watched him reach for something on the top shelf: a fabric-wrapped package that fit in the palm of his hand. *That's the item he hid after his long absence.*

Jax adjusted the towel, then took a seat beside me. "I've had this for a while now," he said, untying the beige twine. "A vendor owed me a favor."

A shimmer of light caught my eye. I stilled. A ring rested in the center of the gray cloth, and not just any ring. It was the same ring I admired during our first outing to the South Village. Slack-jawed, I marveled at the delicate item as Jax rotated it in his hand. Round gemstones, similar to diamonds, surrounded a large center stone that changed colors. The clear gem turned pink depending on how the light reflected.

"I wanted to give you this ring as a thank you"—he held it between his thumb and index finger—"for dealing with my shit over the past year." His eyes found mine. "But perhaps it can mean something more."

Jax slid off the bed and took a knee. Time stopped as he reached for my trembling hand. Even the dust particles floating in the air paused their eloquent dance.

"Elara." The amount of confidence and certainty in Jax's voice caused my spine to lengthen. "I consider our time together as a privilege, because after everything I've done, after the horrific crimes I've committed, I can't help but wonder: How in the hell did I get so lucky?"

I blinked away the tears.

"Physically, you're a beautiful woman, but it's your inner beauty that leaves me breathless. I'm a practical man who doesn't wear his heart on his sleeve. I prefer to internalize my emotions. Relationships fail without compromise, so it's time I let you in, it's time I tell you the truth."

I steadied my labored breathing while Jax tightened his grip around my hand.

"I've never cared for anyone more," he said. "You keep me grounded, and without saying it, you encourage me to be a better man. I don't have to wear a mask around you or put up a front. You see me with compassionate eyes. Elara, you are the *only* woman I want to spend the rest of my life with."

I couldn't speak. I could hardly breathe.

"Our future together is unpredictable. Who knows how much time we have left?" Jax brushed away a tear that slid down my cheek. "So let's make it count." He offered me the glittering token of appreciation. "Elara Dunlin, will you accept this ring as a promise, a commitment to share your life with me?" His brows furrowed. "If we survive the uprising."

I grimaced at the image of Zenith hurling his knife at Jax the night we rescued Idalia. I shifted my weight on the bed. "The first part of your proposal was really romantic. The second part—not so much."

"Forgive me. Like I said, I'm a practical man."

I blew out a tight breath and shut my eyes. *Big decision.*

It is, Elara. You're only eighteen.

I rolled my neck and gritted my teeth. *You show up at the worst times.*

I show up when you need me the most. The masked dealer snickered, its silk mask fluttering around its hidden mouth. *What will your brother say?*

You're right. I can't get engaged at eighteen. I touched my chest; a warmth surrounded my heart. *Or can I?*

No, you can't. It's an absurd idea. I'd go as far as to call it crazy.

But crazier things have happened. I'm living on another planet, starting an uprising against a ruthless dictator who wants to murder me with his bare hands.

Exactly. You don't have time for distractions. Especially those concerning the heart.

Screw it. I glared at the figure lurking in the corner of my mind. *And screw you. I'm tired of making decisions with my head instead of my heart.*

The pleats of its cloak blew in a phantom breeze as it turned its back on me. *Your loss, Elara. Don't say I didn't warn you.*

My eyes shot open. The man with the piercing blue eyes stared back; the man who had turned my world upside down; the man who challenged me both physically and emotionally; the man who gave me the opportunity to discover unconditional love.

Over the past year, we had experienced more highs and lows than most couples face in a lifetime. Our relationship was far from perfect, but it was real, and at that moment, I realized I wanted to share my life with Jax.

I threw my arms around his neck, sending us falling to the ground. His head slammed into the floorboards.

"I'm sorry." I giggled, my hair surrounding our faces.

"Apology accepted."

I eyed the ring in his hand. He moved it closer.

"Do you plan on answering my question?"

"Patience," I teased, pressing my lips against his.

Jax's chest rumbled with laughter until I slipped the ring onto my finger. The silver metal settled between my knuckles, cooling my warm skin. I smiled. It was the perfect fit.

Jax's eyes lit up. "Is that a yes?"

"No."

His face fell.

My cheeks ached from smiling. "It's a *hell* yes."

34

THE FIRE SIGN

The morning sun seeped through the bedroom window, bathing our skin in a luscious glow. I inhaled a deep breath and peeled open my heavy eyelids; the pleasurable effects of the previous night still lingered.

My stomach churned with hunger. Not wanting to wake the Lunin snoozing beside me, I tried wiggling from underneath his arm.

His warm breath grazed my ear as he whispered, "Five more minutes."

I scooted closer, pressing my naked body against his.

Jax brushed the hair off my neck and let his lips wander over my tingling flesh. "Last night"—he paused between each kiss—"gave me a new appreciation for birthdays."

I flipped around to face him, then guided his hand down the curve of my hip. Jax's lips spread into a seductive grin as he watched me drape my leg over the lower half of his body.

"I'm the gift that keeps on giving," I teased, sliding my fingers down the hard planes of his stomach.

"What happened to the sweet, naïve girl I first met?"

"I sent her packing."

"Oh, did you?" Jax rasped, as my hand stroked the hard length of him.

"Mm-hmm." I guided him toward the area he desired, a less-than-subtle reminder of our evening together. "The poor girl couldn't keep up."

"Good thing I can."

He pulled me closer, his fingers gripping my backside. I adjusted the angle of my leg, moving it higher, allowing every inch of him to slide inside me. His lips crushed against mine, and with each thrust, he kissed me harder. Without pausing the steady rhythm, Jax rolled me onto my back and nudged my head to the side. My vision blurred as his lips grazed my neck, and every nerve in my body sparked when his tongue traced the sensitive area near my ear. I lifted my hands to touch his face. I needed that talented tongue of his in my mouth. Jax flicked said tongue before sinking his teeth into my flushed skin. He then grabbed my wrists, pressing them into the mattress. I arched my spine as he pushed himself deeper inside me. The headboard slammed against the wall, my toes curling at the pleasurable sensation that gathered in my core. The moan that escaped my mouth turned into a groan when a fist pounded on the bedroom door.

"It's Cyrus, open up!"

Jax cursed the urgency in my brother's voice. I cursed his poor timing.

"I'm sorry," the Lunin whispered onto my lips. "We'll get back to this later."

I faked a cry. "You owe me. I don't enjoy cliffhangers."

"I'm happy to pay my debt this evening."

"Good man." I winked.

"Open the damn door," Cyrus called.

We scrambled to find our clothes. Jax tossed me his shirt and my undergarments. I caught them with one hand, then leaned over the bed to retrieve his towel. My partner wrapped it around him while hurrying toward the door. The waistband of my underwear snapped against my hip bone right as Jax turned the lock. In walked my brother.

I gasped, covering my exposed breasts with the oversized shirt. "Damn it, Cyrus. Could you not have given us five minutes to get dressed?"

He averted his eyes. "Sorry, sis, it's an emergency." He looked at Jax. "We need you outside—now."

The ex-Collector reached for a pair of pants and a short-sleeved shirt hanging in the closet. Cyrus turned to give him his privacy.

"What's going on outside?" Jax asked my brother, fastening the silver buttons on his fly.

"You'll see."

Jax slipped the shirt over his head and dashed across the room to fetch Zenith's knife from the bedside table. He slid it into his back pocket, then eyed the ring on my finger. "Why don't you stay here?"

I scowled at his suggestion. Not wanting my brother to hear, I lowered my voice and said, "This ring doesn't weaken my position. I won't sit on my ass and play the damsel in distress while you see all the action. I thought we were a team."

"We are." He squeezed my shoulder. "But it's my job to keep you safe."

"Jax," Cyrus called from the doorway. "Samson's waiting. We need to go."

The Lunin spun on his heels and jogged toward my brother.

"I won't sit on the sidelines," I said, reaching for his gray knife in the drawer.

"I know you won't." Jax looked at me over his shoulder. "I'd never ask you to."

As soon as they exited the room, I pulled on some shorts and slid my feet into an unlaced pair of boots. Did I look ridiculous in the oversized nightshirt that hung over my thighs? Absolutely. Much like a child playing dress up.

I brushed off my concerns and hurried down the hallway, eager to catch up with the others. The cool metal brushed against my skin as I slipped the ring off my finger. *Now is not the time to explain the reason I'm wearing jewelry.* I tucked the glittering promise into the tiny pocket sewn inside the larger. You know, the one you never use.

Idalia, Callisto, and Iah stood near the living room windows with their arms crossed, eyes focused on the commotion outside. I made my way to the front door, my boots thumping on the wooden floors.

The heat slammed into my face like an oven set to broil. I shielded my eyes with the crook of my arm and squinted at Samson. The ex-Collector braced himself against the railing, his calloused fingers gripping the chipped wood as if it had wronged him.

Jax stepped beside his comrade. "What's going on?"

Samson jerked his chin at the clearing beyond Iah's front yard. "Look who showed up."

Sharing my brother's powerful Solin vision, I followed my mentor's gaze. A group of young men stood in a tight formation with their heels glued together. *It can't be.*

I breathed hard, observing their pale and tan faces. Shaved heads and a plethora of scars confirmed their identities: Collectors. Their blue and orange eyes stared straight ahead— straight at us.

Jax rose to his full height, then eyed Samson, who nodded in return. Without exchanging words, the two men headed down the porch steps.

I looked at my brother. He looked at Orion. "You coming with us?"

"Might as well. It's gotten pretty boring around here lately."

My brother and I chuckled. A few strides later we caught up to the rest of our party.

"Showing up unannounced takes some balls," Jax whispered to Samson.

The Solin slowed his pace as he approached the group. "I doubt they have any. At least none they're afraid to lose." He gestured to the young men. "They're underage."

Orion and Cyrus expressed their amusement with a loud snort. I rolled my eyes. *I'm working with children.*

Their humor dissolved once they scanned the sea of stone-cold faces. Cyrus took his place on my left while Orion moved to my right. Samson and Jax stood front and center, creating a barrier between us and the group of underage Collectors.

The young men lowered their gaze, refusing to make eye contact with their superiors. Jax's fingers curled into a fist. Samson popped his knuckles, one joint at a time. An eerie silence swept over the two groups.

The former leader of the Inner Circle widened his stance and crossed his arms before addressing the teens. "Things will go south faster than you can blink if someone doesn't speak up and tell us why you're here."

I gulped.

"That's one way to get their attention," Orion whispered.

My brother nodded, shifting his weight.

The young men slid their gaze to the Lunin Collector who stood before Jax. Samson's tongue tapped the roof of his mouth, an auditory demand for the man to comply.

The morning light reflected off the tiny starbursts in the teen's blue irises as he slid a hand into his back pocket. Jax disarmed the Collector in one fell swoop, then tossed the folded blade to Samson who caught it with one hand.

Acting as my personal guard, Cyrus and Orion moved their bodies in front of mine, blocking my view. I glared at their backs. *When did I become the helpless girl?*

I dismissed their chivalry by nudging them out of the way, reestablishing our tight line.

Jax shoved the young Lunin in the chest, and the teen stumbled backward. His peers didn't bother to catch his fall.

"Don't do something you'll regret," Jax spat.

The Collector climbed to his feet, his eyes never leaving the ground. A wicked smirk tugged at the corner of Samson's chapped mouth. It was obvious he approved of Jax's direct approach.

"I'm only going to ask you one more time." The Lunin pulled Zenith's knife from his back pocket and flicked his wrist. "Why are you here?"

Heads turned and eyes widened, the Collectors searching for the quickest escape route.

Samson snickered and pointed the tip of the stolen blade at the young Lunin. "You better start talking, kid." He pinned the others with a lethal stare. "Try to run, I dare you. I'd love to practice my aim on a moving target."

The men froze.

Jax got in the Lunin's face, his fingers rotating the knife's handle. "Did Zenith send you?"

"No, sir. We came on our own."

"How did you find us?"

"We've been walking for days, sir. We heard rumors about you and the twins living up north. I didn't want to risk running into the other Collectors, so we took our chances and headed South."

Jax eyed Samson before asking the young man, "Why did you come?"

"We're tired of being treated like shit."

"You're just realizing that now?" Cyrus asked.

I flinched at my brother's voice. I didn't expect him to jump in on the conversation.

A haze of grief clouded the Collector's eyes as he focused

his attention on Jax's boots. "Archer's death pissed us off, but what happened to our group after you rescued that girl from the basement, well, it's one reason we left." He dared a glance at Zenith's prodigal son. "I'm sure *you* understand why."

Jax's knuckles turned white as he tightened his grip around the knife. The teen hit a nerve—and a massive one at that.

Cyrus narrowed his eyes at the Collector but directed his voice at Samson and Jax. "This could be a trap."

"Well, is it?" Jax snapped at the young Lunin.

The man looked over his shoulder and gave a curt nod to the other Collectors. My eyelashes fluttered watching them obey his silent order. Moving as one, the Solins and Lunins exposed their knives, then dropped them onto the ground.

Orion and Cyrus muttered, "Damn."

Jax shook his head in disbelief. Samson played with the tip of his beard, his orange eyes scanning the group of men.

"Name," Jax demanded.

The Lunin lifted his chin but refused to make eye contact. "Aries, sir."

"Age?"

"Seventeen."

Jax stretched his neck and counted the other members in the group. "Is this all of you?"

"Yes, sir. It's what's left of the Inactive Members." He swallowed hard. "The others didn't make it."

"What did Zenith do?" I asked.

Aries didn't pay me any mind. He just kept staring at Jax's boots.

"The girl asked you a question," Samson drawled.

The teen shifted his weight. "He ordered a mass execution."

I shuddered a breath.

Jax pointed Zenith's knife at Aries and the other Collectors. "Then, how did you escape?"

"Luck of the draw, sir."

"Go on," Samson urged.

"Zenith ordered a mandatory lockdown after the incident. The AMs were the only ones permitted to leave."

Incident? Is that what they're calling it?

Samson balanced the smooth side of the blade on his finger. "Question."

Aries tensed.

"What happened after we left?"

The young Lunin straightened. "It wasn't pretty, sir. After Zenith tended to his wound, he punished the Inner Circle by leaving them in the snow. A few of us snuck outside to watch." He sighed. "There was a lot of blood. It got pretty quiet after a few hours. Most of them were unconscious."

Jax nodded. "What's the health status of Zenith?"

"Sir." Aries popped to attention. "The knife wound you inflicted didn't faze him. He never sat down that night, not even while the doctor stitched him up."

A muscle feathered in Jax's jaw. "Health status of the Inner Circle?"

"Ravi, Levant, and Holmes—K.I.A."

A sly grin crossed Samson's face as he used Arie's knife to pick the dirt from underneath his nails.

With wide eyes, I turned to my brother. "What's K.I.A?"

"Killed in action," he whispered.

"Oh."

"Try to keep up, sis."

The young Collector continued. "Jericho suffered minor injuries. Elio, Oberon, and Ishan made full recoveries. Apollo is off bed rest and Pollux isn't far behind."

Samson and Jax sneered. Hearing the Lunin's name set everyone on edge. A wave of heat surged through me.

I grabbed Cyrus's wrist. "Easy. You'll get your chance to avenge Idalia."

"Sir, you'd hardly recognize him," Aries said to Jax. "Your

fists did more damage than ten men. We didn't think he'd pull through. The doctor told Zenith to make funeral arrangements." The young Lunin snickered. "That didn't go over well. Everyone knows Zenith doesn't respect the dead with a burial."

Jax nodded.

"So," Aries added, "he sent the doctor packing and instructed Elio to take over. Pollux is angrier than ever. No one goes near him."

"Anything else we should know?" Samson asked.

Aries shrugged. "I've never seen Zenith react so violently to a failed mission. After the doctor stitched his wound, he visited the Lower Level. Some of us hid. The younger ones didn't stand a chance. Zenith dragged two boys into the basement, then ordered the AMs to bring him two more at the stroke of every hour. He repeated this routine until after sunrise. He skinned those boys alive and nailed their peeled bodies to the walls surrounding our floor."

My mouth fell open.

Orion clutched his chest and Cyrus muttered, "Sick son of a bitch."

"We didn't sleep that night because their screams kept us awake. The bodies on the wall didn't help. Blood and bits of flesh covered Zenith once he surfaced that morning." Aries's direct tone shifted to somber. "He ordered us to clean up the mess after we collected the skins from the basement."

My blood boiled with rage. Cyrus scrubbed at his face. Familiar with Zenith's brutality, Jax and Samson showed no signs of remorse.

"Zenith locked himself in his personal chamber for over a week," the young Collector said. "We thought he took his own life. Unfortunately, we weren't that lucky. One morning he appeared at our training session and pulled Elio aside. A few minutes later, the Solin informed the AMs of the new ordinance. They sharpened their knives and left for the villages that afternoon."

"How many recruits have they brought in?" Samson asked.

"Around two hundred, sir. With more showing up every day."

I paled. My brother swore.

"This is bad," Orion whispered.

Cyrus nodded. "*Real* bad."

Samson eyed Jax, his expression unreadable. The Lunin clenched his jaw, nostrils flaring. Not pressing his luck, Aries bowed his head and took a step backward.

"Are these men willing to fight for Zenith?" Cyrus asked.

"Yes, sir. More than half volunteered to join the Collectors."

Samson's lips formed a tight line. "This changes things," he said to Jax.

"That it does."

I cleared my throat. "Aries. When did your group leave?"

Ignoring me for the second time that day, he looked at Jax and answered my question. "We left shortly after the ordinance passed." His hands curled into fists. "A traitor in our group informed Archer's brother of our plan. I'm not sure why he told Jericho. I thought he'd let us go considering Zenith ordered Pollux to kill Archer that night."

I gasped, finding Cyrus's hand. He gave it a gentle squeeze, acknowledging the piece Aries added to our life's puzzle. Archer died because Zenith gave the orders.

The Collector's face hardened. "After Jericho reported our treason to Zenith, he ordered the AMs to rectify the situation. Less than half of us got over the wall." He jerked his thumb over his shoulder. "Only eighteen men stand with me today."

"Eighteen?" I stammered. "That's all that's left?"

Aries didn't say a word, much less look in my direction. I huffed a breath. *Am I invisible?*

Our heads turned at the sound of footsteps. Prepared for

another day of training, the men and women in our groups strolled toward us. Their casual pace halted to a stop once they spotted the Collectors standing before us.

I tugged at my brother's arm. "Go tell them it's safe before things get out of hand."

"On it." He motioned for Orion to join him.

The two men jogged to meet the others halfway. Blaze hurried to greet my brother. The light in his amber eyes dimmed once he observed the Collectors standing at attention. Cyrus reached for the child's hand and swung him around, so his back faced Aries.

Mouths moved with sharp tongues as my brother and Orion approached. Cyrus lifted his free hand, silencing the anxious Solins and Lunins.

I turned, hearing Jax ask Aries, "What's Zenith's next move?"

"I'm not sure." The young Lunin paused, picking at a loose thread on his pants.

His hesitation caused Samson to take a step forward. "Then you better figure it out, kid. If I find out you're lying to us, I'll cut out your *fucking* tongue."

Aries swallowed hard, his Adam's apple bobbing in his throat. "Sir, I can't answer Jax's question because we left after the ordinance passed."

Jax observed the men behind Aries. Eighteen soldiers stood tall with their arms held rigid at their sides, eyes averted. I frowned. On the outside, they resembled a well-trained unit, but on the inside, they lacked an integral piece that shaped the heart of all warriors: the act of selfless service. They served Zenith out of fear and escaped the confines of his dwelling to save their own asses.

"If you seek our protection," Jax said. "You've come to the wrong place."

The men didn't budge.

"If you seek a new life and want to join our cause, then surrender your allegiance to Zenith and follow our orders." The Lunin dangled the black knife before their eyes. "If you disobey, I'll wedge this blade in your throat." He inclined his head at Samson. "After he's cut out your tongue. Do I make myself clear?"

"Yes, sir!" they called in unison.

My ears perked up. Jax's intimidation game reflected his time with Zenith. The young Collectors before him never witnessed his high-profile position as the leader of the Inner Circle, but their submissive behavior proved his reputation had proceeded him. The poor teens couldn't even look at Samson; his dark past had also followed him.

I hummed my discord. *This isn't right. Jax shouldn't treat them this way, regardless of his previous position.*

Let the man do his job, Elara.

Shut up.

The masked dealer responded with a quiet cackle.

Fear flickered in the men's eyes. My heart ached for the ones who didn't make it over the wall. It broke for the survivors. I eyed my partner's rigid posture. *What's gotten into him? He knows what it takes to leave Zenith.*

Jax paced in front of the group and tapped the smooth side of Zenith's blade on the palm of his hand while he spoke. "Drop your weapons in a pile near Samson, then form a line for interrogations." He stopped to face the Collectors, his lips curling into a smirk. "Let me give you some advice. Samson can spot a traitor with his eyes closed. The last encounter left him with bloody hands. I'm sure you've learned the proper technique of a clean tongue removal. Am I right?"

"Yes, sir!" they answered.

"The thing is"—Jax rotated the blade in his hand, the silver etchings catching in the sunlight—"Samson uses his own technique."

The color drained from the Collectors' faces.

"That's right," he added. "The bleed out takes a little longer, so choose your words wisely."

Voices reverberated around us as the men yelled, "Yes, sir!"

"Good," Jax sneered. "Now move your asses and get in line."

The men stooped down to retrieve their knives, hurrying to obey the Lunin's orders.

My boot slid forward. "Jax," I whispered, tapping him on the shoulder.

"What do you want?" He didn't bother turning around.

I bristled at his abrasive tone. *Geez. Easy with the Collector attitude.*

Speaking near his ear like an expert ventriloquist, I asked, "Why are you treating them this way?"

Jax grabbed my wrist and spun me around so our backs faced the others. Without saying a word, he escorted me, correction, he dragged me from the group of men.

My brother was too far away to share his Solin strength, so I dug my nails into Jax's skin and hissed, "I'm not a damn dog. Let me go."

He growled, dropping my arm.

I rubbed my sore wrist. "What's with the scare tactic?"

"I refuse to waste time explaining things you won't understand."

I scoffed, tapping the hidden promise in my pocket. "Thanks for the lack of confidence *partner*."

Jax cursed before finding my eyes. "Elara. This is how Zenith treats the Collectors. He teaches them compassion is a weakness. It's etched in their minds at an early age. For once, my dark past gives me the upper hand. They respect my former position. I can use this to my advantage."

My jaw cracked open. "Are you for real?"

"I don't expect you to understand. That's why I didn't want to have this conversation. It's an intimidation game with these kids. They're afraid of me and terrified of Samson. They'll do whatever we ask." He checked the sharpness of Zenith's blade by sliding it over his thumb. I grimaced at the red line that appeared on his pale skin. "Trust me," he added, wiping the blood on his pants. "I know what I'm doing."

"Do you even hear yourself right now? Are you trying to sell me the same bullshit excuse Zenith sold you?" I glared, sarcasm saturating my words. "I guess the apple *doesn't* fall far from the tree."

Jax narrowed the gap between us. "Elara, I'll let that slide. Pretend I didn't hear it." His voice lowered to a threatening growl. "But full disclosure, if you *ever* compare me to that man again, your stupidity won't go overlooked. And this"—he motioned to the two of us—"will end, so I'd advise you to think before speaking. I left that life behind, and if you're unwilling to accept it, then step aside for someone who might."

I breathed hard. I wanted to slap him in the face for speaking to me that way, but he was right. I kept comparing him to Zenith.

My lips moved with an apology, but his quick tongue cut me off. "You can't put yourself in their shoes because you don't know what it's like to be a Collector. You don't—"

"You're right. I don't know what it's like to take orders from a sadistic prick, but you and Samson do." I waved a hand at the group. "These young men want a fresh start. They didn't risk their lives to follow an arrogant leader who treats them with disrespect. They watched the Active Members slaughter more than half of their peers. And if their deaths were anything like Archer's"—my voice cracked—"Lord help them."

Jax shut his eyes.

I pressed on. "If you look past their tough appearance, you can see the pain in their eyes. They're scared, Jax. They're hopeless." I touched his arm. "Please don't use an iron fist to lead them. We can't let history repeat itself."

Jax lifted his chin to the cloudless green sky. The black locks of his hair blew in the breeze as he inhaled a sobering breath. My gaze drifted to his hand, hearing the blade of Zenith's knife fold into the handle.

"Your argument is strong." He looked at me with accepting eyes. "But it's naïve."

"How so?"

"These Inactive Members have lived with Zenith and the other Collectors for years. We can't trust them." Jax pointed to the line of men that formed near Samson. "They're trained killers. It's not a mentality you let go overnight. I'm the perfect example."

Defeated, my posture sagged.

"Elara, I appreciate your concern, but a pat on the back and a warm smile won't ease their troubled minds. This is a transitional phase. They're familiar with following orders. Let Samson and I handle the situation. Let us do our jobs."

"Situation? Is that how you see it? Are these men just another incident to add to your report of injustice?"

"Don't be dramatic." He dragged a hand through his hair. "I can't handle your shit right now."

I fisted my hands. "This is wrong, Jax, and you know it. They're not prisoners of war. Yes, they're trained killers, brainwashed by Zenith, but that doesn't make them less human."

"You say that until they murder us in our sleep."

My leg bounced up and down as I observed the Collectors.

Jax shook his head at me. "Don't even think about it."

"Let me talk to them."

"Over my dead body."

"Now who's being dramatic."

The soles of my boots slid in the morning dew as Jax dragged me farther away from the group.

"Would a leash and collar work better next time?" I spat, yanking my arm free.

"Have you lost your damn mind?" His voice raised. "You can't talk to them. That's a horrible idea."

"Why?"

Jax cursed, dragging both hands down his face. "Elara, you're a smart woman. Why do you insist on acting like a naïve girl?"

"You might want to retract that statement after last night's activities."

"Fine. I'll use the word foolish."

"Screw you."

The corner of his lips twitched. "You already did last night." His smirk grew. "*And* this morning."

My jaw almost hit the grass. "You're an arrogant asshole."

"And you're a huge pain in my ass."

I slapped my backside. "At least *this* ass has a conscience. I'm the only one who cares about the Inactive Members."

"We don't need a martyr on this mission."

"Good. I didn't volunteer to be one."

"Could have fooled me."

I shot him a warning glare. "Do you have anything else to say before I address the Collectors?"

"You're not talking to them."

"Yes, I am."

"Damn it, Elara! That's an order."

"Then charge me with insubordination because I don't take orders from you!"

Jax muttered inaudible words before saying, "Zenith teaches the Collectors that men are superior to women. When I was a child, I specifically remember him telling me that women serve two purposes, and two purposes only." He counted with his fingers. "Pleasure and procreation. Nothing more. They won't listen to what you have to say or show you a sliver of respect. You saw Aries, he won't even acknowledge your presence."

I blew the hair out of my eyes, weighing my options. *Wasted breath. That's all I have to lose.*

A sudden urgency to level the playing field grabbed hold of me. "Women have a voice too," I said, pivoting away from Jax.

He murmured a desperate plea to the universe and reached for my wrist. "Elara. I'm serious. Don't do it."

I dodged his outstretched hand and quickened my pace.

Samson did a double take as I stormed past him, and he tried—he really tried to muffle his laughter watching my lame attempt at whistling with my fingers. Only a silent burst of air rippled off my thumb and index finger. I groaned, my cheeks reddening with embarrassment. *That always works in the movies.*

I recovered with a loud clap. Eighteen heads turned to face me. *There, that's better.* Scratch that. Eighteen vacant expressions stared back. I gulped. Apollo would have been proud that day. The Collector's ice-cold stares screamed *We don't give a fuck about you or the little speech you didn't prepare.*

The masked dealer dragged a jagged claw down my spine. *Elara, let me help you.*

I shivered. *No.*

You need to show them who's in charge.

I rolled my neck. *Go away.*

Very well. I'm here if you need me.

Jax watched me with cautious eyes as I stepped in front of Aries, the unspoken leader of the Inactive Members. I stood tall. If I could get through to him, the others would follow.

"I get it, okay?" The words came out sharper than expected.

Aries didn't cower. He just stared at my chin.

"A few days ago, you saw me as your enemy, and now, here we are." I motioned to Samson and Jax.

The men rocked on the balls of their feet, waiting to pounce if Aries stepped out of line.

"We do things a little different around here," I said. "We treat each other with respect."

Aries drew in a tight breath. The irritated gesture didn't go unnoticed by the ex-Collectors. They took a step forward.

Ignoring their approach, I added, "Respect is a foreign concept to your group. If you want to join our side, you had better grasp it, and grasp it quick. I'd rather not waste time, so let's cut the shit and state the obvious. You don't give two fucks about me, and I sure as hell don't trust you." I eyed the other Collectors in line. "But we have something in common, and it doesn't involve age, appearance, or gender."

I pressed my palm against Aries's chest. He stilled, for two predators with lethal bites bared their teeth at him. I eyed Jax and Samson, silently beseeching them to stay put.

Aries's gaze drifted from the hand I held over his heart to my eyes. I didn't look away. "Courage. That's what we have in common." I patted his chest before lowering my arm. "It took a lot of courage to leave Zenith. You've already lost members of your group. The death toll will continue to rise before this mission ends. We can't guarantee your safety, but we'll do everything in our power to defeat Zenith."

I waited. For what, I wasn't sure, but I kept waiting, observing the line of men. Silence. Not a whisper of agreement or a mutter of understanding. Not an eye roll of frustration or a wicked smirk of amusement. Nothing. They just stood there, toy soldiers on display in life's store. Decorative ones in the glass case not meant for play. The ones with a sign that read *Please do not touch. Ask a manager for details.*

A gust of wind whipped around us. It may have cooled their flushed skin but appeared to entice the flame of doubt to rise within. I sighed. *Doubting a situation is better than fearing it.*

I slicked the stray hairs out of my face and decided on a different approach. "The fear of the unknown sucks," I said to Aries and his comrades. "I have a firsthand account of life's cruel twists and turns." I pointed at Samson and Jax. "And so do they. Like you, those men had a choice. Continue down a path of self-destruction or alter their course and fight for something greater than themselves.

"We can't help you unless you're willing to help yourselves. If you're uncomfortable following our orders, then leave. Beg Zenith for mercy or adapt to life as an ex-Collector in one of the villages." I shrugged. "It's your choice. Both options sound pretty shitty." I tossed up my hands. "But what do I know? I'm just a woman living in a man's world."

Jax hid a smirk while Samson winked at me.

The Collectors shifted their weight, all eyes on Aries. His jaw clenched with enough force to crack a tooth. Jax dashed forward. I blinked at the sudden awareness. Aries wasn't upset. He was awake—alive. A spark had ignited in his blue eyes. One lit by hope, not anger.

My hand shot out, stopping Jax dead in his tracks. "Stand down," I demanded.

He snarled at the order. Samson raised his armed hand, aiming the knife at Aries's chest.

The young Collector cleared his throat before speaking. "Miss, we didn't come all this way to follow another dead end." He offered me his hand. "I've made my decision and speak for the others when I say this, we're not going anywhere."

35

BLADE MASTER

J ax's eyes widened and Samson's arm fell to his side.

I grinned, shaking the Collector's, now ex-Collector's, hand. "You made the right choice."

Aries showed Jax and Samson his palms before reaching into his back pocket. "I think this belongs to you." He offered me a folded blade with a white handle.

"My knife," I said with wide eyes. "How did you get this?"

"I pulled it from Apollo after Zenith went inside to triage his wound."

"Thank you."

I slipped the knife into my pocket and let out a relieved breath once it settled next to Jax's folded blade. I felt complete, like someone had re-attached a missing limb.

The relaxed moment turned tense in a flash. Jax's hand shot out, his fingers curling around Aries's neck. The teen gasped for air, but Jax didn't let up. The heels of Aries's boots slid in the grass as the former leader of the Inner Circle dashed forward. A few paces later, he slammed the young Lunin into a tree. I cursed the familiar image.

"If I give an order," Jax drawled. "I expect your compliance."

I mouthed, "What did I miss?" at Samson.

He just smirked and ran his finger over the smooth side of the stolen blade.

The Lunin didn't fight back. How could he? The poor kid couldn't breathe.

"Did I not order you to drop your weapons in a pile?"

Aries tried to nod. His legs bucked as Jax pushed him farther up the black trunk.

"Then why the *fuck* did you keep that blade hidden in your pocket?"

"Jax!" I hollered. "Let him go."

He brushed off my desperate plea and tightened his grip around Aries's throat. "You deliberately disobeyed my orders."

I wrung my hands. *Please don't kill him.*

Jax looked over his shoulder at the other young men. Their lifeless expressions supported his earlier argument. Over the years, Zenith's cruel ways had desensitized them to violence.

"Rule number one!" Jax shouted.

The men popped to attention and answered his call. "I live to serve my leader."

"Rule number two!"

"My leader's word is law."

My heart hammered in my chest. *This is insanity. What's he doing?*

"Now," Jax hissed. "Remind Aries of rule number eight."

Louder than before the men shouted, "Insubordination equals execution!"

"Very good." Jax sneered. "It appears Aries forgot the Code of the Collectors."

The Lunin struggled to breathe, his eyes bulging. His face had turned a deep shade of purple.

"Shall I remind him how Zenith reprimands those who don't follow orders?"

Silence. The men didn't say a word.

Jax found my eyes. I shook my head and whispered, "Please don't."

He turned his attention back to Aries. "Lucky for you, I'm not my adoptive father."

Jax released the accused. I braced my hands on my knees, steadying my swaying body. Aries clutched his throat as he slid down the trunk of the tree. He gasped and sputtered, the breath of life returning to his lungs.

My head snapped toward Samson. The bastard laughed. He actually laughed at me, as if he approved the jab my partner snuck into Aries's ass chewing.

I flashed him a vulgar gesture, then looked at Jax when he squatted in front of Aries.

"Let me share a little secret," he said. "Samson loves cutting out tongues. I don't." He snickered at the Lunin's wide-eyed expression. "Shocking, I know. It's the logistics that piss me off. I can never decide what to do with the tongue. Do I make the guy swallow it, or do I put it in his pocket as a reminder to follow orders?"

Aries covered his mouth, protecting the muscular organ he used for speech and chewing.

"Do me a favor and make my life easier." Jax gripped the young man's shoulder. "If I give you an order, follow it."

"Yes, sir."

The former leader of the Inner Circle dragged Aries to his feet, then shoved him at Samson. "The kid's all yours."

"Thanks, Jax." The Solin flipped the blade over in his hand. "I was getting bored over here."

Jax nodded at his comrade, then said, "Walk with me, Elara," as he blew past me.

A demand, not a suggestion. *At least he's not tugging at my wrist this time.* I turned to follow.

Once a safe distance from curious ears, I muttered, "Thanks for not killing Aries."

"That was an act. I had to prove a point."

I crossed my arms. "To me or to Aries?"

"To both of you."

"Damn it, Jax. I get it, okay? You're not Zenith. I'm sorry I compared you to him. But was it necessary to rub it in my face with Aries?"

"I didn't rub it in your face."

"Bullshit. I saw the way you looked at me before you spoke to him. You directed that jab at me, not him. Aries did nothing wrong. He could have kept my knife. But he didn't. He gave it back. He offered us an olive branch, and you snapped it in two."

"I did what needed to be done. He disobeyed my orders. I can't let mistakes slide with these guys. All it takes is one slip up. Aries wouldn't think twice about slitting your throat if it meant saving his own ass."

I rubbed the back of my neck, my skin sticky with sweat. "Why can't I wrap my head around this? I hear what you're saying, but it doesn't feel right."

"I'm sure it doesn't. You're a good person. You don't approve of intimidation, cruelty, and senseless violence. I don't expect you to understand the mind of a Collector, nor do I expect you to agree with our ways."

"*Our* ways?" My face fell. "Is it me against you and the Collectors?"

"No. I'm simply stating this is a new way of thinking for you and your brother."

My cheeks puffed. I didn't want to say it out loud but Jax was right. He had lived on Aroonyx for his entire life, along with Samson and the other Collectors. My brother and I were a tad late to the party.

I inhaled a long breath and found his eyes. "You told me to listen to my gut. The quiet voice that speaks from the heart."

He nodded.

"Well, guess what? It says this iron-fist approach is wrong."

The muscles in his jaw tensed.

I held up my hand, urging him to hold his tongue. "You and Samson have mastered the art of scaring the shit out of everyone you meet. It's an impressive feat to witness, and an effective technique—for now. The problem is Zenith has worn these young men to the bone. Mentally, they're exhausted." I reached for his hands and stared at him with pleading eyes. "Things have got to change. And that change starts with you."

Jax groaned and dropped his chin. "I didn't kill the kid. That's progress."

I chuckled, shaking my head at him.

He tucked a fallen hair behind my ear and said, "This is why we make a great team."

"No, we don't. All we do is fight."

"That's not true. We got along great last night."

I scowled at the seductive smirk that played on his lips. "Don't bring the bedroom into this."

"I won't if you stop ignoring the obvious. We do make a great team. We keep each other grounded. You're not afraid to call me on my shit, and I'm not afraid to call you on yours. We might argue more than most, but we always take time to reflect and re-approach the situation with a level head."

"You're right."

"I always am." He winked.

"And you're a smug bastard."

"That too." He rested a hand on his chest and bowed deeply. "And this smug bastard will do anything for his partner."

"So you'll talk to Samson?" My eyes lit up with the possibility. "Convince him to take it easy on Aries and the others?"

"No." Jax laughed. "We can't take it easy on them right now."

I frowned.

"But I promise you this, I'll share your concerns with him after we defeat Zenith."

"Fair enough." I adjusted the waistband of my shorts, the ring digging into my skin. I touched the hidden gem. "Can I tell Cyrus?"

Jax glanced at my hand. "About the ring you're not wearing?"

I pinned him with a long look. "We went for thirty seconds without arguing."

"Perhaps we should try for a minute."

"Let's throw caution to the wind and go for two."

His lips twitched. "Yes, tell your brother. I didn't plan on keeping it a secret."

I smiled and stretched my lips to meet his. He held up his hand, blocking my efforts. "I can't show affection in front of the boys."

My casual expression turned sour. His shoulders shook with laughter. "Your expression." He cupped my face with his hands. "Priceless."

An insult formed on my tongue. It vanished at the touch of his lips. After a quick embrace, he pulled away and inclined his head toward Samson. The Solin pointed the tip of his blade at a Lunin's throat while shouting in his face.

"I should intervene before the kid loses his tongue."

I grabbed Jax's wrist as he turned. "Here." I handed him his gray knife. "Thanks to Aries, I don't need yours anymore."

Jax swiped the folded blade out of my hand only to replace it with Zenith's. I hissed, as if it had scorched my palm.

"Use it as a spare," he suggested.

"No. I don't want it."

He curled my fingers around the handle and jerked his chin at the pile of weapons near Samson's feet. "We have more knives at our disposal. I want everyone carrying a spare."

"Then I'll choose one from the pile because I'm not using Zenith's."

"I need you armed with the best weapons. The knife Idalia

gave you is fantastic and so is mine, but Zenith's is forged with pure Fired Stone. It's the highest quality blade on Aroonyx."

"What the hell is Fired Stone?"

Jax eyed Samson. His posture relaxed when the Solin released the Lunin and moved on with interrogations.

He met my gaze. "Fired Stone is a rock buried deep underground. During Arun's reign, a farmer discovered it while digging a well. Unlike Clear Stone, Fired Stone remains intact if broken apart. The farmer showed his brother, Nash, a skilled craftsman who worked for Arun."

I thought of my history lessons with Jax. "Was Nash the one who designed the knives for Arun after the Seeker brought the plans from Earth?"

"That's correct. Before the discovery of Fired Stone, Nash tried to manufacture the knives out of Clear Stone."

"I'm guessing that didn't go well," I said, remembering how the rock shavings had vanished in Cyrus's hands after he rubbed his palms together.

"No. It didn't. The blade disappeared each time Nash compacted the stone into the mold."

"I bet that irritated the hell out of Arun."

Jax nodded. "Aware of his brother's predicament, the farmer showed Nash the unique properties of Fired Stone. Since Clear Stone was readily available, Nash combined it with the rare Fired Stone and created the first knife. Unfortunately, it had a huge design flaw."

"What was it?"

"The blade shattered any time it connected with a hard object like a tree trunk or a bone. Nash racked his brain, trying to discover a way to strengthen the blades. Arun, being the impatient man that he was, tossed the failed prototypes into the fireplace of Nash's workshop. Once the ashes cooled, Nash retrieved the knives and noticed how the heat had altered the property of the stone, solving the mystery. The blades were no longer brittle." Jax lifted his knife. "When sharpened, they can cut through almost anything."

I eyed Zenith's folded blade. *Tempting.*

"The demand for Fired Stone soared once Nash showed Arun the perfected design. His brother stopped farming and started excavating. No one knows the exact number of blades Nash produced during Arun's reign, but it was enough to arm the Collectors during the Clearing of the Seekers."

"So that means Samson has a Fired Stone blade."

He shook his head. "It's not pure like Zenith's. It's forged with Fired Stone and Clear Stone."

"What about your knife?"

"My blade was custom designed." He showed me the small bumps on the handle.

"I thought those were for decoration."

The Lunin chuckled, running his thumb along the pattern. "No, these act as grips for my fingers. It helps improve my aim." He flicked his wrist. "The blade isn't pure."

"I'm confused. If pure Fired Stone blades were—*are* so valuable, why didn't Zenith have Nash produce more? Why didn't Arun?"

"Executing the perfected design is a tedious job. Others have tried and failed. Nash mastered the technique, but creating a pure Fired Stone blade takes time, time that Zenith had. He didn't mind waiting for Nash to make his knife. And he didn't arm us with Fired Stone blades because he's a proud man who desires rare items that others can't have."

"So he's a sadistic prick and a spoiled brat."

"Excellent description." Jax smirked.

"I'm guessing Arun didn't have this time?"

"No. He needed to arm his Collectors in a hurry, so he settled with the hybrid blades."

I rotated Zenith's knife in my hand. "So this is the only pure blade on Aroonyx?"

"Yes. That's why I want you to have it. It's strong enough to slice through any material."

I touched the scar on my stomach. "It pierced through my coat that night. A hybrid blade couldn't have done that much damage, could it?"

"No. It would have bounced off the material."

"Is Nash still alive?"

"Yes. He lives at Zenith's."

My nose crinkled. "How old is he?"

"I'm not sure. I never met him."

"Jax, you lived at Zenith's for six years. How did you never meet the guy?"

"After Arun's death, Nash closed his workshop. When the disbanded group of Collectors ransacked Arun's dwelling, they stole the original designs and sold them to different black-smiths who agreed to replicate Nash's work for a pricey fee. The imitation knives were shit. The blacksmiths couldn't forge the blades properly. They couldn't figure out Nash's trick. It has something to do with the amount of time he leaves them in the fire."

My eyes grew at this added bit of information.

"Once Zenith gained control of Aroonyx, Nash appeared at his door and offered his services. Zenith keeps his precious items close. He imprisoned Nash in a cell, a workshop attached to his personal chambers. Zenith is the only one who converses with the master craftsman."

"Geez, Jax. Why are you only telling me this now?"

"It never came up."

I gave him a long look.

A smug grin crossed his striking face as he said, "I thought a history lesson on Fired Stone would ease your troubled mind, help you let go of your foolish notions." He pointed at Zenith's knife. "You'll see when you throw it. It never misses its mark."

I swore under my breath, the blade feeling lighter in my hand.

Take it, Elara.

I stilled at the dealer's severe tone. *No. You don't get a say. I make my own decisions.*

Then make the right one and listen to Jax.

The Lunin noted my hesitation. "Take it." He wrapped his fingers around my fisted hand, pushing the folded blade deeper into my palm. "And *don't* be afraid to use it."

36

SOMEWHERE ELSE

"I t's about time you showed up," Cyrus said, gesturing to our training groups. "I tried to calm them down. They won't listen to me or Orion."

I lifted my hand to silence the heated chatter coming from the Solin's and Lunin's mouths. "Jax and Samson have everything under control."

A man shook his head at me. "Those kids are Collectors. We can't trust them."

"He's right," said a Lunin. "What if more show up?"

"I'll deal with it," I said.

"How?" a Solin asked.

"With force."

The man flinched at my sharp tone.

"Easy, sis. We don't need another Jax."

I swore, wiping the moisture off my brow. *With force? Why did I say that?*

"Listen," I said, pointing to the line of men near Jax and Samson. "Those teens are—*were* Inactive Members. They're underage." I found the mothers in the crowd. "A few of them are kids. Each one risked their life to get here, and more than half died trying."

My audience's shoulders sagged, and their eyes lowered to the ground.

"I'm not asking you to accept them with open arms. I'm asking you to see them with an open mind. You won't have to train with them. We'll keep you separated—for now."

The Solins nodded in agreement, while the Lunins watched Aries's group with cautious eyes.

I clapped my hands, distracting them from their curious thoughts. And no—I didn't bother embarrassing myself with another poor attempt at whistling.

"Since Jax and Samson are busy handling our latest recruits, my brother and Orion will work with the men. Ladies, meet me over there." I inclined my head toward a cluster of trees at the other end of Iah's property. A secluded area far away from the ex-Collectors.

The crowd dispersed, but their whispers merged. Skepticism coated their tongues, the uncertainty catching in the breeze. I shut my eyes and inhaled the summer air, my nostrils flaring at the phantom smell of distrust. *Time. Give them time.*

I looked at Blaze clinging to my brother's arm. "You should go play with the other kids."

"No. Cyrus made me a promise."

"Oh, did he now?" I asked, stealing a glance at my twin. He just grinned.

"He said he'd teach me how to use a knife," Blaze said.

"Did you ask your mother?"

"No."

I rested a hand on his shoulder. "Blaze, you need her permission to train with Cyrus."

The young boy dropped my brother's hand and sprinted toward the group of women while yelling, "Mom!"

He tripped over his untied laces, leaving a boot behind. He didn't bother to stop and pick it up.

I cracked a smile. "That kid's hilarious. He reminds me of you."

"I don't lose my boots."

I laughed hard, recalling the morning we trained in the snow outside of Idalia's. "Only when Samson kicks your ass."

"Ha ha. Very funny." Cyrus crossed his arms and scanned my face. "You're extra chipper this morning. Did your time with Jax in the bedroom last night boost your confidence?"

I slapped him in the chest. "I don't kiss and tell."

"The walls are thin, sis. Just saying."

My cheeks burned with heat.

He offered me his hand. "Welcome to the club. We're open year-round and encourage our members to explore the benefits their partners offer." A mischievous grin danced on his lips. "I'm glad you joined."

I knocked his hand away. "Are you done comparing my sex life to a Costco membership?"

His grin grew. "Nope."

"Fine." I pulled the ring out of my pocket. "Does your club offer lifetime memberships?"

Cyrus stammered inaudible words as I slipped it onto my finger.

"Because Jax did when he proposed to me last night."

My response, combined with the added piece of jewelry, wiped the smug grin right off his face. Cyrus grabbed my hand and rotated it back and forth, his eyes wide with a mixture of shock and confusion.

"What did you say?" he rasped.

"I said yes."

"*Elara.*" Cyrus held his head as if he was trying to keep his brain from exploding. "You're only eighteen."

395

My jaw cracked open with mocked surprise. "I am? Thanks for clearing that up. I had no idea."

"I'm serious. You're barely an adult and Jax is—" he paused, his cheeks puffing.

"Jax is what?"

"He's *old.*"

I snorted. "He's twenty-three, not forty."

"Still." He wiggled his fingers at the ring. "*That* is not okay."

My face fell. "Why?"

"Because you hardly know the guy."

"Perhaps, but he's known me for my entire life." I rotated the ring, watching the sunlight reflect off the center stone. "Jax gets me, Cyrus."

"So do I."

I lifted my eyes. "You're my twin brother. That's a given. We can tell each other our private thoughts with a raised eyebrow or a crooked smile."

"It's a pretty cool talent."

"The coolest." I chuckled.

Cyrus let out a tired breath. "You're so young. You have your entire life to meet someone else. What if another guy comes along and hits the mark?"

"Jax already hit the bull's eye with me. The connection we share is—"

"You don't have to explain. I get it." His amber eyes drifted to the Lunin. "You move, he moves. The two of you follow each other like planets orbiting the sun."

I hummed my agreement. I had expressed a similar analogy to Jax after his return.

My brother met my gaze. "Are you sure about this?"

"No. Not at all."

He huffed a breath. "I guess Jax's brutal honesty is rubbing off on you."

"An honest answer is better than a false promise."

"Then you have my blessing."

"Really?"

"Yep. Jax is a good man. He'll take care of you."

"We'll take care of each other."

The breeze rattled the tree branches. Breathing as one, we filled our lungs with the sweet summer air and took a moment of silence. Was it to admire our surroundings or to say goodbye to the old life I left behind? I wasn't sure. Regardless, it felt appropriate.

"It's funny, isn't it?" Cyrus asked.

"What is?"

"Life."

I eyed the vast space, noting the luscious landscape, the women chatting in the shade, the men training with Orion, the ex-Collectors undergoing their interrogations, and my fiancé.

"Last year, we started our senior year of high school," Cyrus said. "We didn't know each other, then Jax showed up and turned our world upside down. A few months later we're living on another planet, starting an uprising against an evil dictator, and now, my twin sister informed me she's marrying said dictator's adoptive son."

I laughed at the absurdity of it all. "Well, when you put it like that our life sounds similar to a serial drama. *Game of Thrones*-worthy, that's for sure."

"Minus the incest."

"True, though Jaime and Cersei kicked some serious ass together."

He nodded, a huge grin crossing his face. "Samson could play the Hound."

"And Jax would make a great Jon Snow."

Cyrus offered me a fist bump. "Nailed it."

"It's the brooding attitude and the hair."

He laughed hard. "I wish we had the dragons."

"They'd come in handy. You could ride Drogon to Zenith's and torch the place."

"That would up my cool with Idalia."

"And with Samson."

My brother scratched the stubble on his chin. "Jax really burst my bubble when he told us magical creatures didn't exist on Aroonyx. I still search the skies, hoping I'll see a dragon or some other badass flying beast."

I squinted at the glowing orb above. "You know what sucks?"

"What?"

"We'll never get to see how the show ends?"

"You might if Jax takes you back to Earth. Speaking of Earth." His eyes grew. "What would your parents say if they heard of your engagement?"

I winced; his words impaled me on an invisible spike sharpened by guilt. I hadn't thought about my parents in days—weeks. The attachment to my old life on Earth lessened with each sunrise and sunset. I swallowed a dense ball of grief.

"Are you okay?"

"I'm not sure," I whispered, rubbing a hand over the cold spot that formed in my chest. "The memories of my life on Earth are fading away."

"Don't sweat it, sis. I bet Jax can jump once we defeat Zenith. He'll take you home."

"He'll take *us* home."

My brother broke eye contact and stared at the swaying branches overhead.

"*Cyrus*?"

He forced a smile. "Yeah, he'll take us home."

"Why are you acting weird?"

"I'm not."

"Liar. You're hiding something from me. Why wouldn't we go back together?"

His posture tensed.

"Just tell me."

"I had this vivid dream."

I gulped, remembering the vision I had of Jax imprisoned at Zenith's. "What was it about?"

"You and Jax were standing behind your house on Earth. Jax looked the same but you looked different."

"How so?"

"You had blonde hair, and your eyes matched Zenith's. One was blue and one was orange."

I grimaced. "That sounds like a nightmare."

"It wasn't. The two of you seemed really happy together, peaceful."

"Did you look the same? Was your hair a different color?"

"I don't know. I couldn't see my body."

"Why not?"

"I wasn't there."

"Where were you?"

"Somewhere else. Somewhere in between."

I blinked and blinked again. Grief trailed his words. A grief I couldn't bear to face.

"Hey." He squeezed my arm. "Don't overthink it. It was just a dream. Remember what I told you after you woke up from that nightmare at Idalia's?"

My heart collided with my head, a battle of gut instinct versus practical reasoning. My head won, moving my lips for me. "I do remember." The words came out clipped—detached. "You said *dreams aren't real.*"

37

PRIDEFUL EYES

The living room appeared darker than usual. Perhaps it was the snow-filled clouds that engulfed the morning sky like dollops of whipped cream blocking out the morning light. Or perhaps it had nothing to do with the weather and everything to do with the ominous tone of our meeting. My nostrils fluttered. The damp logs in the fireplace hissed, filling the house with more smoke than warmth.

"Are you sure about this?" Jax asked Samson.

"It's our only option. Zenith has more men. The remaining citizens living in the villages need to see Elara and Cyrus with their own eyes."

"It's too risky."

Samson ignored Jax's concern and turned to Orion. "What's the latest head count?"

"Two hundred and ninety-six. But one hundred and seventy are willing and able to fight."

The eldest Solin combed through his beard. "And no new recruits have shown up in days. Is this correct?"

Orion nodded. Jax steadied my bobbing leg as I eyed my

brother. His gaze never left Idalia, who sat with her eyes focused on Samson.

"We don't have the numbers," Samson said to Jax. "The men subjected to the ordinance either left their homes escorted by the Collectors or volunteered to join Zenith. We need more bodies: men, women, anyone who can fight."

"Is there anyone left to recruit?" I asked.

"Not the ones affected by the ordinance," Samson answered. "I'm sure there's a handful of women and older men lying low, hoping to avoid confrontation."

"Perfect. And you want us to bring the conflict to them."

"Desperate times call for—"

"What's Zenith's latest head count?" Cyrus interrupted.

Samson motioned to Jax. "What did the scout report yesterday?"

"Surya had to keep his distance because the place was over-flowing with recruits. Zenith has them training outside. From his vantage point, he reported around three hundred and fifty. This number includes Zenith, the Inner Circle, and the recruits he could see."

Cyrus swore, sinking deeper into the couch.

"This is why I'm suggesting"—Samson shook his head —"no, this is why I'm *insisting* we visit the villages."

Idalia bristled at his abrasive tone.

"Sorry, sweetie." He gave her a loving smile, then looked at Jax. "We're running out of time. Our recruits are doing better with their training, but let's be honest, they're not ready for what lies ahead."

My jaw clenched. "So we're sending them on a suicide mission."

"They know what they signed up for, kid."

"He's right," Jax agreed.

I pushed up the long sleeves of my shirt. The frustration that boiled in my veins along with my brother's proximity left my skin surging with heat. "Samson, I've got a bad feeling. What if we run into the Inner Circle?"

"Elara, I don't give a fuck about your feelings right now."

Cyrus and Jax tensed, their protective instincts taking over.

Samson scowled at their rigid postures. "There are only six members of the Inner Circle left. I'll select ten men from Jax and Cyrus's group, the ones who have shown the most progress in their training, and they'll join us on this mission. I'll arm them with the extra knives we confiscated from the Inactive Members." He circled his finger around the room. "Including those ten recruits, we'll have fourteen well-trained men"—he inclined his head toward me—"and one highly skilled woman."

"Orion, do you have a pencil?"

My question tugged at his brows. "Yeah. Why?"

"I should jot down that compliment before I forget it."

Cyrus laughed hard.

"Is there anything I can do to help?" Idalia asked Samson.

He looked at the doctor. "I'm sure Iah needs an assistant while we're gone."

"I do," he called from the kitchen. "I could use an extra hand. You could help me check on the men who injured themselves during yesterday's training exercise."

The beautiful Solin twisted in her chair to see the Lunin. "Sure. I'd like that."

"Hey, Samson?" I asked.

His orange eyes found mine. "What's up?"

"Are we safe, here at Iah's?"

Everyone's heads turned to face me.

"What do you mean?" he asked.

"Zenith saw Orion's face the night we rescued Idalia. I'm sure he knows we're staying at Iah's. Why hasn't he sent the Inner Circle to attack?"

"No one knows where I live," Iah answered. "Remember

how shocked I was to see you and your brother the morning you showed up with Jax?"

"Yeah," I replied. "But Aries found us, and Zenith wants us dead. If I were him, I would have sent the Collectors searching."

Samson climbed to his feet. "That's why I sent runners to the villages."

"What are runners?"

"Men I pay to spread rumors. After we rescued Idalia, I instructed them to whisper our location loud enough for the Collectors to hear." He shrugged. "The last time I checked, Iah lived way up north."

"Ah," I murmured. "That's why Aries mentioned the rumor of our whereabouts."

Samson nodded.

"But Iah's home is south east," Cyrus said.

Our mentor shook his head at my brother. "At least your Solin strength makes up for your lack of intelligence."

My brother blinked. "*Oh*, I get it now."

"Geez, Cyrus," I scolded. "Get your head out of your ass."

He rammed his elbow in my ribs. "Okay, *Samson*."

The eldest Solin clapped Jax on the shoulder as he passed. "I need your help in selecting the men from your group."

"Give me a few minutes. I need to speak with Elara first."

"Don't keep me waiting," Samson said, reaching for his coat hanging on a silver hook. "We've got a long journey ahead of us."

"I won't."

The Solin pulled open the door, sending an icy breeze blasting through the home. The fire expressed its agitation with a thick plume of smoke rising from the chimney.

Jax stood from the couch and motioned for me to follow him through the living room.

I crossed my arms once he stopped in the middle of the

hallway. Bothered by his troubled expression, I asked, "What's wrong?"

"We share the same thoughts regarding Samson's plan."

My heart knocked against my chest. "Then why did you agree to it?"

"I didn't have a choice. If Samson puts his mind to something, he—"

"Risks getting us killed?"

"Shh," he hissed.

I dragged him farther down the hallway, then whispered, "You told me to listen to my gut, and now you're not listening to yours. I thought you said your Seeker's intuition always proves true."

"It does, but Samson ignores my gift. He's a practical man who makes practical decisions. You heard his response when you mentioned *your* feeling. Can you imagine his reaction if I had expressed my concerns?"

I massaged my temples. I had suffered more headaches over the past few months than my entire life combined. With weary eyes, I stared at my partner. "Jax, I have a huge knot in my stomach. Samson wants us wandering around the villages, enlisting more recruits. This is a stupid plan. The remaining villagers won't join our side. Why would they? If the ordinance doesn't affect them, then they're safe in their homes. Not only is this plan foolish, but it's dangerous. We don't know who's lurking around the corner."

"Then don't go. Stay here with Iah and Idalia."

"That will never fly with Samson. He wants the villagers seeing me and Cyrus together."

"Then suck it up. Everyone knows we're in over our heads."

I took a step backward, away from the angered Lunin.

"Forgive me." He sighed, reaching for my hand. "The uprising is wearing my patience thin."

"I'd say likewise, but I had no patience to begin with."

He chuckled, slipping his hand into my back pocket. "Carry these knives in your coat. I don't want you fumbling to reach them."

I took the folded blades from his hand. "Is this how our relationship works now? We're arguing, lying naked in the bed, or discussing where to conceal our weapons."

"It won't always be this way," he said, moving his lips toward mine. "I promise."

"Hey, lovebirds."

I growled at the sound of my brother's voice. Jax pulled away.

"We better get moving. Samson wants us back home before dark."

Jax spun on his heels and headed toward the door.

My brother played with a loose button on his coat, a mindless distraction until Jax passed. Without lifting his eyes, he asked me, "Why the secret meeting?"

I dropped my head and dragged my feet down the hallway. "We've got a bad feeling about this plan."

"It doesn't matter. We have to go."

"You sound like Samson."

"Great minds think alike."

"And foolish minds get people killed."

He frowned.

"Cyrus, promise me you'll be careful today."

"I will."

Our heads turned as Idalia neared. She threw her arms around me. I winced at the sudden impact.

"Promise me you'll be careful," she whispered.

My chest rumbled with laughter. "I just said that to Cyrus."

"And I'm saying it to *you*," she said, locking her eyes onto mine.

"I'll be careful only if you promise to stay busy with Iah. Don't sit in Orion's room all day, worrying while we're gone."

405

"I won't." Mischief flickered in her golden eyes. "I have big plans today."

"With whom?"

"Thea. She hasn't heard of your engagement."

I smiled, rotating the ring on my finger. "I want a full report when I get back."

"I'm happy for you, Elara. You and Jax are a perfect match."

My brother puffed his cheeks, appearing bored with our "girlish" talk.

I shot him a warning glare before saying, "Thank you, Idalia. That means a lot."

"You kids be careful," Iah said from the dining table. "Take care of my son."

I stepped out of the hallway. "We will, as long as he behaves himself."

Orion snickered at my comment, then gave his father a warm hug. "I'll see you later this evening."

"I'll cook a nice stew and have it ready for dinner."

"That sounds great, Dad."

"Love you, son."

Orion nodded, strolled toward the door, then offered me my coat. I slid the knives into the fur-lined pocket.

"That's a good idea," he said, following suit.

"Yeah, it makes them easier to access."

Idalia grabbed Cyrus's arm before his fingers touched the doorknob. He turned.

"Come back to me in one piece," she whispered.

"I always do," he said, kissing her cheek.

I smiled. It warmed my heart to see Idalia accept his tender embrace.

THE BLISTERING cold slapped at our faces while we waited for

Samson and Jax to appear with the others. Cyrus turned up his collar to block the oncoming wind. I tucked my hands deeper into my coat pockets, my fingers grazing the two knives.

The rays of the morning sun couldn't pierce the moisture-filled puffs that blew in from the north. I squinted to see through the fog that cloaked the forest, my warm breath leaving my mouth in a cloud.

My gaze drifted to the white fluff piled high around Iah's property. It reminded me of the cotton batting my mother used to decorate her snow village during Christmas. A swirl of smoke in the distance caught my eye.

I turned to Orion. "Are you sure they're not freezing to death? This weather is brutal."

"The recruits are fine. They have tents, blankets, fires. We already told you, this weather is normal for the people living on Aroonyx."

"Well, I think it sucks," Cyrus said, rocking to stay warm.

"Agreed," I muttered.

Before living on Aroonyx, I assumed Jax's tough guy façade coincided with the reason he appeared unfazed by the elements. That opinion vanished once I met the others. Every inhabitant of my birth planet acted indifferent to the weather.

The comforts I took for granted on Earth were unknown to the citizens of Aroonyx. At first, I viewed their modest approach to life as bleak, undesirable. After spending months immersed in their culture, I learned to appreciate the simplicity of a mini-malistic lifestyle.

"Hey, sis."

Snapped out of my trance, I blinked at my brother. "What's up?"

"What was the last song you heard before we left Earth?"

"Ooh, that's a good one." I shivered, burying my hands deeper into the pockets of my coat. "I think it was 'Mercury,' by Sleeping at Last. You?"

"'Get Home,' by Bastille."

"No shit?" My eyes grew. "The lyrics to that song mirror our current situation."

Cyrus chuckled. "Do they ever."

"You guys do realize I have no idea what you're talking about," Orion said.

"We do," I replied. "After we defeat Zenith, Jax will take us back to Earth, we'll grab our phones, and then you can listen to some tunes."

The Lunin's brows touched his hairline.

My brother flattened the grin on his face before he asked Orion, "How's the cell service on Aroonyx? Iah never gave me the Wi-fi password."

I burst into laughter. Orion glared at the two of us.

Cyrus's grin drooped as he pointed to a group of men strolling toward us. "Here they come."

"Is that Aries?" Orion asked, struggling to see through the white haze.

My brother followed his gaze. "It's hard to tell. I can't see shit in this fog."

"I think it is," I confirmed.

Orion's face squished up with confusion. "Why would they bring Aries? Isn't he underage?"

"Who knows." My brother headed down the porch steps. "Let's go find out."

Our boots sloshed through the snow as we hurried to greet the men.

"And make sure you stay together," Samson said to the group.

The Solins and Lunins nodded, slowing their pace. Roshan gave me a warm grin and adjusted the sleeves of his coat. The others kept their eyes fixed on Samson.

Cyrus flicked his wrist at Aries. "You coming with us?"

"Yes, sir." He popped to attention.

"Don't call me, sir. It makes me feel old." Cyrus scowled at the Lunin's rigid posture. "And stop standing like that. You're creeping me out."

"Yes . . . Cyrus."

"Aries turned eighteen yesterday," Jax said. "His traits are active and he's well-trained in the art of combat. That's why he's coming with us."

Cyrus crossed his arms. "I thought Samson wanted us home before sunset."

"I do, but if we're delayed, we'll need more Lunin eyes to see in the dark while we walk."

I looked at Aries. "Happy belated birthday."

"Thank you, miss."

"Please. Call me Elara."

He lifted his gaze for only a moment before Samson snapped, "And if you want to live to see another day, you'll keep calling me Sir."

Aries popped tall once more. "Yes, sir."

Redirecting the group's attention, Jax asked, "Does everyone have their knives?"

We patted our pockets and nodded.

"I hope you got a good night's sleep," Samson said to the men. "We have a lot of ground to cover in a short amount of time. Keep your bitching and whining to yourselves. We'll start in the East Village, then circle around to the others."

"Solins, keep your eyes peeled," Jax said.

Roshan gestured to the thick haze that surrounded us. "The fog presents a challenge."

"I'm aware," Jax said. "Do what you can to scout the area while we walk." He turned his attention to the Lunins. "Keep a clear head and stay sharp. If we run into any trouble, form a tight line behind me and Samson. Don't split up. We're stronger together."

I struggled to swallow the lump of anxiety wedged in my

throat. Orion caught my eye and tried to ease my discomfort with a dramatic facial expression. The ligaments in his neck protruded and his lips curled into a frown, his eyes bulging. I giggled. Though his effort deserved high praise, his execution lacked credibility. He resembled a croaking frog more than a frightened human.

Samson's eyes slid to Orion, then narrowed at the amusement playing on my lips. "Do you find the logistics of this mission entertaining?"

I held my tongue and lowered my gaze. Orion stared at his boots, suddenly intrigued by his tied laces.

Jax clapped the eldest Solin on the back. "Let's move out."

Samson led the way, and the others fell in line. Cyrus moved to my left, Jax to my right. Orion walked beside Aries, while the rest of our group strolled behind.

"Do you still have a bad feeling?" I whispered to Jax.

He nodded. "What about you?"

"Yep, and it's getting stronger."

"At least we're on the same page."

"What are the two of you whispering about?" Cyrus asked.

"Nothing," I lied.

"Spill it, sis."

A white cloud escaped my parted lips. "Are we ready for this?"

"A casual stroll through the woods?" He flashed me a tiny smirk. "Absolutely."

Orion snickered.

I brushed off their sarcasm. "It's a serious question, Cyrus. Are we ready to tackle the unknown?"

"I stopped asking that question the day we left Earth."

I sighed through my parted lips. The two men I cared for the most moved closer, their pale and tan hands brushing against mine. On my left, a familiar heat surged through me.

On my right, a chill tickled my skin as Jax touched the ring on my finger.

My fire and ice—and I was their air, the element that encouraged the flame and solidified the watery cracks in the foundation.

My eyes glowed with pride as I acknowledged my position. For the first time in my life, I felt special, needed. I glanced at the two men. *They can't do this without me.*

No, they can't.

My fingers slid into my pocket, finding Zenith's knife.

Jax and Cyrus are powerless, Elara.

I lifted my chin higher.

Without you, they don't stand a chance.

A sense of satisfaction washed over me. I nodded, agreeing with the masked dealer. A dangerous mistake.

38

A MORAL DILEMMA

losh. Crunch. Slosh. Crunch. The sounds of boots marching through the snow drowned out the men's mindless chatter. The Solins obeyed Jax's command by scanning the vast forest. Unfortunately, the thickening fog hindered their powerful vision, leaving us walking blindly through the white fluff.

Long minutes passed before we reached our first destination, the East Village. My eyelashes fluttered to see the tiny homes through the haze. The stone and wooden dwellings surrounded a desolate strip of shops; a worn path sliced through the center.

Cyrus pawed at the fog as if a plume of smoke had blown into his face. "Where is everyone?"

"Maybe there's no one left," I answered.

"The East Village didn't have a large population to begin with." Samson looked over his shoulder at Roshan. "Your house isn't far from here, right?"

"It's near the edge of town."

"Is your family there?" I asked.

"No." A sharpness lingered in his tone.

"Where are they?"

"Dead."

"Sorry for your loss," Orion murmured, recovering for me.

Roshan shrugged off his condolence. "My wife died during childbirth. The baby was stillborn. People come. People go. End of story."

The amount of resentment that clung to his words stung my heart. I had never inquired about the Solin's personal life, nor had I spoken with the other recruits about theirs. *Perhaps I should get to know the people risking their lives for us.*

Roshan cleared his throat. "The men affected by the ordinance left the East Village after it passed. Their families stayed behind. I haven't returned since we started training at Iah's."

"Let's go see for ourselves," Samson said.

We sidestepped our way down the hill toward the quiet residences. A few gusts later, our group huddled together, eyes fixed on the home before us. A cracked lantern hung from a hook near the front door. It didn't glow with inviting warmth.

Jax pointed at the chimney. "No smoke. I doubt anyone's home."

"We have to check," Samson said, stomping up the porch steps.

The fragile structure shuddered as he banged his fist on the door. My tongue hissed against my teeth. The lantern crashed onto the Clear Stone floor. Glass exploded around Samson's feet. He swore at the jagged shards, then stormed back down the steps.

Samson repeated this routine twelve times. With four casualties under his belt, he glared at the lantern swinging, taunting him in the breeze. I frowned at the decrepit home. Blocks of Clear Stone had withered to lopsided chunks, forcing the structure to lean to one side, and half the wooden shingles had rotted to black splinters.

I moved closer to my brother, away from the death trap. "That chimney looks like it's about to slide off the roof."

"Mm-hmm." He pulled me to the other side of him.

After five determined knocks, the door hinges squeaked. An elderly Lunin with the skin of a dried prune peered through the crack.

"What do you want?" he spat, his voice was thick with mucus.

Spit sprayed onto Samson's face. He didn't flinch. He just stepped aside and waved a hand at me and Cyrus.

The wrinkles on the man's face deepened. "Be gone!" he shouted, shooing us away. "Traitors aren't welcome here."

Samson gave the door his middle finger after it slammed in his face.

"Well, that went well," Cyrus muttered.

I sighed, fastening the top button of my coat.

"Let's check the vendors," Jax suggested.

After a brisk walk, we spread out, searching the town for recruits.

I sprinted from an apothecary to a hardware store. Not a soul in sight. Baffled, I pressed my nose against the window of a shop that sold yards of fabric. Gray material spooled around wooden planks, the ends covered with evidence of abandonment.

"There's no one here!" I yelled to the others. "Everything's covered in dust."

"Keep trying!" Samson hollered back.

Across the narrow path, Cyrus jiggled the handle of the general store. Roshan tried opening the window of a blacksmith's shop, and the other men knocked on every door in sight.

My eyes grew as I observed the snow-covered ground. "Hey, guys!"

The men turned.

"Look." I squatted and ran my fingers over the grooves stamped into the compacted fluff. "These are our footprints. No one has traveled this path in days." I dusted off my hands. "Not since the last snowfall."

Jax hurried down the stairs of a nearby shop and inspected the boot prints.

"Where is everyone?" I asked him. "It's a ghost town."

"I'm not sure. I've never seen it this quiet before."

"Let's head out to the other villages," said a raspy voice.

I gasped, clutching my chest. Samson had appeared out of nowhere, the fog cloaking him with invisibility.

Jax didn't budge. He just nodded at his comrade. "We'll catch up with you in a bit."

"Don't linger for too long. We need to stay together."

Another nod from Jax before Samson vanished into the haze.

"This shit is crazy," Orion said.

My heart nearly leapt out of my chest for the second time in thirty seconds as he moved beside me. "Good Lord. Why does everyone keep sneaking up on me?"

"Sorry." He chuckled. "At least I'm not a Collector."

"That's not funny."

With a heavy sigh, Jax said, "Orion brings up a good point. This fog presents a huge challenge if we're ambushed."

I gulped at the thought of Pollux and the others.

"Don't worry," he assured me. "I'll keep you safe."

"What if the other villages are deserted?" I asked.

"They can't be." Orion eyed Jax for backup. "More than half of Aroonyx's population resides in the West Village."

"He's right, and if—"

"Jax!"

Our heads turned toward Samson's voice. My pulse quickened at the urgency in his tone.

"Get your asses over here!" he bellowed.

We sprinted across the worn path, our boots sliding through the snow as we rounded a corner. Two Lunins lost their lunch, spraying their boots with chunks of undigested food. A few of the other men stumbled, tripping over their own feet. Aries stood motionless, his face paler than usual. Roshan fell to his knees.

My fingers gripped Jax's arm. He cursed at the top of his lungs while Orion and Cyrus struggled to process the carnage that lay at our feet: a pile of mutilated bodies.

Oh God. My trembling hand shot to my mouth. The horrific sight would haunt me for the rest of my life.

The breeze wafted the rot and decay toward us. I bit my knuckles to keep from vomiting. People rarely discuss the defecation that occurs after a person takes their final breath. The smell is something you never forget. Cyrus gagged, fighting nature's reaction to clear his gut. Orion swallowed hard. The doctor's son had a strong stomach.

Elderly men, women of every age, and children were stacked carelessly on top of each other, their beaten and broken bodies twisted at odd angles. Black and blue bruises lined their tan and pale skin, and their scalps hung off their skulls, ice crystals spreading like cobwebs on the raw flesh underneath. The blood that dripped from their nostrils had dried and crusted with the snot and frozen tears that streaked their faces. Tremors rippled through me. *This can't be real. People aren't this cruel.*

My eyes darted from one corpse to the next, searching for survivors. A pointless endeavor. Lips twisted into pained screams and lifeless expressions stared back. The Collectors had slaughtered them all. The morbid image of sliced throats, removed tongues, and skinned bodies caused my legs to wobble. The sight of a deceased mother holding her decapitated infant sent me to my knees. Jax caught me, easing my shaking limbs to the ground.

"Don't look," he whispered, shielding my face with his hand.

Too late. I couldn't un-see the horrors that surrounded me. I breathed hard. My grief transformed into anger, pushing me to my feet.

"Why?" I cried, tears pooling in my eyes. I gestured to the mound of bodies. "These people were innocent."

Aries nudged a deceased man with the toe of his boot. "They've been dead for days. I'm shocked they went through with it."

Samson's head turned so fast, I thought it would snap off his neck. Jax and Cyrus stilled while Orion muttered, "Oh shit."

"What do you know!" Samson hollered, curling his calloused fingers around the Lunin's coat collar.

Aries's blue eyes bulged. He stammered, trying to string together an answer.

The delay in response only infuriated the Solin. His voice shook with rage as he spat, "The years have left my hands stained with blood. What's a little more?" He reached for his knife, then aimed the tip at Aries's neck. "Tell me everything you know, or I'll slice your *fucking* throat and toss you onto the pile with the others."

"Before we escaped," Aries rasped. "I heard Zenith discussing the new ordinance with Elio."

"And?" Samson's voice raised.

"The families of those who joined the uprising are charged with high treason, so he ordered Elio to send the AMs to the East Village to perform the executions."

I paled. Everything made sense. The abandoned town, the man's reaction when he saw us standing outside his home. I fought back tears. *Hurting those who joined our side isn't enough. The bastard wants to destroy their loved ones.*

I thought of the men staying at Iah's. The majority left their families behind, assuming they were safer at home. My attention snagged on the heap of bodies—again. Quick breaths entered my lungs. *Are these lifeless souls the members of their families?* I reached for my brother's arm. *I'm going to pass out.* He held me steady.

Jax stormed toward Aries like a trained killer locked onto his target. With a flick of his wrist, he exposed the blade of his gray knife and pressed the tip into the Lunin's neck. Blood trickled from the wound.

"Innocent lives were lost." Jax's voice was calm, too calm. "You heard Zenith give the order, yet you didn't share this information during interrogations."

Aries's body shook with fear. He shut his eyes, bracing himself for the painful blow.

"Look at them!" Jax shouted, grabbing him by the hair and forcing his gaze toward the pile. "We could have saved them!"

"I didn't have a confirmation," Aries stammered. "I wasn't—"

Samson pulled him closer, ire flashing in his eyes. "Did you not hear Zenith give Elio the order?"

"Yes, sir, but I didn't think he would follow through with it."

Jax pushed the knife deeper. "How long did you live at Zenith's?"

"Eight years, sir."

"And during this time, did you ever witness a member of the Inner Circle break rule number two?"

Aries's eyes watered with regret. "No, sir. I just hoped—"

"Hoped?" An unstable laugh left Jax's mouth. "Do you mean to tell me, you *hoped* Elio knew the difference between right and wrong?"

"I guess. I just . . ."

"Do we look like fucking idiots?!" Samson barked.

"No, sir."

"I asked you to divulge information that could assist us on this mission."

"And you disobeyed," Jax hissed.

Aries's eyes darted back and forth between the two men; the off-beat rhythm matched my palpitating heart.

"Damn," Cyrus whispered. "They might kill him. Right here, in front of us."

I couldn't speak. Nor could Aries. Fear held both of our tongues.

"Should we intervene?" Orion asked.

My brother huffed a breath. "No. I'm not risking my life for that son of a bitch."

Jax twisted his knife, widening the wound on Aries's neck. "You disobeyed my orders the first day we met." He jerked his chin at the dead bodies. "And now this."

Roshan climbed to his feet, his cautious eyes glued to the ex-Collectors. The other men kept their distance. Their loyalties lay with Samson and Jax, not Aries.

"I'm sorry," the teen cried. "I didn't think they'd go through with it. I didn't—"

"Hold him, Jax."

"No! Please, no!"

Profanity escaped Orion's mouth as the former leader of the Inner Circle moved into position. He kicked the accused in the back of the knees, then grabbed a handful of hair and angled Aries's neck toward Samson. The young Lunin squirmed, desperate to avoid the inevitable. Jax tightened his grip, forcing his compliance.

My brother crossed his arms and scowled at the wet spot forming on Aries's pants.

Samson snickered while checking the sharpness of his blade. "Aries, you withheld information. That's a fancy way of saying you fucking lied to my face." He looked at Jax. "Let's begin with the execution."

My partner nodded.

"No!" Aries begged, tears streaming down his cheeks.

Shit. They're going to kill him. I struggled to catch my breath. *The dead bodies and now this. It's too much.*

Samson turned to the men in our group. "Fair warning. Executions can get a little messy."

Roshan blew out a sharp breath and stood tall. Everyone else's jaws fell open. Aries's shoulders shook with violent sobs. Ignoring his desperate pleas, Samson spit onto the snow and raised his knife.

"Please." My voice sounded smaller than ever. "Don't do it."

"Give me one good reason, Elara."

"We need him on this mission. We need the Inactive Members."

"No, we don't," Cyrus argued. "He's a *fucking* traitor."

"I have to agree with your brother," Samson said.

I took a step forward. "He made an honest mistake. That doesn't make him a traitor."

Samson adjusted the grip on his knife. "A mistake that cost him his life."

My fingers clenched my scalp. *I can't watch.*

"Wait." Jax grabbed Samson's wrist, stopping the blade before it pierced the main artery in Aries's neck. "Elara's right. He has a voice with the others. We don't have the numbers. His group is small, but they know how to fight. If we kill him, they'll abandon our side."

"I don't give a fuck if he has pull with the other Collectors at Iah's. He disobeyed our orders."

"Then teach him a lesson," Jax said, tapping Aries's lips with the smooth side of his blade.

Before I could inquire, Samson reached into Aries's mouth and sliced off a piece of his tongue. The Lunin hollered in pain.

"Now swallow it," Samson said, offering him the chunk of flesh.

My stomach churned. Orion and Roshan exchanged a slew of curse words.

Blood dripped out of Aries's gaped mouth as he stared at the Solin's outstretched hand.

"Do it!" Samson yelled.

Between the mutilated bodies and the oily residue that stained Aries's teeth, I had to look away. *I'm going to be sick.*

"Easy, sis," Cyrus soothed. "It'll be over soon."

The blanket of snow near Samson's boots. Yes, that's a safe place to look.

Nope. Drops of blood splattered the white fluff. I cursed, lifting my gaze back to the unfortunate Lunin. He stretched his trembling fingers to reach the tip of his tongue.

"I'm not a patient man," Samson snapped. "You have three seconds to comply or I'll shove it down your throat."

Aries snatched the piece of flesh, cracked open his jaw, and tossed it into his mouth.

"Swallow," Samson demanded.

The teen shut his eyes and obeyed.

Another man emptied the contents of his stomach. Roshan stepped aside, keeping his boots clean from the projectile vomit.

Samson glowered at the sick man and used Aries's coat to wipe the blood off his blade. He gave Jax a long look. "We're working with a bunch of pussies."

My partner didn't respond. He just released Aries and walked away.

The injured Lunin collapsed onto the snow. He ripped a piece of fabric from his shirt and applied pressure to his now shorter tongue.

"Let this be a warning," Samson said, crouching beside him. "If you ever lie to me again, I'll cut off your *fucking* head."

Aries's eyes watered. The pain overwhelmed him as he mouthed, "Yes, sir."

"We move!" Samson hollered. "Now."

I stood motionless, mind blown by the events that unfolded

in the East Village. I pointed to the dead. "What about the bodies? We need to bury them."

Samson didn't stop his quick pace or bother to look back at me when he said, "They're gone, Elara."

"He's right." Cyrus gave my shoulder a loving squeeze before following our fearless mentor.

I turned to Jax. "We can't leave them like this."

He stomped his boot, the ice crystals compacting under his weight. "The ground is frozen solid. We can't dig that many graves. We don't have the tools."

"Then burn them," I pleaded. "Start a fire."

"We can't." His severe tone left no room for argument. "The smoke will attract attention. Zenith will know we were here."

I chewed on my nails, my eyes bouncing between the rotting corpses. They stopped on the decapitated infant. I choked back a sob. "This is wrong, Jax."

"I know it is." He motioned to Aries. The young Lunin sat with his head in his hands, blood spilling through the cracks of his fingers. "The entire situation. It's all *fucking* wrong."

39

THE IMMORTAL TWIN

The cold nipped at my bones with each weary step that led me farther from the souls we left behind, the souls we couldn't save.

A veil of grief hung over our group, the heavy train dragging in the snow behind us. The casual exchange of words had ceased. The determined attitudes had faded. Everyone appeared lost in the maze of their troubled thoughts. A deep line had formed between Roshan's brows after he saw his friends' mutilated bodies tossed into a pile like forgotten laundry. The dark skin around his knuckles had turned pale; he hadn't stopped clenching his fists since we departed. The massacre in the East Village left the men on edge. The Solins expressed their anger with set jaws and narrowed eyes, while the Lunins internalized their emotions with faraway looks.

The stillness of the forest added an eerie quality to our endeavor. The black tree limbs didn't scratch or fight with each other, the emerald leaves didn't shiver, and the phantom wolf didn't howl. Nature's conductor had paused its symphony.

I wiggled my numb toes and rolled a ball of lint in my pocket. "This is taking forever."

"How much farther?" Cyrus asked.

Samson pointed to a village beyond a cluster of trees. "We're here."

I stretched my neck to get a better look. Rows of houses surrounded the town center. "It looks bigger than the East Village."

"It's the second largest," Samson said, pivoting to face us. He ran a hand over his beard and let out a long breath. "I don't have a clue what to expect, especially after what we saw earlier."

The men tensed.

Samson shot Aries a glance filled with malice. "Let's hope they caught wind of what happened to the others and made it out alive."

He inclined his head toward the desolate town. The men followed, but I froze. "Did you guys hear that?"

Fourteen men spun on their heels and reached for their knives.

"Where?" Jax asked, scanning every tree in sight.

I pointed at twelve o'clock. "There."

"Show yourself," Samson demanded.

Slosh. Crunch.

Blades flipped out of handles. Jax held up a fist, commanding us to hold our formation. I sucked in a sharp breath, my pulse thumping in my ears.

"I'm only going to ask one more time!" Samson yelled. "Come out, come out, wherever you are."

Silence.

"You don't want to play hide-and-go-seek with Samson," Jax said. "His knife moves faster than your feet."

The threat worked. With great caution, a blond head poked around a wide tree trunk. Two amber eyes darted back and forth before stopping on my brother. I grimaced. Cyrus swore under his breath and Jax shook his head.

"*Blaze*," Cyrus scolded. "What the hell are you doing here?"

The boy dashed through the snow, the tails of his oversized coat fluttering behind him. The extra-long sleeves hung over his tan hands, leaving only his head exposed to the elements.

Cyrus squatted before the child. "Why did you follow us?"

"I heard Samson and Jax talking to Roshan. I wanted to be brave"—his eyelashes fluttered at my brother—"like you."

Blaze's pouting lips along with the quiver in his voice caused Cyrus to mutter, "Lord help me." He sighed through his nose. "Have you been trailing us the entire time?"

The boy nodded.

"Perfect." I scoffed, eyeing the others. "We had a kid following us and we never knew it. Who else is lurking in these woods?"

The men shifted their weight, blue and orange eyes searching for hidden Collectors.

Orion moved closer, the muscles in his face tense. "Blaze, did you go into the East Village with us?"

"No. I got tired of walking, so I stayed on the hill and waited for you to leave."

Everyone let out a relieved breath. Everyone but Samson.

He spit a wad of yellow phlegm onto the snow before taking a knee beside my brother. "Kid, there's brave and then there's stupid." He flicked Blaze in the forehead. "And your decision to follow us was *fucking* stupid."

I winced at the unnecessary word Samson added to the sentence. He gave the boy another flick, sending him toppling over.

Cyrus caught the child by the collar of his coat. "Easy. He's just a kid."

"And a stupid one at that," Samson said, climbing to his feet. "I don't have time to babysit, Cyrus, and neither do you." He shooed Blaze away with his hand. "Get out of here."

"We can't send him home," Roshan argued.

Samson pinned the Solin with a fierce stare. "Why the hell not?"

"Come on, man. We've been walking for hours. It's too dangerous."

"Boy-wonder should have realized this before he snuck off."

"I'm sorry," Blaze whimpered. "I wanted to help."

I rested my hand on his shoulder. "You could have helped by staying with the other children at Iah's."

"Does your mother know you left?" a Lunin asked.

The child bit his lip.

"*Blaze.*" Roshan's patient eyes narrowed. "You know how she worries. She'll think something bad happened."

"I'm sorry." He blinked away the tears. "I couldn't ask her. She would have never let me go." He kicked the snow with his boot. "I was bored. It sounded like an adventure."

Cyrus palmed his brows. "Kid. We're not on vacation. This is work. Dangerous work. I won't tell you what we saw at the East Village but—"

"They're dead, Blaze," Samson interrupted. "Your friends: Sol, Alba, Aftab, the baker who gave you those sweet rolls from his shop. They're all dead. Slaughtered by the Collectors."

The child's throat bobbed, his lip quivering.

"Samson, that's enough," Jax said.

"No. That was his village. He needs to hear the truth." The Solin squatted before the trembling boy. "You think you're so tough, following us through the woods, pretending that stick is a knife." Blaze's mouth gaped as he touched his pocket. "Well, guess what? You're not of age, you weren't invited, and you're not welcome, so get the hell out of my face."

A tear rolled off the boy's cheek.

"I'll take him home," Orion suggested. "Make sure he gets there safely."

"Get your ass back in line," Samson snapped.

Orion bowed his head in submission.

426

Roshan touched his chest. "Let me take him."

Another Solin lifted his hand. "I'll go too."

"No." Jax's voice raised over the others. "Splitting up is not an option." He shot Samson a stern glance. "We can't let a child wander through the forest on his own. He comes with us. End of story."

My brother stood tall. "I agree with Jax."

I nodded.

"Is this how that democracy thing works?" Samson asked, his eyes sliding between us.

"It is." I looked at the men in our group. "All in favor of Blaze coming with us, say *aye*."

The word rolled off twelve tongues and stumbled off half of another.

I flashed Samson a smug grin. "The ayes have it. Sorry, old man."

He sneered at Blaze. "You are to be seen and not heard. Do I make myself clear?"

Blaze popped to attention and shouted, "Yes, sir!"

Aries rolled his eyes at the child, then adjusted the bloodied cloth in his mouth.

"The kid's a pain in my ass," Samson grumbled, storming toward the North Village.

"Here." Jax reached into his pocket and offered Blaze his spare knife. "I want you to keep this in your hand at all times."

His eyes glowed with excitement. "I will."

"If we run into any trouble, stay close to me and Cyrus, okay?"

The boy nodded, marveling at the folded blade. Roshan poked him in the back, urging him to follow Samson.

I nudged Jax with my hip as we walked. "That was nice of you."

"See? I'm not always an asshole."

Cyrus clapped him on the back. "You're a lot nicer now that you and Elara are—"

"Don't finish that sentence," I warned.

"I will." Orion chuckled.

My cheeks flushed with heat. Jax kept his gaze forward, a smirk tugging at his lips. Cyrus's light-hearted expression dissolved once Blaze opened his mouth.

"Hey, Aries. Have you killed anyone?"

"Blaze." I wagged my finger in his face. "Don't ask him that."

The boy shrugged, his eyes fixed on Aries. The Lunin humored him with a shake of the head.

"What about you, Jax? I bet Zenith made you kill a lot of people."

"Dude. What did my sister just say?"

Blaze ignored my brother and tugged at Jax's arm. "Is it more than ten?"

My partner tensed.

"Little man." Cyrus grabbed the child's hand and lifted him to the empty space beside him. "Cool it with the questions."

Samson pointed ahead. "We've reached the main path. Keep your eyes and ears open."

"What about Samson?" Blaze asked. "I bet he's killed a bunch of people."

The Solin whipped around, glaring at the boy through tiny slits. "I know you're stupid, but are you deaf?"

The boy frowned, the blond mop on his head swishing back and forth.

"Not another word from that overactive mouth of yours."

"Sorry. I forgot." He lifted his eyes and only his eyes at Samson. "But have you"—his voice lowered—"killed anyone?"

I grabbed Samson's wrist as he moved to backhand Blaze. "Don't be mean."

He ripped his hand away from me, then moved his face inches from the boy's. "Yes. I've killed lots of people. Lots of little shits, just like you." Blaze gulped. "So I'd advise you to shut that trap of yours before I add you to my list."

Blaze eyed my brother, who gave him a wink in return. He rolled his little shoulders, lengthened his spine, and pressed his lips together, pretending to lock them with an imaginary key.

Orion and I did a horrible attempt at hiding our laughter. Watching a seven-year-old stand up to Samson provided us with much needed entertainment. The Solin cursed the two of us before spinning on his heels.

Jax chuckled, taking my hand. "And to think, the day's still young."

THE HAUNTING images we saw in the East Village added to our anxiety as we hurried down the beaten path that sliced through the center of town. After a head nod from Samson, we scattered, searching the shops for recruits.

My brother dragged his feet up the steps of an abandoned storefront while murmuring, "Here we go again."

Like before, he jiggled the handle, then pounded his fist on the aged wood. My eyes darted to a window above the shop. I froze. A woman stood behind the glass with her arms crossed and jaw clenched. She shifted her gaze between me and my brother before glaring at Jax. Connecting the dots, she pulled the curtain shut.

"They're in there," I said, gesturing to the blacked-out window. "But they won't come out."

"Do you blame them?" Orion whispered near my ear. "I'm still wondering if we'll stumble upon another pile of bodies."

"Roshan and Aries scouted the edge of town," Jax said. "We're good. It's all clear."

Cyrus swatted the fog and stepped beside the Lunin. He

pointed at the window. "Do you think they hid from the Collectors?"

"No." Jax scratched his five o'clock shadow. "The ones left behind are the families of those who joined Zenith."

"I guess the others heard about the massacre and left before the AMs showed up," I suggested.

Orion stared at me with wide eyes. "I wonder who told them. There was no one left in the East Village."

"Perhaps it was the old man in that dilapidated house," Jax said.

My cheeks puffed. "I hope he got the message to the other villagers."

"Yeah, we need a win," Cyrus said.

"Don't start celebrating," Samson muttered. "We have two more villages to scour. Keep trying the other shops."

Knobs turned and fists knocked on each store that bordered the main path. The spark of hope flickering inside our group dimmed with each failed attempt. After long minutes of the mind-numbing routine, we crowded together, watching Samson approach a shop with boarded windows.

Cyrus elbowed me in the ribs. "Ten bucks says no one answers."

I shut my eyes, listening to the quiet voice that struggled to speak over the masked dealer's incessant chatter.

Someone will answer the door, Elara.

I smiled. "Twenty says it opens."

We shook hands. A moment later, my prediction proved true.

"I'll take my payment in full after we return to Earth."

"Beginner's luck," Cyrus muttered.

A man, close to Samson's age, flung open the door. His pale blue eyes observed our group before locking onto the Solin who stood before him.

"Why are you here?" His voice sounded groggy, as if he had

woken from a long nap. "I already told you. I'm not getting involved in this shit."

"Things have changed. We need to talk."

"No. It's too risky."

Samson wedged his boot between the door and the frame to keep the wooden panel from slamming in his face. "Come on, Castor," he drawled. "Dangerous shit never stopped you before."

"Twenty bucks says he's an ex-Collector."

I huffed a breath at my brother. "Keep your money. I agree."

Jax nodded, folding his arms across his chest.

The thick cloud that left Castor's mouth matched the color of his neatly trimmed beard. His eyes bounced between me and Cyrus one last time before inviting Samson inside.

I stayed close to Jax as we stepped over the threshold. My muscles twitched at the drastic change in temperature. Burning logs glowed in a fireplace at the far end of the shop, its heat warming my numb face. The men sighed with relief and took off their coats. I blinked, then blinked again. The fog had hindered my ability to share my twin's Solin eyesight.

I noted the vast space as I unfastened the buttons on my coat. Gray bags with wide shoulder straps lined the walls. Neatly folded shirts and pressed pants rested on a circular table at the center of the shop. I admired the simplicity of the standard wardrobe on Aroonyx, my fingers grazing the muted fabrics. No bright colors, designs, patterns, or unique textures. No denim, corduroy, or leather. I had yet to see a woman wear a dress. There were no sandals, sneakers, or heels—just boots. I unfolded a long-sleeve shirt and searched for a tag. No price and no stickers to mark a size.

The men warmed their hands around the stone fireplace. A puddle of melted snow pooled around Blaze's boots as he inspected a basket of coiled belts and scarfs.

My head turned when I heard Castor ask Samson, "Why did you bring them here?"

The Solin tapped his lips with his finger, then called Orion's name. The Lunin tossed his coat onto the growing pile before jogging across the room.

"What's up?" he asked.

"I'm taking Jax, Elara, and Cyrus upstairs to speak with Castor. Keep an eye on the men while I'm gone. Make sure they don't run off or do anything"—he motioned to Blaze—"stupid."

The child struggled to breathe. He had tied a scarf around his neck like a noose.

Samson shifted his gaze to Orion. "What we saw in the East Village rattled the men's nerves. Do something to distract them."

"Got it," Orion said, hurrying to rescue Blaze from the large duffle bag that had fallen off a hook and landed on his head.

"Help," he cried, his voice muffled under the heavy fabric.

"Castor, let's chat upstairs. We need some privacy."

The shop owner motioned to the staircase behind the counter. He grabbed a pair of eyeglasses and cleaned the lenses with his shirt before stomping up the wooden steps.

"Elara, Cyrus," Samson called. "Let's go. You too, Jax."

In a single-file line, we marched up the stairs that led to a narrow hallway. The simple architecture of the old building reminded me of Idalia's. Creaking floorboards, black walls, and dust bunny colonies blotted the chipped baseboards—but that's where the similarities ended. Something felt off, wrong. My pulse quickened the farther we ventured down the hallway. *Nope. I don't like this.*

Deep grooves and swirls lined the walls. I clung to Jax's arm, terrified at the thought of what we might see. Magical creatures didn't exist on Aroonyx, so claw marks were out of the question.

"Fingernails," Jax clarified as if reading my mind.

"What the *fuck*?" Cyrus moved closer.

Castor stopped in front of a closed door. More grooves covered the wooden panel, only this time they formed a picture. A stick figure hung from a tree with the word *Daddy* written beneath it.

I squeezed Jax's bicep. "I don't want to go in there."

"Me neither," my brother whispered.

Jax's eyes never left Castor. "Keep your knives close. I don't know who this guy is or the reason we're here."

I patted my pocket, grateful I didn't remove my coat.

Taller than Samson, Castor ducked his graying head so it didn't hit the top of the doorframe as he stepped into the room. We followed the two men inside. The heat of another crackling fire blasted my face.

The quaint loft served its purpose well. A round table rested on a dust-covered rug in the center of the room, and a full-sized bed was pushed against the back wall. The sheets, splattered with murky stains, were twisted into a loose ball, and someone had draped the frayed comforter over the window as a makeshift curtain. I eyed the kitchen. The sink overflowed with food-crusted bowls and plates; a damp and dirty rag hung lopsided on a silver hook.

I didn't want to touch the chairs, much less sit on one. But life enjoyed testing me. I stifled my complaints when Castor told us to make ourselves comfortable.

Cyrus's face squished up in disgust as he brushed bits of rotten food and crumbs from the wooden seat. Samson didn't bother removing the unwanted leftovers from his. He just collapsed, the weathered wood creaking under his weight. Jax dusted off the chair that faced the door, then motioned for me to take a seat. Though the lack of cleanliness made my skin crawl, my legs rejoiced the much-needed break. My partner didn't sit. He stood behind me with one hand shoved in his pocket. I didn't have to peek inside to know his fingers gripped the handle of his knife.

Reminding me of a disgruntled server at a restaurant, Castor grabbed a dirty bowl from the kitchen sink and filled it to the brim with withered pieces of dried meat before tossing it onto the table, a poor attempt at a hospitable gesture.

My nose wrinkled at the foul-smelling offerings. My brother snagged a handful of the tender strips marbled with fat. I groaned, watching him toss the gray pieces into his mouth. His eyes bulged. He covered his mouth and tried not to gag as he swallowed. My amused expression fell flat once Castor took a seat and narrowed his eyes at Samson.

"Why did you come here? I can't help you."

"Can't or won't?"

"Both."

Samson twisted in his chair to face the Lunin. "Joining our side is the right thing to do—and you know it."

"It's the right thing to do if I want to get myself killed. Did you hear what happened in the East Village?"

"Yeah, we saw the bodies."

Castor sighed, pushing his glasses farther up the bridge of his nose. "Then you understand the reason I want nothing to do with this mess."

Samson pinned him with a long look. "You don't have any family to protect. It's just you."

This comment appeared to hit a nerve with the Lunin. "I'm warning you Samson, *don't* push me."

"Damn it, Castor!" The Solin slammed his palm on the table, the bowl of shredded meat wobbling from the sudden jolt. "When did you become a pussy? You never cowered before Arun. Why would you with Zenith?"

"I'm not afraid of Zenith. Things are different now. I'm not going down that path again."

I observed Castor's features. His tall and lean build fit the mold of every other Lunin on Aroonyx, but the bone structure that shaped his pale face, and the distinct shade of his light blue eyes reminded me of someone I had met. I leaned closer, my forearms sticking to the residue on the wood. *But who?*

Curious, I asked, "How do you two know each other?"

"We worked as Collectors for Arun," Samson answered.

My twin caught my eye and mouthed "Told you so."

I shrugged. Nothing surprised me anymore.

Speaking to me but looking at Samson, Castor said, "I left that old life behind."

"So did I, but sometimes the past follows you into the future." The Solin pointed at me and Cyrus. "And these two came with it."

"That changes nothing. Blood is blood, regardless of who spills it. I've moved on. I enjoy living a simple life."

"In this shithole?"

Castor may have scowled at Samson's remark, but a sadness clung to his words when he said, "Yeah. It's all I have left."

"Fine. Stay here and keep beating yourself up about the past. It's not like you tried to stop him."

Castor's lips curled into a snarl as he leaned across the table. "*Fuck you* for putting that shit on me. I did everything in my power to keep him from going to Zenith."

I stilled. Cyrus reached for his knife, and Jax placed his body between me and the enraged Lunin.

Unfazed by the verbal attack, Samson rested his back against the chair and crossed his arms. "He's your son. After all the fucked-up shit he's done, I'm shocked you won't help us stop him."

"How can I stop him?!" Castor yelled. "He's a grown man. He has no remorse for the crimes he's committed. He has no regrets." The Lunin tossed his glasses onto the table, then massaged his temples. "In my eyes, my son died a long time ago."

My tongue moved without conscious thought. "Who's your son?"

435

Castor hesitated. His pupils constricted as he met my gaze. "He's a Collector. A member of the Inner Circle."

I paled. Jax's fingers gripped the back of my chair.

"What's . . . his name?" Cyrus stammered.

The Lunin cleared his throat before looking at my brother, a lifetime of regrets clouding his eyes. "His name is Pollux."

40

BLOOD TIES

B lood rushed to my head, blurring my vision. *No. No. No.* I palmed my eyes. *This is not okay.*

The fingernail marks on the walls, the disturbing picture carved into the bedroom door, the eerie chill that crept up my spine as we walked down the hallway. *This is Pollux's home—the place he grew up.* My body recoiled at the thought. I clutched my hands near my chest.

With wide eyes, Cyrus sprung to his feet. Jax exposed the blade of his knife while I stayed glued to the wooden seat. I could hardly breathe, much less move.

Samson lifted a hand. "Stand down. Castor hasn't spoken to his son in years."

I blinked at the Lunin. *How did I not make the connection? He looks like an older version of Pollux.*

Jax took out his angst on the top rail of my chair, the aged wood cracking under his death grip. My brother handled the news worse than my partner. The muscles in his face quivered with rage. His desire to avenge Idalia sent a burst of heat rushing through me. I slid a finger under the collar of my shirt.

He pointed the tip of his blade at Castor. "Your son is at the top of my shit list. That makes you number two."

Samson rolled his eyes. "Cyrus, put the knife away before you get yourself killed. Castor has enough blood on his hands to last a lifetime."

I flashed my brother a stern look.

A growl rumbled in his chest. He took a seat, then stabbed the knife in the table. I flinched, watching the handle sway back and forth.

Samson arched a wiry brow at my brother. "What did this table ever do to you?"

Cyrus leaned in his chair and folded his arms across his broad chest, refusing to look at the Solin.

"When was the last time you spoke with Pollux?" Jax asked Castor.

It wasn't a casual question, but the start of a stern interrogation.

"A few years ago."

"Where?"

"The West Village."

Jax widened his stance. "What was the purpose of your visit?"

Castor hummed while scratching the short hairs of his beard. "Let me think." His eyes grew with mock surprise. "His devotion to his father." He snapped his fingers. "Yes, that was it. Pollux wanted to express his love for me. Or perhaps, he wanted to reiterate how much he hates me. How much he despises his shit father. And just maybe, he wanted to remind me of the reason he's kept me alive. To watch me suffer. To destroy the lives of those around me."

My partner exhaled a long breath.

Castor cleaned a smudge off the lens before slipping on his glasses. He shifted his gaze around the room as he spoke. "I'm aware of the horrible things Pollux has done over the years. My son isn't right in the head. He never was. Even as a child, he gravitated toward the darkness. I tried to stop him from going to Zenith. He joined the Collectors out of spite because he blamed me for his mother's death."

"What happened to his mom?" I touched my throat, my voice sounded strangled.

"I killed her."

Cyrus swore. I blinked and blinked again.

"Not with my bare hands," he corrected. "She couldn't handle my coping mechanisms."

Confusion raised my brows.

"Most days were tolerable," he added. "The others not so much. The darkness from my past would blind me." He adjusted his glasses. "I couldn't see straight."

I gulped. *I doubt that comment has anything to do with his eyesight.*

"It felt like I was reliving the murders—the tortures I committed while working for Arun. I couldn't get the images out of my head. It made me angry, so I lashed out at Pollux and his mother." Castor stared at nothing. His voice sounded hoarser with each word that left his mouth. "I'm better now. Back then the flashbacks came on strong. The night terrors drove me mad. I'd wake up with the sheets soaking wet, the base of my skull throbbing as if someone carved a trench through the middle of my head."

Samson hummed his understanding while rubbing the back of his neck. I frowned, wondering if he suffered the same side effects as his comrade.

"I met Lilith shortly after I left the Collectors," Castor said. "I only married her because she got pregnant." Resentment filled his eyes. "Lil was a weak woman. She never fought back when I beat the shit out of her, and she never lifted a finger to protect Pollux.

"I thought a family would distract me from my past." His

lips pursed. "It only made things worse. Pollux kept to himself. Stayed out of my way, but Lil took everything personally. She said my flashbacks were a punishment for the crimes I committed. She told me to suck it up, to be a good father. Her behavior left me feeling isolated. I struggled to process the emotions. I should have talked to someone, asked for help." He shrugged. "I was a proud man back then. Too proud. Eventually, my pride bit me in the ass."

He paused. We waited.

Castor's eyes drifted to the bed. "We had a daughter named Stella. She was four years younger than Pollux. One night she wouldn't stop crying."

Cyrus's spine straightened, and a muscle feathered in Samson's jaw. He turned his head in the opposite direction.

"I didn't mean to kill her," Castor said. His voice lacked emotion. "I just wanted her to stop crying." His haunting eyes found mine. "Babies are such fragile things. Her neck snapped so easily."

Cyrus muttered a slew of curse words and scrubbed at his face. Jax didn't say a word, his expression unreadable.

"Stella's death caused Lil to snap. She wouldn't touch me, much less look at me. Hell, she even abandoned her own son. She spent hours pacing the hallway, talking to herself. I'd find her fingernails covered in blood."

The claw marks in the walls. I blew out a small breath and wrapped my arms around me.

"The years passed and we became two trapped souls, stumbling with the motions of life. Hollow shells just biding our time."

My partner rested his hand on my shoulder and gave it a gentle squeeze. A reminder to count our blessings. Like Castor, Jax had struggled with the demons of his past. Both men had faced the darkness. Only one had the courage to walk through it.

"She used one of my old knives to do it." Castor pointed at the bed. "That's where I found her."

My eyes followed his extended hand. As if approaching a devastating car crash, my morbid curiosity moved my gaze to the discolored floorboards near the bed. My heart thundered in my chest. Cyrus scooted his chair closer to mine—away from the evidence.

"She severed both arteries," Castor said, running a finger over his wrist. "I don't know how she did it." His cheeks puffed. "Poor Pollux, I found him sitting next to her body, playing with the knife." He waved a hand around the room. "The kid used her blood to paint twisted shit all over the walls. It took me a week to clean it up." His attention snagged on the door. "There wasn't anything I could do with the picture he carved in the wood."

The hangman. The word daddy. I shivered and looked at my brother.

His eyes grew.

I nodded. *Yeah, I want to get the hell out of here too.*

Cyrus lowered his gaze and stared at the cracks in the table while I twisted the loose button on my coat. *No wonder Pollux is so screwed up. His abusive father killed his sister, and his mother went off the deep end.*

As usual, I spoke without thinking. "Do you love your son?"

Jax stiffened, Cyrus choked on his spit, and Samson sat taller.

"Love is a fragile thing," Castor answered.

"No, it's not," I argued. "Unconditional love can't be broken."

He removed his glasses and rubbed his weary eyes. "I wouldn't know."

"Did you ever care for Pollux?" I pressed.

"I'm not sure. It's been a long time since I thought of him as my son."

"Do you wish you could change the past?"

"Is that a trick question?"

I shook my head.

"Of course I do. My entire life is one big regret."

"Then do something to make it right. You didn't have the power to save your son, but you can help us save the others, the young Collectors blinded by Zenith." I reached across the table and touched his hand. "Your life isn't over. It still has a purpose."

Castor inhaled a long breath, then let the air whoosh out of his lungs. He turned to Samson. "You taught her well. She speaks with the passion of a true leader."

"I taught her how to fight physical battles." Samson flashed me a small grin. "Elara taught herself how to win the mental ones."

His compliment stained my cheeks.

Castor pushed up the sleeves of his shirt. "There's not much keeping me here. Most of the vendors closed after the incident in the East Village. There's only a handful of people left."

"When did it happen?" Samson asked.

The Lunin looked at his old friend. "Four days ago."

My fingers dug into my palms. "We could have saved them," I said, to no one in particular.

"Don't dwell on the hypothetical, kid," Samson said. "It's not worth your time."

As much as it pained me, I had to agree with him. We could have warned the villagers had Aries shared the information he overheard, but he didn't.

"Think of how long it's been since we've gone on a mission together." A mischievous grin spread across Samson's face. He wiggled his eyebrows at Castor. "It might be fun to stir up some trouble."

"We stirred up plenty in the old days."

"Yeah, but back then Arun ran the show. He wrote the rules." His grin grew. "This time we write our own."

"I'm listening."

"A change is coming, Castor. I can feel it." He inclined his head at me and Jax. "And so do they. This is our shot at redemption."

Castor folded his glasses and dropped them into his shirt's pocket. He eyed everyone in the room before extending his hand to Samson. "All right, I'm in."

The Solin beamed, sealing the Lunin's fate with a firm shake. "I hope you haven't forgotten how to use a knife."

Castor reached into his pocket, exposed a sharp blade, and hurled it through the air. A loud thud confirmed it connected with the door. My jaw almost fell into my lap.

"Damn," Cyrus murmured, spinning in his chair.

Samson clapped his friend on the back and stood from the table. "Perfect aim. Just like the old days."

"I'm surprised you doubted me."

"I never did," Samson said, freeing the embedded blade. "I just wanted to see the kids' reactions."

"Dude." Cyrus spun back around, his eyes growing. "I've never seen anyone expose a blade that fast."

I touched the scar on my stomach. "It's obvious you haven't seen Zenith in action."

My brother grimaced. "Sorry, sis."

"Elara's right. Zenith's throwing skills outmatch us all." Samson tossed the Lunin his folded blade. "But Castor can hold his own against Oberon and Jax."

"Is that a challenge?" my partner asked.

Castor rubbed his beard as he sized up his competition. "Only if you think your aim is better than mine."

"Uh oh." Cyrus's eyes darted between the two men. "I think someone needs a demonstration, Jax."

The former leader of the Inner Circle held Castor's gaze

when he said, "Shall we see if that reputation of yours precedes itself?"

Jax chuckled and circled his throwing arm, warming the muscles.

Oh boy. Let the games begin.

My brother leaned back in his chair, balancing it on two legs. "This will be fun to watch."

"It will," Samson said. "For me and your sister. You get to help with the demonstration."

"Wait. What?"

Cyrus's head slammed onto the tattered rug after Samson kicked his chair out from underneath him. A cloud of dust exploded around his body. He coughed, waving the particles out of his face.

"Get off your ass and go stand by the door," Samson demanded.

"No. I'm not playing your twisted game."

"It's not up for discussion."

I chuckled watching Cyrus drag his feet across the room.

He shot me a vulgar gesture before pressing his spine against the door. "Keep laughing, sis."

"Don't worry, bro. I'm right here, just a few feet away."

He scoffed at the words he shared with me during the courage exercise.

"That was required training. This"—he jerked his chin at the men's knives—"is unnecessary."

"It's necessary entertainment."

"I want to be an only child."

My lips slid over my teeth. "Where's that Solin courage?"

"Shut your mouth."

"Spread your legs," Samson said.

The color drained from my brother's face. "Why?"

"We need to see who has the better aim," Castor answered, checking the sharpness of his blade.

"Then aim for my head. Not my balls."

"Are they still in there?" Samson squinted at Cyrus's pants. "Your behavior says otherwise."

I covered my mouth, muffling my laughter. Jax snickered, his fingers rotating the handle of his knife.

"Castor, you're up first."

"For the record"—Cyrus shielded his manhood with both hands—"I hate all of you right now."

"We love you too, bro."

The eldest Lunin raised his armed hand. "Try not to move." He released the knife.

Samson's favorite four-letter word flew out of my brother's mouth. He repeated said word after the blade pierced the wood. It landed only inches from his protected area.

"This is not okay," he said, refusing to look at the near miss.

"You're up, Jax," Samson called.

My partner nodded and moved into position. I couldn't stop laughing.

Cyrus cracked open his eyelids, squinting at Jax as if he was the sun. "I want to have kids one day. Don't screw up my chances."

"I'll keep that in mind."

Jax inhaled a steady breath, then let the blade fly. It landed above Castor's knife, a hairsbreadth from my brother's white knuckles.

"*Fuck* this!" Cyrus stood on his toes, lifted his hidden jewels and shimmied his body over the wedged blades. "Jax wins. We're done playing target practice."

Castor took the loss with grace and shook my partner's hand. Cyrus collapsed onto the chair, only after checking his pants for phantom tears in the fabric.

Samson muttered inaudible words as he watched my brother adjust himself for the fourth time in thirty seconds.

445

"Not to be a buzzkill," I said to Jax. "But shouldn't we wrap this up?"

He nodded. "I don't want us wandering around in the fog at night. It hinders our Lunin vision."

"How so?" I asked.

"Imagine walking through a room filled with glowing smoke. The lights are on, but the visibility is poor."

"This is true," Castor said. "Lunins can't see shit in the fog at night."

I eyed the door. *Perfect. Now I'm even more anxious.*

Castor strolled toward the closet. "Let me grab a few things before we head out."

Samson tossed a handful of dried meat into his mouth while watching his friend prepare for his new mission.

The Lunin stuffed a backpack with a handful of wrinkled clothes, worn socks, and a tattered belt that had seen better days. He then threw on a heavy coat, tossed the bag over his shoulder, and grabbed a black wooden box off the top shelf.

Castor removed the lid and rested it on the table. Jax and Samson nearly tripped over their feet to get a better look, their jaws hanging open. My brother and I exchanged quizzical glances, then craned our necks to see what the ex-Collectors were drooling over.

"Well, I'll be damned." Samson reached into the box. "If it isn't my old friend." He balanced the foreign object on his two fingers. "Hello lovely. I haven't seen you in over twenty-five years."

41

A SEEKER'S INTUITION

"Is that an Origin blade?" Jax asked, his eyes growing in wonder.

"Yep." Samson offered him the dagger. "And so are the rest."

"Damn," Jax murmured. "I've never seen one with my own eyes."

I reached into the box, careful not to cut myself on the elongated weapons. "What's an Origin blade?"

"The first design Nash created with Fired Stone," he answered.

My mouth gaped as I recalled my history lesson with Jax.

"Why are they so long?" Cyrus asked. "And why don't the blades fold into the handles?"

Samson looked at my brother. "Arun followed the designs the Seeker brought from Earth."

"They resemble daggers from the Middle Ages," Cyrus said to me.

I nodded, rotating the handle.

"We didn't use them for long," Samson added.

Castor's shoulders shook with laughter. "Remember what a pain in the ass it was trying to get your knife out of the holster?"

Samson snickered, grabbing a belt crafted with leather-looking sheaths. "I can't believe you kept all of this shit."

"Call me nostalgic." Castor smirked. "But they might come in handy."

"Yeah, if I want to stab myself," I said, noting how the blade matched the length of my forearm. "I'll keep my folded knife."

"It's a safer option," Samson said. "Arun figured this out after a Collector tripped and stabbed himself in the groin. That's when he ordered Nash to change the design."

I picked up a handle without a blade. "What happened to this one? Did it break? I thought hybrid blades were strong."

Castor watched Samson. Grief clouded the Solin's eyes as he pointed at the useless weapon in my hand. "That was Janus's blade."

Cyrus's ears perked up. "Idalia's father?"

He nodded, then held out his palm. "Elara, let me see your knife."

I reached into my coat pocket and handed him the white weapon with the twin moons engraved on the handle. Samson's shoulders sagged after he exposed the blade.

"What's wrong?" I asked, bothered by his reaction.

He brushed off my concerns, his eyes fixed on the crescent moons. "Janus met Helen after he left the Collectors. His reputation followed him around the villages, so he had this knife made to keep her safe."

"Yeah, Idalia told me."

"But did she tell you this knife is an Origin blade?"

"No."

He motioned to the bladeless weapon in my hand. "Janus paid a blacksmith to create a folded design using the Origin blade of his dagger. He didn't want Helen walking around town with one of the cheap imitations."

My mouth gaped at Jax. "Did you know about this?"

"Yes, that's why I let you keep that knife. If it wasn't a hybrid blade, I would have insisted you take mine, along with Zenith's."

Castor's brows touched his hairline. "Zenith's?"

"Show him," Samson said.

I pulled the black knife from my pocket.

The eldest Lunin wiggled his fingers, eager to touch the mysterious weapon. "Let me see that thing."

I dropped it into his open palm.

Samson pointed to the silver etchings on the blade. "She's a beauty, isn't she?"

"You can say that again." Castor checked the weight, balancing it on his finger. It didn't teeter. "How's its aim?"

A burst of air shot out of my mouth. "Good and it's sharp as hell. That blade sliced through my coat and my stomach without slowing down."

Castor grimaced, handing me the knife.

"I'm glad everyone's familiar with Fired Stone." Cyrus dug in the box. "Meanwhile, I don't have a clue what the hell y'all are talking about."

"It's a long story," I said.

"Then give me a summary, sis."

I slipped both blades back into my coat pocket. "Nash was . . . *is* a master craftsman who creates the finest blades. He worked as a free man under Arun's reign, but Zenith has him imprisoned in a cell attached to his living chambers. The Collectors carry hybrid weapons: blades forged with Clear Stone and Fired Stone. They're strong and effective. Zenith has the only pure Fired Stone blade on Aroonyx. It can slice through anything."

"What about the knives on the black market?"

"They're stolen hybrids or imitation blades blacksmiths tried to forge." I snapped my fingers. "Do you remember

Aarush's knife? How easily Samson broke the blade?"

He nodded.

I looked at Jax. "I'm guessing that was an imitation?"

"Yes. An easy way to tell is by checking the integrity of the blade. Hybrids won't snap unless you use the proper tools."

"Even with a Solin's strength?" Cyrus asked.

"They won't break. The combined materials are too strong."

My brother slipped a hand into his pocket. "What kind of blade do I have?"

"A hybrid," Jax confirmed. "The ones Idalia kept in that box were stolen or purchased from the black market."

My brother smiled as he rotated the handle. He appeared to have a new appreciation for his knife.

"Should we arm the recruits with the Origin blades?" I asked.

Jax's head swayed back and forth. "It's too dangerous. The blades don't fold. I don't want them stabbing themselves like Castor and Samson's old pal."

"Yeah, but we can't send them into battle unarmed," Cyrus argued.

"We're not," Samson countered.

"Yes, we are. The knives surrendered by the Inactive Members aren't enough to arm our recruits."

"That's why we'll arm them with the extra blades Aries and his men brought with them," Jax said.

The lines on my forehead wrinkled. "I'm confused. What extra blades?"

"Aries is smarter than he looks. He ordered his men to visit the weapons room before they left Zenith's. That's why he lost over half of his group. The sacks were too heavy. They struggled to lift them over the wall. It slowed them down."

I blinked at the turn of events. "When did Aries tell you this?"

"A few days after they showed up. He wanted to make sure

he could trust us before disclosing where they hid the sacks of knives."

"I see," I muttered, still disturbed by the attack on the young men.

"Well, I'm taking a few of them with me," Castor said, fastening the belt around his waist. "I always preferred the weight and length of the Origin blades."

"Sounds good," Samson said. "Do you mind carrying my old one? I might use it on the battlefield."

He nodded, slipping the dagger into a sheath.

"Meet us downstairs when you're ready," Samson added.

"I won't be long," Castor replied.

Eager to leave Pollux's old dwelling, my brother and I dashed out the door and down the hallway while Jax and Samson strolled behind. I did a doubletake once our boots touched the last step. The men in our group lay sprawled on their backs. Their chests rose and fell with relaxed breaths, their eyelids twitching with signs of deep sleep. Orion rested near the fireplace with his hands tucked underneath his head. His full lips moved with a story of his father's early career as a doctor. Blaze had his cheek pressed against Roshan's chest. A puddle of drool had formed on the Solin's shirt. Both the child and the man were out cold.

Samson swore under his breath and pushed past me and Cyrus. He kicked Orion in the thigh, knocking his crossed legs apart.

"What are you doing?" he snapped. "It's not story time. I told you to calm them down, not put them to sleep."

Orion muttered his apologies while scrambling to stand. The rest of the men stirred. They stretched and rubbed the sleep from their eyes. A few yawned as they observed their surroundings.

Samson scowled at the men he hand-selected. "Now that you're rested, perhaps we can continue with our mission."

His sharp tone acted like a shot of espresso. The men hopped to their feet and hurried to retrieve their coats.

I turned to face the Solin. "We haven't tried the homes in the North Village."

Castor emerged from the stairwell and spoke for Samson. "It's not worth our time. The villagers joined Zenith or they're at Iah's. The families of your recruits already left, and the ones who stayed behind won't participate in the uprising."

I sighed, heading toward the door. My pace slowed noting Jax's narrowed eyes. "What's wrong?"

"Nothing."

"Don't lie to me. What is it?"

"That feeling is getting stronger."

A cold sweat formed on my palms. "I thought it would disappear after the disaster in the East Village."

His lips formed a tight line.

"Should we skip the West Village?" I asked, my stomach twisting into a knot.

"Samson won't allow it."

"If this feeling has nothing to do with the pile of bodies, then what is it?"

"It's not what." His voice lowered. "It's *who*."

My lips moved to inquire, but Castor cut me off. "Go catch up with the others. I need to lock up the store."

Jax reached for my hand and guided me toward the exit. He didn't let go as we followed the others.

"The fog isn't lifting," Cyrus said.

"I can hardly see." Orion waved his hand through the haze. "Is it getting worse?"

"I can't tell."

"Make sure we stay together at all times."

Blaze looked up at Jax. "What about me?"

"Stay close to Cyrus."

The boy popped to attention mid-stride. "Yes, sir!"

Aries's shoulders tensed. I could see the irritation written on his pale face. The injured Lunin spit blood onto the ground every few paces. He didn't chat with the other men. Not that he could with half a tongue.

I wanted to investigate the *who* Jax had mentioned, but his stone-cold expression acted as a shield, guarding him against my question.

Blaze did a wonderful job at keeping the mood light. He never stopped talking to my twin. He told him how fast he could run, how much taller he was then the other Solin boys his age, how he couldn't wait to turn eighteen, and how he longed to be his little brother.

My heart warmed watching Cyrus nod his head with enthusiasm. He threw in an exaggerated facial expression when Blaze boasted of his popularity among his peers and gasped while listening to him declare himself the funniest kid on Aroonyx.

Under the circumstances, Cyrus displayed more patience than most. He answered Blaze's endless questions with a smile on his face.

"Yes, the trees on Earth have brown bark and no, it's not soft and fuzzy."

"*Brown?*" The child's nose crinkled. "That's weird."

"And we have lots of bugs." Cyrus walked his fingers up Blaze's neck. "Big creepy spiders with long legs and sharp fangs."

The child squealed, squirming in his boots. My brother mimicked the sounds of a crane and lifted Blaze off the ground. A deep belly laugh followed.

He lowered him beside Orion, and said, "Why don't you ask him how to set a broken bone? I'm sure he'd love to discuss the world of medicine."

Orion shot my brother a weighted glance, then forced a smile once Blaze started another round of twenty questions.

I turned to Jax. "He's a funny kid, isn't he?"

My partner loosened his grip around my hand. "Do you enjoy spending time with children?"

"Yeah, I love kids." My mouth slammed shut. *Perhaps I should clarify.* "I don't want any right now. Maybe when I'm older." *Maybe?* I cursed in the quiet space of my mind. *What if he wants kids? Shit. That never came up in his proposal.*

I watched Jax out of the corner of my eye. His expression remained blank. He didn't smile. He didn't frown. He just nodded and kept his gaze forward.

"What are those?" Cyrus asked.

My head turned. A fence constructed from blocks of Clear Stone enclosed a massive field. I rubbed my eyes, wondering if they were playing tricks. A herd of animals had crowded together, their long snouts rooting in the snow for food.

I tugged at Jax's arm. "We don't have those on Earth."

"They're called grazers," he clarified.

I stood on my toes to see over the others. "Are they friendly?"

"Samson!"

The Solin spun around at the sound of Jax's voice. "What's up?"

"We're getting close to the West Village. Why don't we take a quick break? Let the men regroup before we start the third leg of our journey."

Samson eyed our group. "You heard the man. Take five."

The men spread out. Some chatted while others checked the sharpness of their blades. Aries stood alone, leaning against a tree, the blood-soaked rag dangling from his hand.

"Come on," Jax said to me and Cyrus. "It's time for a field trip."

Orion inclined his head at Samson. "I'm gonna hang with

the others." He flashed me a smug grin. "Have fun with the grazers, Elara."

Blaze grabbed my brother's hand and dragged him through the snow. I hurried after them, eager to inspect the mysterious animal.

The boy climbed the fence, swung his legs over the side, then patted the space beside him. My brother chuckled; his tall stature allowed him to rest his forearms on the top of the enclosure.

I wedged the toe of my boot in a crack in the wall and lifted myself higher, my eyes glowing with excitement.

The grazers resembled the crossbreed of a horse and a llama. Gray wool covered their muscular frames. A darker strip of the fuzzy fur outlined their ears and flowed down the length of their spines. The color lightened to a heather gray once it touched their hindquarters. The solid pattern shifted to elaborate swirls, decorating their powerful legs in a unique design.

"Wow," I whispered. "They're beautiful."

The animals snorted and snuffed, their onyx hooves pawing the ground in search of hidden grass. A slender female lifted her head and sniffed the air. A white cloud left her nostrils as she swished her tail.

Blaze wiggled his fingers and clicked his tongue. The elegant creature trotted toward him.

"So this is the world's most resourceful animal," Cyrus said, letting the grazer's lips inspect his palm.

Jax nodded, scratching the female behind her ear. She leaned into his touch. "These beauties provide us with wool to make clothes, stuffing for beds, pillows." He paused, brushing her white mane out of her eyes. "And their meat is a staple in our diet."

I frowned. "But they're so docile."

"So are cows," Cyrus argued. "That never stopped you from eating them on Earth."

My lips drooped even more.

"Don't worry." Jax laughed. "Every part gets used. The grazer's hide provides us with long-lasting bags, boots, and belts."

My brother's brows etched together as he pushed himself off the fence. "Wait. Is that what I ate at Castor's today?"

"But you eat cows on Earth," I said, mocking his voice.

"And I'm okay with that. Cows taste good. The meat I ate today tasted like shit."

"You enjoyed the ribs at Idalia's," Jax said. "And you love Iah's stew."

"Well, the dried meat tasted horrible."

Jax shrugged. "Brain is an acquired taste."

"Dude." Cyrus's face turned a light shade of green. He slid his boots away from the animal. "Please tell me you're joking."

"Not this time."

My brother bit his knuckle and swallowed hard. My shoulders bounced with laughter as I stretched my arm to touch the grazer. She flicked her tail, rolled her head, and with a loud snort, galloped toward the herd. Hooves thundered under the magnificent beast, misting my face with snow.

I stood slack-jawed, stunned by the animal's skittish behavior.

"Grazers don't like women," Jax said, dusting off his hands.

"That's not funny." I glared.

"It's true." Blaze hopped off the fence. "They hate girls. Men are the only ones who can raise them."

I pouted. The female glanced over her shoulder at me. Her long lashes fluttered over her steel-blue eyes as if saying, *Nice try, sweetheart.*

"No sad face, sis. I'm sure Jax can buy you a toy grazer to cuddle with."

I patted my brother's stomach as I walked by. "At least I didn't eat its brain."

The greenish hue returned to his tan complexion.

"I love the brain," Blaze said, sprinting past us.

"And I'd love for you to stop talking," Cyrus muttered.

Jax and I shared a good laugh and headed toward the group.

Orion's smug grin reappeared once I approached. "Did you enjoy your time with the grazers?"

"Bastard. You knew they hated women."

"I can't give away all of our secrets."

I responded with an eye roll.

He looked at Jax. "You'll never guess what one of the guys told me."

"Spill it. I hate guessing games."

"Fair enough." Orion dragged a hand through his hair. "He saw Aarush wandering the woods near Iah's."

Jax folded his arms across his chest. "When?"

"Last night."

The lines on Cyrus's face hardened as he eyed my partner. "What was he doing out there?"

Jax didn't respond, his mind reeling with unspoken thoughts.

My pulse quickened. "I hope he's not working for Zenith."

"He might be," Orion said. "Remember how pissed he looked the night he challenged Jax to a duel."

My partner shook his head. "Joining sides with Zenith won't avenge his father's death. He watched Elio beat his mother to a pulp after I . . ." He didn't bother finishing the sentence.

I nodded. "Why would Aarush team up with the man who —" My heart dropped into the pit of my stomach. *The man who manipulates those around him. The man who twists the truth to get his way.*

I reached for Jax's arm, my knees wobbling.

"Elara, what's wrong?" he asked.

"The bad feeling." I clutched my chest, thinking of the men,

457

women, and children at Iah's. "It was a warning—a warning for us to stay."

Cyrus and Orion moved closer, their blue and orange eyes darting between me and Jax.

I fought to get the words out, tears welling in my eyes. "Jax, you said Zenith is always ten steps ahead of everyone else. What if Aarush is a spy? What if he's been watching, waiting for us to leave, so he could give the signal to Zenith?" I breathed hard. "The signal to send the Collectors to attack our group when they least expect it. When we're not there to protect them."

A four-letter curse word shot out of Jax's mouth as he dashed past me. I locked eyes with Cyrus, then Orion.

The Solin whispered, "Idalia," and the Lunin whispered, "Dad."

The fear of the unknown acted as a vice grip around my pounding heart. Together, we sprinted after my partner.

Samson's pupils constricted as he listened to Jax share my theory.

"Maybe Elara's wrong," Castor suggested. "That's an elaborate suspicion."

"You bring up a good point," Samson said.

Jax shook his head, disagreeing with the ex-Collectors. "We can't take any chances. You saw how they slaughtered the families in the East Village. That's child's play compared to what they'll do to the men and women in our groups."

"My dad." Orion's breath quickened.

Samson's hands curled into fists, the vein on his neck pulsating. "I'll rip out their *fucking* throats if they touch Idalia."

Cyrus could only nod; rage had clamped his jaw shut.

"We need to head back to Iah's—*now*," Jax said.

"This stays between us. We can't confirm Aarush is a spy." Samson gritted his teeth, his orange eyes narrowing at Jax. "I don't make decisions based on your damn *feelings*. You know how I feel about that Seeker shit."

"Elara's not a Seeker. She observed the obvious and expressed her concerns."

I blinked at Jax, surprised to hear him twist the truth. I stopped blinking once I realized his motive. Samson was a practical man who made practical decisions. He wouldn't alter our course for a gut feeling, but he would for logic.

"What's the fastest way to Iah's?" I asked.

"Through the West Village," Orion answered.

Jax nodded. "We'll go through the center of town to save time."

Samson's whistle pierced through the men's muffled voices. "Gather around," he demanded.

Roshan grabbed Blaze's hand and hurried to meet us. The others weren't far behind.

"Plans have changed. After speaking with Castor, I've realized our chances of finding new recruits is slim to none. We'll cut through the West Village and make our way back to Iah's."

The men nodded, believing the lies that Samson fed them.

He looked at Aries. "We need to have a little chat."

The young Lunin dropped his head and ambled toward Samson. I grimaced. *He's going to ask him if he knows about Aarush.*

My partner nudged me in the arm. "Let's go."

With little enthusiasm, my boots moved forward. I eyed the milky sky and pleaded with the universe. *I can't handle any more deaths. Please keep our recruits safe.*

"My dad's too old to fight." Orion's words came out in a tight whisper. "He can't defend himself against the Collectors."

I touched his hand. "Let's try to stay positive. Maybe Aarush isn't a spy. Maybe my theory is wrong."

"And if it's not?"

"Then we failed them," Jax said. "And it's all my fault."

My head turned. "Why would you say that?"

"You know why." His voice raised. "If I hadn't murdered his father, he wouldn't seek revenge. If your prediction proves true, then once again, I'm left with innocent blood on my hands. Once again I'm—"

"Just stop!" Cyrus snapped. "I don't want to talk about this shit anymore."

"Easy." A river of heat flowed through me. "I'm sure Idalia will be okay."

The muscles in his face twitched. "You don't have the power to predict the future, so stop pretending that you can."

Orion lifted a finger to his lips. "Keep it down."

My chin hit my chest. He gave my hand a gentle squeeze, then let it go once Jax interlaced his fingers around my other.

We slowed our pace and walked alone, trailing the men.

"At Castor's, you told me your feeling involved a who, not a what. It's about the recruits at Iah's, isn't it?"

"No. That's your intuition, not mine."

"Then who is it about?"

Jax refused to meet my gaze.

I tugged at his arm. "You can't keep this a secret. Just tell me."

His head turned; his blue eyes filled with grief. "The bad feeling is about you, Elara."

42

NOT A WARM WELCOME

I spun him around to face me, my body quivering with fear. "And you're only telling me this now?"

"We have to keep moving."

I tripped over my feet walking sideways. "Why did you keep this from me?"

"I didn't want you to worry."

"Damn it, Jax! That's all I do these days. Did you not think I could handle the bad news?"

He tossed up his hands. "These feelings don't paint a clear picture of the future. It's like I'm staring at a blurred map. The outline is there, but the details are missing."

"You should have at least told me, so I could prepare—"

"Prepare for what?"

"Torture, imminent death?"

He gave me a long look.

"Don't say it," I hissed. "I'm not being dramatic. I'm being practical. We saw a pile of bodies today and your adoptive father wants me dead. This is real life. *My* life. The West Village is a stone's throw from Zenith's. I bet it's swarming with Collectors."

"Not if they're at Iah's."

"Thanks for putting my mind at ease."

"I wasn't trying to. I thought we were being practical."

"It's not funny."

"I'm not laughing, so keep your ass glued to my side while we walk through the village. Do you understand?"

I tapped my hand to my forehead in a mocked salute. "Sir, yes, sir."

SAMSON HELD up a fist once we reached the edge of the West Village. I shared my brother's powerful vision and observed the Lunins and Solins strolling through town. They carried cloth-wrapped packages, baskets of supplies, and nodded their salutations to one another as they passed.

"Why is everyone so chill?" Cyrus asked.

"Our recruits came from the other villages. I doubt the latest turn of events affected these citizens," Samson answered. "This village is too close to Zenith's. I bet the men subject to the ordinance didn't put up a fight when the Collectors came knocking. They probably joined willingly."

Orion shoved his hands into his pockets. "So how are we supposed to cut through town without blowing our cover?"

"Not a damn clue."

I needed to swallow. I couldn't. An impending sense of doom choked me with its invisible hands. I unfastened the top button of my coat.

"I want us to stay in a tight formation," Samson added. "Jax and Cyrus, flank Elara. Castor, you're next to me." He locked eyes with Orion. "You, Roshan, and Aries lead the others. Stay close, only a few paces behind us."

"What about me?" Blaze asked. "Jax said I should stay close to Cyrus."

"He doesn't have time to babysit. Go bother someone else."

"Blaze," Roshan called. "Come stand by me and Aries."

The boy pouted but obeyed the command.

Our group inhaled a shared breath as our boots touched the main path. A long exhale later, we encountered our first villager: a Solin carrying a sack of grain. The woman paused to let us pass, her golden eyes lifting. Trepidation smeared her flawless complexion, hardening the soft features of her face. I thought a warm grin would ease her apprehension. It had the same effect as if I had snuck up behind her and shouted *boo*. She dropped the sack, its contents spilling onto the ground, then sprinted toward the opposite end of town.

"Next time, try not to smile, sis."

I glared at my brother. "I didn't get our father's dimples. Why don't you try working that charm of yours on the next villager?"

Jax ignored our banter. He kept his gaze ahead, eyes peeled for trouble.

Every few strides, people scattered, doors slammed shut, and curtains drew closed.

"I wonder if this is how it feels to be a Collector?" Cyrus whispered to me.

"I bet it does."

"Look at how fast they get out of our way."

"Keep your mouths shut," Samson hissed.

A few strides later, we passed the Union Services building. I nudged my brother. He nodded, acknowledging my unspoken thoughts. My unwavering determination to rescue Jax propelled me forward the night we traveled with Archer. This time, fear led the way.

"Take a left," Samson instructed. "We'll sneak through the back. Keep a low profile."

We turned and followed a deserted path through the

outskirts of town. Tall trees bordered our right, the backsides of shops on our left.

I pointed to the ground as we rounded a corner. "The snow's a lot deeper out here. I don't see any footprints."

The men followed my gaze. This momentary distraction nearly cost us our life. We almost ran headfirst into a group of men strolling in the opposite direction, the thick haze hiding them from view. Our tight formation jolted us to a stop.

Fuck. My eyes drifted to the Lunin standing front and center. My vision blurred. I couldn't breathe.

Thick purple scars disfigured the man's fair skin. His deformed nose sat two inches in the wrong direction, and a massive gash sliced through his eyebrow. Someone had stitched the wound too tight. The messy operation pulled the Lunin's brow to the middle of his forehead; the coarse hairs sprouted like overgrown weeds between the sutures. His patchy beard couldn't hide the damage to his cheeks and jawline.

With a feline grace, Samson and Castor moved beside Cyrus. The other men tightened their ranks. I reached for my white knife, but my trembling hand prevented me from holding the damn thing. Fear hopped in the driver's seat and engaged the emergency brake. I froze, for there stood Pollux and the rest of the Inner Circle.

43

A TWISTED REFLECTION

Pollux eyed his father, his misshapen nostrils flaring. This subtle advance triggered Samson and the others to expose their knives.

Jax slid his boot forward and drawled, "You're outnumbered."

The burn scars on Elio's face stretched as he sneered at his former comrade.

"There are six of us." Pollux jerked his chin at Samson and Castor, then glared at Jax. "And only three of you. The rest of your men aren't a threat. Hell, they don't even look the part." He stole a glance at Apollo and Elio. "I wish more of our friends could have joined us."

The Solins snickered their agreement.

Pollux shifted his gaze back to our group. "But they're a little busy right now." Malice flickered in his pale blue eyes. "The massacre at the East Village was a training exercise to prepare the Collectors for their mission at Iah's."

I paled. Callisto, Idalia, Iah, and the faces of our recruits swirled in my mind, the names I never learned etched on rows of headstones. Orion's body swayed. My brother and Jax cursed; the bleak reality of my theory proved true. Roshan shifted his weight while concerned whispers rolled off the men's tongues.

"That's right," he said, noting our pained reaction. "This is what happens to traitors. They die a slow and painful death." The Lunin looked at Jax. "And thanks to *Aarush* your friends are doing this as we speak."

"You'll pay for this," Cyrus growled.

The wave of heat that zipped through my veins almost knocked me over.

Pollux and Elio laughed at my brother while Oberon cleaned his nails with his knife. Apollo's cheeks puffed. The Solin appeared bored with the vicious banter. The other men watched us with ice-cold expressions. Jericho stood there, tracing our figures with the blade of his knife. I shuddered. *I wonder if he's the Collector who enjoys skinning his victims alive.*

Pollux wiggled with mock excitement as he eyed my brother. "Ah. The illusive twin speaks. Are you ready to play with the big kids now? Or should we anticipate another disappearance?" He looked at me. "Elara, I hate to break the news." His lips drooped into a pout. "But your brother is a fucking coward."

I gripped the handle of my knife, ready to defend my blood with actions rather than words.

Castor stepped forward. "Stand down, son. You're asking for nothing but trouble."

"Don't waste your breath on me, old man. Your time is coming—sooner than you think." Pollux turned his attention back to my brother. "Now, where was I? Ah, yes. Your lack of courage."

"He's not a coward!" Blaze yelled.

Roshan hollered the boy's name. My partner's arm, along with my own, shot out a moment too late. The boy tripped over his untied laces as he charged the Inner Circle, his tiny hand still clutched around Jax's spare knife. Samson wrapped his strong arms around my brother, holding him back.

Pollux observed Blaze with a morbid satisfaction smeared across his face. "And this proves my point. Cyrus has children standing up for him." He spat onto the ground. "Pathetic."

The child aimed his knife at the Lunin's gut. "I'm not afraid of you."

"You're not?" Pollux took a knee and directed the tip of the blade at the main artery in his neck. "Then do it. Make your friends proud and kill me."

I eyed Jax and Castor, hoping someone would intervene. The two men kept their attention focused on the unspoken leader of the Inner Circle. My brother twisted in Samson's arms, desperate to free himself.

Blaze's hand trembled, the knife brushing Pollux's skin.

"Go on," he encouraged, pressing the blade deeper.

The boy gasped at the blood dripping from the self-inflicted injury.

"Why are you hesitating?" the Lunin taunted.

Apollo squatted before the boy, balancing his weight on the balls of his feet. "You're making us Solins look bad." His ginger-colored eyes flickered with intimidation. "I'm giving you an order, son. Plunge that knife into his neck."

"You heard the man." Pollux snickered, tugging on his collar. "Do it."

Blaze's chest rose and fell with sharp breaths. His eyes darted between the two men. The blade in his hand became a black blur. The poor child couldn't stop shaking.

"Look at him." Elio crossed his arms and shook his head in disappointment. "What a pussy. I guess he's a blond-haired Lunin."

Pollux's lips curled into a dramatic pout, and in a patronizing tone, he said, "Awe. Are you scared of the big bad Collectors?"

The child whimpered, his eyes brimming with tears. Castor dashed forward to help Samson restrain my brother. They held his arms behind his back, holding him in place, but they couldn't stop the morbid threats that flew out of his mouth.

My hands vibrated with so much heat I thought my skin would melt off my bones. Sensing my emotions stir, Jax took action and held me in a tight hold. Aries gripped his knife, and the other men formed a tight line behind us. Orion and Roshan scooted their boots closer to the Inner Circle. Samson's fierce gaze halted their approach. Pollux dangled Blaze's life before our eyes. One wrong move would send him to an early grave.

"Do it!" Pollux yelled.

Blaze stumbled backward, the knife falling from his hand. As if the evil duo had practiced the move a hundred times, Pollux grabbed the child, spun him around, and shoved him toward Elio. The Solin caught him with one hand, yanked Blaze's hair, and angled his head toward the sky.

My entire group hollered, "NO," when Elio raised his knife.

I bucked under Jax's tight grip. "Let me go!"

"Stop," he demanded. "You'll make it worse."

"We have to save him," I cried.

"Elio!" Samson's voice bellowed around us. "Release the kid."

"He doesn't take orders from you." Pollux adjusted the cuff of his sleeve. "The boy comes with us."

I choked back a sob.

"So help me God," Cyrus said, spit spraying from his mouth. "If you lay a *fucking* hand on him."

Pollux lifted his eyes. "I'd love to help Jericho peel the boy's skin from his body." He shrugged, flicking a loose thread off his coat. "But I can't. We can't. Zenith wants to perform the executions himself. We're just gathering the stragglers."

The cruel and heartless words shook Blaze's shoulders with sobs.

Pollux shut his eyes and pinched the bridge of his nose. "Elio, crying gives me a headache. Make it stop."

The Solin lifted Blaze's chin higher and slid the blade across his neck with enough force to draw blood.

"Pollux," Castor said, fighting to restrain my brother. "That's enough. He's just a boy."

"Like you give a fuck. When I was his age you tied me to a chair and cut me with your knife for fun, remember?"

The memories of Castor's past drained the color from his face. "*Son—*"

"I'm just doing my job," Pollux interrupted. "Stop pretending you care if this child lives or dies. It's too late to make amends. You're still the useless piece of shit father you were back then."

"Pollux, this is your last chance," Samson warned. "Let the kid go, or we let go of Cyrus and Elara. I'm sure the twins will be happy to remind your pal how their little trick works."

Elio gritted his teeth and slid another line across Blaze's neck. A mixture of pain and terror stained the child's face. Tears wet his cheeks and snot dripped from his nose.

Apollo, Jericho, and Ishan tightened their formation. Oberon circled his throwing arm, warming the muscles in his shoulder.

An unexpected villager turned the corner. The man did a double take at the inevitable brawl, then spun around with his hands held in a surrender stance.

Save the child, Elara. Before it's too late.

I rolled my neck, the dealer's voice slithering through my mind. *How?*

Use Zenith's knife.

No. I can't.

But you must. It's the only way.

I swore under my breath, struggling in Jax's arms. *Get out of my head.*

I can't. You and I . . .

Pollux's tongue tapped the roof of his mouth, distracting me from my internal banter. "Here's the problem," he said to Samson. "Elio's hand will slip and slice the boy's throat if your group attacks. The child comes with us and that's final."

"No," I growled. "He's not going anywhere with you."

The Lunin flashed me a grin that oozed cruelty. "Elara, you *are* a feisty little thing." He licked his lips, his eyes roving over my body with ill intentions. "I can see why Jax keeps you around. I bet you're a screamer in the bedroom."

Bile crept up my throat. My partner went rigid; the tendons in his arms had turned to stone.

"I hope you put up more of a fight than the other girls," Pollux said. "It's quite boring if they don't, and it annoys the hell out of me when they just lie there crying, begging me to stop." He shot a casual glance at Cyrus. "Idalia was just a meaningless fuck. That bitch had it coming to her, but with *you*"—wicked laughter rumbled in his chest, the sadist emerging—"I plan on taking my sweet ass time."

Jax shoved me to the side and lunged at his arch rival. Before I could blink, Orion dashed forward and tackled Jax, taking him to the ground. My fight-or-flight instinct moved my feet to help my friend restrain the enraged Lunin.

Cyrus thrashed his body, fighting to break free while calling Pollux every foul name in the book. The hostility burning in Samson's eyes made me wonder if he'd release my brother and assist him with ending Pollux's life. The threats continued to fly out of my brother's mouth. The milder ones included: hanging Pollux by his intestines and nailing him to a tree by his balls after removing the part he used as a weapon against women.

Orion and I struggled to keep Jax from ripping Pollux apart with his bare hands. I begged him to stand down, but the darkness had grabbed hold of him.

"Don't do it," Orion said. "They'll kill Blaze."

Pollux tapped his blade against his scarred palm. "He's right. I'll give the order." He sneered at Jax. "Try that shit again. I dare you."

Accepting the challenge, my partner lifted his gaze. If looks could kill, Pollux would have dropped dead in the snow. *Shit. He's not backing down.*

I eyed Orion and mouthed, "Hold him."

He nodded and adjusted his grip. It didn't do a damn bit of good. Jax squatted, taking us with him, then threw out his arms as he stood, sending us toppling over.

Pollux raised his hand, a silent command to end Blaze's life. Elio directed the knife at the boy's artery—a kill shot. Roshan sucked in a sharp breath and held it. Jax didn't attack. He just stood there, his chest rising and falling.

A wicked cackle left Pollux's mouth as he lowered his arm. Elio rolled his eyes, irritated with the change in orders.

"Good boy, Jax," Pollux chided. "Now get your ass back in line."

Having spent countless hours training together, Samson knew Jax's mannerisms better than most. He swore, watching his comrade rise to his full height. Even Apollo and Oberon acknowledged the unspoken warning. They moved closer, preparing for battle.

"Please don't do something stupid," I whispered. "Think of Blaze."

Jax answered me by baring his teeth at Pollux. "Let's end this. Right here, right now. You versus me. My men won't intervene, and neither will yours. We fight to the death."

My heart dropped into the pit of my stomach.

The unspoken leader of the Inner Circle scoffed at the suggestion. "I won't play your games, Jax."

"Why? Because you're afraid to lose?"

Pollux's face twitched. "No. Because your games are boring as fuck. Killing you is too easy. Where's the excitement in that?"

471

His eyes drifted to me. "I have big plans for the three of us." They slid back to Jax. "After I've tortured you to the brink of death, you get to watch me fuck your little bitch. I'll even let you hang out while Jericho and Elio join in on the fun." He smirked at the men beside him. "You guys don't mind sloppy seconds, do you?"

They snickered, their eyes scanning the more sensitive areas of my body. Orion held onto my arm to keep me from falling to my knees.

Jax took another step forward. "Come find me when you're done cowering behind your false threats."

"I think you were the one who said don't confuse a threat with a promise."

"Then hear me when I say this: The next time we meet, I promise to make you swallow your threats, along with your fucking tongue. And then, I'll saw off your limbs one at a time and use your intestines to stitch them back together. Elio and Jericho can watch. Though that might present a challenge if I carve out their eyes." He looked at Cyrus and Samson. "You guys don't mind helping me out, do you?"

An evil grin crossed the Solins' faces. They nodded their approval.

Pushed to his limit, Pollux charged. Apollo grabbed him by the wrist, holding him back.

"Don't forget. We're under strict orders from Zenith," he reminded him. "Don't fuck this up."

"Get your hands off me! That's an order."

"Then stand down," Apollo demanded, yanking his arm.

Oberon whispered near the Lunin's ear. "Zenith will have our heads if you disobey his orders."

Silence. Not a swaying tree limb, not the crunch of snow—nothing. Just mind-numbing silence. Pollux and Jax glared at each other like big cats securing their territory. Blaze's terrified expression snagged my attention; the masked dealer expressed its concerns.

The boy is good as dead if they take him to Zenith's.

I shut my eyes. I couldn't watch the child suffer. *What can I do?*

I told you, Elara. Use the knife.

What good will that do?

Use your powers.

My eyes shot open at the sound of Elio's voice. "Pollux, I'm getting blood on my hands. I just washed them after killing the last traitor we captured."

"Let's go," Apollo said to the Lunin. "We did as Zenith asked. We bought the men time." He pointed his knife at Blaze. "And as a bonus, we got the boy."

His words siphoned the air from my lungs. *Men. The other Collectors sent to murder our friends at Iah's. Zenith didn't dispatch the Inner Circle to kill us. He dispatched them to create a diversion. It was a trap. One we never saw coming.*

Moisture filled my eyes as I looked at Orion and Cyrus. They made the connection. The Lunin braced his hands on his thighs, he couldn't catch his breath. My brother's body went limp. Samson and Jax cursed, for we had lost the battle.

"They played us," I whispered to my partner.

"Yes, we did," Pollux said, his eyes glowing with a victory. "My men work quick. Rule number three . . ."

"I do not pity the weak," Elio and the others answered.

"And that's exactly what those traitors in the East Village were—*weak*. I'm sure by now, the pile of corpses at Iah's is twice that size."

"You won't get away with this," Roshan said through gritted teeth.

"I already did." Pollux stomped his boot on the compacted snow. "Good luck burying the dead. The ground's a little hard."

The scars on his face pulled tight as he smiled at Jax. "Perhaps a fire will do. Let's go."

Moving as one, the Inner Circle spun on their heels. Elio dragged Blaze by his hair through the snow. The child sobbed, screaming my brother's name.

"Jax, we have to do something."

"No." His fingers wrapped around my arm. "We can't."

"But Zenith will kill him."

"Listen to Jax," Samson said, still struggling to restrain my brother. "Both of you." He shook Cyrus. "There's nothing we can do to help that child. He's gone."

My heels slid through the snow as Jax pulled me farther away from the hysterical child. "No!" I cried. "I won't leave him."

"*Elara.*" Jax's tone switched from stern to severe. "You're not making this any easier on me."

"We have to go." Orion's voice sounded a mile away. "My father—" His words faded.

As if leaving a funeral, Roshan and the others hung their heads and turned their backs on Blaze. Aries looked over his shoulder at me, his expression blank.

Do it, Elara. End the madness by using Zenith's knife.

Why his?

It's a pure Fired Stone blade.

My mind reeled with curious thoughts. *How will that help?*

Use your powers and find out.

A pained sob from Blaze kicked my ass into gear. *You're right. Let's do this.*

I compelled my body to relax in Jax's arms. Convinced I wouldn't run after Blaze, he let me go. Samson followed suit, releasing my brother. Their mistake.

I reached for Cyrus to absorb his power. The warmth rushed from one side of my body to the next, concentrating in my free hand. A heartbeat later, my fingers found Zenith's knife. I opened the floodgates, heating the handle with invisible flames. Once the fur-lined pocket of my coat started smoking, I inhaled a ragged breath and exposed the blade.

Cyrus's nostrils flared at the stench of burning hair. His tear-filled eyes grew once he noticed the knife in my hand. As if I held a branding iron fresh out the fire, the weapon glowed with warmth. The blade had changed colors from black to a vibrant orange streaked with gold.

My twin gasped. "Elara, what are you—"

"I'm sorry," I whispered, dropping his hand. "I won't leave him."

Hearing these words caused Jax to pivot and reach for my armed hand. Months of combative training allowed me to dodge his pursuit. I spun around and dashed toward the Inner Circle. Though their backs faced me, I could see Elio and Blaze through the fog.

Jax lunged and hollered, "Don't!"

I sidestepped the Lunin. Another near miss. I had to throw the knife before it cooled. My partner yelled for Samson and Cyrus to help. Boots skidded to a stop as I raised my arm.

"Elara, no!" The desperation in Jax's voice made me hesitate.

Do it, Elara. Aim for the base of the skull.

The hesitation vanished. *Consider it done.*

And before anyone could stop me, I unleashed hell. Death's prelude whistled through the air, the high-pitched solo ending with a loud thud. Elio staggered, his fingers loosening around the strands of Blaze's hair. As if piercing a block of soft clay, the glowing blade sliced through the flesh and bone that protected the Solin's spinal cord. The handle, the only part of the knife exposed, swayed from the forceful throw. Blood, and lots of it, poured from the wound. The hint of color left in Pollux's face drained as he watched his partner in crime fall to the ground.

The masked dealer cackled louder than ever, its black claws clinking with delight. *Well done, Elara.*

My extremities went numb as I stared at Elio's dead body. Relief didn't wash over Blaze when he met my gaze. Fear clouded his amber eyes.

Oh, God. What have I done? My legs buckled, sending me to my knees.

Like the other men around me, Oberon stood slack-jawed, baffled by the turn of events.

He pointed at Elio while whispering to Apollo, "How the *fuck* did she manage that? No one can sever a spinal cord by throwing a knife. Not even Zenith."

Apollo shrugged, his eyes wide with disbelief.

Cyrus slid on his knees through the snow, then rested a hand on my shoulder. "Sis, are you okay?"

I grimaced; his gentle touch sent another surge of heat zipping through me. Bracing myself, I pressed my palms into the ground. The ice crystals hissed at the sudden change in temperature. My body sank deeper, a puddle forming around me. A shaky breath later, I sat on a blanket of wet grass, six inches lower than everyone else. I looked at Pollux, tears pooling in my eyes.

He stumbled backward into Apollo.

"I'd advise you to release the boy," Samson said, waving a hand at the melting snow. "Unless you want to hop into the grave with your pal."

A tangible fear grabbed hold of Pollux. His eyes darted back and forth between me and Elio.

Samson grinned at his reaction. "Smart kid. Now run along and tell Zenith we refuse to cower. Regardless of the dirty games he plays." He pointed the tip of his knife at me and my brother. "The next time we meet, the twins come for his blood."

Oberon snarled, and without Pollux's approval, he shoved

Blaze toward Samson. The boy sprinted past me and Cyrus, then jumped into Roshan's waiting arms.

Pollux glared at me through tiny slits. "Your days are numbered, Elara."

And without saying another word, he stooped down, pulled the knife from Elio's skull, and jogged toward Zenith's. The remaining members of the Inner Circle hurried after him. We watched them go until they disappeared in the haze.

Silence. My old friend, silence had returned. I couldn't speak. The only part that could move were my eyelids. They closed.

The masked dealer sauntered into the private room of my mind and held its slender arms behind its back. *I'm proud of you, Elara.*

Why does your voice sound familiar?

You'll see. It stifled a laugh, the mask shifting around its hidden face. *You did the right thing.*

We did it together.

No, you did this. You murdered Elio.

But you told me to do it.

It shook its head. *You make the rules. I never told you to kill the man. I only told you to use the knife.*

My heart slammed against my chest watching the dealer untie the silk mask. *What are you doing?*

Showing you the truth.

What truth?

The truth you're afraid to see.

The cracked foundation that housed my sanity shattered and turned to dust once the dealer revealed its identity. *No, it can't be.*

Fair skin, dark brows, and a pair of blue eyes stared back. The dealer's full lips, *her* lips, spread into a wicked grin as she observed my reaction.

No. No. No.

477

The young woman tossed the mask to the side. *That's better. I no longer have to hide.* She combed her thin fingers through the locks of her black hair before meeting my gaze. *You and I are one and the same. We always have been.*

I gasped, staring at my reflection—a twisted version of myself.

A switch flipped. The lights went out. *Welcome to the darkness, Elara.*

44

ASHES TO ASHES

The troublesome effects of psychological trauma extend beyond the human mind. Physical ailments include stomach upset, headaches, racing pulse, and muscle tension. I experienced each symptom, along with the emotional shock of committing cold-blooded murder. Regardless of my heroic efforts, I had killed a man—and he never saw it coming.

Thick tears, salted with remorse, stung my eyes. The darkness that consumed me triggered a pained scream. On hands and knees, I crawled toward the deceased Solin. *I can fix it. I have to fix it.*

Jax called my name. I refused to turn around.

My pale fingers turned red as they grazed the gaping wound. *I can fix this.*

Desperation and illogical thoughts guided my hands. I scooped up the blood-stained snow around Elio's skull and compacted the injury. Jax begged me to stop. I couldn't. My mind toed the edge of insanity.

Fix it. I picked up an oily clot of blood. *Fix it.* My fingers trembled as I pushed the mass into the wound. *Fix it.* I scowled.

The warmth of the red ooze melted my efforts. It dripped from the hole, pooling in my palm.

"Elara." My partner grabbed my shoulders. "He's gone."

"*No.*" A guttural voice, one not my own, caused him to stumble backward. "I can fix it."

"Stop," he begged. "This is madness."

"Trust me. I can fix it. Watch." I rolled Elio onto his side. As if a taxidermist had replaced his eyes with marbles, two lifeless orbs stared back. Snow stuck to his face. The thick stream of blood that dripped from his mouth cut a valley through the ice crystals.

"See." I gathered more snow. "I can fix it."

"Sis." Cyrus took a knee. He couldn't hide the quiver in his voice. "What are you doing?"

"I'm fixing it," I snapped. "What does it look like I'm doing?"

"He's gone. *Elio* is gone."

"No, he's not!" The demon inside me spoke once more as I rolled the Solin back onto his stomach. I grabbed my brother's hand. "We can fix it."

"No, we can't. Our powers can't raise the dead."

"Maybe they can." I held my blood-soaked palm over the wound.

"Elara stop it," Jax demanded.

"Shut up! I need to focus. I need to fix this."

Orion and Samson approached with great caution.

The Solin whispered to Jax, "What the hell is she doing?"

"Fuck if I know."

Orion repeated the four-letter curse word as he watched Elio's skin smoke. Cyrus twisted to get away from me, but I held his hand tighter. The tether that secured my sanity had snapped.

"Sis, please." His voice cracked. "You're scaring the shit out of me."

Each vertebrate in my neck popped when I rotated my head

to face him. I smiled, releasing more heat from my hand. Defeated, his chin hit his chest.

The skin around Elio's wound melted—and then it melted some more. Moments later my palm pressed into his spinal cord. I refused to let up. The heat continued to flow. My hand went deeper, feeling the bones warm—crack. *Fix it. Close the wound. Fix it.*

"Elara is experiencing shock," Orion said. "She's not thinking straight."

"We have to go," Samson said. "The men are losing their shit. One already took off because his wife and kid are at Iah's. I've got to check on Callisto and Idalia."

Hearing her name caused my brother to rip his hand away from mine. The heat subsided. Now frantic, I kneaded Elio's flesh, pressing it into the wound. The melted skin stuck to my fingers like hot glue. I didn't mind. I continued my morbid craft project until I could no longer see the hole.

"There." I wiped my hands on my pants. "Now he can wake up."

"Do it," Jax said to Cyrus.

My brother lifted me off the ground, threw me over his shoulder, and ran, abandoning the murder scene.

I hollered my protest, kicking and screaming. He didn't flinch when I pounded my fists on his back and he never stopped running when I begged him to put me down.

The men in our group continued their quick pace until their burning lungs forced them to a brisk walk. Long minutes passed before I gave up the struggle. Exhausted, my body went limp, my chin knocking against my brother's back.

No one dared to speak. Blaze stayed close to Roshan and held a hand over his wounded neck while they trudged through the shin deep snow. Every few strides, Aries stole a glance in my direction. Samson gave him a stern look and inclined his head at Jax. The Lunin ceased his observation, noting the faraway look in my partner's eyes. The day's events had caught up with him. With a set jaw and clenched fists, he trailed behind Cyrus and the other men. Was it guilt for the recruits at Iah's or grief for my actions that cloaked him in darkness? Who knows? Perhaps it was a mixture of both.

"I'll put you down if you promise not to run off," Cyrus whispered.

I didn't answer.

Pressing his luck, he slid me off his shoulder. After stretching his sore neck and circling his arms, he cupped my face and said, "Everything is going to be okay. *We* are going to be okay."

"Fuck you."

Cyrus blinked.

I took a step backward and looked over my shoulder at Jax. "Fuck all of you."

The Lunin grabbed my wrist before I blew past Cyrus.

"Don't touch me," I hissed, yanking my arm away.

Samson turned. Cyrus motioned for everyone to keep walking. He took his own advice after noting the ferocity in my gaze.

Once alone, Jax said, "You did nothing wrong."

My chilled palm slapped him across the face, sending his head flying to one side. He didn't block the unexpected attack.

Slowly, he rotated his head to face me. "Elara—"

"I killed a man!" I hollered, shoving him in the chest. "With the knife *you* gave me. I heated the blade. I could have never done that with my knife."

"Hybrid blades are forged with Fired Stone. I bet you could repeat that trick with any knife."

"A trick?" My eyes almost fell out of their sockets. "A trick that killed a man! I could have saved him, Jax. I could have fixed it had Cyrus not—"

"Stop it!" His voice erupted with anger. "You can't bring people back from the dead."

"You don't know that."

He shook me by the shoulders. "Yes, I do. This isn't a fairy-tale, it's real life. You're in shock. It's normal to act irrational—"

"Irrational?" My voice raised an octave. "I saw a pile of dead bodies today. I murdered a man, and now I must face whatever happened at Iah's." My voice trembled. "I can't take any more hits to the heart."

He pulled me into his arms. I buried my face into his chest and sobbed.

"The first kill is always the hardest," he whispered, running his fingers through my hair. "Don't focus on Elio's death. Focus on the life you saved."

"It's not that easy." I wiped the snot from my nose and widened the gap between us. "I did nothing but trade one life for another."

"Blood gets spilled on the battlefield. You knew we would face great challenges."

"I didn't think those challenges involved murder."

"This is war, Elara. Soldiers on Earth fight to protect their country and their loved ones. How is what you did today any different?"

Daggers shot out of my eyes. "I'm not a soldier! I didn't volunteer to join the military and deploy to war."

He arched a brow. "You didn't?"

I shook my head.

"You didn't volunteer to leave Earth and stand against Zenith?"

Jax's words sliced through my emotional shield. I shut my eyes. Each bone-chilling moment on Aroonyx replayed in my mind. Jax's brawl with Cyrus, his confession, the unexpected morning with the Inner Circle, the attack at the spring, the tense weeks spent at Idalia's, Archer's untimely death, Jax's turbulent recovery, his crazed desire to choke the life out of me. The images wouldn't turn off. *Make it stop.*

I pressed the heels of my palms into my eyes. Faster and faster, the memories flashed and flickered. The weeks I spent worrying about Jax, the feeling of abandonment, rescuing Idalia from Zenith's, her painful recovery, the mound of bodies in the East Village, the fear of what I would find at Iah's. *No.* I saw stars as my palms went deeper. *It's too much.*

I looked at Jax. "I can't do this."

He paled, watching me slip off the ring.

I dropped it in his hand and curled his fingers around the glittering promise. "It's over. I'm not strong enough to stand by your side." A tear rolled off my cheek. "Find a new partner and tell the people to find a new leader."

Jax shook his head, his hand still outstretched. "I don't want another partner, and the people don't want me, Cyrus, or Samson leading them." He lifted my chin. "I won't let you give up on this mission, and I sure as hell won't let you give up on us."

Our breath formed a familiar cloud. The same cloud that brushed my lips the day Jax left, only this time he stood on the receiving end.

"You don't get a say in this," I said, ice lacing my words.

Jax blinked. His expression mirrored my own the day he abandoned me.

Twisting the knife deeper, I whispered near his ear, "Let me share a bit of advice you once gave me."

He swallowed, bracing himself for the verbal attack.

"Stay the hell away from me."

No one stopped me when I stormed past the men, and no one asked why I chatted with the masked dealer—chatted with myself.

"I'll make sure Idalia, Iah, and Callisto are okay, then head to the cliffside."

"Why there?" I asked myself.

I shrugged in response. "It seems appropriate."

"Are you calling it quits with the uprising?"

"Yeah, I'm not qualified to lead the people. I tarnished my record." I kicked a fallen tree branch. "I'm a murderer. I'm no better than Zenith."

"That was an impressive shot."

"I know, right? How the hell did I do that?"

"Don't take all the credit. I suggested you heat the blade."

"I'm glad you did. Did you see how easily it slid through his skull?"

"Yep. That's why I wanted you to use Zenith's knife."

The unstable laughter that shook my shoulders turned into violent sobs. "Why did you make me do it?"

"Don't blame me. You threw the knife."

"I hate you."

"Better hated than ignored."

I used the sleeve of my coat to wipe the tears off my cheeks. "What about Cyrus?"

"He'll be fine. He's the stronger twin."

"And Jax?"

"He deserves a better partner."

"Who? Thea?"

"Maybe."

"Fuck you."

"Sorry. That was low."

My jaw slammed shut when I heard Cyrus and Jax whispering.

"Dude, this is freaking me out," Cyrus said. "She's been talking to herself for over ten minutes."

"I know," Jax said. "I'm worried too."

Cyrus lowered his voice. "Why was she trying to close Elio's wound? He was dead—like *really* dead."

"Desperate people do desperate things."

"She's in shock," Orion reminded them. "My father can give her some medicine." He paused, trying to gain his composure. "If he escaped the Collectors unharmed."

I heard a hand clap on someone's back. I assumed it was my brother comforting Orion.

"Should I give her a hug?" Blaze asked. "My mom says hugs are quiet thank-yous."

Samson huffed a breath. "Shut your trap, kid."

"No hugs, Blaze," Cyrus said. "Just leave her alone."

The fog had lifted, yet the blistering cold slapped at my face. I welcomed the discomfort, enjoyed the painful tingling on my skin.

"They're concerned about your mental health," I said to myself.

"That's another reason I'm leaving. They can't waste their time worrying about me."

"You're right."

A crooked smile broke at the corner of my mouth. "I'm always right. You were the one who told me that, remember?"

"I did."

I could feel my brother's eyes drilling a hole in the back of my skull.

"Did your first kill screw with your head?" he asked Jax.

"A little, but I never verbalized my emotions."

"Me neither," Samson said. "Maybe talking with someone is a good thing." He cleared his throat. "Even if that *someone* is herself."

"People process trauma in different ways. Some keep it bottled up, while others . . ." Orion's voice trailed off as the phantom wolf howled its warning.

My nostrils wafted at the strong scent of burning wood. The

men froze. My head snapped up. In the near distance, a large plume of smoke drifted across the evening sky. The culprit wasn't the small fires our recruits built to keep them warm on the winter's night. No. A structural fire had caused the gray haze. My knees wobbled. Only one family lived in a house that far from town, the house I called home.

45

DUST TO DUST

T he men sprinted past me toward Iah's, a slew of curse words and gasps falling out of their mouths. I clutched my throat. A knot tied by the hands of grief had lodged in my esophagus.

I can't do this. I can't handle any more deaths.

Sorry. The story isn't over.

The sound of Idalia's name catching in my brother's throat snapped me into action. Adrenaline lightened my heavy legs, sending me dashing after the men. The smell of burning wood grew stronger once I approached the familiar location.

I didn't think my eyes could shed any more tears. I was wrong. A pile of corpses came into view. Unlike the ones in the East Village, the Collectors had tossed the poor souls onto the smoldering remains of the quaint home. The stomach-churning smell of singed hair and melted flesh wafted toward us.

I fell to my knees, unable to tear my gaze away from the horrific sight. The bodies of our recruits formed a teepee of death. Their charred skin flaked, their scalps hung off their skulls, their clothes melted to their bones. I bit my knuckles and looked away, only to see Samson lunge for Orion. It took all of his strength to keep the Lunin from crawling through the ashes.

"DAD." He screamed the three-letter word until he lost his voice.

My brother collapsed beside me and breathed, "*Idalia.*"

Her name ping-ponged off Orion's painful cries. I sobbed into my hands. *This can't be happening.*

The men in our group scattered. Most ran toward the camp-sites in search of their loved ones. A few stuck around to help Castor, Jax, Roshan, and Aries search the smoking remains. They hissed and swore; the glowing embers scorched their hands as they removed the shingles and blocks of Clear Stone off the bodies.

A Lunin shrieked. He recognized the face of a deceased woman—his wife. The man tried lifting her burnt corpse off the pile. Her brittle leg bone snapped in two. Castor shielded the distraught Lunin from the devastation while Aries collected the pieces of his wife.

Blaze shook my brother's shoulders. "Where's my mom?" he cried. "I want my mom."

"I don't know, kid." He slid the boy onto his lap and held him close. "I don't know."

A moment later, Roshan removed a burnt door from the pile. He sighed before directing his voice at Cyrus. "His mother's gone."

"NO," Blaze screamed. "I want my mom!"

Cyrus restrained the frantic child; the whites of his eyes had turned a bright shade of red.

The skin around Roshan's knuckles thinned as he gripped the remnants of the door. He threw it across the yard. "They're gone," he rasped. "They're all gone."

"No," Jax said. "This can't be everyone. Keep searching."

The harsh reality knocked the wind out of Samson. He

released Orion and sank to his knees, a cloud of snow exploding around him.

"No." His chest moved with labored breaths. "Not my Ida."

Cyrus's tears soaked the top of Blaze's hair as he rocked him back and forth.

I buried my face in my hands and cried with him. *They can't be gone.*

My gaze lifted when Jax cursed. He had identified another corpse. His fingers clung to a chunk of the ashen roof. Orion approached. Jax hesitated to show my friend what hid underneath.

"Show me," he demanded.

"No," Jax argued. "You shouldn't see this."

The doctor's son grabbed the crumbling wood out of Jax's hand and tossed it to the side. He would have fallen onto the pile of bodies had Aries not caught him.

My hand shot to my mouth, muffling a scream. The charred remains of a man sat tied to a chair. His melted flesh masked his identity, but the singed medical bag in his lap confirmed the bitter truth. *Iah.*

I had witnessed my fair share of horrors while living on Aroonyx. Nothing compared to watching Orion sob onto the shoulders of his father's skeleton. The doctor who delivered me and Cyrus, who saved Jax's life, who tended to our injuries, was dead. The man who fed us, who clothed us, who treated us like his own children, was gone *forever.*

Jax bowed his head and rested a hand on Orion's quivering back. The other men formed a circle around the deceased and his grieving son.

"Come on, sis." Cyrus choked back a sob and climbed to his feet. "We should pay our respects."

Blaze clung to my brother's chest until Roshan opened his arms. The elder Solin patted the child's back as he walked away from the home.

I leaned into my brother, wishing it were day so I could feel his warmth. With a heavy heart, I stared at Orion—and only Orion. I couldn't bear to look at his father. I wanted to remember Iah smiling—laughing. Not a burnt skeleton strapped to a chair.

We stood in silence for long minutes. Sharing our memories of the doctor's life could wait for another day. The bones of others lay at our feet. It felt disrespectful to grieve the loss of one man and not the others.

The winds gathered the smoke in a tight funnel. It spun in endless circles, just like the regret-filled thoughts in my mind. I looked up. The twin moons didn't smile. They hid behind the thick snow clouds in the evening sky.

The men continued to search for our friends. I didn't help. I just stood there, swaying in the breeze with the tree limbs. *Where were Callisto's and Idalia's remains? At the top of the pile? At the bottom? Somewhere in between?*

My mind twisted irrational thoughts into plausible justifications.

This is your fault. You should have stayed at Iah's. You should have listened to your gut.

But Jax insisted that we go.

Then blame him. It's his fault Aarush sought revenge.

"I've counted forty-seven," Roshan said.

My head snapped up.

"So did I," Jax replied. He stole a glance at the Lunin who clung to his father's remains. "Before we left Orion gave us the latest headcount."

"Two hundred and ninety-six," Roshan confirmed.

Jax nodded, his eyes searching the vast area. "Then where are the others?"

"Sir, most of the bodies are unidentifiable," Aries said. He rotated the scorched face of a child, then pointed to a cluster of hair stuck to Blaze's mother. "It appears these are women and children."

"A few are men," Castor said, frowning at the gender-revealing parts of another corpse.

Samson closed the eyes of an elderly man with half a face. "We need to find the others."

"Let's start at the campsites and—"

The gasp that left my mouth interrupted Jax. Heads turned. A flash of gold snagged our attention. *Impossible.* A beacon of hope, a lighthouse in a storm, shone brightly. *Idalia.*

Samson reached for Jax. He steadied the Solin, allowing him to catch his breath. My brother fell to his knees and expressed his gratitude to the universe.

I tripped over the dead while running to greet her, then threw my arms around her neck. I squeezed her tighter and tighter, refusing to let go.

"We thought you were dead," I cried.

She didn't pull away. Her tears soaked my shoulder. Two sobs later, Samson, Cyrus, and Jax appeared. Idalia wiped the moisture off her ash-stained cheeks, then jumped into the eldest Solin's arms. He held her against his broad chest, his muscles quivering with relief. Idalia repeated this routine with Cyrus and Jax before she spoke.

"We tried to fight back." She sniffled. "They came out of nowhere. There were so many."

Jax crossed his arms and widened his stance. His time for grieving had ended.

"Where did they attack?" he asked.

"By the spring. Everyone scattered. Some ran off, but the recruits you trained stood their ground."

A hint of pride flickered in Samson's eyes.

"Fifty or so didn't make it," she added. "The Collectors worked fast."

I gritted my teeth, remembering Pollux's similar comment.

Jax struggled to swallow. The guilt was choking him. He cleared his throat, his fingers rubbing the spot near his Adam's apple. "Was Aarush fighting with them?"

"I'm not sure. I was speaking with Thea when they attacked." Idalia's lips pursed as she eyed my bare ring finger. "I tried keeping everyone in a tight formation, but it didn't last for long."

Cyrus pointed to the dried blood crusted on her cheek. "Did you fight?"

"Yeah. Why wouldn't I?"

He stumbled over his words. "I didn't know you could."

Samson shot my brother an incredulous look. "You didn't think I'd teach the girl I helped raise how to use a knife?"

"Oh." Cyrus scratched at the stubble on his chin. "I guess not."

Idalia tossed her matted hair over one shoulder. "We set up a makeshift camp because the bastards burned most of the tents along with our supplies. The men collected the dead. We have them lined up near the spring so the families can grieve. We can't bury them." She lifted her boot. "The snow is too thick, and the ground is frozen solid. I think we should build a fire." Her eyes watered as she inclined her head at the fallen structure behind us. "After the Collectors set the house ablaze, they tossed the bodies of the elders, women, and children onto the flames." She burst into tears. "I tried to get him out. I really did."

My brother shut his eyes while Jax inspected the fresh burns on Idalia's skin. We hadn't even noticed the damage or the singed sleeves of her coat.

"Sweetie." Samson rested a hand on her shoulder. "Can you tell us what happened to Iah? Orion's a mess. I don't know if he'll recover from this one."

She wiped her nose before saying the words I never wanted

to hear. "They beat him, tied him to a chair, then set the place on fire."

"When?"

"Late this afternoon. I was helping him with his rounds. He told me to take over for a few minutes because he needed to check on the stew he was cooking for dinner."

My shoulders caved inward. *The stew. The fucking stew killed him.*

She brushed away a tear. "They attacked right after I finished wrapping a man's arm. I don't know how much time had passed, but the smoke caught my attention. I told Callisto—"

"He's alive?" Samson asked.

"Yeah, he's fine. He suffered minor injuries."

A unanimous sigh moved through our small group.

Jax touched her arm. "What did you tell Callisto?"

"To protect the others," she rasped. "I had to get to Iah. I used a chair to break the front window because the Collectors had barricaded the door." She touched the bubbled flesh on her palms. "The backdraft nearly took me out. I felt so help-less." Her tears flowed once more. "I could see him, but I couldn't get to him. Flames had engulfed the living room."

Samson pulled her close and stroked her hair. "It's okay, sweetie." He eyed me out of his peripheral vision. "Some things in life are out of your control. You tried to save him and that's what counts."

A tiny cloud of frustration left my nostrils. I wasn't an idiot. The Solin comforted Idalia with advice he directed at me. I glared at my mentor. *It doesn't matter. I killed a man.*

Idalia pointed at the collapsed house that was no longer a home. "If it's any consolation, I think the smoke killed Iah before the flames. He looked peaceful, as if he was sleeping."

"Orion should hear this," Cyrus suggested. "It might give him some closure."

Samson nodded. "Then tell him."

My brother's cheeks puffed as he stared at the grief-stricken Lunin.

"I'll do it," Idalia said, dusting the ashes off her sleeve.

Our heads turned when Aries approached. He stared at the ground as if finding the courage to speak.

"Spit it out," Samson snapped.

His injured tongue tapped against his teeth. "Can I ask her a question?"

"Make it quick."

The young Lunin lifted his gaze and found Idalia's eyes. "Did any of my men—" Unable to finish the sentence, he dropped his head.

"Fight alongside the Collectors?"

He nodded, then lowered his head even more.

She smiled, hooking a finger under his chin. "No. They fought to protect us."

46

WHAT GOES AROUND

Aries squeezed his eyes shut. Samson clapped him on the back, and Jax nodded his approval. Without saying the words, the two men had initiated the young Lunin into our group. His men proved themselves worthy. As their leader, the silent praise fell on him.

The silver lining in our haze of devastation vanished once Idalia said, "They killed a lot of your men. Callisto is tending to the wounded now."

Aries looked at Samson. "I should check on them."

"Cyrus and I will go with you." Samson turned to my brother. "You can help me calm them down."

Cyrus shook his head. "The recruits won't listen to me. Elara should speak with them."

"I can't." Once again, my voice sounded foreign on my tongue. "I have nothing to say."

Jax met my gaze, a muscle feathering in his jaw. Ashamed, I looked away.

Coming to my aid, Idalia said, "You and Samson figure it out. I'm staying with Orion." She turned and jogged toward our grieving friend.

"Samson, take Roshan and the other men with you." Jax's tone left no room for argument. "Elara and I will catch up later. I want to start another fire and let it burn out."

"Why?" Cyrus asked.

"We can't transport the bodies to the spring. They'll fall apart. You saw how that leg snapped. Also, I don't want the recruits seeing their loved ones in that condition. Look how it affected Orion."

"Then do it," Samson said.

He cupped his hands and called for Roshan. Blaze's red-rimmed eyes found mine as they passed; his head was draped over the Solin's shoulder. His little fingers stretched to reach mine. It took every ounce of energy to lift my hand. Our chilled skin touched for a split second before Roshan's long strides carried the child away from me. Blaze's kind gesture didn't bring me peace, it only brought me pain.

Orion floated by me and Jax like a damn ghost. His skin tone had turned a sickly shade of gray, and the light in his sapphire eyes had dimmed. He cradled the charred medical bag against his chest, the half-melted stethoscope dangling over his ash-covered wrist.

Once the men's silhouettes blurred in the distance, Jax motioned for me to follow him toward the house. "Come help me build the fire."

"No. I'm not looking at Iah's body again. Why would you suggest such a thing?"

"Because it's time to face your fears."

"Face my fears?" My hands curled into fists. "That's all I've done since stepping foot on Aroonyx."

"You haven't faced shit. Over the past few months, you've experienced a handful of traumatic situations. Well, guess what? So have I, so has your brother. But instead of walking through your fears, you keep avoiding them." He flicked his wrist at my rigid posture. "Like you're doing now. You refuse to talk to the people, and now you're refusing to give the departed a proper burial." He narrowed the gap between us. "Elara, you can't ignore your responsibilities. The people need you to lead them—"

"To what?!" I yelled, gesturing to the collapsed structure. "An untimely death? We don't have the numbers. We don't stand a chance against Zenith. I won't give them false hope. It's over." I poked him in the chest. "*You* and *I* are over. I have nothing left to give you. The girl you fell in love with died today. You should probably move on."

His jaw cracked open. "You promised to stand by my side until the very end."

I flung out my arms like a game show host. "Well, here we are."

"Bullshit. This isn't the end."

"Doesn't matter. I never made that promise, Jax. You did."

"You accepted my proposal."

"I felt pressured." Lies. "I never wanted to marry you." More lies.

"Says who? You or the voice inside your head?"

I stilled. *How does he know?*

Ignore him. You need me. Don't let him destroy us.

Shh. I won't.

I rolled my neck and straightened my spine. "You know nothing, Jax."

"Really?"

Hit him hard, right where it hurts.

"No. This is all your fault. Iah and the others would still be alive had you not murdered Aarush's father. You're sick with guilt, and instead of dealing with it, you're pawning it on me. Twisting my words, trying to make me feel crazy or unstable—"

"Do you hear yourself right now?" His eyes grew wide. "*I'm* making you feel crazy. Try again, Elara. Maybe the voice in your head can answer this time."

"Screw you."

His lips formed a tight line. "Yes, guilt weighs on my shoulders when I think about what happened today, but I refuse to listen to the darkness that tugs at my mind. I played that game, the game you're playing now, and you know where the voice led me?" He didn't wait for me to respond. "To the edge of a cliff."

He reached for my hand. I pulled away.

"Elara, you are treading on dangerous ground. The voice you're hearing has no power over you, so please, stop listening to the madness." He pressed his palm into my chest. "And start listening to the truth inside your heart."

Don't listen to him. He's trying to rip us apart. End this. Do it now.

"I don't want to talk to you anymore."

"Then let me take you to see your brother. You should talk to someone before it's too late."

"No," I hissed. "I'm not going anywhere with you."

"Please." He held out his hand. "Let me help you get through this."

"I don't need anyone's help. Especially yours."

The whites of his eyes turned red as he whispered my name.

"How many ways must I say it, Jax! It's over. Get the hell out of my life. I never want to see you again."

I didn't stick around to see his reaction. I spun on my heels and sprinted through the forest, leaving the man I loved behind.

47

CROSSING OVER

I didn't chart a course or keep track of how far I ran. I just kept running.

You made the right choice.

No.

Yes you did. You don't need Jax anymore.

Go to hell.

I'm already there.

My Lunin endurance guided me deeper into the forest. I avoided the spring, unwilling to see the grieving recruits, unwilling to smell the stench of death's rotting breath.

I slowed my pace once I approached the Moon Drop clearing that I visited with Orion. The snow clouds blocked my view of the twin moons. I cursed the gray puffs, taking a cautious step closer. *There's only one way to find out.*

A shower of snow dusted the top of my head as I pushed a low-lying tree limb out of the way. I ducked under another. After brushing the ice crystals from my lashes, I observed the stunning yet ominous site.

Moon Drops glowed at my feet, their soft petals fluttering in the breeze. The glittering orbs hovering in the center of the rose-shaped blooms hummed with a life source powered by an unseen energy.

I scowled, strolling toward the edge of the cliff. For once, nature's metaphor had missed the mark. *Figures.*

Disregarding my fear of heights, I lowered myself onto the ledge and swung my legs over the side. My heels tapped the hard surface as I watched the gray waves crash against the jagged rocks below.

I frowned. *Will it hurt?*

Probably. That's a long way down. Are you sure you want to jump?

I shrugged. *There's no point in sticking around. I should have stayed on Earth and never got involved. I'm the one to blame. Archer, Iah, Blaze's mom, the recruits, hell, even Elio. They're dead because of me.*

If you're to blame, then so is your brother.

No. He had a normal life until I screwed it up.

Correction. Until Jax screwed it up. Blame him.

I'm tired of blaming others. I'm ready to end it.

Interesting.

I scooted my body farther over the vertical drop, my fingers gripping the thin sheet of ice. A piece of the Clear Stone ledge broke apart. I counted to four before it splashed into the water.

Are you sure you want to do this?

I yawned. *Yeah. They don't need me anymore. They never did.*

Why don't you wait until sunrise? Make it a symbolic gesture. Do it when the Moon Drops dissolve. Leave the world with a little flair.

Another yawn. *Fair enough. They're always calling me dramatic. I might as well give them a show.*

I lay on my side and curled into a ball, hiding my face in the warmth of my coat.

Sleep.

I nodded. *Just a quick nap.*

No. Sleep long and hard.

I STUMBLED THROUGH THE CLEARING, the thick fog hindering my vision. *Ouch.* I hopped up and down, holding my stubbed toe. *Why do I keep tripping?*

Again, my boot knocked against something hard. I didn't stop to investigate the buried object or the blood-stained snow.

I pawed at the haze. *Where am I?*

The darkness inside didn't answer.

"Hello?" I touched my throat. As if I had shouted into a vast cavern, the word echoed around me.

A silky voice answered, "I'm here."

"Jax?"

I followed the sound of his call. Another hidden object snagged the toe of my boot.

Irritated with the distraction, I jiggled my foot. No luck. I stooped down to touch the trap that held the toe of my boot in place—Samson's gaped mouth. His body was buried in the snow. *Oh, God.*

I lost my footing and fell backward.

"Help!" I cried, wiggling my leg. "I'm stuck."

"Then get unstuck," the man answered.

I used my free leg, pressing the sole of my boot on Samson's lifeless face. I pulled hard. His jaw snapped in two. My hands slid in the snow as I scooted away from his rotting corpse. I bumped into another frozen object—Castor. Someone had carved his eyes from his sockets, blood dripped from the gaping holes. *What the hell?*

I scrambled to my feet, only to trip over two more mutilated bodies—Idalia and Callisto.

"This way," the man encouraged. "You're safe with me."

I ran, leaping over the dead. The number of bodies

increased. One turned to two, and two turned to four. The piles grew higher, each obstacle spaced a few feet apart. I climbed, clawed my way up and over their broken limbs and pained expressions. After long minutes, I reached the end. Only it wasn't the end. It was the start of another pile. I trembled, observing the massive structure. My eyes drifted to the top.

A man stood with his gray boots pressed into Jax's and Cyrus's chests. Their necks were snapped at odd angles, their mouths open mid-scream. My legs gave out. The half-Solin, half-Lunin smiled at me, his blue and orange eyes glowing.

"Thank you, Elara. Abandoning your loved ones assisted me with my efforts." Zenith motioned to Cyrus and Jax. "They didn't put up a fight." He shrugged. "Not that I care. I just thought you should know."

"I didn't abandon them," I argued. "I'm still here."

Zenith jerked his chin at my body. "Are you?"

I looked down. A pained cry flew out of my mouth. My pale skin had turned transparent. I touched my chest, my hand slid right through me.

"It's over, Elara. I've won."

You were too weak to stop him. You never stood a chance.

Zenith snickered at my defeated expression, his fingers playing with the handle of his knife.

A quiet voice hummed near my heart. The one that always whispered, the one I usually ignored. *They're wrong, Elara. They're both wrong.*

"Please." I bowed my head and clasped my hands, a posture of surrender. "I need help. I can't do this alone."

You have me. You don't need anyone's help. You said so yourself.

I was wrong.

No. Don't listen to your heart. Listen to your head. Listen to me.

"Please," I begged, tears pooling. "I'm asking for help."

You stupid girl! You stupid, foolish girl.

I ground my teeth, my wicked thoughts clawing at the back of my mind.

It's time for you to go.

You can't get rid of me. I'll always be here, even if you throw yourself off that damn cliff. Your physical death won't separate us. It can't. Your soul will live forever and so will I.

But I have a choice, and I choose the light.

Miracles happen every day, though they're easily overlooked. We expect a grand gesture or an elaborate display, confirmation that our prayers were answered, confirmation that the universe had spoken. A sudden awareness lifted my eyelids. Sometimes it's a gentle tap on the shoulder, a quiet whisper in your ear, or a gentle nudge in the right direction. For me, a jolting realization slapped me upside the head.

"I choose to let go of the darkness."

As soon as I verbalized my intention, a blinding light pierced through the fog. A woman appeared. She moved with angelic grace, the black waves of her long hair cascading over her shoulders. Her sapphire blue eyes sparkled as she whispered, "Well done, my precious girl."

Zenith snarled and aimed his knife at the mysterious woman. Her gaze never left me as she disarmed him with a wave of her hand. The half Solin, half Lunin dived for his beloved weapon. He slid down the pile of bodies, his fingers stretching to reach the black blade.

I climbed to my feet, my brows raising with confusion and wonder.

The woman cupped my face and rotated my head to meet her gaze.

"It's just noise," she said. "Don't listen to the noise."

Slack-jawed, I stared at the Lunin's familiar features. Fair skin, dark brows, black hair, and deep-set eyes. I blinked. Was I gazing into a distorted mirror?

"*Mom?*" My voice cracked.

She nodded. "I can't stay for long."

"Why? How are you here?"

"I've been trying to get through to you, but your head got in the way of your heart." She brushed a tear off my cheek. "You stopped listening to the truth."

More drops of regret flowed once I recalled my argument with Jax.

"He's a good man, sweetie."

"I know, and I screwed it up. I screwed everything up." I sobbed into my translucent hands. "Mom, I killed a man."

"To save an innocent life."

The strands of her hair floated around her face as if gravity didn't apply.

"I'm no different from him," I said, gesturing to Zenith. "He's a murderer and so am I."

Desperate to find his knife, the leader of Aroonyx tossed bodies off the pile.

My mother watched him carefully before speaking. "You are not the same, my child. You acted out of love, not hate."

"It didn't feel that way. The voice inside my head sounded angry."

"The mind reacts to emotion." She touched my chest; her hand didn't move through it. "Your heart reacts to the truth. Don't close yourself off to it. Don't close yourself off to me."

I wrapped my fingers around her hand. "I won't. I promise."

The darkness swirled, its voice screaming, begging me to listen. I rolled my neck. For once, I ignored the incessant chatter.

I eyed the dead bodies. "Is it too late to save the people of Aroonyx? Is it too late to save my relationship with Jax?"

She flicked her wrist. The pile vanished, along with Zenith.

I shuddered a breath.

My mother locked her eyes onto mine. "It's never too late to rewrite your story."

At that moment, the sun peeked over the horizon. Its glorious rays burned through the remaining fog, basking the clearing in a majestic glow. The snow melted. My mother's bare feet hovered above the emerald grass. I inhaled a breath of the summer-kissed air and surrendered to the beauty of life. I surrendered to the grace that pulled me from the depths of hell.

"Can you give your brother a message for me?"

I nodded.

"Tell him his courageous act won't go overlooked."

"What does that mean?"

"Give it time, my child. Your story has just begun."

My pulse quickened as I observed my fading body. "But how do I rewrite my story? Where do I begin?"

Her lips spread into a warm grin. "Exactly where you left off."

"I need to help the others. How do I get back?"

"It's simple." She kissed my forehead. "You wake up."

48

WAKING UP

Elara, *it's time to wake up.*

My eyes shot open. A dizzying blur of rocks and water filled my vision. The upper half of my body hung over the cliff's edge. I was sliding, slipping into an unmarked grave.

Well, shit. I want to live and now I'm falling to my death. My fingernails cracked and bled as they clung to the icy ledge. I summoned my core strength and pushed myself away from the impending doom below.

I crawled to the center of the Moon Drop clearing, then rose to my feet. My mind raced with images of the life-altering dream. I patted my body, relieved to feel the weight of my coat and the firmness of my cold flesh and bones. My gaze drifted to the evening sky. The clouds parted, revealing the full moons, their bright glow merging with my well-lit surroundings.

I'm alive. I let out a relieved breath. *And I'm ready.*

Curious, I waited for the darkness to emerge. Waited for its loud protest. Silence. A warmth enveloped my heart. I smiled, touching my chest. *I hear you, Mom. I won't forget.*

I dashed through the clearing, careful not to disturb the Moon Drops. I needed to find Jax. I needed to make things right.

With a clear head, I approached the spring. Samson and Castor paced in front of the deceased recruits. The Solin motioned to a corpse. The Lunin shook his head, then pointed at another. Cyrus caught my eye. He was helping Aries rebuild the tents the Collectors destroyed during the ambush. Their pale and tan hands worked together to patch the burns and tears in the fabric.

Idalia's blonde hair swished back and forth as she darted from one injured recruit to the next. Callisto hobbled behind her, a blood-stained bandage covering his thigh. They brought water to the lips of those who couldn't lift their heads and applied makeshift bandages to bleeding wounds.

Roshan assisted Thea and Oriana with the handful of uninjured survivors. Blaze and his grieving friends sat in a circle with their legs crossed. A middle-aged woman used elaborate hand gestures as she described a depiction of the afterlife. She called it beautiful, peaceful, calming. The choice words didn't resonate with the children. How could they? They watched the Collectors murder their mothers and fathers before their eyes.

Friends expressed their condolences to one another while women knelt beside their fallen husbands, brothers, and sons. Tears rolled off their colorless cheeks, moistening the lifeless ones below.

I turned my head and found Orion sitting near the edge of the spring. I cursed. He still clung to his father's medical bag. I wanted to throw my arms around him and share a good long cry, but I knew better. He needed time alone to heal.

Death and devastation surrounded me. I refused to listen to the darkness that vied for my attention. Instead, I focused on the new voice that warmed my heart, my mother's voice.

You'll get through this, Elara. One day at a time.

Yes, yes, I will.

I flinched hearing Samson call my name. He hurried toward me.

"What's up?" I asked, meeting him halfway.

"I've got some news."

I rolled my shoulders and stood tall. "Tell me. I can take it."

"Are you sure?"

"Listen." I touched his arm. "I know I acted crazy after Elio's death. I've been fighting an inner demon for months. The events today just—"

"Woke it up?"

I laughed. "Yeah, you could say that. But I took a power nap and now I'm good."

"A nap?" He shook his head. "Is that what you were doing? I was wondering where you went."

"Yep. I took a little snooze."

"A nap slayed your demon?"

"Mm-hmm. It was a productive sleep."

He scratched his beard. "So you made peace with your first kill?"

"I wouldn't call it peace. Acceptance is a better word. I'm not proud of my actions, but I rescued Blaze. And if I'm honest with myself, I'd do it all over again to save that little pain in the ass."

Samson chuckled and reached into his coat pocket. "All right, kid. You're ready for your next mission." He offered me a gray scroll. "This came while you were gone."

"What does it say?" I asked, rubbing my thumb over the seal.

"I don't know. I didn't read it. The scout said it was for your eyes only."

"What scout?"

"Zenith sent someone to deliver the message." Noting the

frantic look in my eyes, he added, "And no, he wasn't armed. He just handed me the scroll and said, *Elara must break the seal*."

My posture sagged. "So it's from Zenith."

"Clever girl. I'm glad that nap sharpened your mind."

I gave him a sidelong look. "Should I open it?"

"It's your call."

Throwing caution to the wind, I cracked open the black seal and read the words aloud.

This ends tomorrow.
Meet me at the Village Center once the sun reaches its highest point in the sky.
Zenith

SAMSON SCOFFED, snatching the letter from my hand. "A man of few words." He turned it over, searching for a hidden clue. "I figured he'd pull some shit like this after the attack."

"How many recruits do we have left?"

His lips formed a tight line as he scanned the campsite. "Not many."

"Give it to me straight. What's the head count?"

"We lost over a hundred."

My jaw cracked open.

"And a handful ran off during the ambush."

"So how many will fight?"

"That's a great question, Elara. We have one hundred and twenty capable bodies. But how many of those men and women still support our cause? The attack rattled their nerves. It rattled their trust. We weren't here to protect them." He shook the scroll. "Zenith might play a dirty game, but he excels at winning. He hit us hard with the ambush, and now he wants to end this while he's ahead. He knows our men are battle worn —exhausted."

I blew a stray hair out of my face. "Our scout reported he had around three hundred and fifty men. I'm trying to stay positive, Samson, but the numbers are not in our favor."

He nodded, handing me the letter. "That's why you should talk to the recruits. They could use a little motivation."

"Motivation?" I cleared my throat and pretended to address a crowd. "Attention everyone, you have a 99.9-percent chance of dying tomorrow. See you then."

Samson rolled his eyes. "You inspired them once. You can do it again."

"Fine." I groaned. "I will. But first I want to—" My words faded as Idalia approached.

"Hey, Elara." Her eyes lit up. "You look like you're feeling better."

"She took a nap." Samson snickered.

Idalia's brow furrowed.

"I'll tell you about it later," I said. "But yes, I'm doing much better now."

"Good. I'm happy to hear it." She shifted her gaze between me and Samson. "Can I talk to you guys about Orion?"

"How is he?" I asked. "Did you explain what happened with the fire?"

"I did." She sighed, tossing her hair behind her back. "I don't think it helped."

"Why do you say that?"

"Because he said he doesn't want to fight Zenith."

"I wish he'd change his mind." I offered her the scroll. "We could use his help tomorrow."

"Is this what the scout brought?" she asked Samson.

He nodded.

Her eyes grew as she read the cursive lettering. "Well, this changes things."

I watched Orion sift through his father's charred medical equipment. "Why won't he fight? Is he too sick with grief?"

"No, that's not it." She handed me the note. "He wants to honor his father's legacy by helping the wounded men and women." She pointed at Callisto, who tended to a large gash in a man's abdomen. "Some injuries are severe. We could use a doctor."

"Let him stay," Samson suggested. "It's a healthy distraction for the kid. I want men of sound mind on the battlefield."

"Speaking of sound minds," I said, scanning the area. "Where's Jax? I need to speak with him."

Idalia frowned, cocking her head to one side. "I thought he was with you."

"He was but . . . *shit*."

"Elara, what's wrong?"

Ignoring Idalia, I grabbed Samson's arm. "When did the scout arrive?"

"About an hour ago."

My nails dug into his sleeve. "Was he alone?"

"Yeah."

"Are you sure?"

The color drained from Samson's face.

"Elara." Idalia's voice cracked. "Where's Jax?"

I breathed hard. The parchment crinkled as I curled my fingers around Zenith's note.

"Which way did the scout go?" I asked. *Don't say toward the house. Please don't say toward the house.*

"Back the way they came." Samson's voice came out in a tight whisper. "Toward the house."

Oh God. My head spun and vision blurred.

Acknowledging my unspoken concerns, Samson hollered Cyrus's and Castor's names, then bolted past us toward the campsite.

Idalia's lip quivered. "Was it a trap? Did they take Jax?"

"They can't." My head shook back and forth. "Not after the

things I said to him. Not after I . . . I'm sorry," I cried, turning away from her. "I have to go."

"Elara, wait! You can't search for him on your own."

I had no choice. I sprinted toward the last place I saw Jax—the heartbreaking spot where I abandoned the man I loved.

49

THE WALK THAT LEADS TO NOWHERE

I yelled Jax's name until my boots reached the front lawn. *Where is he?*

Another desperate call scratched my sore throat. "Jax!"

No answer. I spun in circles, snow spraying in my wake. My eyes darted from one patch of splattered blood to the next. Were they a sign of struggle between Jax and the Collectors or evidence of the recruit's sufferings? I couldn't tell.

I shielded my face from the heat and smoke that engulfed the pile of bodies. *Did he start this fire or did someone else?*

So many unanswered questions. So many regrets.

"Elara! Where did he go?"

I turned, hearing my brother's voice reverberate through the quiet space. He sprinted toward me; the color drained from his tan complexion.

"I don't know," I cried. "He's not here."

Samson tensed as he approached the lawn. Castor and Idalia were not far behind.

"Cyrus," he ordered. "You and Idalia search the south end of the property. Castor and I will head north." He cupped his hands and directed his voice toward me. "Elara, stay here in case Jax returns."

I gave him a thumbs-up, though I wanted to turn it upside down. *If he returns?* My knees wobbled. *The Collectors won't let him go.* I blinked back tears. *He's gone.* I melted into the snow as the others hurried to search their assigned locations.

The wind blew a plume of smoke, sticking bits of ashes to my damp lashes. I rubbed my aching chest. *What happened to "rewrite your story?"* The tears fell. *This isn't my idea of a fresh start.*

Long minutes passed. Long, agonizing minutes crawled by one silent tick at a time. The lower half of my body went numb because I never shifted my weight, and snot dripped from my nose because I never bothered lifting a hand to wipe it away. I blinked and blinked again. The ashes that drifted from the house, courtesy of the unforgiving winds, scratched at my eyes. I did nothing to ease my physical discomfort. I just sat there, wallowing in despair. *They took my partner—again, and this time it's all my fault. He'd still be here had I not listened to the darkness, had I accepted his help.*

Look.

I ignored the gentle voice.

Trust your heart, Elara.

I lifted my gaze. Glowing embers and smoke stared back.

Look again.

My head turned. Out of the brush walked a man, his arms swinging by his sides. The Lunin's clothes weren't torn, and his pale skin was free of blood. He kept his gaze forward while he walked, the twin moons reflecting in his piercing blue eyes.

I choked on a sob and rose to my feet. Stiff from sitting for so long, the muscles in my legs protested the quick movement. An ugly cry twisted my facial features as I dashed toward the Lunin.

He did a double take, then winced at the sudden impact when I threw myself into his arms.

"What's wrong?" Jax asked, stunned by my reaction.

I didn't answer. I held him in a tight embrace, soaking his chest with drops of salted relief. My hands slid over his back, his shoulders, and his jawline. Rough fabric, hard muscle, coarse hairs: confirmations that he existed.

"Elara." He tried to pull away, but I forced him closer, and he winced again. "Why are you so upset? What happened?" He stretched his neck, scanning the front yard. "And why are you out here alone?"

"The scouts," I sobbed, burying my face deeper. "I thought it was a trap. I thought they took you to Zenith." On the verge of hysteria, more sobs shook my shoulders. "I thought you were—"

"*No*," he soothed, stroking my hair. "After I started the fire, I took a walk to clear my head."

I looked up. "You didn't see the scout?"

"What scout?" He reached for his knife. "Should I patrol the area?"

I motioned for him to put away the blade. "Zenith sent a scout to deliver a message. I overreacted because Samson said he headed toward the house—toward you."

"What was the message?"

I offered him the crumpled scroll.

Jax scowled at the cursive lettering. "Then so be it."

The gray parchment fell from his fingers. It drifted in the breeze before landing near the burnt home.

"I'm so sorry." My lip quivered with guilt. "I never meant to say those horrible things."

"I should have let you rest before voicing my concerns."

"No. You did nothing wrong. I needed a good kick in the ass."

He chuckled as I wrapped my arms around him.

With my cheek pressed against his beating heart, I said, "*Now* I understand why you left that day. Facing your inner demons is something one must do alone."

"Taking the initiative to chart one's course is required, but asking for guidance helps keep you on track."

I smiled, thinking of my plea to the universe, thinking of the help I received.

"I knew you were struggling with the demon inside your head."

I pulled away. "How did you know?"

"Your body language."

"Really?"

He nodded. "Your eyes glazed over, and you'd roll your neck. I had a similar experience. Remember the twitch that plagued me?"

My jaw cracked open. "You heard a voice too?"

"Yes, and that's how my body reacted to it. It spoke to me for years. The voice got louder once Pollux took me to Zenith's, and after I woke up at Iah's, I started listening to it. The darkness drove me into the pit of despair. That's the reason I left."

"I see why you did." I bit my lip and tapped my temple. "I can still hear that bastard calling for me. Like it's whispering behind a closed door. I'm trying to ignore it."

"It's best not to condemn it. Just see it for what it is—mindless chatter. Sometimes the voice inside my head will offer advice." He snickered. "I just smile and say thanks, I'm good."

A warm cloud left my parted lips. "That's a practical approach."

"I'm a practical man." He winked. "The voice will shut up if you don't give it any power."

I hummed my agreement, relieved that the voice no longer controlled me.

Jax brushed the hair off my shoulders. "I'm glad you walked through the darkness."

"Me too. A little nap goes a long way."

He angled his head. "Now who's being cryptic?"

I laughed, the tension in my body loosening. "I'm just trying to keep up with Master Yoda."

His teeth grazed my forehead as he kissed me; his lips had spread into a wide grin.

"Can you forgive me for saying those awful things?"

Another gentle kiss warmed my flesh. "Yes. I'll always forgive my beautiful pain in the ass."

"Thank you." I stood on the tips of my toes and traced the outline of his jaw with my lips, then kissed every inch of his unshaven skin. "Can I have my ring?"

Jax's chest rumbled with laughter. "What am I going to do with you?"

"Whatever you want, but first, I want my ring back." I batted my lashes. "Please."

He tapped his chin as if considering his options. Moments later he reached into his pocket.

I spread out my fingers, encouraging him to slip it on.

He hesitated. "I'll give it to you under one condition."

"Which is?"

"Promise me you'll never take it off."

"What if I need to clean it?"

A smirk tugged at his lips. "I was speaking figuratively."

"Deal."

I turned after Jax slid the ring onto my finger. Cyrus and Idalia jogged toward us with their hands tossed in the air.

"Where were you?" My brother panted. "We've been looking everywhere."

Clutching the cramp in her side, Idalia said, "Samson's pissed. I've never seen him so worried."

Jax rested a hand on his chest and bowed. "I'm honored."

"Dude," Cyrus chided.

"My apologies," he replied.

"Did Elara tell you about the letter from Zenith?" Idalia asked.

"She did."

My brother scrubbed at his face. "We don't have the numbers, Jax."

"I'm aware. We'll make do."

"Make do?" My eyes grew. "They'll slaughter us."

"Perhaps, but we're out of time. We must fight. Zenith chose the Village Center for a reason."

"Why there?" Cyrus asked. "I assumed he'd want the home field advantage."

"He wants to put on a show. Let the villagers witness the consequences of not obeying him."

"A show?" My brows raised. "In front of what audience. There's no one left."

"There are plenty of citizens living in the West Village, and a few in the North and South. Zenith planned it this way. He only makes a move if he has the upper hand."

"No shit," Cyrus snapped. "He slaughtered half of our recruits to get that upper hand. We're outnumbered three to one."

"The logistics no longer matter," Jax countered. "I don't care if he outnumbers us ten to one. The citizens of Aroonyx must see us take a stand against their leader. If we ignore his invitation, he'll hit us again—*harder*, and he'll continue this insanity until only two people remain: you and your sister."

I eyed my brother. He kept his attention focused on the Lunin.

"Then he'll drag you into the Village Center and slice your throats in front of everyone."

A sigh slipped through Idalia's lips. "Thank you for the visual, Jax."

A casual shrug. "I only wanted—"

"You son of a bitch!"

Everyone flinched. Everyone but Jax. Samson grabbed him by the collar of his coat, spun him around, and shoved him in the chest. He staggered backward into Cyrus.

Samson's hand shook as he pointed a finger at Jax. "The next time you pull a stunt like that, I'll cut off your *fucking* head."

Cyrus and Idalia grimaced, but the Lunin struggled to keep his composure.

"Forgive me, Samson." He recovered. "Next time, I'll ask permission before taking a walk."

The Solin glared. "You better wipe off that smug-ass grin before I do it for you."

"Yes, sir."

Samson spun on his heels and shouted, "No more walks!"

Castor chuckled, hurrying to keep up.

"I'm serious." He held up his index finger. "Not a single stroll."

Idalia covered her mouth, muffling her giggles.

Cyrus met my gaze. "I think Jax is Samson's favorite."

"Awe." I smiled at the Lunin. "The teacher's pet."

"More like the teacher's most improved," he muttered.

Our humorous expressions faded once Idalia pointed to the full moons. "It's getting late. We should head back. Elara needs to speak with the recruits."

I nodded, though a part of me dreaded the conversation.

Jax nudged me in the arm. "Why don't you walk with your brother? I need to chat with Idalia."

I stole a glance at Cyrus. He shrugged, then offered me his arm. Amused by his chivalry, I curtsied before slipping my hand through the loop.

During our stroll, we chatted about our first day at school and the eye-opening drive to Crystal beach. A few laughs later, our topic of discussion switched to our time spent on Aroonyx.

"It's quite the contrast, isn't it?" I asked, stooping down to collect a handful of snow.

"Yeah, it's like we've lived two separate lifetimes."

"And we're only eighteen."

"But I feel thirty."

I snickered, compacting the fluff into a tight ball. Cyrus snatched it from my hand and chunked it at a tree. It exploded into a white mist.

"Do you think the recruits will fight with us tomorrow?" I asked.

"I hope so. Can you imagine the look on Zenith's face if we showed up with just a handful of people?" He curled his lips into a dramatic scowl and stared at me down his nose.

I chuckled. "Oh, the shame."

"That sounded like something Jax would say."

"He's rubbing off on me."

"That's not a bad thing. You're a lot stronger now. I'm proud of you."

"Why?"

"Because you hit rock bottom and climbed your way out."

My cheeks puffed with a mixture of emotions. "I had some help."

"Regardless, you slayed your inner demons."

I remembered my mother's request. *His courageous act won't go overlooked. Should I tell him now or later?*

I grabbed my brother's wrist, stopping our casual pace.

"Uh oh. Why the long face, sis?"

"I want you to make me a promise."

"Which is?"

"Don't do anything stupid on the battlefield."

"Like what?"

"Like get yourself killed."

His jaw clenched. "I can't make that promise."

"Why?"

521

"Because we can't predict the future. You heard Jax, Zenith won't stop until we're dead." He rested a hand on my shoulder. "I'm your older brother. It's my job to protect you."

"You're my twin. We're the same age."

"Iah told me I came out first." He flashed me a smug grin. "So, technically, I'm older and wiser."

I rolled my eyes.

"I'm serious." Cyrus tightened his grip. "If push comes to shove, I won't hesitate to finish the mission."

"I'm aware of this," I said, blinking away the tears. "And that's what scares me."

"Jax and Samson won't hesitate either."

"That doesn't make me feel any better."

He shrugged. "This is war, sis. Tomorrow we go to war. You took World History. Hell, you sat next to me in class. Soldiers die in battle. We could all die tomorrow."

"Thanks for the reminder, bro. I'll start carving our headstones as soon as we get to camp." I pretended to chisel the air with an invisible pick and hammer. "Here lies Elara Dunlin, sister to Cyrus Lofton, engaged to Jax—" I paused. "Well, shit." My hands fell to my sides. "I don't even know his last name."

Cyrus laughed at my defeated expression.

"Stop making fun of me," I scolded. "Why haven't I asked him?"

"That's an important detail to overlook. What if it's something weird like Nithercott or Portendorfer?"

I pinned him with a long look. "Did you just make that shit up?"

He laughed harder. "No. Those are real surnames. Tim Nithercott and Ned Portendorfer work for my dad."

I couldn't hide my amusement. "I hate you so much right now. I'm asking him tonight."

"Elara Portendorfer." Cyrus shook his head. "Your poor kids."

"Stop," I begged, slapping him in the arm.

"Not a chance."

He continued the name game for the rest of our stroll.

"Are you done?" I asked, unable to keep from laughing.

"For now." He threw his arm over my shoulder. "I'm going to miss this."

My boots slowed. "Miss what?"

"Joking around with you."

"Why would you stop?"

"Because tomorrow life gets a little more serious."

50

DON'T LET GO

"I'm shocked Thea offered us her tent."

"And to think"—Jax kicked off his boots before unfolding a thick blanket—"you were so quick to judge."

I scoffed, unfastening the buttons of my coat. "She's still a bitch. Did you see the way she rolled her eyes at me?"

"Try taking the high road, Elara. Thea fought hard to protect those who couldn't fight today. Idalia said she proved herself during the ambush."

"Fine," I grumbled, untying my laces. *Time to switch the subject.* "Why did you want to chat with Idalia tonight?"

After smoothing a fold in our temporary bedding, Jax collapsed onto his back. The air rushed out of his lungs as he tucked his arm underneath his head. "No reason." He stared at the fabric ceiling while he spoke. "I just wanted you and your brother to spend some quality time together."

My face squished up. "Why?"

"Earlier this afternoon, he voiced his concerns regarding your mental health."

I hummed my understanding and lowered myself onto the

blanket. Jax gathered my hair before I rested my cheek against his chest.

"Cyrus is making me nervous."

"Why?" he asked.

"A while back he had this vivid dream about us standing outside my home on Earth."

"Why does that make you nervous?"

"Because he wasn't there." I swallowed. "He said he was somewhere else, somewhere in-between. And anytime I bring up Zenith, he switches the subject or tries to make me laugh."

Jax ran his fingers through my hair. "Perhaps it's a coping mechanism. People process stressful situations in different ways."

"Maybe." I inhaled a long breath. "But I keep getting the impression he's trying to say goodbye."

"Tomorrow is a life-changing day. Anything can happen."

I lifted my chin and rotated my neck to face him. "Why does everyone keep telling me this? I get it, okay. People die in battle."

"Easy, Elara."

"And what if it's just us fighting tomorrow?" I didn't wait for him to respond. "You saw the recruits' reactions after I gave that speech tonight." I slid a hand over my face, changing my smile to a stone-cold expression. "Blank, lifeless. They have no desire to fight. They think it's a lost cause."

"It's not."

"Obviously, but they don't agree with us. I tried to inspire them. I tried to explain the importance of this mission. The words went in one ear and out the other."

Jax patted his chest, encouraging me to lie down. I agreed.

"Elara, they're still in shock from the ambush. You told them to sleep on it. Give them time to make their decision."

"Time? We're out of time. Sunrise is in a few hours."

"And shortly after, this war will end."

I faked a cry and draped my leg over his lower half. "And then what?"

He patted my thigh. "We start a life together."

"*If* we survive."

My face slid off Jax's shirt as he propped himself up on his elbows. I rolled onto my back.

"What have I told you about fearing the future?"

I lifted a finger to my lips, hearing my brother's voice rise outside of our tent.

"No. Idalia and I will sleep in this one. You and Castor—"

"Have you lost your fucking mind? You're not sleeping in the same tent."

My eyes grew at the severity in Samson's tone. Jax strained his ears.

"Why not?" Cyrus pressed. "We're adults."

"I wasn't born yesterday. You're an eighteen-year-old boy with one thing on your mind."

"Samson, I would never touch Idalia without her consent."

"Good, because if you did, I'd cut off your balls."

Jax snickered at the threat. I covered my mouth, smothering the laughter.

"Idalia will share a tent with Thea and Oriana. You get to cozy up with me and Castor."

My brother huffed a breath. "That's not fair. Jax and Elara—"

"Life's not fair, and I'm not her father."

I looked at Jax, my brows touching my hairline. "Father?"

He averted his gaze.

"I need Jax focused tomorrow," Samson added. He cleared his throat and directed his voice at our tent. "I'm sure Elara will be more than happy to assist with his concentration."

I mouthed, "Oh . . . my . . . God," at my partner.

He just smiled.

"What about my focus and concentration?" Cyrus argued. "I'm fighting too. I don't know the last time I—"

"Then use your hand because that's all the action your ass is seeing tonight."

"You're an asshole."

Samson chuckled. "That's the consensus."

"And you snore. I won't sleep a wink."

"Ten minutes until curfew. Castor and I could use a foot massage after our long day. Ignore the bunions."

"You're disgusting," Cyrus said.

A hand clapped someone on the back.

"Nine minutes left. Don't be late."

Cyrus grumbled a slew of curse words and stormed off.

"Samson might be my new hero," I said to Jax.

"Don't let him hear you say that. He'll use it to his advantage."

"True."

A seductive smirk tugged at the corner of Jax's mouth. He pulled me closer.

"Should I obey Samson's orders?" I walked my fingers down his abdomen, stopping at the first button on his pants. "Assist with your concentration?"

"I thought you didn't take orders?"

My hand slid over the visible impression my suggestion had left, and I admired the hardened length of him. "Perhaps we should get some rest before the big day." I stretched and pretended to yawn before settling beside him.

Jax traced the curve of my leg while he spoke. "It's unfortunate Samson didn't give me the orders."

"Why?"

He nudged me onto my back, his hand bypassing the fortress of silver buttons on my pants. "Because I always obey."

My breath hitched. I sucked in my lower abdomen, giving him ample room to work. My vision blurred with lust as his fingers

527

circled the desired area. I bucked my hips, an invitation for him to further explore. He accepted, slipping his longest finger inside me. My pulse raced. Without pausing the back-and-forth motion, he leaned the upper half of his body over mine and silenced the pleasurable moan that escaped my parted mouth. I kissed him hard, my nails gripping the swell of his bicep. His gentle yet assertive touch lured my legs to open wider. He inserted another curious finger, sending me closer to the brink of ecstasy.

I fumbled with his buttons, silently cursing the lack of zippers on Aroonyx. His pants needed to come off and my one-handed approach had failed the daunting task.

"These need to go," I demanded, tugging at the fabric. "Like now."

"Consider it done," he whispered.

The Lunin removed his moistened fingers. My groan turned into a moan when the heel of his calloused palm grazed my throbbing area as he went to unfasten his pants.

Irritated with the pause in foreplay, I rose to my feet and hurried to undress. The sound of Jax's sensual voice halted my efforts.

"Don't." He slipped off his pants and tossed them to the side. A heartbeat later his shirt landed on the pile. "Let me do it."

Like an overzealous volunteer, I raised my arms.

The muscles in his stomach contracted as he shook his head at me. "Patience, Elara."

My glare softened once he kneeled before me. I drank in the sight of his naked body, noting the faded injuries that colored his pale skin, the cords of muscle that created his attractive physique. My eyes landed on his erection—the part I *needed* inside me.

As if agreeing with my private thoughts, Jax kissed the tingling flesh of my stomach before pulling off my shirt. One of his hands cupped my breast while the other unfastened the clasp. It fell onto the floor. He followed the curves of my body before freeing me from the restricting fabric that shielded my lower half.

Jax slipped a finger under the waistband of my underwear. He snapped it against my skin. Reminding me of my earlier words, he said, "These need to go."

I nodded. He tugged on the thin material, and his eyes glazed over with need—a craving desire as he watched the remaining article of clothing slide down my legs. I held onto his shoulders, steadying my quivering body. Jax rested his hands on my backside while his lips traced my inner thigh. I breathed hard. Only a few more inches to go. I directed his head toward the spot that beckoned his oral touch. He obliged. I almost lost my balance.

His tongue, damn that glorious tongue, moved in lazy circles. He flicked it between rotations, pushing me further over the edge. I twisted the soft locks of his hair and arched my lower back, the sensation overwhelming me. His hands gripped me harder as he devoured every part of me. The burning tension in my thighs increased once Jax's fingers slid inside once more.

"Don't stop," I begged.

The moment approached, and the world spun. I shut my eyes. His tongue continued its fierce rotation while his fingers went deeper.

Words filled with desperation rolled off my tongue. "*Please* don't stop.

Jax pulled away before I reached the finish line. *Bastard.* I wanted to punch him in the nose for disregarding my request.

"That's not fair," I rasped.

A lazy smile spread across his face as he watched my heavy eyelids blink, the evidence of my pleasure dripping off his chin.

"I'm not done with you yet." He wiped off his mouth and pulled me onto his lap, wrapping my legs around him.

My frustrations vanished after he guided every inch of his hardened length inside me. His name formed on my tongue in a breathless whisper. I clung to the taut muscles of his back. He went deeper, his lips caressing the scar on my neck. He lifted and lowered my hips, finding a steady rhythm while I found his mouth. Our tongues danced around each other, the stress of the day forgotten.

My teeth nipped at his lip as he adjusted his grip. "I want more," I whispered into his skin. "I *need* more."

Jax indulged my fantasies by lowering me onto the blanket. He kissed every inch of me, starting from where he left off between my legs. I grabbed his hair, urging him to join me up top. His lips followed an imaginary path along my trembling body. They traced my naval, the scar on my abdomen, then slowed at the curve of my breast. His tongue found my nipple while his thumb circled the other. Every nerve sparked. The heat rushed through my veins. *If he keeps this up, I might burst into flames.*

Jax lifted his head and observed the view from above. "God, you're beautiful."

My lip quivered as it hit me. I was staring into the eyes of the man I loved; the man I wanted to share my life with. *Will he survive tomorrow? Will I?*

Tears welled in my eyes.

"Are you okay?" He rolled off of me. "Was I hurting you?"

"No." I sniffled, covering my face. "I just feel sad."

"Why?" He brushed away a tear that escaped my finger barricade. "What's bringing you down?"

"The thought of this being our last night together."

"Let's stay positive."

I peeked through the cracks of my fingers. "I don't even know your full name."

His shoulders shook with laughter.

"Stop," I scolded, slapping him in the chest. "Why haven't you told me?"

"Surnames don't exist on Aroonyx."

My jaw cracked open. "What?"

"I'm teasing you." He chuckled. "I guess it never came up."

"Please tell me it's nothing weird like Portendorfer."

He couldn't stop smiling as he ran his fingers along my bare flesh. "Elara Portendorfer. That name might raise a few brows during formal introductions."

"Oh, no." My pulse quickened. "You *do* have a strange last name. That's why you haven't told me.

"No. I'm just testing your patience."

I knocked his hand away. "You tested it plenty on your knees."

"I just wanted a taste. I planned on pleasing you in other ways." He winked, pressing himself against my leg.

"I'll let you finish where you left off." I held up a hand, stopping him from resuming the dominate position. A seductive smirk crossed his striking face once I slid my body on top of his. "*After* you tell me your last name."

"Very well."

I gazed into his piercing blue eyes, the locks of my hair framing our faces. "Go on," I pressed, letting the warmth between my legs glide along his hardened length.

Jax growled his desire and encouraged me to resume our earlier activity by thrusting himself at me. I raised my backside, declining the invitation.

"I'm still waiting," I whispered, tracing his ear with my tongue.

"It's Caspen." He breathed. "Jax Caspen."

Relief filled my eyes as I met his gaze. "That's not a weird name."

"I'm glad you approve. It will be yours soon."

I blinked. *Elara Caspen. Yes, I can work with that.*

I lowered my hips, giving him access to the area he desired. Our bodies moved as one. His hands directed my lower half while I braced my palms on his rock-hard pectorals. The favored position would allow us to achieve climax, but his mouth was too far from mine. I slid my hands up his chest and leaned over him, crushing my lips against his. I didn't mind the friction from the coarse hairs of his beard or the friction from below that left me panting. Between sounds of pleasure, he whispered my name while I whispered explicit language into his ear. The tension in his biceps signaled me to stop talking. Release quickly approached my partner. *Shit.* I needed three more seconds to join him at the finish line. *That's his ass if he leaves me stranded.*

As if hearing my hidden concerns, Jax moved my hips faster, pushing me into first place in our imaginary race.

The physical release slowed my speed but the emotional connection I shared with my partner steered me into the lane of bliss. My teeth sank into his shoulder, drawing blood. I'm sure the entire campsite heard me shout my enthusiasm, but at that moment, I didn't care.

Without breaking the connection, Jax rolled me onto my back. Pleasurable tremors rippled through me. He thrust himself deeper, his hips pounding against mine. My spine ignited with an icy heat. I clawed at his back, the sensation building—*again. How is that possible?*

I wanted to ask him the simple question, but the words couldn't form on my tongue. I wanted to look at my partner, enjoy the glorious show, but my eyelids felt like lead weights. Hell, my entire body had gone numb with elation.

The loud moan that left my mouth took me by surprise. A heartbeat later, Jax followed my lead. He shut his eyes and pulled out. I smiled at the goosebumps that rose on his biceps and held him close when he tried to roll over, a common courtesy he always performed.

"It's fine," I whispered.

I didn't care about the mess. I welcomed it. Jax lay on top of me, our bodies glued together by sweat and proof of our intimate time together.

Not wanting to cause me discomfort, he slid onto the blanket and pulled me into his arms. "I love you, Elara," he whispered onto the back of my neck. "More than you'll ever know."

"And I love you, Jax Caspen."

"Are you cold?"

"I'm not sure," I answered. "Everything feels numb."

An amused breath left his mouth as he reached for the edge of the blanket. He tossed it over the lower half of our bodies, then lifted my head before resting it in the crook of his arm. I scooted closer, the lines of my body merging with his.

"Better?"

"Mm-hmm," was all I could manage.

He gave my hand a gentle squeeze. "Get some rest. Tomorrow is a big day."

I hummed another murmur of agreement, ignoring the fearful thoughts that haunted my mind. I refused to let them ruin my evening with Jax. *Not now. You can worry about life later.*

With dreamland within reach, I asked, "Can we sleep like this all night?"

"If it pleases you."

"It does. I want to remember this moment forever."

"As do I." He gathered my hair and brushed it off my neck before pressing his lips onto my tepid skin.

"Then hold me," I whispered. "And don't let go."

And so, he did.

51

THE PROMISE

I gasped, sucking in a breath of the frigid air. Like a protective barrier, Jax's arms locked around me, holding me tighter.

"Elara," he whispered. "You're dreaming."

I watched the fabric of the tent wall flutter in the strong breeze, then squinted at the sunlight leaking through the cracks of the flimsy doors.

Morning. It was morning; the day our lives would change.

I flipped over to face Jax, the vivid images zipping through my mind.

His smile turned sour after noticing my troubled expression. "Bad dream?"

"No, just weird."

He draped the blanket over my shoulder. "Do you want to talk about it?"

"We were sitting under the bridge near Starbucks. You touched my hair and said *it's different, but I think I like it.*"

He lifted a brow. "And?"

"And that's it. I woke up."

"Sounds terrifying."

I shot him a stern glance. "I never said it was a bad dream."

"Then why are you worried?"

"I'm not."

He returned my earlier glance.

"Okay, fine." I groaned, scrubbing at my face. "Maybe I'm a little worried."

"Explain."

"It felt real. Too real." I twisted a lock of my hair before checking for split ends. "Sitting under the bridge, talking to you, like I am now."

"Is being on Earth together such a horrible thing? Perhaps it was a sign."

"Of the universe playing a cruel trick?"

"Or perhaps"—Jax interrupted my grooming efforts by kissing my knuckles—"you dreamed of getting another haircut."

My nose crinkled. "I'm never cutting my hair again."

"You could shave your head, and I'd still think you were beautiful."

"Well, aren't you charming this morning?"

The grin that swept across Jax's face confirmed the memories of our evening still lingered. He slipped a hand around my waist and pulled me closer, pressing my naked body against his. "Last night was amazing."

I expressed my shared sentiments with a kiss. His tongue parted my lips, but my words stopped him from going any further. "Can I ask you a question?"

"Sure." He adjusted the part that stirred from our quick embrace. "What's on your mind?"

"Samson." I bit my lip. "Is he Idalia's biological father?"

"I'm sworn to secrecy."

My mouth gaped. "I knew it. That's why he's so protective. And that's why he corrects himself each time he says my—"

"Shh. Keep your voice down. This isn't public knowledge."

My eyes sparkled with curiosity. "Spill it. Did Janus know? Does Idalia? Does anyone?"

"It's not my secret to tell."

"*Please.*" My hand slid down the planes of his stomach, resting on the hard length of him. "I won't say a word."

"Stop." His fingers curled around my wrist. "Your seductive ways won't assist you with this mission. I don't cave under pressure."

"Fine," I growled, flipping onto my back.

The callouses on his palm grazed my flesh as he rubbed a hand over my bare stomach. "Ask Samson. If you're lucky, he might tell you."

"Why? Because if I die today his secret is still safe?"

His wandering fingers paused their pursuit. "Elara, that was both dramatic and slightly morbid."

"Sorry." I swallowed a lump of anxiety and found his eyes. "I'm not ready."

"You don't have a choice. Time's up. Our entire lives have led us to this moment."

"Oh geez. You sound like Cyrus."

He shrugged. "I'm simply stating the obvious."

"Well, the obvious sucks."

"True." He tucked his arm underneath his head. "Elara, I don't want to dampen the mood—"

"In a few hours, we fight Zenith. The mood is already dampened."

His dark brows etched together. If my partner were standing, he would have crossed his arms and widened his stance. I braced myself for the lecture.

"First, you need an attitude adjustment." He flicked my downward facing chin. "You can't fight Zenith with your eyes fixed on the ground."

I stuck out my tongue. "Says who?"

"Says his adoptive son and your combative superior."

I looked at the back of my skull. "Here we go."

"That's right, so pay attention."

He sat up and took me with him. I shook off the brain fog before meeting his gaze.

"You must stay strong on the battlefield. Not just for yourself, but for the recruits willing to fight."

"*If* they fight."

"Stop spreading negativity." His casual tone switched to stern. "It's contagious. You can't act this way in front of everyone today."

"Fine." My lips spread into a fake grin. "Is this better?"

"No. Now you look demented."

I punched him in the gut, then cursed hearing the tent doors rattle. Jax tossed the blanket over our naked bodies.

"Elara," Samson snapped from outside the makeshift dwelling. "Get your ass out here."

"Why?" I reached for my bra. "What's going on?"

"Don't ask stupid questions. Put on your damn clothes and come see for yourself."

My cheeks flushed when I recalled the loud moans and pleasurable cries of the previous night's escapade. Jax smirked, handing me my shirt and pants.

"Samson won't let me live this down, will he?"

The Lunin chuckled, fastening the buttons on his fly. "Probably not. One time he caught me in the woods with—"

"I don't want to hear about the time you screwed some girl in the woods."

"Wow." His eyelashes fluttered. "I was going to say he caught me making out with a girl, but your dramatic mind assumed the worst—as usual."

I threw him his shirt, hitting him square in the nose. "Asshole."

"At least we went a few hours without arguing last night."

I raised an imaginary glass in celebration and slipped on my boots. "Here's to progress."

Jax returned the gesture by slapping me on the ass, leaving my right cheek throbbing. "And to many years of practice."

"I'm not getting any younger," Samson called.

After Jax helped me with my coat, I inhaled a sobering breath and ducked to exit the tent. I shielded my eyes from the morning light and shivered at the frigid wind that crept down my collar. Nature's surprise attack felt like a gentle kiss compared to the fierceness in the blue and orange eyes that stared back.

I gulped. Over a hundred men and women stood dressed, prepared for battle, their pale and tan fingers gripping the handle of their knives. The crowd didn't cower when Jax moved beside me. They were ready.

"We stand with you," Roshan said, gesturing to the recruits. "All of us."

My eyes drifted from one brave soul to the next. "I applaud you for finding the courage to stand together. I know you're exhausted and disheartened. And so am I. The odds aren't in our favor. We're outnumbered and we don't have a clue what to expect once we arrive on the battlefield. The fear of the unknown scares the shit out of me, and the thought of losing more loved ones makes me want to vomit."

The crowd shifted their weight.

I inclined my head at Jax. "This man taught me the benefit of brutal honesty. Sometimes it sucks to hear, but it's necessary to move forward, so I won't stand up here and ease your troubled minds with false promises."

I observed Orion and Idalia, then looked at my brother. "I've learned many things while living on Aroonyx. I learned how to fight and how to stand up for truth." I eyed Samson and Jax. "I learned to accept my friends, regardless of their past, and I learned to accept the decisions I've made, whether the universe deems them forgivable or not. But the most valuable lesson I've learned is this: love is the source of our power. It never falters, and it never fails.

"Today our lives will change. Hope brought us together and hope will guide us through this challenging time. I'm honored to fight by your side today, and so are the men who stand beside me. We will stop at nothing to defeat Zenith." I wiped a rogue tear that slid down my cheek. "My brother and I will stop at *nothing* to finish this mission, and if we die trying, then so be it."

Silence. Only the swaying tree limbs dared to interrupt.

Samson took a step forward. "Say goodbye to your loved ones. We leave for the Village Center in a few minutes." He observed the injured men and women who gathered around the recruits. "We'll send word once it's done."

With a collective nod, the group dispatched. A tiny smile broke at the corner of my mouth watching the Solins share words of encouragement with the Lunins. The simple gesture that curled my lips upward wasn't a sign of joy. No, it was a sign of acceptance.

Samson nudged me in the arm. "I'm proud of you, Elara. You've really grown since we first met. If I was a family man, I'd hope to have a daughter like you."

More tears stung my weary eyes. Samson's candid words tugged at my heartstrings. I never realized how much I loved the old bastard.

"Thank you," I said, wrapping my arms around him. "For everything."

"Anytime, kiddo."

The coarse hairs of his beard scratched my cheek as I whispered, "Over the past few months, I've missed my dad . . . a lot. You helped fill that void." I pointed to Idalia. "She misses her father too. It's unfortunate she doesn't know he's standing right here."

He stilled.

"No, Jax didn't tell me," I reassured him. "I figured it out on my own."

The Solin let out a long exhale. "I can't tell her the truth—not yet."

"Your secret's safe with me."

He folded his arms across his chest and watched Idalia as he spoke. "Janus and I were inseparable when we worked for Arun. And it stayed that way after we left the Collectors. He met Helen a few seasons later." He smiled. "She went everywhere with us. I tried to ignore my love for that woman, but I couldn't hide it. She meant everything to me. Helen never judged me for my dark past and she had this laugh." His throat bobbed, grief saturating his words.

I eyed Samson out of my peripheral vision. My chest caved. I always saw him living the bachelor life. I never imagined him loving someone with his whole heart.

"Helen's laugh could brighten a darkened room." His eyes glazed over with memories of the past. "Like Idalia, she was a stunning beauty."

"Did Janus know?"

"No, we never told him the truth."

"How did it happen?"

He gave me a sidelong glance. "Do you really need that talk after your activities last night?"

My cheeks burned with embarrassment.

He snickered. "I didn't think so."

"You know what I was implying," I said. "How did he not know the two of you were—"

"*Fucking?*"

I grimaced. "Having an affair works too."

He shrugged. "One night, the three of us were hanging out after the bar closed. Janus got tired, so he went upstairs. Helen and I kept drinking and talking about random shit. I almost fell out of my chair when she leaned over the table and kissed me."

I blinked hard. "She made the first move?"

"Yeah, and I pushed her away because it was wrong." He sighed, rubbing a hand over his beard. "But then she started crying and confessed her true feelings. She spent years waiting, hoping I'd say—*do* something before they got married." He huffed a breath. "I never thought she'd choose me over Janus.

"Listening to her that night made me realize I was a damn fool for ignoring the obvious, so I forgot my best friend, I forgot I was staring into the eyes of his wife. Hell, I even forgot to play it safe." He met my gaze. "We had a wonderful time together, but the guilt we experienced afterward ruined everything."

"Helen never told Janus she had an affair?"

"No. We swore to take our mistake to the grave. It would have crushed Janus. He was a good man. I wasn't."

I craned my neck to see Idalia chatting with Blaze and Cyrus. "Are you sure she's your daughter? Helen and Janus were sleeping together too."

"I'm certain. We have matching birthmarks on our backs and shoulders."

I nodded. "And she has your nose."

"Now you know why I helped Helen raise Idalia after Janus's death."

"What happened to the Collectors who murdered him?"

A wicked smirk tugged at his mouth. "I cut off their heads while they slept, then dropped their bodies at the door of the other Collector they worked for."

"Thanks for the imagery."

"You asked, I answered."

I crossed my arms. "So that's why Callisto stepped aside after Helen passed."

"Yep." He swallowed hard. "And now we're done discussing

my fucked-up life. Go say goodbye to Orion. He was asking for you earlier."

I squeezed Samson's hand before jogging toward the Lunin. *What do I say to a man who lost his father? I'm sorry? Time will heal? He lived a full life?* I cursed my shallow condolences.

Using actions rather than words, I embraced him in a warm hug. He went rigid. I didn't let go.

"I'm sorry for your loss," I whispered. "Your father was an amazing man. We all loved him."

"Thanks." His chest quivered with grief. "I'll honor his legacy by healing the wounded."

I cupped his chilled face and found his red-rimmed eyes. "I think that's a wonderful idea. Helping others is a great service to ourselves. You're a strong man, Orion. I know you'll get through this."

A smile fought the vacant expression that masked his face. "Spoken like a true leader."

"Half the time I talk out of my ass."

"Most leaders do." He clapped a hand on my back. "Keep it up. It suits you, Elara."

I gathered my hair into a high ponytail and observed the wounded around the spring. "Are you going to be okay working alone today?"

"I'm not alone. Callisto's leg is still bothering him. He can't fight, so he'll stay and help me care for the injured." He jerked his chin at Cyrus's mini-me. "And I'm sure Blaze will keep me distracted with his endless questions." He lowered his gaze. "Are *you* going to be okay on the battlefield today?"

"Do you want the truth?"

"Over a lie? Sure."

"I'm trying to stay strong," I said. "But my insides have turned to mush. The thought of losing Jax or anyone else makes me want to cry, and the thought of failing the people of Aroonyx makes me want to crawl into a hole and die."

"Wow. That was a little dramatic."

"If you haven't noticed, I'm an expert at the dramatic approach."

A grin followed a squeeze on my shoulder. "Elara, regardless of the outcome, you've failed no one. You gave the people hope, and that's more than Zenith's ever done."

"Spoken like a true friend."

Tears pooled in Orion's eyes as he looked at Cyrus. "Take care of each other out there. Don't do anything stupid."

Before I could respond, Orion spun on his heels and walked off. The breeze whipped around me, loosening a sheet of snow from a low-lying branch. The white fluff stuck to my lashes. Carelessly, I brushed it away. *Why are goodbyes so heartbreaking?*

"Because we're programmed to think goodbyes mean forever."

I flinched at the sound of Jax's voice, my eyes wide with wonder. "Are you sure your Seeker powers don't include mindreading?"

He shook his head. "I can't hear your thoughts. I just know you better than anyone else." He extended a hand toward the tent. "Idalia gave us a fresh change of clothes. I'm going to get dressed and sharpen the spare knives. Meet me inside once you're done making your rounds."

I murmured, "Okay," as he kissed the top of my head, then turned, hearing Blaze call my name.

The young boy threw himself into my arms. I stumbled backward. Jax steadied me before giving us some privacy. I lowered myself to the ground, taking Blaze with me.

"Thanks for saving my life," he cried.

"Did Cyrus tell you to say that?"

"No." He sniffled. "I wanted to tell you the day it happened, but you looked so angry."

I used my sleeve to wipe the snot dripping from his nose. "I was angry—with myself, but not anymore."

The child burst into tears. "Don't go. I don't want you and Cyrus to die."

I rocked him in my arms. His desperate plea nearly ripped out my heart. "It's our job to protect you and your friends. After the battle is over—"

"We'll adopt you," Cyrus said, kneeling beside us.

The moisture in Blaze's eyes dried as he stared at my fearless twin. "You would?"

"How 'bout it, sis? You could use another brother."

"Absolutely." I grinned. "We'll make it official once we get back."

Blaze's lips drooped into a pout. "Won't you need Zenith's approval?"

"Not if he's dead."

I shot my brother a stern look and mouthed, "Don't scare him."

He rested his hands on the sides of Blaze's face. "Let me give you some advice I shared with my sister." The boy rose to his full height. "Everything is going to be okay. *You're* going to be okay, kiddo."

My heart warmed. Leave it to Cyrus to calm a frightened soul.

I fluffed the blond mop on Blaze's head. "I'm leaving you in charge while we're gone. Stay strong for your friends. They need a good leader."

Blaze popped to attention and said, "Yes, ma'am," before hurrying to catch up with his peers.

My brother draped an arm over my shoulders. "I'll miss that kid."

"You'll see him later."

Cyrus didn't respond. He just gave me a loving squeeze and said, "See you in a few, sis."

I STAYED silent while I dressed. An unforced laugh escaped my mouth once I observed my partner's wardrobe. "We match."

He smoothed a crease in the long-sleeved shirt that covered his torso, then snickered at the discolored patches on our pants. "Uniforms for battle."

My lip quivered with fear. Jax took the folded blades from my hands and slid them into my coat pockets before wrapping his strong arms around me. I shut my eyes. *Please. Let us live to see another day.*

I wanted to ignore the inevitable and stay lost in his embrace for eternity, but an unspoken truth pulled us apart. As if taking a mental picture, Jax traced the features of my face with his fingers. I did the same with him, my thumb grazing his full lips. He smiled, and I smiled back.

Our story wasn't written on the pages of a book—not yet at least. We couldn't cheat or skip ahead to see if our characters got a happy ending. No. We experienced each moment as it happened: the good, the bad, the victories, the failures. Our life was more than black words typed on crème-colored paper. It was a colorful journey. One we shared—together.

Jax pressed his lips against mine, then whispered, "It's time, Elara."

I nodded. "I can face anything with you by my side."

"And I can with you. But promise me you'll keep moving forward if I can't uphold my end of the bargain."

I felt the color drain from my face. "Why would you say that?"

"Just promise me." Another gentle kiss touched my lips.

A ball of grief blocked my airway. I cleared my throat and rubbed the ache in my chest as I whispered the words he wanted to hear, the words I struggled to say. "I promise."

PART III

DISCOVERING THE TRUTH

52

UNTIL THE VERY END

We ventured deeper into the forest, closer to the Village Center—closer to Zenith. Samson instructed the recruits to enjoy their walk, take some time to get to know one another. Over a hundred faces scowled at the ridiculous suggestion. I kicked a fallen branch. *Get to know each other? Why? So they can watch their new pals die in battle?*

I shook my head at the Solin. It's not like they volunteered to take a casual hike through the woods. They volunteered to fight the leader of Aroonyx and his army of trained killers.

My brother looked at Jax, a mischievous grin tugging at his lips. "Are you focused this morning?"

The Lunin responded with a smirk.

"Don't start," I said to Cyrus.

"Were you trying to rub it in last night, or did you want everyone on Aroonyx to hear your explicit activity?"

I glared. Jax's smirk grew as Cyrus imitated the pleasurable sounds he heard coming from our tent.

"Don't tease her," Idalia scolded.

I smiled at the beautiful Solin who strolled beside my brother. "Thank you. I'm glad someone has my back."

"Always."

Keeping a straight face, I asked Cyrus, "Did you enjoy spending time with your hand last night?"

"Go to hell."

I shrugged. "I've already been there. It's overrated."

Our heads popped up hearing Samson call for Aries. The group halted its casual pace, but the ex-Collector dashed forward, his boots sloshing through the snow.

"Scout the area," Samson ordered. "I want a headcount and a detailed description of their formation." He slapped Aries on the back. "Make it fast. The sun is nearing the highest point in the sky."

"Yes, sir."

My pulse quickened as I watched the young Lunin dash ahead. I turned to Jax. "Are we at the Village Center?"

"Yes. It's just over that hill."

I rested a hand on my hip, struggling to fill my lungs.

"You okay, sis?"

"Yeah." I choked on the lie. "I'm cool."

Cyrus spoke to Jax behind my back. "She really is a horrible liar."

"Mm-hmm. It runs in the family."

My brother cleared his throat and shifted his gaze forward. Like a stealth surveillance camera, my head swiveled between the two men.

Jax threw a verbal jab at my twin. But why? My lips moved to question said jab but paused once I noticed Aries jogging toward Samson.

I tried eavesdropping on their private conversation, but the howling winds muffled their voices. Aries used his hands while he spoke, tracing squares out of thin air.

A white cloud shot out of Samson's nostrils. He shut his

eyes, then motioned for Aries to get back in line. I rocked on the balls of my feet as the Solin neared. The lines on his face hardened and his lips pursed. Jax reached for my hand, for he too could see the defeat in our mentor's eyes.

"They're down there." Samson raised his voice for everyone to hear. "All of them."

The crowd muttered their shared anxieties. My brother cracked his joints, sending a burst of heat through my veins.

"The numbers haven't changed," Samson added. "Aries counted over three hundred men. Each one is armed and ready to fight."

"Shit," I muttered.

Idalia caught my eye and mouthed, "It's okay."

I repeated the curse word. Cyrus grabbed my free hand and held it tight. Jax recoiled. Without knowing it, I had released a small amount of heat.

"Sorry." I grimaced.

"It's fine." He showed me his uninjured hand. "Good practice."

I faked a cry at his little joke.

"Let me explain the logistics," Samson said. "As suspected, Zenith gathered the remaining citizens of Aroonyx to watch the mayhem unfold. They're standing out of harm's way. He has assembled the Collectors and recruits in a tight formation. The underage boys are on the front lines."

Jax huffed his irritation. Samson nodded, acknowledging Zenith's disregard for innocent lives.

"At the back of the formation awaits the Inner Circle." Samson paused before disclosing the most valuable bit of information. "They're guarding Zenith."

My nails dug into Cyrus's hand.

Samson lifted a finger. "We have one goal to achieve today. Get Elara and Cyrus to Zenith."

The recruits nodded.

"Failing this mission isn't an option."

More heads bobbed up and down.

The Solin looked at me and my brother. "Unlike Zenith, you won't hide behind those who fight for you." He pointed to the space in front of him. "You'll lead us into battle."

I gulped.

My brother spoke for the both of us. "Yes, sir."

Samson paced while he addressed the group. "Cyrus and Elara, I want you front and center. Castor and I will flank your sides. Jax and Aries, watch our six. Roshan, create a tight formation with the men who joined us in the villages, and stay a few paces behind." He stretched his neck to find his daughter's eyes. "Idalia, I want you and the rest of the recruits marching in staggered lines of ten. Keep the gaps tight."

She nodded, her golden eyes flickering with determination.

"Now go!" he barked.

The men and women moved into position. Jax's fingers grazed mine before taking his place behind me and my brother. He circled his throwing arm, while Aries triple checked the sharpness of his blade.

Castor adjusted the holster that housed the Origin blades. He offered Samson a dagger, the one he was instructed to keep safe. The Solin tossed it to Idalia who caught it with one hand, then asked his old comrade for another.

"Remember," he said to us over the bustle of the recruits. "Zenith has kids on the front lines. Spare them if you can. I'm sure they'll scatter once the fighting begins. Save your strength for the Active Members."

Postures shifted. The Solins stood tall, their orange eyes glowing with courage. The Lunins shared a nervous breath, but they never cowered. Seeing their dedication lifted my spirits and propelled my feet forward once Samson gave the signal.

My heart thundered in my chest as we reached the top of the hill. Using our unique bond to communicate, I expressed my concerns to my brother with wide eyes and raised brows. *Are we ready for this?*

He flashed me his pearly grin. "Yeah. We've got this, sis."

I held my breath and scooted my boots closer to the unknown. The ice-kissed wind slapped at our faces, and the gut-wrenching site below punched me in the gut.

"We're screwed," I muttered.

"I second that," Castor said, his eyes growing in disbelief.

Death had disguised itself as a snow-covered clearing. Hundreds of armed recruits stood with their shoulders touching, hands glued to their sides. Like Roman spectators at the Colosseum, the citizens of Aroonyx waited at the far end of the field, eager to watch the bloodshed.

I shared my brother's powerful vision and searched for Zenith. A short inhale later, I found him standing behind the Inner Circle. My heart skipped a beat.

Cyrus gritted his teeth, his eyes narrowing on Pollux. The Lunin chatted with Oberon. I shivered, and it wasn't from the blistering cold. *I'm sure they're discussing the horrible ways they plan on torturing us.*

Zenith stayed silent. He slid a finger back and forth over the smooth side of his pure Fired Stone blade, the blade I used to kill Elio.

The half Solin, half Lunin opted for a thick, long-sleeved shirt instead of a coat. A skilled seamstress had woven flecks of silver into the dark fabric, the same shade to match the etchings on his blade. I couldn't find a crease in his charcoal-colored pants. It appeared he had dressed for the occasion. I glowered at his attire. *What an arrogant prick.*

A sheen coated his jet-black locks, the afternoon light shimmering off each perfectly placed strand. His hair didn't budge when a gust of wind whipped through the clearing. My head tilted. *Does hair gel exist on Aroonyx?*

I cursed his flawless complexion. A fresh shave left his

bronze skin looking smoother than a baby's ass, and the cords of muscle in his chest tightened as he rolled his toned shoulders.

"Do you think Rico's down there?" Cyrus asked.

Snapped out of my trance, I looked at my twin.

"I bet he got jealous of Blaze and joined sides with Zenith."

A smile escaped, though I fought the urge to laugh. "Now is not the time to joke around."

"Sorry." He winked. "I wanted to see you smile one last time before—" His voice faded.

Zenith had lifted his head, his blue and orange eyes staring right at us. I gasped. Cyrus swore. The air rushed out of Jax's lungs.

His adoptive father flashed me the tiniest smirk—a cruel gesture. His lips moved. Pollux turned to his leader. A moment later the Lunin fisted his unarmed hand and spun around to face us. Though Pollux lacked Zenith's Solin vision, he glared at our location on the hill. The other members of the Inner Circle stopped their mindless banter and tightened their formation. Apollo cracked his neck while Oberon warmed up the muscles in his arm. Jericho and Ishan exchanged a cautious glance, then fell into line.

Shit. I wiped the cold sweat off my palms. *This is really happening.*

Zenith nodded at Pollux. The Lunin shouted a command. *Oh fuck.* Over three hundred men popped to attention with their arms raised in a rigid salute. Their vicious expressions and quick response time reminded me of Hitler's Gestapo.

Agreeing with my unspoken thoughts, Cyrus muttered, "Great. It's like we're reliving an altered version of Earth's history."

Samson squeezed my shoulder and repeated the ominous words Jax shared earlier that morning. "It's time, Elara."

My hand trembled as it slipped into my coat pocket. I

grabbed a spare knife, knowing I should save my white one for later. I looked over my shoulder at Jax. He didn't smile. He only nodded his approval. The time for encouragement had passed. We had reached the final battle.

My partner, the true warrior of the story, wore his scars like badges of honor that day. His spine lengthened as he inhaled a steadying breath, and his pale fingers gripped the handle of his gray knife with enough force to snap it in two.

Samson lifted his hand and hollered, "On my signal!"

Moisture blurred my vision when I found my brother's eyes. The amount of courage that radiated out of his being rippled through the entire group. Everyone felt it. Even our adversaries at the bottom of the hill. They shifted their weight, fear consuming them.

"We stay together," Cyrus whispered.

I forced a head nod once Samson gave the orders to start the war. "Together, until the very end."

53

YOU, NOT WE

As Samson predicted, most underage Collectors fled to the woods in search of sanctuary. We penetrated their loose formation, pushing the braver, more foolish adolescents out of the way.

A young Solin had the audacity to direct his blade at Cyrus's chest. My twin sidestepped the attack, grabbed the boy's wrist, and twisted it 360 degrees until the bone snapped. The injured fell, cradling his broken wrist.

Castor scooped up the boy's knife and tossed it to my brother. They never slowed their mad pursuit through the clearing.

Even under the deadly circumstances, I dodged the underage men, refusing to harm the innocent. But this didn't apply to everyone. My head snapped to the right, a Solin catching my eye. *Aarush.*

"Cyrus!" I yelled.

He turned, slowing his pace. His nostrils flared as he followed my extended hand.

"Let's go!" He sprinted toward the traitor.

Disregarding Samson's orders, I broke the formation and

took off after my brother.

The teen's eyes were wide with panic. One of our recruits had knocked him to the ground. He cowered as my twin reached down and grabbed him by his throat.

"*You*," Cyrus hissed.

Aarush clawed at my brother's hand, his bronze complexion turning a deep shade of purple.

"You son of a bitch!" He dragged the young Solin to his feet. "You're the reason they murdered our friend. You're the reason they slaughtered our recruits."

The accused tried to shake his head. My brother lifted him higher until his toes dangled above the snow.

"Don't lie to us," I warned. "You betrayed us—all of us."

"I had no choice," he sputtered. "Zenith threatened to kill my mother."

Cyrus's face squished up with confusion.

"Let's hear him out," I suggested.

With great reluctance, my brother lowered Aarush. He then curled his fingers around the collar of his coat and pulled him close. "Start talking."

Aarush swallowed hard, his eyes watering from the aftereffects of the brutal hold. "I never wanted this to happen."

"Bullshit," Cyrus argued. "Jax murdered your father, and you sought revenge by selling us out to Zenith."

"No." He rubbed his swollen neck. "That's not the reason."

Cyrus directed his knife at the main artery in Aarush's throat. "You've got thirty seconds to come clean."

The young man struggled to speak. "After the meeting, I went home and spoke to my mother. Yes, we were angry with Jax, but even more so with Zenith. A few days later we decided to put the past behind us and join your side."

"Why?" I asked.

"Because it was the right thing to do."

My shoulders sagged, and Cyrus lowered his knife.

"But the Collectors arrived before we got a chance. My mother fought to protect me. Once they started beating her, I surrendered to the ordinance. It didn't matter. They wouldn't let up." Tears welled in his eyes. "Sharing valuable information was the only way I could make them stop."

"So you told the Collectors where we were hiding," I said.

Cyrus's eyes darted between Aarush and our recruits. They pressed forward leaving the three of us behind—alone in a snowy mist.

"No. I told them I'd tell Zenith *if* they stopped beating my mother." Aarush paused before shuddering a breath. "They dragged us to his dwelling. He wanted the details: specific coordinates, headcounts, names of recruits"—he met my gaze —"your health status."

I touched the scar on my stomach.

"He needed a spy," Aarush added. "So he threatened to kill my mother if I didn't volunteer for the job."

My heart ached for the young Solin, but my teeth gritted at the thought of our friend's charred body. "That's why you were scouting the area around Iah's property yesterday."

"Yes." He choked back a sob. "I've been watching you for weeks."

Cyrus swore again. My chin hit my chest.

"And once Zenith heard you left for the villages with a group of men, he executed my mother and forced me to join the Collectors."

My brother had a dangerous side to his personality, but he wasn't a ruthless killer. He let go of Aarush. "The bastard waited for the most opportune time to attack us," he said to me.

I nodded, a hole punched in my heart.

"I'm so sorry," Aarush cried. "I had to protect my mother." He showed us his empty hands. "I dropped my knife as soon as the battle started. I choose your side. I want to make things right. I want to fight for—"

Aarush never finished his sentence because an Origin blade pierced the back of his skull, silencing him forever. The violent murder left the tip of the long dagger jutting out of his gaped mouth. A thick river of blood flowed down his chin, splattering the snow below.

I gasped, scooting away from the horror that filled my vision. Cyrus swore and caught the teen's lifeless body as he slumped forward.

My gaze drifted upward, finding the person responsible for such brutality.

"For Iah," Idalia hissed, ripping the blade out of Aarush's skull.

The sickening sound turned my stomach inside out. She didn't bother cleaning off the knife. Bits of flesh and blood dripped off the forged stone as she tossed her braided hair behind her back. Cyrus lay Aarush face up in the snow, hiding the entry wound. It appeared less gruesome that way.

She angled her head at the deceased, satisfaction glowing in her golden eyes. "It's time to get to work."

She pointed at our recruits in the near distance. They plowed through the underage men, a battering ram of sheer determination. Samson hurled a teen five feet through the air, knocking out three more while Jax disarmed two boys at once. Roshan collected the fallen blades, tossing them to Aries as he ran.

"They're doing this for you," Idalia reminded us. "They're clearing a path. Now get your asses to Zenith."

We didn't need a paternity test to confirm her blood relation to Samson. She was her father's daughter.

Without delay, we followed our friend into the midst of chaos.

A BLUR of bodies danced around me. I struggled to see through the chaos, searching for the Active Members.

"Where are they?" I shouted at Cyrus.

"I don't know." He hopped over a boy curled into a ball. Fear had left the poor child incapacitated. "I can't see shit now that we're in the thick of it."

"They're up ahead," Jax said, shoving a young Lunin to the side.

I breathed hard, winded from the long sprint. My burning side begged me to stop, but I kept running. I had to.

After long minutes of dodging frightened boys and scaring those brave enough to attack, I heard Samson yell, "The next group comes for blood!"

Our chests rose and fell with quick breaths. We had reached the next stage of battle: the Active Members and Zenith's recruits. Men, not boys.

I scanned their tight formation, taking a mental inventory of the Solins and Lunins who wanted us dead. Rows of twenty, over ten rows deep. My eyes flickered up and down their lines trying to get an accurate headcount. *Shit. We're outnumbered two to one.*

As if hearing my inner dialogue, Cyrus grabbed my hand, sending a burst of heat rushing through me. These men differed from the underage boys we left in the snowy wake behind us. Fear didn't flicker in their eyes. They didn't cower in our presence. They stood tall with smug grins, eager to plunge their knives into our beating hearts.

I eyed my brother, curious why they didn't charge. He shrugged. It appeared they had orders to attack after we made the first move. Our boots scooted closer—closer to where Zenith hid behind his personal guard.

I glanced at the persimmon-colored sun in the cloudless sky, wishing it would burn through the shared tension that encapsulated the two groups.

Cyrus pointed his blade at a Solin barring his teeth. Jax and Aries stepped forward along with Castor and Samson. The men surrounding me had transformed into a lethal unit. They would stop at nothing to complete the mission.

I shut my eyes and listened to the gentle voice inside my heart.

It's time, Elara.

I know. Everyone keeps reminding me.

Then what are you waiting for?

Answering for me, my brother charged the Collectors. The sound of bodies colliding echoed through the clearing like a crack of pins in a bowling alley. Nothing could have prepared me for the morbid soundtrack that followed. Pained screams, guttural shouts, and gurgling blood filled my ears.

The gory images painted by the Grim Reaper's hands rivaled the most gruesome battle scenes on film. The silver screen showed the viewer the director's cinematic vision. Life's stage didn't work that way. There were no cuts or edits, no rubber weapons or special effects makeup. Choreographers didn't stage the violence and carnage, and the bodies that collapsed weren't actors or stuntmen. They were unfortunate souls who writhed in pain from the wounds they suffered or souls who slipped into the afterlife.

I tripped, nearly faceplanting into the snow after avoiding a near miss. Jax grabbed my wrist and shoved me toward my brother before jamming his knife into the side of a man's neck. He slid the blade forward, severing the man's trachea. I didn't bother turning around. The hiss of blood spraying from the wound confirmed my partner had donned the mask of a killer.

Samson and Castor worked as a team, slicing through the crowd. The Solin made the kill shot and the Lunin disarmed the dead, recycling the knives. I marveled at their impressive skills. A mist of blood followed the two men as they fought their way deeper into the formation.

My chin snapped toward the sky. A Solin had grabbed a handful of my hair and yanked me to the ground, knocking the wind out of me. He straddled my waist. Remembering my training, I tapped my foot and lifted my hip. My escape maneuver fell short once the man backhanded me across the face. Stars, lots and lots of silver flecks exploded in my vision. I cursed the blood seeping from my wound. His knuckles had ripped the skin above my cheekbone.

"Bastard!" I yelled.

"Whore."

I spit in his face. "That's all you've got?"

Poor decision on my part. He struck again, splitting my bottom lip wide open. I slid my tongue over my teeth, making sure they were intact and accounted for.

The features on his face hardened as he raised his knife over my heart. He hesitated, a white mist spraying his face. Cyrus had slid through the snow and grabbed my left hand. I reached with my right, aiming for the most accessible part of my attacker's body—his abdomen. The man hissed. I had melted the fibers of his shirt to his flesh. My hand went deeper, sinking into the hard planes of his stomach. His eyes bulged, a cold sweat forming on his brow. My brother used this distraction to his advantage and disarmed the Solin, then shoved him off of me.

"Thanks, bro," I rasped, reaching for his extended hand.

"Anytime, sis."

We bobbed and weaved through the clearing. A Lunin threw a knife at Cyrus. He avoided the projectile object by crouching, taking me with him. To the naïve eye, the maneuver appeared unplanned. It wasn't. Months of training had prepared us for that moment. I grabbed our attacker's leg as he ran by, sending him cursing and tumbling face first into the snow. He rolled on the ground, cradling his scorched shin bone.

Cyrus pulled me to my feet and laced his fingers through

mine, securing his grip. We observed the devastation that unfolded before our eyes. Our recruits had scattered, lost in a violent sea of fists, knives, and blood. Cyrus searched for Idalia while I searched for Jax. I blinked and blinked again. An obscure image of the Grim Reaper hung in the shadows, the sunlight reflecting off its black scythe. *What the hell?*

I flinched when Jax darted past us. He hurled a knife over his shoulder. It punctured his target's lower abdomen, stopping the man dead, literally, in his tracks. Roshan appeared and grabbed the embedded blade, ripping it from the torn flesh. The lifeless man fell to his knees. The image of Death nodded and floated over the blood-stained clearing to collect the dead.

Idalia's screams turned us in the opposite direction. A Solin had restrained her in a ground hold. Another held a sharpened blade to her neck.

We sprinted after our friend.

Cyrus adjusted his grip on my hand. "Hold on tight, sis."

Reminding me of an Olympic shot-put competitor, he spun in a circle, allowing nature's momentum to propel me forward. I stretched my leg, slamming my boot into the armed attacker's face. He flew backward, blood spraying from his fractured nose.

I stretched to reach the man who held our friend and pressed my vibrating palm into his face. His skin smoked and bubbled, his eyelids sticking to my fingers. Overwhelmed with pain, the Solin collapsed, burying his disfigured features into the snow.

My brother hurried to assist Idalia—an unnecessary gesture. With lightning speed, she hopped to her feet, and after kicking the burn victim in the ribs, five times to be exact, she unleashed hell on her other attacker's crotch. The man hollered at the top of his lungs. Adding insult to injury, she twisted the toe of her boot into his balls. Cyrus grimaced.

I cursed watching Samson storm toward us. A lethal rage flashed in his orange eyes as he noted the deep gashes on his daughter's face. He bent down and grabbed the unburned attacker by the hairs on his head.

"Please," the man begged. One of his hands held his broken nose, the other his crotch. "I—"

Death silenced his desperate plea. I had never witnessed a decapitation. It's not something I had on my bucket list. Samson's Solin strength combined with the Origin blade severed the man's head in one fell swoop.

He held it in the air, a morbid trophy on proud display. The fighting ceased for a shy moment. Everyone observed the horror frozen on the man's face: his contorted features, gaped mouth, glossy eyes. Their gazes shifted to the red tendrils of muscle and ribbons of veins that dangled in the breeze. Clots of blood dripped from the base of the trophy onto the snow. Samson flung the head into the crowd. One of our recruits, a woman, squealed as it rolled over her feet.

Our mentor wiped the dagger on his pants, then nodded at Idalia. She flashed him a wide grin and inclined her head at the madness of the crowd. The father-daughter duo left me and my brother standing with our jaws hanging open.

"Did that just happen?" Cyrus asked me.

I nodded, staring at the headless corpse. "It sure did."

A familiar grunt shifted my attention. *Jax.*

Two Lunins held my partner's arms outstretched while a Solin sat on top of him, pointing a blade at his heart. I dashed forward, aiming a spare knife at the man's stomach. A breath later, he winced. His fingers trembled as he touched the embedded blade. Jax bucked his hips, rolling the wounded man off of him. He then lifted his arms, flipping the Lunins onto their backs. Like a pump-action rifle, Jax punched each man in the temple, rendering them unconscious. Without delay, he reached for the handle of my spare knife and sliced open the Solin's gut. The man choked and sputtered, then fumbled with his slimy innards. Unscathed, Jax sprung to his feet and disappeared into the chaos.

A surprise attack sent my brother staggering forward. Two Solins had snuck up behind him. A third grabbed the tails of my coat. He yanked the fabric hard, slamming my head onto the compacted snow. More stars exploded around me. My vision cleared in time to see the loathing in my attacker's eyes.

"Zenith will award anyone who brings him your head."

I needed to keep him distracted so I could access my knife. I wiggled while asking, "I thought he wanted me alive? I thought he wanted to murder me with his bare hands?"

"Not anymore," he snarled. "You're going to make me a very rich man." He raised the back of his hand. "After I beat the shit out of you."

He struck me repeatedly. The bones in my face cracked and shifted. Blood trickled down the back of my throat. I twisted underneath his weight, stretching my fingers for the hidden lifeline in my coat pocket. This man's reaction time surpassed my first attacker. He struck again. I squinted to see through the murky haze that clouded my vision, the ringing in my ears deafening. The Solin had a shaved head, a plethora of scars on his tan flesh, and a copper sunburst shining in his eyes. I stilled, recognizing the Active Member. Go figure. It was Inan, the Solin Collector who interrogated me at the bar the night I heard the rumors of Jax's death.

I hollered his name, bracing myself for another blow. "Stop!"

"Awe." He paused mid-swing. "You remembered, how sweet." His fist collided with my bruised and busted face once more.

Tunnel vision signaled my loss of consciousness. *Don't pass out. You can't pass out.*

Gritting my teeth, I reached for my twin. He lay feet away

with his arm outstretched. My fingers touched the snow and nothing more. *Shit. He's too far away.*

I sucked in a sharp breath and held it as Inan prepared for the knockout blow. He froze, his fist inches from my face. A tremor rippled through him, and his eyes widened with shock, blood dripping from his mouth. I looked up to find Aries standing beside the Collector, a stone-cold expression masking his pale features. He pushed the blade deeper into the man's neck, puncturing his trachea. Aries then shoved the Solin to the side and helped me stand.

"Thank you," I panted, spitting a wad of iron-rich mucus onto the snow.

Concerned filled his blue eyes as he assessed my injuries.

"I'm fine." I waved him away. "Go help the others."

"Yes, ma'am," slipped off his half tongue as he hurried to assist Roshan with a group of bloodthirsty men.

Samson and Castor rescued my brother from the two Solins. One attacker made the foolish mistake of rushing the latter. The Lunin pulled a dagger from his belt and sliced the man from his navel to his neck. Samson whirled on the other Solin, plunging an Origin blade into the back of the man's skull. I looked away, already familiar with the efficiency of his kill shots.

I went for a spare knife. The restricting fabric limited my arm movement. *Screw it. I'd rather freeze than bleed to death from a knife wound.*

After shoving the four remaining lifelines into my back pockets, I tossed the coat to the ground.

I searched for Cyrus, my eyes drifting from one bloodied recruit to the next. I glanced at the deceased surrounding my feet. The stark-white clearing had turned into a muted canvas slathered with various shades of red. I needed to swallow but my heart lodged in my throat. Hundreds of lifeless eyes stared back: the departed souls who fought to defend Zenith and those who fought to defend us. I did the math. We were losing the battle . . . and losing it fast.

I spun in circles, shouting Samson's name. *Where is he?*

A stone's throw away, I saw him fighting for his life. Four men had circled my mentor, blood dripping from their blades. Samson held a hand over a deep gash in his upper thigh. A man lunged from behind, stabbing him in the shoulder. Samson swore and collapsed onto his knees. The attacker nodded at his peers, signaling the men to restrain the wounded.

I raised my knife and aimed for the leader of their group. A massive Solin knocked it out of my hand when he tackled me. My ribs cracked, the pain radiating in my chest. Jax came to my aid. Seeing me injured flipped a switch, waking the demon of his past. No clouds moved across the sky, but a shadow hung over my partner. His pale fingers curled around the man's throat, and without breaking a sweat, he crushed my attacker's windpipe. *POP.* The sound sent a shiver down my spine.

"Samson . . . *fuck,*" I cursed at the bone shards poking my lungs. "He needs our help."

Jax shook his head and pointed at the Solin. "Not anymore."

I turned. Samson had pulled the knife from his shoulder and slit the Lunin's throat. Like a sprinkler, the man's blood fanned in a wide arc. Samson wiped the oily residue from his eyes while Castor charged the other men. Armed with two Origin blades in his outstretched hands, he twirled in a tight circle. The daggers sliced through the men's necks without delay. More blood sprayed from the fatal wounds. With a wild look in his eyes, Castor squatted. The tip of one blade touched the snow, staining it red, while the other pointed toward the sky. I gulped. He reminded me of a high-profile assassin who had hit his mark. After a short pause, he stood upright, spun the daggers in his hands, then slid them into the holster.

I looked at Jax. "And I thought Samson was the one with the mad skills."

Ignoring my comment, he ripped off the bottom half of his shirt, fastened the gray fabric around my broken ribs, and pulled it tight.

Warmth stung my eyes. "Damn it, Jax. That hurts."

"Sorry. It will help ease the pain when you inhale." He found my eyes. "Let me know if you feel winded. Broken ribs can puncture the lungs."

I adjusted the makeshift bandage, my teeth sinking into my busted lip. "Great. I'll try not to die before I see Zenith."

"Good girl." He winked and gave my forehead a quick kiss. "Let's go. Your brother and Idalia just caught up with Samson and Castor."

Each step hurt like hell, but I trudged on.

Cyrus acknowledged us with a curt head nod, then hissed at Idalia. She tried dabbing the blood that dripped from his split eyebrow. He motioned for her to stop.

"It's getting quiet," I said, grazing the broken bones in my face.

Castor nodded. "That's what happens after people die."

I waved a hand through the air. "Yeah, but *our* people are dying." My voice quivered with grief. "They're *all* dying."

"Both sides have suffered a great loss," Jax said. "Look around you, there are more bodies on the ground than those left standing."

The Solins in our small group scanned the clearing. Their lips moved, counting the pairs of men and women who fought for their lives.

"Seventy-seven?" Idalia suggested.

Jax hurled a knife at a Collector who tried sneaking up on us. The sudden impact of the blade sent the man toppling over.

"Seventy-six," Jax corrected, dusting off his hands.

My brows raised, squeezing more blood from my injuries. "That's it?" I stumbled over my words. "Zenith had over three hundred men. We had one hundred and twenty."

"This is war, Elara. People die."

I clutched my chest; each breath was more painful than the last. "This isn't war!" I cried, my eyes narrowing at Jax. "It's a *fucking* massacre."

"Easy, sis. We need to stay focused."

"He's right," Idalia said. "Don't focus on the dead. Focus on what you must do to secure Aroonyx's future."

Jax nodded at his friend's wisdom, then pointed at Samson's wounded leg and shoulder. "You good?"

The ex-Collector swatted the blood saturating his upper thigh. "Just a scratch." He rolled his neck, indifferent to his injured back. "We must get the twins to Zenith."

My partner rose to his full height and locked eyes with Castor. "The three of us will form a tight line. Push through their defenses, act as a shield to protect Elara and Cyrus."

My brother scoffed. "Shield, my ass. We fight together or we don't fight at all."

Samson shot my brother a stern look. "No. We can't screw this up. We'll cut through the stragglers." He shot a quick glance at his daughter. "Idalia will watch your backs. You and your sister must stay alive—at all costs."

Defeated, my brother stared at the love of his life.

She stood on the tips of her toes, and whispered, "I love you," near his ear before kissing his cheek.

He shut his eyes as she moved behind him, preparing for the final round of battle.

Fear held my boots in place. I grabbed my brother's wrist. "I can't do this."

"Yes you can."

I shook my head, panic consuming me.

"Elara, you must." He grabbed me by the shoulders. "Look at me."

I refused.

"Look me in the eyes," he demanded.

I lifted my chin.

"I wasn't honest with you earlier." He struggled to say the words that formed on his tongue. "It's time I come clean."

A vice grip clamped around my heart.

"Everything is going to be okay, sis. *You* are going to be okay."

My lip quivered. *You,* not we. He had altered the first word of the second sentence. Before I could question my brother, he turned me to face our mentor.

"We stop at nothing to get them to Zenith," Samson said to Castor and Jax.

The men inhaled a shared breath, their pale fingers gripping their knives.

No. I wanted more time with my brother. I needed to ask why he removed himself from our life's puzzle. I never got the chance because he pulled me forward once the ex-Collectors dashed toward the Inner Circle.

As promised, the three men sliced through the fading crowd. They moved as one. A snake with three heads. Each strike was more deadly than the last. The fierce determination they displayed that day lightened the heavy burden I carried on my shoulders.

"There they are," Cyrus panted, pointing ahead.

Idalia took one look at Pollux and slowed her pace. I didn't blame her—no one did. My friend was the strongest woman I had ever met, but even steel can bend under pressure.

"Find Roshan and the others," I said to her over my shoulder. "We need backup."

She nodded and sprinted in the opposite direction.

Samson watched her go before finding my eyes. "We'll handle the Inner Circle." He motioned to the citizens cowering behind their leader. "Lift the veil, Elara. Show them the monster hiding behind Zenith's facade."

I tried lengthening my spine, but my broken ribs foiled my

efforts. Instead, I gave a thumbs-up to my fearless mentor. A *fucking* thumbs-up.

"Cyrus," Jax said. "Leave Pollux to me." A demand not a suggestion.

My brother nodded, his eyes never leaving the sadistic Lunin. I shuddered a breath. The thought of another bloody brawl between the two men left me lightheaded.

"*Elara*," Pollux called, his eyes roving over me. "Are you going to stand there all day?" He licked his lips. "I hate it when a woman keeps me waiting."

54

DEATH'S CRUEL HANDS

The late afternoon sun mocked us with its hope-filled rays, and the phantom wolf howled, its invisible tongue licking our faces with each icy gust. I observed the citizens standing on the sidelines, their eyes bouncing between us and the Inner Circle.

The battle cries in the clearing dimmed to painful murmurs. *Did Idalia find Roshan and Aries? What about Thea and Oriana? Are they alive?*

Zenith silenced my unspoken questions by flashing me a victorious grin. I shivered, recalling my vivid dream. Pollux's scarred lip curled into a snarl as Jax took his place beside me, and his menacing expression grew at the sight of his father reaching for another Origin blade. Samson moved to my brother's left. A trail of blood followed. I eyed my mentor. His injury was more than just a scratch, but he refused to let the pain show.

Zenith met my gaze, his long fingers playing with the handle of his knife. Without breaking eye contact, his lips moved with words we couldn't hear. Pollux and Apollo nodded, then stepped aside to let their leader pass. The Inner Circle tightened their formation, their eyes fixed on our armed hands. Oberon stood tall. One wrong move, one misstep on our part, would send his blade flying.

The crowd stilled watching their leader narrow the gap between us. Not an ounce of fear flickered in his blue and orange eyes. His boots paused, only feet away from where we stood. He widened his stance and his wicked grin grew as he rotated the blade of his knife, sunlight reflecting off the silver etchings.

"Nine years," he said, without lifting his gaze. His voice was smoother than the silk that had hid the dealer's face. "I have waited nine, very long years for this day."

"That makes two of us," Jax countered.

I blinked. *Are my ears playing tricks?*

Their diction was a perfect match. The night we rescued Idalia, Zenith uttered one word and nothing more. It wasn't enough to catch the striking similarity between him and Jax's voice. Living with his adoptive father had affected my partner in more ways than one. The way he conducted himself in front of a crowd, his rigid posture, his cool and calm demeanor, his method of communication. These were the side effects of living with a man who wanted to mold his protégé into an altered version of himself.

Zenith inhaled through his nose and lifted his eyes. "Hello, my son. It warms my heart to see you . . . *well.*"

Jax mirrored his posture and drawled, "*Father.*"

A hush fell over the crowd. The Inner Circle and the men beside me tensed. Jax was playing a game with the leader of Aroonyx. A *very* dangerous game.

"I've missed your company."

My partner shook his head in disgust. "If only I could say the same about you."

Zenith lifted his chin, a challenge glimmering in his eyes. "Is this how you repay me?" He waved his knife at our fallen recruits. "You manipulate my citizens and convince them to overthrow the man who raised you as his own?" He blew out an exaggerated breath. "I'm disappointed, Jax. I rescued you from a home of betrayal."

"No. You kidnapped me and murdered my parents."

Mouths gaped. It appeared the citizens were unaware of Jax's early childhood.

Zenith sighed. Pollux smirked as if he could hear the words forming on his leader's tongue.

"My poor naïve child." His eyes locked onto Jax. "That's not how the story goes. Aelius paid me a visit and confessed he harbored a Seeker in his home. For a handsome fee, your 'father' surrendered his claim as your guardian."

I grabbed my partner's wrist, steadying his swaying body. The news nearly knocked him off his feet.

"He informed your mother the day the Collectors removed you from your home." Zenith twisted the emotional knife deeper by pointing to the eldest member of the Inner Circle. "Apollo was there. He heard your father say, *Kyra, it's for the best. The boy will bring shame to our family.*"

"Lies," Jax spat. "You murdered my parents."

"Because they trespassed on my property." He stole a glance at Apollo and Oberon. "If you require verification, ask your old comrades. They assisted with the executions."

Jax staggered backward. I tightened my grip.

"Kyra wanted to return the rehoming fee I paid your father."

Rehoming fee? My stomach twisted into a sickening knot. Zenith spoke of the transaction as if Jax were a dog he had adopted from a shelter.

"She begged for your release," he added. "Deals, *especially* those signed in blood, can't be breached. I planned on turning her away, but your father arrived, unannounced, and demanded I rip up our agreement." He snickered. "My citizens don't make demands. I refused and your parents attacked." He gave a casual shrug. "My men are trained to protect their leader."

Cyrus swore under his breath. I stood motionless, stunned by the turn of events. Zenith had outsmarted us all. He kept this information hidden from Jax for a reason. An emotional blow would leave him vulnerable. This was the ace he hid up his sleeve.

"Don't let him get under your skin," I whispered to my partner. "He—"

Zenith cut me off by raising his hand. "My loyal citizens." The crowd stirred, all eyes on their leader. "Allow me to further explain why I gathered you here today." He flicked his wrist at Jax. "My son. He's the reason we're here."

Men stretched their necks to get a better view. Women held their children closer.

"I raised Jax in a loving home," Zenith added. "Gave him a life others could only dream of living."

I gritted my teeth. *Liar.*

"And nine years ago, he returned my generosity by disobeying my orders. He failed a mission, failed it on purpose, to punish me." He observed the innocent bystanders. "To punish *us.*"

An evil smirk twitched at the corner of Apollo's and Oberon's mouths. Pollux chuckled at Zenith's twisted truths. A lifetime of frustrations scooted my partner's boots forward. His spine straightened, chin lifted, and eyes narrowed on his adoptive father.

Unfazed by the silent threat, Zenith glowered at me and Cyrus while he spoke to the people. "I knew the twins would bring danger to Aroonyx. I could feel it in the depths of my soul. That's why I sent Jax to remove them from the equation. The thought of killing two newborn babies caused me terrible heartache." He gestured to the corpses spread around the clearing. "But as you can see, ending their lives would have saved hundreds. I based my decision on the love I have for each and every one of you."

My jaw cracked open at the absurdity that left his mouth.

The citizens nodded. They agreed with the lies he fed them on a silver spoon. *No wonder he's ruled Aroonyx for over sixteen years. Samson and Jax were right. He's brainwashed them all.*

I fisted my hand as Zenith continued his charade.

"Do you not live in peace?" The question wasn't open for discussion. "I passed the new ordinance to protect you from outside threats." Another flick of his wrist at me and my brother. "Threats that jeopardize your safety. Arun made the foolish mistake of taking advice from others. Be grateful your leader listens to one voice." He tapped his temple. "The voice of reason."

"The guy's a *fucking* lunatic," Cyrus whispered.

My head bobbed in slow motion, baffled by the insanity that rang in my ears.

Hypnotized by the wolf in sheep's clothing, the people glared and sneered at our group. A low growl rumbled in Samson's chest. Castor spat onto the snow.

Zenith eyed his deceased Collectors who lay sprawled around the clearing. "Jax is responsible for these deaths," he said. "He disobeyed my orders and kept the twins alive by hiding them on Earth." He looked at the crowd. "My *son* betrayed me. He waited for the twins to come of age. He waited to bring them to Aroonyx so he could start an uprising right under my nose. These traitors want to destroy our world. Those twins want to destroy *us*."

The wind whipped through the clearing. No one shivered or adjusted their coat. Hell, I didn't have a collar to shield me against the icy blast. I just stood there—trapped in the verbal battle.

"As your leader, it's my job to protect you," Zenith said.

"Treason is a crime punishable by death. Unlike my son, I will complete the mission and execute the guilty party."

Silence. Even my ragged breathing paused. Zenith made his move. He verbalized his intention to end our lives.

Pollux's lips slid over his teeth. Victory was within reach. The men beside me inhaled a long breath of the afternoon air. A moment later, four white clouds left their mouths.

"Let this be a warning," Zenith said to his loyal followers. "Those who challenge my authority don't live to tell the tale."

Trepidation and uncertainty clouded the Solins' and Lunins' eyes. Throats bobbed at the severe threat. Their brows furrowed at the Inner Circle, then raised once they looked at us. *Are the twins the lesser of the two evils? Is this the question they asked themselves?*

The sun cast a mysterious glow around Zenith, illuminating the truth. My head tilted at the sudden awareness that grabbed hold of me. I finally understood the big picture, the reason the people followed their leader with blind eyes. They didn't know any better. They believed the lies; they believed the madness. It had to end. *I* had to end it.

I took a step forward. "Enough." My voice sounded stronger than expected. "The only traitor here is *you*." Zenith's jaw clenched as I pointed at his chest. "You hide behind fabricated words. Lies you shove down the citizens' throats."

Cyrus and Castor muttered, "Oh, shit."

Samson snickered. Jax's lips didn't budge.

Stunned that I found the courage to speak, Zenith blinked once—twice. Jericho's and Ishan's jaws hung open while Apollo and Oberon sneered. Pollux waved goodbye, dragging the smooth side of his blade across his neck.

My arm raised at the same time Zenith's mouth moved. The crowd gasped at my dangerous gesture. I refused to let him interrupt.

"This isn't the leader you deserve," I said to the men and

women. "The pages of Earth's history are filled with delusional dictators. They annihilated millions of innocent lives for their own selfish reasons. Zenith is no better."

"You see." His voice raised over the howling winds. "This is why I must end their lives. These twins know nothing about Aroonyx. They want to corrupt our world with Earth's skewed view of society. They want—"

"No!" I barked. "I won't let you twist my words."

Zenith snarled. A woman in the crowd held her swaddled infant closer to her breast. The taut features of her face softened once she met my gaze.

I looked into her eyes, and said, "We wish you no harm. We are the light that stands against the darkness."

"Deceit laces her words," Zenith spat.

"Elara don't push him," Jax pleaded, wrapping his fingers around my wrist.

"I don't care." I jerked my arm free. "The people need to hear the truth."

He cursed, warming the muscles in his throwing arm.

"I'd advise you to hold your tongue," Zenith said to me.

Ignoring his threat, I pressed on. "Let me explain the reason Zenith sent Jax to murder me and my brother. He never saw us as a threat to Aroonyx. He saw us as a threat to himself. We were born during the bi-lunar eclipse. The rare event made him paranoid. He feared our powers would overshadow his." I pointed my knife at Zenith. "His decision to remove us from the equation wasn't based on the love he had for his people. It was based on fear, desperation. He wanted to protect himself, not you. That's why Jax rescued us. He knew the truth. His Seeker's intuition guided him to do the right thing. He—"

"Silence!" Zenith's voice bellowed around us.

Cyrus grabbed my hand. His power shot through me. The handle of my white knife vibrated and warmed in my palm. The smug grin on Pollux's scarred face vanished. The time for verbal jabs and snide remarks had ended. This was war, and I had woken a sleeping giant.

If the loathing in Zenith's eyes had hands, they would have reached out and snapped my neck in two. A strand of his perfectly placed hair fluttered in the breeze, and with zero emotion or inflection in his voice, he said, "This ends now."

"Yes, it does," Jax responded. "Your reign ends today."

Zenith shook his head. "You're outnumbered."

"No, you are." Jax flashed his adoptive father a grin that oozed confidence. "There is only one of you"—he jerked his chin at me and Cyrus—"and two of them."

Zenith's body quivered with a hidden rage that boiled to the surface. Pollux stepped beside his leader, their arms touching.

"Bring me his head," Zenith ordered.

Pollux's amused expression resurfaced. "Yes, sir." He held his hands behind his back, moved closer to his leader, and asked, "What about Samson and Castor? The twins?"

"Kill them. Kill them all."

Eyes widened with fear. Mothers shielded the faces of their children while men exchanged curious glances. I scoffed. They had come for a show, and now they cowered, afraid to watch the finale.

Pollux gave the signal that unleased the Inner Cirlce, Hell's blood-lusting hounds.

"Together," Cyrus whispered to me. "We end this *together*."

I nodded, ready to accept our fate. "Don't let go of my hand."

"Never."

The sight of Ishan charging Samson dropped my heart into the pit of my stomach. It drowned in the murky depths of the unknown when Pollux lunged at Jax.

My head snapped toward Oberon. The Lunin slid his boots through the snow, gaining speed with each quiet step. I swore as he raised his armed hand. We didn't have a shield to block the attack.

A different blade whistled past me and my brother. Oberon dodged the projectile, and before I could exhale, he hurled his own knife at the man standing behind us. The gut-wrenching sound of gurgling blood followed a loud thud. I whipped around to find Oberon's blade wedged in Roshan's trachea.

No. I dashed toward our dying friend.

Cyrus hollered my name, his strong hand holding me in place. "Don't. We must stay together."

I met Idalia's tear-filled gaze. "I'm sorry," she mouthed, closing Roshan's lifeless eyes. "I'm so sorry."

My lip quivered. She had returned as promised. A handful of our recruits went blade to blade with the remaining Collectors.

My brother spun me around to face the man who had murdered our friend. Oberon reached for another knife. Cyrus altered our earlier routine and lunged, pushing me ahead of him. I reached for the Lunin. The ligaments in my arms stretched, the muscles in my side ripped, splintering my broken ribs.

I gasped for air. Only shallow breaths entered my lungs. Without a second to lose, I released every drop of heat onto Oberon's face. He toppled over, hollering in pain. I didn't stop until the hairs on his head smoked and the cartilage in his nose turned to ash. His body convulsed with shock before collapsing onto the ground. Convinced that Death had collected its next victim, I lifted my hand and showed Zenith the melted skin dripping off my palm.

The color drained from his face. He had yet to see our trick with his own eyes.

I lifted a brow, challenging the half Solin, half Lunin. "You wanted a show." I flung the rubbery flesh at him. "How's that for an opening act?"

Zenith barred his teeth. He turned to Apollo. "Kill the girl first. Make her brother watch."

"Yes, sir." He cracked his neck. "It would be my pleasure."

"Get ready," Cyrus whispered, sending a burst of heat through me. "This is it."

I struggled to breathe while searching for my partner. I couldn't take the final steps without seeing his face. He wrestled with Pollux in the snow, their fists flying with bone-breaking punches. *Where are their knives?* I scanned the blood-stained area. *There.* Jax's blade lay feet away from their rolling bodies—but where was Pollux's weapon?

Apollo strolled toward us without a care in the world. A malicious grin crossed his unshaven face as he showed us his palms and wiggled his fingers. He didn't need a knife to end our lives. He planned on using his brutal strength.

With two daggers plunged in his lower back, Ishan dragged himself through the snow. Blood dripped from his parted lips. He reached for his leader's hand. Zenith scowled and stepped over the dying man as if he were a fallen tree limb.

A blur of color snagged my attention. Samson and Castor circled Jericho, taunting him with cruel threats. I blinked. *Pollux, Apollo, and Jericho are the only ones left.*

I wheezed, gripping my side.

"Sis." A deep concern saturated Cyrus's words. "Are you okay?"

"Yeah. I'm good." It was a lie worth telling. "Let's finish this."

We took a step closer to Apollo. He splayed his arms, encouraging us to attack.

Jax shouted my name. The amount of desperation in his voice caused our heads to turn—including Zenith's.

Cyrus dropped my hand. Jax slid through the snow, his eyes wild with panic. He reached for the knife Pollux aimed at my heart. But he was too late. The blade soared threw the air. Only it wasn't Pollux's hybrid blade that spun toward me. It was

Zenith's. The image of them standing side-by-side with their arms touching and Pollux holding his hands behind his back flashed before my mind's eye. *They switched knives without us knowing.*

Without warning, Death's cruel hands reached out and altered our destiny. My body slammed onto the ground, for my brother . . . my fearless twin had pushed me out of harm's way. The hands of time slowed as Cyrus fell to his knees, and life's clock stopped ticking when he touched the pure Fired Stone blade wedged in his heart.

Moving faster than one could blink, Jax grabbed his gray knife and plunged it into the side of Pollux's neck. He twisted it hard. The Lunin choked on the blood pooling in his throat. His pale fingers reached for the handle but Jax slid the blade forward, nearly severing his arch rival's head. Only in death could Pollux hold my gaze. His lifeless eyes looked the same. The light didn't dim after he inhaled his final breath. How could it? It was never there to begin with.

On trembling hands and knees, I crawled to my brother's side, Idalia's blood-curling screams ringing in my ears. Someone restrained the distraught Solin, but she continued to shout Cyrus's name.

The fighting ceased. The citizens of Aroonyx stilled. Zenith stretched his neck around Apollo to get a better look. He smiled at the embedded blade.

The whites of my brother's eyes turned red as he stared at the cloudless sky.

I found his hand that searched for mine. "I'm here." My voice cracked. "I'm right here." I reached for the handle of the knife.

"No!" Jax lunged and grabbed my arm. "Don't pull it out. He's running out of time."

I burst into tears, patting the blood-soaked area around the injury. "No. He can't leave me."

My partner bowed his head. This mournful posture sent me over the edge. *No.* Tears streamed down my face. *This isn't how the story ends.*

Cyrus struggled to breathe. With each inhale the muscles in his chest contracted around the blade. I fought with my own injury. My lungs felt more useless by the second, the slivers of bone went deeper with each violent sob. But none of that mattered. My other half, my best friend was *dying.*

I cupped my hands around his face and stared into his amber eyes. "Everything is going to be okay, remember? *We*—" My throat bobbed as I recalled how he altered the simple word.

Cyrus turned his head to face Jax, and through half breaths, he said, "Take care of my sister."

My partner squeezed his hand until his knuckles turned white. "Now and always."

"No." I rotated his head back to face me. "You can't leave me. I won't let you." More sobs shook my shoulders. "I can't do this without you."

Blood trickled out of Cyrus's mouth. He winced, lifting a hand to brush away my tears. The moisture slid down his fingers.

"You will." He pressed his palm against my cheek. "Ask Jax, he knows the truth."

My eyes narrowed at my partner. He swallowed hard, bowing his head once more.

"The night he rescued us." Cyrus coughed, choking on his blood. "The night he had that intense feeling. It had nothing to do with me. It had everything to do with you." He rested a hand over my heart. "This is your journey, sis. It always has been. *You* are the only one who has the power to defeat Zenith."

I rested my forehead on Cyrus's chest, my vision blurring with grief. A montage of vibrant memories played in my mind: my brother describing his strange dream, Jax and Samson mentioning a change in the air, the reason my partner never questioned why I absorbed Cyrus's power. I shut my eyes. And the words my mother wanted me to share with her son. My heart shattered. It wasn't a dream. It was another vision.

Our mother knew what Jax had known all along. My brother's path ended before my own.

The heartbreaking reality draped over me like a weighted blanket. "Cyrus, please," I begged. "You can't leave me. Not like this."

In a soft murmur, he asked the universe for more time.

"*Please*," I cried, wiping the blood off his chin.

He grabbed my hand. "Can you do something for me, sis?"

I nodded.

"Once Jax takes you back to Earth, find my father and tell him I love him." His eyes welled with tears. "Tell him I forgive him."

"I will." The words caught in my throat. "I promise."

Blood seeped from the wound as Cyrus fought for his last breath. I used my free hand to stroke the side of his face.

"I spoke to our mother," I whispered.

He blinked, trying to stay conscious.

I bit my lip. I had to stay strong. I had to give him the message. "She wanted me to tell you something."

He squeezed my hand, clinging to the final moments of life.

I pressed my cheek against his and spoke near his ear. "Your courageous act won't go overlooked."

I sat up, sensing a tangible peace move through Cyrus. The flecks of gold in his eyes ignited with an enteral flame that would burn long after his physical death.

Four simple words left his parted lips. "I love you, sis." Four words I'd remember forever.

The warmth inside me faded faster than the setting sun, for the hero of the story had taken his final breath.

55

A VISITOR FROM THE PAST

And just like that—my brother was gone.

I wrapped my arms around him and let the tears flow. Every sob pushed my broken ribs deeper into my punctured lung, and every faint breath I inhaled lacked the required oxygen I needed to stay alive.

I looked at Jax. He looked at the shirt tied around my hidden injury, the grayish hue of my grief-stricken face, and my labored breathing. A deep red shaded the whites of his eyes. I didn't need to verbalize the obvious.

"No." His voice quivered. "It's not your time."

Zenith tossed his head back to the evening sky and roared with laughter. He had won, and everyone acknowledged his victory. The sounds of battle faded. The anxious citizens stilled. Even the phantom wolf retreated, leaving an eerie stillness behind.

"Elara," Jax pleaded. "You must stay with me."

His features blurred. I fluttered my lashes and shifted my gaze to Cyrus. He looked peaceful with his eyes closed, as if he was far away in dreamland. *I'll see you soon, bro.*

Death's icy fingers tapped on my shoulder; black spots exploded around me.

My partner reached for my hand. "Elara, please. Don't leave me."

Zenith raised his voice to address the crowd. "This girl is"— he paused—"*was* weak. Her brother died, so she lost the will to live. Is this the leader you wanted? One who lacked power? One who lacked courage? *I* am the true—"

I stopped listening because his words faded. *Tired. God, I'm so tired.*

I closed my eyes and rested my forehead on my brother's chest. "Together," I whispered. "Until the very end."

The darkness slammed into me, but the bone-chilling cold that followed consumed me entirely. I surrendered to the negative emotions that surfaced: guilt, apathy, grief, fear, desire, anger, pride. They swirled in an endless circle of suffering stemmed from my own misgivings.

The truth. Accept the truth, Elara.

I welcomed the afterlife with open arms, but it pushed me away, sending me tumbling into the void. The judgments I harbored for those around me zipped through my consciousness. As if seeing through another's eyes, the truth shone forth: The Inner Circle and the Collectors lacked understanding. That's why they acted with their heads and not their hearts. Zenith was nothing more than a troubled man who lacked compassion and forgiveness. And the citizens followed him out of blind innocence.

An excruciating pain, an invisible pickaxe, chipped at the layers of falsehood, revealing the truth, one grueling hit at a time. My body writhed from the physical anomaly. I clutched my brother's chest, my nails digging into his cold flesh. Jax swore and slid his hands over my back, unsure how to help. More laughter rumbled in Zenith's chest.

Elara. The gentle voice hummed around my heart. *Stop*

resisting the pain.

I gritted my teeth. *How? I can't breathe. It feels like my bones are breaking.*

Remember Jax's lesson. Let it be there.

I focused on my throbbing face, the broken bones, my shattered ribs, and the hole in my lung. The discomfort pulsed from one injury to the next. There was no beginning and no end.

Let it be there.

"I'm trying," I cried, bearing through the pain.

The voice inside my heart split in two. *I'm here, sis.*

Life's clock started ticking, and it didn't stop. My brother was with me.

Surrender to the pain, sis. Surrender to it all.

And so I did.

I let go of everything: the pain, the emotional suffering, the expectations, the fear of the unknown, the regrets. But more importantly, I let go of the bullshit. And when I did, something magical happened.

The warmth that left my body after Cyrus's death resurfaced and surged through me with enough force to knock me on my ass. My jaw clenched. With each beat of my pounding heart, the heat grew, *healing* my injuries. The hidden flames cauterized the gap in my lungs, fused my broken bones, and sealed the gaping wounds on my lips, cheeks, and brows.

I kept my face buried in Cyrus's chest. The heat danced across my skin. Goosebumps trailed behind. The internal flames crawled up my spine, concentrating in my head. My nose crinkled at the strange sensation. As if someone had combed my hair with a brush made of hot needles, the nerves in my scalp sparked. The warmth slid down my forehead and brows. I pawed at the tingling behind my eyes, and when I opened them, the tiny fibers on my brother's shirt were crystal clear, magnified.

I lifted my head. Jax stumbled backward, his eyes bulging with disbelief. The crowd gasped and shuffled closer.

"Impossible." Zenith shuddered a breath.

I turned. Samson and Castor stood with their mouths hanging open, arms dangling by their sides. Jericho shrugged at Apollo. The eldest Solin just shook his head.

"Elara," Jax stammered.

I spun around. He pointed at my face.

"What's wrong?" I asked.

"You're alive." He blinked. "And you're—"

"I'm what?"

A four-letter curse word shot out of Jax's mouth as he scooted farther away from me.

A man in the crowd nudged a woman beside him. "Look at her hair!"

Out of my peripheral vision, I noticed the strands floating around my face. I gulped. They moved like my mother's in the dream.

"Jax?" My eyes grew once I noticed it change color. "What the hell is going on?"

He couldn't speak. He just kept pointing at my head.

Another innocent bystander said, "How did it change color?"

I snatched a floating strand to get a better look. *Holy shit.*

My hair was no longer black. It matched my brother's blond locks. Baffled by the new change, I glanced at my hands. They were still pale. I patted my half Lunin, half Solin body, examining the healed injuries.

"Elara, I'm—"

"Is it night?" I interrupted Jax, rubbing my eyes.

He nodded.

I scanned the citizens of Aroonyx. A cool glow illuminated their pale and tan bodies. I still had my Lunin vision, but I could make out every detail. I could see each freckle, birthmark, and scar on their shocked faces. I noticed the fine stitching on their clothes, the tiny scuffs on their boots. I looked beyond the clearing. My powerful Solin vision allowed me to see the veins in the emerald leaves and the grooves in the smooth bark of the trees. I blinked and blinked again. They were over a mile away.

Jax snapped his fingers to get my attention. "Elara, your eyes. They look like his." He jerked his thumb at his adoptive father. "One's blue and one's orange."

"What?" I pressed them with the heels of my palms.

He swore again once I dropped my hands. "And they're glowing. Your *eyes* are glowing."

Zenith breathed hard. "No." He repeated the word.

I leaned over my brother, held Jax's hand, and released a drop of heat. He hissed. From my perspective, it felt like a small amount, but the fiery river that coursed through my veins left his palm beet red. He raised it for everyone to see. Murmurs rippled through the crowd and boots shifted closer.

"Well, I'll be damned," Samson said, loud enough for Zenith to hear. "It all makes sense."

I eyed Jax for clarification.

He touched my brother's arm. "Cyrus gave you a gift before he left." A large grin swept across his face. "He passed his powers to you."

"No!" Zenith shouted.

Samson and Castor lunged for the knife, but it had already left Zenith's hand. Thump. The blade pierced my abdomen. Thump. Another one entered my side. I sank deeper into the snow, blood dripping from my mouth.

The crowd turned into an angry mob. They pumped their fists and hollered their complaints, appalled by their leader's unwarranted attack.

Jax crawled toward me. I stared at the embedded blades. Though evidence of injury seeped from the wounds, I felt no discomfort. I held up my hand, halting my partner's pursuit. Grief with a hint of confusion consumed him as his eyes darted from one knife to the next. The invisible flames gathered around the new wounds. With a steady hand I removed one blade, then the other. The internal bleeding healed; the sliced skin melted together. Not a visible scar remained.

We exchanged a knowing look, and at that moment, the two of us assembled a crucial piece of my life's puzzle. Cyrus had passed me his powers and so much more.

I opened the floodgates. The knives in my hands vibrated with heat. Traces of Fired Stone in the hybrid blades glowed and pulsated. Red and orange lightning bolts flickered and flashed along the smooth surface.

I pointed both knives at Zenith. Fear, and lots of it, clouded his eyes. Without using my hands, I stood. My legs were stronger now. My Solin strength had transformed my lean muscles into toned, more shapely cuts of living steel. The snow melted underneath my feet. I shifted my weight and rose to my full height. The white-blonde hairs on my head hovered around my face. A mirage of heat rippled out of my body, a weapon to wield at my command, a shield to protect those in need.

Zenith snarled and hurled a knife at Jax. I shifted the mirage toward my partner. The drastic change in temperature nearly knocked him off his feet. He flinched as the blade bounced off the invisible barrier. Sounds of awe and wonder moved through the crowd. Jax no longer stood on a blanket of snow. He stood on the emerald green grass.

Zenith seethed with rage. The muscles in his face twitched. He gritted his teeth and reached for another knife. No luck. He was out.

"Apollo!" he called. "Give me your blade."

I smiled at the desperation in his voice. Jax tilted his head as if seeing me for the first time. Absorbing Cyrus's powers had transformed me into a lethal weapon forged by fire and ice. My Solin and Lunin traits didn't fight for the spotlight. They worked together. The heat ignited unwavering courage while the chill calmed my rising temper. I had the physical strength and mental clarity to complete the mission.

I inhaled a long breath of the evening air, shut my eyes, and verbalized my intention to the universe. "I'm ready for my new role in life. I'm ready to free the people of Aroonyx."

The universe responded by cloaking me in total darkness. My body recoiled as if falling into a deep sleep. I gasped. *No way.* My eyes shot open. *It can't be.*

I spun in circles, my boots slipping on the dry mulch. The elongated limbs of the pine trees rustled in the gentle breeze. I stopped mid-rotation. An owl rotated its head 180 degrees, its claws gripping the rough bark. Brown, not black. I covered my ears as it let out an ear-piercing shriek. Nature sounded louder than I remembered. The majestic bird swooped down and snagged an unexpected mouse. Crickets chirped, frogs croaked, and a family of opossums scurried through the dense brush.

I braced my palms on my thighs and slowed my heavy breathing. I was back on Earth, standing in the exact spot where I held hands with my brother and Jax before we jumped to Aroonyx.

"It's been a long time since I've seen another Seeker."

My hair fell out of my face as I lifted my head. An elderly man stood before me. Tall and well-built for his age, his broad shoulders raised with a relaxed inhale. The wrinkles on his tan face deepened while his pumpkin-colored eyes examined my features.

"You're different from the others."

Still dazed that I was standing on the trail, I stammered, "I'm sorry. What did you just say?"

"The combination of your hair color and skin tone." He frowned. "You're not like the other Solins and Lunins."

I eyed a blonde strand hovering near my temple. *Stop doing that. Just act normal.*

The piece obeyed my silent command and fell onto my shoulders.

I cleared my throat. "It's a recent change."

The old man steepled his fingers under his chin. "A lot has changed over the years."

"I'm not trying to sound rude," I said, shooing a mosquito that flew into my face. "But who in the hell are you?"

"Forgive me. It seems I've forgotten my manners. Allow me to introduce myself." He offered me his hand. "I'm Saros."

My jaw almost unhinged from my skull. *Saros?* He said his name like a passing thought. But he was no passing thought. He was Saros, the first Seeker, Arun's most trusted advisor, the man sent to Earth to search for weapons, the man Taurus blamed for destroying his relationship with Arun. Saros was the reason Taurus adopted Zenith, the reason he tortured him, the reason Zenith grew into a murdering lunatic, the reason he destroyed the lives of my loved ones.

My eyelids moved in slow motion. I was staring at the catalyst who ignited years of bloodshed. The heat pulsed through my veins. The mulch smoked under my boots. Saros stole a glance at the strange phenomena, his brow furrowing.

I pointed my finger at his chest. "You better start talking."

Sis.

I lowered my arm.

Are you forgetting Orion's lesson?

I blew out a tight breath in response to my brother's voice.

Blame is an endless circle. Don't get trapped in the past.

Saros twisted the cufflink on his navy-blue collared shirt. "It appears you have some resentment toward me."

"Yes, and I don't like the taste, so can you clear the air and answer a few questions?"

"Of course."

"How are you standing here?"

"My legs are stronger than they look."

I lifted my eyes and only my eyes. "I'm not in the mood for jokes. How are you standing on this trail, right here, right now?"

"That's an interesting question. One I'm still trying to answer." He slid his hands into the pockets of his black slacks. "Tonight, I was sitting in my loft, enjoying a macchiato with a good book. *Power vs. Force.* Have you heard of it?"

I shook my head.

He shrugged and rocked on the balls of his feet. "Suddenly, this familiar feeling, this awareness grabbed hold of me. I closed my book, walked to the window and observed the city skyline. I thought of my birthplace, and suddenly, I found myself standing here." His head turned as he observed the surrounding pine trees. "But this isn't Aroonyx and its not Central Park, so I'm guessing I'm no longer in Manhattan."

"No. You're in Houston, Texas."

"Ah. That would explain the humidity."

"Wait." I waved my hands in front of my body. "You can jump between different places on Earth?"

"I never tried until tonight. I guess I can."

"How long have you been standing here?"

"Not long. I heard the sound signaling your arrival."

The loud pop that sounds like a gunshot? The sound I heard each time Jax appeared out of thin air? The sound only I could hear?

Again, I stumbled over my words. "You can hear it too?"

He chuckled at my wide-eyed expression. "Yes. It's a Seeker trait. The pop alerts other Seekers that one of their own has arrived."

My time on Earth with Jax replayed in my mind. I had inquired about the strange sound, but he disregarded my claim, telling me he heard nothing. I gasped, assembling another piece of my life's puzzle. *Jax has never heard the popping noise because he's never seen another Seeker jump. I could hear it—I can hear it because . . . holy shit.* My eyes grew wider as I accepted the reason I stood on Earth. *I'm a Seeker.*

The trail spun.

Saros held my elbow. "Are you okay?"

"Yeah." I took a few deep breaths. "Just give me a minute."

I shut my eyes. It was too much to process with them opened. The gut feelings, the intense emotions, the battle between my head and my heart, the unspoken connection I shared with Jax. They weren't Lunin traits. They were Seeker traits.

My knees wobbled.

"Easy, child," Saros soothed. "When was the last time you jumped?"

"A while ago. I've never done it on my own."

"I see. So this is a new gift you've discovered."

"Yeah. About five minutes ago." My shoulders sagged with a deep exhale. "Saros, where have you been?"

"Here . . . and there, but mostly here."

Great. He's equally cryptic as Jax. "What is that supposed to mean? Why are you on Earth? Why haven't you returned?"

"It's a long story."

"Then summarize." My tone was sharp. "Horrible things happened after you left. Arun lost his damn mind and slaughtered the Seekers."

"I'm aware."

"How? You've been hiding on Earth."

"No. Never hiding. Just stuck."

I folded my arms across my chest. "Can you elaborate?"

"Arun instructed me to jump to Earth so I could investigate the new tools the other Seeker discovered. I agreed and learned these 'tools,' though efficient in slicing through grazer's hides and assisting with other domestic tasks, could be altered into weapons. I couldn't wrap my mind around the reason Arun wanted to design something that could harm others. Aroonyx was a peaceful place, and so were its people.

"Ignoring the tug pulling at my heart, I continued my research. I learned how Earth's leaders struggled with temptation once they acquired weapons. I learned of the devastation and destruction that follows. Do I share this information with Arun? Do I tell him of the horrors I discovered? Those two questions caused me many sleepless nights."

"So what did you do?" I asked, pushing up the sleeves of my shirt.

"There's a saying, *if you don't know, don't.*"

"Ah, so you stayed on Earth."

A haze of regret clouded his eyes. "Yes, but the days passed, and the guilt gnawed at me. As Arun's advisor, I had a responsibility to keep him informed."

"So you went back to Aroonyx."

"I tried, but I couldn't jump."

"Why?"

He watched me carefully. "You already know the answer."

I hummed my understanding. "Your intention."

"Yes. I never wanted to harm the citizens of Aroonyx, but I obtained information that could. Hurting others is a selfish act."

"Wait. I thought a Seeker could jump if their intention was pure. Are you saying it's based on the collective?"

"We're all connected. The choices we make affect those around us." He smiled. "It's not as personal as you might think, my dear."

"You have an interesting way with words."

He shrugged. "Words are but fragmented sentiments. Tiny impressions with everlasting meanings, strung together to create a singular thought."

My brows tapped my hairline. "And that went right over my head."

He chuckled, patting my arm. "Fear not, my young Seeker. Clarity isn't bound by the limitation of words."

Right. No wonder Arun named him his personal advisor.

The thin hairs on his head danced in the warm breeze, and the crow's feet around his eyes creased as he squinted to see me in the dark. "I'm guessing you have more questions?"

"I do. How old were you when you got stuck on Earth?"

"Twenty-seven."

I calculated the time differential between the two planets. Time on Earth moved twice as fast as on Aroonyx.

"Arun died twenty-seven years ago," I said. "That's fifty-four years on Earth. Twenty-seven plus fifty-four is eighty-one."

His lips spread into a warm grin. "You have a sharp mathematical mind, but you didn't factor the years I lived on Aroonyx after Arun's death."

I tossed up my hands. "I thought you couldn't get back?"

"Not at first. I tried, every single day. And on the ninth sunset of my tenth year, I finally jumped."

"How? Why that day?"

"The intention shifted. Arun had passed. His death released me from my obligation. I no longer had to share my knowledge of weapons, knowledge that could harm others."

"How long did you stay on Aroonyx?"

"Sixteen years."

I rubbed my eyes. "Saros, how did you live there with no one seeing you? You were Arun's most trusted advisor. That's a high-profile position." My pulse quickened when I thought of Zenith's adoptive father. "What about Taurus? Was he still alive?"

His brows etched together. "How do you know about Taurus?"

I swallowed a lump of grief. "A doctor by the name of Iah told me he was jealous of your relationship with Arun."

"How is Iah?"

"Dead." The lump resurfaced. "Zenith's Collectors murdered him."

"I'm sorry. He was a wonderful apprentice. Taurus was a very troubled man, and yes, he was jealous of my friendship with Arun. Everything went south after he visited with Zenith."

"Iah mentioned the impromptu meeting. He said it didn't go well."

"My job was to advise Arun. I sensed a darkness in the child and saw Taurus's intention. He wanted to use Zenith as leverage to repair his broken relationship with Arun. I shared my thoughts. Arun always respected my wisdom, so he turned Taurus and the child away."

"Well, you did the right thing because Zenith became a monster."

"Yes, he did." Saros sighed. "Zenith blamed me for the way Taurus treated him. He blamed me for turning him away. When Taurus died, I knew Zenith had murdered him."

"So that's why you kept a low profile. You knew Zenith would seek revenge."

"Yes, so I observed from a distance. I noticed a drastic change in the people's attitudes. The last few years of Arun's reign combined with the Clearing of the Seekers left them jaded. They shut down, lived quiet lives, kept to themselves." He rubbed the white stubble on his face. "The people spent eleven years without someone looking over their shoulder. That changed once Zenith gained control of Aroonyx."

"I'm not surprised."

"I never trusted the man, but I was curious, so I stuck around to watch—listen. For the first five years of his reign, Zenith acted like a true leader. He fooled the citizens into believing they chose the right man for the job. It wasn't long before he showed his true colors. He passed strict ordinances, re-formed the Collectors, and raised the taxes.

"A part of me felt responsible for Arun's demise. I wanted to make things right. I wanted to help the citizens rid themselves of Zenith, so I got on my knees and expressed my intention. I said, *I'm ready for my new role in life. I'm ready to free the people of Aroonyx.* A second later, I stood on Earth."

"Saros." My eyelashes fluttered faster than the Solin's hair blowing in the breeze. "I said those exact words right before I jumped."

"History has a funny way of repeating itself."

I huffed a breath. "I guess it does."

"I returned to Earth at the age of fifty-three, and I've been stuck here ever since. I've spent twenty-two years searching for a way to bring peace to Aroonyx. That's why I'm not eighty-one," he added, flashing me a tiny smirk. "Fifty-three plus twenty-two is seventy-five."

I dragged a hand through my hair. "Saros, I lived on Earth for eighteen years. Why are we only meeting now?"

"Timing is everything." He rested a hand on my shoulder. "It appears our paths have crossed for a reason. *You* are the peace I've been searching for."

I smiled at the play on words. "And *you* are the missing link that will close the gap between me and the people." I curled my fingers around his wrist and found his eyes. "You can be my voice—my advisor." I tightened my grip. "Our people are in grave danger. Each second we spend on Earth pushes them closer to the brink of death. Zenith threatens to destroy everything innocent and pure. Hundreds of men and women lost their lives today. My twin brother sacrificed himself to save me —to save Aroonyx. And now I must finish the mission. With your help, we can fulfill our obligation to the universe. We can free the people."

"Then what are we waiting for?" Saros stood tall, his Solin courage shining forth. He eyed the hand that held his wrist. "We have a date with destiny. Let's not keep her waiting."

56

THE DEAD & THE DYING

My fingers stayed glued to Saros's wrist, even after our feet touched Aroonyx's soil.

The old man gasped as he took in the sights and sounds. Battle cries, images of the dead and the dying, the frightened citizens huddled together. I worried the chaos might send my new friend into cardiac arrest.

My eyes narrowed at my brother's lifeless body. Someone had removed Zenith's knife from his chest. I looked around the clearing; the hidden flames inside me gathered like a burning tidal wave.

Idalia and Aries fought alongside the remaining members of our group, their blades slicing at the Collectors. Samson and Castor hopped over Jericho's corpse while dodging a swift and brutal attack from Apollo. My eyes drifted to Zenith. The skin around his knuckles thinned as he adjusted his grip on the pure Fired Stone blade. He circled Jax, his boots sliding through the snow.

Saros tugged at my arm. "What should I do?"

"Get behind me," I instructed.

After stepping in front of the Solin, I looked at the crowd, who stared at me with dumbfounded expressions. Apparently, they had never seen a Seeker appear out of thin air.

"Everyone," I called to them. "Get behind me. Now!"

Without delay, they dashed toward us and formed a tight cluster behind Saros. I focused my attention on the mirage of heat that rippled out of me, then flung the invisible shield over Saros and the citizens. They winced as the heat slammed into them. Beads of sweat dotted their brows, an elderly man clutched his chest, and a young child squatted to touch the melting snow.

My hair lifted off my shoulders and floated around my face when I shouted Zenith's name.

Everyone froze. The fighting ceased. Without lowering his armed hand, the leader of Aroonyx turned his head. His tan face paled once he noticed Saros standing behind me.

Jax spun around. "*Elara?*" His tongue tripped over the simple word. He blinked and blinked again. "You're a Seeker?"

"Yeah. Small world, huh?"

He glanced at Samson, who shook Castor's arm with enough force to dislocate his shoulder.

"Saros," he cried, pointing at the mysterious visitor. "Castor, it's Saros."

"No!" Zenith spat. "Saros is dead. That's impossible."

The Seeker moved beside me. Quick to act, I redirected the shield to protect him from the man who wanted us dead.

"I'm alive." Saros raised his voice so everyone could hear. "And thanks to"—he paused, then moved his lips near my ear —"it's Elara, right?"

I nodded. I never told him my name.

He cleared his throat. "And thanks to Elara, I have returned."

"Lies," Zenith said. "This man is a liar."

"The only liar is you," Saros countered. His eyes never left Zenith as he spoke to the citizens. "Many rumors are true. Arun sent me to Earth to learn everything I could about the tool a Seeker had discovered." He pointed at Zenith's knife. "But it wasn't a tool. It was a weapon."

The crowd glared at their leader.

"Having this knowledge kept me trapped on Earth, but I returned after Arun's death."

Zenith's nostrils flared.

"That's right," Saros added. "I lived in hiding for sixteen years, observing, listening. I sensed your ill intentions, and once you gained control, I watched them unfold before my very eyes." He shifted his gaze to the people. "I jumped back to Earth and spent twenty-two years searching for a way to help you free yourself from this man. And today, I found that help." He reached for my hand and held it in the air. "This young woman is the answer."

I squeezed his hand, a small gesture of appreciation. His words sparked a flicker of hope in the citizens.

Zenith's chest rose and fell with quick breaths. His eyes darted from one living soul to the next before stopping on the dead scattered throughout the clearing.

I laughed. I actually laughed, relieved to see the simplicity of it all. Before that moment, I had categorized the surrounding people into two different groups: good versus evil. But in reality, there was only one group—a singular entity. I laughed again. *How did I not see it?*

People make the best decisions they can. For months, I had preached those words to my brother and Jax. For months, I thought I understood the true meaning behind those words. But looking around the clearing that day, observing the confused faces on both parties, decoded this powerful message. Brainwashed or not, the Collectors fought against us because they believed they were doing the right thing. Blinded or not, the people followed Zenith for the same reason.

Forgiveness. I smiled at life's little secret: the key that unlocks the dualistic mind, the reason one sees through eyes of acceptance rather than the eyes of judgment. A wise man once said, *Forgive them, for they know not what they do.* And I would because *that* was the truth.

"You're an old ignorant fool," Zenith hissed at Saros.

"Old I might be, but a fool, I think not." He continued to address the crowd. "Zenith rules with an iron fist forged by cruelty and fear. He lacks the courage of a powerful leader and makes decisions based on his own selfish agenda. This is the reason you stand in a blood-stained field today." He lifted my arm higher. "Elara does not support this man, and neither do I."

Jax's name got caught in Idalia's throat when Zenith grabbed him by the collar of his coat. The heat rolled and gathered inside me as the half Solin, half Lunin pressed the blade of his knife against my partner's throat.

Jax went rigid. He didn't dare challenge the man whose combative skills outmatched us all. One wrong move would deliver him into the Grim Reaper's arms. Samson and Castor exchanged an anxious glance while Zenith's lips curled into a malicious grin. He wiggled the blade. A trail of blood dripped down Jax's neck, staining the gray fabric of his shirt.

Before my brother's death, my palms vibrated with heat. Now, my entire body shook uncontrollably. I needed to release the internal flames. It was hot. Too hot.

"Easy," Saros soothed, eyeing the sweat trickling down my face. "Remember, timing is everything."

Zenith directed his voice at the men and women who stood behind me. "You will prove your allegiance and bend the knee." He grabbed hold of Jax's hair and jerked his chin toward the evening sky. "If you refuse, this man dies, along with every child here today." His voice lowered to a growl. "Do *not* make the grave mistake of challenging my authority."

A head nod at Apollo signaled the assault. The Solin shouted orders at the Collectors.

My shield had deflected Zenith's earlier attack, but it wasn't an impregnable wall. The Collectors walked right through the rippling mirage as if it didn't exist. Women screamed and clawed at the men ripping their children from their arms. Fathers tried to defend their families but collapsed from hard blows by Zenith's trained killers.

Samson cursed, watching mothers beg and plead with the Collectors. Moisture filled Saros's eyes. This wasn't part of the plan.

The Collectors held their knives at the hostages' throats. Sobs, screams, and ear-piercing cries of children echoed around us.

I looked at Jax. "What do I do?"

He shut his eyes. And that's when I remembered the wisdom he shared with me under the bridge. A desperate man will stop at nothing to get their way. Zenith wasn't requesting the citizens' compliance. He demanded it. And if they disobeyed his orders, he'd kill every child on Aroonyx.

He yanked Jax's chin higher and shouted, "Bow!"

The love for their children sent every parent to their knees. A dark shadow hung over Zenith as he repeated the three-letter word. He kept saying it. He refused to stop. Citizens without children bowed. The future of Aroonyx dangled before their eyes. Our remaining recruits looked at me for guidance. They sought approval to bow before the man who had destroyed the lives of those around us.

I touched my chest, searching for the voices inside my heart. *I need help. What am I supposed to do? If I attack, Zenith will kill Jax, then order the Collectors to kill the children. If I bow, he might kill them out of spite.*

A soothing warmth cradled my heart. *Use your gifts, Elara. It will shatter their weapons and lift the veil.*

Literally or figuratively?

A burst of heat sent my hair blowing in every direction. Sweat slid along my spine.

Why don't you find out for yourself, sis?

Okay. Let's do this. I inhaled a sobering breath and stood tall. *You got my back, bro?*

I flinched. An invisible hand rested on my shoulder. *Always, now go kick some ass.*

I shifted my features into neutral and met Jax's gaze. He blew out the smallest of breaths, preparing for the inevitable. I couldn't let him see the card I hid up my sleeve. But Samson caught a glimpse. He must have noticed the flicker of courage burning in my eyes because he winked, giving me the silent approval I needed to take the biggest risk of my life.

Playing his part, Samson plastered a look of defeat on his face and took a knee, then motioned for Castor, Idalia, Aries, and our recruits to join him. Tears welled in Idalia's eyes. She hesitated but followed her father's unspoken orders after I gave her a subtle head nod. Aries's cheeks puffed. He tossed his knife to the ground. The others repeated the submissive gesture. Shoulders sagged and heads lowered as the men and women of Aroonyx bowed for their leader. Even Saros sank to his knees.

Victory didn't soften the features of Zenith's face. Disdain twitched the muscles in his jaw. "And then there was one," he hissed, scowling at my upright position. "Bow, Elara or I slit Jax's throat and give the orders to execute the children."

I didn't budge.

He tilted his head. "Perhaps you want more innocent blood on your hands."

With pleading eyes, Jax mouthed, "Do it."

My partner valued his own life, but he valued the future of Aroonyx more. He knew his adoptive father better than anyone else. He knew if I didn't obey, Zenith would saturate the clearing with children's blood.

More sweat formed on the back of my neck. I let the heat build. Each beat of my pounding heart urged the hidden flames to grow. With a steady leg, I slid the toe of my boot behind me.

Silence followed, save for the squeak of the damp grass I had disturbed. I lowered my head and crossed my arms in an X, holding them over my chest.

"Yes." Zenith laughed. "You will bow before the true leader of Aroonyx."

I lifted my gaze. His elated expression vanished.

"No." I stopped my knee from touching the ground. "I will never bow to a man who receives pleasure from watching others suffer. I will never cower before a man who threatens innocent lives."

Before Zenith could slide the blade across Jax's throat, I splayed my arms and released every drop of heat. A tangible wave shot out of me and rolled through the clearing, engulfing everything in its wake. As if I had detonated a nuclear bomb, an explosion sounded, the ground shuddered, and the snow melted from the thermal radiation. The blast knocked everyone off their feet. The Collectors lost their grips on their captives, the men and women on their knees toppled over, and Zenith flew over fifteen feet with Jax in his arms.

Crack. Crack. Crack. My eyes darted to the hybrid blades that shattered in the Collector's hands. Their jaws hung open as they fumbled with the brittle shards that no longer posed a threat. Mothers crawled toward their children while fathers lunged at the unarmed Collectors. Chaos ensued. Fists flew and bones crunched. The Collectors didn't stand a chance. I learned another valuable lesson that day. The love of a parent is a fierce thing to behold.

Jax and Zenith scrambled to their feet, the latter swearing at the top of his lungs. The blade of his precious knife had turned to ash and blew away in the breeze. Jax stilled as the memories of his past brushed his cheek, staining his face with relief. With wide eyes, he rotated the handle of his gray knife. Samson and Castor blinked, showing Jax their intact weapons. Idalia and Aries reached for theirs. Thea shrugged, snatching her own blade. I smiled at the twin moons engraved on my white knife. The blast had destroyed Zenith's and the Collectors' blades. It left ours untouched.

"Elara." My partner gestured to everyone around him. "How did you do this?"

I ignored him, along with the other curious eyes that watched my every move, and took a step forward, and then another. Noting the confidence and determination in my gait, Jax moved his body in front of Zenith to protect me from his adoptive father's wrath. Apollo, the surviving member of the Inner Circle, rushed to his leader's side.

His advance didn't slow my pace. My boots churned beneath me as I gained speed.

Jax held up his hands, motioning for me to stop.

"Move!" I hollered. "This is between me and Zenith."

Jax tried to argue, but my Solin strength knocked the wind out of him. My palms connected with his chest, sending him soaring through the air, crashing near Samson's feet. My mentor didn't offer him assistance. He just stood there with a huge grin on his face, his eyes glowing with pride.

"Get out of my way," I said to Apollo.

He never got the chance to argue because I summoned my power and blasted him with a wave of heat. The Solin flew farther than Jax. Castor dodged the near-miss, then snickered as he pulled another Origin blade out of his holster.

Zenith didn't hesitate. He lunged, his eyes flickering with vengeance. I faltered, slipping on the slick grass, then spun around and unleashed another wave of heat through the palms of my hands. He stumbled but didn't fall. I hit him again—and again. Each burst slamming into his chest. Though sweat doused his brow and the sudden rise in body temperature reddened his cheeks, the man refused to stand down.

"It's over!" I released more heat. "Your time as ruler . . . is over."

He bared his teeth and spat, "No."

I shut my eyes, wielding the weapon that stirred inside me. "If you don't surrender, I'll force your compliance."

"I will *never* surrender to you."

My eyes shot open. "Then so be it."

The heat left my fingertips in long tendrils. I moved my hands, guiding the serpent-like flames toward Zenith. With a flick of my wrist, they lashed at the half Solin, half Lunin. He fell to his knees, shielding his face. Like hungry adders, the glowing ropes wrapped around Zenith's neck, then slithered under his shirt. They sparked and hissed at the cool touch of his skin.

I tilted my head. The extensions allowed me to feel the hard planes of his chest and abdomen; they paused on his pounding heart. I sent more of the reddish-orange whips toward his wrists and ankles. Zenith hollered at the restraints holding him in place. His flesh didn't melt. It cracked like the blade of his knife. I tightened the fire-infused ropes, watching his skin chip away one flawed flake at a time.

Overwhelmed with pain, Zenith collapsed onto his back. I moved closer and stood over the man I once feared, Jax's wisdom echoing in my mind. *A person of true power doesn't control others. They stand up for truth and lead with selfless intentions. They refuse to let their own wants or needs hinder the greater good. A powerful person looks at a situation for what it is, not for what they desire it to become. You and your brother are more powerful than Zenith will ever be.*

I looked at Cyrus's body, then back at Zenith's, noting the

stark contrast. *Jax was right. Zenith is nothing more than a coward who hides behind the façade he's created.*

I shook my head in disappointment. "Stand down, Zenith." A hint of desperation lingered in my voice. I needed him to yield. Murdering the man would accomplish nothing. The people needed to witness his surrender. I gathered the ribbons of heat and guided them to his face. "It's over, Zenith. You've lost."

His skin split apart. A tendril reached for his wrist when he lifted his hand. I was too late. He tossed a small capsule into his mouth and cracked it open. My nostrils flared at the familiar scent of menthol and lavender. *Minlav.* My arms fell to my sides, and the flames extinguished.

"I lose by my own hands," he said, choking on the black foam that overflowed out of his mouth. "Not yours."

Zenith's body jerked and twitched with convulsions. The concentrated dose of Minlav had attacked his vital organs. Blood penetrated his eyes, pooling in his tear ducts before dripping down his cheeks. I didn't look away once he emptied the contents of his stomach, and I didn't offer assistance when the fear of death surfaced, causing him to scream for help. I had no antidote. And even if I had, he wouldn't have taken it. Regardless of how much he fought with the afterlife, Zenith wanted to end his.

I nodded at Death when it approached. Not a gesture of victory. A gesture of acceptance. Its black cloak fluttered in the phantom breeze as it scooped up a shadow of Zenith. The dark figure continued to writhe and beg for mercy as Death carried it across the clearing, disappearing into the oblivion. I frowned at the empty shell it left behind.

As if they had waited over sixteen years to breathe, the citizens of Aroonyx sucked in the evening air. Their bodies swayed and over half dropped to their knees, the relief intoxicating.

I stared at Zenith's body and envisioned the verbiage on his headstone: *Here lies a man who lacked the courage to face his darkest fears, a man who refused to recognize the truth.*

I slid my hands into my pockets. The hairs floating around my head fell onto my shoulders as I let out a deep sigh. *Zenith had a choice, and he chose the path that led to nowhere. He chose the easy way out.* Another sigh slipped through my parted lips. *Or at least he thought he had.*

Hearing footsteps, I lifted my gaze. Saros, Jax, and Samson took their places beside me. We stood in silence, processing the emotions that surfaced. There were no tears of remorse or tears of joy. Just four vacant expressions blinked at Zenith. We inhaled a shared breath, then exhaled our resentments and frustrations. We had completed our mission. We had freed the people of Aroonyx.

The citizens formed a circle around our small group. Even the Collectors dared to join us, save for Apollo. He kept his distance, his orange eyes fixed on the former leader of Aroonyx.

I closed my eyes and searched for my guides.

Thank you, Mom. Thank you, Cyrus.

Silence. I touched my chest. Though a gentle vibration still hummed near my beating heart, the voices had vanished. I looked at Jax, a tear rolling off my cheek.

"People come into our lives at a specific moment," he said, "and they leave once that moment has passed. It's not personal, it's not unremarkable. It just is what it is."

I nodded, then shifted my attention to Saros when he nudged me in the arm.

"My dear." He inclined his head at the citizens. "They seek your approval."

My eyes grew watching the crowd stirred. *Oh no. What are they doing?* Everyone, including the Collectors, took a knee.

"No." I motioned for them to stand. "Please don't bow to me."

A woman lifted her head. "It's not a posture of surrender.

It's a posture of gratitude. You freed us from a lifetime of servitude."

I eyed Cyrus's body, the men beside me, and our recruits before finding her eyes. "I couldn't have done this on my own. It was a group effort."

She flashed me a warm grin and said, "Spoken like a selfless leader," then lowered her head once more.

Samson eyed Jax, and Jax eyed Saros. The men nodded at one another, then took a knee. Warmth stung my eyes as I observed the fearless Solin who encouraged me to stay on my path, the first Seeker who would help restore peace to Aroonyx, and the Lunin with the piercing blue eyes. The man who always believed in me, the man who refused to let me give up, the man who loved me with his whole heart.

I acknowledged the fallen member of our group. The agonizing grief I experienced during Cyrus's death had vanished because I knew the truth. He had moved on.

A few heartbeats later, the citizens stood. They rubbed their weary eyes and observed the bodies sprawled around the clearing. One by one, they hurried to assist the wounded and collect the dead.

Jax grabbed Samson's arm, stopping him from hurling his knife at Apollo. "Let him go."

The Solin scoffed. "Have you lost your damn mind? That's Apollo, not some average Collector."

"He's not a threat," I said, watching him dash toward the tree line that skirted the clearing. "Let him live out his days in hiding."

Samson grumbled his complaints and lowered his arm. "Don't say I didn't warn you."

"Noted." I tapped my toe against Zenith's boot. "I'm tired of fighting. We've seen enough bloodshed for a lifetime."

"I'm proud of you, kid. You did good today."

"I did what needed to be done."

"And *that* makes all the difference."

I shrugged, though a smile tugged at my lips.

Samson turned his attention to Saros. "Why don't you help me check on the wounded?"

"I'd like that." He removed the cuff links from his dress shirt. "Elara, could you keep these safe for me?"

I nodded. He dropped a matching pair of opal twin crescent moons into my hand. I opened my palm for Jax to see. He smiled. The homage to the celestial bodies proved that Saros had missed Aroonyx, and the bounce in his step confirmed he was thrilled to be home.

Jax's face fell. Curious, I followed his gaze. Castor sat in the snow beside Pollux. An emotional dam broke open after his pale fingers closed his son's eyes. Perhaps it was years of pent-up anger or guilt that shook his shoulders with violent sobs. Perhaps it was both. Whatever the cause, Castor let go of his pride that day; he let go of the resentment he harbored toward the man who had caused others pain, and held his son in a tight embrace.

I turned to give him privacy only to find Idalia kneeling over my brother. She rested her cheek on his chest and held his hand while she wept. I wanted to comfort my friend, but she needed time alone to grieve.

Out of habit, Jax brushed the scar on his palm. His thumb paused its mindless pursuit. The gesture warmed my heart. After all these years, it appeared my partner finally got the closure he needed.

I glimpsed the amethyst-colored sky, noting the twinkling stars and the twin moons. For the first time, I felt at peace standing on Aroonyx.

"Well." Jax sighed, breaking the comfortable silence. "This has been a very interesting day, Elara."

A white cloud of amusement left my mouth. "Yes. Yes, it has Jax."

"I'd love to express my affection but honestly"—he eyed my fingers as if searching for the glowing tendrils—"I'm slightly terrified of your new powers."

"Get your ass over here," I said, pulling him closer.

He tensed.

"Stop it," I scolded. "I won't burn you. I can control it now."

He shot me a sidelong glance and jerked his chin at the blonde strands that lifted off my shoulders. I cleared my throat, a silent command for my hair to obey. The strands fell limp once more.

"See." I flashed him a smug grin. "It listens."

The line between his brows deepened. "It?"

"Yeah. I think it reacts to my emotions."

"Then remind me not to piss you off." Jax snickered. "I don't want to make *it* mad."

"Rico." My eyes lit up. "That's what I'll call it."

Jax huffed a laugh. "Cyrus would be proud." His smile drooped. "I'm sorry for your loss. Your brother was a great man."

"Yeah." I swallowed hard. "He was the best."

Jax laced his fingers through mine. "Elara, I'm amazed at how well you fought during the battle and how well you're handling your brother's death." He looked at Zenith. "Words can't describe the amount of courage you showed tonight. I'm so proud of you."

"I think Cyrus passed me his courage, along with his powers."

"Or perhaps he showed you what was there all along."

I let go of Jax's hands to wipe a tear that rolled off my cheek. "Death is an interesting part of life."

"Yes, it is. One impossible to avoid."

"It's an event people fear the most."

"Why?" he asked.

It wasn't a question Jax needed me to answer. It was a question he wanted me to ponder.

I found his eyes. "People grieve the loss of a loved one because they fear the loss of love, but *love* is impossible to lose. It's not found outside of ourselves." I rested my hand over his heart. "It's found within, and it's ours for the taking if we're willing to accept life's greatest gift."

A large grin swept over Jax's unshaven face. "Wise words spoken from a wise woman."

"Cyrus's death didn't break the strong connection we shared." The warmth surged through me and concentrated near my heart, verifying my observation.

"And why's that?" he asked, his eyes twinkling with the unspoken truth.

I stared at my brother and smiled. "Because even in death, there's no separation."

57

LIKE WE ALWAYS DO

Long days and short weeks. Those words described the passage of time after the uprising. The citizens of Aroonyx bonded and grew stronger during the long hours of tending to the wounded and collecting the dead.

We buried Cyrus near the windmill on the hill. His headstone rested beside our biological mother and father. The ones who had supported him from the beginning expressed their love and appreciation for his dedication to our mission.

After the service ended, I kissed the tips of my fingers and pressed them to the etching on his headstone, then whispered, "See you on the other side, bro."

I turned, feeling a tug at my arm.

"I miss him so much," Blaze cried, his eyes rimmed in red.

I squatted and held the child in a warm embrace. "I know. I miss him too."

"Why did he have to die? Why did my mom?"

"There are some things in life we can't explain, kid."

"It's not fair." He stomped his foot in the snow and crossed his arms. "Cyrus said he'd adopt me as my little brother."

"I still can."

"Really?"

"Sure. I mean most of the time people adopt children, not siblings, but we can start a new trend."

He sniffled. "What about Earth? Aren't you going home?"

Home. The word tugged at my heart. I eyed the abandoned dwelling were my biological mother gave birth to me and my brother. "I haven't decided yet."

"Oh." Blaze stared at his boots. "Okay."

I kneeled before the child and rested my hands on the sides of his face. "Do you remember what my brother told you before he left for battle?"

He shrugged.

"Everything is going to be okay. *We* are going to be okay."

"How can you know for sure?"

I smiled, thinking of my twin's courageous act. "Because everything works out in the end."

Blaze wiped the snot from his nose and stood tall.

"Here." I reached into my back pocket. "Cyrus would want you to have this."

Blaze's eyes grew with excitement, though he hesitated to take the folded blade. I dropped it into his hand.

"I promise I'll take good care of it," he said, grinning from ear to ear.

"I'm sure you will."

"Do you think I'll grow up to be like Cyrus?"

I nodded. "And maybe one day you'll be the leader of Aroonyx."

His jaw cracked open. "That would be so cool."

"Anything's possible."

Blaze wrapped his arms around my waist and gave me a tight squeeze. "See you around, Elara. Don't get stuck on Earth."

My laughter faded as my lips curled into a frown. *Shit. That thought never crossed my mind.*

The boy ran toward Samson and reached for his hand. The grumpy Solin scowled but humored the boy with a lackluster high five, then found my eyes and motioned to Idalia.

The poor girl sobbed in Orion's arms. She struggled with the emotions that surfaced after my brother's death. We all did, but she took it harder than anyone else. Jax had shared words of wisdom, and I had shared words of comfort. Unfortunately, they fell on deaf ears.

Orion was the only one who got through to her. They bonded during those emotional days by staying up late, swapping stories about Iah and Cyrus, and comforting one another.

"ELARA, sunscreen doesn't exist on Aroonyx. If we stand in the sun any longer, your skin will burn."

I glared at Jax, the hairs lifting off my shoulders.

"Apologies, Rico." He hid a smirk and showed me the palms of his hands. "We've been standing on this damn cliffside for hours. Your skin is turning red, and I'm bored out of my mind."

"Boredom is a good thing. Weeks ago, that word didn't exist in our vocabulary."

My partner raised his arms to block the sun from my face. "Yes. This is both efficient and comfortable. I'll just stand here and act as your human sunshade."

I swore under my breath and shook my arms, the sweat dripping off my elbows. "I'll do it. Just give me a few more minutes."

"No. You've had more than enough time. We've gone over this every night for the past three weeks." He motioned to the vast body of water. "Just do it. Jump."

I gritted my teeth. A mirage of heat rippled out of me, slamming into Jax. He hissed, his forehead dotted with moisture.

"Sorry." Acting as a vacuum, I sucked the invisible wave back inside me. "Rico doesn't like it when you pressure me."

Jax shot me a weighted glance. "Don't blame this on Rico."

"Fine." I wrung my hands. "I'm just scared it won't work."

"Why wouldn't it work?"

"My intention."

Jax scoffed, tossing the hair out of his eyes. "Elara, your reason for returning to Earth is selfless. You promised Cyrus you'd speak to his father, and your adoptive parents deserve to hear the truth about your military ruse. You've been away from Earth for over a year. Cyrus gave Coach Burnell twelve letters to mail to your mother and father. By now they've stopped getting them. Sooner or later they'll learn the truth: you never went to boot camp."

I scrubbed at my face. "What am I supposed to say? Hey guys, it's me, Elara, the girl you raised as your daughter for eighteen years. Sorry, I lied about joining the military. I was hanging out on another planet with my fiancé."

Jax snickered.

"It's not funny," I scolded. "This is a horrible idea."

"No, it's not."

"What if *you* can't jump?"

"My intention is selfless. I'm not going on vacation. I'm going to support you on the final leg of your journey."

"What if I get stuck on Earth?"

A smile played on his lips. "Then you're on your own."

"Asshole."

He winced as my knuckles slammed into his shoulder. "Easy with the Solin strength."

"Then stop antagonizing me."

"I will, once you stop procrastinating."

I stuck out my tongue. "You'd miss me if I got trapped on Earth."

"I'd miss our nightly activities."

I flashed him a vulgar gesture.

He grinned, taking my hand. "Can we go now?"

"Fine," I grumbled. "How do I do it? Do I think of my parents or my obligation to Cyrus?"

"We've already been through this, fifty-seven times. Just hold your intention in your mind."

I looked at the cloudless green sky, filled my lungs with the summer air, and envisioned my adoptive parents, then thought of the promise I made to my brother. *Home. Where is home?*

A moment later, I flinched at the jarring sensation of jumping between worlds. Jax dropped my hand. I covered my ears, the auditory stimulation overwhelming me. Birds chirped, squirrels scurried up the branches of the tall pine trees, and children's laughter echoed in the familiar space. A motorcycle zipped around the street corner, its engine roaring to life as the driver shifted gears. My head turned. The repetitive beep of a garbage truck reversing sounded nearby, along with the subtle hiss of sprinklers watering the yellowing grass.

"Go figure." I pointed at our feet. "We're standing where you stood the night I saw you outside my bedroom window."

Jax lifted one boot, then the other. "Nothing surprises me anymore, Elara."

I lifted my chin to the blue sky. The rays of the afternoon sun warmed my face, the smell of terpenes carried by the summer breeze wafted into my nose. I inhaled the comforting aroma. *Oh, how I've missed Earth.*

My casual expression shifted to concern once I saw my hair hovering around my face. "How am I going to explain this to my parents?"

"Hmm." Jax tapped his chin. "Static electricity?"

I pinned him with a long stare. "Okay, smartass. Are you going to stand there and rub a balloon over my head while I chat with my mom?"

"If it pleases you."

"You know"—I strolled past him toward the front of my house—"not long ago I found your suggestions helpful."

"And now?"

"I find them irritating as hell."

Jax snorted and stepped over a fallen branch. "Forgive me. I thought you wanted us on the same page." He slapped my backside. "You've been a pain in my ass all year. I'm returning the favor."

"Bastard."

"Language." He clicked his tongue. "Your adoptive parents won't appreciate that new mouth of yours."

"Okay dad, I'll—"

The verbal jab faded at the sight of my mother. She sat in the front yard near a pile of mulch with her back facing us. The short strands of her blonde hair fell into her eyes as she spread her gloved fingers through the dirt. I tilted my head, watching her reach for a shovel. *When did she take up gardening?*

My heart nearly leaped out of my chest when I noticed my father standing on a ladder with his arm outstretched.

"Emily," he said, gesturing to a newly installed hook. "Do you want the begonias here or over there?"

She shielded her face from the bright rays. "I'm worried the afternoon sun will hit them too hard if we hang them over there."

He swung the basket of yellow flowers through the air. "So, here?"

She nodded before digging another hole.

I squeezed Jax's arm, my eyes welling with tears. *Hanging plants and wondering where to put them. God, I've missed the simplicity of living with my parents.*

"Go on," Jax whispered. "Say hello."

I rubbed the sweat off my palms and took a hesitant step forward. "Mom?" My voice cracked.

"A little louder," Jax encouraged.

My parents turned, hearing his voice. As if an apparition had appeared, my mother's eyes grew wide while my father clung to a rung of the ladder. I held my breath. Over twelve months had passed on Earth since my departure. *Did they receive the letters I wrote? Did they believe I joined the Coast Guard? Did they ever contact the base?*

Their stunned reactions made me question everything.

My mother held a trembling hand over her quivering lips and climbed to her feet.

"Honey?" My father hurried down the ladder. "Is that you?"

I sprinted across the front lawn and threw myself into their arms. My father kissed the top of my head and expressed his gratitude to the universe while my mother sobbed hysterically, her dirt-stained gloves digging into my back.

"We were so worried. We haven't received a letter in months."

I let out a relieved breath. *I can't believe it worked. Remember to thank Coach Burnell.*

"The last letter said you were working as a health services tech aboard a cutter," my father added. "This threw us off because you never mentioned studying medicine in A School."

I grimaced. Jax had instructed us to keep it vague. Apparently, I had left out a key part of my pretend military career.

"I wanted to speak with your recruiter," my mother said, wiping her eyes, "but I never got his name. The local recruiting office didn't help. They couldn't do anything unless we knew the location of your base"—she lowered her gaze—"which you never told us."

"Right," I murmured.

"I was about to contact our local congressman to see if he could offer us assistance."

"Mom. I think it's best we go inside. I need to explain—"

"The reason you bleached your hair?" she asked, scowling at my blonde locks.

I bit my lip, compelling the strands to stay put. "It's a recent change."

She squinted at my scalp. "Your stylist did an amazing job because I can't see the roots."

My shoulders shook with laughter. She had reverted to her overbearing self in two seconds flat.

"And your eyes." She moved her nose inches from mine. "Why are you wearing only one orange contact? Is this a new trend on social media?"

I laughed again. "No, it's permanent."

"And your muscles." She gasped, squeezing my bicep. "Bootcamp served you well. You look like a fitness model now."

"That's a recent change too."

My father twirled me around, observing my new appearance. "The hair and eyes are a unique look. Does your superior on the vessel allow you to treat patients this way?"

"*Dad*, it's not like I have blue hair and tattoos all over my body."

"No, but—" He paused, his eyes drifting toward Jax. "Honey, why is that man staring at us? Is he a friend of yours?"

I nodded, waving him over. Jax ambled across the lawn with his hands shoved in his pockets and his chin held high. I eyed my mother's sheepish grin. *Oh geez. Here we go.*

My father rolled his eyes at his wife's blushing cheeks. Once Jax took his place beside me, I slipped my arm through his. "Mom . . . Dad." I wiggled my ring finger. The glittering promise sparkling in the sun. "This is Jax, my fiancé."

My mother clutched her chest. My father almost choked on his spit.

Quick to recover and smoother than most, Jax extended his hand to my father. "It's an honor to meet the man who helped raise such a respectful daughter."

My father stammered inaudible words and shook my partner's hand.

"Let's go inside," I suggested. "We have some news I want to share."

My mother's lips pursed as she motioned for us to lead the way. Dreading the conversation, I dragged my feet toward the front porch.

"Rog," she whispered. "If Elara tells us she's pregnant—"

"*Mom.*" I whipped around. "Why would you say that?"

"Because we haven't seen you in over a year, and suddenly you show up with a strange man on your arm and a ring on your finger. What else am I supposed to think?"

"Mrs. Dunlin." Jax touched his chest. "I consider myself a gentleman. Rest easy knowing Elara is not with child."

My father gave him a curt head nod. "Good answer, son." He looked at his wife. "Emily, I like him already."

Jax bowed his head, then urged me to step over the threshold.

"A gentleman?" I whispered to him. "Is that what you call yourself?"

His mouth gaped with a mocked offense. "You doubt my claim?"

"I do."

"My method of impromptu birth control makes me the perfect gentleman."

I shut my eyes, his snarky comment staining my cheeks red.

Jax snickered at the family photo hanging in the entryway. "I forgot you wore braces."

"I didn't. I covered my mouth anytime I spoke because the kids at school wouldn't stop teasing me."

"Come on you two," my mother said, interrupting my trip down memory lane. "Let's go pick out a name for my grandchild."

I rolled my eyes, following her toward the kitchen.

"I see who inspired the dramatic side of your personality," Jax murmured, nudging me in the side.

I glared. He just laughed.

"Do you guys want anything to eat?" my father asked, offering us bottled water from the fridge.

"No, we're good." I smiled, twisting off the cap. *Geez. I took everything for granted on Earth.*

The four of us lowered ourselves onto the chairs surrounding the dining room table.

Sharing my lack of patience, my mother drummed her nails on the wooden surface. "Spit it out, Elara."

And that's exactly what I did. I spent three hours explaining everything that happened after I left home. She shot me a stern look once I came clean about the self-defense classes I never took, and my father's jaw almost hit the table after he heard the reason behind my military ruse. I struggled to verbalize the heartache and suffering I experienced while living on Aroonyx and held back tears when I mentioned Cyrus's selfless and courageous act.

With my emotions drained, I rested my elbows on the table and massaged my brows. Jax folded his arms across his chest and leaned back in his chair, his blue eyes shifting between me and my adoptive parents.

Hearing the truth left them speechless. My mother stared at the swirled knots in the table while my father pinched the bridge of his nose.

After several heartbeats of uncomfortable silence, he lifted his gaze. "Honey, I'm having a hard time believing any of this. A strange planet? Time travel?" He blew out a long breath while glancing at Jax. "Are the two of you on drugs?" He reached across the table for my hand. "If so, we can find a treatment center that—"

"No," I snapped. "We're not taking drugs. I know it sounds crazy, but it's the truth. I didn't believe Jax when he first told me. It wasn't until he brought—" I paused, looking at my partner.

He nodded, offering me his hand. "Your daughter has something she wants to show you," he said to my parents.

"What is it?" my father asked.

"Proof that life exists on another planet," I said. "We'll be right back."

My mother lifted her head. "Where are you going?"

"Please don't freak out," I begged. "And don't call the cops or run to the neighbors."

We vanished before she could argue our sudden departure. Jax and I dashed toward the clearing where we shared our first kiss. In one fell swoop, I plucked two Moon Drops from the emerald grass, grabbed Jax's hand, and jumped back to Earth. I couldn't help but laugh at my parents' bewildered expressions. I'm sure I looked equally baffled the first time Jax appeared before my eyes.

I handed them the beautiful flowers and took a seat while my partner shared the familiar story of the Moon Drop. A single tear slid down my mother's cheek when he explained the flowers' transformation at sunrise.

My throat bobbed. The retelling resonated on a deeper emotional level than it did the first time. Jax's theory of the Moon Drops changing forms rather than disappearing reflected Cyrus's passing. I closed my eyes, feeling the warmth move through me. Though I could no longer hear his voice, I knew my brother was near.

Long minutes passed before my parents accepted the truth: for the past year, their adoptive daughter had lived on another planet with her twin brother and the man she now called her fiancé, the man who had acted as their daughter's silent guardian for her entire life.

My pulse quickened as I checked the time. "We have to speak to Cyrus's parents."

With little enthusiasm, my parents rose to their feet.

"Jax," my father called.

"Yes, sir."

"I'd like to speak with you alone."

He nodded, then followed my father into the foyer.

I frowned at my mother when she turned to face me. "Please don't cry again."

"I can't help it." She sniffled. "After hearing how Zenith wanted to—" She covered her mouth, unable to finish the sentence.

"I'm so sorry," I said, holding her close. "I should have never lied to you and Dad."

"I understand why you did. I'm just glad you're home."

Home. The word I struggled to define.

"I haven't decided if I'm staying on Earth."

More tears pooled in her eyes. "Sweetie, you just got back."

"I'm aware." I rotated the ring on my finger. "But things have changed. The citizens of Aroonyx need guidance. Jax needs—"

"I don't care what they need. You've done enough for those people. You risked your life. Your brother lost his." Her eyes narrowed at the Lunin down the hallway. "If Jax cares for you, he'll let you stay on Earth."

"Mom. That's not how our relationship works. Jax respects the decisions I make, and I respect his. It's a partnership, not a dictatorship. Trust me, thanks to Zenith, I learned the difference between the two."

Her posture sagged in defeat. "Just promise me you'll think it over."

"I will."

My head turned at the sound of my father's voice. "One more hug before you go?"

I wrapped my arms around him and smiled at the familiar scent of Speed Stick and aftershave.

"Why don't you guys come over for dinner after you speak with Cyrus's parents?" he added. "We can fill you in on our uneventful year and catch up on *Game of Thrones*. I haven't watched it since you left."

I chuckled, remembering my conversation with Cyrus. *You might find out what happens if Jax takes you back to Earth.*

"Dad, I wish we could, but"—I looked at my mother—"Jax and I have a lot to discuss after we meet with Cyrus's parents."

She nodded, approval flickering in her eyes.

"Oh, I see," my father muttered.

"Let them go, Rog. I'm sure they'll visit soon."

"Mr. Dunlin, Mrs. Dunlin," Jax said, shaking their hands. "It was a pleasure meeting you both."

"Likewise, son."

My mother forced a smile. "Take care of my daughter."

"We'll take care of each other." Jax locked his eyes with mine. "Like we always do."

58

HOME

We kept to ourselves after we turned into Cyrus's gated community, the weight of my decision growing heavier with each step.

Do I stay on Earth or return to Aroonyx? Saros can guide the citizens. He's more than qualified. I frowned. *But he's so old. Jax doesn't want to lead the people, and Samson . . . well, he's Samson. That won't work.* I sighed, watching the strands of my hair dance in the phantom breeze. *What would Cyrus do?*

Jax stayed quiet but brushed his fingers against mine every few strides. He knew I was struggling with my decision.

I groaned, observing the guard shack.

"What's wrong?" he asked.

I pointed at the man who sat with his plump arms resting on a desk, his brown eyes fixed on the computer monitor. "The guy can be a real asshole. Last time I had to lie to get him to open the gate."

Jax ignored my concerns and motioned for me to follow. I held my breath as he rapped his knuckles on the glass.

Without moving his gaze from the zombies occupying his

computer screen, the man slid open the window, and asked, "How can I help you?"

"I need to speak with the Loftons."

The guard turned his head, his eyes widening. "Jax Caspen." He stuck his hand through the window. "It's been a long time, my friend. How the hell are you?"

My jaw cracked open. *How do they know each other?*

"I'm good, Darius. How's Izelle and the rest of the family?"

"Ize's doing great. Marcus is still a pain in our ass, but the grandkids make up for it. Carl just started pre-school and Kayla had her first dance recital."

Jax smiled at the man. "Kids grow fast."

"You should stop by for dinner sometime. Ize always finds a way to add you to the conversation." His voice raised an octave as he mocked his wife. "How was work? I'd love to see that Jax Caspen and those eyes of his."

My partner chuckled, shaking his head at Darius.

"Swing by," the guard added. "She'll make her famous casserole."

"I'll see what I can do. In the meantime, tell her I said hello."

Darius jerked his chin at me. "Who's your lady friend?"

"This is my fiancé, Elara."

I shook the guard's hand.

"It's a pleasure to meet you Elara."

Before I could return the salutation, Jax said, "She's Cyrus Lofton's twin sister."

Darius dropped my hand. "I never knew Cyrus had a sister." His dark eyes shifted between the two of us. "How's military life treating him?"

I looked away, my throat tight with grief.

"I see." He pressed the button that opened the gate. The motors whizzed to life. "Don't let me delay your visit."

I kept my mouth shut until we rounded the street corner.

"All this time, I thought you hid in the shadows, spying on me and Cyrus." I clicked my tongue. "Little did I know you were breaking bread with Darius and his family."

"It's not like I could run to the bank and make a withdraw. My survival depended on my charm and good looks."

I gave him a sidelong glance. "How many Earth friends do you have?"

"A few."

"Should I prepare for more impromptu meetings?"

"No. I don't plan on taking you to the bar tonight."

"The bar or the gentleman's club?"

His smirk grew. "I needed a thorough investigation of Earth's inhabitants."

"You're ridiculous," I chided. "I bet your number grew exponentially during your visits."

He shrugged, then smoothed the hairs that hovered around my head. "Rico doesn't like it when you get jealous."

I shoved him hard, sending him flying over the sidewalk and into the brush. His hands shot out, stopping him from slamming into a tree.

"You're so aggressive these days," he said, dusting off his palms. His eyes roved over me. "It's kind of sexy."

"Are you done?"

He grabbed my hand and kissed my knuckles. "Yes, until later this evening."

A girlish giggle rattled in my throat. "I have a question, Jax Caspen."

"And I have an answer, Elara Dunlin."

"What if I stayed living in Maine and never moved to Texas? How would you have brought me and Cyrus together?"

"I orchestrated the entire event. I'm the reason your father got the job offer."

My boots stopped mid-motion. "How in the hell did you manage that?"

"I can't tell you all my secrets."

"That's not fair. How did you do it?"

"I have my ways, and that's all I'll say." Jax inclined his head at the massive dwelling that rested before us. "Now, it's time to get your head in the game."

My heart dropped into the pit of my stomach once I noticed Cyrus's black Camaro parked outside one of the six garages.

"I don't think I can do this," I whispered.

"You can and you will because you made a promise to your brother." Jax led me across the circular driveway. "Honor your commitment, Elara."

Sweat lined my palms as Jax knocked on the front door. A second later, it cracked open. A petite woman dressed in a uniform poked her head around the metal frame.

"May I help you?" she asked in broken English.

"Can I speak with Cyrus's parents?" I asked.

Her brown eyes scanned my troubled expression.

"Who is it, Gloria?"

I flinched at the familiar voice: Cyrus's adoptive mother.

"No sé. Es una chica."

Heels clicked on the marble floors. The quick pace matched the rhythm of my thundering heart. The woman moved away from the door once Cyrus's mother appeared.

She scowled at the two of us and flicked her wrist at the sign hanging near the doorbell.

NO SOLICITING

"We're not selling anything," I said. "We're here about your son."

She paled. "You're not wearing uniforms. Are you with the military?"

"No. My name is Elara. I'm Cyrus's twin sister, and I *really* need to speak with you and your husband. It's urgent."

Her voice trembled as she turned her head and yelled, "Chris! Get over here."

"I'm in a meeting, Julie," he yelled back. "Can't it wait?"

"No. It's an emergency, get off the damn phone!"

A loud clang confirmed that Chris had either dropped his phone or thrown it across the room. Jax tensed, preparing to play mediator.

"Come inside," Julie encouraged.

My partner nudged my arm and pointed to the crystal chandelier hanging above the foyer.

"Wow," I whispered. "I bet it cost more than my dad's car."

"Probably."

Two long hallways followed by a sharp left turn led us into a parlor that resembled the set of a historical drama.

"Make yourselves comfortable," she said, gesturing to the couch.

Is that a joke? I winced as my backside landed on the misleading cushion. The piece of furniture was nothing more than a decorative chunk of discomfort, and an overpriced one at that.

Chris entered the room with a scotch in hand. He sat on the leather club chair nestled near the elaborate fireplace while his wife perched her thin frame on the edge of an armless seat beside him. Like a high-born lady, she held her hands in her lap and crossed her ankles, not her legs. The woman's spine was straighter than the framed pictures hanging on the walls.

Chris watched us with curious eyes as he swirled his glass, the stainless-steel ice cubes clinking in the amber liquid.

I rubbed my sweat-lined palms on my shorts. Jax cleared his throat, a silent request for me to keep Rico in check. Not taking any chances, I slipped the black hair tie off my wrist and secured my locks into a messy bun.

The grandfather clock in the corner reminded us that no one had spoken. Each swing of the golden pendulum increased the building tension. *Just do it. Say something.*

I sucked in a sharp breath, and before my tongue could

move a different uniformed employee stepped into the parlor. The air rushed out of my lungs. I wanted to kiss the woman for saving me from the conversation I dreaded.

Her full lips spread into a warm grin, exposing a large gap between her front teeth as she offered us an assortment of bite-sized cakes and tea. Not one for grandeur, Jax scowled at the delicate cup she placed in his hand. He then poked at the mini iced scone she added to his saucer. I bit my lip to keep from laughing.

"That will be all," Julie said. "Leave us."

As if the queen had spoken, the woman bowed her head and walked backward until she reached the double doors. I hid an eye roll at the unnecessary formalities. *I can't believe Cyrus grew up surrounded by servants. He never acted like a snob, and he always treated his peers with respect.*

I scooted to the edge of the couch. "There's no easy way to tell you this, so let's start from the beginning."

THE TEA in Julie's cup dripped onto the floor. Her hands hadn't stopped shaking after I explained the reason her son returned to his birthplace. Chris muttered his disbelief and headed toward the beverage cart. Cyrus had mentioned his father enjoyed watching C-SPAN, golfing with his old college buddies, drinking with his ex-Marine pals, and reading historical fiction. A practical man, a no-nonsense fellow. That's how Cyrus described his father.

"Chris, I'm not lying," I said.

He huffed a breath, snatching the half-empty bottle of Macallan with the number eighteen stamped on the label. "So you want me to believe"—he paused, filling his glass to the rim —"my son never joined the Navy?"

"Yes."

"And you expect me to believe he's living on another planet?"

I swallowed hard. "He *was.*"

The amber liquid sloshed onto the floral rug as he waved his drink around the room. "Then where is he now?"

"I'll tell you after you accept the truth. Your son was born on Aroonyx."

"You have no proof." His voice raised. "I'm a businessman, Elara. I won't invest in a company unless I've done my due diligence. I know nothing about you or your boyfriend or the crazy shit you keep telling me."

"*Chris*, please," Julie whispered.

He waved her away.

"Fine." I grabbed Jax's hand. "You want proof. Watch this."

The Moon Drops supported my claim, but our disappearing and reappearing act closed the deal with Cyrus's father. He tipped back his head and drained the glass in one long swig. The leather cushion sighed as he collapsed onto the chair. Julie sat there stunned—speechless.

Jax held my hand while I shared the highs and lows of living on Aroonyx. He tightened his grip once I reached the final battle.

Julie struggled to accept her son's fate. She whimpered the word *no* as she wept.

The Scotch had stained Chris's cheeks red, but the color faded when the clock struck six. Ding. Ding. Ding. He grew paler by the second. Ding. Ding. Ding. He turned a sickly gray. With his jaw clenched, he stared at the intricate designs on the coffee table.

"Chris." I inhaled a shaky breath and braced my forearms on my thighs. "I understand you and Cyrus had a strained relationship, and I'm aware you didn't part on good terms." Tears stung my eyes. "But before he passed, he asked me to deliver a message."

The somber man lifted his eyes. "What message?"

"Tell my dad I love him, and I forgive him."

Chris stilled, his eyes brimming with grief. His shoulders shook as he dropped his head into his hands.

I never wanted to break the news to Cyrus's parents. His father's painful reaction proved the reason behind my hesitation.

"I've seen my fair share of battles," Jax said. "And your son's courage rivaled the bravest of men. Don't forget, Chris, you helped raise him."

Cyrus's father didn't acknowledge Jax's compliment. He just sat there with his head in his hands.

The heat stirred inside me. Without giving it much thought, I rose to my feet, walked across the room, and rested my hand on Chris's shoulder.

"Do you feel that?" I asked.

He flinched at my vibrating palm.

"Even though you can't see him"—I released more heat —"you need to trust that he's still here."

Chris tried controlling his emotions, a failed attempt.

"Excuse me." His voice cracked as he stood. "I need a few minutes alone."

I nodded, watching him exit the room.

Black rivers of mascara streaked Julie's face. I touched her arm and kissed her damp cheek before whispering, "It's time for us to go."

She looked me square in the eyes, her pointed nails gripping my warm flesh. "Thank you," she cried, "for telling us the truth."

I smiled, squeezing her hand. "It's the only thing that frees us from despair."

"Did the meeting go better or worse than you expected?"

"Worse," I said, stepping over a crack in the sidewalk. "Their reactions broke my heart."

"They need time to heal."

"I'm just glad it's over."

Jax hummed his agreement.

"What should we do now?" I asked.

"This is your world, Elara. You call the shots."

"Speaking of shots. I could go for a double espresso."

"Excellent." His lips twitched. "There's this popular spot down the road. Warning. They take their coffee very seriously." His smirk grew. "Hell, they even write codes on the cups."

"I hate you right now."

He chuckled, wrapping a stray hair around my bun.

"And even if I wanted to submit to your humiliation, I can't."

"Why?"

"I don't have any money."

"I do."

"How? Did Darius slip you a handful of ones to visit the club later?"

"Not this time." He slid his arm around my waist and pulled me close. "But your dad gave me some cash."

During the long stroll to Starbucks, we revisited our final moments with my brother.

"Why didn't you tell me your vision had nothing to do with Cyrus?"

"It wasn't a vision," he argued.

"Fine. Then why didn't you mention your *feeling*?"

"I did—sort of. That night, under the bridge."

"No. You said you experienced that feeling once you looked at me *and* Cyrus."

He grimaced. "I guess I added his name to the mix."

"Yeah. Why?"

"It felt like the right thing to do."

A wave of heat rippled out of me. Jax recoiled from my touch.

"But I clarified on the night of my confession," he said. "Remember when we were sitting by the rock near the cliffside?"

I nodded.

"I said *you* were the reason I left the Collectors."

"But you left out my brother dying."

"Elara, we've been through this. You're a Seeker. You should understand these 'feelings' better than anyone else. These glimpses of time, these intuitive moments, they don't give us a clear image of the future. I had the utmost confidence you and your brother would make the journey together, but in my heart, I knew you, alone, would defeat Zenith."

"But I didn't defeat him on my own. Without Cyrus's help, we'd all be dead."

Jax sighed. "You're right. Perhaps I sensed your brother's journey would end before yours. He accepted his fate after he had that vision."

"What vision?"

"Cyrus pulled me aside one afternoon and voiced his concerns regarding the vivid imagery he had of us standing behind your house."

"He told me that was a dream."

The Lunin shrugged. "Vision, dream? You've had similar experiences, have you not?"

"Yeah, I have."

"Afterward I shared my thoughts and expressed my own concerns. Your brother was a smart man. He knew what he signed up for."

The internal flames rolled inside me. "So the two of you kept this from me."

"Yes. We did it to protect you.'

"I didn't need protecting Jax!"

His eyes narrowed at the glowing whips that slithered out of my fingertips. I fisted my hands, extinguishing the flames.

"I needed"—I brushed away a tear—"I *want* . . . my brother."

My partner shut his eyes before pulling me into his arms. "Hey, it's okay. I understand you made peace with your brother's death, but it's normal for these emotions to surface. It's only been a few weeks. I get it," he added, pinching my bicep. "You're a tough girl now. Hell, I wouldn't fuck with you."

I cracked a smile.

Jax lifted my chin. "Regardless, never feel the need to wear emotional armor around me, Elara. We all have shitty days. I'll support you until my last breath, even if you and Rico continue to threaten me with your sorcery."

"Stop it." I laughed. "I'm not a witch."

"You said it, not me."

I sent a burst of heat into his chest. He hissed.

"Don't push me," I teased.

"I wouldn't dream of it." Jax winked, then gestured to the steep ravine near the bridge. "Should we take the trail this time?"

"No. Let's live a little."

I BURST into a fit of laughter once we stepped over the threshold. The overly friendly cashier who wrote her number on Jax's cup during our first visit to Starbucks stood behind the counter.

My partner delighted at the opportunity of making me jealous. He stepped in front of me and flashed the woman a seductive grin before ordering two shots of espresso. Her green eyes glazed over with lust as she tapped the computer screen. Jax braced his palms on the counter and flexed his biceps while jerking his chin at the seasonal drinks listed on the chalkboard.

His performance didn't go unnoticed. With flushed cheeks, the giggling girl rambled about her love of sparkling herbal teas.

I tapped my foot and cleared my throat.

Not skipping a beat, Jax leaned across the counter and said, "The color of your apron really brings out the emerald flecks in your eyes."

And just like that, the poor girl lost her composure. She fanned her beet red face and eyed the barista who worked beside her. The young man wiggled his eyebrows and mouthed, "Get his number."

Oh, hell no. Refusing to let Jax win, I slid my body in front of his and rotated my ring while I spoke to the lovestruck cashier. "Forgive me. My fiancé hit his head earlier this week. He's been talking out of his ass all day. The doctor said caffeine will help lift the brain fog. Can you double those espresso shots?"

"Of course," she said, reaching for two cups. "I'm sorry he's unwell. I hope the espresso helps."

"I'm sure it will," I said, swiping the ten-dollar bill from the Lunin's outstretched hand.

It took every ounce of restraint to muffle my laughter while we finished the transaction. Jax hid his own amusement by biting his lip.

With a smug grin on my face, I snatched the invisible trophy out of my partner's hands and strolled to the other side of the counter, not bothering to collect my change.

I RESTED the empty cup on the stone surface, then leaned my head on Jax's shoulder. The summer breeze kissed my flushed skin. I eyed the underside of the bridge. Cars zipped by overhead, their tires bouncing over the tiny gaps in the concrete. I appreciated the evening sounds. Crickets chirped, frogs croaked, and cicadas called for their mates.

Jax ran his fingers through my hair. "It's different, but I think I like it."

I blinked, remembering how he uttered those exact words in my dream.

"Is it true?" he asked. "Blondes have more fun."

I moved my lips toward his. "You tell me."

Jax indulged me with a few deft sweeps of his tongue before he pulled away.

I frowned at the deepening line between his brows. "What's wrong?"

"Elara, your happiness means everything to me." He tapped the center stone of my ring. "So I refuse to let my selfish desires sway your decision. You don't have to marry me. You can stay here on Earth and start a new life."

The sincerity in his voice stung my heart like a hot poker. I loved that man with every part of my being. The thought of us not being together brought tears to my eyes.

"You won't entertain us living on Earth together?"

He shook his head. "This isn't my planet. I'm out of my element here."

"I was out of my element on Aroonyx, but I adapted."

"Out of necessity. Not out of choice." He shifted his weight. "The ex-Collectors need help. Samson and Castor lack the patience to rehabilitate those kids. I have plenty. The day Aries showed up, you insisted the change starts with me. Well, here I am. I can help transition them back into society, and I can help them walk through the darkness."

I shut my eyes. *Jax Caspen. The selfless warrior. That should go on his headstone one day.* I faked a cry. *What should I do? Do I stay or do I go? If I stay on Earth, I could live with my parents, attend the local community college, get a mindless job, transfer to a public university, date a bunch of random dudes, get my heart broken, graduate, start a new career, find a husband, have a few kids, and live a simple life. Or I can return to Aroonyx, marry my true love, help pick up the broken pieces Zenith left behind, and live a life filled with uncertainty and mystery.*

I stared at my partner. "Jax, I lived an easy and predictable life before I met you."

He swallowed—hard.

"And then you showed me a magical world filled with mystery, danger, and enough heartache to last a lifetime."

He grimaced. "The odds aren't sounding in my favor."

I gave his hand a loving squeeze. "I wanted to give up, toss in the towel, but you never stopped believing in me, and because of you, I believe in me for the first time. You are my life partner. Where you go, I go."

The tension in his shoulders dissolved. "So you're willing to leave everything behind for the unknown?"

"It wouldn't be the first time."

He laughed. "True, though life on Aroonyx will be much different this time around. We have a lot of work to do."

"We'll figure it out."

"Just like we always do." He winked.

I inhaled the evening air, savoring my final moments on Earth, the planet I once called home.

I closed my eyes. *Am I making the right choice?*

A gentle vibration warmed my heart.

Thanks, bro. I needed that.

I looked at Jax. "Let's get the hell out of Dodge."

"You lost me on that one, Elara."

"Then how about this?" I kissed his knuckles. "Let's go home."

His piercing blue eyes lit up as he whispered, "I thought you'd never ask."

FIFTEEN YEARS LATER

I t was hot, and I was sweating. After living on Aroonyx for over a decade, I still hadn't acclimated to the heat. The legs of the wooden chair sank deeper into the grass as I leaned forward to adjust my dress. Sweat had glued the pale fabric to the underside of my thighs.

"He looks nervous," I whispered to Jax.

"It's a big day."

"It took him long enough to ask her."

"Orion waits for the most opportune time to make his move," he teased, nudging me in the ribs.

I chuckled, remembering the day Orion kissed me before Jax arrived after his long absence. My eyes grew. *That feels like a lifetime ago.*

"Here she comes," he said, rising to his feet.

The crowd followed my partner's lead and turned to see the bride. Men smiled and women murmured their approval as Idalia walked down the aisle lined with Moon Drops. She had pinned her blonde locks in a messy up-do. Tiny braided strands framed her face. The elegant crème-colored train of her dress trailed behind her, brushing the emerald grass.

With tear-filled eyes, I admired my beautiful friend. The rays of the summer sun bathed her tan skin in a rich glow, and the light reflected off the golden flecks in her irises once she spotted Orion. He stood tall with his hands clasped in front of him, his grin growing wider as his betrothed moved closer.

Samson escorted his daughter down the aisle, patting her hand every few steps. He came clean and told Idalia the truth about their family ties. To everyone's surprise, she accepted Samson with open arms and an open heart.

"She looks gorgeous."

Jax nodded and hooked his arm around my waist. "Though not as stunning as my wife."

"You're getting smoother with age."

"And you're getting sharper. Are you sure Cyrus didn't pass you his humor along with his powers?"

I rubbed my chest, smiling at the warmth buzzing around my heart. "Maybe."

The man overseeing the ceremony encouraged the audience to take a seat. I rested my head on Jax's shoulder while he played with the silver rings on my finger. We stayed silent, listening to Idalia and Orion exchange their wedding vows.

My cheeks puffed at the quiet argument beside me. I lifted my finger to my lips. "Shh. Stop talking."

"He won't stop kicking me."

I nudged Jax. "Talk to your son; he's driving his sister crazy."

His head turned, and in a firm but hushed voice, he said, "Cyrus, leave your sister alone."

"Yes, sir," the boy murmured, tucking his feet underneath his chair.

I grinned, observing our Solin twins. Their physical features mirrored each other beautifully, but emotionally they sat on opposite ends of the spectrum. Our daughter Kyra, who we named after Jax's mother, kept to herself and internalized her emotions. Like her father, she preferred to observe rather than participate. Unfortunately, her Solin temper caused her to overreact and lash out at anyone who got in her way—her brother being the main target.

A mental clone of his uncle, Cyrus led and never followed, he spoke his mind, stood up for the kids at school who got bullied, and kept us laughing with his witty sense of humor.

After Idalia and Orion finished exchanging their vows, the officiant called for my participation. Smoothing a wrinkle in my dress, I strolled toward the newly minted couple and kissed them both on the cheek before taking my place beside the overseer.

On Aroonyx, it was customary for the leader to give their blessing during a ceremony. Couples no longer needed union approval to marry the love of their life because the leader had no right to intervene with matters of the heart.

I verbalized my joy-filled sentiments, wished the couple years of happiness, then returned to my seat.

The man acknowledged my kind words before sharing a closing statement with the elated couple. "May you always find the light in the darkness, may love guide your hearts, and may you honor your happily ever after." His lips spread into a warm grin. "It is my greatest privilege to pronounce you man and wife. Orion, you may kiss the bride."

Idalia's eyes brimmed with tears when her husband said, "I love you."

The crowd erupted into applause once he pressed his lips against hers.

Jax tossed my long, braided hair behind my back and in his silky voice he whispered, "And *I* love you."

WE SPENT the afternoon celebrating the newly wedded couple. Bite-size meats, vegetables, and pastries lined the wooden tables. Mugs of Maragin clinked together and laughter filled the vast space.

My gaze drifted to a cluster of trees. Kyra sat alone with her arms crossed, knees tucked into her chest, and brow furrowed. I sighed. *Why is she pouting?*

I scanned the area for my other child. His white teeth flashed in the sunlight as he played tag with a little girl. The young Lunin squealed, zigzagging through the crowd.

My head turned when I heard Orion and Idalia approach. I raised my cup of Maragin. "To many years of happiness."

"Thank you, Elara," Idalia said, bustling the train of her dress.

"Are you excited about next week?" I asked Orion.

"No. I'm nervous as hell. It's surreal to think it's finally opening." He rolled up the sleeves of his dress shirt. "The permit took forever to finalize."

I grimaced. "I apologize for the delay. My hands are tied with the approval process."

"It's not your fault. You've done more than your fair share to support this project."

"It's a project I believe in. A medical center is a huge facility to open and an even bigger responsibility to run. Your father would be proud of you, Orion."

His throat bobbed. "I wish he could have been here today."

"I'm sure he's smiling at the two of you right now."

Lightening the mood, Idalia slipped an arm around her husband's waist. "I still can't believe I married a doctor. And not just any doctor—but *the* doctor on Aroonyx."

"You chose the winning combination." He puffed out his chest. "Brains and good looks."

I snorted and rolled my eyes at him. "After all these years you haven't changed."

"I might be older, but I'm still young at heart."

"Elara."

I looked over my shoulder. A Lunin stood near a table, vying for my attention.

"Duty calls," Idalia said.

I huffed a breath. "I'll catch up with you guys later."

"See you around, Elara."

I spun on my heels and headed toward the man waiting to speak with me. He rose to his full height.

"What's on your mind, Rigel?"

"I want to discuss a new invention that will assist with the heating and cooling of homes and establishments."

"That sounds promising."

He fidgeted with a button on his blazer. "Could you work your magic and push it through?"

I pinned him with a long look. "Rigel, I won't use my position to cut corners. This invention is no different than the others. It must go through the approval process with the General Council before it's implemented."

"I understand." The Lunin blew out a frustrated breath and met my gaze. "But this is big. Think of the new medical center. The patients' comfort should be considered."

"And it will be. I'm sure the council will motion for its approval. We're at a wedding, Rigel. This isn't the time or the place to discuss business."

"You're right." He bowed his head. "Forgive me."

MY TEETH SANK into a soft dinner roll as I observed the content faces of the guests. The citizens of Aroonyx lived happy and peaceful lives. As I had predicted, my life with Jax was filled with uncertainty and mystery. The two of us returned, eager for a fresh start. The Transition, as the people called it, lasted a few turns of the seasons. Shortly after, a unanimous vote named me the new leader of Aroonyx, and with Saros's help, we formed a government.

Each village nominated a handful of people who formed a Village Council, and those members created the General Council, who worked directly with me and Saros—my most trusted advisor. This group oversaw ordinances, education, and health care. Every item that landed on my desk went through a lengthy approval process and ended with a vote.

Our first task was Zenith's dwelling and what to do with it. The General Council passed Saros's suggestion without argument: tear it down and build a memorial for the people who lost their lives during the uprising. A carpenter crafted a wooden bench and placed it in the shade of a tree. He even inscribed a silver plaque with a quote by my brother.

Everything is going to be okay. We are going to be okay.
−Cyrus Lofton

BEFORE ZENITH'S body turned cold, Jax and Samson hurried to free Nash from his cell. They returned empty-handed.

"Where is he?" I had asked them.

"Gone. We broke down the door and found a blazing fire in the hearth, a warm cup of tea, and knife molds scattered around the table." Jax tossed up his hands. "But no Nash."

"How did he escape?"

Samson eyed me and Jax.

My mouth gaped. "Do you think Nash is a Seeker?"

Jax shrugged. "How else would he have gotten out of there? Saros jumped after Arun's death. Perhaps Nash's intention shifted after Zenith's passing."

I hummed my understanding, and the three of us left it at that.

A handful of Seekers emerged after the uprising. Together, we formed a Seeker Council and worked alongside the General Council. We focused our efforts on technology. The people valued my and Saros's extensive knowledge of Earth, so we helped select inventions that would benefit Aroonyx. Teams presented different ideas to the General Council and debated which items deserved priority.

I never replaced Saros after he passed. The first Seeker died in his sleep, and the carpenter etched his name and quote beside my brothers on the silver plaque.

> *Timing is everything.*
> *–Saros*

I USED the crook of my arm to shield my eyes from the setting sun while I reflected on my position.

The first ordinance we passed stated the term limits for a leader. The elected official could serve Aroonyx for four years, exceeding no more than four terms. After fifteen years of self-less service, my time as the leader had reached its final year.

"The kids are growing up fast."

I nodded, watching Samson limp toward me. His leg never fully recovered from the injury he suffered during the final battle.

I stole a glance at my son, who stood chatting with Idalia and Orion. "They sure are."

"Don't they have a birthday coming up soon?"

"Yeah. I can't believe they're turning ten."

Samson ran a hand over his beard. "Damn, I'm getting old."

"We all are."

"You're still a kid to me," he said, knocking my shoulder with his.

"And you're still a grumpy old bastard."

He chuckled under his breath. "Some things never change."

I wrapped my arms around his waist and leaned my cheek against his chest. "Idalia seems happy."

"Orion's a good kid. He'll take care of her."

"Yeah, he will. He loves your daughter more than life itself."

"And he gets to deal with me if he fucks it up."

I shook my head at the Solin. "You're the world's scariest father-in-law."

He snickered, twisting his beard into a cone.

Cyrus's blond head snapped toward Samson. Weaving through the crowd, he dashed toward his favorite Solin and raised his fists in the guard position. Samson humored my child by motioning for him to strike his palm. Cyrus faked a left jab before punching my old mentor in the gut. He cursed the unexpected attack.

"*Cyrus*," I scolded.

He laughed before chasing after the Lunin girl once more.

"That boy of yours will send me to an early grave."

"Never. He loves his grumpy gramps."

"Don't call me that."

"I didn't give you that nickname. If you have a problem with it, file your complaint with the twins."

A smile broke at the corner of his mouth as he glanced at Kyra. The girl remained glued to the tree. "She's the only one allowed to call me that name."

"Figures. The two of you are connected at the hip."

"She's a pain in my ass. Just like her mother."

I scoffed at his little jab.

"I better head out," he said, squeezing my shoulder. "I promised Castor I'd meet him for a drink later."

"Tell him I'm sorry about today."

"He understands. Blood ties run deep."

I nodded. Ally or not, Idalia refused to let Pollux's father attend her wedding.

"See you around, kiddo."

"Take it easy, Samson."

I flinched as Jax's fingers pinched my side. He grabbed my hand and spun me around, fanning the pleats of my dress.

My eyes roved over the fitted long-sleeved shirt that hugged his biceps. "Hey there, handsome."

He pulled me close and whispered, "Hey there, beautiful."

His lips brushed mine for only a second before Cyrus bolted past us.

"Ew," Cyrus complained. "Don't be gross."

I cupped my hands and directed my voice toward our son. "One day you'll have a girlfriend and you won't think it's gross."

Cyrus's shoes slid across the fine blades of grass. He turned, a tiny smirk curling on his lips. "I already have a girlfriend."

My jaw cracked open. "Is she the Lunin you keep chasing?"

He winked before dashing after the black-haired girl.

I looked at Jax with wide eyes. "What are we going to do with that kid?"

"Send him to live with Samson."

I laughed hard, my gaze drifting to Kyra. I frowned. *What's with the sour face? She's had a foul attitude for weeks. Jax should speak with her.*

That thought slipped from my mind as I watched a Solin walk toward us. Tall, with broad shoulders, the man oozed enough confidence to turn heads. His white-blond hair danced in the summer breeze, and his amber eyes sparkled in the late afternoon light. He flashed Jax his pearly grin and extended his hand. I did a doubletake every time I saw the young man. He looked exactly like my brother.

"How's it going, Blaze?"

"It's going well, sir."

I gave him a warm hug and asked, "Are you ready for your exam tomorrow?"

"I think so."

Jax clapped him on the back. "You're ready."

Blaze's lips buzzed with uncertainty. "The competition is stiff. Over ten Protectors applied for the job. I've spent weeks studying the material. I even made the mistake of asking Samson to quiz me."

Jax crossed his arms and widened his stance.

"It's not the physical part of the test that concerns me." Blaze faked a jab at Jax. My partner didn't flinch. "It's the written part."

"I'm sure you'll do fine," I said.

After we established the General and Seeker Councils, we formed a group sworn to protect the citizens. Resembling a combination of firefighters and police officers on Earth, these men and women provided selfless service to their community. Unlike the Collectors, the Protectors wore uniforms and followed strict guidelines. Each recruit spent two years studying the art of combat while learning the rules of engagement.

The Protectors adhered to an honorable code of conduct and continued their education after graduation, staying up to date with training and certifications. After Samson retired, Jax accepted the nomination of Chief of the Protectors. He excelled in his position, and every member held him in high regard.

"Trust me," Jax said, "you'll pass the test."

Blaze shoved his hands into his pockets. "If you say so."

"Deputy Chief." I nodded my approval. "That's a high-profile position."

"Thanks, Elara. I'll rest easy tonight."

I laughed. "No pressure."

Blaze groaned, dropping his head. "Now I'll go home and study until my brain explodes."

"Don't stay up too late," Jax said. "I need my new Deputy Chief rested for his first day of work."

Blaze's heels clicked together as he popped to attention. "Yes, sir."

"Dismissed."

The Solin did an about-face, then jogged toward the tree line.

"It's getting late." Jax pointed at the twin moons glowing in the evening sky. "We should get the kids home. They have school tomorrow."

I nodded, eyeing Rigel. He spoke animatedly with a member of the General Council.

"I could use a good night's sleep," I said. "I have a strong feeling I'll find my desk piled high with paperwork tomorrow."

"It always is."

I shrugged.

"Why don't you sleep in tomorrow," he suggested. "I'll drop off the kids before I go to work."

"The school isn't on the way to the station."

"I have to stop by the Village Center and give a speech to the graduating recruits before overseeing the Deputy Chief exam."

"I thought Aries was giving the speech."

"No. Samson wants me there."

"He's retired. He doesn't get a say."

Jax laughed hard. "You try telling him that."

"We're so domestic now," I said, motioning to the two of us.

Jax snickered and gave me a quick kiss before jogging to collect the twins. He snatched Cyrus right before he pounced on his sister. Our son giggled and squirmed until Jax tossed him over his shoulder. He then reached for Kyra's hand. Her eyes glittered in the moonlight as she smiled at her father.

My heart expanded with the love I had for my family. Jax won the award for parent of the year—parent of the decade.

His patience outmatched mine, and he raised our children with a firm but gentle hand. With an open heart and an open mind, he listened to every word they said, never breaking eye contact. Cyrus and Kyra had a deep respect for their father. At times, I wondered if they preferred him over me.

"Hey, Mom?"

I blinked, turning my attention to our daughter.

"When can we visit Grandma? I want to see if she's feeling better."

I sucked on my lip and eyed Jax. He nodded, aware that her question had tugged at my heartstrings. Over the past year, my adoptive mother's health had declined, so my father hired a hospice nurse to assist with her care. Cancer hit her hard, but it hit me and my father harder. It brought my mother great joy to see her grandchildren and the pureness of this intention allowed us to jump back and forth between Aroonyx and Earth.

"We'll pay her a visit soon," I said.

Kyra braided her blonde hair as she walked, her mind distracted with unspoken thoughts.

"Can we spend the night?" Cyrus asked, still draped over Jax's shoulder. "Grandpa promised I could finish watching that old *Game of Thrones* show."

My head snapped toward him. "Please tell me he didn't let you watch that."

He grinned in response.

"*Cyrus.* That is not an appropriate show for children."

"Don't be so dramatic, Mom."

I glared, the invisible flames tapping at my fingertips.

"How about *Star Wars*?" Jax suggested.

"Fine," Cyrus grumbled.

Our family strolled through the forest toward the small house on the hill near the windmill. After we returned to Aroonyx, Jax and I renovated the abandoned home. It took over five seasons to finish the damn project because we lacked the modern tools found on Earth, but we managed, thanks to Samson and Castor's help.

THE FIRST SNOWFALL arrived a few weeks after Idalia and Orion's wedding. I watched the ice crystals twirl outside our bedroom window while Jax read the weekly reports.

"Anything new?" I asked, tracing the maze of scars on his abdomen.

"No, not really." He turned the page. "There was a minor incident today between two vendors in the South Village, but Blaze followed protocol and brought the guilty party to the station."

I lifted my cheek from his chest. "He takes his job as Deputy Chief pretty seriously, doesn't he?"

"With good reason. It's a tough position. Blaze is responsible for seventy-five Protectors. If anything goes wrong, he reports to me."

I grimaced.

"Don't give me that look," he said. "I'm not Samson. I won't chew his ass if he fucks up."

"So the heated argument with your previous Deputy Chief was just a fluke?"

"That was one time, Elara."

"Fair enough," I said, lying back down.

"I can't scare off Blaze. I need him to take over my position one day."

I sat up. "You're not thinking of retiring, are you?"

"Not yet." He tossed the stack of papers onto the nightstand. "But sooner than later. I'm getting too old for this shit."

"You sound like Samson. You're thirty-eight, not sixty."

"I'm almost thirty-nine," he corrected. "I've spent over twenty-five years training people in the art of combat."

My face squished up. "Well, when you put it like that."

"See, I should retire."

"But leaving the Protectors means leaving your uniform behind."

He flashed me a seductive grin. "Is that a problem?"

"Mm-hmm." I hooked my leg around his waist and straddled the Lunin.

He rested his hands behind his head and let his eyes wander over my body.

"I find a man in uniform very attractive," I said, sliding my fingers up the hard planes of his stomach.

He jerked his chin at the closet. "Should I put it back on?"

"Why bother?" I asked, tracing his ear with my tongue. "I'll just take it off again."

Jax gripped my waist and moved my hips to the desired location. "I'm okay with that."

I kissed him long and slow while my hand searched for the part that firmed against me. I hit my mark only for Jax to lift me off of him.

"I can't believe I forgot to tell you," he said, his eyes wide with excitement.

I slapped his chest, irritated with the delay. "Can't it wait?"

"No. Guess who I ran into today?"

"Who?"

"Apollo."

I stifled a loud gasp. "*No.*"

"Yes."

"Where?"

"Near the cliffside. During my rounds, I saw a man standing dangerously close to the edge, so I went to investigate. I nearly had a heart attack when he turned around."

"What did you do?"

"Elara, I wish you could have seen my face. Out of habit, I reached for my knife."

"That's understandable, considering your last encounter with Apollo."

He shrugged, eyeing the scar on the palm of his hand.

"So what happened next?"

"Nothing. We just stood there, staring at each other and then he said, *Oh, how the tables have turned.*"

"What the hell does that mean?"

"Not a clue, though it sounded like a warning."

My face fell. "Why didn't you bring him to the station for questioning?"

"*Elara.*" He shot me a sidelong look. "I had no backup. Apollo is the strongest Solin I've ever met. If I tried to restrain him, he would have tossed my ass over the cliffside."

"Thanks for the imagery, Jax. Now I'll lose sleep wondering if Apollo has something hiding up his sleeve."

"Don't overreact." He smoothed the hairs that hovered around my face. "Apollo didn't attack. Hell, he didn't even threaten me. He just turned around and walked away."

"I don't care. It still bothers me. Tomorrow I'm speaking with the councils."

"No, you're not." His voice raised. "This is out of the councils' jurisdiction. As Chief of the Protectors, I'm granted the right to oversee any and all issues involving security on Aroonyx."

"I'm aware of your rights, Jax. I wrote the damn law."

"Then maybe you and your councils should review it."

The glowing ropes snaked out of my fingertips and sparked through the air while I argued, "This is Apollo we're talking about. An ex-member of the Inner Circle, the man who tried to kill us on multiple occasions. We have kids now, Jax. I won't take any chances."

"Then let me do my job."

I pressed my palms into the comforter, the thick fluff smoking. "I will if you let me do mine!"

Jax cursed, draping an arm over his eyes. I gritted my teeth. Our job titles rarely conflicted, but when they did, the gloves always came off.

"Are we fighting?" he asked, peeking around his elbow.

I shut my eyes, calming the rising flames. "You'd think by now we could go longer than ten minutes."

Jax frowned at the ashes that puffed into the air as he fluffed the comforter. "That's the second one you've destroyed in three weeks. At this rate, I'll have to work overtime to pay for your outbursts."

I scrubbed at my face. "I'm sorry."

He laughed, pulling me into his arms. "What am I going to do with my little witch?"

"Don't call me that."

"Sorceress? Enchantress?"

I pinched the underside of his bicep. "Keep it up. If you're not careful, I'll start acting like one."

"Start?"

I zapped him with a burst of heat. He just laughed.

"Now back to Apollo. Where do you think he lives? We haven't seen him in fifteen years."

"Who knows?" he said. "Maybe he learned how to swim and lives on a nearby island."

"I wonder what's out there."

"Out where?"

"Across the water. We can't be the only inhabitants on Aroonyx."

Jax stayed quiet, running his fingers through my hair.

Long minutes passed before I asked, "Does the uprising feel like another lifetime?"

"Yes. Time's a tricky thing. Zenith's death feels like forever ago and the twin's birth feels like yesterday."

"I agree."

Jax covered my lower half with the singed comforter.

"Speaking of Kyra," I added. "I'm worried about her."

"Why?"

"She's been so quiet lately. I think she's afraid to tell us what's on her mind."

"She is her father's daughter."

"True, but something's going on, I can feel it."

"I'll talk to her tomorrow."

"Good, because you're the only one who can get—"

My voice trailed off as the bedroom door cracked open.

"Mom, Dad?" Kyra called. "Can I come in?"

I sat up and looked at Jax. "Why do we have a door? They never knock."

He chuckled, then directed his voice toward the entryway. "You can come in, kiddo."

Kyra lowered her gaze and shuffled her bare feet across the hardwood floors. Jax lifted our daughter onto the bed. She squeezed her petite frame between ours.

"Bad dream?" I asked her.

"No. I can't sleep."

Jax brushed her blonde hair off her shoulders. "Why not?"

"The voice inside my head won't shut up."

I paled. *Oh no. Not the dealer.*

Jax tensed, but kept his attention focused on our daughter.

Forgetting Kyra was an underage Solin, I reached for the lamp on the bedside table.

"I don't need the light on," she said.

I stilled, my fingers resting on the switch. "You're a Solin, you can't see in the dark."

"Yeah, I can."

My head turned in slow motion. Jax blinked, equally shocked by this bit of information. "Honey, how does the room look right now?" he asked.

"The same as it does in the day."

"Is it well lit?" I pressed.

"Yep. Like moonlight is shining on everything."

I mouthed, "What the hell?" to Jax.

He shrugged, his eyes growing.

"I can see even better during the day," she said.

"You can?" I stammered.

"Yep. I can see the veins in the leaves on the top branches of the trees and the swirls on the grazers' fur all the way from the playground."

I swallowed. The man who raised grazers lived over a mile away from the school.

"I told Cyrus I had my Solin traits." Kyra fisted her hands. "He called me a liar, so I pinned him on the ground, just like Grumpy Gramps taught me, and showed him my strength."

My brows tapped my hairline as I met Jax's gaze.

"She's only nine," he mouthed.

I pinched the bridge of my nose, unable to wrap my mind around our daughter's claim. Not only did she obtain both Solin and Lunin traits, but she acquired them before she turned eighteen. I inhaled a long breath and pushed the darkness I sensed around my daughter into a quiet room in the back of my mind.

Noting our baffled expressions, she asked, "Am I in trouble?"

"No," Jax answered.

She sighed, scratching at the burned handprint on the comforter. "This is why I've been acting weird. I was afraid to tell you. These girls at school overheard my conversation with Cyrus, and one of them started this stupid rumor, and now no one will talk to me."

"What rumor?"

She turned to face me, her bottom lip quivering. "They're calling me the new Zenith."

A low growl rumbled in Jax's chest. My nostrils flared.

People could throw their verbal jabs at us, but one wrong look at our kids sent us both over the edge.

I spun her around on the bed and lifted her chin. "People fear what they don't understand. You're a good person, Kyra." I paused. Who was I convincing? Her or myself? I wasn't sure. Clearing my throat, I added, "Hold your head high and be proud of who you are."

"Your mother's right. I spent my younger years dealing with the harsh judgments of others. We can either listen to the bullshit or ignore it. The choice is yours."

She giggled at the curse word he slipped into his speech. I shot Jax a stern glance. He winked.

I lifted the covers and patted the space beside me. She obliged, making herself comfortable.

"Do you want to hear a secret?" I asked.

She nodded.

"I discovered Cyrus was my twin brother after I turned eighteen."

Her nose crinkled. "What?"

"That's right. And guess who told me the news?"

"Uncle Cyrus?"

"Nope. Your father."

Her little mouth gaped. "How did Dad know he was your brother?"

"Now that's a very long story." I chuckled.

"Will you tell me?"

I paused, observing our curious daughter. Wise beyond her years, Kyra exuded a level of maturity that mirrored my own at her age.

Sensing my desire to connect with our daughter on a deeper level, Jax said, "Elara, she's a little young to hear the details of that story."

I smiled, tucking a stray hair behind her ear. "No, she's ready."

Jax kissed the top of our heads before swinging his legs off the bed. "Then I'll leave you to it."

I lifted my head off the pillow. "Where are you going?"

"To check on Cyrus. And besides"—he looked over his shoulder and smiled—"this story is best told by the author."

"I love you, Jax."

"And I love you. More than you'll ever know."

After the door closed, I fluffed our shared pillow and pulled the blanket over Kyra's shoulder. "Are you warm, comfortable?"

She nodded, her blue and orange eyes glowing.

"Then let's go back and start from the beginning. Once upon a time, a man closed his piercing blue eyes and jumped."

ACKNOWLEDGMENTS

You're still reading? After all those pages? I'm honored. Thank you for joining me on this journey. I hope you enjoyed the story half as much as I enjoyed writing it. *Passage of Time* took two years and eight drafts of sweat and tears to complete. Whew. Now I get a break. Just kidding. I have three more books in the series to publish. More on that later. Right now, I want to thank the beautiful souls in my life who encouraged me to stay on my path.

God. Without His guidance these books would have never happened.

J.C. & Doc—my spiritual team for life. Thank you. Thank you. Thank you. We did it.

Sunny, you are my light in the darkness.

My husband, the man who inspired a key character in this series, the man who has always believed in me, the man who never lets me give up, the man who loves me with his whole heart. J, you are my partner for life. I love you more.

My son, E. You are my everything. Thank you for the constant interruptions while I write. Without you, mommy would never take a break.

My advisor and best friend, C.L. Ashton. What would I do without you? You are my breath of fresh air. You keep my chin lifted and my spirits high. You are the friend I always wanted and the friend I'm grateful to have. Friends don't let friends eat late night cookie dough.

My mother and stepfather. Thank you for being the world's best Nana and 'buelo. Thank you for giving me the time to write and for loving E. I love you dearly. Get the bus ready.

My father, the man who inspired Samson. I love you to the moon and back.

My author soul sister, April Woodard. Thank you for loving my characters and laughing with me about the highs and lows of the self-published world. We'll get to 10K one day, girl.

My ninja publicist, Loolwa Khazzoom. Thank you for kicking my ass into gear and believing in me.

My family and friends. Thank you from the bottom of my heart for your love and support.

Captain Von Trapp, I appreciate your guidance with medical terminology and combative maneuvers. You are the biggest badass I know. Thank you for your selfless service to our country.

My unofficial mentor, Jay Kristoff. Thanks for opening my eyes to the darkness. I'm sure my readers appreciated your influence.

George RR Martin, thank you for giving me the courage to kill my characters in unimaginable ways.

Tiffany White, thank you for polishing these books to perfection.

The following people have watched my journey from the beginning and have showed me a lifetime of encouragement and support.

Lucy Castro, Derek Buckler, Ashley Rafiner, Allen Cheesman, Jessica Snelson, and Josh Langlois.

A HUGE shout out to the artists who helped shape the

scenes and dialogue in this book. Bastille, Sleeping at Last, Aquilo, The Moth & the Flame, Seafret, Ruelle, Ludovico Einaudi, Sean Redmond, Amber Run, Hidden Citizens, and Ramin Djawadi.

My readers, you are the reason I keep writing these stories. Thank you for the kind messages, the shares on social media, the endless words of encouragements, and the positive reviews.

I wanted to the write *The End* after the last line in the story, but how could I? It's only the beginning.

Printed in Great Britain
by Amazon

54261504R00404